It's Wrong for Me to Love You:

Renaissance Collection

It's Wrong for Me to Love You:

Renaissance Collection

Krystal Armstead

www.urbanbooks.net

Urban Books, LLC
300 Farmingdale Road, NY-Route 109
Farmingdale, NY 11735

It's Wrong for Me to Love You: Renaissance Collection

ISBN 13: 978-1-945855-37-5
ISBN 10: 1-945855-37-1

First Mass Market Printing August 2018
First Trade Paperback Printing August 2017
Printed in the United States of America

10 9 8 7 6 5 4 3 2 1

This is a work of fiction. Any references or similarities to actual events, real people, living or dead, or to real locales are intended to give the novel a sense of reality. Any similarity in other names, characters, places, and incidents is entirely coincidental.

Distributed by Kensington Publishing Corp.
Submit orders to:
Customer Service
400 Hahn Road
Westminster, MD 21157-4627
Phone: 1-800-733-3000
Fax: 1-800-659-243

It's Wrong for Me to Love You:

Renaissance Collection

by

Krystal Armstead

Acknowledgments

Because of my supporters' love and dedication to me, I have to dedicate this book to them.

Words cannot express how thankful I am for Racquel Williams and Carl Weber for taking a chance on me. I appreciate the opportunity to work with you and look forward to accomplishing greatness!

I would also like to take this time to give thanks to the following people who believed in me enough to read my writing before it was even published: Angela Vega, Wendy Palmer, Krystal Brackett, Sara Stephens, Charita Warren, Tanya Felder, Markiesha House-Woodson, Rhomesha Peterson, Danika Glass, Chaynia Dawkins, Coquenia Cooper, Mashawn Anthony, Brittany Derden, Yolanda Henderson, and Jamie Artis. You all took the time to actually read my thoughts. Your belief in me means more than you could ever know. I will *always* love you all!

Since I have been a published author, I have met some wonderful people! This wouldn't even be possible without them: Robin Michelle Watkins, Michelle Neal, Mesha Turner Latrese Washington (that's my cousin, y'all!), Nicki Ervin, Shonda Midgette, Octavia Carter, Elysia McKnight, Glenda Daniel, Kasey Smith, Shyalice Oates, Monique Franklin, Fallon Hampton, Allison Smith, Latonia Peterson, Natasha West, Monique Gray, and all of my reader homies in my reading group, "Krystal's Motivation"!

Thank you to my mother and father, Jennifer and Conrad Artis Jr. We have not always seen eye to eye, but you have always been there to support me. Nothing I can ever do can repay you both for all that you have done for me, but I promise to make you both proud!

This book is for my four beautiful children, Jada, Adrian, Jordan, and Angel. See, babies, dreams really do come true! This book is also for the missing pieces of my heart, my beautiful three stepdaughters, Jamie, Jasmine, and Anglie. I love you all like you are my own, even if you don't see it.

And last but definitely not least, my husband, James. I would not have accomplished this book without you. You are the motivation for *every* male character in this book! I put characteristics that

I love about you in some, and characteristics that I hate about you in others! Without good, bad, happy, and sad times that we shared, I would have never been inspired to tell my story.

Thank you all for your support. Thank you, God, for the opportunity.

A'ight, y'all, *let's do this!*

Chapter 1

The Unexpected

Ne'Vaeh

I swear, we do some stupid shit when we're young and in so-called love. It's like the part of our brain that contains common sense completely shuts down, and the part of our brain that is completely delusional takes over. Whom can we blame? Our parents, who never took the time to make sure we didn't make the same mistakes that they did? Our friends, who couldn't wait for us to fuck up just so they could bask in our misery? The boy who made you love him when he knew that he wasn't the type of guy you should give your heart to? Or yourself, who should have known better?

My name is Ne'Vaeh Washington. Juanita Washington gave me that name because she said that when she gave birth to me, her life was the complete opposite of heaven. January 1, 2015, was the worst fuckin' day of my life. However, it goes back further than that. . . .

I was a freshman attending Howard University in our nation's capital. I was a straight-A student, the vice president of the Student Government Association, a member of the National Honor Society, and a soloist of the Gospel choir. I occasionally went out clubbing and drinking, and I may have smoked a blunt or two every now and then. For the most part, I kept my head in the books and didn't let anything distract me from my goals. I was determined to do something with my life, and I was determined to find love again, wherever it was.

Though I feared love and shied away from it, I had this burning, physical sensation of desiring it. I guess you can call it hunger. I mean, there was this boy who set my soul on fire every time that he entered the room. I'm telling you, he had me to the point where just one glance at him sent sweat trickling down my back. Just the thought of him made my mouth water. He looked so delectable that I would have done just about anything to get just one taste of him, just to see how he felt in my mouth. That was the way Aaron Whitehaven made me feel. The only problem was . . . He was my best friend's boyfriend, and I should have known better.

I only had one good friend. Her name was Charlene Campbell, Charlie for short, and she was the best friend I ever had. She was the total opposite of me. I was a short, petite girl with brown skin and dark, shoulder-length hair. I had a mouthful of breasts and barely a handful of ass, but Charlie? She was about five foot seven, with the perfect Coke-bottle figure, and legs and ass for days. She had long, dark brown hair and a toasted-almond complexion. Her skin always looked as if she'd just had a facial. She barely wore any makeup unless it was lip gloss, which drew attention to her plump, perfect, pouty lips. On her worst day, she looked better than most people looked on their *best* day. She looked, talked, walked, and even breathed like a model. Everyone wanted to look like her and live the life that she did, me included.

I'd known Charlie ever since the first grade, and she'd always been the most popular girl in school. I don't think there was a male athlete that she hadn't dated, fucked, sucked, kissed, or dismissed. She was my girl, but the way she played the field always bothered me. She never knew when to quit—that was, until Aaron made his debut. . . .

I'll never forget . . . It was a Thursday, spring semester of our junior year in high school, 2012. I was sitting next to Charlie, fourth period, in African American History, a class taught by the whitest of white men, Mr. Jimmy Porter. We were in class, laughing at Mr. Porter's jokes, which were actually funny for a change, when Aaron strolled through the classroom door.

Charlie grabbed my arm, her light eyes looking in the same direction that every girl in the classroom was looking. "*OMG*, look at *that!*" she whispered, digging her American-manicured tips into the skin of my forearm.

My eyes followed him as he strolled his way over to Mr. Porter to hand him a sheet of paper, probably a note from the principal, assigning him to our class. Aaron stood about five foot ten. He had a peanut butter complexion, and dark, wavy, close-cut hair. He was dressed in black and white, from his hat to his Nike shoes. He had the smoothest walk. The brutha had a swag that nobody could deny. I watched as Mr. Porter pointed in my direction, telling Aaron to sit in the chair behind me. My heart pounded in my chest as he looked at me. Our eyes met. I could feel my cheeks turning red. Aaron grinned as he walked toward me.

I braced myself as he sat down behind me. As he sat, it was as if every female in the class, single or not, turned in their chair to face him, Charlie included.

Charlie scooted to the edge of her seat and cleared her throat to get his attention.

Aaron looked at her.

"I'm Charlene, but everybody calls me Charlie." She smiled, sticking her chest out even further.

That's not all they call you, I thought to myself.

"What's up, shorty? I'm Aaron." His voice was music to my ears.

"And *this* is my BFF, Ne'Vaeh—heaven spelled backward." Charlie threw her pencil at me to get my attention. "Ain't that the coolest name you've ever heard?"

I felt a tap on my shoulder. My heart nearly shot out of my chest. I turned around in my chair to look into his eyes—those gorgeous eyes.

"Heaven, huh?" Aaron grinned.

"Your . . . Your eyes are green. . . ." I stuttered, not sure what else to say to someone who *had* to know how good he looked.

Charlie giggled. "So," she looked at Aaron, "what are your plans for tonight?"

The girl couldn't wait to get the first taste. She couldn't wait to sink her fangs into his neck.

Two weeks didn't even go by and the two were already a couple. You wouldn't see one without the other. I never told her how angry I was with her for stealing his heart before I even had the chance to have a full conversation with him. I never told her that I wanted that boy more than anything.

They dated for over two years. In high school, they were voted most popular, most attractive, best-looking couple, most athletic, and they were chosen as prince and princess at the junior prom and fuckin' king and queen at the senior prom. Aaron made the basketball team in no time. Upon graduation, he received an academic *and* athletic scholarship to the University of Maryland, College Park. Charlie ended up at Morgan State University. I ended up at Howard University. As different as both Charlie's and my lives were, we tried to remain close. When she wasn't with Aaron, she was at my dorm in D.C. *talking* about Aaron.

As time went by, we spent more time on the phone and less time together. It seemed like the only time she came around sophomore year in college was so I could help her with her homework or study for exams. Her life was dancing, cheering, and Aaron. She was in love, and she wasn't letting him go. They were the perfect couple, and I was alone. Aaron wanted Charlie, and I wanted *him*. Damn . . .

There I sat alone in my dorm on a Friday night, the weekend of homecoming, fall 2014. I was supposed to be at the homecoming game, and I was supposed to attend the dance, being that I was the vice president of the SGA. I just couldn't bring myself to party that weekend, though. Charlie invited me to attend her homecoming at Morgan State a few weeks earlier, but plans had changed. Charlie's uncle had passed away that week, so she flew home to Texas where her uncle was going to be buried. She was devastated, and I felt for her. I lost my brother six years earlier, and I swore on my life that I would never attend another funeral.

Charlie and I had been texting each other on our iPhones that whole day. It was 8:30 p.m., and I sat at my desk typing on my Dell laptop when my cell phone rang.

I looked over at it and then held it in my hands. I didn't recognize the number, but I answered it anyway. "Hello? Ne'Vaeh speaking. . . ."

"What up, Heaven? What'cha been up to?"

My heart palpitated in my chest in sync with every syllable uttered through his lips. I couldn't believe it was Aaron's voice on the other end. He had never called me before. I could never go on double dates with him, Charlie, and whatever loser they'd try to hook me up with. I couldn't even look at the boy longer than a few seconds, because my eyes had a tendency to want to undress him. I went speechless for a second or two.

"Heaven, are you there?"

"Yeah . . . Yeah, I'm here. . . ." I stuttered.

"Good, 'cuz I am too. Come downstairs. . . ." He hung up his phone.

My mouth dropped open as I took the phone from my ear. I just sat there, staring at it. I felt like I was in the Twilight Zone. I couldn't believe he'd called. He never called. Up until that point, Aaron and I hadn't even had a one-on-one-conversation.

I put the phone down. I was dressed in a black tank top and black boy shorts, so I threw on some sweats, grabbed a hoodie, snatched my keys, and headed out the door. I was so anxious. I couldn't wait at the elevator, which seemed to be taking longer than normal. I shot down four flights of stairs and out the lobby of my college dorm.

There stood Aaron, leaned up against the side of the building. He was dressed in his gym clothes—a dark blue hoodie, baggy, dark blue sweatpants, and white Air Force Ones. He stood up from the building as he saw me walking toward him.

My heart fluttered in my chest as I approached him. I stood before him, arms wrapped around myself. My hair floated in the wind as it flew past us.

Aaron looked down at me as he licked his lips. "What up, Heaven? What's good with ya?"

Ever since the day we met, I don't think that boy ever called me by name, but I loved it. It was our thing.

I looked up at him. "*You* tell me. It's home-coming weekend. Why aren't you out with your friends?" I didn't understand why he'd driven over forty-five minutes to go see someone he hadn't so much as had a forty-five minute conversation with.

Aaron just looked at me.

I looked at him. "Why'd you come here?"

"You never go out with me and Charlie when we go out. I tried hooking you up with my boy, and you won't give a nigga a chance. You're cold, sweetheart." Aaron shook his head at me.

I resented that. "*I'm* cold? No, what's cold is you and Charlie trying to hook me up with a dude who was like twenty in the eleventh grade, eats with his mouth open, has six baby mamas, and who laughs at his own corny-ass jokes. His breath smelled like sweaty gym socks, and he wouldn't even supersize my fries when we went to Burger King because he said some lame shit about how he likes his women 'pretty in the face and slim in the waist'!" I rolled my eyes. "Where did you meet *that* idiot? *Y'all* were wrong for *that* shit."

Aaron threw his head back in laughter. "I swear, I didn't know any of that shit about him! I knew the dude had a few kids, but *damn!* Well, forget about Trey—what about Keon? He's a good dude, no kids, no baby-mama drama, and I hear he's been diggin' you since y'all were in the eighth grade."

I shook my head. "No way. Thank you, but *no* thank you. I appreciate your concern for my so-called love life, but don't even bother hooking me up with *anybody* else, because you apparently have absolutely *no* taste in men."

Aaron grinned. "I guess not. Hey, you can't be mad at me for tryin'. I just don't wanna see someone like you alone. . . ."

I looked up at him. "S . . . Someone like me? What do you mean?"

He avoided the question. "So, what'cha doin' tonight? Aren't you the vice president of SGA?

You're supposed to be at the homecoming. If you're not gonna go to the homecoming, you should at least kick it with your boy, Aaron. Come kick it with me. . . ."

I was speechless. I didn't know what to say to him. I would have given anything two-and-a-half years earlier for him to ask me to hang with him. Just to be in the same room with him. Breathing the same air as him was too deep. I was in love with that boy, but he wasn't mine, and it broke my heart. The smarter half of me wanted to walk away, tell him I was working on a fifteen-page paper for my Humanities 101 class. However, the part of my heart that beat for him took over my body. He was Charlie's boyfriend—my *best* friend's boyfriend. That meant that he was off-limits. Untouchable. She was out of town, and he was alone.

"Why are you here asking me what I'm doing tonight? We never speak. You've never called me. You've known my number ever since junior year in high school. We never hang out. The only time you talk to me is when you're trying to hook me up with one of your lame-ass friends. So, I guess you're lonely tonight, and you needed someone to talk to since your girl's gone. Is that it? The only reason you came is because she's gone, right? Admit it." I had to be honest.

Aaron licked his delectable lips. "To be honest, yes."

He didn't beat around the bush.

My mouth dropped open a little. I didn't expect him to be *that* honest.

"What I'm trying to say is . . ." Aaron tried to correct the way his words came out. "There are some things that I need to talk with you about. I never get the chance to talk with you, because I'm not trying to make Charlie upset. We both know that her jealous streak is hell-a-crazy. I don't wanna come between you and your best friend, but . . ." Aaron took my hand in his, and my heart melted. "We need to talk. So, come for a ride with me."

I nearly lost my breath. I quickly slipped my hand from his. He had driven nearly an hour to see me—how could I look into those pretty green eyes and tell him no? "But . . . I'm not dressed. . . ." I whispered, looking down at my outfit.

Aaron smirked. "Neither am I. I just left the gym with my boys." His eyes traced my lips. "C'mon. We can just go chill, get something to eat, or we can go kick it over at my crib since my roommate is gone for the weekend. We can do anything you wanna do. We can go anywhere that you wanna go. I just got paid today, so you can chose wherever you wanna go, and I got you.

Just come with me . . . please. . . ." Aaron pleaded, taking my hands again, holding both my hands in his.

My whole body blushed. I could feel his heart beating through the palms of his hands the blood rushing through his veins. He was just was nervous as I was. Aaron had more power over me than he knew. From that day we met in Mr. Porter's class, I wanted him. Now, there he was, asking me to go back to his apartment with him. Should I have gone out with him that night? No . . . but I did.

It was 10:30 p.m. when we arrived back at Aaron's three-bedroom apartment in Parkville. We had stopped at Taco Bell for a late-night snack and brought the food back to his cozy apartment. We sat at the bar, facing each other. I tried to hold my composure as he watched me eat. He had his eyes on every piece of food that slid through my lips.

I looked up at him. "What?" I blushed, licking the sour cream from my fingers.

"Y . . . You have a little sour cream on your lips. . . ." He put his hands on my face, swiping the sour cream from my lips with his fingertips.

I watched him as he licked the sour cream that he took from my lips from his fingers. Charlie had herself one sexy man, but for whatever reason, he felt the need to come to me. What wasn't she doing for him that had him coming to me that night?

Aaron kept watching my lips.

I looked at him. "Why do you keep looking at me like that?"

"What, I can't look at you?" Aaron's eyes searched my face. "I haven't seen you in months. . . ."

I tried not to smile. Over his shoulder, I caught a glimpse of a picture of Charlie on his refrigerator. I looked back at him. That picture snapped me out of my trance. I had no business there with him that night. "Why'd you drive so far to talk to me? Since *when* do me and you *ever* hang out, Aaron?" I asked.

Aaron cleared his throat. "I . . . ummm . . . I asked Charlie what she thought about marriage a few days ago."

I instantly lost my appetite. I placed the nacho that I was about to pop into my mouth right back in the bag. I looked at him as I wiped my fingertips on a napkin. I just knew that whatever he was about to say was something I really didn't want to hear.

"The thing is, as soon as the words came out of my mouth, I thought about you . . ." Aaron looked at me.

My heart jumped in my chest. "You . . . You thought about *me?* Why?" I was stunned. Definitely not what I expected to hear from him.

"I . . . ummm . . ." Aaron was nervous as hell. He was struggling to find the words to whatever it was he had to tell me. "I've been avoiding you, trying to hook you up with my boys, trying to spend as much time as I could with Charlie, trying my hardest not to look at you when you come around. . . . From the moment that I met you junior year, I wanted to ask you out. I wanted you bad as hell, but I didn't think you wanted the same thing, so I never approached you."

I nearly swallowed my own tongue. I hopped up from the bar stool, shaking my head, not believing my ears. "No, no, you can't be telling me this now, Aaron!" I wanted to cry and punch that muthafucka at the same damn time. "You're my best friend's boyfriend, and you're telling me right now—today—that you have feelings for me? Why the hell would you want me when you have someone as beautiful as Charlie? You have *got* to be joking! Is this some type of sick, cruel joke?"

Aaron got up from the stool, reaching for my hand. "Baby, calm down and just hear me out."

I pulled from him. "No! You shouldn't have told me this!"

"It doesn't even matter how I feel about you—it ain't like you feel the same way. It's not like you ever talked to me. You haven't so much as tried to carry on more than a three-word conversation with me. You don't look at me, you don't talk to me, you don't laugh with me, and you don't acknowledge me. I know I'm wrong for saying this, but I wouldn't have ever gotten to know Charlie if you would have taken some interest in me. You had to feel me staring at you the day we met. The fact that I was dancing with *you* and not her at our senior prom didn't ring a bell? I only got to know Charlie to get to know you, but you never let me," Aaron explained.

I wasn't going to let that boy make me cry. The words that came from his lips stung like a muthafucka. "So, what did my best friend say when you asked her to marry you?" I looked up into his face.

Aaron looked down at me. "I didn't ask her to marry me. I just told you that I asked shorty what she *thought* about marriage. I asked her if she could see herself spending the rest of her life with me. I asked her if she was still in love with me, and do you know what the girl did? She laughed at me. She said she was too young to be thinking about spending the rest of her life with anyone. She said she loved me, but marriage was the furthest thing from her mind. I felt stupid as fuck for even bringing the shit up—I should have stuck with my first mind and kept the shit to myself. She doesn't feel for me the way that she used to. At first, I thought she was just being cold because her uncle just passed away, but I know that wasn't it, because she left me that night and went out to the club with her girls. Yeah, I feel for the girl, but a part of me can't help but wonder what it would have felt like to be with you. That's why I call you Heaven. I know that heaven is what it would have felt like to be with you."

My heart fluttered in my chest. I wanted to be angry with him, but my heart wouldn't let me.

"Don't be mad with me, Heaven. I just have regrets. I've been with Charlie going on two years now, and I know I'm not who she wants to be with. I know that she isn't the girl who I want to be with either. I don't even know why we're dragging this relationship out, because it's not going anywhere. In high school, she was funny, she was flirty, she was sexy, she was popular, she was interested, and we looked good together. Knowing her helped me get on the basketball team as quickly as I did. Knowing her helped me get scholarships and grants to college. I think she used me just as much as I did her." Aaron paused a moment, then said, "She doesn't love me, Heaven, and I don't love her."

I shook my head. "Aaron, I don't need to be hearing this," I whispered.

"I'm sorry if I'm not supposed to be talking to you about any of this, but I couldn't hold in the way that I felt anymore. When I asked Charlie about marriage, I knew in my heart that I wanted her to say exactly what she said. Charlie and I don't belong together, but me and you? I know we could work something out." Aaron spoke softly.

My eyes began to water, and I knew the tears were coming. "You could have anyone in the world, Aaron—why would you choose me? Why would you choose your girlfriend's best friend?"

Aaron's eyes traced my lips. "Because you complete me."

I shook my head. "Complete you? You don't know *anything* about me."

Aaron grinned. "Your favorite color is blue. I know because every time you get dressed up, you wear royal blue all the way from your hoop earrings to your stilettos. Your favorite restaurant is IHOP. You always order scrambled eggs with extra cheese, turkey bacon extra crispy, two pancakes, and hash browns. You don't hang out

with your girls as much as you used to in high
school. You'd rather kick it in the library, in the
farthest corner, just you and your Dell laptop.
Your favorite candy is Haribo Gummy Bears—
you go through at least two packs in a day. You
were raised by your aunt and Miss Campbell.
Your mom is in prison. You haven't seen your
sister since you were thirteen. Your brother
passed away. Your first boyfriend was a dude
named Jamie—you dated him for about two
years until he moved to Memphis, Tennessee,
the summer before your sophomore year. You're
shy. You keep to yourself. You're not easily
persuaded. And you wish people would know
the way that you feel without you having to open
up your mouth to say a word. Now, wouldn't you
say I know a *little* something about you?"

I just looked at him. He didn't hit the nail
on the head exactly, but he was close enough.
I don't even think Charlie paid me that much
attention. For someone who only saw me once
in a blue moon, he sure did pay close attention
to details. "How . . . How did you know about
Jamie?" was all I could say.

"I have my sources, but don't worry about all
that." Aaron looked down into my face.

Jamie was my first love, my first kiss, my
first hug, my first touch, my first everything.

We made love for the first time before he left me to move to Tennessee. He took a piece of me with him when he left me, a piece that I thought I would never get back. I loved that boy *hard*. I never thought I would love anyone else again. It wasn't until Aaron walked in my classroom door that day that my heart began to beat again.

"Why didn't you just tell me how you felt about me back in high school, Aaron?" I asked.

"Everyone kept telling me that you were still in love with Jamie. I didn't wanna be the rebound nigga, so I did what any man would do—I went for what was available." Aaron licked his succulent lips. Oh, I wish he'd stop doing that.

"Well, you're about a year and a half too late, Aaron. You picked a fine time to tell me how you feel about me." Tears lined my lashes.

"Well, tell me something—how do you feel about *me?*" he asked.

I backed up a little. "What?"

"Stop being scared and just tell me how you feel about me. It's just between you and me." Aaron held my hands, pulling me closer to him.

My heart thumped against my rib cage. I slid my hands from his, backing away from him again. "I'll tell you how I feel. I *feel* like you could've told me how you felt about me a *long*-ass time ago! Maybe a good time would have been before you started dating my best friend! Or maybe before you started telling her that you loved her! Or maybe before you started having sex with her! Or better yet, before you became the strongest, longest, most faithful relationship that she's ever had! No matter what she may mean to you, I *know* that you mean the world to her! You're all she ever talks about, all she ever dreams about, all she ever brags about! She probably said that shit to you a couple of days ago because you scared the shit out of her when you brought up marriage. Charlie is beautiful, but she has been dogged out and has been played just like an average girl. Guys hit, split, and quit her ass just like they do everyone else! She thought you were different, but you're obviously not!"

Aaron frowned a little, though he didn't deny that what I was saying wasn't true.

"Okay, fine, you wanna know how I feel about you? Fine, I'll tell you. I've had feelings for you ever since I looked into those pretty green eyes of yours that day you stepped into Mr. Porter's African American History class our junior year in high school. I got lost in your eyes, and I still haven't found my way back. I hadn't felt that way about anyone but Jamie." I looked up at him.

"After he left, it's like my heart stopped beating. It didn't beat again until I met you."

Aaron looked at me for a minute or two as he tried to find the words to respond to what I had just said. "Why-Why didn't you tell me how *you* felt?" He stumbled over his words a little.

"Because my best friend didn't hesitate to let every female know that you were hers and only hers. You were hers from the moment she spotted you in class that day. She's happy with you—happier than I've seen her with anyone. She's happy with you, so I'm happy *for* her. And if she knew how I felt about you, it would kill her." My eyes grew mistier with each second that I looked up into his face, so I looked away. "So, Aaron, if this is all you brought me here for tonight, you might as well take me back to Howard so I can work on my paper."

Aaron shook his head. "Nah, you're with me tonight, and tonight, my boy, Maxwell, is throwing a party. We don't gotta get all dressed up or anything—it's more of a get-together. You know, people drinking, dancing, playing cards, and shit. Just roll with me."

I looked up at him, into those irresistible eyes. Why didn't I just walk away, stick with my first mind, tell him to forget about me, tell him I couldn't be his friend, and tell him it hurt to know how he felt about me?

Instead of going with my better judgment, I went into his bathroom, threw on a little makeup, did a little something with my hair, and made sure my lip gloss was poppin'.

Aaron took me to his friend's party that night. My eardrums vibrated like a snare drum from the bass coming out of the stereo speakers. Chicks were throwing their asses, twerkin', grinding as hard as they could against the crotch of the males' jeans, sweating out their perms, dressed in next to nothing. The males were holding on for dear life to the women's hips as they were thrust back against the wall. Blunts were being passed around, along with alcohol of every sort. Cigarette and weed smoke filled the room. All in all, it was a typical frat party.

The party was a little too much for me, and I tried to slip away unnoticed, while Aaron was talking and laughing with his friends. He caught my hand just as I tried to sneak past him, and he pulled me back to him.

I looked up at him.

"Hold up, ma. Where you goin', Heaven?" He spoke over the music.

"Outside, where I can breathe and hear myself think. I need some air. Besides, I seem to be a little overdressed for this type of party." I rolled my eyes as a girl in a halter-top and what looked like fuckin' boy shorts walked past us. I looked back up at Aaron. "This ain't even my scene. I don't know why I'm here! Not to mention, there's a lot of people coming here that I know from Howard." I slid my hand from his.

"So?" Aaron took a sip from his cup.

"*So?*" I watched his lips as he drank. "What do you mean 'so'? You're not mine, so I have no business being here with you. You're dating Charlie, and everyone here knows it. What does that make me look like, Aaron?"

Aaron's friends looked at me.

Aaron lowered his cup from his lips. "Like you came to have a good time."

I shook my head. "I can't do this." I backed away.

"Hold up, shorty. Let's go outside." He took me by the waist.

We stood face-to-face outside on Maxwell's balcony. I wrapped my arms around myself. I looked up at Aaron as he drank the last sip of Hennessy from his cup. I shivered, hands tucked in the sleeves of my Old Navy hoodie.

Aaron looked at me as he tossed his cup in a small trash can in the corner of the balcony.

"That hoodie is cute, but I know you ain't warm in it. You wanna wear my coat, shorty?" He didn't even wait for me to answer. He took off his coat and placed it over my shoulders.

"This is hell-a-awkward, Aaron," I whispered, looking up at him.

Aaron looked at me as he leaned over, resting his forearms on the balcony railing. "How do you think that *I* feel telling you everything that I said to you tonight? I feel stupid as fuck."

I looked at him. "So . . . How do you expect me to react to you now that I know how you feel? Aaron, you're with Charlie. That, alone, is hard for me to deal with. Now I have to deal with the fact that my best friend's boyfriend wants to get to know me better. And the worst part about this whole situation is that . . . I wanna get to know you too, more than you could ever know."

Aaron's eyes sparkled under the moonlight.

I laughed to myself, thinking of the lonely nights I spent thinking, dreaming, and yearning for Aaron's touch. "Do you know that I used to dream about you?"

Aaron just looked at me, his green eyes searching my face.

"I wanted you in the worst way, but I knew better. Not to mention my heart hasn't fully recovered from that summer before sophomore year when that jerk left me. Your friends weren't lying. It took me years to get over Jamie. Sometimes, I'm not really sure I'm over him, but I've learned to deal with the fact that he's never coming back." My vision was getting hazy. I tried to fight back the tears.

Aaron laughed a little. "So, you *are* still in love with him?"

I shook my head. "A heart never fully recovers from the pain of losing someone, Aaron, if that's what you mean. He left me when I really needed him. I never got any closure, but I'm good. When I met you, my heart started to feel something again. I think that you are amazing. I used to go to all of your basketball games. I didn't see anyone else out there on that court but you. The way you would glide across the hardwood floor of that basketball court looked as if you were floating on air." I leaned over the balcony next to him.

Aaron looked at me, his eyes searching my face. "You make me sound like a star."

"You *are* a star." I looked away from him. "Charlie doesn't know how lucky she is to have someone like you. And this right here, us talking this close, is teasing the hell out of me. I don't want a damn snack, Aaron—I want a whole *meal*."

Aaron laughed a little.

My eyes sparkled. "You laugh, but I'm dead serious. I'm in love with my best friend's boyfriend. Ain't *this* a bitch?"

Aaron looked at me. "Yeah . . . It is."

I really wanted to cry because the more I stood there next to him, breathing in the same air that he was breathing, the more I wanted him to be mine. I was in love with him, and that alone was wrong.

I looked back at him. "Can we get out of here? I don't care where we go. I just can't risk anyone seeing us together and word getting back to Charlie. I don't wanna hurt her," I whispered.

Aaron looked at me as he took his keys out of his pocket. "Yeah, let's roll out before I get too drunk to drive."

I felt awkward being alone with Aaron that night. No matter where we went, I felt uncomfortable. We ended up going back to his apartment. We sat in his weight room that night, dressed in a tank top and sweatpants. We talked about everything you can think of that people talk about when they're trying to get to know more about each other. I found out more about him that night than I had in the past two years I'd known him.

"I had no idea that you could cook!" I squealed. "That's so exciting! I can't believe Charlie never told me that! If I had a dude who could cook, bruh, I'd be telling everyone who *didn't* have a man who could cook that I had one who could!"

Aaron grinned, sitting down next to me on his exercise bench. He handed me a bottle of Lipton's green tea. "I was raised by my five aunts and grandmother—hell yeah, your boy can cook. You name it, and I'll cook it. I'll have to invite you over for dinner some time." He threw his left leg over the bench and sat facing me.

I blushed a little, holding my hoodie in my hands. "Aaron, this is the hardest thing I've ever done. I've been feeling you from day one. It was just a fantasy of mine to be sitting here, this close to you, breathing the same air, smelling your cologne, listening to your sexy voice. I could have never imagined that you actually wanted to know me the same way that I wanted to get to know you. I never would have thought you felt for me what I feel for you. I haven't felt this way in a long time. This is so wrong, but it feels so right. And all I can think about is you touching me."

Shit, I guess all Aaron needed was an invitation. He took the hoodie and bottle of tea from my hands and placed them on the carpet.

He held my hips, pulling me closer to him, in between his legs.

My heart pounded in my chest, thumping against my rib cage. I hadn't been touched in four years the way that he touched me that night. "Aaron, no, we can't." I wanted to cry.

Aaron's said, "I can't keep my mind off touching you either. I wanna kiss you too—can I do that?" He held my face in his hands.

Before I could pull away from him, his lips were pressed against mine. His silky lips embraced mine, and I nearly melted. His lips were so smooth and delicate. The insides of my thighs began to twitch and tingle, and I could feel my panties instantly dampen.

I pulled my lips from his, getting up from the bench as fast as I could. "Take me back to my dorm, Aaron! I'm not even supposed to be here!" I cried, rushing toward the door.

Aaron got up from the bench, catching me by the arm before I could reach the door to escape. He pulled me back to him.

I looked up at him as he held my face in his hands. My body was on fire. I dreamed of that moment, and there it was—a reality. A *cruel* reality. Tears slid down my face as he slid his hands around my bare waist. The warmth from his hands soothed my soul. He loosened the drawstring to my pants as he gently sucked on my bottom lip. He was killing me.

I pulled my lips from his and shook my head at him, my heart pounding and my lungs gasping for air. "Aaron, this is wrong—what are we doing?" I panted. "You have a girlfriend—she's my *best* friend! She took me into her home when I had no place else to go!" I could hear my cell phone vibrating in my purse, and I knew it was Charlie.

Aaron's eyes searched mine as he slid my pants over my hips. "Heaven, I apologize, but I've been wanting to do this for over two years—can I just touch it? That's all I wanna do."

I shook my head, my chest heaving in and out. I was breathing so hard, I thought I was going to hyperventilate. My lips were saying, "No, I can't do this," but my body language was screaming, "Yes, just *take* it, dude, *all* of it."

"That's it, Heaven, I promise." Aaron's eyes hungrily searched my face.

I looked up into his face, lips trembling, and body shaking.

He slid my panties over my hips, and they fell to the floor. I looked at him as he looked down at the Brazilian wax that I had done a few days earlier. He bit his lip as if he couldn't wait to get his hands in my pussy. He looked back up into my eyes, and then lifted my body up, wrapping my legs around his waist. He walked back over to the bench, holding me up by my thighs. He sat back down on the bench, gripping my thigh with one hand and the other hand gripping my behind.

"Why would you wanna start something that there's no way we can finish, Aaron?" I whispered, tears already sliding down my face.

"I ask myself every day why I didn't start *sooner*." His eyes focused on my face.

Tears continued to cascade down my cheeks. I shook my head, "Why are you doing this to me?"

"All I wanna do is touch you, shorty. That's it. I just wanna hear you scream. And when you come, I'll stop. I promise. So, will you scream for me?" He slid the index finger and middle finger of his right hand inside of me, making sure to swirl his fingers along the way, all the way, until his fingertips tickled my cervix.

Beads of sweat instantly formed along my hairline. "Aaron!" I moaned, grabbing on to his biceps with what little strength I had.

"How does it feel?" His hand rested on my behind and outer labia, as his fingers gently massaged the walls within me. The insides of my thighs were slippery wet, and fluid trickled down them.

"Why-why does something so wrong have to feel *so* good, Aaron?" I stumbled over my words, tears tumbling down my cheeks. I sunk my nails into his biceps. "Aaron, please stop. You have no idea what you're doing to me." My thighs began to tremble, and every blood vessel in my body began to twitch.

Aaron took his other hand and began to massage my clit.

My whole body trembled, and I screamed with delight.

"I'm not gonna stop until I feel that pussy come on my fingers, Heaven." Aaron gently kissed my trembling lips. He started to massage my clit a little faster and pumped his fingers in and out of me at the same time.

My whole body jumped, and the veins between my thighs pulsated. Aaron continued to rub and penetrate my insides with his fingers until I let out a sigh. I exploded from the inside out. My legs trembled uncontrollably against his waist.

Aaron stopped rubbing my clit but continued to penetrate my body with his fingers until I screamed and came all over again. The walls over my pussy caved in, pulsating around his fingers.

My body fell against his, and I laid my head on his shoulder, as my whole body pulsated. My vagina cried out in ecstasy all over his fingers.

His whole hand was saturated. I cried on his shoulder. I lifted my head from his shoulder, looking up into his face. His fingers still rested inside of me. My sugary walls throbbed around his fingers.

Aaron slowly took his fingers from out of me; then he slid those exact same two fingers inside of his mouth. He sucked the sticky fluid of my vagina from his fingers, satisfied with its taste. "*Shit,*" he whispered. "You taste just like I imagined you would."

Tears covered my face. I felt guilty as hell, and it was blatantly obvious that Aaron was ready for more. Though I wanted his hands, lips, tongue, and dick all over me, I knew what I was letting that boy do to me was wrong, *dead* wrong.

Aaron gripped my thighs tightly in his hands, as he licked his lips.

My lips trembled. "Aaron, this is wrong, and I want you *so* bad, but this is *so* wrong."

He started to loosen the drawstring to his pants as if he didn't hear me.

"Aaron!" I cried, pushing him, stopping him from loosening his pants. "Take me to my aunt's house *now!*" I got up from his lap, going over to where my panties and pants lay on the floor.

He sat there on the bench, catching his breath. He watched as I cried to myself, putting on my panties, then my sweatpants. I slid into my socks, then into my Nikes. I kneeled down to tie my laces.

Aaron got up from the bench and walked over to me.

I stood up, backing away from him. I could smell myself all over him.

He caught my hand, pulling me closer to him. "Heaven," he whispered to me.

Tears stained my face.

"Heaven, I love you," he whispered.

I cried aloud, pulling from him. I had been waiting over two years to hear him say those words to me, but when he finally said those three words, it hurt like nothing I'd ever experienced.

"Take me to my aunt's house *now,* Aaron! I'm not supposed to be here! Why did I let you bring me here? Why did I let you touch me like that? Why?" I cried. "Why am I in love with my best friend's boyfriend? This isn't supposed to be happening!" I pushed him.

Aaron looked as if he wanted to cry as well. He knew that what we did was wrong and that there was nothing we could do to take it back.

"Aaron, this is the *last* time that anything like this will *ever* happen!" I sobbed. "I don't wanna see you, I don't wanna talk to you, and I don't wanna know you!"

Aaron shook his head. "You don't mean that."

"I love you, and I'm not supposed to! You touched me, and you weren't supposed to! You're not supposed to love me when you're with my best friend, Aaron! We don't belong together! You got who you need! Forget about me—forget about us!" I pushed past him and walked out of the room.

Aaron dropped me off at my aunt Joyce's house that night. We didn't say one word to each other on the ride over. My mind was racing. I silently cried to myself, wondering how I could let Aaron touch me and kiss me the way that he did. He licked the juices from my vagina from his fingers. He tasted my insides, and he liked it. He enjoyed pleasing me, and no feeling had ever felt better. I couldn't erase the thought of it from my mind. I could still feel his fingers inside of me, and I could still taste his tongue inside of my mouth.

When we got to my aunt's house, I darted out of the car, slamming the door behind me, and I raced up my aunt's porch steps without even saying good-bye to the poor boy. I couldn't even look at him after what we'd done. I didn't have to knock at my aunt's door. She stepped out of her new black BMW, dressed in a black Gucci dress with matching stilettos. I knew she'd just gotten home from one of her many hot dates.

I stood there on the porch as she approached me.

"Baby, what's wrong?" she asked, and then looked across the yard at Aaron's maroon Chevy Impala speeding off the down the street.

I cried, throwing my arms over her shoulders. I cried my eyes out, burying my face in her neck.

Chapter 2

Closer

Ne'Vaeh

I sat down on the leather sofa in my aunt's living room the next morning. I didn't get any sleep the night before, and it was going to take a gallon of cappuccino to keep me awake all day so that I could finish my Humanities 101 paper.

My cousin Renée sat down next to me, handing me a cup of toasted almond cappuccino. She was a tall, sexy, brown-skinned girl with hazel-brown eyes and shoulder-length curly hair. Seemed like I was the only one not blessed with hips and ass. Renée looked like a got-damn stripper, her body was so bad. Women paid thousands to have a shape like hers.

She looked at me as I took the cup from her and held it to my lips with both hands. "So," she hesitated, "Mama says you came over late last night."

I nodded, taking sips from the mug.

"We're like sisters, Ne'Vaeh. You know you can always talk to me," she assured me.

I looked at her. She was right. When Aunt Joyce took my brother, sister, and me in for those months my mother spent in rehab, it was Renée who kept me from pulling my hair out. She was there to comfort us. If it wasn't for her, I would have never made it through junior high and some of high school. She never left me alone when I was feeling down. When I needed to talk, she was always there to listen, so I had to tell her about Aaron.

I turned to her as I placed my cup down on her glass coffee table. I took a deep breath to calm myself. "Well, you know Charlie's boyfriend named Aaron, right?"

Renée looked at me and nodded. "Hell yeah, I know him! He's the finest boy on the basketball team at College Park! His ass is gonna end up getting drafted! Charlie says there are already about two or three teams after his ass right now! What about him?"

I sighed, not sure how to tell her what Aaron did to me the night before. "He-He came to my dorm room last night. He said he needed to talk to me. He's *never* come by to talk to me. We've known each other going on three years, and we have *never* talked one-on-one."

Renée looked up at me. She scooted to the edge of her seat as if she were bracing herself for what I was about to tell her.

I hesitated. "He-He took me to his apartment. I wasn't feeling it, so we went to a party. I wasn't feeling *that* because too many people I knew started walking through the door. We ended up *back* at his apartment. No one was there but the two of us. And while we were there, he told me that he wishes he would have chosen me instead of Charlie." My eyes dampened.

Renée's eyes widened. "Ne'Vaeh, *tell* me that you didn't sleep with that girl's boyfriend!"

I hesitated. "No, but it was close enough."

"*How* close?" She folded her arms.

I looked at her. "He licked my pussy juice from his fingers—*that's* how far it got, Renée."

Renée shook her head in disgust, not really sure what to say to me. She was pissed—more like disappointed—at me. She looked at me. "Charlie loves that boy—you know how much that boy means to that girl! You let the nigga play in your pussy? Charlie is gonna kick ya ass!"

"I love him too, Renée!" I cried. "What was I supposed to do when he touched me? What was I supposed to do when he kissed me? What was I supposed to do when he told me that he loved me? I've wanted that boy from day one, and when I finally had him to myself—telling me that he felt the exact same way about me—what was I supposed to do? He knew what he was doing to me! He made it feel *so* right, when he *knew* it was wrong!"

Renée looked at me, her eyes sparkling. "You're my baby cousin, and I love you like you were my own little sister, so I'm just gonna have to say this to you: you are stupid as hell if you actually think that this situation is gonna work out in your favor. Your best friend's boyfriend—*really*, Ne'Vaeh? I'm twenty-six years old, and I have *never* seen a situation like this work out. Charlie's gonna end up hurt, Aaron's gonna end up hurt, and *your* ass is gonna end up hurt! You've been through so much shit in your life, and Charlie has been there through a lot of it to help you through it. And this shit is how you repay her? You're a whole lot smarter than this shit, Ne'Vaeh! I don't even know why you're crying."

Tears slid down my cheeks, but I quickly dried them away. "I don't wanna hurt Charlie. I told Aaron that I can't see him anymore. And I know that after what happened last night, I'll never be able to look Charlie in the eyes again. How could I do this to her? How in the hell did I fall for my own best friend's boyfriend?"

Renée shook her head at me. "Ever since Jamie left, girl, you have been totally lost. My girl, Kristina, said she saw him a few weeks ago when she went to visit her cousin at Memphis State. She said Jamie even asked about you."

I shook my head, heart palpitating in my chest. The sound of his name still sent blood rushing to my heart. "Can we *not* talk about Jamie right now, Renée?"

Renée sighed, getting up from off of the couch. "C'mon, cuz, let's go get something to eat. You know I can't talk about depressing shit like this too long. Let's go get our grub on."

I looked up at her, tears saturating my face.

She looked down at me and grinned. Renée's heart didn't know how to withstand pain, hurt, or anger. She wouldn't allow herself to feel any type of misery. Whenever she felt even the slightest twinge of any emotion that she couldn't handle, she'd snap right out of it. I loved how she was able to turn her emotions on and off like a light switch. She hated pain, and she refused to let herself experience it. She held my hand, pulling me up from the couch.

***

Renée called up a few of her friends that morning to join us at IHOP. They sat there laughing and talking about the crazy situations that they happened to get themselves out of that week. I, on the other hand, sat there pushing my food around on my plate, trying to figure my way out of *my* crazy situation.

Renée eased her laughing when she noticed that I wasn't eating. "I thought that was your favorite meal," she commented.

I looked down at the scrambled eggs with extra cheese, turkey bacon extra crispy, two pancakes, and hash browns that sat on my plate, untouched. Aaron knew what I ate for breakfast. He knew so much about me, when I barely knew him.

"Ne'Vaeh, food is *not* free. I paid nine eighty-nine for that meal. Shit, that's over three gallons of gas!"

Her friends giggled. Renée could literally "make a dollar out of fifteen cents." She was the cheapest person I knew. She brought her own food to the movie theater, used every drop of toothpaste, diluted hot sauce with water, and only bought clothes off the clearance rack. She was one of those girls who counted out seven fifty in pennies at the register. She was embarrassing, but homegirl was never broke.

I looked up at her. "I'll eat it, and if I don't, I'll pay you back. No worries."

"Ne'Vaeh, Charlie is supposed to be going with me tomorrow morning to pick up a few things for your party. I tried calling her, but she's not answering my calls. When is she coming back?" Kristina asked. Kristina was a pretty, brown-skinned, big-boned girl with a round face and deep dimples. She was in graduate school at College Park, maintaining a 3.8 GPA.

I looked at her. "She's supposed to be here tomorrow morning at eleven o'clock."

Renée looked at me. She knew that I hated the thought of Charlie coming back so soon. I didn't know how I was going to face her after what I'd done with her boyfriend.

Kristina looked at me, and then over my shoulder. She squinted her eyes to get a better look at what she had spotted. "Hey, isn't that Aaron?" she asked, pointing in the direction she was looking.

My heart fluttered in my chest as Renée and her friends turned in their seats to get a good look at the famous Aaron Whitehaven. I didn't even have to turn around to know that it was him. The whole restaurant clapped their hands and cheered for him and his entourage as they walked through the dining area.

Renée looked at me. She knew that I felt uneasy. "Girl, come with me to the restroom real quick."

I nodded, springing up from my seat. I turned around just in time to see Aaron walking right up to my table. I gasped, placing my hand over my chest as he walked up to me.

Aaron stood before me, dressed in a white Polo shirt, dark denim jeans, and fresh white Nikes. He looked fresher than a muthafucka, fine as hell, but the boy still wasn't mine.

"What up, Heaven?"

I was speechless, out of breath. My mouth fell open, but nothing came out.

"Oh, so you don't see the rest of us sitting here?" Renée's friend, Adina, rolled her eyes, popping a grape from her fruit cup into her mouth.

Aaron looked over my shoulder at our table, and then at Renée. "Hello, ladies. How's breakfast? Y'all bought enough food—damn, is there anything left for me and my boys?"

The girls giggled.

Renée rolled her eyes. "We were just about to bounce. We got a lot of business to attend to today. So, if you'd excuse us. . . ."

Aaron looked at me. "Can we go somewhere and talk?"

I shook my head, my bottom lip trembling. "I don't think that's such a good idea, Aaron."

"What do you have planned for today, ma?" he asked.

"Why you worrying about all that? Her plans ain't with *you*. She's comin' with me and my girls to Hair Expressions. Her birthday party is tomorrow, so a full makeover is on me. If you ain't payin', don't worry about where she's goin'." Renée folded her arms. There she was again, being her usual loud, talk-so-the-whole-wide-world-hears-her, smart-ass self.

"Damn, Renée—why you gotta treat the boy like that? He just asked the girl a simple question." Kristina shook her head at Renée.

"I'm just sayin', why's he worried about what she's doin'? He ain't goin' with us." Renée looked up at Aaron. "You need to be worried about what *Charlie's* doin'. My cousin is turning nineteen tomorrow. We're throwing her a big birthday party tomorrow. We still have a lot of setting up to do, and *you're* holdin' us up."

I sighed. I was turning nineteen, not really an age to look forward to. You're on your way out of your teens, but still not of legal age to drink. However, with cousins like mine, getting drunk was never an issue. Renée and her friends planned to take me to a club that Sunday night. I swear, Renée knew every bartender in Maryland, D.C., and Virginia, so getting drunk was *not* going to be a problem. I needed a drink. Shit, I could have used a whole *bottle*.

"Am I invited?" Aaron whispered to me.

"*Hell* no," Renée spoke up for me, irritating the hell out of me.

"Renée!" I exclaimed. "Damn, I can speak for myself!"

Renée looked at me, folding her arms, weight shifted on to her left leg. *Oh, so now you wanna just talk to him?* was written all over her face. I knew she wanted to call me out in front of him for getting loud with her, but she remained as calm as she could.

I turned to Aaron. "Aaron, today is really not a good day. My family has a lot planned for me, I have a term paper to finish, not to mention, *Charlie* is flying back in town in the morning, and I am supposed to be meeting her there. So whatever it is you need to talk to me about will have to wait until another day."

Aaron wasn't backing down. "C'mon, Heaven. You know we need to talk, and you know what we need to talk about. You're not gonna be busy all day and night, shorty—don't try to play me. If you don't come find me, I'm coming to find *you*."

I knew he wouldn't back down. From what Charlie told me about him, when Aaron had his mind made up, it was made up, and there was no changing his mind. The night before proved how determined he was to get what he wanted. I couldn't spend the rest of my day worrying about what Aaron had to say to me.

I turned to Renée. "Renée, I'll be right—"

Renée shook her head, cutting me off. "*No,* Ne'Vaeh! What the fuck! We have hair appointments! Whatever he has to say to you is irrelevant in this situation, and you know it! I had to book these appointments a fuckin' month and a half in advance! If we miss this appointment, Ne'Vaeh, I swear to—"

I cut her off, "Renée, please, stop, okay? I'll be right back. I promise."

I stood outside the restaurant, facing Aaron. I looked up at him. "Aaron, why did you show up here this morning?" I asked.

He looked down into my face. "Because I knew you'd be here."

I shook my head. "I mean, really, though? In front of my cousin and her friends? You know how much those bitches run their mouth about everyone's business but their own! I can't do this with you today, Aaron." I turned to walk away from him.

He held my arm, pulling me back to him. "Heaven, please don't walk away."

I pulled from him.

"Just hear me out, shorty," he pleaded.

I looked up at him.

"I, ummm . . . I couldn't stop thinking about last night. I apologize if what I did hurt you, Heaven. I don't wanna hurt anybody. That's not what I'm here for. I'm here to be with you, sweetheart—I know in my heart that you're the one that I wanna be with."

My eyes sparkled.

"I'm sorry if me being in love with you scares you, but it's how I feel, and it was killing me to hold it in." Aaron reached for my hands, but I pulled away. He sighed. "C'mon, Ne'Vaeh, just hear me out."

Once again, tears slid down my face, but I wiped them away as quickly as I could. "I don't wanna hear you out because you're not hearing *me!* I can't have a relationship with my best friend's boyfriend, and you shouldn't even wanna *put* me in this situation! You should have kept this shit to yourself! You shouldn't be in love with your girlfriend's best friend!" The tears kept coming.

Aaron tried to dry my face, but I pushed him away. "Well, tell that to my heart, Heaven. You think I wanna feel this way about a girl who's like a sister to my girlfriend? How I feel isn't lust. I'm not just saying I love you just to be saying this. It took me over two years to build up the strength even to tell you how I feel, Heaven. And to prove to you that I'm not playing, that what I'm saying is real, I'm breaking up with Charlie tomorrow night."

My eyes widened, and my heart was pounding as if it were going to shoot straight out of my chest. "Wh-what did you say? You're gonna do *what?*"

"I'm gonna tell shorty it's over," he restated.

"On my birthday? And why would you do that to her when she just lost her uncle?" I exclaimed.

"Well, when do you suggest I tell her? Is there *really* a right time to tell someone good-bye?" Aaron's eyes searched mine.

I hesitated—I wasn't sure what to say to that.

"I can't be with someone when I'm in love with someone else. It's wrong." Aaron's eyes watered.

I just stood there crying. Charlie was there for me ever since we were six years old. My so-called mother, Juanita, was an alcoholic. She'd drink until she threw up; then she'd drink some more.

When she wasn't drinking, she was mixing all sorts of prescription medication together. She'd pop pills all day long, which would put her to sleep for days at a time. All sorts of people would run in and out of our house. My sister even got molested and sexually assaulted in the process. Even after she was violated and my brother kidnapped, social services still didn't step in. In fact, my mother's doctor continued to prescribe her Percocet for her so-called back pain.

One night, Juanita drank so much and popped so many pills that she damn near lost her mind. She'd abused my brother, my sister, and me all of our lives, but that night, she beat my little brother so bad that he didn't wake up the next morning. My sister ran away that night, and my mother went to prison the next day. I haven't seen my sister since my little brother died six years ago. I was thirteen, Kevin was nine, and Autumn was sixteen at the time. Aunt Joyce couldn't take us in anymore. Uncle Sean—her husband at the time—was getting tired of my mother and her problems. Aunt Joyce cared about my mother and us more than she did about him and his needs. It was too much for him, and he couldn't care less if social services stepped in and put us in foster care.

Charlie's mother wasn't having it. Miss Theresa Campbell, a single mother of four children, took me into her home. They treated me like family. I came to the Campbell house with a book bag that contained a toothbrush, toothpaste, a hairbrush, a bar of Ivory soap, three outfits, and three pairs of underwear, two bras, two pairs of socks, and a diary from Hallmark. Charlie got her mother's credit card and took me shopping for a whole new wardrobe. She spent her allowance on making sure my hair, fingernails, and toenails were done. No friend of hers was going to go around looking tore up from the floor up.

Charlie couldn't relate to what I was going through, but she knew her friend was hurting, and she did whatever she could to keep a smile on my face. There were nights when I cried myself to sleep because I missed my brother and prayed that my sister was somewhere alive. There were nights that I woke up from the same recurring nightmare that I had about finding my brother dead in his bed. Charlie would stay up with me, holding me in her arms, singing me to sleep. Charlie was my mother and my sister, and I couldn't forget everything that she had done for me. Aaron was everything to her. She swore she won her a trophy when she snatched Aaron up. How could I take her happiness when she did all she could to restore mine?

I looked up at Aaron, tears gliding down my cheeks.

Aaron looked down at me. "Ditch your people and ride with me."

I shook my head. I didn't even have to turn around to know that Renée was standing in the glass double doors behind me with her arms folded—I could feel her glare burning a hole in the back of my neck.

"I'll pay to have your hair done, Heaven. Please." His eyes traced my lips.

I shook my head. "Please don't break up with that girl, Aaron! She doesn't deserve this, and you know it." I backed away from him. "Aaron, I gotta go."

Renée and her crew walked through the doors to my rescue. Renée walked past me, linking her arm with mine. I looked back at Aaron as she pulled me off with her.

I sat at my computer that night, working on my Humanities paper. I was finally making progress when there was a knock at my dorm door. I stood up to get it. I thought it was my RA coming by my room to tell me to turn down the music, so when I answered the door, I didn't even bother to look through the peephole. I opened the door . . . and before I could open my mouth to say anything, Aaron walked through, the smell of Ralph Lauren cologne trailing behind him. He made his way over to my bed, sat down, and leaned back against the headboard, making himself at home.

I closed the door and leaned back against it. That boy was killing me oh so softly. . . . He knew it too.

"Aaron, what part of 'we can't do this' don't you understand?" I exclaimed.

"The 'can't' part," he grinned.

"And how the hell did you even get in here?" I asked.

"You know who I am, shorty—you think I really have to *ask* if I can get into a female's dorm? They just ask *me* who I'm there to see, and they let me in, baby girl."

I rolled my eyes. "Sweetie, you can't stay here. I have work to do tonight. I already know that I'm not gonna get any work done this weekend with my party goin' on and everything. I don't have time for this right now."

Aaron sat up in the bed, taking his hat from his head. He was dressed in South Pole—a white shirt and dark denim jeans. His Nikes were clean and scuffless. He was looking fine as wine, and he knew it too. "What do I have to say to get you to go out with me tonight? I mean, look at you—you got your hair done, nails done, toes done. You're looking too good to stay in, Heaven. Let's go to the club. We can go with a group of my friends so nobody will think we're there together, bae. C'mon."

I shook my head, walking over to my desk to plug in my laptop because the battery was dying. "Aaron, don't call me 'bae.' And you got a lot of nerve comin' here after what happened at IHOP."

Aaron reached for my hand and in an instant, I was sitting on his lap. My heart pounded in my chest as he slid his hands around my waist.

"I meant what I said when I told you that I can't be with Charlie anymore. I'm breaking up with her tomorrow night. I know you ain't tryin' to hear that, but it's the truth."

"You can do whatever you want, Aaron, as long as you don't break up with her because of me," I whispered. "We can't be together, so stop torturing me like this!"

Aaron's hands gripped my waist. "I shouldn't even ask you to be my girl when my soon-to-be ex-girl is your best friend. I'm wrong for that, and I apologize. When Charlie asked me out on that first date, I should have told her that I wasn't feelin' her, but that I was feelin' *you*."

I got up from Aaron's lap and turned to him.

He stood from the bed, looking down into my face.

I looked up at him. "We were wrong for what went down at your apartment, Aaron, and you know it. You are such a freak."

Aaron grinned, biting his lip. "And you like it too, don't you?"

"You know what you're doin' to me, Aaron—I don't have to tell you. I'm just asking you to *think* about what you're doin'." I looked into his eyes.

Aaron pulled me closer to him by my waist. "I *have* thought about it, trust me."

I blushed. "Slow down, Aaron, that's all I'm asking. Stop calling me, stop coming by my dorm, stop teasing me, stop looking at me like this, stop touching me like this. This is too much. So just keep your hands, your eyes, your hormones, and your thoughts off of me, Aaron."

"C'mon, Heaven, I promise I'll get you back here in time to finish your paper," he pleaded.

I shook my head, looking up into his face. "Sorry, Aaron, but no."

He sighed. "Heaven, okay, I'm just gonna be honest with you. Yeah, you know I wanna fuck the shit out of you. Yeah, I wanna kiss you, touch you, taste you, be with you. Just let me take you out tonight and let whatever happens just happen. I promise you that if you don't enjoy yourself with me tonight, I'll leave you alone. I won't call you, I won't text you, I won't e-mail you—I'll keep my distance. I'll back off."

My eyes glistened, and my heart raced. My mind kept telling me, *No, don't go out with that boy because he's nothing but trouble. Look at him, look how fine he is. He knows you want him. He knows his touch makes you weak. He knows his very presence makes your panties wet.*

But my heart—my heart wasn't trying to hear that shit that my mind was saying.

Aaron went to his car to wait on me while I got dressed. I threw on some stilettos, some skinny jeans, a spaghetti-strap shirt, and a dark denim jacket. I grabbed my purse and keys and darted out the door. I knew what I was doing was crazy, but I went along with it anyway. About ten of Aaron's friends met us at the club that night. There were so many people there that no one really noticed that I was there, sitting at the bar with Aaron. Aaron and his crew knew the owners of the club, not to mention the bartender was Aaron's best friend and roommate's cousin. So you already know the bartender kept the glasses full all night.

Aaron's friends were scattered throughout the club, having a good ol' time. Meanwhile, I sat there at the bar, trying to drown the thoughts of Aaron playing between my thighs from my head. It had taken me years to get over losing Jamie. I did everything that I could not to let anyone else into my heart, but there I was, my heart infatuated with even the mere thought of Aaron. He was amazing, perfect in every way. What did Charlie do to push him to me?

"Heaven, you good?" Aaron was grinning, sipping from his glass. "You having a good time?"

I nodded, taking a gulp of whatever sweet-tasting alcoholic drink the bartender gave me. "Umm-hmm."

I turned to him a little. "If Charlie didn't leave town this week, when were you gonna tell me about your feelings for me, Aaron?"

He didn't respond. He just drank from his glass.

I rolled my eyes. "Charlie must have really done something bad for you to build up the nerve to talk to me, Aaron. And don't try to blame it on the fact that she turned your idea of marriage down either."

Aaron just looked at me for a few seconds before responding. "She just wasn't you, that's all."

I shook my head. "You have to do better than that, Whitehaven." I pushed my bangs from my eyes.

Aaron sighed. "I just got tired of lying to myself, Heaven. I got tired of telling myself that I could make it work with her. I got tired of hearing about muthafuckas that she slept with. I got tired of getting into fights in the locker room with niggas who used to sleep with shorty. It would have been nice to know why she was so popular *before* we became official, know what I mean? How the fuck would you feel if you were dating someone, and every time you turned around, bitches were in your face, telling you how, when, and where they fucked your dude? You'd get tired of defending your relationship too. . . ."

I shook my head. Well, Charlie didn't actually give anyone a chance to tell the boy the truth about her. She cuffed the man thirty seconds after he walked into our classroom. He was "hers" thirty seconds into their first conversation. It wasn't my place to tell Aaron that his girl was Superhead, was it?

"When I asked around about you, everyone said you were a good girl. That after Jamie left, you put up this wall, shutting everyone out. When I asked about Charlene, muthafuckas got quiet. It wasn't until I got cool with Ashton that his girl, Alisha, started telling me the truth about the girl I was with." Aaron took a sip from his glass.

I looked at him. True, Charlie should have told him the truth about her history, but I mean—come on—Aaron was fine as hell. He was talented, smart, and charming. Everyone loved to be around him. Up until he approached me about his feelings, he was a one-woman man, despite all the hoes that were up in his face every day. Most girls would have done exactly what Charlie did—keep their past a secret.

"Nobody's perfect, Aaron. That girl changed for you. She would lie, die, and fight for you. Charlie loves you, you know she does." I took another sip, my glass almost on E.

"Nah," Aaron shook his head, "she loves dancin', kickin' it with her friends, partyin', cheerleadin', clubs, fame, attention, recognition, makeup, and shit." Aaron looked at me as I drank the last sip from my glass. "I'm glad you decided to kick it with me and my people tonight, Heaven. It's good to see you open up a little. That dude, Jamie, did some serious damage, ma."

"Excuse me," I signaled the bartender to come over. "I need another drink. Anything sweet." I looked at Aaron. "I'm *really* not in the mood to talk about him. In fact, I haven't talked about him in over four years, and I'm not about to start talking about him now with you—*especially* with you." The bartender slid me a Strawberry Daiquiri topped with whipped cream and a cherry.

Aaron watched as I plopped the cherry in my mouth, then started to drink from the glass. "I can hear your heart, Heaven. It needs someone." He shook his head at me.

I fought back the tears. I knew that I needed love, but Aaron belonged to someone else. He was right. I did need to talk to someone about my feelings. Charlie was always too busy to talk to. The only thing she was concerned with when it came to me was helping her pass. Renée was about the only one who didn't make me feel like shit when I brought up Jamie's name years earlier. I didn't hang around Alisha or her girls that often because they were always running their mouth about other people's business, and I didn't have the time to get caught up in their shit. My family members were more concerned with my education than with my heart. I didn't have anyone other than my therapist to talk to, and she didn't do shit but say "Hmm" while probably writing, *"this bitch is crazy"* on her notepad.

Aaron looked at me, waiting for me to say something about Jamie.

I shook my head. "I don't know what to say other than I loved him, and he left me. I gave my heart to him, and he left me, Aaron. One night we were making love, the next day he was gone. All I know is when I woke up, he wasn't next to me. I woke up to his sister throwing my clothes at me, telling me that I had to get dressed and get the fuck out of her house. I was a few months shy of turning fifteen. True, I had no business having sex. But the look on her face when she told me that her brother deserved better than me is still imprinted in my mind. She always thought I was holding him back, that he lost focus when we started dating. No, he lost focus when his own family didn't support him or his dreams. I know you've seen him on TV, playing college football. He's doing the damn thing now. I don't know what motivation he has now, but I guess his sister was right—all he needed was to get away from me to complete his goals." Tears began to slide down my cheeks.

Aaron's eyes traced my face. "Nah, Heaven, there has to be more to that story."

I shook my head, drying my face. "Well, whatever it is, I hope the nigga is happy, because I'm miserable! I don't know how to love or be loved!

It's been four years, and the only person I've managed to fall for is my best friend's boyfriend!" I put my glass to my lips, drinking it to the last drop.

Before I could wipe the whipped cream from my lips, Aaron held my face in his hands, wiping the cream from my face with his thumbs. Yet again, he licked the cream from his fingers.

"And cute little shit like that doesn't help, Aaron," I sighed, still holding the glass in my hands.

He laughed a little. "Heaven, I told you that I was gonna show you a good time tonight, and that's what I plan on doing. So, do you wanna dance with me?" He took a sip from his glass then set it on the bar.

I looked up at him as he licked the liquor from his lips. My favorite love song came on serenading the club at the very moment that he asked me to dance. My heart was racing, my lips and hands were trembling, and my stomach was doing fuckin' backflips.

Aaron grinned, taking the glass from my hands and setting it on the bar. He got up from his seat, then pulled me up from mine by my hands. He led me out onto the dance floor. As soon as we were in the middle of the crowd, he turned to me, pulling my body up against his.

We hadn't danced together since our senior prom, and even then, it wasn't to a slow song. I went to prom alone, and I didn't have anyone to dance with. Aaron grabbed me off the wall and took me out in the middle of the dance floor. I had to admit, he had the moves. He could dance his ass off. He loved to have fun. He was always smiling, and I always loved that about him.

That night at the club, there we were, hormones raging, hearts racing, palms sweating. Aaron gripped my hips in his hands, and I lay my head up against his chest, listening to his heartbeat. I danced with him until my feet hurt. I drank with him and his friends until I couldn't stand on my own. I hate to admit it, but I had a great time with Aaron that night. He didn't flirt with me, he didn't try to kiss or touch me inappropriately, and he didn't act as if we were anything other than friends. I hadn't opened up about my feelings for Jamie in years, and it felt good to talk to someone who actually gave a damn about my feelings.

I enjoyed myself a little too much that night, because it wasn't until around 2:30 that morning that I decided that I had had enough. I accidentally grabbed the wrong set of keys that night when I left my dorm room—I grabbed my spare car key instead of grabbing my room key. There wouldn't be anyone at the front desk of the dorm to let me in at that time of night. I had no choice but to go back to Aaron's crib with him.

Chapter 3

Getting into Heaven

Ne'Vaeh

The last thing I remember from that night is waking up on Aaron's sofa. I pushed my hair from my face, looking up to see Aaron asleep on the couch across from me. I peeled myself from the sofa. My head was throbbing. My shoes and jacket were off. I stood from the couch only to fall straight back to the floor, hitting my knee on the damn corner of the coffee table. I didn't let out a peep, but the sound of me knocking against the table and falling to the floor woke Aaron from his deep sleep.

His eyes opened. After seeing me on the floor, he instantly sat up from the couch and got up, making his way over to me. He helped me from the floor, even though I was trying to push him away. "Too much fun last night, huh, Heaven?" he smirked, helping me back to the sofa.

I looked at him as I pushed my hair from my face. "I bumped my knee on your fuckin' coffee table," was all I could think of to say.

Aaron laughed aloud. "Which knee—this one?" He started rubbing my left knee with his big, warm, strong hands.

My whole body blushed, and I pushed his hand away. I looked up at him. He was dressed in a wife-beater and gray sweats. He smelled as if he had just stepped out of the shower, like fresh Irish Spring.

"What-what time is it?" I asked.

He looked at me, then down at his watch. "It's 7:30."

"Someone should be at the front desk at the dorm to let me in around 8:00, so maybe we should get going. I have to get dressed. I have a long day. I had a little too much to drink last night, and my head is pounding. My party is tonight, so I have to do something to get rid of this migraine," I said, watching Aaron's eyes trace my lips.

"Let me fix you some breakfast before we roll out, shorty." He got up from the sofa.

I sighed, slowly getting up from the sofa, careful not to bump my knee again on the way up. "Aaron, please, just—"

"Don't act like you're not hungry." Aaron made his way over to the refrigerator. "It won't take me long to hook up some French toast, eggs, and bacon, shorty."

We sat side by side on Aaron's couch that morning eating breakfast. The French toast was amazing, made from scratch. The eggs had been scrambled just right, and the bacon was crisped to perfection. We both sat there eating, not saying a word to each other. I looked up at Aaron, just when his tongue slid across his silky lips, licking away the maple syrup that coated them. Instantly, thoughts of Aaron sucking my pussy juice from his fingers flashed through my mind.

Aaron felt me looking at him. "Is the reason why you haven't slept with anyone these past four years because you've been waiting on me, Heaven?"

My heart jumped in my chest. "What? What makes you think that I haven't slept with anyone?"

Aaron smirked, looking up at me.

My whole body blushed. "You know, you're real fuckin' arrogant, Aaron." But it was true. Though I knew I couldn't have Aaron, I wanted him badly. I found myself comparing him to everybody who tried to get my number. If a man didn't walk, talk, think, act, or even smell like Aaron, he didn't have a chance.

Aaron grinned. "I'm just sayin', Heaven. A nigga can just tell."

I rolled my eyes. "For your information, I *have* slept with someone before, Aaron. I told you that shit last night. Yeah, it's been a few years, but I'm in *no* way waiting on you to take my virginity. That was taken years ago, *thank you,* Mr. Ego."

Aaron laughed a little then continued eating.

I sat there, eating nervously. He knew he was driving me crazy. He knew that I wanted his lips all over mine. He knew that I wanted him to fuck the shit out of me. I tried my damnedest to remain calm, but my emotions were draining through my pores. My palms began to sweat. My limbs began to tremble. It soon became difficult to swallow.

Aaron laughed a little watching me struggle to cut the French toast into little pieces. He took the fork from my hand and started cutting the French toast for me. He looked up at me, turning to face me, and he held the fork up to my lips.

I shook my head.

"Open your mouth, shorty," he whispered.

My lips trembled as I opened them, and he slid the moist French toast through my lips.

I chewed and swallowed hard as I watched him eat from my plate.

Aaron looked at me as he licked syrup from his lips again. "You know I can't stop thinking about that night I touched your pussy, Heaven."

I shook my head, holding my hand over my heart. "Please, Aaron, no, I'm begging you not to do this." He was driving my hormones up the fuckin' wall. "You did such a good job last night of *not* bringing that up. Please, don't bring it up now."

"Your pussy was so tight, wet, sticky, and sweet. That fat pussy tasted like butterscotch . . . shit. Got a nigga's dick hard just thinking about it."

I snatched my fork back. "C-can we *not* discuss this right now? What are you doing, and *why* are you doing it to me? You know you need to stop."

Aaron grinned as his cell phone rang in his pocket. He took it out, looked at it, touched the screen to answer it, then held it to his ear. "Yo?" he answered.

I looked at him.

"Where you at, nigga?" He looked down at his watch; then he looked at me. "Nah, Charlie's not here, but I *do* have company. . . ."

My heart pounded in my chest.

"A'ight, nigga, you just make sure you have my bottle of Grey Goose that you and your fuckin' cousins drank up the other night. Ha-ha, my ass. Have my shit when you get here, a'ight?" Aaron pressed "end" on his phone, then set his phone on the coffee table. He looked at me.

I looked at him.

"My roommate is on his way over with some friends. Said he'd be here in fifteen. We probably gonna fire some shit up, shorty. Not sure if you get down like that or wanna be here for that, but—" He stopped talking, seeing me reach for my purse, shoes, and jacket.

I stood from the couch.

Aaron looked up at me. "Where are you goin' so fast?"

"Back to the dorm. You said that your roommate, Ashton, was on his way over. He and Charlie are like best friends! I don't care what y'all are smokin' on. I don't wanna be here when I'm not even supposed to be here with you." My eyes searched his. "Not to mention, Charlie's flight will be in soon, and Renée is supposed to be picking me up in a few hours to get ready for the party."

Aaron shook his head, standing up from the couch. He reached for me, but I pulled away. He sighed, shaking his head at me. "I just want to say Happy Birthday, baby."

My eyes moistened over. "Thank you."

"Come upstairs with me to my room real quick before you leave—I got somethin' for you."

I shook my head. "Dude, no!"

He grabbed me by the hand anyway, pulling me out of the living room and up the stairs to his room.

Aaron's room was warm and cozy. His bed was dressed in a chocolate-brown and olive-green comforter and quilt. His headboard, footboard, nightstand, desk, and dresser were cherry wood. Posters of his favorite sports stars and beautiful Victoria's Secret models were all over his walls. It was nice to see a black man actually have pictures of *black* women on his wall. He had all of the latest electronic gadgets, from his 42-inch flat-screen TV, to his PlayStation, to his laptop, to his desktop computer, to his stereo system—*everything* was up-to-date.

I looked over on his nightstand, and walked over to it, picking up a picture he had in a frame of Charlie and me together. We were all hugged up, posing, on the day of JV cheerleading tryouts, freshman year in high school. I have to admit, we were looking pretty fly that day. I laughed to myself.

I looked up at Aaron as he walked over to his closet. He must have had fifty boxes of

Jordans stacked on top of his closet shelf, and I don't think he could even fit any more clothes in there. He bent down to pick a gift bag off the floor of his closet. Then he stood back up straight and turned around, walking toward me with the bag.

I looked at him as he held up the sparkly bag. I set my jacket, shoes, and purse on the floor, then took the bag from his hand.

My whole body blushed. "Wha-what's in the bag?"

Aaron grinned, biting his lip, as I reached into the bag.

First, I grabbed a gold box that contained a pair of platinum hoop earrings. Then I pulled out a red velvet box that had a platinum "Heaven" charm hanging from a platinum necklace. Two diamond-studded angel wings enclosed the name.

I looked up at him, tears already sliding from my cheeks. I reached in the bag to pull out a tight-fitted, thigh-high, Coogi sweater dress with a hood, size five. My eyes widened. That dress was three-hundred-fifty bucks at the mall! I know Coogi is a nineties thang, but I loved Coogi, and he knew it too. That gift bag had to contain at least $800 or more worth of gifts.

I looked up at him, not even knowing what to say except, "Why? Why would you spend all of this on me? It's too much. I can't accept this." I started to put everything back in the bag.

Aaron caught my hand.

I looked up at him, tears racing down my face by now.

Aaron shook his head. "Your cousin already told me that I wasn't invited to your party, shorty, so this is the least I can do, since I can't be there."

"Are you kidding me?" I dried my tears, but more followed right behind them. "The *least* you can do? I can't afford things like this. A Coogi dress? I saw this dress at the mall last week, *wishing* I had a dress like this. I couldn't even afford to try the dress on!"

Aaron laughed a little to himself.

I looked up into his face as he held my face in his hands and dried my tears. "Why do you have to be so fuckin' amazing?"

"Are you gonna wear this to your party? Do you have shoes to match the dress? If not, I can go get you some." Aaron's eyes searched mine.

I blushed a little and shook my head. "No, you've done enough. Thank you. I'm sure I can work out something."

"So, you like everything? I don't have such bad taste after all, huh?" Aaron smiled, taking the bag from my hands.

My heart beat stronger for him in my chest as he took the bag and removed the dress from it. He placed the bag on the floor, threw the dress over his shoulder, then pulled me closer to him by the belt loops on my jeans. After that, he started to unsnap my jeans.

I caught his hand. "Whoa, what are you doing?"

"Try this on for me. I wanna see you in it. I can't see you in it tonight, so I just thought I'd get to see you in it now." His eyes traced my bare shoulders.

I sighed. What could it hurt? Whether I was dressed or undressed, Aaron was going to think what he was going to think. It was obvious the man had a vivid imagination. He saw me in the dress before he even gave it to me. He knew my size just by looking at me. He'd never seen me in a dress that tight, but he knew I'd like it.

I unzipped my pants and stepped out of them. I slipped my shirt over my head and tossed it on the floor.

Aaron pulled me closer to him by the elastic waist of my panties, but I put my hands on his chest, pushing him away. He laughed a little as I snatched the dress from his shoulder.

I turned around and walked over to the full-length mirror on his wall. I could feel his eyes roam all over me. I pulled the dress over my head and slid it over my breasts, waist, hips, and over my butt. I looked at my reflection in awe. I looked hot. The V-neckline was low, showing the right amount of cleavage. The dress hugged me in all the right places. I turned around to Aaron, who was already walking toward me.

"So-so what do you think?" I whispered as he pulled me closer to him by my waist.

He gripped my dress in his hands. "I got Magnums, shorty," he whispered back. "I mean *lots* of 'em."

I tried to back away, but he was gripping my dress tight. "You know, just because you bought me a dress doesn't mean you're gonna get some pussy, Aaron. I just wanted to throw that out there."

"So then, what's it gonna take, shorty?"

I shook my head. "Aaron, don't do this, please. I have to go. Thank you for everything, but you *know* this is wrong."

He let go of me, and I pulled the dress up and over my head and walked back over to the bag and my clothes on the floor. I placed the dress back in the bag and picked my jeans up off the floor.

Aaron walked back over to me. "Heaven, ever since that night we kissed, all I can think about is putting this dick inside of you. I keep imagining what my dick going in and out of that pussy must sound like. Yo, I wanna make that pussy *cry*. Shorty, there are so many things I wanna do to you," he had the nerve to tell me.

I started to cry again, about to slide my feet into my pants when Aaron grabbed my arm and took the pants from me, tossing them back to the floor. I tried to pull away from him, but he pulled me closer to him.

"Heaven, you *know* I want you." His eyes glistened. "I mean, not just in this way, but in *every* way."

I looked up at him, lips trembling, as he slid his hands up my back. He unhooked my bra. I shook my head, trying to back away from him, but he moved with me. "Aaron, this is wrong! You *know* this is wrong!"

He held both straps to my bra, pulling the straps from my arms, and from my body. "Heaven, you can't tell me that you don't want me as much as I want you. You *know* you want this dick."

I did. I *did* want the dick, but I still tried to resist him.

I reached for my bra, but he tossed it over in the pile with my jacket, shoes, and purse.

"Aaron, we can't do this," I cried as he slid his shirt over his head, then pulled the drawstring to his pants. He dropped them to the floor then stepped out of them.

Aaron pulled me closer to him. In an instant, I was in his arms, legs wrapped around his waist, and he was carrying me over to his bed. He lay me down on his bed, his body hovering on top of mine, and he gently kissed my lips.

My body melted in his arms. He felt so good. Every hair on my body stood straight up. Every inch of my body was burning hot. My clit was throbbing. My pussy was already dripping wet.

I held his face in my hands, pulling my lips from his. I looked into his face. I could feel his heart beating against my breasts.

"Please, Heaven, I need this. I need you." He gripped my waist in his hands. "If you never wanna see me again, just please, be mine for this one moment." I could feel his dick through his boxers.

I looked into his eyes as he sat up and reached for his nightstand drawer. My body trembled. Aaron stood from the bed, dropping his boxers. I watched as he bit open a Trojan, then slid it on his thick, long, hard, curved penis. He didn't give me a choice. He didn't hear my cries. My body language was all he paid attention to.

I sat up from his bed as he tugged on the reservoir tip of the condom to make sure there was enough room for his semen. That thing was *huge,* and there was no way that I could brace myself enough to be able to handle it. I shook my head as I tried to get up from the bed. "Aaron, we can't do this to her!" I cried out.

Aaron held my thighs, pulling me toward him, causing me to fall back on the bed. He quickly slid my panties from my body, down my thighs, over my calves, and past my ankles. He tossed them on the floor then climbed on top of me. "Heaven, you already knew when you came in this room that I wanted this pussy. You already knew what was gonna happen," he whispered, gently kissing my lips.

"Aaron!" I screamed out, as he held my body against his by my hips. "Wait wait *wait!* I can't—I can't do this!" I cried, feeling like I was going to have a heart attack.

Aaron gently kissed my neck as he gripped my thighs. He didn't hear my cry for him to stop. "Can't" wasn't in his vocabulary. "No" wasn't a word he understood. He was going to take my pussy, no turning back. He knew I wanted his body, even though I was terrified.

"Sshhh," he whispered as he reached down to hold his dick and slide it into me.

I shut my eyes as tightly as I could and gripped his biceps.

He pushed his way through me, stretching my vagina like a speculum.

Before I could scream out in agony, his lips were caressing mine. I dug my nails into his back as tears slid down my cheeks, soaking his pillow.

Aaron slid himself all the way into me. He stopped kissing me, then looked into my face.

I looked up at him and watched as he eased his way out of me, snatched off the condom, tossed it on his nightstand, then slid his way back inside of my wet pussy. He didn't even ask whether I was on birth control.

I cried, "Aaron, what are we doing?"

He started to stroke, and my soul was on fire. He dug deeper and deeper into me. He kissed my lips as he brought my vagina to tears.

"Heaven, I love you. Shorty, I knew you would feel like this," he whispered in my ear.

I just cried, locking my legs around his waist.

It felt too good, too amazing. I was floating on air.

"*Got-damn. Shit.*" His body became moist. "So, *this* is what Heaven feels like."

I screamed out in pleasure, holding on to him.

Just when he threw my legs over his shoulders, about to work the shit out of my pulsating pussy, the door to his room flew open.

"Eh, Aaron, where is the—" His roommate Ashton and his girlfriend Alisha were standing in the doorway, mouths dropped open.

"Got-damn, muthafucka!" Aaron yelled. "Don't you knock?"

"My bad, A!" Ashton was shocked and embarrassed as he slammed the door closed. There was a pause, then loud whispers. "Oh, what's up, Ne'Vaeh?" Ashton hesitantly said.

I cried out as I pushed Aaron off me. I heard Ashton and his girl whispering between themselves as they walked away from the room.

Aaron sighed as he got up off me, sitting on his bed. He reached for me to help me up off the bed, but I pushed his arm away. "Heaven, baby, I'm sorry," he whispered.

I looked at him, tears brimming, threatening to spill over. My pussy was still throbbing. We barely got it in that morning, but my pussy was already sore. Though I was angry and embarrassed, I couldn't help but think about what my body would feel like had we gone all the way to the finish.

"You're 'sorry,' Aaron? *Sorry?* Your fuckin' roommate and his girl just walked in on us fuckin'! I know both of them! I've been going to school with Alisha since third grade! You think she doesn't know that your girlfriend is my *best* friend? Do you really think that she's not gonna say anything to Charlie? She fuckin' *hates* Charlie! And forget Alisha—what about *Ashton?* He grew up with Charlie! He's gonna tell her!" I cried, getting up off the bed.

Aaron watched as I went over to my clothes and rushed to put everything back on. He didn't know what else to do except put his clothes on as well.

I put my clothes on in a minute—tops. Aaron stood there in his clothes as he watched me slide into my shoes and slide my arms through my jacket's sleeves. I picked up the gift bag and walked up to him to hand it back to him.

Aaron looked at me as if he was hurt. "What are you handing me this for, shorty?"

I shook my head, tears rolling down my face. "This doesn't belong to me. It was a great thought. It was a wonderful gift. I don't deserve anything like this."

Aaron shook his head. "Shorty, I can't take this back to the store. This stuff is nonrefundable, Heaven."

"I don't care what you do with it, Aaron, I just can't take it. Give it to Charlie or some other girl, for all I care! And stop calling me 'Heaven'!" I cried.

Aaron shook his head, taking all of the gifts out of the gift bag, and taking my large purse from my shoulder.

I tried to get my purse back from him, but he pushed me away.

He shoved the dress and jewelry down in my purse. He looked up at me and handed my purse back to me.

I snatched my purse, putting the strap back over my shoulder.

His eyes glistened as he reached for me, but I pulled away. He knew that I was hurt, angry, and embarrassed out of my mind. He also knew that I loved each and every inch of him that morning. He had entered my soul that day as well as my heart. I was in deeper than I wanted to be. He reached for me again, pulling my body up against his. "Shorty, they won't say anything, I can promise you that," he assured me.

I shook my head, tears saturating my face. "I can't believe I let you do this to me! I'm smarter than this! I know better than this shit! Aaron, why didn't you just stop when you heard me *crying* for you to stop?"

I shook my head, looking up into his face. "I can't even be mad at you. What was I thinking, coming to your bedroom, when you made it perfectly clear two days ago that you wanted to get me naked? I'm so fuckin' stupid."

"Baby, nobody thinks any less of you." Aaron dried my face with his big warm hands.

I looked into his face. "But I think less of *myself*, Aaron. What am I doing here?" I cried aloud.

"This is where you wanna be. This is where you *need* to be." Aaron placed my hand over his heart, then placed his hand on top of mine. His heart beat strong against his rib cage. "You feel this? *You* did this to me, shorty. Not Charlie, not anybody else but *you*."

My heart skipped a few beats. I slipped my hand from under his. "I-I have to go, Aaron." I didn't know what else to say.

"Let me at least drive you back to the dorm. It's the least that I can do," he suggested.

I backed away from him, shaking my head. "No, no, you've done enough. It's obvious that we don't need to be alone together. I'll just catch the bus back." I turned away from him, about to walk toward the door when Aaron pulled me back to him.

I looked up at him as he pulled me close, up against his chest, and he gently kissed my lips. My knees grew weak. My stomach was doing all sorts of twists, flips, and somersaults.

"I love you, Heaven. I'm sorry, but I love you," he whispered in between kisses.

I held his face in my hands. He held my waist in his hands. I could feel his pulse through his lips, through his hands, through his skin. I was lost in the moment . . . that was, until there was a knock at the door to his room.

"Umm, Aaron, uhhh, ya girl, Charlie's on the phone," Ashton hesitated through the other side of the door.

I cried aloud in Aaron's mouth as I pulled my lips away from his.

His eyes glistened. "Baby, I'm sorry," he whispered.

I opened the door, rushed past Ashton down the hallway, and raced down the stairs. Just when I opened the door about to rush out into the cold, Alisha was finishing a Newport, on her way back into the house.

She grinned at me as she flicked the cigarette butt into the grass. "Where you off to in such a hurry, Cutie?" She exhaled smoke through her nostrils. Just like Aaron, I don't think she'd ever called me by my name ever since I met that girl.

"I'm gonna miss this bus if I don't hurry." I was nearly out of breath. "You know how them fuckin' bus drivers will have you chasin' their ass down the street."

"I know that's right. These bus drivers around this muthafucka are ratchet as hell. I'll give you a ride." Alisha's looked at me. "It's too fuckin' cold to be waitin' on a damn bus. Fuck *that* shit. And what you look like walkin' up them bus steps in fuckin' stilettos?"

I hesitated.

"C'mon, I'm headed in your direction anyway. I gotta go to my mom's crib to get a change of clothes. Your cousin invited me to your party—I gotta go get cute. I know your shit is gonna be off the chain tonight! I can't wait!" Alisha grinned, nudging me in the shoulder.

My eyes glistened. I just knew she thought I was a damn slut for fuckin' my own best friend's boyfriend.

Alisha rolled her eyes, pulling me by the arm off the porch along with her to her car. "Girl, c'mon, and stop actin' childish."

We cruised down 495 in her burgundy Dodge Charger, on our way to my dorm. I needed to attempt to get some sleep before my cousin picked me up at noon. She was supposed to be taking me to lunch with the family and with Charlie who felt like family. My intentions were to meet up with Charlie at the airport at 10:00, but after what happened that morning with Aaron, there was no way that I would be able to face her that soon. I had to get myself together. My emotions were running wild. My mind and heart were racing.

Alisha glanced at me while she was driving. She was probably *the* most popular girl from middle school all the way through senior year in high school. She was dark-skinned with long, sleek, shiny black hair. She had the prettiest smile and the smoothest skin. Not to mention, she was thick as hell and had an ass like *whoa!* which made her a favorite among the guys. She and Charlie always bumped heads. Neither of them were fans of the other. Alisha always called Charlie the blue-eyed devil. She had been accusing Charlie of sleeping with Ashton junior year after homecoming. Ashton and Charlie both denied it, but Alisha knew in her heart that the man she had been with since seventh grade had been unfaithful. She'd found an earring similar to one that Charlie had lost around the same time, in the backseat of Ashton's car. She even found an empty condom wrapper in Ashton's pants that night. She was in love, but she was no fool.

"You know, I never liked Charlie, right?" Alisha stated.

I looked at her, eyes puffy and all.

She grinned a little, glancing over at me.

I shook my head, knowing that she was trying to make me feel better, but I was in no mood for jokes. "Alisha, I'm *really* not in the mood. Please talk your shit about Charlie some other time, okay?"

She glanced at me. "So, you're embarrassed because me and my man caught you fuckin' *Charlie's* man this morning, huh?"

I didn't say anything. I just gazed out of the window.

Alisha sighed. "Not that you owe me—or anyone else for that matter—an explanation, but . . . Did you sleep with Aaron to get back at Charlie for something?"

I looked at her, shaking my head. "No. What has Charlie ever done to me?"

Alisha ignored the question. "Do you like Aaron?"

I shook my head. "I don't just like him, Alisha, I *love* him."

"Then you didn't do anything wrong." She glanced at me.

My eyes widened. "How could you say that? Charlie *loves* Aaron!"

Alisha smirked. "Are you serious? You have no idea, and I'm not gonna be the one to tell you."

I looked at her. "What do you mean?"

Alisha laughed a little. "Let's just say that Aaron is the farthest nigga from her mind right now. I told Aaron back in high school that he should've hollered at *you*, but no, he had to listen to his boys, who told him that you were still stuck on Jamie. Aaron told me back then that he liked you. Maybe *I* should have been the one to tell you. I don't even know why you're crying about this shit. You should be happy!"

There the tears were, freely flowing down my face again. "Happy? You're trippin'. I don't care what you say, Alisha—I'm wrong for this shit."

"Well, I tell you what, I know *Aaron's* not feeling bad about it. He's been talkin' about breaking up with Charlie for weeks. He talked to the girl about marriage, and she dissed him. He probably was just sayin' the shit to see what she said, but that's beside the point. She doesn't care about him. Probably only got with the boy because she knew that *you* were feelin' him first." Alisha glanced at me again.

I shook my head. Why was everyone bad-mouthing my best friend? "She's not even like that, Alisha. We must be talking about two completely different Charlies. The Charlie that *I* know has been my best friend ever since elementary school. When no one else took the time to be there for me, she was there. My mother murdered my brother and beat my sister until she ran away. Haven't seen my sister in six years, and though I miss her, Charlie has done one hell of a job playing her part. Charlie has always been supportive, and she's always had my back. She feels like family to me, and for me to go and do something like this to her . . ." I fought back the tears. "I don't even deserve to have her as a friend."

Alisha shook her head at me. "You'll find out soon enough, Cutie. She's not the girl you think she is. I'll just leave it like that, because I already know that whatever I say, you're not gonna believe me."

I just looked at her. Alisha was always the gossip queen of our clique. I didn't have time for her drama today. Whatever she had to say about Charlie didn't matter at that moment.

I sat nervously in my dorm room that day around noon. It took me at least two hours to find something to wear. I hung the dress that Aaron gave me on a hanger on the knob of my closet door. I must have walked past that dress fifty times before breaking down and deciding to put the muthafucka on. I slipped the dress over my head, pulling it down past my waist, and over my hips. Then I slipped my feet into a pair of burgundy stilettos, glossed some burgundy lipstick over my lips, and slid the strap to my matching Coogi purse over my shoulder. My hair still managed to stay intact. All I had to do was separate the curls a little with my fingers. I looked at myself in my full-length mirror. I was lookin' good, but I felt like shit.

I sat there shaking my leg nervously when my cell phone vibrated on my lap. It was a text from Renée, telling me that she'd pulled up outside my dorm, and for me not to take all damn day because the family was waiting for me at Venus, a soul food restaurant owned by my cousin, rapper and superstar Darrick "D-Allan" Allan's ex-wife, Jade Abdula-Matthews. It was an honor that she would even let all twenty-five of us dine at her restaurant on such short notice, let alone free. She was in town for the week, and I couldn't believe I was going to get the chance to meet her. Seeing her around usually meant that Cousin Darryl, Darrick's fraternal twin, would show his face. I didn't see much of him these days. He'd taken a break from producing records and went straight to working with film. He was married to Anastasia Jones, one of the hottest singers, dancers, and choreographers there was. She was phenomenal, and I hoped that she would show up at my birthday party as well.

"I cannot believe you missed your own birthday breakfast this morning." Renée rolled her eyes at me as I got into the passenger seat and closed the door behind me. "You had my ass up at seven-thirty this morning, and I don't wake up that early unless I'm goin' to work."

"Sorry, girl." I looked at her, "I didn't wake up until almost eleven."

Renée looked at me as we drove off, out of the parking lot, away from my dorm. "Oh, yeah, I forgot—you *did* say that you were working on that term paper."

I glanced at her. I had forgotten all about that damn paper. I would be pulling an all-nighter this weekend to finish it, that was for damn sure.

"And your girl, Charlie, called me, telling me that she had been trying to call *you* all morning. Her flight just got in a few minutes ago. Their flight was delayed this morning, and she didn't want you showing up to the airport when she wasn't going to be there. She said she would be at the hotel around one o'clock to help set up."

My heart began to race in my chest. I couldn't face her—there was no way I could face that girl after what I'd done. I shut my eyes as tightly as I could, trying to fight back the thought of Aaron's lips pressed against mine. I could still feel his warm dick inside me.

"Cute dress." I felt Renée looking me up and down.

I opened my eyes, my heart nearly popping out of my chest. Damn, that bitch never misses *anything*, always peepin' shit. Ol' nosy ass. "Huh?" I gulped.

"What? Don't 'huh' me. The dress—it's awesome!" Renée laughed a little. "The perfect party dress!" She looked at me again. "Wait a minute. I saw that dress at the mall. That freakin' dress was like $400! Where the hell did you get that kind of money to spend on a dress, when you're not even working full time?"

I swallowed hard. "Girl, you know I'm broke as hell. It was a birthday gift."

Renée glanced at me. "A birthday gift? Whose nose do you have *that* wide open for them to get you a dress that cost damn near half a grand?"

I remained quiet. She got on my damn nerves always figuring shit out.

The girl slammed on her brakes in the middle of traffic.

My heart nearly stopped in my chest as the car behind us slammed on its brakes to avoid hitting her. I swore my damn heart slammed against my rib cage. "Damn, Renée! You're gonna give me fuckin' whiplash!" I squealed. "Are you fuckin' crazy?"

Cars were honking their horns as they passed around Renée's stopped vehicle.

She gave them all the middle finger as they drove by her, cursing her crazy ass out. "Man, fuck them." She looked back at me, her light eyes searching the expression on my face for clues as to who could have bought me the dress. "Aaron." She pointed in my face. "Aaron bought you that dress? And those earrings! And that necklace?" She covered her mouth. "I mean, fuck! The necklace says 'Heaven' on it! Who the fuck is the only one who calls you that? That is a *dead* giveaway!"

I put my hand over my heart in agony. I couldn't bring myself to talk about what happened that morning, but cuz was forcing me to talk to her about it. "Please, Renée—please start this car before someone runs us off the road."

Renée shook her head at me, "What did you do to him?"

My eyes widened. I looked at her. "What? What did *I* do to *him?*"

Renée finally came back to her senses, put the car back in gear, and began to drive down the street again. "What did you do to get that muthafucka to buy you a dress *that* sexy and *that* expensive? Did you suck his dick or some-thing?" She gasped. "You fucked him, didn't you?"

I shook my head. "No."

Renée looked at me, pursing her lips.

"He fucked *me*." I sank back in my seat. "He fucked me *good* too, Renée."

Renée shook her head, "O-M-muthafuckin' G! I can't believe this 'Jerry Springer,' 'Love and Hip-Hop' type shit! You should have given him the dress back!"

"I tried!" I exclaimed. "I tried to give it back, but he wouldn't let me. When he kissed me, I told him to stop. When he undressed me, I tried to push him away, but he just . . ."

Renée glanced at me. "So, the muthafucka just forced his shit on you? The muthafucka just *took* the pussy? That nigga *raped* you, Ne'Vaeh!"

I shook my head at her before she got into her head that Aaron raped me. "Renée, see, that's *not* what I said. I knew what I was doing when I went to his room, I knew what I was doing when I tried on the dress, and I knew what I was doing when I got naked in front of someone who made it perfectly clear that he wanted to have sex."

She just continued to shake her head. She was pissed off.

"Renée, I love him." I started crying.

She sighed, frustrated with me. "Girl, *why?* You are too smart and too beautiful to want anybody's leftovers, no matter how muthafuckin' fine he is or no matter how much money the brotha is about to be making in the very near future. You have so much potential. There are so many men that want you. I've seen the kind of men that approach you, and I've seen you turn each and every one of them down. And for who? A man who belongs to someone else? Ne'Vaeh, *why?*"

I look at her, tears trickling down my face. "I loved Aaron the very moment that I ever laid eyes on him. I was going through *hell,* and Aaron looked like an angel. There was a connection to that boy from the start. I had no idea that he felt the same way that I did until just two days ago. For almost two years, I have been holding in the fact that I was in love with him. He barely looked at me, and I thought he didn't notice me. I thought he didn't care. I thought he would never see me. As bad as I feel for letting my emotions overrule my common sense . . . I just couldn't stop him from kissing me, touching me, undressing me, and loving on me. I hadn't been touched in four years, Renée! If it wasn't for Ashton and Alisha walking in on us this morning, I'd probably still be in his bed, in his arms."

Renée's eyes widened. "They walked in on y'all fuckin'? Ne'Vaeh, sweetie, you're in for the rudest, most fucked-up awakening, I'm sorry to tell you. I'm telling you, sweetie, stay away from that man. You had your fun, you got laid, you woke the pussy up from her nap, you got some dick, but it's morning. So, 'as you slept the night away' with Aaron, you both 'forgot to face one simple fact'—he belongs to someone else—and that someone else is your best friend. The same best friend who took you in when your mama abandoned you, and you didn't have a fuckin' pot to piss in. She's back in town, so the next time that you decide to visit his bed, remember that Charlie sleeps in that bed too. Charlie gave you a home. I suggest you keep that shit in mind the next time you decide to wreck *her* home."

I cried because I loved Aaron, but . . . I respected Charlie just as much, if not more. She was like a sister to me. I couldn't hurt her when all she'd ever done was try to protect me from hurt. I loved Aaron, but he belonged to Charlie. What was I supposed to do when *my* heart belonged to Aaron? He was going to break up with her. I believed him when he told me that he would do it at my birthday party.

He hadn't talked to me in over two years, and as soon as he got the opening to tell me how he felt, he jumped for the chance. He was serious. As if my life wasn't hectic enough, I had to go and make things even more complicated.

Chapter 4

Gonna Fuck Him

Charlene

"Here, honey, let us help you with those bags. Why are you carrying these bags by yourself? Heather, come carry these bags for your sister. Jorge, come hold this." Aunt Stacen took my Coach carry-on bags and purse from me, passing them off to my little sister and brother.

I sighed, rolling my eyes. "C'mon, Aunt Stacen, really? My *purse?* I can't carry my own *purse?* I'm pregnant, not crippled. Got-damn, people, stop treating me like I'm fuckin' handicapped." I took my purse back from my sister.

"Charlie!" my mother exclaimed. "Watch your mouth!" My mother pranced over to the baggage conveyor belt in her Chanel sandals. "We're only trying to help. Keep acting like you don't need anybody. In a few months, when this baby comes, you're going to wish you weren't so bitchy to the people who were just trying to look out for you." Mother grabbed her Gucci suitcase from the conveyor belt. She looked at me, her blue eyes searching my face. She was so disappointed in me, but I was more disappointed in myself.

Mama hadn't said too much to me since she found out that I was pregnant. I took the pregnancy test one day in my sister's bathroom, and carelessly, I left the applicator on Heather's sink. Mind you, my baby sister is thirteen. Mother happened to walk into Heather's room and found the applicator, and you know she went *straight* off on my sister. I had to tell her that the pregnancy test was mine; then she went straight off on *me*.

My eyes began to water. "Mama, I'm sorry. It's these hormones. I'm trippin'. I appreciate your help, but you know how I am."

Mama's eyes searched my face. "So, when are you going to tell Aaron about this baby?"

I looked at her, my heart skipping a few beats. Tell Aaron? I dreaded the thought because I was too young for a baby. I'd already planned to get an abortion when Mama found the applicator, but Mama made it perfectly clear that it was my mistake, and I wasn't going to make the baby pay for something that I did. I also dreaded the idea because I knew in my heart that Aaron wasn't the father of my baby. Let me tell you how I pretty much played myself. . . .

It was August 15, about two weeks before sophomore year in college started for the fall 2014 semester. My girls from the cheerleading squad and I took a trip to Miami just because. Sometimes, we took trips just to unwind from all of the hard work that we had been doing throughout the year. We did everything from tournaments, to fashion shows, to community service, to football games, to basketball games, to TV appearances. We deserved to relax and unwind. We all needed a relaxing getaway under the sun. Especially me—I just needed to get away *period*.

I needed to escape Maryland. I needed to get away from the responsibility of babysitting Ne'Vaeh, plain and simple. Even though we were in separate colleges, my mother and the rest of the family still expected me to keep up with Ne'Vaeh. They felt sorry for the girl. It was more than sympathy. They loved her as if she were their own, especially my father's side of the family. My father died of a heart attack when I was six years old. My sister was just born, and my mother was devastated. I knew Ne'Vaeh's pain of losing someone that she loved. Ne'Vaeh lost a brother, a sister, a mother, and never knew her father. My father was everything to me. Losing him did serious damage to my heart and to my life. No one bothered to notice. From the moment Ne'Vaeh stepped into my life, she'd won my family's heart. When her mother went to prison for killing her younger brother, my mother stepped up to the plate and took Ne'Vaeh in. Ne'Vaeh's mother, Juanita, used to be best friends with my mother when they were in high school, according to my grandmother. They were the original Salt-N-Pepa. My mother was white, and Juanita was black. Whatever happened to split the two apart, no one talked about it, but I'm pretty sure it had something to do with a man. It always does.

The squad arrived in Miami at 1:15 p.m. that day. I was so happy to get away from Maryland, away from Ne'Vaeh, and away from *Aaron*. Yes, I know, Aaron is wonderful. He is the epitome of the perfect man—someone *else's* man. He didn't love me. It was obvious that he was in love with someone else. He tried his damnedest to love me, but he couldn't, and I desperately wanted him to. He was a great guy, don't get me wrong, but there was absolutely no passion in our relationship. Sure, we looked phenomenal together. Every night out together felt like a Red Carpet event, but whenever we made it back to our separate apartments, he stayed on his side of the bed, and I stayed on mine.

Aaron didn't pay me attention anymore. We made "like," not love. He had the most amazing sensuous lips, yet he never kissed me. He had the softest hands, yet he never touched me. Whenever we had sex, I'm pretty sure he didn't even reach orgasm. After a few strokes, sometimes, he would just get up and go to the bathroom. When we had sex, it was like he was thinking about someone else the whole time. Sometimes, he would just stop, pull out, and go to sleep. Nothing I did turned him on. I showed up to his apartment one night with nothing on but Burberry stilettos, a Burberry raincoat, and a black lace thong from Victoria's Secret. Do you think he cared? No. The nigga took one look at me as I opened my coat, and said, "Charlie, its thirty-two degrees outside. Are you trying to get sick?" Yep, he wasn't cheating on me . . . but it was sure to come.

I needed to get fucked, if not loved. My trip to Miami was going to help that shit happen. There was always something going on in Miami. That night, there was going to be this huge college football party at a hot new club in Miami Beach. I stepped off the plane that afternoon with one thing on my mind—fuckin'. Aaron and I hadn't had sex in over three months. I needed a fling, a one-night stand, a hit it—split it—and—quit it. I didn't give a fuck, just something to let me know that someone actually wanted to spend some sort of time with me. Men hit on me all the time, but I wanted *Aaron* to want me. I wanted him to need me, but he didn't, and I was tired of it.

"Ladies, we're going to the College Football Fiesta tonight at nine-thirty," Alisha announced to all fifteen of us that afternoon in the lobby of the Hilton Hotel. "I have three limos picking us up at nine-thirty *sharp*. Dress to impress, divas, because some fine, hot, sexy, soon-to-be-drafted-into-the-NFL men are going to be there tonight!"

All the girls cheered, whooped, and hollered.

I looked up at Alisha and rolled my eyes at her.

Why I had to be cursed by ending up at the same college on the same cheerleading squad with that bitch, I don't know. Yeah, I slept with a lot of guys in my day, but she had in her head that

I had sex with her boyfriend, Ashton. Ashton and I grew up together and lived next door to each other, until my mother moved when I was twelve years old. Though he might have had feelings for me, he never told me so, nor treated me like anything other than a sister. I was wild, I was loose, there was no taming me. Ashton didn't have time for that shit. He tried to keep me out of the trouble that I always seemed to be searching for. I would party *hard*, even to the point where I'd get so high and so fuckin' drunk that I would wake up in places, having no idea how I got there. Imagine waking up sore and buck naked, lying next to a man, woman, or men and women you didn't even know. Yeah, that was your girl. Ashton would often come to my rescue. He saved me from wild fraternity parties on *many* occasions.

I started having sex at the age of thirteen. I lied about my age to a nineteen-year-old guy who was in college. I can't even remember dude's name. All I remember is the feeling. He adored me, he admired me, and he lusted after me. I didn't realize then the muthafucka was a pervert. All I cared about was the fact that he lusted after me. The guy blew up my phone for weeks, looking for some more of me. I ignored his phone calls. He wanted some sort of relationship, as sick as that sounds. I just wanted a rush.

I believe that between the ages of thirteen and sixteen, I had to have had sex with at least fifty or more guys, all ages, sizes, and colors. I had a reputation. I was good at what I did. I was trying to fill the empty space in my heart with something—anything. I was afraid to love, even though I desperately wanted it, and when I met Aaron, I knew I had to change. I didn't want to be that girl who was great at giving lap dances, who was great at giving head, who could eat your girl's pussy, who could take on four guys at a time. I can't even begin to tell you the amount of shit me and my girls got into with men and women of all statuses in life. I'm talking senators, doctors, lawyers, judges, *every* muthafucka who held some type of political position. And this is while we were only in high school. I couldn't be tamed, but that day that Aaron stepped into my classroom junior year in high school, I knew it was time to change. I wanted Aaron from the moment that I met him. I knew I had to have him. He was beautiful, he was talented, he was sweet, he was amazing, and he was sexy as a muthafucka. I didn't give a damn who else wanted him. He was going to be *mine*. I was determined. Thirty seconds into our first conversation, I asked him out on a date.

I introduced Aaron to Ashton junior year in high school, and they clicked from the start. I was so excited when they decided to be roommates. I had my "brother from another mother" and the man who I loved with every inch of me.

Aaron treated me like royalty when we first met, which had my emotions soaring high. I didn't know much about Aaron, but what I did know was that he was from a very wealthy family. His parents lived back in California, so he stayed with his aunt, who was in the military, right up until he moved in with Ashton. I didn't know why his relationship with his parents was so strained, but he didn't want anything from them or anything to do with them. Aaron was an amazing basketball player, destined to achieve greatness. I knew I could help him get to high places in no time. I introduced him to college basketball coaches and college scouts from all over the country, some of which I had slept with, of course. I got him a great job working with my uncle at an engineering company. I introduced Aaron to a life he wouldn't have known otherwise. He held me on a pedestal for the first six months or so into our relationship.

That was, until he discovered who I was. No one gave a damn about my sex life until Aaron came along. He made me want to change. I wanted to forget my past, but no one else wanted me to forget. Almost everyone—including Alisha—decided to put me on Front Street in front of Aaron. They couldn't wait to let him know the name of every guy and girl I screwed around with in college. They told him about my adventures in the boys' locker room. They told him about my fling with the art teacher. They told him about the time I was caught giving head to the assistant basketball coach in the boy's bathroom. They told him about the three-month relationship I had with Carla, this beautiful Puerto Rican girl who was a sophomore in college—she knew how to eat pussy until your toes curled and eyes rolled to the back of your head. They even told him about the group sex tape I was in on my sixteenth birthday. Aaron was disgusted. We almost broke up, but he gave me a chance. Though he didn't leave me, he was no longer the same. He hadn't touched, kissed, looked at, or spoken to me the same since he found out the truth about me, and I started hating myself.

That afternoon, I snuck away from the squad and went out on the town on my own. I didn't feel like going to the spa with them, listening to them brag about all the shit their men bought for them. I walked along the sandy beaches of Miami, did a little shopping, and got my nails done. Then I went out to eat. I sat alone at a small restaurant, just staring at my cell phone. Aaron hadn't called or texted me *once* to even see if I was okay or that I made it safely into town. Ne'Vaeh had called at least six or seven times, though I ignored her calls. I rolled my eyes every time the phone rang and her name appeared on the display. She loved me like her sister. She adored me. I loved her too, but I hated her just the same. It was as if my family replaced my father with her. It seemed as though my mother took her in to help distract her from missing my father. I resented Ne'Vaeh for throwing all of her weight on top of the weight that I already carried. I was responsible for that girl, and I hated it. I needed a life outside of her. She had me trapped. I tried my hardest to avoid her in college, but she'd find her way to me. Man, that week in Miami felt like freedom.

"Charlene Campbell, got-damn, I *know* that ain't you!" a familiar, deep, sexy voice exclaimed over my shoulder.

I looked up to see Jamie "Memphis" Green looking back at me. I stood from the table in shock as he turned my body around to face him then threw his arms around me, squeezing me oh so tight. Oh my God, his body was so soft and warm. And he smelled so good.

Jamie Green was Ne'Vaeh's first and only boyfriend. She was in love with that boy, from the top to the bottom of her heart. It nearly killed that girl when he left her back in high school. There he was, standing before me, tall, milk chocolate, handsome, delectable, looking good enough to eat. His hair was close cut. His eyebrows and goatee were perfectly trimmed. He was dressed in a clean, crisp, white T-shirt and ankle-length khaki shorts. Fresh Air Force Ones were on his feet. I could see how chiseled his body was through his shirt. He looked a-maz-ing, *got-damn*.

"Oh my goodness! What the fuck!" I covered my mouth, giggling.

Jamie laughed a little.

"OMG, how you've grown up! You're not Li'l Memphis anymore!" I watched him smiling. "Boy, what are you doing here?" I exclaimed.

"I'm here with the football team. You know I'm at Memphis State right now, right? I'm sure you seen me doing my thang on TV." Jamie smiled, showing his dimples, pearly whites and all.

I looked at him, rolling my eyes, shaking my head, "Humph, still cocky, I see. I have my own life, Jamie. Don't nobody got time to be watching your conceited ass on TV."

Jamie laughed a little. He had the most gorgeous smile. He was still sexier than a muthafucka, and he knew it too. "So, what are *you* doing here?" he said as he licked his lips.

"Vacationing with the squad. You know we've been doing it big since freshman year in high school." I smiled up at him.

Jamie looked around for the squad. "Where they at? Who's here with you now?"

"They went to some spa. I had to get away from them. *Alisha's* the captain of my team. Yeah, you *know* I'm hatin' that. I ditched the crew. I'm here on my own," I responded.

"You wanna kick it with your boy today? I mean, if you're not too busy. You look busy."

My heart skipped a few beats. I didn't know what to say except, "I have a boyfriend."

Jamie laughed a little to himself. "I have a girlfriend—what's your point?"

I looked up at him. "My point is I don't think it's appropriate to be alone with you, Jamie. You might not be good at keeping your hands to yourself. I've heard about you. You know it's a small world. Cheerleaders talk. And most of their talk is about you and your dick." I looked him up and down a little, pursing my lips.

"Oh, it's like that, huh? I haven't seen you in, what, three-and-a-half or four years. We've known each other since second grade, shorty, and you can't come chill with me, get some lunch, go to a movie, or hit up a mall real quick? That's fucked up." Jamie held my hand, pulling me a little closer to him.

I looked up at him. His intentions were probably very innocent, but shit, *mine* weren't. He looked too hot and too damn tasty. If wherever he took me to didn't have a lot of people there, oh yeah, I was gonna fuck the *shit* out of him.

"We need to talk, catch up, and shit. I miss y'all, man. My niggas are having a barbeque at my man's beach house around six o'clock; then they're heading over to that college football party at this club. Call your girls, tell 'em to meet up with you. My team would love to see your girls, man." Jamie grinned, still holding my hand.

I looked up at him. I really wanted him to ditch his crew, take me back to his hotel room, and fuck my pussy *dry*. I should have been thinking about Ne'Vaeh at that time and how much she would have loved to hear from him. When he left her, she cut off all contact with him. It was his choice to move to Memphis to live with his father. He didn't have to go, but he did, and she felt abandoned.

I should have been thinking about her, but I was only thinking about my own needs at that time. Someone finally wanted to spend some time with me, and I wasn't about to pass that up.

Of course, Alisha had something to say about Jamie's invite. She sat down alongside me on a bench outside of the beach house belonging to Jamie's friend that evening. I'd never seen such beautiful scenery. The man's house was so peaceful, so serene. It was as if Jamie's friend, Alonzo, lived on heaven's beach.

"I cannot believe that you just *happened* to run into your best friend's ex, almost 1,100 miles away from home." Alisha laughed to herself, crossing her legs, showing those fat-ass thighs the niggas loved oh so much.

I rolled my eyes at her. That bitch always had something smart to say to me. "Look, just because you're captain of this team doesn't mean you're captain of my fuckin' life, Alisha," I snapped at her.

She laughed aloud. "Whoa, let me keep my opinions to myself then! All I'm saying is that when you saw Jamie, the first thought on your mind should have been Ne'Vaeh, and not yourself. She loved that boy with all of her heart back in the day. She cried for nearly two years over him leaving her, or did you forget that?"

I looked at her. A twinge of guilt stung my heart. I couldn't care less about Ne'Vaeh when I ran into Jamie. All I cared about was my own selfish, horny needs. Jamie was making me feel the way Aaron used to make me feel. Aaron had made me feel like royalty when we first started dating, and I needed that old feeling back, even if it was from my "sister's" ex-boyfriend.

"He's been all over you since we've been at this party." Alisha couldn't help but notice. She looked at me, her brown eyes searching my face for remorse. When she found none, she shook her head. "I don't give a fuck how you feel or don't feel about Aaron, but *Ne'Vaeh* loves you like a sister, Charlie. The kind of friendship y'all have doesn't come around that often. You really wanna fuck that up by fuckin' with her heart? I don't too much care for you, and you know that, but Ne'Vaeh is good people. You've known the girl since third grade. Don't do this shit to her like you did to me. . . ."

Alisha made tears fall from my eyes. I dried them as fast as I could. The bitch fucked up my relationship because she thought I was fuckin' her man, Ashton. Okay, I will admit one thing: I sucked his dick. It was more of helping him out than it was sexual. He was about fourteen years old. We were chillin' in his room, doing homework as usual. We were watching some movie that had a sex scene in it, where a woman went down on this guy. Ashton looked at me, asking me how it felt. I told him I didn't know because I wasn't a guy, but if he wanted to know what it felt like, I would show him. I sucked him off for five or ten good minutes before he busted in my mouth. I went to the bathroom, brushed my teeth, and that was it. We never talked about it again. I'm sure he never told her about it, though I figured he asked her to do it to him the same way that I did.

I couldn't care less about what Alisha had to say about what I chose to do with my life.

"I've done a lot of wild shit in my time, but I never fucked any of my friends' men, and I didn't fuck yours, Alisha. You didn't have to go telling Aaron all about my past, because it was none of your fuckin' business. Thanks to you, Aaron won't fuck me, touch me, kiss me, talk to me, or fuckin' *look* at me!" I stood up from the bench.

A slight grin grew across her face. "Why are you mad at me—because *you* chose to be a ho in high school? Be mad at yourself, shit. *You* should've never fucked with my man, Charlene. I told you I was gonna get you back."

"Trust me, bitch, if I wanted Ashton, I'd be with him, believe that shit! You worry about your fake-ass life and stay the *fuck* out of mine." I stormed away from her and passed Jamie, who stood alongside his friends near the grill.

Jamie caught my arm and pulled me to him, looking at the dried-up tears on my face. "What's up, ma? What's wrong?"

I looked at him, tears lining my lashes. "I'm not feeling this. I'm leaving. Y'all have fun with the squad. Trust me, that sexy li'l Puerto Rican chick named Lailah, the skinny white chick named Nicole, and Rita, that thick-ass, dark-skinned chick will fuck you *and* your team's brains out. Have a fuckin' ball." He loosened his grip on my arm, and I walked away.

I went inside the house to grab my jacket and purse. It was about 7:15. The night was still young. The party was just getting started, and Alisha had to start fuckin' with me, fuckin' up my mood.

The door slid back and in came Jamie. I looked at him as I slid my purse over my shoulder.

"Wanna talk about it, shorty?" he said softly, his eyes searching my face.

I shook my head, "Nah, not really. I don't know what I was thinking, going on a trip with

Alisha's ol' hatin' ass. I'm taking the first flight up out this bitch tomorrow morning, believe that!"

Jamie laughed a little. "You gonna let Alisha chase you away from a good time, shorty?" He shook his head. "Nah, man, you can't go. How long were you supposed to be here in Florida?"

I looked at him, "A week. Why?"

"Because I'm not ready for you to leave yet. . . . You could stay with me for about four days." Jamie looked into my face.

My heart jumped. "With-with you? Seriously?"

He nodded. "Why not? I have a few television appearances this week, but that's about it. I'm free. We leave in five days. I wouldn't mind the company. I'm staying at my cousin's house on the other side of the beach. He let me stay in it for the week, while he's away on business. I'm all by myself, shorty. C'mon, stay with me."

I looked up at him, hormones jumpin', and pussy already starting to throb in my panties. "You promise not to touch me?"

Jamie laughed to himself, "Yo, I don't make promises that I can't keep."

"Whatever, Jamie. I just need to get out of this house *now*. Alisha is gonna make me fuck her ass up. Always talkin' shit." I looked up into his face.

"Let's roll, then, shorty. I'll try to be on my best behavior. You shouldn't look so good if you don't want anybody to touch you. I'm just sayin'." Jamie looked down into my eyes.

Boy, he was turning me the hell on.

I rolled my eyes, trying to play off my attraction to him. "I can't believe I'm actually contemplating your offer. I know better than this."

Jamie grinned a little.

He took me back to the hotel to get my luggage. Then he took me to a movie that night. We sat close, shoulders touching. His hand rested on my knee as we ate popcorn out of the same bucket, laughing at the same parts, and getting upset at the same parts. It felt like a real date. He treated me as if he cared about me. He knew I was hurting about something, and he did everything that he could to make me smile. When his phone rang, he didn't even look at it to see who it was. I was his number one focus at that moment, and I needed that desperately.

We sat on the steps outside of his cousin's beach house that night smoking, drinking champagne, and eating fresh fruit. I was feeling *real* nice. The wind blew through my hair. I loved the salty, yet sweet smell of the air.

Jamie laughed after reminding me of our many memories in middle school. "Man, we had some crazy times back in middle school, shorty!

I don't even know how the fuck I passed! My ass was foreva' skipping school and shit!" He took a hit from his Newport 100. "Remember Mr. Nelson's art class? We used to throw paint at that nigga! And remember smokin' weed in the back of the gym?"

I slid the cigarette from his lips, then put it to mine.

Jamie looked at me and grinned.

"Those were some good times, boy!" I laughed, "Those were the good ol' days. Those days are *long* gone. I'd give anything to get those old days back, I'm tellin' you." I took a sip of champagne.

Jamie exhaled deeply. "Shit, you ain't *never* lied."

There were a few moments of silence.

"Are-are you happy?" Jamie hesitantly asked.

I looked at him, shaking my head. "No. Not really. This time right here with you is the happiest I've been in a *long* time," I admitted. "You?"

Jamie shook his head, taking his cigarette back from me. "I thought I wanted this life, but it's not what it's cracked up to be. I got muthafuckas thinking they control me and shit. I got my manager, then the agent, then the coach, then my endorsers, then my professors, then I got my family asking me for shit when they ain't ever did a *got*-damn thing for me. I love playing football, don't get me wrong, but I don't have time to enjoy the game anymore. Everything is happening so fast. Endorsement deals, television appearances, muthafuckas asking to write a book about my life, radio interviews, magazine photo shoots, parties—it's almost unreal. You know, I've been through so much bullshit in my life. I don't have the support from my family—shit, if you even wanna call them backstabbing, dysfunctional muthafuckas *family*. My dad tries to be supportive, but you know he's sick, which is the whole reason why I moved back to Memphis."

I looked at him, shaking my head. "I never knew that, Jamie." I'm pretty sure Ne'Vaeh didn't know that was the reason that he left either.

Jamie nodded. "Yeah, shorty. I wanted to get to know my father before he . . . ya know. Basically, what I'm saying is that I don't have the support that I need to keep myself motivated to make it through all of these changes and to stay focused on my goals. If it weren't for my coach, teachers, and all y'all believing in me, I would be back on the streets. Coach Jackson believed in me, working the shit out of me to improve on my skills. I have everything that I could ever want, and more except—" He stopped.

I looked at him.

He looked at me, his brown eyes sparkling under the moonlight. "I have this girl who wants all of the perks of this lifestyle, but isn't willing to deal with all that *comes* with this lifestyle, ya feel me?"

I rolled my eyes. I knew what the hell that meant. "You're cheating on her, huh?"

Jamie laughed aloud. "Is *that* what you call it?"

I just looked at him. "Really? Sticking your dick in a bitch who's not your girlfriend? Yeah, honey, that constitutes cheating. Y'all niggas kill me."

Jamie took a hit from his cigarette. He shook his head. "I just can't see myself with one woman."

I shook my head. "No, you just haven't found the woman that you want yet. You haven't found that *one* woman yet who makes you wanna settle down."

"I had a girl once who I just knew I wanted to be with foreva'." Jamie shook his head to himself.

I looked at him.

He looked at me. "So-so, how is she?"

I knew Ne'Vaeh's name would come up sooner or later. I wanted to avoid that subject, but I should have known Jamie well enough to know when he wanted to vent about the past. So, I let him vent.

"She's still Ne'Vaeh. All school, no play. Since you left, niggas don't stand a chance with her. She talked about you for two years straight after you left. She was really hurt. Took her a minute, but she learned to deal with the fact that you weren't coming back. I know you stopped calling because she never returned your calls, but I think you should call her sometime. She hasn't forgotten you, and I think she would wanna hear from you, boo." I sipped from my champagne flute.

Jamie shook his head. "Nah, shorty wouldn't wanna hear from me. She's mad at me for leaving her. Shorty, you know, she's the only girl I ever loved. Everybody else—the girl I'm with now, included—was just a substitute. I never forgave myself for leaving her to stay with my dad, but . . . I had to go. My father came looking for me. He knew I needed him. Ne'Vaeh couldn't understand where I was coming from because she was tired of people abandoning her. I didn't mean to fuck shorty up the way I did, but I had to do what I had to do for *me*. This girl I'm with now . . . shit, I tried to love her, but you know how it is. Your mind can't tell your heart what to do, you know what I'm sayin'?" Jamie's eyes sparkled.

I nodded, taking the rest of champagne left in the bottle to the head.

Jamie looked at me. "So what about you?"

I glanced at him before popping open a bottle of gin. "What *about* me?" I opened up a bottle of orange juice. I shook my head, not really in the mood for talking about my nonexistent love life.

"From what I can remember, you're not that much different than me, shorty." Jamie blew smoke through his nostrils.

I rolled my eyes, pouring a little gin in my orange juice. "People *can* change, Jamie."

"*Can* they?" He flicked his cigarette out into the sand, then sat back against the stair rails facing me.

I nodded. "Hell yes. I met someone in high school. *He's* the reason I wanted to change. I *had* to change. He saved me from myself. I mean, damn, you remember the old me, right?"

Jamie laughed aloud. "Is this a trick question? You *really* want me to answer that?"

I rolled my eyes, watching him laugh at me. "Yeah, okay, it's obvious that you do. Yes, you're probably the *only* guy on the football team that I didn't fuck, and that was only because I have known you all my life and because you were Ne'Vaeh's man."

Jamie smiled a little.

"I had a few issues going on back then, I'll admit to that. I craved attention, fame, recognition, and dick. It wasn't until junior year of high school that I met Aaron." My eyes started to glisten while I was thinking about him. "I didn't give a fuck *who* else wanted that man. The moment I saw him, I knew he was mine. I didn't even give the nigga a chance to ask me out—I asked him out on a date within the first thirty seconds of our first conversation!"

Jamie shook his head at me, taking the orange juice bottle from my hand. "Yeah, that's typical Charlene Campbell."

"I just go for what I want, Jamie—you know how I do," I whispered, taking the bottle back from him.

"So, what's the problem now?" Jamie watched as I took a gulp of orange juice.

I swallowed hard, holding the bottle firmly in both hands. "From the moment I met Aaron, I knew I wanted and needed to change. I gave up my whole lifestyle the moment I set eyes on him. I erased all the male contacts in my cell phone that weren't family members, I threw away all my provocative clothes, I took all of my revealing pictures off of My Space and Facebook, I had some of my nude tattoos removed, and I threw away my homemade porno tapes. I did a *major* transformation. I didn't leave a trace behind of who I was before we met . . . or so I *thought,* anyway." My eyes swelled up with tears.

Jamie already knew the deal. "Hatin'-ass bitches."

I nodded, "Shit, niggas, too. Nobody wanted me to forget that life. They let Aaron know *every*thing about me from day one. At first, he didn't let what they were saying bother him because he knew that people make shit up when they don't want to see a person happy. But more and more people approached him about me, and he started to question me. As long as I was that slutty, fuck-you-and-your-friends, fuck-you-and-your-girl cheerleader that I was, everything was all good. As soon as they saw that I wanted to change because I met a man who *made* me wanna change, oh, all hell broke loose. I made a lot of mistakes. I did a lot of shit that I had no business doing with a lot of men who were already in relationships with some girls that I knew. I have changed drastically, but nobody supported me except for Ne'Vaeh. I know I was an embarrassment to that girl, but she never turned her back on me."

I exhaled deeply then continued. "Alisha's bitch ass told Aaron *everything* about me. She's pissed because she thinks I fucked Ashton. Okay, yeah, I sucked his dick back in the ninth grade, but that was it. Okay, maybe I fucked up, but I didn't deserve this shit! Just when I meet a guy who I want to be with, my past comes back to haunt me. Aaron hasn't left me yet, but it's coming."

Jamie shook his head, "Nah, shorty. If he wanted to leave you, he would have left when he first heard the shit. How long you been with him?"

"It'll be three years in January," I replied. "Not long enough to think that he's gonna stay with me. He won't touch me, kiss me, fuck me, look at me—*nothing*."

"Everybody has problems, shorty. No relationship is perfect." Jamie took a pack of Newports out of his pocket.

"I miss him . . . I miss *us*." I took a sip of orange juice. "I want the old Aaron back. The one who used to hold me, kiss me, make love to me, see me. All he sees is the old me. I'm not that girl anymore, Jamie. I *swear* I'm not that girl anymore." Tears started to slide down my face, and I quickly dried them. "Oh my goodness, I'm sorry. You don't wanna hear this bullshit."

Jamie put a cigarette to his lips and lit it. He shook his head, inhaling. He exhaled smoke from his lips and nose. "Nah, shorty, you're good. I'm here to listen."

I shook my head, taking another sip of alcohol. I was getting tipsy as a muthafucka. "My life is *not* how I want it to be right now. Your life seems so calm and peaceful. Look at this beach. Oh my goodness."

Jamie smirked, "Peaceful? No, my life is *not* peaceful, shorty. Are you serious? I *never* get to chill like this. If you hadn't come over here, shit, my homeboys would be here, bringing about seven or eight groupies with them. I would be in the hot tub right now fuckin' about three or four females. Shit is hard work."

I rolled my eyes. "TMI, Jamie. *Seriously?* Who wants to hear some shit like that?"

Jamie laughed a little. "Just keepin' it one hunnid."

I rolled my eyes. "Whateva, Jamie. That orgy shit is old and played, I'm sorry. After awhile, you'll get tired of itchin' and going to the gynecologist every other week. *Trust* me."

Jamie laughed a little to himself.

It was quiet for a few seconds.

He sat there looking at me, watching me drink. "So," he hesitated, "when *is* the last time you and your man—Aaron, is it—had sex?"

I looked at him. "Like three months ago."

Jamie's eyes grew huge. "Whoa."

I nodded. "Yeah, I know, right? And even longer if you're talking about *good* sex. Shit, when we *do* have sex, he doesn't even kiss me, touch me, or look at me. He just bends me over, doesn't even want to see my face. He hits it then quits it. I can't even remember the last time that we spent time together like me and you are doing right now. I can't even remember what his lips feel like on mine." My eyes watered again.

Jamie looked at me. He heard the pain in my voice. He reached over and took the orange juice from me before I could take another drink.

I dried the tears that began to fall again.

Jamie stood up, pulling me up with him. He pulled his shirt over his head.

I looked at him, my drunk heart pounding in my chest.

"Let's go for a swim." He pulled me closer to him by my shirt and started to unbutton it.

I just looked into his face as he removed my shirt from my body. "A swim?"

Jamie grinned as he unbuttoned my pants, his hands grazing against my belly button ring. He undressed down to his shorts and began walking past me, Polo boxers showing. "C'mon, shorty." He walked off the porch, across the sand, to the water.

I watched him undress all the way to this boxers. My heart raced in my chest as I undressed down to my violet Victoria's Secret push-up bra and low-rise panties. I walked down the porch steps and across the sand and stood in the wet sand, the water washing up against my feet. I was a little scared to go into the water any deeper, though I had been thinking about wading in that water *all* day, if you know what I mean.

Jamie signaled me to come in farther. "Feels good, right?" he whispered as I walked toward him.

The water was above his waist, and just below my breasts.

I faced him, tears lining my lashes. "What would your girl think if she knew you were alone like this, with a half-naked girl as fly as me, on a beach?"

"Shit," Jamie grinned, "she's probably sending me a text right *now* that says, 'your ass better not be alone on a beach with some little bitch'!"

I smiled a little. "You're a trip. . . ." I was terribly nervous. I knew where the night was going, and at that moment, I wasn't so sure I was ready to go there. I was starting to miss Aaron, and I was starting to think about how Ne'Vaeh must have felt when she was alone with Jamie. He was so charming and so charismatic. Everything he did felt good. He was so sexy, his skin looked so soft, and his lips looked so moist. Jamie was still the same old Jamie. He was who I used to be two years before. He had no problem getting a girl into bed with him. He was so smooth. He knew all the right moves.

I looked up at him. He wasn't even thinking about his girl or Ne'Vaeh. "You didn't even tell me your girlfriend's name. She must not mean that much if you can't even tell me her name."

Jamie grinned. "Why you wanna know her name? You want her number too, so you can call her and tell her where I am and what I'm doing? While we're at it, how about you give me Aaron's number, so I can call him and tell him that I have his girl here with me and what I plan on doing with her in just a few minutes."

I laughed nervously. He always was a smart-ass. "All I'm saying is that I remember how much in love with Ne'Vaeh you were back in high school. You can't tell me that you don't miss her or even think about her."

Jamie looked at me. "I try my best not to think about her too much. I have a girl—*Pamela*—now. I'll admit, I do find myself thinking about what could have been, but . . . but who *doesn't* do that shit?"

My eyes sparkled. I wished someone felt that way about me. "Do-do you still love her?"

Jamie's eyes sparkled back. "I haven't talked about shorty in years. I want to keep it that way, Charlie, you feel me?" was his response. He loved her. I could hear it in his voice and the way he kept trying to avoid the topic of her. He just didn't want to admit to himself that despite all the women he'd had in his life, his heart still belonged to Ne'Vaeh. A woman he hadn't seen in four years.

"Well, I love Aaron. I'll admit my life wasn't right for a long time, and my past is just coming back to kick me in the ass, but I just want someone to look at me and see me for who I really am, and what I really need. Aaron never saw me. He never saw past my looks. He never saw my heart. He never tried and as soon as he heard about—not *saw*—a side of me that he didn't like, he turned his back on me. Like I said before, he hasn't left yet, but the time is coming." I lowered my head.

Jamie shook his head, looking down at me.

I shook my head back. "He's ready to give up on me, and I wish the muthafucka would just dump me instead of stringing me along. I'm so tired of feeling this way, Jamie. I wanna be happy. I wanna feel good about life."

"What did you come here for tonight, outside of leaving the party before you beat Alisha's ass?"

I just looked up at him.

"Did you come here to talk about Aaron or to forget about that muthafucka for a few days?" His hands slid around my waist.

My heart skipped a beat. I looked up at him. "Jamie, I haven't slept with anyone *but* Aaron in over two years, since the very day I laid eyes on him. But yet, when he looks at me, all he can see is that girl who slept with hundreds of people. I know I fucked up, Jamie. I know I don't deserve someone like him. But I just need him to see the person that I am now. Why can't he see me, Jamie? Me, just me!" I cried.

"C'mon, shorty, don't cry." Jamie tilted my chin so our eyes could meet. He tried to dry my tears, but I took his hands from my face.

I shook my head. "Jamie, I'll be okay."

He ignored me because he knew I needed affection. He surrounded me in his arms. He gently kissed my neck, and my whole body trembled. I could feel his heart beating against my chest. His body was so silky, smooth, and warm, and oh, he smelled so good. His muscular arms were so strong. His body was amazing. He held me close against his body. I could feel his dick rising, poking me in the stomach.

Jamie sucked on my neck until I couldn't take it anymore. I giggled, trying to pull away, but he wouldn't loosen his arms or his lips, and I laughed aloud.

"Jamie, stop!" I squealed.

He laughed, removing his lips from my neck.

I dried my tears of sorrow, which had turned into tears of joy. "Oh my goodness, Jamie! You still know how to make a girl smile even when she's upset. But you *did* promise me that you'd keep your hands to yourself, and you didn't keep your promise."

He looked down into my face. "No, I said that I would *try* to be on my best behavior. I tried to keep my hands to myself. I swear I tried. But listening to you talk about what your man's not giving you is only giving me ideas of what I would do if I had the chance, and since you're here with me, I *do* have the chance."

I so needed the affection that he was giving me. I needed someone to make me smile and make me laugh, even when times were bad. I hadn't seen Jamie since I was fifteen, and here he was, four years later, making me feel like no time had passed between us. He'd never crossed the line, never hit on me. He never so much as even looked at me in a sexual way. And despite how my life was back then, he never judged me or called me out of my name.

I looked up at him as he lifted my body up, wrapping my legs around his waist.

He held me close against his body. "It's just you and me tonight. Nobody else is here with us. My girl, Pamela, isn't here. Your man, Aaron, isn't here, and your best friend and my ex-girl-friend, Ne'Vaeh, isn't here. It's just us. I think we could both use a vacation away from stress. I think you came here because you wanted to get fucked."

I blushed a little, not wanting to admit that I needed some dick. A girl who used to know how to make a nigga come in his pants just by danc-ing with him needed to get laid? I was ashamed of myself. I had completely changed for Aaron, and where did it get me? I was still being judged as if I were that same girl, so what was the point of changing?

"I can't lie," Jamie gently kissed my lips. "When I ran into you today, seeing how fine that ass was lookin' in those tight-ass jeans, yeah, I wanted to hit it. But once we started talking, and I could see that you were in pain, I knew what you needed more than anything was to feel some affection. I want to make you feel good, Charlene. I've known you since elementary school. You've made mistakes. Shit, we all have. You're human, shorty. You've grown a lot too. I can see that. You've changed for a muthafucka, who can't even see that. He didn't know you like

I knew you, shorty. I see you, Charlene. I *really* see you. You're *more* than beautiful. You're a woman who owned up to her past and made an effort to change. So even if that muthafucka can't see you, *I* see you, Charlene."

Tears slid down my face as I felt Jamie unsnap my bra.

I helped slide it from my arms and held it in my hands. I nearly lost my mind as he kissed my breasts, sucking my left nipple into his mouth. He sucked on my nipple until my pussy started throbbing.

I held his head in my hands, running my hands across his smooth, low-cut fade.

He kissed all the way up to my lips, and I nearly lost my mind as his lips touched mine. He held me tighter against him. We nearly ate each other's lips off at that moment. I hadn't been kissed that way in so long. I needed him, *all* of him that night. He ran his fingers through my hair. He tugged on my hair just a little. He gripped my behind as he carried me back toward shore. We made it halfway across the beach to the house, when he got down on his knees and laid me on the sand, hovering over the top of me. He gripped my thigh in one hand and slipped my panties down with the other. I helped slide them off my body. Then I helped him slide his wet boxers off.

Jamie lay down between my legs. He didn't waste any time sliding his hard dick inside of my extremely wet pussy. I sunk my nails into his shoulders as his tongue penetrated my lips, and his dick penetrated my soul. Our wet thighs slapped together as he pumped in and out of me.

"Jamie!" I screamed out, "Please . . . fuck me," I cried.

"Your pussy feels so wet . . . so warm. . . . *Fuck*, this shit is good," Jamie whispered between kisses. His body shivered as he pumped deeper inside of me.

I held on to him as he dug into my soul—and then abruptly pulled out of me and sat up.

I sat up, nearly out of breath. I looked down at his dick. It was still nice and hard, covered in my pussy juices. He didn't bust yet, so why did he stop?

"Wh-what's wrong? Oh my gosh, why did you stop?" My chest heaved in and out, as I watched him pick up his boxers, along with my panties and bra.

He looked up at me and held my hands, pulling me up off the wet sand. "C'mon." He led me to the house.

We walked up the steps into the beach house. Jamie tossed his boxers and my underwear on the couch. I stood there naked as I watched him walk over to the stereo to turn it on. The sounds of R&B singer Jamie Foxx flowed through the speakers.

I smiled nervously, eyes already full of tears, as Jamie walked over to me.

He looked down into my face as he held my hips, then gently kissed my lips.

I cried in his mouth. His hands, his lips, and his body felt so good up against mine. He backed me up against the wall, lifted my body up, and I wrapped my legs around his waist.

Jamie braced my body up against the wall as he slid himself inside of me and began to grind to the music. I moaned as Jamie sang in my ear. With every stroke, my pussy spit fluids down his thighs. His dick was saturated.

"How does it feel, Charlie?" he moaned, pumping harder.

I sighed. "Like fuckin' magic," I cried out passionately.

"Tell me you like it." He pounded to the rhythm of the drums in the song.

"I *love* it." I dug my nails in his shoulders.

"If I taste that pussy, would you put your lips on this dick? Your lips are so thick and juicy. I wanna kiss those lips between your thighs like a muthafucka, shorty. And I want these lips"

Jamie gently kissed my lips, sucking on my bottom lip just a little, "on this dick. I know that shit would feel good as fuck, and I promise to make that pussy purr over and over in my mouth. Can we make that happen tonight?"

I burst out in tears. I loved every bit of the way that Jamie was making me feel inside and out that night, but I was angry at the same damn time.

Jamie watched the tears slide down my face. He stopped stroking me but still held my legs around my waist, bracing me up against the wall. "Do you want me to stop?"

I couldn't stop crying enough to respond to him.

Jamie pulled himself out of me, then lowered my feet back down to the floor. He looked down into my face, his body still pressed up against mine. "Why are you crying? What am I doing wrong?" he whispered.

I looked up at him, shaking my head. "What? No, Jamie, you're not doing *anything* wrong. You're-you're doing everything just right, just perfect. I wish I had more of this each and every day."

Jamie knew what the problem was. He wasn't Aaron, and he knew how much that I wished that he were. I was in love with Aaron, yet Aaron was far from being in love with me. And I was there making what felt like love to a man that my own best friend once loved with all of her heart for years.

Jamie held my face and dried my tears. "Charlie, 'til this day, you are still one of the hottest, finest women that I have ever met."

I shook my head, rolling my eyes. "Whateva, Jamie, you don't have to flatter me."

He shook his head, "Nah, nah, I'm not just saying that. Man, all them niggas in middle school and in high school wanted your ass. And it wasn't because you was fuckin' some of them, shorty—it was because they was in love with you. You're sexy, smart, talented, and you're beautiful. Your lips, eyes, hair, skin, ass, thighs, shit, your pussy—*everything* about you is sexier than a muthafucka. If I wasn't constantly on the road, didn't already have a girl, and if your best friend wasn't my ex, I swear to you that I would do whatever it took to make you mine. You know I couldn't care less about your nigga, right?"

Tears trickled down my face.

"I've known you since elementary school. I don't give a fuck about your past. You're a beautiful person, Charlie, real talk. We've been friends for a long time, before it even came down to this moment. That nigga, Aaron, is crazy. If he doesn't love you the way that you want him to love you, maybe it's time that you let him go and stop wasting your time. And stop crying. The Charlene Campbell that *I* know never cried over no nigga. You know better than that shit, ma."

I looked up at him as he backed up and pulled me to him by my hands. He turned my body around then held me by the waist, grinding his body up against my booty. I began to grind my booty and hips up against his dick, in time to the music.

He kissed my neck, rubbing his hands across my stomach, hips, ass, and between my legs. I gyrated my hips up against his dick until pre-come began to drip from the tip.

"*Shit*," he moaned, turning my body around to face his.

I looked up into his face.

Jamie held my hands, leading me into the bedroom. He sat down on the bed, pulling my body in between his legs. I sat down on his lap, swinging my legs around, facing his body. I lifted my ass a little, holding his dick, easing it inside of me. I looked down into his face, and he looked up at me, biting his lip. He held on to my hips as I began to bounce on his dick. It was the perfect size . . . not too big, not too long, not ginormous. It was just right, and it curved to the left just a little.

Jamie gripped my waist, damn near digging his nails into my skin. He moaned as I rode him. "*Charlene.*" Jamie called out my name as I locked my knees around his waist and rode him until he couldn't take it anymore. He held my waist, signaling me to stop before I made him come. We quickly switched positions. He lay me down on the bed, lying between my legs.

My tears saturated the pillow as Jamie began to dig deep into my pussy as if he was digging a hole, digging for buried treasure. Deep sex, yeah, that was what I needed. Jamie pumped in and out of me. I gripped his ass in my hands.

I was just about to come. Jamie felt my body begin to moisten and the walls of my pussy begin to tighten. Then, he pounded harder. I cried even more as my body jerked. We came together, as he bit down on my neck.

All Jamie's weight fell on me as his heart beat strong and steady in his chest. I held on to him as tightly as I could. His body felt so warm against mine. I inhaled his scent. He smelled so good.

Jamie buried his face in my neck. "*Damn . . .* Baby?"

"Hmmm?" I fought back the tears, loving the sound of his voice in my ear.

"How many more days do I have you?" He gently kissed my neck.

Just when I was about to answer, I heard my cell phone ring in my purse. The ring tone was my favorite old-school song, "Come Talk to Me." It was Aaron.

"Aaron!" I whispered excitedly, butterflies fluttering in my stomach.

Jamie laughed a little to himself as he pulled out of me.

I couldn't get to my phone fast enough. I almost tripped over my own two feet. "Hello?" I answered the phone, damn near out of breath.

"Hey, baby, what's up?" Aaron's voice was music to my heart.

"Nothing much. Just chillin' with my people. Ran into a few old friends." I laughed nervously.

"Sorry it took me all day to call. I had basketball practice, I had to work, and then I went out to get some drinks with the fellas. You enjoying yourself? I mean, are you behaving yourself?" I could hear him exhaling, which meant he was smoking. I hated that. Aaron hid his health from the team, but he hadn't outgrown his asthma. He just had a doctor who knew he was good at playing basketball and didn't want to ruin his career.

I looked up, watching Jamie make his way to the bathroom. I knew I was making him feel uncomfortable. "Ummm, yeah, of course, I'm behaving myself. I haven't whooped Alisha's ass yet, if that's what you mean. She's still breathing, so everything is all good."

Aaron laughed a little. *"So, how long are you gonna be in MIA?"*

"A few more days." My eyes glistened. I was starting to feel a little guilty because he actually sounded like he missed me.

"When you get home, Charlie, we need to go out and have some fun. I'm tired of working twenty-four-seven, not spending any time with my girl. I wanna take my baby out and show her off. When is the last time that we went out and had some fun?"

I smiled a little to myself as I began to cry. "Like four months ago." I could hear people talking and the faint sound of music playing in the background. "Where are you?"

He hesitated. *"In the restroom at Purple Panties."*

I rolled my eyes, drying my face. Purple Panties was a new strip club that the basketball team went to on a damn near daily basis. I knew most of the hoes who worked up in there, and they damn sure didn't make all that money they made by just dancing. Those bitches got buck-ass naked onstage, damn near fucked dudes onstage, and went with about two, three, or even

four guys to the "champagne room." I don't give
a fuck what Chris Rock said—there *is* sex in the
champagne room.

"Oh my goodness, Aaron, you know I hate
when you go to that fuckin' club. Please wash
your hands when you leave there if you touch
any of those girls." I reached for my bra and
panties. "And do *not* take your ass in that champagne room, do you hear me?"

*"Hey, Charlie, I gotta go. I'll give you a call
tomorrow, a'ight?"* Aaron acted as if he didn't
hear my comment.

I sighed, "All right, Aaron. I love you, baby."

I waited to hear an "I love you" back. But I
waited in vain.

"Talk to you later, babe." He hung up.

I just sat there on the floor, phone still to my
ear. The tears started rolling again.

"Everything all right, shorty?" I heard Jamie's
voice behind me.

I took the phone from my ear, quickly drying
my tears. I stood up, turning around facing
Jamie. He was dressed in his wife beater and
Ralph Lauren boxers.

I nodded, faking a smile as I slid back into
my bra and panties. "Everything's all good," I
whispered.

"You in the mood for another drink?" Jamie
walked past me, over to the kitchen area.

"Yeah, sure. I could use a drink or two." I ran my fingers through my hair anxiously. I went over and sat at the bistro table, watching Jamie as he took out a bottle of Grey Goose from the fridge.

"Jamie?" I called out.

He looked at me as he reached into the cabinet for two glasses. "What's up?"

"Thank you for tonight," I whispered. "I really needed this."

He looked at me and smiled a little. "Did I warm you up enough to go back to your man?"

I looked at him, shocked that he would imply that I actually used him. "Oh, so, you think I used you? That's not what this was, Jamie. You have a girl like I have a man, so before you wanna go throwing up those types of comments—"

Jamie laughed, cutting me off. "Shorty, I'm just sayin', though, you couldn't get to the phone quick enough. Pamela has been blowin' up my phone all day long, and you haven't seen me answer the phone *once*. As a matter of fact, you haven't seen me check my phone *once* to see who it was. I just know it was shorty because she calls me three times back-to-back, then texts me about three times back-to-back, then sends me a message on Facebook about three times, then calls again back-to-back for about an hour straight.

The girl blows my phone up when I don't answer. I have a life outside of her, man. Aaron's ass didn't call you all day, and as soon as he did, you nearly broke a toe trying to answer the phone. What did you expect me to say?" Jamie sat down at the bar next to me. "You sprung, shorty. The nigga's got you *sprung*."

I hesitated. "So, maybe he does, okay? I guess I'm still looking for something that's not there. I need him to need me, and he doesn't." I shrugged.

"Shit, it is what it is, shorty." Jamie popped open the bottle. "And if it's not, well, then, shit, it's just not. And you don't need that shit. You deserve love, Charlene. You don't deserve bull-shit. It's about time you start realizing your worth. You fine as a *muthafucka*, Charlene. You deserve so much better." He poured me a glass then poured a glass for himself.

I took the glass.

Jamie held up his glass to toast me. "To five days together. No worries. No drama. No boy-friend. No girlfriend. No bullshit. No *crying*. Just fun, smoking, drinking, shopping, and fuckin'. Just you and me. Fuck everything else. A'ight?"

Tears lined my lashes. I nodded, holding my glass up to him. "I'll toast to that."

The week went by fast, *too* fast. I didn't want it to end. Jamie and I went out on the town. I went with him to just about all of his TV appearances that week. I went with him to two parties. We went to four or five movies that week. In public, we were old friends catching up. But in private, shit, we were like two lovers who had spent months apart. We had sex at least three or four times a day. I ended up staying with him the entire week. He wasn't lying when he said that he was a celebrity. He made time for me when he really didn't have the time, and it felt great. We were inseparable that week. I was having a great time, and I really didn't want to leave him. He had my body on fire whenever he touched me. He sparked a flame inside my soul that Aaron hadn't even bothered to tend to. I felt with him what I wanted to feel with Aaron. Jamie was more than a friend at that moment. I waded in waters too deep, and I was drowning in it.

Chapter 5

Deeper

Charlene

I met back up with the cheerleading squad just in time for our flight to leave.

Alisha folded her arms as I walked up to the squad. She tapped her Prada shoes against the terminal floor. "Well well well, look who finally decided to grace us with her presence. If it isn't Queen Charlene," she hissed.

I rolled my eyes, flipping my hair over my shoulder. "Alisha, I am not in the mood for your shit today, so you need to back the fuck off."

"For real, Charlie, where have you been?" Kelissa asked. Kelissa was a short, petite, brown-skinned girl with long hair and hazel eyes. She didn't too much care for Alisha either, but she always took her side to avoid confrontation. "Half of the clubs that we wanted to get in wouldn't even let us in without you, the 'Redbone Bombshell.' You wanna fill us in on where you were?"

I looked at Alisha. They all stood there waiting on me to respond. I shook my head. "Last time I checked, my daddy was dead and my mama was in Maryland. I'm grown, and I don't have to answer to none of y'all bitches. I went and spent some time by myself. I had to get away from y'all to avoid opening up a can of kill-a-trick on a few of y'all, okay?" I rolled my eyes.

"Excuse me," I heard a sweet, gentle female voice call out over my shoulder.

I turned around to see bright, Colgate-clean teeth gleaming at me. She was the color of soft caramel, with long, dark, silky hair and bright brown eyes. Her lips were full and glossy. She was about five foot five, with a Coke-bottle figure and dressed very classy. She wore a white button-down shirt, tight smoky-gray pants, and a gray scarf around her neck. She smiled at me, handing me a brown leather wallet. "Sweetie, you left this in the cab. I was just about to get in when I saw it in the backseat. You were in such a hurry. I don't think you heard me calling out to you."

I hesitated, taking the wallet from her. "Thanks, hon. Oh my goodness, girl, my *life* is in this wallet!" I laughed a little.

Alisha pointed at her. "Hey, you look real familiar."

The young lady smiled. "Yeah, some of you all do too."

"Wait a minute, I know you." Lailah, the Puerto Rican cutie in the squad, stepped forward. "You're captain of the cheerleading squad at Memphis State! I saw you doing your thing at one of y'all's basketball games in Charlotte last year when I went to visit my cousin last season! Your team has mad skills! Y'all make that shit look effortless!"

The young lady shook her head. "No, we just work our ass off. We have our flaws, trust me. We just know how to dress it up a little on the court." She looked at me. "I know who you are too. Seen you at a few competitions. I think my boyfriend even said he went to school with you."

I looked at her, and my heart skipped a beat, for what reason, I don't know. Seems like my body caught on to the situation before my mind did. "School with me? What did you say your name was?"

She smiled, holding her hand out to shake mine. "Oh my goodness, I'm so rude. I'm Pamela

Rhodes, trying to be Pamela Green, if you know what I mean."

Alisha loved the expression on my face. She laughed a little. "Green—as in *Jamie* Green? Yes, girl, I went to school with him freshman year in high school. Shit, Charlene here practically grew up with him. How *is* he doing?" Alisha elbowed me a little, waking me up from my daze, and forcing me to pick my jaw up from the floor.

"Great! He's here on a few television appearances. We took separate vacations. Thought I'd surprise him. I'm here with my parents for a few days." Pamela smiled sweetly. "I'm sure y'all have seen him and his teammates."

"Oh, I thought that was him at that basketball party about a week ago. Nope, didn't say much to him, though. Charlie, did you speak to him?" Alisha grinned at me.

The squad giggled.

I shook my head nervously. "Girl, I probably wouldn't recognize him if I did. Haven't seen him in years, but when you do see him, tell him I said hi."

Just when I thought the situation couldn't get any worse, we all caught sight of Jamie and a few of his teammates walking toward us. You should have seen the look on his face when Pamela went running up to him, jumping into his arms.

She was happy to see him, not even stopping to wonder why he showed up at the airport when he didn't even know she was arriving. She was there to surprise him, and he was there to say good-bye to me.

Jamie looked over her shoulder at me, as she hugged him around his neck. We never exchanged numbers. I planned to leave things the way they were, but apparently, he wanted something more. We both agreed that week was just that week—something we both needed—well, maybe me more than him. I didn't see a need to get his number, since I was going back to Maryland to deal with my own situation. Up until that point, I wasn't even feeling bad about cheating on Aaron with Jamie, especially after Aaron called me from the strip club and couldn't even tell me he loved me over the phone. However, when I saw Pamela hugging Jamie as if he was the most important person in the world to her, I felt like a true slut. She held on to him the same way that Ne'Vaeh once held on to him. I couldn't help but think that sleeping with Jamie was the worst thing I could have done to a woman who didn't deserve that.

"Shorty, what's up? What are you doing here?" Jamie was as shocked to see Pamela as I was shocked to see him show up at the airport.

Pamela let go of Jamie, slapping him in the shoulder playfully. "Sweetie, my mom came here to visit my aunt, who's having a baby in a few days. I just wanted to surprise you! You must've been real busy since you weren't returning any of my calls!" Pamela looked over at me and saw me staring straight back at Jamie. She looked at Jamie. "What are you doing here, Jamie? I didn't tell you I was flying in."

Jamie looked at me, then back at Pamela. "Oh . . . My homies wanted to come wish the ladies luck this coming basketball season. A few of the girls from the squad showed up at the party the fellas threw at a club last week. They was just stopping by to give their number to a few of the ladies on the squad. Ain't that right, fellas?"

They nodded behind him, agreeing and spread out, walking up to the ladies on my squad.

One of Jamie's teammates stepped to me, handing me a folded-up sheet of paper.

I took it from him, grasping it in my hand while glancing at Jamie over his shoulder.

Pamela looked at me. "What was your name again? Charlene, is it?" She turned to Jamie. "Jamie, this is Charlene. She said she went to school with you."

Jamie nodded, "Yeah, we did." He looked at me. "You were friends with Ne'Vaeh, right? Tell her I said what's up when you see her."

I nodded, clearing my throat, "W-will do."

Pamela pulled on Jamie's arm. "Sweetie, we need to get going. My mother is waiting. Tell your friends you'll catch up with them later. It was nice meeting you all."

Passengers boarding flight IG F8122, please report to the passenger service center at this time.

"Well, that's us, fellas." Alisha hugged and kissed one of the players on the team. "It was nice meeting some of y'all and reuniting with a few of y'all! The party was off the fuckin' chain! Until the next party, y'all!"

The girls hurried over to the flight attendant to hand over their boarding passes.

I couldn't move. My feet were planted on the ground.

Jamie looked back at me as Pamela locked arms with him, leading him away from the passenger terminal. He winked at me, and my heart melted.

"C'mon, Charlie!" Kelissa grabbed my arm, pulling me off to board the plan.

We stuffed our carry-on bags in the compartments above our head and sat down in our first-class seats. Just when I sat down at the window, finally able to breathe again, Alisha sits her big butt beside me.

I looked at her, rolling my eyes. "I thought Karla was supposed to be sitting next to me, Alisha."

"We switched seats, boo. I thought I would enjoy sitting next to you." She grinned.

I looked at her. I smelled a blackmail coming on. "What the fuck do you want, Alisha?"

"I know you fucked Jamie, Charlene Campbell." She glared at me, pointing at my face with her American-manicured pointer finger.

"And how the fuck—"

Alisha put her hand in my face, cutting me off. "Don't try to play me, bitch. You walk different, talk different, skin glowing and shit. And I saw the way he looked at you. You fucked your best friend's ex-boyfriend, and instead of being ashamed, you're actually falling for the nigga."

I hated that bitch, but she was right. "Like I said, Alisha, what the *fuck* do you want?"

"I want you to quit the cheerleading squad," she grinned.

My eyes widened. "You must have lost your fuckin' mind if you think I'm going to give up something that I have been working my whole life for!"

Alisha couldn't care less. "You have until homecoming game to give up your pom-poms, boo, or I'm telling Ne'Vaeh. And it's as simple as that."

I shook my head at her. "You have no proof that I slept with Jamie, the same way that you have no proof that I ever slept with Ashton's ass, trick."

Alisha looked at me as if she wanted to smack me in the face for even bringing up Ashton's name. "I don't? Back in high school, you had niggas callin' their girl 'Charlie' every time their girl gave them head, and why? Because you were giving them niggas head. You had them niggas asking their girls to swallow that shit, and why? Because *your* nasty ass was swallowing that shit. When I gave Ashton head the first time, the nigga called me 'Charlie,' and why is that, bitch?"

I sat back in my seat, looking out the window. I couldn't even deny what the bitch was saying. "I'm not quitting the team. I don't give a fuck what you say. You have no proof of that shit you talkin'." I looked back at her, my eyes glistening. "*No* proof."

"What's on the note Jerry handed you? Did you even *look* at it?" Alisha asked.

I hadn't looked at it, and I didn't even realize that I still had it in my hands. I hesitated. What did I have to lose by opening the note? I unfolded it.

Alisha leaned over to take a peek. "'*I can still feel your lips on it. Until the next episode. 901-761-3228, Jamie G.*'" She looked at me.

I looked up at her, swallowing hard. That nigga Jamie, boy, I tell you . . .

Alisha was disgusted. "Ol' nasty-ass bitch. Still suckin' dick. You a dick-sucker. You'd probably suck mine too, if I had one."

"Shut up, Alisha." I rolled my eyes, folding the note back up. "Keep talkin' shit."

"Homecoming game, Charlie." Alisha shook her head at me.

It was the second week of school at Morgan State, and we were behind on cheerleading tryouts. I was going through my own personal issues and really wasn't in the mood for being one of the judges on the panel that chose which girls were worthy of being on our cheerleading squad. I had an eye for talent, which is why I was on the panel, but I really wasn't feeling it that day. Alisha had already warned me that I only had a few months to come clean about my affair with Jamie.

Four weeks had passed since Miami, and I found out just a few days before tryouts that I was pregnant. I wasn't exactly sure how I was going to deal with the situation. I'd avoided any contact with Ne'Vaeh, and I made it a habit to seduce Aaron from the very day that I found out that I was pregnant. If I decided on keeping the baby, I had to get the timing right. Aaron kept his promise of trying to spend more time with me. However, it wasn't until the night that I found out that I was pregnant that I finally came around to sleeping with him. Though I loved the attention from Aaron, a part of me couldn't help but wish that I was back on that beach with Jamie.

"Girl, are you all right?" Dana, the assistant cheerleading coach, nudged me in my shoulder that afternoon at tryouts.

I snapped out of my daze. "I'm good." I looked up into her pretty brown eyes, faking a grin. "I'm good."

Her eyes searched mine. "Mm-hmm. Well, we need to make a decision. We should have had a decision like *yesterday*, and your ass is sitting over here daydreaming. We have games and tournaments coming up in like two weeks, and we don't even have our squad together yet. I'm tired of UMBC and Howard showing us up. I wouldn't be surprised if some of them bitches from College Park show up here today, *just* because they know we're having tryouts. Alisha is *pissed*, okay? And I really ain't trying to hear her mouth today."

I looked over at Alisha, who was in the middle of the basketball court, choreographing the cheers for the tryouts.

I rolled my eyes. "Man, fuck Alisha, okay?"

Danita, who sat to my left, laughed a little. "Girl, we have been dealing with y'all's drama since middle school. How long are you two gonna let that old shit dictate your lives?"

I looked at Danita, who seriously needed to get those thick-ass eyebrows tweezed before she wanted to try to check somebody. "'Old shit'? *Please,* okay? She is *still* trippin' off of that shit with Ashton. *Her* ass is the one who can't leave the past where it is. She's been accusing me of fuckin' her man for the past five years. . . ."

Dana looked at me. "Well, wasn't it *you* who told me that Ashton ate you out in the ninth grade?"

Danita burst out in laughter.

I elbowed her then looked back at Dana. "What? I *never* told your ass no shit like that! I told you that I sucked *his* dick. *Please* get your facts straight. See, that's how rumors get started. Sucking a boy's dick doesn't mean that he reciprocated the favor, *nor* does it mean that there was any penetration involved. Alisha wasn't suckin' his dick to his satisfaction, so, hey, he came to me."

Danita rolled her eyes. "Okay, *Superhead,* and you wonder why the girl can't stand you. She loves that boy. Call it what you want, but *sex* is sex. Suckin' and fuckin' are the same damn things, if you ask me."

"Well, nobody *asked* your ass, Danita." I rolled my eyes.

Danita shook her head. "Alisha can destroy you, and you know it. Fuckin' with someone's man in any type of way is suicide. Trust me. Y'all *know* that I know." Danita pulled back her hair that covered her left ear. You could still see where the doctors sewed her ear back to her damn head.

In the eleventh grade, Danita got into a fight with this Puerto Rican chick named Marcia. Marcia was the hottest, most talented dancer of the senior graduating class that year. Danita was fuckin' Marcia's boyfriend, Carlos, nearly six months before Marcia caught the two. She'd seen Carlos's car parked in front of a Motel 6. She went to the front-desk clerk to ask what room he was in. The clerk barely got the words "room 206" out before Marcia rushed off to the room. She got to the room, damn near out of breath, but as calmly as she could, she knocked on the door. She heard a woman's giggle behind the door. She knocked again then stood to the side of the door so the person wouldn't see her through the peephole. Danita's stupid ass opened the door, sticking her head out. As soon as she turned to see Marcia's face, it was too late. Before the bitch could run back inside and slam the door, Marcia grabbed her by her hair. If the housekeeping cart hadn't blocked Marcia from throwing Danita's ass over the railing, Danita's ass would have been dead. Before Carlos could even make it out of the room, Marcia had pulled out her got-damn knife and cut Danita's ear slap off.

I shook my head at Danita. "That's your crazy-ass life, Danita. Not mine. Nobody told you to fuck Marcia's man. She's the only girl in a family of eight boys. You knew she'd fuck your ass up on sight, no questions asked. You lucky she didn't throw your ass over the railing, you crazy bitch."

Danita laughed, shaking her head at me. "All right, Charlie, keep talking that shit. That might be you one day."

I rolled my eyes. "Please, Alisha ain't shit but talk. I knew Ashton all my life. We're just friends, regardless of whether Alisha wants to believe me. I ain't got shit to prove to her, and I *damn* sure ain't got shit to prove to y'all bitches, either."

Dana shook her head at me too. "Well, whatever. All I'm sayin' is that as bitchy and as loud as Alisha can be at times, she is cool people. Best damn captain that we could ever have on our team. You know she's leaving us in January to be a Laker Girl, right? She's going places. Where the hell are *you* going?"

I should have known that she would stick up for Alisha. I mean they *are* cousins.

I rolled my eyes.

Dana thought I was a slut too. The only reason she even hung around me was because I had connections. The reason why she really didn't like me was because she liked Ashton but never had the chance to be with him because he was with her cousin, who was "going places." Shit. Who gave a damn? Okay, *I* gave a damn. I was pregnant and scared as a motherfucka. My mom tried to convince me not to have the abortion, but at that point, I wasn't so sure. Hearing that Alisha was living her dreams was tearing me the hell apart. My reputation had gotten the best of me. I was turned down from damn near every dance audition that I went to because there were at least two judges on each panel that I'd got into it with in high school because of cheating with their man, or they were friends with the person whose man I slept with. Nineteen and my life was already shot to shit. I had no idea how I was going to get my life back. What was I going to do with a baby? Jamie's baby at that?

"You know what?" I got up from the table, but Danita grabbed me, pulling me back down. I pulled from her. "That shit with Ashton was five fuckin' years ago. We were kids. Yeah, Alisha was fuckin' him, but she wasn't *suckin'* him. So he came to me, his best friend, who, at that time, would do *any*thing for him. Yeah, I was a ho back then. Yeah, I fucked and sucked the whole basketball team! Are you happy now? Y'all can judge me if you want, but that is the past. I've changed. I moved on, and I am *not* that girl anymore! I've been with Aaron since January, junior year, spring 2012. It's almost fuckin' 2015 and y'all hoes are *still* talkin' about the same old shit! Y'all bitches helped Alisha make my life a living hell, and yeah, maybe I brought it all on myself. Aaron barely wants shit to do with me! I damn near have to rape the boy to get him to have sex with me now!"

Dana laughed a little.

I glared at her. "Oh, you wanna laugh, do you?"

She straightened up. "My bad, you're right. It's not funny. And you're right, we're wrong as hell."

"If I wanted Ashton, I could have him. Alisha needs to let that shit go and stop putting ideas in everyone's head about me." I shook my head in disgust.

Danita looked at me, tapping her pencil on the table. "Oh, okay, so I guess she's wrong about Jamie too, then, huh?"

I damn near swallowed my tongue. "Wh-what?"

"She *said* she guesses Alisha is wrong about Jamie too, then, huh?" Dana was always a fuckin' cosigner.

Danita nodded. "Alisha said that you went missing from the squad for the whole week y'all were in Miami. Said you may have been chillin' with Jamie the *whole* damn time. Wasn't Jamie your bestie's man a few years ago?"

Just when I started to answer Danita, stomping and chanting echoed throughout the gym. We looked up to see about ten girls, dressed in tight blue, tiny T-shirts and black leggings steppin' across the hardwood floors, forcing our squad and the girls trying out for our squad out of the way. Hair flippin', booties poppin', hips gyratin', flips, twerkin', feet stompin'—shit, they were *killin'* it—and made our squad look like beginners. It didn't take me long to notice the big dark blue "M" embroidered across their breasts. My eyes widened. It was the Memphis State cheerleaders.

My heart pounded in my chest as about ten dudes wearing blue and white sport coats made their way into our gym, standing back up against the wall. I looked back over at the cheerleaders, who were seriously showing us up, and I saw Pamela dancing in the center of the squad, chanting her ass off. I looked back over at the ten guys standing up against the wall, only to see Jamie staring straight back at me. My heart skipped a beat. He winked his eye at me.

I looked over at Alisha, who stood, posing with her arms folded across her chest. She looked back at me . . . and winked her eye at me too.

I shook my head at her as the Memphis State cheerleaders' showdown came to a close. Our squad had no choice but to clap for them, even if it was a forced clap. We could hate if we wanted to, but we had to admit they had skills. I'm pretty sure the girls who were trying out for our team wished they went to Memphis State.

"Well well well, looky here." Alisha walked up to Pamela, who stood with her hands on her hips in front of her squad. "If it isn't Pamela."

Pamela grinned, breathing heavily. "What's up, girl? You know we had to pay y'all a visit to show y'all how the South gets down and dirty."

Alisha nodded. "Oh well, that *was* dirty as hell, showing up here when we have tryouts going on. What are y'all doin' here anyway?"

"My baby is in town visiting his sister." Pamela signaled Jamie to come over.

Alisha looked over at me, signaling us to come over too.

I shook my head, but Dana and Danita each took an arm and pulled me up from my chair. "O . . . M . . . G," I whispered, with my hand over my chest.

Dana laughed a little, letting go of my arm, making her way around the table. "It's showtime, ladies."

We made our way to the middle of the floor, just in time to meet Jamie and his boys.

"So, how long do y'all plan on staying here?" Kelissa approached the Memphis State athletes. "Shit, y'all know y'all can't leave town without us showin' *y'all* asses up at the Q party tonight."

Pamela and her squad nodded. She grinned, teeth looking like she just hopped out of the dentist's chair. "Well, we're here all weekend. We could use a little practice for nationals. We don't mind putting y'all skills to the test at your *own* school!" Her team laughed along with her.

"Well," I finally caught my breath. "It has been nice watching y'all kick our asses today, but I gotta get going. I still haven't gotten all of my schoolbooks for the semester, so . . . I'll holla . . ." I turned to walk away.

Kelissa caught my arm. "Charlie, we're supposed to be going shopping, girl! I don't got shit to wear to the Q party tonight!"

I glanced at Jamie, then looked back at Kelissa. "Girl, I'll catch back up with you. I'll call you when I leave the bookstore."

I hurried off to the bathroom before the chunks started to rise in my throat. I just knew I was going to throw up all over the floor. I could feel my stomach burning, and I could feel the tension building in my chest. I burst into the stall, kneeling down over the toilet, and instead of vomit spewing from my mouth, tears spilled from my eyes instead. How could I have been so stupid? I knew in my heart that I was in love with Aaron, but when I saw Jamie standing there in his letter jacket, looking good enough to eat, my body was on fire. There I was, pregnant with his baby, knowing good and damn well that there was no way I could keep his baby *and* keep Aaron without telling Aaron that he was my child's father.

I did end up going shopping with Dana, Danita, Kelissa, and Lailah that evening. They were pressed to get dresses with our school colors, orange, blue, and white. I ended up buying a tight, backless, royal blue minidress.

I wasn't in any mood to go to a fuckin' Q party. The fraternity party scene was played out to me. Not to mention morning sickness was kicking my ass twenty-four-seven. I played it off as best as I could, but even the squad knew something was up when I didn't want anything to drink later. They danced their asses off that night, paying the Memphis State crew back for making us look bad at tryouts.

I sat at the bar, cheering from the sidelines. Jamie sat with his crew at a far corner of the club. I can't tell you how many muthafuckas were drooling over me that night. Some were hot, some *really* not. I *was* looking good in my D&G dress. My hair was slicked up into a bun. Silver hoop earrings hung from my ears. My makeup was flawless. The stilettos I had on made it look like I had legs for days. Despite how good I knew I looked, I wasn't in the mood for anybody being all up on me, smelling like sweaty balls and liquor.

Jamie caught sight of me as I took a sip from my ginger ale. I set my glass down on the bar table and quickly got up as I saw him rise in his chair. I wasn't sure where he was off to, but just in case the nigga decided to be bold and talk to me in a room full of people in front of his girl, I made my way to the bathroom.

I stood at the mirror, set my purse down, and took out my cell phone. Aaron hadn't called me once that night. Ne'Vaeh had called several times, and I had yet to return her calls. I had only looked that girl in her face about two times over the course of four weeks, and it was only because I needed help studying for calculus. I hadn't seen her since I found out that I was pregnant. There was no way that I could face her after what I had done. If I was any type of friend, I would have called the girl and told her that Jamie was in town. However, the selfish part of me actually was glad that he showed up when he did. I had to find a way to talk to him about my situation. I never called him once in those four weeks. In fact, I threw away his number the day that he gave it to me at the airport.

"So, that's how you do a nigga, huh?" I heard a deep male voice over my shoulder.

I looked up to see Jamie standing in the door to the ladies' room. My eyes widened as I backed up against the counter in shock. "Jamie, what the fuck are you doing in here? Are you *seriously* bringing your ass into the ladies' room like somebody isn't gonna walk up in here and see your ass?"

Jamie grinned as he approached me, looking down into my face. "Why didn't you call a nigga?"

I looked up into his face, eyes coated in tears. "You need to get out of here before someone sees us, Jamie! What if your girl walks the fuck up in here? How are you gonna explain this shit to her?"

Jamie reached and opened the door to a stall, and he went in, pulling me in with him by my dress. I pulled away from him as he closed the stall door behind him.

My heart pounded in my chest as I pushed him in his. "You have *some* fuckin' nerve showing up to my school with your girl and shit, Jamie! You don't love Pamela, that's cool. But I am actually in love with Aaron, a man who has a hard time trusting me because of shit like this!"

Jamie looked down into my face. "We have known each other since elementary school. Took us damn near twenty years to finally sleep together. We spent a whole week together. It wasn't just about sex. We're friends, shorty, *more* than friends."

I shook my head. "I don't know what we are now, Jamie, but we're not friends. Your girl is out there, Jamie. What would she say if she knew about this? I have a boyfriend. Jamie, we *just* had sex this morning! You don't see anything wrong with fuckin' Pamela, then turning around that same day fuckin' somebody else?"

Jamie gripped my dress in his hands and slid it up, exposing my panties. "I haven't *touched* Pamela since the day I touched you, shorty," he whispered.

Tears slid down my face. He knew just what to say. He knew just what I wanted to hear. He knew just what I needed in my life.

I shook my head, lips trembling as he unbuckled his belt, unbuttoned his pants, and dropped them to the floor. Only Jamie Green would actually have the nerve to have sex in a public bathroom, in a club where his girl was just a few steps outside the bathroom door.

I tried to resist him as he held my hips, lifting my body up, wrapping my legs around his waist, bracing my body against the door of the stall. I could feel him pulling his dick out through the hole in the boxers. He didn't take my panties off; he just pulled them bitches to the side and pushed his way through.

I squealed a little bit as he bit down on my neck and began to work the hell out of me, digging into me like a shovel. He gripped my thighs as I held on to his shoulders, trying to hold in the screams.

Jamie moaned, "Charlene, *shit*." He whispered my name, thrusting his pelvis. He worked me as if we were dancing to the music outside the door.

My pussy held on to his dick with all her might. Though she was wet as a muthafucka, she was gripping for dear life. She held on to him as if she never wanted to let him go. When I came, my body fell limply against his. He held my body against the door and worked me until my legs went numb. When he came, he let out a long sigh in my ear. Our hearts pounded against each other's chest, and he just held me for a moment. He looked up at me, and I looked down into his face as he pulled out of me and gently let my body down to the floor.

I pulled my dress down as he pulled his pants up.

Tears slid down my face as I watched him buckle his belt.

Jamie dried my tears and gently kissed my lips. "Damn," he whispered. "I swear, your pussy feels good as a muthafucka. Feels like the best place on earth to be, shorty."

I gently pushed him away, then opened the door to the stall. Just when I walked out of the stall, Alisha and Kelissa walked into the bathroom. My heart literally stopped beating, and I froze in my tracks.

Alisha stopped in the doorway when she caught sight of me. She was in as much shock to see me walking out of the stall, with Jamie following behind me, as I was to see her walking in the bathroom on us.

Kelissa wasn't paying us any attention at first, too busy digging in her purse. "Girl, I can't believe my period had to come on tonight of all—" She abruptly stopped talking when Alisha held her hand up to her face. Kelissa looked up at us. Her eyes widened. "What the . . . Charlene? *Jamie?*" she squealed.

Alisha shook her head, folding her arms across her chest. "Fuckin' in the fuckin' bathroom? Y'all cheating muthafuckas couldn't get a room somewhere?"

Jamie laughed a little. "What's up, Alisha?"

Alisha glared at him. "Y'all are some triflin' muthafuckas. Pamela is out there lookin' for your ass, Jamie." Alisha looked back at me. "And Ashton just called me, saying him and Aaron were on their way here. And quit all that got-damn crying, Charlie! Your ass wasn't crying when you were fuckin' that nigga! No, wait, I take that back. I heard how he does. The dick put you to tears, huh, bitch? Ol' nasty, trashy, sleezy, classless—"

I rolled my eyes, drying my tears from my face. "Shut the fuck up, Alisha."

Kelissa shook her head at me. "Charlie, what are you doing? Jamie fucks *everybody!* Y'all in here fuckin' in the bathroom and shit, when his girl is right out there on the fuckin' dance floor? This shit is fucked up! You haven't changed since high school, Charlie! You want people to look at you differently, but you're *not* different! Alisha never lied about you, dummy! Your reputation doesn't *need* words! I *told* Aaron he couldn't turn a fuckin' ho into a housewife! I *told* him he couldn't tame a bitch who had a pussy hole that was miles long!"

Before I could get in her face, Jamie pulled me back. "Hold up, hold up. Y'all comin' down real hard on somebody like y'all shit don't stink. Alisha, didn't you pay the judges at Charlie's last audition *not* to choose her, even after she was already chosen?"

I looked at Alisha. "What's he talking about?"

Alisha glared at him.

Jamie nodded. "Yeah, Charlie, *you* were supposed to be a Laker Girl, not this bitch."

Before I could even reach out to strangle the shit out of Alisha, Kelissa got in the way. I pushed her out of my way, but Jamie pulled me back by my arm.

Alisha laughed aloud. "Hey, it's not like you would be able to keep the job anyway due to your . . ." she pointed at my stomach, "little *situation.*"

Both Kelissa and Jamie looked at me.

I shook my head at her. I should have known that bitch would have eyes on me at all times, even at the fuckin' hospital. I should have known she would look at my hospital records after we had our physicals for cheerleading the week before school started. If that bitch opened her mouth, I was going to knock her got-damn teeth out.

Alisha grinned. "See, at first, I was going to lay *all* your shit bare in front of the whole school, in front of the whole squad, in front of Aaron, in front of Ne'Vaeh. But then I found out from a friend of mine, who works as a physician's assistant at the University of Maryland, that you might have a little *situation* that might just prevent you from dancing or cheering for Morgan State—or *any* state, for that matter, for a long time." Alisha approached me, getting all in my grill, just daring me to touch her. "I was going to be the one to hang your ass, but I thought I would just stand by and let you hang yourself. Oh, I am *really* going to enjoy watching this shit."

I pushed her out of my face. "Alisha, you got one more time to get in my face."

Jamie pulled me back again.

Kelissa shook her head. "I don't know what the hell Alisha is talking about, and I *really* don't wanna know either. All I'm saying is a lot of people are going to get hurt. I'm sorry I said that shit to Aaron about turning a ho into a housewife, because I'm no one to judge, but Aaron is a great guy, who anyone would love to be with. Jamie, on the other hand," Kelissa rolled her eyes over to him, who stood there nonchalantly with his hands in his pockets, "has groupies lined up and down the East Coast." She rolled her eyes back over to me. "You're wasting your time with him. And you're gonna ruin a good friendship and a relationship in the process. You're too pretty to be *this* fucked-up in the head. I'm gettin' up outta this bathroom before Pamela comes in here." Kelissa threw her hands up, walking out of the bathroom.

Alisha walked over to the mirror to take a look at her flawless face and smooth her edges down with her hands. She looked at my reflection in the mirror.

Jamie looked at me. "Shorty." He grabbed my hand.

I looked at him, tears lining my lashes. I slid my hands from his. No matter how much I couldn't stand Alisha and the rest of the girls on the squad, I knew they were right. I shook my head at Jamie, putting my hand in his face before he said another word. "Jamie, please, just go."

Jamie looked over at Alisha, who stood at the mirror, arms folded across her chest. Jamie shook his head, then looked back at me. "What you do with your life is nobody else's business, shorty. There's no ring on my finger, and there's no ring on yours. Until Aaron puts a ring on it, you can do whatever the fuck you like. All I'm saying is . . ." he kissed me on my forehead, "you deserve better than what he's giving you."

My lips trembled as I watched Jamie walk out of the bathroom. I didn't want to break down and cry again in front of Alisha, but I couldn't hold back the tears.

Alisha sighed, going into the bathroom stall, and tearing a wad of toilet paper off a roll. She walked up to me, handing me the tissue.

I looked up at her, reluctant to take it from her hands.

She nodded, shoving the tissue in my hands. "Stop all that punk-ass crying. And here, clean your face, Charlene—we have a lot of appearances to make tonight."

I dried my face, shaking my head in disgust. I couldn't believe I was destroying my life, all over the need of attention, love, and affection. If I hadn't been such a ho, maybe Aaron wouldn't have treated me as such. He wasn't cheating on me at the moment, but he was cold, and it was only a matter of time before he found whatever it was that he was looking for. What I was looking for in Jamie, I had no idea. Jamie was a playa. Everyone knew that shit. He was arrogant and conceited, but he was compassionate, loving, and charismatic. He knew just what to say. He knew just where it hurt. He knew just where to touch. He was everything that I needed in Aaron.

"I know how you feel, Charlene." Alisha went back over to the mirror and dug through her handbag.

I walked up to the mirror, standing alongside her. "How could you possibly know how I'm feeling right now, Alisha?"

Alisha looked at me, shaking her head. "You don't think I know what it's like to be with a man who doesn't show you any kind of attention? Whose eye is always on another girl? Who wishes that I was someone else? Do you think *my* life is perfect? You were just the first bitch to screw around with my man, but you damn sure weren't the last!"

I just looked at her, not sure what to say.

"Nothing I do to that muthafucka in bed has topped whatever it is that you did to him. I know in my heart that Ashton loves me, but for a man as fine as him, one woman just isn't enough." Alisha shook her head again.

I didn't know what to say, except, "Alisha, why don't you leave him?"

Alisha looked at me as if I were crazy. "What? Ashton is going to medical school. He's going to be a doctor, making all kinds of bread. He's been good to me in ways that no one can imagine. All men cheat. I haven't met one who doesn't . . . except *your* man. And that's why I'm so pissed at you, Charlene! You think I don't need to be loved, held, touched, and fucked from time to time? Ashton would rather go to the strip club than to spend time with me! He's a *man*, Charlene. They disappoint us sometimes, they hurt us sometimes, they make mistakes sometimes, but if you do right by them, they'll eventually turn around. You wanted to pay Aaron back for not loving you and look what you did to yourself. Pregnant by your best friend's ex-boyfriend."

I cried harder.

Alisha shook her head at me. "Does she even *know* he's in town? Or did *you* want all of his time? Does the nigga even know you're pregnant with *his* baby?"

I shook my head. I couldn't even look her in the face. "I'm not keeping it, Alisha."

Alisha's eyes widened. "Not keeping—" She couldn't even get the words out. She shook her head at me. "So you're just gonna get rid of it and act like this shit between you and Jamie never happened?"

"What do you expect me to do, Alisha? I have worked my whole life to become a dancer! You stole my chance with the Lakers, and it's all good because I'll get another chance. I can't have this baby, Alisha." I dried my tears.

Alisha glared at me as she shook her head. "You always were a selfish little bitch. Everything is all about you. Whether or not you keep this baby, your problem is not going away. I suggest you tell your boyfriend and your best friend the truth before it's too late. Y'all need to stop playing before someone fucks around and gets hurt."

Why didn't I listen to Alisha? While we were at a party in downtown Baltimore that night, I heard one of Jamie's old teammates mention that he was staying at the Hilton downtown. I don't know what inside of my heart, mind, and body told me to go to him that night, but I did. I wasn't even thinking about the fact that Aaron was blowing up my phone or that Jamie might have had company that night. I was tired of thinking about Jamie. When I slept with him in

Miami, I had no idea that I would fall as deep as I did.

There I was, at three-thirty in the morning, knocking on the door to Jamie's hotel room. The door flew open, and a bitch dressed in nothing but Jamie's tank top answered the door.

The bitch grinned, flipping her blond hair over her shoulder. "Yes, may I help you?"

I immediately went into defense mode. "Did I *ask* for your help? I'm here to see Jamie."

"Shorty, who's at the door?" I heard Jamie's deep voice coming from down the hall.

I pushed past the bitch, walking into the hotel room. And there were three other females sitting on the couch, smoking, drinking, all dressed in next to nothing. A few of Jamie's boys were sitting at the table playing cards, drinking, and smoking too. Jamie came down the hallway from the bathroom. He stopped in his tracks when he saw me standing there in the living room, arms folded, eying the groupies on the couch.

"Shorty, what's up?" He approached me. "What'cha doing here at three-thirty in the morning? You know your man's probably wondering where his girl is."

"And what about Pamela? Does she know y'all got all these hoes up in here and shit?" I looked around at everyone. "I don't think she'd be too happy to know that her man is out here fuckin' bitches and shit when you probably have her waiting for you in another hotel room!"

Jamie laughed to himself. He knew I was jealous. "You need to clear your mind about somethin', Charlie?"

I shook my head at him. "You told me that you hadn't touched Pamela since the day that you touched me, but what you *didn't* tell me was that you were fuckin' *other* bitches! True, you don't owe me any explanation, but I thought I actually meant something to you, Jamie! This here proves that I don't. You made me feel special, and I'm pretty sure that's how you got these hoes to come here to see you tonight." Tears welled up in my eyes and slid down my face.

Jamie's eyes glistened. "Charlene, you already know my lifestyle." He grabbed my arm before I could walk away. "Shorty, you *have* a man. What are you doing here questioning me about what I do, when you're not even supposed to be here?"

I just looked up into his face, lips trembling and speechless.

"What do you need me to do, shorty? We got a room full of people and you talkin' to me about shit I don't think you want everyone to know about. Do we need to talk in another room or what?" Jamie's eyes traced my lips.

I hesitated as he grabbed me by the hand.

Jamie and I stood face-to-face in one of the bedrooms in the suite. I was angry with him when I had no business even being there.

"Where's your man at, Charlie?" Jamie's eyes searched mine.

"At his place, calling me every ten minutes or so," I whispered, drying my eyes.

"So, what are you doing here? Why are you not at his place, cuddled up with him? You don't need to be here. You don't need to see this side of me." Jamie shook his head at me. "Go home, Charlie."

I shook my head. "You knew what you were doing when you pulled me in that bathroom stall today. You knew from the moment that you touched me that my body was yours. I can't even have sex with Aaron without thinking of you, Jamie! My body is addicted to yours, even though my heart belongs to him. Whatever this is that you're doing, it has to stop. If we're just friends, then that's all we're gonna be, Jamie. From here on out, we're just friends, and nothing else. I can't deal with this kind of confusion. You either want me or you don't. There is no got-damn in between with me!"

Jamie nodded, eyes sparkling. "I feel you."

I turned to walk away from him when he pulled me back to him. I looked up into his face as he kissed me. My lips trembled in his.

Jamie's lips let go of mine. "Just a friendly reminder that you *are* special and the fact that you had to come to me to find that out says a lot about the nigga you're with." Jamie's eyes searched mine. "You need to leave that mutha-fucka. You deserve better than this. Better than having to go to someone else, just to feel some sort of affection. There's someone else out there for you, shorty. It's not me, it's not him, but it's somebody."

I wanted to tell Jamie then that I was pregnant with his baby, but how could I, when he was basically telling me that there was nothing between us but sex? I should have taken Jamie's advice about leaving Aaron alone, to find someone who truly valued me, but I couldn't. Not just yet. One way or another, I was going to have the man that I wanted, and at that point, I wasn't even sure who that man was.

Chapter 6

Trapped

Charlene

The week before homecoming, Aaron took me out to a fancy restaurant. No friends, no team-mates, just the two of us. It had been awhile since he had taken me out on a date. I still hadn't seen Ne'Vaeh face-to-face and had only spoken over the phone to plan her birthday party. I was a little over two months pregnant and not sure when I was going to tell Aaron. I still maintained my figure, and the only thing on me that had gotten any bigger at the moment were my breasts. I knew Aaron noticed it because he couldn't stop staring at them.

That night at dinner, Aaron asked me what I thought about marriage. It scared me out of my mind. I knew that I was pregnant with Jamie's baby. I knew that he would be pissed if he found out the baby wasn't his, and I knew he would leave me if he found out. All I could think about was Jamie at that moment and how I was going to tell him. The last thing on my mind was marriage, and it wasn't because I didn't want to marry Aaron, because I did. It was because I knew I was in the wrong, and I didn't deserve to marry him. I knew I broke his heart when I told him that marrying him was the last thing on my mind, that my career was more important than us, and that I wasn't even sure if he was the guy I wanted to marry. Maybe a small part of me was trying to push Aaron away before he left me. Maybe a small part of me wanted to make my situation easier.

That same week, my uncle passed away. My family and I flew to Texas to attend his homecoming. I was devastated. Uncle Carlito was my favorite uncle and my father's little brother. He was the youngest of ten children. He stayed with us until I was about thirteen years old. He was more like an older brother to me, than he was my uncle. He taught us how to play soccer, how to fight boys, how to fire weapons, how to fish, how to make a campfire. . . . He was going to be missed. I hated the fact that I couldn't see his face and talk to him about my problems. I was avoiding him throughout my entire pregnancy because I knew if I called him on the phone, he would hear in my voice that something was wrong. Rest in peace, Uncle Carlito.

I had finally started talking to Ne'Vaeh again, or at least texting the girl on a regular basis. Two months had gone by, and I hadn't contacted Jamie, nor had he reached out to me. However, the day I arrived back in Maryland from Texas, I got a call from Kelissa telling me that Jamie was going to be in town for the week. Why she felt the need to tell me, I had no idea. And why I couldn't contact Ne'Vaeh *or* Aaron the day I arrived back in Maryland, I didn't know either. Neither one showed up to the airport to meet me as planned. Neither were answering their phones, either. I had to contact Renée, Ne'Vaeh's cousin, just to know what was up. Once I had arrived in Baltimore, I agreed to meet Renée at Venus around one o'clock to help them finish decorating for the party.

I got in a cab that afternoon, as my sister and brother placed my bags in the trunk. My whole family was going to a family get-together at my aunt's house. I planned to meet Aaron for lunch, but he wasn't answering my calls. I tried calling Ne'Vaeh to wish her a happy birthday, but she never picked up her phone either. I asked the cabdriver to take me over to Aaron's crib. I was going to shower and change before heading to Venus. My flight was already late, and I knew that by the time I got to Venus, they would probably be finished setting up the ballroom for the party. Renée told me that the family was meeting there around twelve-thirty for Ne'Vaeh's birthday lunch. She was really hoping I'd show up in time to eat with them, but I wasn't in the mood to converse with Ne'Vaeh's fake-ass family. Renée and her family were cool, but the rest of the family never supported her because of the way they felt about her mother. Why they decided on showing up years after the fact, I had no idea.

I could smell the Purple Haze in the air as I stepped out of the cab, upon arriving at Aaron and Ashton's apartment. I rolled my eyes as I walked around to the trunk of the cab to get my bags from there. Aaron and his friends were so busy sitting, smoking, and laughing on the balcony that they didn't even notice that I pulled up. Ashton strolled out of the front door of the apartment building just in time to help me.

"What's up, sista?" he called out, running up to meet me at the cab.

"Hey, Ashton." I smiled at him as he approached me.

He kissed my cheek. "Girl, let me get those."

"Thanks, boo." I sighed. I looked up at Aaron as he passed a blunt to Amina, this light-skinned chick who made it a habit to show up to the crib whenever she knew weed was involved. I wasn't really sure what to think of her. I wasn't really worried about Aaron sweatin' her. He didn't even seem to have an interest in red chicks, myself included. Every poster on his wall of a model was either brown or dark-skinned.

"Well, I see why Aaron hasn't been answering his phone." I rolled my eyes. "How long have they been here? Have they been out here smoking *all* day?"

Ashton looked at me as he closed the trunk. "Nah." He put the strap to my overnight bag over his shoulder and pulled the handle on my suitcase so he could roll it down the walkway. "How was your trip?" he asked.

I looked at him, shaking my head. "Saw a lot of family I haven't seen since I was like four or five. Had some laughs and a whole *lot* of tears. You know how much I loved Carlito. He was like a father to me. He will be missed."

Ashton nodded. "Yeah, shorty, I know. I wish I could have been there with you, but I just got this job down at the hospital and—"

I cut him off. "Please, Ashton, you don't have to apologize." We started walking toward the apartment building. "You have always been there for me. I didn't want anyone seeing me falling out, crying over Carlito's body in that casket anyway. I don't even wanna talk about it."

We got to the building, and Ashton opened the door to let me in. We walked up a flight of stairs to his apartment, and again, he opened the door for me. The smell of butter and cinnamon smacked me in the nose the moment we entered the building and nearly suffocated me upon walking into the apartment. "Oh my goodness . . . *Mmmm*." I followed the smell into the apartment. "Y'all niggas were cooking French toast this morning?"

Ashton shook his head, carrying my luggage into the apartment. "Shit, not me. You know I can't even boil water."

I looked at him, setting my purse on the coffee table. The apartment was so nice and tidy, smelling like Pine Sol and carpet cleaner, which was *so* not the usual. Usually, their apartment smelled like sweaty gym socks, cigars, and Newports. "Damn, so y'all cooked *and* cleaned? Y'all must have had company over."

Ashton set my luggage alongside the coffee table. He looked at me, then came over and sat by me on the sofa. "Nah, shorty, I ain't had shit, and I ain't cooked shit. And I damn sure didn't clean this apartment. Shit, niggas come in this bitch all day fuckin' up shit. Eating up all the snacks. Most of the time, Aaron has the whole basketball team up in this bitch. Alisha helped Aaron clean a few days ago. Guess she got tired of shit lying everywhere."

I rolled my eyes. "Ashton, why the fuck you lyin'? Alisha wouldn't clean up after y'all grown-ass men."

He just looked at me.

I really didn't even want to know. Alisha admitted that Ashton was slinging his dick around the tristate area. As much as Alisha got on my damn muthafuckin' nerves, I had to admit that she was beautiful. Her body looked amazing. Weren't too many teenage women who had big breasts, a tiny waist, a phat ass and thick thighs. She looked like a stripper. Alisha dissed niggas left and right for Ashton, and meanwhile, he was playing the field.

I rolled my eyes. "I'm not even gonna ask. Y'all niggas make me sick. How much pussy does one nigga gotta have? Y'all always claiming hoes ain't loyal; then you turn around and do shit to *make* her not be loyal to your sorry ass!"

Ashton laughed to himself. "So, you think it's *me* who's cheating on my girl?"

I looked at him, feeling like I was talking to Jamie. "Ashton, do we *really* even have to play this game right now? As much as I can't stand your girl, a nigga would have to be real stupid to even *look* at another girl, when they have a girl who looks like that! Alisha is a knockout! Ashton, why would you cheat on her?"

He looked at me. "Charlie, it's not cheating when your girl knows about it. You don't have to understand what me and my girl have going on, because that's *our* thing. I don't have to answer to you or anybody else. I use protection. I wrap my shit up. If I'm gonna give into my weakness from time to time, I play smart about it. I might bring a girl or two over, give them the dick, then I send her 'bout her business, simple as that. I know my worth, and I know these chicks around here make a career out of getting pregnant by athletes and doctors and shit. I'm going to college to play ball, *and* I'm going to medical school. I really don't give a fuck if you think I'm triflin' or not, Charlie. I *love* Alisha, and the last thing I wanna do is hurt her. We can't have sex, shorty, which is why we *don't* have sex."

I looked at Ashton, a little puzzled. "What do you mean you 'can't' have sex?"

He looked at me, shaking his head. "Just forget it, yo. Let's just leave it at that, shorty. I've said too much already. We *all* have our secrets. There are skeletons in everyone's closet, including *yours*."

My heart skipped a few beats. "Wh-what is that supposed to mean, Ashton?" I stuttered.

He just looked at me for a few seconds. "I think that's a conversation you need to be having with Aaron. I try not to get in grown folks' business."

I shook my head. Alisha and her big-ass fuckin' mouth. "Ashton, I love Aaron, okay? If I tell him about Jamie, he'll leave me alone with this baby! A baby that I don't even want! A baby that I am *so* not ready to have!"

Ashton looked confused. "Jamie? Jamie who? I didn't say anything about no 'Jamie.' And you're *pregnant*? What?"

I was stunned into silence. He wasn't even talking about Jamie. The expression on his face proved he had no idea what in the hell I was talking about. Alisha had kept her big-ass mouth shut for once, and I had opened mine too soon.

Ashton's looked at me. "Charlie? What are you talking about?"

I sighed. "Ashton, yes, I'm pregnant. About eleven weeks pregnant."

Ashton wasn't even sure what to say. His brown eyes searched my face. He shook his head at me in disbelief.

I started to cry because I was in a fucked-up situation, though there was really no use in crying. I created the storm, yet I was the one upset when it started to rain. Man, that Karma is a mean bitch.

Ashton thought to himself for a minute then looked at me, watching the tears slide down my face. The look on his face changed from disbelief to *I-know-what-the-fuck-you-did*.

"Charlie, Alisha mentioned this morning that she was going to surprise Ne'Vaeh with someone from her past tonight at her birthday party. I have known shorty for a long time, and I know that there's only two people that she might want to see right about now, and that's her sister who ran away six years ago or Jamie *Green* who left her about four years ago. Is *that* the Jamie you're talking about, Charlie? Tell me *he's* not the Jamie you're referring to, shorty."

I dried my tears. I couldn't even look Ashton in the face, but I could feel him looking at me.

Ashton put his hands on my face, turning my face toward his. "Charlie, look at me. Tell me what's goin' on. C'mon, shorty, I'm your boy."

I shook my head, taking his hands from my face.

"Eh, yo, what's goin' on?" Aaron's voice shook both of us.

Ashton got up from the couch.

I sat there, drying the tears from my face.

Ashton laughed the tension off. "Nuthin', bruh. Your girl was just curious about why you didn't save her any French toast this morning. You know that's her favorite, man."

Aaron looked over at me. He saw my wet cheeks. He wasn't buying it. "Uh-huh. Charlie, meet me in the bathroom, a'ight?"

I nodded my head, unable to look up at him. I stood from the couch, watching Aaron's back as he walked back toward the bathroom. I began to dig through my luggage for a pair of jeans and a ribbed tank top.

I could feel Ashton's eyes on the back of my neck. "Charlie, you're really not gonna tell me what's going on?"

I shook my head in frustration, standing back up from my luggage, clothes in my hand. "Ashton, just drop it, okay?" I started to walk toward the bathroom when he grabbed my arm. I looked up at him.

Ashton shook his head. "You might not wanna tell me what's goin' on, but trust me when I tell you that you aren't the only one who has some explaining to do." He let go of my arm.

When I stepped into the bathroom, Aaron sat on the edge of the bathtub smoking a cigarette. The shower water was running. The smell of Caress soap filled the bathroom, and I knew Alisha hadn't left the apartment too long ago. I tried to hold my breath, and not breathe in the smoke.

"Please," I coughed, "could you put that shit out? You have fuckin' asthma, Aaron, and I know second-hand smoke kills too. . . ."

Aaron exhaled smoke from his nose before tossing the cigarette in the toil et. He looked higher than a muthafucka as he watched me undress. Though he looked fine as hell in his wife beater and sweats, I couldn't help but notice he wasn't dressed to leave the house.

"Are you going to Ne'Vaeh's birthday lunch *or* her birthday party tonight, Aaron?" I unsnapped my bra, pulling it from my arms. My breasts popped out of my bra like biscuit dough popping out of a biscuit canister. Damn, I needed a bigger bra. In two months, my breasts had gone from just barely a C-cup to a damn D-cup.

Aaron's eyes were fixated to them. He didn't take his eyes off them the entire time I undressed. "Nah, I wasn't invited."

I rolled my eyes, sliding off my panties. "Aaron, I would like to *not* have to dance alone this year at Ne'Vaeh's party. You know every time Renée throws a party for anyone, she has that damn couple's dance." I climbed into the shower.

He sighed. "How was Texas, shorty?" He brought up another touchy subject to avoid the touchy subject that we were already on. For some reason, Aaron never went to any of Ne'Vaeh's parties. I shouldn't have been surprised that he didn't want to go to this party.

"Shitty as any funeral would be, Aaron." I stood under the shower, rinsing my hair before applying floral-scented shampoo to it. "Don't try to change the subject, Aaron. Why the hell do I always have to go to this girl's birthday parties by myself? What do you have against her? You don't like my girl or something? You're always avoiding her or any conversation about her." I lathered the shampoo, massaging my scalp with my fingertips. "You never like any of my friends, Aaron!"

"Charlie, I have nothing against your girl. I just don't go where I'm not invited, shorty. It's that simple. But if you want me to go with you, all right, I'll go. What time are you going to her party?"

I rinsed my hair. "Well, I was supposed to be there a few hours ago." I washed my face. "Speaking of a few hours ago, I was blowing up your phone all morning, and you didn't answer. As a matter of fact, I called both you *and* Ne'Vaeh, and *neither* of you answered."

Aaron was silent, *too* silent.

"So, you have no words, right?" I began to lather soap all over my body.

He sighed. "Charlie, you wanna talk about not answering calls, huh? Why did you avoid *my* calls the entire week that you were gone? Why did you laugh when I mentioned getting married? And why didn't you tell me that you were thinking about transferring to Miami?"

I looked up to see Aaron peeping at me from behind the shower curtain. He always did answer a question with about two or three questions of his own. That was his way of reversing the blame. I wasn't in the mood for his games when I was already feeling really shitty.

"Look, Aaron," I rinsed the suds from my body, "I was going through a whole lot in Texas. I didn't feel like talking to *anyone*." I turned off the shower. "When you asked me what I thought about marriage, I had just found out that my uncle passed away. I was in my feelings, I was emotional, and I wasn't thinking straight. Of course, I love you and would love to be your wife someday, but now isn't the time." I wrung out my hair.

"I applied to colleges outside of Maryland because I'm sick of this place. I cannot seem to get away from my past, and I'm tired of it getting thrown in my face. The University of Miami was the first college to accept me. The only person I even mentioned it to was Dana's big-mouthed ass. I didn't think it even mattered to you one way or another. You could give a fuck if I stay here. Your mind always seems to be on everything else *but* me, Aaron. You don't care if I leave Maryland. You probably wouldn't even notice." I stepped out of the shower onto the rug.

Aaron made a face at me as if he didn't know what in the hell I was talking about. He watched me grab a towel and wrap it around my body. "Charlie, where is all of this coming from? The fuck you mean I wouldn't notice? How the fuck could you think I don't care if you leave and go to Florida?"

I looked at him. "Aaron, we both know this relationship is in no way what it used to be. You don't have to pretend to love me anymore. You stopped loving when Alisha and the rest of her bitches told you about my slutty past! Yeah, I was a freak. Yeah, I fucked everybody! Yeah, I was a ho! Yeah, you deserve better!" I squealed.

Aaron sighed. "Charlie, I can't do this shit. . . ." He ran his hands over his head, frustrated as hell at the way that I was acting.

I looked up into his face. "Can't do what, Aaron? It's like every time we have a conversation, you avoid telling me how you really feel! You don't wanna go with me to Ne'Vaeh's party, and I need to know why."

Aaron looked at me. He took a deep breath. "Charlie, I gotta do this. I know it's not the right time, but then again, it's never the right time to tell someone that it's time."

My eyes grew misty. "Time for what, Aaron?"

He didn't say anything. He just turned and walked out of the bathroom.

I followed behind him, grabbing his arm. He pulled away from me. "Time for *what,* Aaron?"

Aaron stood against the hallway wall. He couldn't even look at me.

My heart thumped against my rib cage. It was time to say good-bye. I could see it in his face. We both knew it wasn't going anywhere. We both knew it was over. He wanted to make the first move. I couldn't let him leave me without an explanation. "Why, Aaron?"

He still couldn't look at me. "I just don't feel the same way that I used to feel about you, and it doesn't have shit to do with what Alisha or her friends said about you. It's just me, Charlie."

I shook my head. "Hell nah! No, it's not you. It's someone else. Who is she?"

Aaron finally looked up at me. "Does it really matter, Charlie?"

I pushed him in his chest. "Yes, it fuckin' matters! I want to know why the only man who I have ever loved isn't in love with me anymore! There has *got* to be someone else! You don't kiss me, you don't hold me, and you won't fuck me! I have to basically get you drunk or act like I'm one of those got-damn strippers to get you to touch me!" I pushed him again. "Fine. If you wanna be free, just go! I can take care of this baby all by my damn self!"

Aaron looked at me, catching my arms and stopping me from pounding on his chest. "What did you just say?"

I looked up at him, tears sliding down my cheeks. The words had just exploded out of my mouth. I wasn't even thinking. I sure as hell didn't plan to tell him until I couldn't hide the pregnancy anymore. The look on his face when he heard the words come out of my mouth broke my heart. I wasn't sure if he was concerned or if he was hurt at the fact that the woman that he wanted to leave was pregnant with his baby. Regardless, I had thrown a wrench in whatever plan that he had.

"I'm pregnant, Aaron," I cried.

He let go of my arms. He just stood there stunned and looked at me. "How long have you known about this?"

I dried my tears. "Oh, what does it matter? This doesn't change the fact that you want to leave me, Aaron! I'm too young to have a baby! I don't even want this baby, and you want to leave me to take care of it alone?"

Aaron shook his head at me. "You knew about this baby when I asked you what you thought about getting married? You have been acting strange as hell for about two months, Charlie, and it's because you knew you were pregnant and you weren't even gonna tell me? Why, Charlie? Why would you keep this shit from me?"

"Because I didn't wanna have this baby!" I yelled, walking past him into his bedroom.

Aaron followed behind me. He stood in the doorway as he watched me dig through his dresser drawers for a bra and panties.

"The day I went to the abortion clinic to get rid of it, my mother showed up, cursing out everyone at that clinic! She made everyone there feel like shit! I didn't wanna have a baby in this situation, Aaron! I'm in love with a man, and I'm pregnant with a baby that's not—" I stopped talking, then looked up at him. "That's not wanted."

Aaron's eyes glistened. "A baby isn't in my plans right now, Charlie, but that doesn't mean you have to kill it either. I'll take care of what's mine, shorty. That includes you *and* the baby."

I broke down and cried. "Aaron, please don't leave me!" I sat at the corner of his bed, turning my back to him. I couldn't even face him. How could I when I basically just stopped the man from leaving me because he believed that the baby inside of me was his? I was wrong, and I knew I was going to pay for it one way or another some day.

Chapter 7

A Bitch Named Karma

Charlene

By the time I made it to Venus, Ne'Vaeh's entire family was there. The restaurant was covered in blue and silver balloons. I should have known that a few cameras would be there. Superstars Darryl Allan, Anastasia Jones-Allan, and Jade Abdula-Matthews were in the place. Darryl barely came to Maryland after he moved to the ATL years ago. It wasn't until a few years back that Ne'Vaeh even knew that Darryl Allan was her cousin. She found out on her sixteenth birthday when we went to one of Anastasia's concerts in D.C. Renée introduced us to Darryl Allan backstage. He said that he found out from his grandmother that Ne'Vaeh's mother was his mother's half sister. Ever since he found out Ne'Vaeh was his cousin, he made it his business to look out for her whenever she needed it. Though she had a hard time adjusting to the fact that she had a cousin that was a celebrity, they still kept in touch. Most people would have been milking the shit out of their multimillionaire cousin, but not Ne'Vaeh. The girl could sing her ass off, but she never told Darryl about it. Couldn't have been me, shit.

Ne'Vaeh was looking *very* sexy that day in her Coogi dress. I know Coogi was the nineties look, but she was making it look real fly. She was bringing Coogi back. The dress hugged her in all the right places. She was a short li'l girl, but that minidress and those heels made her look at least five foot eight that night. Her makeup was flawless. Her skin was glowing. She sat at the far end of the table, between Renée's mother and Anastasia Jones-Allan. Ne'Vaeh looked a little tense. She barely hugged me back when I hugged her that afternoon. She looked like something was bothering her real bad. She sat there, chin in hand, with laughter all around her.

I swear, every time Anastasia or Darryl opened their mouth to say anything, a damn camera was flashing. The media has no damn respect for privacy.

"So, Ne'Vaeh," Anastasia set her wineglass down, "I heard from your cousin, Renée, that you have an *angelic* voice. I've been looking for a background singer for *months*. So, any time you wanna show me your skills, let me know. And any time you want a break from school, come holla at'cha girl." Anastasia winked her eye at Ne'Vaeh.

Ne'Vaeh laughed to herself, shooting Renée a quick glare. "Thanks, cuzzo, but *no* thanks. I'm going to college, then to law school. Singing in the choir is something I do to keep God in my life when I'm not in church."

Renée's eyes widened. "'No thanks'? What the . . . girl the fuck's wrong with you? Are you crazy? *Anastasia Jones-Allan* just ordained you her got-damn backup singer! Hell yes, Anastasia, she'll rock the fuck out of that microphone! Mama, I'm sorry, but your niece has some issues that I needed to set straight!" She put her hands up, surrendering before Miss Joyce got in her ass about her language.

We all laughed a little.

I looked at Aaron, who leaned back in his chair, looking a little uncomfortable to be there with us. I elbowed him to sit up in his chair, but he didn't budge. I rolled my eyes at him.

"So, cuz, tell me why I don't see a man sitting at your side today." Darryl chimed in with his wife. Miss Joyce elbowed Darryl in his rib cage. "What? Aunt Joyce, I'm just sayin', look at her. My cousin is *beautiful,* with a *capital* B. So why doesn't she have a man?"

Aaron finally sat up in his chair, as if he was waiting to hear the answer to the question as well.

Ne'Vaeh glanced at Aaron. She laughed nervously, looking at Darryl. "Wow, really? What's this? Embarrass-the-hell-out-Ne'Vaeh-on-her-birthday? Gee, thanks, cuz."

Ne'Vaeh's cousins laughed a little.

Darryl made a face. "Nah, cuz, what? I'm just concerned, shorty. You look sad as hell on your nineteenth birthday. I haven't seen my baby cousin smile in *years*. I just know your family and friends have some fun planned for you tonight. I'm only gonna be able to party with y'all for about an hour tonight. And while I'm here, I wanna see my cousin have some fun. I don't wanna see you sitting alone on your special night, cuz."

The family nodded in agreement.

Ne'Vaeh's eyes glistened. "I appreciate that, Darryl. And I'm *not* alone—I have y'all here with me today." She grabbed Anastasia's hand in hers and cameras flashed. "Oh, goodness, that's annoying. Cuz, could you please tell them to stop taking fuckin' pictures? How do y'all live like this? *Sheesh*."

Anastasia smiled, squeezing her hand. She signaled the camera crew to get lost with her other hand.

"Lunch was amazing, Jade. And thank you all for coming." Ne'Vaeh tried to fake a smile. She looked over at Aaron. "Even those who weren't invited."

I looked at Aaron.

Aaron grinned at her, nodding in agreement, winking his eye at her. It was the first time that he had smiled all day. That moment really had me feeling some type of way. I wasn't sure what to think.

Lunch was awesome. There was nothing better than freshly cooked seafood, dessert, and wine for an afternoon meal. Ne'Vaeh tried her best to enjoy her much-needed time with her family. After lunch, her family members presented her with their gifts. Darryl, Anastasia, and Jade stuck around for a little while. Aaron left to go pick up his bonus check from work. And a few of the family members left to get a few more things for the party. That afternoon, those remaining presented Ne'Vaeh with her gifts. She was in tears opening them all. She got everything from an iPad to a Rolex. Darryl handed her the last gift. It was a gift from her mother. Ne'Vaeh finally looked at me that afternoon. It was the first time that her mother had reached out to her in six years. She got up from the table, then hurried off to the bathroom.

Renée rose from her chair. "Oh, poor baby . . ."

"Wait," I rose in my chair too. "I'll go get her."

"Ne'Vaeh, sweetie?" I crept into the bathroom, hearing Ne'Vaeh sobbing in one of the bathroom stalls.

"Please, Charlie, leave me alone, okay?" she cried.

I sighed, approaching the stall where her voice was coming from. "Well, I can't do that, hon. You have a room full of people who are *so* happy to see you today." I opened the door, seeing Ne'Vaeh sitting on top of the toilet seat. I grabbed a wad of tissue from the roll and started dabbing her cheeks. "Ne'Vaeh, oh my goodness, you're going to ruin your makeup! You look gorgeous! Please, stop crying before you ruin this masterpiece called 'your face'!"

Ne'Vaeh laughed a little, taking the tissue from my hands. "Please, Charlie, let me sit here alone and cry, okay? I really don't feel like talking."

"Sweetie, your family came from all over the U.S. to wish you a happy nineteenth birthday. I know your mother was the last person you wanted to wish you a happy birthday, but, hey, that's life. Full of surprises, some good, some fucked-up." I leaned up against the wall of the bathroom stall.

Ne'Vaeh looked up at me, "Charlie," her lips trembled. "It really hurts being alone."

I shook my head, "Sweetie, you know Darryl didn't mean any harm by what he said."

Ne'Vaeh nodded. "I know he didn't. But he reminded me of how lonely I am when he brought up the fact that I don't have a boy-friend. I know he didn't mean any harm, but that didn't make it hurt any less. I'm nineteen years old, and I haven't found love. Love *never* loves me like it's supposed to! I can never have what I love, or love always ends up hurting me. I'm sick of this disappointment. I'm so sick of this pain. When is it *my* turn to be loved? I wanna be loved too, Charlie! Not the kind of love that hurts, but the kind of love that heals old wounds. That makes you smile even when you're mad. That you don't have to show where it hurts because he already knows. That knows when I need him to hold and comfort me. And that lets me know with every waking moment he can't live, breathe, eat, sleep, *exist* without me." Tears slid down her cheeks again. "Charlie, I *need* love. My mother *hated* us with every inch of her soul. She hated life. When she failed at taking her own life, she took my little brother's. Your mother saved my life. My aunt Joyce saved my life. And for that, I will always love them both. I have not one mother, but I have *two* mothers." She handed the small gift box from her mother back to me. "And neither one of their names is Juanita Washington. Fuck that bitch."

My eyes glistened. Ne'Vaeh was in so much pain. I could hear her pain in her voice, and I felt so guilty inside for what I had done. Jamie was just what she needed at that moment. He was amazing. Though a part of me had started to fall for him, I knew what I was feeling was mainly lust. He was sexier than a muthafucka, he knew the right things to do, he knew the right things to say, and he knew just where it hurt. Everything that Ne'Vaeh said that she needed, Jamie was the man to give it to her. Though I had started to develop feelings for him, a small part of me hoped that Jamie showed up to her party tonight. She needed him. She needed him *so* badly.

"Okay, babe, let's clean you up, then go back out there with your family to enjoy the rest of your lunch. You got your makeup bag?" I pulled her up from the toilet seat, taking her by her hand over to the bathroom sink.

"I'm so sorry for breaking down like this." Ne'Vaeh continued to cry as I dabbed her face with Kleenex. "Maybe I drank too much."

I swept her hair from her face. "Where did you put your purse so we can fix this makeup?"

Ne'Vaeh pointed to the drawer. "Renée said she put some makeup in the drawer this morning for me. I guess she knew I would cry when I saw Juanita's gift."

I dug in the drawer for some mascara, concealer, and pressed powder. "We just need to touch you up a bit and we're good."

The tears just kept rolling down her face, which made it impossible to apply any makeup. Black tears slid down her cheeks.

I sighed. "Sweetie, trust me, I know how you feel. Love hurts like a muthafucka. I wish I didn't feel the way about Aaron that I do." I didn't want to turn the conversation to me, but I wanted her to know her life wasn't the only one that was a wreck.

Ne'Vaeh looked up at me, her tears slowly subsiding.

"Our relationship has changed. Hasn't been the same since Alisha's bitch ass outted my past. I act like everything is so perfect between me and Aaron, but it's not, girl. For a long time, we didn't kiss, touch, hug, fuck, or look at each other—*nothing*. It wasn't until like two months ago that we actually started having sex again after going without it for like three or four months straight." I looked at Ne'Vaeh and the expression on her face.

She held her stomach, looking like she was about to throw up. She braced herself up against the bathroom sink.

"Are you okay?" I asked her.

She nodded, tears lining her lashes. "Yeah, I guess I'm a little queasy from all that wine I drank."

I sighed. "Well, I could use a drink or two or *three*. Aaron and I almost broke up this morning."

Ne'Vaeh looked at me. "W-what? *Almost* broke up? What is 'almost broke up'?"

I shook my head, "Yeah, girl, I believe he had a whole speech down too. He was about to give me this whole never-the-right-time-to-say-good-bye-but-I-gotta-make-the-first-move-

Chris-Brown shit." I laughed a little to hide my pain. "Well, that was until I told him that I was pregnant."

Ne'Vaeh put her hand over her heart as if she was about to have a heart attack. The girl nearly stumbled over her own two feet.

I caught her before she fell up against me. I helped her over to the vanity seat. "Whoa, Ne'Vaeh, are you okay?"

Her whole face flushed. She didn't respond. Her body was completely limp. I braced her body up against the wall, then hurried to the bathroom entrance to call for help. Renée was the first to enter the bathroom. Anastasia, Jade, the aunts, and the few female cousins that were in the restaurant rushed in behind her.

"Go get some water, ma!" Renée rushed over to Ne'Vaeh's limp body over on the vanity seat. She held her cousin in her arms. "Oh my goodness!" She struggled with all of her might to hold back any tears. "What happened, Charlie?"

I was stunned. I had never seen Ne'Vaeh pass out before. "I-I don't know! We were just talking, and she fainted! She fell up against me! What's wrong with her? I have never seen her pass out before!"

"She was diagnosed with heart failure a few months ago, Charlie." Miss Joyce came back with the water, handing it to Renée. "She had numerous surgeries as a child. She was born with several holes in her heart, sweetie, and the left side of her heart isn't pumping properly. We really shouldn't have even let the poor girl have any wine today. Oh my goodness—that present from her mother—I don't know what we were thinking."

"Heart failure?" I was shocked. I had no idea, and Ne'Vaeh never mentioned anything to me about having any health issues. All those times she went in for surgeries growing up, I thought she was getting her tonsils or her appendix removed. I knew she said her heart was broken, but I didn't know she meant it literally.

"Miss Joyce, we were only talking." I shook my head, watching Ne'Vaeh's aunt try to help resuscitate her.

Anastasia sat on Ne'Vaeh's other side, fanning her. "Well, whatever you said to the child had to have been something serious for her to just pass the hell out!" She looked up at me, dark, luminous lashes surrounding her brown eyes. "What were y'all talking about? What did you say to her?"

Jade took her cell phone out of her purse. "Should I call the ambulance? I mean, she looks really bad, y'all!"

Renée looked up at me, curious about what I said to her cousin that would make her pass out cold. "*Well?*"

I swallowed hard. I really didn't want to tell them about me being pregnant, but the cat was already out of the bag. "I don't know what I could have said to upset the girl! Nothing I said to her was really that devastating that she would fall the fuck out! We were talking about her mother, about love, about me being pregnant with Aaron's baby."

"Lawd." Renée sighed, shaking her head at me, patting Ne'Vaeh's cheeks to make her come to. "C'mon, baby, please . . . Snap out of it, cuz."

"Like I said, do we need to call 911?" Jade repeated frantically.

Renée looked at me, shaking her head as if I had done something wrong. "Nah, sweetie, no ambulance is needed. She'll be fine. I guess baby girl just heard some news that she wasn't ready for, that's all."

Ne'Vaeh came to. As soon as she opened her eyes, looking into Renée's face, she started bawling her eyes out in her cousin's arms.

Renée sighed, her eyes growing misty. "Okay, everybody out. I got it from here."

Everyone, me included, was stunned. We wanted to see if Ne'Vaeh was okay, but Renée was adamant about us leaving them alone.

"C'mon, now, everybody get the fuck *out!*" she exclaimed.

I just stood there alongside the sink, watching everyone exit the bathroom.

Renée looked up at me, rolling her eyes, "OMG, Charlie, what part of 'get the fuck out' didn't you understand? The 'get,' the 'fuck,' or the 'out'? You always were kinda slow!"

I made a face at her. Ne'Vaeh had been living in my house for years, and I couldn't hear whatever conversation the two of them were going to have? I was just as much family as anyone else there was. Hence, the fact that I was invited to the *family* luncheon.

"Look, Renée, I'm the one who made her pass the fuck out! I don't know what I said to upset her, but I need to be here to comfort her." My eyes grew misty, watching Ne'Vaeh bawl.

Renée shook her head. "Nah, sweetie, you really don't need to hear this. Please, let us talk alone."

I put my hands up, surrendering. I had lost that battle. Renée wanted me out of their business, so I stayed out of their business.

Needless to say, the party was turned *all* the way up that night. Seemed like the ballroom was filled beyond capacity, once everyone found out that Anastasia Jones and Darryl Allan were in the spot. The celebrities were there for a good hour and a half before leaving that night. By then, everybody was already tore up, even Ne'Vaeh, who sat alone at the bar. She had recovered physically from the incident that happened earlier, but mentally, I'm not so sure. I wasn't sure what was going on with her, and I was afraid to ask. I sat at a table with Dana, Danita, Kelissa, Monique, Raya, and Kai, keeping an eye on Ne'Vaeh, making sure she didn't drink too much. It was almost time for the couples' dance. Renée would pick a random love song and have the DJ play it to calm the mood a little bit. She made her way over to the DJ, and Aaron had finally made his way over to me.

Kelissa grinned. "Yeah, ladies, it's about that time. Let's go find our men."

They got up from the table, making their way out onto the dance floor just in time for my favorite song, "You Gotta Be." My heart nearly jumped out of my chest. I absolutely loved that song, but I knew someone who loved it more. I looked over at Ne'Vaeh, who sat, face in hand, in tears. I looked back at Aaron.

Aaron looked at me. "What's up, shorty?" He spoke over the music.

I leaned over and whispered in his ear, "Please, go dance with her."

Aaron looked at me, then over at Ne'Vaeh. He shook his head, looking back at me. "Nah, Charlie. Trust me. She doesn't wanna dance with me."

I nodded. "Please. Look at her. She needs it."

Aaron hesitated before getting up from the table. He made his way over to the bar. He whispered in Ne'Vaeh's ear, over her shoulder. Ne'Vaeh turned around in her chair, stood up, and pushed Aaron out of her way before walking past him.

I stood in my chair. *What the hell?*

Aaron grabbed her arm, pulling her back to him. She tried to pull from him, but he pulled her close, surrounded her in his arms, and the girl started crying her eyes out up against his chest. Though I couldn't hear what Aaron was saying, I know I saw him mouth the words, "Baby, I'm sorry" in her ear. Now, what the dude was sorry about and why he was calling her "baby," I had no fuckin' idea. However, something in my heart wouldn't let me pass off that moment as nothing. Before I could make my way over to the two, someone grabbed my arm.

I turned around to see Jamie Green looking me dead in the face.

My heart fluttered in my chest. "Jamie, what the hell are you doing here?" I exclaimed, forgetting that Kelissa mentioned that he was in town.

Jamie smiled, platinum teeth gleaming. "Shorty over there invited me." He pointed over to Alisha, who was over by the loudspeaker, dancing with Ashton.

I glared over at her. Alisha caught sight of me looking at her, and the bitch winked at me. Ol' messy-ass bitch. I knew Ashton said that she planned to invite someone from Ne'Vaeh's past as a birthday surprise, but the day was already hectic enough. I didn't have time for drama. Yes, Ne'Vaeh needed Jamie, but by the looks of things, I wasn't so sure Jamie was who she wanted.

I looked at Jamie, then back over to the bar where Aaron and Ne'Vaeh were supposed to be. I had lost sight of them. I searched the room with my eyes until I caught sight of them on the dance floor. The two were more like hugging than dancing. They were barely moving. Looked like the two were both crying to me. What the fuck was going on?

I looked up at Jamie. "I need your help," I said as I leaned over and whispered in his ear.

Jamie nodded. "What's up?"

I pointed over to Aaron and Ne'Vaeh on the dance floor. I looked back up at Jamie. His eyes were coated in tears. I'm not sure how he felt seeing the love of his life hugged up with another man, but I knew I was feeling some type of way watching the love of *my* life hugged up with another woman. Though I had walked myself into that situation when I asked Aaron to comfort her, I didn't like what I was seeing. Something was telling me that this dance was not just a dance.

"I take it that's your man, huh?" Jamie looked back at me.

I nodded. "Yeah. I guess."

"So, why is *she* dancing with *your* man?" he questioned my logic.

"She needed it, Jamie. The girl is hurting. You should have seen her today. She's been crying and moping around *all* damn day." I looked up into his face. "I told my man to dance with her because I thought she needed to feel *someone's* arms around her. She needs love, Jamie."

"Who's love? *Aaron's?* I thought *you* needed his love." Jamie looked back at the two on the dance floor.

I looked over at them. Ne'Vaeh lifted her head from resting on Aaron's chest. She looked into his face, and he looked down in hers. He dried her tears. I watched as his eyes searched her face, as if he wanted to kiss her, but instead of kissing her, he swiped his thumb across her lips. Oh, I was *so* done. That was enough. There was something going on.

I was about to step out onto the dance floor when Jamie caught my hand. I looked up at him. Oh, I was mad. Aaron never touched me or held me the way that he was holding her. He cared for her. He hadn't so much as spent five minutes of his time with that girl; yet, there they were—close enough to kiss. I was ready to fight—ready to beat a bitch's ass over my man—heart problems or not.

"Charlie, be easy. Damn! You stay ready to fight someone." Jamie looked down into my face.

My eyes widened. "What? *Look* at them! Do you see what *I* see? That nigga *never* touches me like that!"

Jamie grinned a little bit. He leaned over and whispered in my ear. "How can you really be mad at them, shorty, for dancing, when we *both* know that a lot more than *dancing* happened between us?"

I looked at him, coming to my senses . . . just a little bit. I was already fragile, and I knew that

Aaron wanted to break up with me. I had trapped him with a baby that he didn't even know wasn't his. "Jamie, I *don't* want him dancing with her." I was furious.

Jamie held my hand, leading me out onto the dance floor. Ne'Vaeh's back was turned to us as we approached them on the floor. Aaron caught sight of us walking toward them, then loosened his grip from Ne'Vaeh's hips. She turned around to see Jamie approaching her, me following close behind him.

It took her a few seconds to register who he was and when it registered in her mind, I think it registered in her heart as well. Her lips trembled. She looked up at Aaron, who was looking right back at her. His temples twitched a little.

"Aaron, it-it's Jamie." She talked over the music, looking back up at Jamie. "Jamie," she whispered to herself, looking at her long-lost love.

Jamie held her hand, pulling her to him. "Happy birthday, li'l Ne'Vaeh." His eyes glistened under the ballroom lights.

Ne'Vaeh slid her hand from his, then looked at me. "What's going on?"

"Surprise!" I heard Alisha's voice over my shoulder. She ran up to Ne'Vaeh to hug her around her neck.

Ne'Vaeh wasn't sure how to react. I'm sure the last person she expected to see was Jamie. She hadn't seen him or talked to him in four years. She had just learned to deal with the fact that Jamie was never coming back to Maryland—and there he was, standing there before her, looking like a sexy piece of milk chocolate.

"Look who I found, honey!" Alisha glanced at me, then looked back at Ne'Vaeh. "All the way live, from Memphis, Tennessee!"

"Jamie, what are you doing here?" Ne'Vaeh was obviously upset that no one bothered to ask her how she felt about seeing Jamie again after so long.

"Just came by to see what was up with my first love. I must say, shorty, you are looking fine as a muthafucka in that dress. C'mere, shorty. Give me a hug. Let me hold you." He pulled her close in his arms.

Ne'Vaeh broke out in tears.

Aaron looked crushed. He watched Jamie holding her, gripping her waist in his hands. He watched Ne'Vaeh crying in his arms.

Ne'Vaeh pulled from Jamie, pushing him off her. "Four years, Jamie! I haven't seen your ass in *four fuckin'* years, and you think you can just stroll up in here like you didn't just up and leave me?"

Jamie just looked at her, not sure what to say.

Ne'Vaeh looked at Alisha. "How could you all do this to me today? On my muthafuckin' birthday!" She stormed off past us, pushing her way through the crowd of people.

Alisha sighed. "Well, *that* didn't go as planned."

"Yeah, shorty, you *think?*" Aaron shook his head. "I don't know why women don't think before they do shit. How do y'all figure she wanted to see this muthafucka?"

Jamie had to laugh at the fact that Aaron was talking about him as if he wasn't standing right there.

Alisha rolled her eyes. "Whatever, Aaron. Fine. Y'all want me to take the blame for how she feels, as if *y'all* don't have shit to do with this? Okay, I'll take the blame. This is *my* fault, so *I'll* go get her." She hurried off to find Ne'Vaeh.

There I stood, between Aaron and Jamie. Aaron looked at Jamie. Jamie looked at him. Aaron knew what Jamie once meant to Ne'Vaeh. By the look on Aaron's face, I wasn't so sure what Ne'Vaeh meant to *him,* but it was obvious by the way he looked at Jamie that he didn't appreciate him ruining their sensual moment.

"What's good, Aaron?" Jamie grinned. "I heard a lot about you, man."

"Well, I haven't heard shit about you, nigga, other than the fact that you smashed the girl, then bounced." Aaron was defensive.

Jamie laughed a little. "Hold up, homie. Forgive me if I'm wrong but, uh, you seem a little offended that I'm here. Now, if Charlene is your girl, why does me coming here to see *Ne'Vaeh* got you feeling some type of way?"

I pulled Aaron away from Jamie by his arm. It didn't take much to piss Aaron off, and from what I remember about Jamie, he was on the same page—Anger Management 101.

Aaron pulled from me, getting back in his face. "Muthafucka, I don't gotta explain a *muthafuckin'* thing to you. Anyone can see that Heaven has been through enough bullshit. Your ass hasn't stepped foot in the girl's life in four years; then you pop up out of the blue like she's supposed to greet your ass with open arms?"

I looked up at Aaron. Since I've known him, he's always called that girl 'Heaven,' and it always bothered me, though I never said anything.

Jamie looked at me. *He* knew it bothered me. He looked back at Aaron. "What do you know about 'Heaven'? Why is 'Heaven' any of your concern, Aaron? I don't see her here with anybody. Is she here with *you?* Because I thought you were here with *her*." He pointed at me. "You wanna explain to your girl here why you're in your feelings about a girl—who's *not* your girl?" Jamie grinned. "You have a woman as fine as Charlie, and you worried about her best friend? Fill her in on that, my nigga."

Aaron looked at me, his eyes glistening, temples twitching. "Charlie, I told you that I didn't wanna come to this party. I knew it was gonna be some shit. If you wanna stay here and reminisce with your friends, cool, but I can't do this shit." He walked past me.

"Aaron!" I tried to grab his hand, but he pulled away, making his way through the crowd, and out of Venus. "Oh my goodness, this night couldn't get any worse!"

Jamie shook his head at me. "Shorty, you got bigger problems than you know."

I looked up at him. "What do you mean?"

Jamie looked at me. "There's a reason why he calls her 'Heaven,' shorty. Seems to me like 'Heaven' is where he wants to be." Jamie walked past me toward the bar.

I just stood there in the middle of the dance floor, heart pounding. I wasn't going to make any assumptions until I found out from the horse's mouth. I was feeling guilty for my own actions, which probably had me questioning Aaron's.

Aaron never so much as brought up Ne'Vaeh's name, unless he was trying to hook her up with one of his friends. I had no idea why he all of a sudden cared about her feelings. He'd been calling her Heaven from the day he met her. If he wanted her from day one, then why did he take *me* out instead of her?

Would you believe that Ne'Vaeh left her own birthday party? Turns out, she asked Renée to take her back to Howard. Jamie stayed until the party was over. Aaron went wherever he went and didn't answer any of my phone calls. I stayed until one o'clock when the party was officially over. The girls invited me to the club with them, and I agreed, though I was in no mood to party. I knew Jamie would be at the club with the whole damn football team. Judging by the fact that his phone didn't ring or vibrate all night long, I'd assumed that things were over between him and his girlfriend. I didn't have time for any more drama. I had problems beyond repair. Aaron was in his feelings about Jamie's encounter with Ne'Vaeh, and I was in my feelings about Aaron's encounter with Ne'Vaeh. Something was going on, and I was going to get to the bottom of it.

Just as I was about to leave Venus with the girls, Ne'Vaeh's aunt runs up to me with Aaron's coat. "Sweetie, Aaron left this at the table this afternoon. . . ." She handed me his coat.

I thanked her, taking the coat from her.

Just when she handed me the coat and walked away, what looked like a receipt fell from the coat pocket.

"What's that?" Danita asked as she bent over to pick the piece of paper off the floor. "Looks like a receipt." She handed the receipt to me.

I looked at it. It was a receipt from the new Vintage Urban Hip-Hop Outlet at the mall. The shit in that store was too damn expensive for the average person. I shopped in the store from time to time when I felt like splurging, but it had been a few months since I stepped foot inside that store.

Dana took the receipt from my hand. "Three hundred seventy-eight dollars and forty-two cents, Coogi Sweater Dress with Hood?" She looked at me after reading the receipt.

I looked at her, taking the receipt from her hand, reading it for myself.

"Didn't that receipt come from *Aaron's* pocket?" Danita asked.

Dana looked at me. "I haven't seen you wear no damn Coogi sweater dress with no damn hood. As a matter of fact, you don't even *wear* Coogi. Who the fuck *still* wears Coogi?"

My heart started to pound in my chest. I knew who did.

That funky bitch.

Kelissa looked at me. She knew too. "*Ne'Vaeh* had on a Coogi sweater dress with a hood tonight."

Tear instantly lined my lashes. I looked at Danita.

Danita shook her head. "I told you. That bitch Karma always shows up just in time."

Chapter 8

Drink a Little Bit

Ne'Vaeh

"Ne'Vaeh, sweetie, you need to pull yourself together. Do you really want him to see you like this?" Renée exclaimed.

I was hurt. I cried like a baby in my cousin's arms that afternoon, in the bathroom at Venus. I couldn't believe that Charlie was pregnant with Aaron's baby. I mean, Aaron and I had *just* had sex that morning. He'd just told me that he was breaking up with her. He'd just told me that *I* was the one who made his heart beat. The fun had just begun—and then it was over, just like that. I hadn't felt so lost, so hurt, so confused, so angry since Jamie left me some four years earlier. I hated love, and obviously, that bitch hated me.

Renée held my face in her hands, drying my tears. "You need to dry these tears because there is really no use crying over this! Baby, didn't I tell you that this would happen? Didn't I? Why are you so shocked? Why are you falling out in front of the damn girl? Why are you not owning up to the fact that *you* are the other woman, *she's* not? I told you that your weekend fling wouldn't last, boo! I know you love that boy. Trust me, I know what love looks like, but he is *hers*, do you hear me?"

I shook my head at her. "Why doesn't love . . . love me, Renée? Why does it always hurt me? He doesn't love her, Renée! He loves *me!*"

Renée shook her head back at me, still holding my face in her hands. "Sweetie, his love for you isn't gonna stop that baby from being born. It's not gonna change the fact that your best friend is in love with that boy, despite how you feel about him. Y'all had two years to get this shit straight. If the nigga loved you like he says he does, he wouldn't put you in this position. If he loved you the way he says he does, he would'a manned up and asked you out in high school. It's too late for you two, boo. You gotta move on."

I looked up into her face, tears dripping from my face, on to her hands. There was no denying that my cousin was right. I was in love with

Aaron for two years and had to live with the fact that he was with my best friend every day. Once I finally got the chance to spend some time with him alone, it only took him two days for him to have me sprung. The fact that Aaron and Charlie were together was devastating enough. The fact that there was a baby in the picture took away my consciousness. As soon as the words came out of Charlie's mouth that afternoon, my whole body completely shut down. I didn't know how I was going to live, knowing that Charlie was going to give birth to a part of Aaron. Anastasia's offer to move to Atlanta and possibly sign on to her record label was looking pretty damn good right about now.

I could barely think straight the rest of that night. The liquor was taking over me. I drank until I could barely move. I sat at the bar in Venus, sitting alone at my own birthday party. Tears slid down my face as I sipped from a bottle of Budweiser.

"Heaven, will you dance with me?" I flinched at the sound of Aaron's voice over my shoulder.

I jumped up from the barstool. I wanted to slap him dead in his face, but instead, I pushed past him. "Get the fuck away from me, Aaron!"

He grabbed my arm, pulling me back to him.

I looked up into his face, shaking my head. "Aaron, go back over there and dance with your baby's mama!"

Aaron shook his head, pulling me closer to him, surrounding me in his arms.

I buried my face in his chest. "How could you do this to me?" I sobbed. "You said you loved me!"

"Baby, I'm sorry." He whispered in my ear, "I'm sorry you had to find out like this."

I lifted my head from his chest, looking up into his face. "Aaron, what is it you want from me? We can't be together when you're having a baby with my best friend!"

Aaron looked like he was on the verge of tears, but he manned up. He let go of me and took me by the hand, out into the middle of the dance floor, where we faced each other. He grabbed my body by my hips and brought me closer to him. I slid my arms over his shoulders as Aaron looked down in my face. His lip was trembling. He didn't know what to say. His words came out in tears. I cried aloud, burying my face in his chest.

"Heaven, I love you. This doesn't change that. I'm sorry. I swear, I didn't know," he whispered in my ear, drying the tears from my face. "I'm not ready to be a father, especially to a girl

I know I don't wanna be with. I wish that *you* were the one having my baby, shorty. You know I'd rather be with you, Heaven, don't you?"

I looked up into his face, my heart fluttering in my chest.

He looked down into mine, his eyes searching my face. I thought he was going to kiss me, right in front of everyone. To top it off, the drunken part of me actually wanted him to . . . but he didn't. He just held my face in his hands, drying my tears. His thumbs grazed against my lips.

"Aaron, you-you are *so* wonderful. And I wish I would have told you sooner," I whispered, looking into his face as he put his hands back on my hips.

I looked up at him, watching the look on his face change from remorse to frustration. He let go of my hips, and I turned around to see Charlie standing there, arms folded, alongside . . . It took a few seconds to realize who the man beside her was because my whole body seemed to go numb. Flashbacks of middle school raced through my mind. Flashbacks of the happiness, sadness, pain, anger, and loneliness flashed through my heart. There I was, staring in Jamie's face again after four years. He looked amazing, like a model fresh off the cover of *GQ* magazine. He stood there, dressed in all white from head to toe. His skin was smooth, chocolate, and flawless. When he held my hand, I could feel his pulse. I snatched away before my soul connected with his again. He had left my heart to fend for itself, then, out of the blue, he pops up at my birthday party four years later. In just three days, my life was turned upside down. I went from being lonely to being confused, to being angry. I had no choice but to leave my own party.

I didn't make it halfway up the sidewalk when Alisha comes running behind me. "Cutie, where are you going?" She caught up with me.

I turned around to face her. I wanted to slap her dead in her face, but instead, I cursed the bitch out. "Why the *fuck* would you invite Jamie?"

"Oh, sweetie," Alisha grabbed me in her arms and hugged me. "I didn't mean to hurt you, I swear! I just thought you needed to see him. I ran into him a few months ago in Miami. One of his teammates gave me his number. A few weeks ago, I called him and told him that I wanted to surprise you. It wasn't easy getting him to come. He said you wouldn't wanna see him. I guess he knew more than I did. I thought you would at least be a little happy to see him, Cutie. I didn't know you would be this hurt." She let go of me.

"He-he looks so *good*. *Why* does he have to look so fuckin' good?" I sobbed.

Alisha laughed a little. "I know, boo, I *know*."

"I found out today that Charlie's pregnant." I dried my tears.

Alisha just looked at me, not really sure what to say. She hesitated, "S-she told you that she was pregnant?"

I nodded, "Yeah. She said that Aaron and her were about to break up this morning until she told him that she was pregnant with his baby."

Alisha giggled a little. "Aaron's baby, huh? That's funny as hell."

I didn't see anything at all humorous about the situation. "Alisha, you know how I feel about him! You saw us fuckin' in his bedroom! Charlie is like a sister to me, and this was the *last* thing that I wanted to do to her! My cousin's wife asked me to go on tour with her, and I'm seriously considering it. I can't stay here anymore. It was bad enough loving Aaron when I didn't know how he felt about me. Now that he told me how he felt and he *showed* me how he felt, there's no way I can live with this. I couldn't breathe when Charlie told me that she was pregnant with Aaron's baby, Alisha. I passed the fuck out right in front of her! When I woke up, I was looking right into the face of the person who *told* me that I was only going to end up hurt! I straight up ignored her—and look what the fuck happened!"

Alisha shook her head. "Girl, you need a drink."

I looked at her, wiping my tears that just wouldn't stop coming down. "Alisha, I drank enough for at least ten people tonight."

"Hey, cuz!" Renée came scurrying down the sidewalk in her heels. "Where do you think *you're* going? Oh my goodness, did you see *Jamie's* fine milk-chocolaty ass up in there?"

I shook my head. "Girl, you just answered your own question with another question. I gotta get outta here."

Renée looked frustrated. "Ne'Vaeh, why are you gonna let your emotions run you from your own birthday party? Do you know how long it took me to plan this shit? Do you know how much *money* I spent on these decorations? You lucky Jade Allan let us get this spot for free, or I would kick your ass right about now!"

I put my hand in her face. "Renée, I had a long day. I need to get the fuck outta here. Now either one of you are gonna drive me back to Howard, or I'm gonna walk. I'm sure some perverted muthafucka will be glad to pick me up and give me a ride."

Renée rolled her eyes, grabbing me by the arm. "You are too damn dramatic. C'mon, but I'm not taking you home, boo. I know *just* the place."

***

We ended up going to a late-night karaoke bar. I was in no mood to sing, but I always did enjoy watching people making a fool of themselves, trying to keep up with words to songs that they'd never heard. It's funny as hell watching an old white guy rapping to Lil Wayne. The shit you see in Baltimore.

The three of us sat at a corner booth in the far corner of the club, eating vodka Popsicles, the bartender's specialty. It was really strange to see Alisha hanging out without her little entourage.

"That bartender looks real familiar." Alisha pointed over to the light-skinned bartender.

Renée nodded, taking a bite of the Popsicle. "She's Amina, my best friend's little sister."

Alisha shook her head, "Nah, I know her. She comes over to Ashton's crib every now and then to smoke with the crew. As a matter of fact, she was over there today." Alisha looked at me. "She came over to the crib after *you* left."

She just had to remind me about that morning. I sank back in my chair. "See, I was just about to thank y'all for taking my mind off my stupidity, but never fuckin' mind, Alisha."

Alisha laughed a little. "Girl, I don't even know why you're trippin'. I mean, besides the fact that you think Aaron got your girl pregnant."

I looked at her. "What do you mean I 'think' Aaron got her pregnant? You know what, Alisha? I'm not even gonna get into this shit with you. Let's just chill and get some more drinks. Matter of fact, I'll go up to the bar and get us some. What y'all drinkin'?"

Renée looked at me, looking like she wished she hadn't invited instigating-ass Alisha to come. "Girl, just get me a rum and Coke."

"Make that two." Alisha winked at me.

I rolled my eyes, getting up from the table. I made my way over to the bar. The place was crowded. The bar was surrounded with people, but Amina caught sight of me and signaled me to come to the front of the bar.

"Hey, sweetie!" Her red lips formed a smile. "What'cha drinking?"

"Three rum and Cokes, please." I sat on a stool at the bar.

Amina looked at me as she mixed the drinks. "You're lookin' real nineties fly in your Coogi today."

I grinned a little. "Thanks, boo."

She smiled, setting the drinks on a small tray. "Girl, a mutual friend called a few minutes ago. I hope you don't mind that I told him you were here."

I looked at her. "Friend? What friend?"

"So you just up and leave your own party, Heaven?" I heard Aaron's voice over my shoulder.

I looked up to see him looking down into my face, his green eyes glistening under the bar lights. I hopped up from the stool, turning around to face him, my heart flickering in my chest. "Aaron, I'm not with this shit tonight. Y'all muthafuckas already ruined my birthday party! Now you're here to ruin the only peace I've had all fuckin' week? Why would you show up here?"

Aaron pulled me to him by my hand. "Shorty, can we go somewhere and talk?"

I slid my hand from his. "No! What is there left to talk about, Aaron? You're having a baby with my best friend! What is there left to discuss?" I walked past him, heading out of the bar. I really couldn't have the whole bar in my business.

Aaron followed behind me. "So you're just gonna ignore me? You're just gonna walk away from me?" He grabbed me by the arm once we got outside of the club doors.

I pulled away from him then pushed him in his chest. "Aaron, why are you doing this to me? I told you this morning when you kissed me that this was wrong! That touching me, kissing me, making me feel like I was someone special was *wrong!*"

"Ne'Vaeh, is this muthafucka bothering you?" I looked up to see Renée walking out of the bar. Alisha came close behind.

I looked back up at Aaron. "No, he was just leaving."

Aaron looked at me.

Renée walked over to my side, hands on her hips. "I can't believe you would bring your ass here! Now, it's bad enough that you took advantage of this girl when you knew how she felt about you, but then you have the nerve to *still* pursue her after she just found out that you got Charlie pregnant?"

Aaron looked at her as if he was really losing his patience with her. Every time she saw him, she had a nasty attitude. "Look, Renée, you need to stay out of this shit. Now, I'm trying to respect my elders, but you keep overstepping your boundaries."

Renée's eyes widened. "*Elders?* Oh, so now I'm old? Overstepping *my* boundaries? Nigga, you have me *fucked* up! Muthafucka, *you* overstepped your boundaries when you fucked my cousin when you knew you had a girl!"

Alisha had to step in. "Whoa. Hold up now. I mean, she had a part in this too, while you're talkin' all this shit to Aaron. He didn't force her to have sex with him!"

Renée looked Alisha. "Oh, really? Let's see." Renée looked at Aaron. "Aaron, did she tell you no?"

I pulled Renée from him before she got in his face. "Renée, please, just leave it alone."

Renée pulled from me, stood her ground, and got right up in Aaron's face. "I asked you a fuckin' question. *Did* she tell you no?"

Aaron's eyes glistened. He looked at Renée then looked at me. "I know I was wrong, but I had to have her."

I rolled my eyes. Renée was always in my business, and I had to admit, it was pretty fuck-ing aggravating at times. "C'mon, y'all, let's just end this conversation before we take this too far."

Renée was already fired up, and there was no stopping her. "You are a triflin'-ass muthafucka! You know the girl hadn't had dick in like four fuckin' years! You knew it wouldn't take much to get into her panties! You could have had any girl you wanted, so why would you choose your girl's best friend? Why?"

Aaron just looked at Renée. He had had enough of her. "So, God hired you to be my judge, right? How the fuck are you gonna judge me *or* your own cousin when the nigga you dealin' with *now* has a fuckin' girlfriend *and* a fuckin' baby on the way? How the fuck is a side chick gonna try to give relationship advice? Get the fuck outta here with that bullshit, ma."

Alisha just stood there, sipping her rum and Coke from a straw, with her eyes lit up like she knew some shit was about to go down.

"Why are you bringing this shit up? What you got going on with my cousin has nothing to do with me!" Renée pushed him in his chest.

"Well, the way I feel about your cousin doesn't have shit to do with you either!" Aaron exclaimed, trying his best not to push her ass back.

"The hell it doesn't! Why are you out here talking to her? There's no way that y'all can be together when that girl is pregnant! I'm not gonna let you string my cousin along!" Renée turned to me. "Ne'Vaeh, sweetie, please use your head! What do you think is gonna happen to you if you continue to mess with Aaron? He claims he loves you now, but how do you know how he'll feel once this baby is here? How do you think Charlie will feel once she finds out that you've been fuckin' her man behind her back?"

I looked up at Aaron. Everything in my mind was telling me that the way I was feeling was wrong, but my heart had no common sense whatsoever.

"Heaven," Aaron grabbed my hand, "I didn't mean for any of this to happen. I swear I didn't know that Charlie was pregnant! You know I was gonna break up with her this morning. I was gonna end it until she told me that she was having my baby. I didn't want this. I'm not ready to be a father. In my family, most of the men had unplanned children with women who they didn't plan on being with. Even my own father. He married my mother at seventeen because she was pregnant. My father is from England. His family is big on reputation. When you get someone pregnant, they expect you marry the girl."

I looked at Aaron, my heart pounding in my chest.

"Aaron, no!" Alisha exclaimed. "You're gonna let your parents tell you who you need to marry? You're a grown-ass man! No, don't do this! Not with Charlie! I'm telling you!" Alisha looked at me. "Ne'Vaeh, say something!"

I shook my head. What could I say? I was wrong in all types of ways. I deserved for Charlie to be pregnant with Aaron's baby. I deserved for her to jump the broom with him right in front of my face.

"Heaven, I have to do the right thing. I wasn't raised to walk away from my responsibility. I love you. I have never loved *anyone* the way that

I love you. I should have stepped to you in high school. Baby, I'm sorry." He held both of my hands.

"Well, it is what it is. And it's already done." I slid my hands from his.

Renée held my arm. "C'mon, Ne'Vaeh, let's go back inside. Let him go."

I turned around to walk back inside the bar.

"Heaven," Aaron called my name.

I turned back around, heart racing, a sharp pain in my chest.

"If it's all right with you, I wanna finish where we left off this morning." Aaron's green eyes shone under the streetlights. "Heaven, we may never have this opportunity again. So come with me. *Fuck* your cousin *and* what she has to say about it."

I looked at Renée, who stood there with her arms folded across her chest.

She shook her head at me, pretty much done with my heart and me at that moment. Then she threw her hands up, finally surrendering. "Fuck what *I* have to say about it? You know what? I'm done. If all you want from this boy tonight is sex, then I'm not gonna judge you. Go ahead. Fuck his brains out. All I'm saying is Charlie *is* gonna find out. I just hope Aaron is worth the drama that she's gonna bring, because you *know* the bitch is gonna bring it. Karma goes *both* ways, cuz. You just remember that shit." Renée stormed back inside the bar.

Alisha looked at me, not really sure what to say. She looked at Aaron. "I told you to tell her how you felt back in high school, Aaron. This shit is gonna get messy, *real* messy." She turned around and walked back into the bar as well.

I turned to Aaron, looking up into his face.

His cell phone rang in his pocket. He ignored it, looking down at me instead.

"Aren't you gonna answer it? You already know it's Charlie callin' you, wondering where you're at. You can't just ignore her calls, Aaron." I shook my head.

"She'll be all right. I got something I gotta do. I may never get this chance again." His eyes grew misty. "I know I'm wrong, Heaven, but I'm really feeling some type of way about Jamie showin' up here to your party. I know you're not my girl, but you're not his either." His eyes hardened. "Charlie didn't like the way that I was defending you, and I really don't give a fuck, Heaven. *She* should have been defending you. She knows the nigga broke your heart, yet she and Alisha thought it was cool to invite the muthafucka to your birthday party."

"I don't think Alisha meant any harm by inviting Jamie. Why she invited him, I'm not sure, but I don't think her intentions were to hurt me."

"My agent's cousin owns the Courtyard Marriott in Alexandria. Some friends are there now, throwing a party in the ballroom. We can go there, show our faces, get a dance in, have a few drinks, then bounce. I plan on gettin' drunker than a muthafucka. I ain't gonna be able to drive, shorty. My manager reserved me a suite in his name—we can go chill there. I need to stay there for a few days to clear my head. I need to think. I need to figure out how I'm gonna tell my aunt and my parents." Aaron ran his hands across his head anxiously.

I shook my head, looking into his shimmering eyes. "Look at the mess we've made, Aaron."

I didn't know the kind of family that Aaron was raised in, but apparently, everyone else did. Even Alisha knew his parents would want Aaron to marry Charlie to "protect his reputation." It took me until our high school graduation to finally meet his family. His father was a handsome white man from England. His mother was breathtakingly beautiful. Her bronzed skin looked as if the sun had kissed it. She was Arabian and Senegalese, and one of the most beautiful women that I had ever met. I saw instantly where Aaron got his green eyes. Her eyes looked straight through you to your soul. She couldn't care less about me when she met me at our high school graduation, but she immediately took to Charlie.

Aaron's parents lived in California. When he got into some sort of trouble, hanging out with the wrong crowd, they sent him to live with his father's half sister, who was an officer in the army, stationed at Fort Meade. From what I knew about his family, I wasn't exactly the type his family would have accepted. I wasn't "paper bag" light or from a rich, prestigious family. I was the brown-skinned daughter of a poor drug addict, who didn't know which one of many lays fathered her three children.

I was put in a pretty tough spot. I was in love with a man who was untouchable in every aspect. It was obvious by the look on Charlie's face when she mentioned being pregnant that Charlie was afraid of losing Aaron. I had no idea their relationship was a mess. I hadn't been around Charlie or her friends in years to know anything about the rumors that caught Aaron's attention. From the moment the two had started dating, I'd tried to keep my distance. My heart had been sealed shut for years before Aaron came along. Jamie had ruined every man's chance at breaking my heart. I swore the day that he left me that I would never fall in love again. However, from the moment I looked into Aaron's eyes that day in my African American History class, my heart was his.

There we were, cruising down the street in Aaron's candy-painted maroon Chevy Impala. The late-night slow jams played on the radio. The fact that it began to rain didn't help brighten the mood either. My cell phone was on vibrate, but it was ringing off the hook. Family members were blowing up my phone, calling, texting, leaving voice mails. Even Jamie happened to get ahold of my cell phone number. The dude left three voice mails, and I deleted each one of them, without listening to the messages. Alisha called, Renée called, even Darryl and Jade called. The only one who I expected to call hadn't called even once. Charlie was feeling some type of way about me that night. I knew it wouldn't be long before I would have to deal with her wrath, regardless of whether she knew something was going on.

I couldn't handle any more drama from anyone that night. I looked over at Aaron, about to ask him exactly what friends were going to be at this party. Aaron was deep in thought, temples twitching. I knew he was angry with himself but probably angrier with the family tradition that he would be forced to follow. I grabbed his hand in mine, kissed it, then held it up against my chest. I wanted to tell him that everything was going to be okay, but I wasn't so sure how things would turn out myself. All I knew was that Aaron and Charlie were going to be married, and I was going to have to watch.

We got to the party within an hour and fifteen minutes. The parking lot was packed. It was about 11:00 that night. To be honest, his friends' party was a lot better than mine was. I at least felt welcome at their party. There was no drama, no family asking me why I didn't have a man, no presents from Juanita, no pregnant best friend, no cousins making me feel guilty about my feelings, no old boyfriend, no tears, no pain, and no heartbreak. We drank, we danced, and we had a great time. I made it through three slow dances and three Long Island Iced Teas before Aaron had to call it a night. I don't think he could take any more skin-to-skin contact that night without wanting to undress me.

Chapter 9

The After-Party

Ne'Vaeh

We made our way down the hotel hallway toward the suite that Aaron's coach and manager reserved for him that night. Aaron's hand trembled as he slid the key card into the key slot. He opened the door, and we walked in. I was in awe walking into the hotel suite, which was more like a two-bedroom apartment. Fresh roses were in every vase. Scented candles were scattered around the living room, down the hallway, and all over the kitchen. The hotel room smelled like the cleaning crew had just left. The carpet smelled like Carpet Fresh, the wood floors in the hallway looked like they'd just been mopped, and the furniture looked like it had just been polished. I felt like I was on my honeymoon, and I wasn't even the one who was about to get married.

Suddenly, I felt like shit.

I turned to Aaron as he slid my jacket from my shoulders.

He tossed the jacket on the sofa. "Shorty, I am drunk as *fuck!*" He laughed a little.

I nodded in agreement. My vision was a little blurry, and I could barely stand up straight. "Yeah, boo, I had a little too much to drink myself. Not to mention all the weed that you and your homeboys smoked around me got me feelin' like *I* was the one chiefin'!"

Aaron smiled a little. "It's been a long day. I mean a *very* long day. I'm staying here for a few days because I ain't trying to go back to my apartment. I don't wanna deal with Ashton's mouth or run into Charlie. You can stay with me for a few days if you want to, shorty. You know you need a break."

I sighed. I did need a fucking break. Not just from school, but from "Mama" Renée. She was always on my ass about *every* decision that I made. Not saying that I didn't need it, but just like Aaron said, her life wasn't up to par to be talking about anyone else's. "What about a change of clothes, Aaron?"

"I already got you." He grinned. "There's an outfit in the back room for you. You know, some sweats, a tank top, a pair of Reeboks. C'mon, shorty, let's get in the shower."

He was too amazing, and the more I was around him, the more I hated my life. I never got what I wanted or what I needed. Everything that I wanted seemed to be out of reach. There I was, alone in an expensive hotel with my best friend's soon-to-be-fiancé. I wanted that boy more than I've ever wanted anything. It was hard to enjoy the moment when I knew it wasn't going to last forever.

"So, you just knew that I'd give in and come here with you tonight?" I looked up into his face as he grabbed me by the waist, pulling my body up against his.

Aaron licked his lips. "Nah, but I was hoping you would ditch your cousin and roll with me. She's miserable, shorty. Any decision that you make, she'll have something negative to say about it. Let's just enjoy the moment. We can drink a little bit more if you want. We can get in the hot tub. We can fix something to eat. Whatever you wanna do, it's totally up to you tonight, Heaven." He gripped my dress in his hands.

Our eyes held their gaze as he slid my dress up over my head then tossed it on the sofa. I stepped out of my heels. Then he held my hand, leading me down the hallway to the bathroom. The bathroom was huge, about the size of my old bedroom at Charlie's house. Large, scented candles surrounded the huge tub, which was in the center of the bathroom. Everything I needed to take a shower sat in a basket on top of the sink's countertop—bath sponge, vanilla-scented bath wash, shampoo, a bar of soap, face wash, washcloth, and towel.

"H-how did you know what my favorite body wash is, Aaron?" I exclaimed.

Aaron smiled at me before walking over to the shower. "You remember the other day when I had you in my weight room, and I was playing in your pussy? Well, I still remembered the scent you left on my fingers. It smelled like a mix between vanilla and butterscotch. I couldn't find butterscotch at the store, so I went with vanilla."

He knew just what to say to get my adrenaline pumping and my hormones raging. Even though he had me feeling some kind of way about him, my emotions were overpowered by the guilt of being infatuated with my best friend's boyfriend. I stood there, barely able to move as Aaron slid back the frosted glass door, then turned the shower on. Steam immediately filled the bathroom.

My heart pounded in my chest as he sat down on the toilet seat to untie his shoes. He kicked them off, then slipped his shirt over his head, tossing it on the floor. He pulled off his tank top, then stood up to unbuckle his pants. He looked up at me, noticing that I wasn't undressing along with him.

He walked over to me and pulled me closer to him by my hands, snapping me out of my "what-the-fuck-am-I-doing" daze.

"Heaven?" He looked down at me.

I looked up at him, bottom lip trembling. "M-maybe we shouldn't do this, Aaron," I whispered. "Haven't we done enough already?"

Aaron shook his head, letting go of my hands, removing the belt from his pants. "Nah, we haven't." He unbuttoned his pants, dropping them to the floor. I watched as he slipped off his socks, then his boxers. He looked down at me as he slid his hands around my waist, then up my back to unhook my bra. "Just forget about everyone else. Right now, it's just you and me. Charlie doesn't even *exist* right now, if you ask me."

The steam in the bathroom caused my curls to go limp. My damp hair hung just below my shoulders. Aaron gently kissed my lips, running his hands up and through my hair, yanking it just a little. My body was on fire, and I felt light on my feet. I would say that I was floating on air, but I was really floating on weed and alcohol. I had been drinking nonstop all day, and my body was feeling it. I didn't have the strength to resist Aaron that night, and he knew it too. I grabbed the body wash, loofah, shampoo, then followed him into the shower. I'd barely lathered my hair or body when Aaron turned around to face me. My whole body trembled under the showerhead that night. I was feeling all types of emotions, mostly heartbreak.

Aaron held my face in his hands, looking down intently. "Heaven, baby, I know you're upset with me."

"Yes, I am, Aaron! If you wanted me in high school, you should have just said so!" I exclaimed. "I would have done anything you would have asked me to! I was in love with you from the very first moment I saw you! You were *so* beautiful! Oh my goodness, Aaron, if you would have asked me back then, I was *so* ready!"

Aaron sighed, shaking his head to himself. "Shorty, I had no clue. You barely even *looked* at me! I got with Charlie because I didn't think I had a chance with *you*."

I shook my head, looking up into his face. "Well, now, you have the girl of your parents' dreams. The woman your mom and dad would want you to be with. She's having your baby, whether or not you like it. I love you, I really do, but you belong to Charlie! I don't know what is going wrong in y'all relationship, but I promise, I am *not* the answer."

Aaron shook his head in disagreement. "Nah, shorty, you *are* the answer. I have loved you for almost three years but was too afraid to get rejected by you. Shorty, you were so mean and stuck-up in high school!" He laughed a little.

I blushed. "No, Aaron, I was *not* mean or stuck-up. I was just hurt. Someone who I loved hurt me when he left me, so I kinda kept my guard up. But you broke down my walls, Aaron. Like now, for instance. I'm naked in a shower with my best friend's soon-to-be husband, and for what? To get heartbroken all over again?"

"I never meant to hurt you, Heaven. Just when I decide to tell you how I feel about you, Charlie tells me she's pregnant. I mean, she told me *right* when I was about to break up with her, shorty. The girl wasn't even planning to tell me because she didn't plan to keep the baby. But as soon as I tell her it's over, yo, shorty drops the news on me."

I continued washing my hair. "Well, Aaron, any woman in her right mind would say just about anything to keep you."

Aaron looked at me as he continued to lather his body in Lever 2000. "I can't stand the fact that your dude, Jamie, is here. The nigga had me ready to pop off in that bitch tonight, I'm tellin' you. He knows the way I feel about you. Even hinted to Charlie that I was a little 'too concerned' about him coming to see you."

I looked up at him.

Aaron looked down at me, pulling me closer to him. His body was so silky, so smooth, and so warm. "I missed out on my chance of being with you the way that I wanna be with you, which is why I brought you here tonight. If I can't have you forever, I thought I should at least get to spend some time with you for just a little while." His heart beat rapidly against mine. He gently kissed my lips, and I nearly melted in his arms. His kisses soothed my soul, instantly taming my heart and my mind.

"Let's just—" I whispered in between kisses. "Let's just go to bed. I just want you to hold me, please. That's pretty much all I can handle tonight."

He lifted me up in his arms, wrapping my legs around his waist as he opened the door to the shower and walked out, carrying me out of the bathroom.

We were soaking wet, suds dripping everywhere. He carried me into the master bedroom, sat down on the bed, then lay back, holding me against his body. He gently kissed my neck as I buried my face in his. Having sex was the furthest thing from either of our minds at that point. I think we were both too drunk to perform that night. Our drunken asses fell asleep right there, wet as hell.

I awoke early that morning to the smell of pancakes, bacon, and eggs. My head was pounding. For a minute I forgot where I was until I sat up, looking around at the hotel room, remembering the events that had happened the night before. I looked over at the alarm clock on the nightstand. It was 6:15 a.m. I had class that morning at 11:00, and I had to finish my term paper, which was due the next day.

A white robe sat on the chair in the corner of the room. I got up from the bed then walked over to the chair to put it on.

"Aaron?" I called as I walked down the hallway to the kitchen.

There he stood over the stove, in his tank top and boxers. Oh my goodness, the boy had a body on him. He was chiseled and cut as if someone had carved him out of stone. He was a little cocky, yes, but in an adorable kind of way. The more I looked at him, the sadder I became. He wasn't mine, and he was supposed to be, and that shit was eating me up.

He looked over at me as I sat down at the kitchen table.

Two wineglasses, both filled with orange juice, an ice bucket with a bottle of champagne, ketchup, syrup, salt, and pepper sat on the table. I was in awe. I looked up at Aaron, shaking my head at him. "Oh my goodness, what time did you wake up to do all of this?"

Aaron grinned. "Man, you look beautiful when you wake up in the morning."

I rolled my eyes. "Aaron, please. I know I have the breath from hell right now, and my hair looks like a bird's nest." I ran my fingers through my tangled hair, which was still damp. "I look like something from *The Nightmare Before Christmas* right about now."

Aaron laughed aloud. "Girl, you're somethin' else! Never did know how fine you are." He walked over to me with two plates stacked full of food and set the plates on the table.

Bacon, eggs, pancakes, sausage, and hash browns were on my plate. He was too much.

Aaron looked at me as he handed me a fork and a knife.

I took the utensils from him. I knew from the moment we started eating that I wasn't going to make it to class that morning.

"Do you have classes today, Heaven?" Aaron dug in.

I nodded, cutting my pancakes into small pieces.

"You goin' or you hangin' out wit'cha boy today?" he asked, already knowing the answer to that question.

"I don't feel like facing the world just yet, Aaron," I whispered back.

He agreed. "Me neither, shorty."

"But I *do* have a term paper that I really need to work on today. I've been trying to get it done all weekend." I looked up at him.

"There's a laptop in the other room, shorty. Everything you need is right here."

I dried the tears that slid down my cheeks. Yeah, I'm a crybaby. Get over it. "I don't wanna waste time crying or feeling sad. Just once, I would like to feel happy and loved, even if it's only for a day or two. Let's talk, let's laugh, and let's drink. Today, I'm yours. So whatever you wanna do, just ask, or better yet, just do it."

Aaron grinned. "A'ight. Let's hurry up and eat."

Aaron lay on the bed watching TV as I blow-dried, then flat ironed, my hair that morning. He wasn't lying when he said that he had everything that I needed for me at that hotel. He bought me a full change of clothes and sexy lingerie. I stood at the mirror admiring myself in the silk burgundy bra and panties that he bought me.

Aaron looked up at me as I unplugged my flat iron.

I walked over and sat beside him on the bed.

He pulled me closer to him by my hips. I knew he was scared of where his life was going. I knew he had no clue about what he was going to say to his family about Charlie. I don't think it was so much the baby that bothered him. I think it was more of the fact that since Charlie was pregnant with *his* baby, he would be forced to marry someone who he wasn't in love with.

"I got a call a few days ago, shorty, from my agent. He said that there were a few teams that wanted me. It was just a matter of which team offered the most on my contract." He looked into my face.

My eyes lit up. It was the best news that I had heard all weekend. "That's great! Wow, so, which team do you wanna go with?"

He shrugged. "I don't know. It all depends on Charlie now. I would like to go with LA, or overseas, but we'll see." He swept my bangs from my face.

I smiled, happy as hell for that boy. "That's amazing, Aaron! I'm so happy for you. See, I *told* you that you were a star!"

Aaron laughed a little to himself. "A star, huh?"

I looked into his face. "You don't seem too happy about this, Aaron. Why don't you sound happy about joining the NBA? Your parents would be so happy for you!"

He shook his head. "Nah, not really. I haven't even told them. As a matter of fact, my parents thought I was going to school to be a doctor. My father even had medical schools picked out for me already, shorty. Hanging out with the fellas from the basketball team is what got me kicked out of school in California. I got caught selling drugs for my homeboy back in South Central."

I shook my head. "Aaron, why the hell were you selling drugs? And why the fuck were you even hanging out in South Central? Word around town is your father is some sort of royalty, and your family has money for centuries to come!"

He sighed. "I know, Heaven. I wasn't the one selling drugs. It was my homeboy. He was from the hood. He was gonna be the first in his family to graduate high school and go to UCLA on a full athletic scholarship. The nigga had skills. I knew that if I took the rap for him, my father would just pay my way out and send me to another school or some shit. My boy, Timothy, didn't have it like that. He didn't have a chance. Now, he's in UCLA, doin' the damn thing, making damn near straight-As. His family is proud, while my parents can barely look at me. And the fact that Charlie is pregnant isn't gonna help fix the situation either. I'm basically fucked."

I wasn't sure what to say. I had no idea that he had so much going on. "Ummm, do you really have to tell your parents that Charlie is pregnant?"

Aaron laughed a little. "Heaven, my parents are gonna know the only reason I'm marrying Charlie is *because* she's pregnant. They know I don't love that girl. If I don't marry her, that will be one more thing they'll be disappointed in me for."

"Everything that you do isn't gonna make someone else happy. I learned that a long time ago when I would do everything in the world to try to make Juanita smile when she was depressed." I swept my hair from my face. "There were times when she wouldn't get out of bed for weeks. There were times when we had to beg family members for food because sometimes, the only thing we had in the refrigerator was baking soda and Budweiser."

Aaron's eyes searched mine, a sympathetic look swept across his face.

"Juanita hated us, Aaron. My little brother and my older sister were the best siblings anyone could ever have. I loved them so much. I would get the shit beat out of me for trying to stop Juanita from beating my brother, all because he kept stealing money out of her purse to go buy food from the corner store. My sister was beautiful . . . legs, hips, and ass for days. She had long hair, caramel skin, light eyes. I think every one of my mother's boyfriends molested her, and my mother never gave a fuck. She probably traded my sister for drugs. Who knows? All I know is only *one* of her boyfriends tried me," I hated to admit.

Aaron's temples twitched. "What did the nigga do to you?"

I looked at him. "Let's just say I made it out of the house alive that night. About the only thing Juanita ever taught me to do was how to fire a gun. One night, when her boyfriend tried to climb into my bed naked, I reached under my mattress, pulled out the gun, and shot the muthafucka right between his legs. My mother came home that night to find an ambulance and the police outside of our home. She never forgave me for that night, even though I told her that he tried to rape me! She drank herself into a deeper and deeper depression. She watched another boyfriend rape my sister, and the bitch ended up killing my brother. Aaron, I have been through hell!" I shook my head, stomach in knots. "If it wasn't for Renée or for Charlie, I wouldn't be here talking to you right now. I would have blown my brains out the day my brother was murdered!"

Aaron held my hands, kissing both of them. He wasn't sure what he could say that could take away any of the pain that I still felt inside.

I looked at him. "Jamie helped me through a lot too. We grew up together. We only dated for about two years. He was my best friend. A huge part of me died when he moved to Tennessee to live with his dad. He just up and left me, not really saying good-bye. I had lost so much, Aaron. I lost my father who I never knew, I lost my mother who never wanted to know me, I lost my brother who loved me with all of his heart, I lost my sister who couldn't handle what had happened to her, and I lost Jamie who was my sunshine after the storm."

Aaron's eyes traced my lips.

"I'm sorry for talking about this. I said I wanted to be happy today, and here I am bringing up the past. Aaron, it's just that I need love. I don't want your pieces. I have been getting bits and pieces of people all of my life." My eyes searched his. "Don't I deserve to be happy, Aaron? Don't I?"

Aaron gently kissed my lips. "Yes, shorty, you deserve the world."

I looked into his face as he kissed my lips again. "Oh my goodness, my heart could have really used your touch back then. I seriously doubt that you would have left me feeling as if love doesn't exist. Everything about you is love, Aaron. I wish I would have felt some of this sooner."

Aaron's eyes traced my lips once again. "I don't know what Jamie's reason was for leaving you, but that nigga was crazy to leave someone like you. I would have protected you. I would have done whatever I could to make sure I kept a smile on your face, Heaven. I would do anything I could to repair your heart. You would have been happy with me, Heaven, I promise you that." He ran his fingers through my hair. "I'm not even gonna lie. The only time you would feel a little pain would be when I was drillin' that pussy. I would have fucked the *shit* out of you in high school . . . shit, probably middle school too!" He smiled a little.

I shook my head, drying my tears. "You're so stupid," I laughed.

"I'm serious, shorty. You deserve to be happy. I wish I wasn't so intimidated by how I knew you felt about Jamie. You were so *fine*, so pretty, so cute. I tried approaching you in school, but every time we were face-to-face, I lost my nerve." Aaron held my hips. "If I would have known that you were feeling me too, this whole situation would have been avoided." His lips caressed mine, his hands gripping my hips. "C'mon, enough of the talkin'. Let's put in some work."

I stood from the bed, unhooking my bra.

Aaron slid my panties past my hips, across my thighs, down my calves, and from my feet. He slipped his tank top from his head and pulled his boxers off. He scooped me up in his arms, wrapping my legs around his waist, laying me down on the bed, his body on top of mine. We kissed passionately until he couldn't take it anymore. He reached for a condom from the nightstand. I watched him tear it open, then slide it on. I held on to him as he slid his way inside of me. I bit down on his neck as he dug through me. He had a fist full of my hair, and he tugged on it a little. My whole body was burning hot. It didn't take long before we both broke out in a sweat.

My pussy was so wet. Aaron's heart beat against my chest. He took my breath completely away at that moment. All I could do was take in his air. He pumped my pussy until it was dry. I felt my cervix shift in all sorts of directions. I whimpered and I cried as he dug into me. I gripped his ass in my hands as he stroked my body. Just when I couldn't take it anymore and begged him to stop, I could feel his dick throbbing inside of me. And then, all his weight fell on top of me.

We had sex that entire afternoon. I needed it, though the entire time we spent together was pointless. Kissing him, touching him, holding him, suckin' on him, fuckin' on him, stroking him, riding him. . . . It was all pointless. I knew he loved me. He had to. He knew he would have to deal with Charlie as soon as he saw her. He had been avoiding her calls since the night before. Meanwhile, Renée, Alisha, and damn near the whole dance squad was blowing up my phone. People I hadn't talked to in years were calling, asking me why I hadn't shown up

to class. I think I even got a call from one of
Aaron's teammates. I knew then that everyone
was calling me just to see where Aaron was.

While Aaron slept that afternoon, I worked
on my term paper and finished it within two
hours. At about 2:30, Aaron awoke from his nap
and went to the grocery store to pick up a few
items. I guess the boy wanted to seduce me with
his cooking. He made shrimp pasta, rolls, salad,
steak, and potatoes. Oh my goodness, the boy
made love to me with his cooking. I had already
been sipping on Siren Songs all afternoon, and
I was drunk as hell. We laughed, we drank, we
smoked, and we ate. Then we had sex. A *lot* of
sex.

Aaron and I had sex on a chair out on the balcony. We had sex on the kitchen table. We had
sex on the recliner. We had sex in the hot tub.
He had sex in my mouth. I had sex in *his* mouth.
We had sex in the shower. I was too drunk to
remember if there was another round after that,
that afternoon. All I knew is that I woke up on
the bathroom floor, condom wrappers stuck to
my back. My whole body was sore. I could barely
drag myself up off the floor. I could barely walk.
I could feel my pussy lips throbbing, swollen
between my legs. Needless to say, yeah, he
murdered the pussy. I peeled the empty condom

wrappers from my skin, tossing them in the trash can. My sweatpants and tank top sat in a corner. I walked over, picking them up off the floor.

"Aaron?" I called out, walking down the hallway, pulling my tank top over my head. As I slipped into my sweatpants, I felt a breeze coming from the living room. The smell of a Newport hit me in the face. Aaron was outside smoking on the balcony.

He looked up at me as I slid the door open wider to go outside to join him. He grinned at me as I sat down. It was dark out. The moon sat high in the sky.

"What time is it?" I asked, sitting across from him.

"It's 9:30." He exhaled smoke from his nostrils. He saw me squirming a little in the chair, trying to figure out a way to sit that was comfortable. "You all right, shorty?"

I looked at him, trying not to show any signs of pain on my face. "Just trying to get comfortable. The pussy is a little swollen."

He laughed a little, leaning back in the chair, the very chair that we had sex in. He didn't look too happy. He looked like something was bothering him.

I hesitated. "Do you want to be left alone? I mean, I can go back inside if I'm disturbing you."

Aaron shook his head as he exhaled smoke through his nose. "Nah, you're good. I'm just thinkin', that's all."

"About?" I swept my bangs from my face.

"You." He put his cigarette out in the ashtray.

My heart palpitated in my chest. "What about me?" I asked.

"What's gonna happen to you? I mean, what are you gonna do?" He sat up in his chair.

I was confused. "Do about what, Aaron? What do you mean?"

"I called Charlie." He ran his hands across his close-cut hair.

I suddenly felt like shit again.

"Told her that we needed to talk in the morning." His eyes grew misty.

I got up from my chair, about to head back into the hotel.

Aaron got up from his chair and grabbed my arm, pulling me back to him.

I pushed him off me.

He exhaled deeply. "Heaven, we knew this was coming. Did you really think I was gonna be able to face her without having to explain to her where I've been these past few days?"

"Aaron, whatever you decide you wanna do with her, that's your business. I really shouldn't be, and I really don't *wanna* be hearing this." My voice trembled.

Aaron tried to fight back the tears. "It's not fair to myself, Charlie, or the baby to marry someone who I am not in love with, just to save my family's reputation or so that the person who my parents think is the 'perfect fit' for my family can inherit their money. Charlie's not stupid, shorty. She's been blowing up my phone since I left your cousin's restaurant last night. The only reason why she even agreed to meeting me in the morning is because she has a doctor's appointment tomorrow and wants me to go with her."

I was so hurt hearing him talk about her. There was no use in crying over him. There was no use in being mad at the situation. He wasn't mine to begin with. The past two nights with him didn't change that.

"Charlie couldn't care less about my family's tradition. She might say fuck me *and* my got-damn family tomorrow when we speak. She already cursed me out over the phone! After I get her to calm down, and if she wants to get married, then I'm calling my parents."

I laughed a little. "*If* she wants to get married? *Really,* Aaron?"

He looked confused. "What do you mean?"

"Charlie *loves* you, Aaron. I don't give a fuck *what* you do. The girl is in love with you. Now, she might hate *me* after this, but *you?* No, boo-boo, she's not going anywhere any time soon. I really think you could get away with murder right about now and the girl would probably say 'the muthafucka deserved it.'" I swept the bangs from my face. "So, go 'head, and pick your girl out a nice ring. Something at least three or four karats—probably princess cut—most likely in a platinum setting. You know Charlie hates gold or anything too flashy. But I'm pretty sure that your family has some sort of ring that they pass down through generations, huh?"

Aaron looked surprised that I talked about his situation so calmly.

I shrugged. "What do you want me to say, Aaron? The sex today was *beyond* amazing. I can barely feel my legs right now!"

Aaron laughed a little, though I know he was hurting inside just as badly as I was. "Yeah, that pussy *still* has a nigga dazed."

"But despite how good it feels to be with you, we know this is wrong. This is it. After tonight, it's back to reality." I sighed, hair blowing in the wind behind me.

Aaron hesitated for a minute, as if he had something to say, but didn't know how to say it.

I looked up at him. "What?"

He looked into my face. "I found out today why your boy Jamie is here for a week."

I looked up into his face, heart pounding against my rib cage. I shook my head. I really couldn't care less why Jamie decided after four years to show his face back up in Maryland. I knew I wasn't the reason why he showed up. He had missed four of my birthdays already. I knew I couldn't have been the reason he'd come back.

"Word on the street is his new agent works out of Baltimore. Come May, your boy will be drafted into the NFL. I heard the Ravens want him, but that's just what I heard." Aaron looked at me, waiting for a reaction.

I was highly upset. "What the hell does that have to do with me? I don't give a fuck what team Jamie ends up playing for. His life is not my concern anymore; hasn't been for four years, Aaron."

Aaron knew I was hurt by the entire situation. Jamie was the last person I wanted to see, let alone hear about. "You gonna meet up with him this week, shorty?"

I was getting really irritated with the whole subject. "Aaron, why are you asking me about Jamie? Why are you even bringing him up, that's what I wanna know?"

"I'm just sayin', shorty, what are you gonna do the rest of your life? Be alone?" His eyes glistened. "You know it pains me to say this shit, but maybe you should give dude a try. The way he got all defensive at your party proves the dude still has feelings for you."

My lips trembled. I fought back the tears. "The only thing worse than being alone is to even *think* about being with him! I can't even believe that you're suggesting this!"

"You just said last night at your own birthday party, in front of your cousin, that you weren't lonely, but we all know that's bullshit, Heaven. You wanna be with somebody. You want love. Even before I knew that Charlie was pregnant, and I told you that I would leave her for you, you pushed me away. You're afraid to get hurt, and that's cool, but someday, your heart has got to give." Aaron pulled me closer to him by my hands.

I looked up, shaking my head. "Aaron, today, you kissed my lips—the ones on my face *and* the ones between my legs. You massaged my shoulders, my back, my butt, my thighs, and my feet. You sucked on my fingers, my neck, my shoulders, my nipples, *and* my clit. You gently pulled my hair. I put scratches on your back. I wrapped my legs around your neck while you tongue fucked my pussy. I came in your mouth, and you came in mine. We took a shower together. You ran your fingers through my hair. You made my pussy cry just as you said you would. Tears of joy trickled down my thighs. Aaron, we made long, wet, passionate, hot, sticky, sweaty, nasty, crazy, drunk *love*."

"Yeah, it felt like magic, that's for damn sure." Aaron shook his head to himself.

I slid my hands from his. "If I can't feel the way I felt with you today *every* day, then I don't wanna feel that way at all. I don't know what I'm gonna do, Aaron, but moving on to someone else isn't gonna heal my heart. You have me wide open, like literally. The fact that Jamie is coming back in town doesn't change the fact that he left me four years ago, without looking back. He never came to visit, let alone wrote me any letters. I could give a fuck if Jamie is here or not. He's toxic, and I'm not going anywhere near him."

"Heaven, the reason why you're still hurting over dude is because you still love him. If you didn't, it wouldn't hurt so badly. You'd be like 'fuck it, fuck *him*.'" Aaron's eyes maintained contact with mine as he spoke.

I shook my head. "Aaron, I *really* don't wanna talk to you about Jamie, okay?"

He nodded. "A'ight. I'm sorry for bringing him up, but you're gonna have to face the dude sooner or later. Can't run from dude for too long, and I already know it won't take a week before he comes looking for you. You didn't see the look on his face when he confronted me about you. Dude still has feelings for you."

I sighed. "I need a drink." I ran my fingers through my hair anxiously.

Aaron grabbed my arm, pulling me closer to him. "Nah, let's get in the hot tub again." He looked down, eyes tracing my lips.

I nodded, heart pounding in my chest as he held my hand, taking me back inside. He had my heart ready to explode. His touch, his kiss, his voice, his smell, his very presence drove me crazy. Aaron had me like Kia up in that bitch. Dude licked, sucked, and fucked my *everything*. I rode that dick that night as if I was never going to get that dick again, literally. Charlie made sure of that. The sad part was that Aaron was right about Jamie. He'd come for me eventually. It's funny how niggas don't want you until they see someone else is interested in you.

Aaron didn't take me back to the dorm until early the next morning. At about 7:00, we got up, got dressed, and ate breakfast. I felt like I was on death row, eating my last meal before an execution. I already knew I was about to face the firing squad that morning. I had been avoiding Renée since the incident at the karaoke bar. She was bound to show up at my dorm that morning. I had a 10:00 Humanities class. I wasn't sure what time Aaron had to be in class, but he sure as hell looked like he wasn't in the mood for anything educational that day either. He must have gone through about half a pack of cigarettes that morning. I've never seen him smoke that much.

"You're not going to class today, Aaron?" I asked, watching him light up another Newport.

He looked at me, shaking his head. "Nah. I'm about to hit the gym, then roll up on shorty. She's got a 10:00 appointment this morning. Depending on how that goes, I might show up to my 1:00 Physics class." Aaron watched me as I folded the Coogi dress he had bought me. "I don't think I got the chance to tell you how good you looked in that dress."

I looked up at him.

"Shorty, you looked *good* in that dress. Fine as a muthafucka." His eyes searched mine.

I blushed a little. "Thank you, Aaron."

"You got everything?" he asked, walking toward the door.

No, I didn't have everything. I didn't have my head together. I didn't have my emotions together. I didn't have my dignity. I didn't have my pride. I didn't have my self-esteem. I didn't have my strength. I didn't have *him*. I was a complete mess. I had no idea how I was going to recover mentally, physically, or emotionally.

I shrugged. "I guess so, Aaron." I placed my dress, heels, jacket, and the toiletries that Aaron bought in the bag that the clothes I was wearing came out of.

Aaron approached me, handing me the clean pair of panties and bra that I had on the night of my party.

I took them from him, lips trembling as I placed them in the bag. I couldn't even look up at him. "I had a *really* nice time, Aaron. I can-I can still feel you all over my body. I can still feel you inside of me."

Aaron tilted my chin so our eyes could meet, and he gently kissed my lips, sucking on my bottom lip just a little. "No matter what happens from this day forward, just remember, Heaven, that I will always love you. *Always*."

Aaron dropped me off at my dorm room that morning. When I opened my mouth to tell him good-bye, tears and pain came out instead. He leaned forward to kiss me on my forehead, then on my lips, then on my wet cheeks.

My lips trembled as he gently kissed my lips again. I held his face in my hands as his lips caressed mine. He felt so wonderful, so amazing, and so comfortable. I loved him. As brief as our encounter was, it was going to take every ounce of strength I had to give up and walk away from him. It took everything in me to pull my lips from his that morning. I didn't want to let him go.

Aaron held my hands to his lips, softly kissing them.

"Heaven, everything is gonna be okay," he whispered.

I struggled to smile. "My heart has been broken into so many pieces. Too many pieces to pick up, too many to count, too many to put back together. Kind of like dropping a vase on the floor—even when you put a shattered vase back together, there is always a piece missing, even if it's the tiniest piece." I dried my face because it was time to stop crying. "How can I mourn the loss of something that was never mine to begin with? I have no choice *but* to be okay with this. I ruined my own chances at a relationship with you. I shouldn't have been so shy and insecure. Charlie is *beautiful!* I didn't think I could compete with her! I never thought you would choose someone like me over someone like her!"

Aaron shook his head. "Heaven, you are sexy as hell. Your chocolate skin tone is mouthwatering, yo. Yes, Charlie is a beautiful woman aesthetically, but the connection was never there, and we both know that."

I shook my head at him. I couldn't handle being in his presence any longer. "Charlie loves you, Aaron. So you're just gonna have to learn to love her back, for the sake of this soon-to-be beautiful baby. See you around, Aaron." I couldn't get out of that car fast enough. Oh my goodness, why didn't anyone tell me that love would hurt this fuckin' bad?

Chapter 10

The Reunion

Ne'Vaeh

I dodged the firing squad for a few days, and I mean just a *few* days. I sat in a far corner of the library that Friday, studying for a statistics test I had that afternoon. I mean, I was just sitting there, minding my own damn business when a pair of size six-and-a-half heels comes stomping across the lobby of the library. I sank back in my chair, trying to bury my face in my notes, acting as if I didn't see Renée's crazy ass stomping toward me, like Ms. Sophia from *The Color Purple*.

"Okay, so now you're gonna not only ignore my muthafuckin' phone calls and texts, but you're gonna sit there, lookin' like you haven't slept in days, acting like you don't see me standing here in front of you too? Ne'Vaeh, act as if I won't get loud up in this muthafucka if you want to! You *know* I know how to get you and me both barred from somewhere! Act brand new if you want to, boo-boo!" Renée's voice already started to rise.

I rolled my eyes, looking up at her from my iPad. "Oh, hey, girl. What's up, Renée?"

Renée's eyes widened. "*'What's up?'* What's up? No, what's up with *you?* I've been worried sick about you *all* fuckin' week! Why have you been ignoring my fuckin' calls? I know you seen my texts! *And* I sent you like twenty messages on Facebook!"

My eyes filled with tears. She was right when she said I looked like I haven't slept in days. I hadn't. I hadn't had any sleep since I fell asleep that Monday night in Aaron's arms. It took everything I had every morning that week to crawl out of bed. I must have taken a whole bottle of sleeping pills. I'd had a prescription for sleeping pills ever since the day I found my brother's body lifeless in his bed. It took years to fall asleep without seeing his face. Now, here I was, unable to get Aaron's face out of my head. I couldn't get my mind to register the fact that I wasn't around him that week. In my mind, I could still smell, taste, hear, feel, and see Aaron.

I couldn't even say his name aloud without crying. I thought about him every second. I couldn't help but wonder how his conversation with Charlie went the morning he dropped me back off at the dorm. I kept one of the towels from the hotel, the towel that he dried off with after we got out of the hot tub. Oh, it smelled just like him. I draped the towel across the pillow on my bed, burying my face in it, crying in it every night. I hadn't even spent a week alone with Aaron, but the time that I did spend with him had embedded memories in my mind, heart, body, and soul. I could still feel him kissing me, touching me, biting me, sucking me, inside of me. I can admit, yeah, I was sprung. I had no idea how I was going to get over him, but I had no choice but to move on, and I was probably going to need counseling to do it.

I looked at Renée. "I really didn't feel like talking to anybody, okay? My fuckin' birthday was a fuckin' disaster. I'm gonna have to start going back to my damn therapist, just to get over the events that occurred that night. And you know I hate that bitch."

Renée sat down at the table across from me. She was dressed in a tight sweater that showed a little too much cleavage, and tight black denim jeans. She always did dress to impress. I don't even think that girl owned one pair of fuckin' sweatpants. Even when we went to the gym, she would find the shortest shorts. They might as well have been panties, and the tightest, tiniest tank top to put on. Always had to be the sexy one in the crew. You would have never thought by looking at her that she was pushing thirty because she fit right in with the teenagers.

"So," she looked at me, "how was the *after-party?*"

I looked at her, not sure really how to respond. I figured when all else fails, play dumb. "*What* after-party?"

Renée pursed her lips. "Bitch, don't make me slap the shit outta you."

I rolled my eyes. "Renée, you know, there are three rules to business. Number one, I mind my business. Number two, you mind *your* business. And number three, stay the *fuck* outta mine."

Renée laughed aloud. "Oh, okay, I see, using my own shit on me, huh? So, you got dicked-down by Mr. Whitehaven, and now you think you're a full-fledged woman? Okay, I got you. Well, I just thought I'd let you know that Charlie knows about your little love affair."

I just looked at Renée, my heart beginning to speed up.

Renée nodded, "Yeah, she found the receipt for that damn dress you had on last weekend in Aaron's jacket pocket. He admitted that he bought the dress, those damn earrings, *and* that necklace that you *still* have on for your birthday. He didn't admit to her that y'all slept together, but Charlie isn't stupid. The nigga was MIA from Sunday night until Tuesday morning. She knew where the fuck he was at. She knew where the fuck *you* were at. She has connections, Ne'Vaeh. You just remember that."

Tears slid down my face, but I quickly dried them away.

"Girl, I must say, though, Charlie slapped the living *shit* outta that muthafucka when he showed up that Tuesday morning!" Renée laughed to herself.

I looked at her, putting my iPad down. "How do *you* know this?"

She looked at me. "Because I was there, honey."

"Since when do you start hanging around Charlie?" I asked.

Renée shook her head at me. "Since *your* ass stopped answering your fuckin' phone, and I needed to find out where the fuck you were! Charlie is more pissed than a muthafucka at you! But for some reason, and I can't quite put my finger on it, she hasn't beat your ass yet. Or at least attempted to. I mean, as much as I'm pissed at you, I wouldn't let anything happen to you."

My heart was racing. "What-what happened after she slapped him, Renée?"

Renée shrugged. "I don't know. All I know is that she planned to take me with her to her appointment because she really wasn't ready to face Aaron. When he showed up, her ass blanked out on him—she was kicking, screaming, and slapping him! It took her cousin, Tyra, and me to pull her off Aaron! She fell to the floor crying, and the funny thing is that Aaron started crying too. I don't think the dude was crying over her being upset with him. I think he was crying over what happened with *you*."

Thoughts of Aaron's stroke flashed through my mind.

"Aaron asked us if we could give them some privacy for a few minutes. We stepped outside. Twenty minutes later, Tyra went back in the house to make sure everything was cool. She came back outside and said . . . Well, let's just say that he said something *and* did something that the girl needed to get over it." Renée knew she was telling me everything I didn't want to hear, but she continued talking. "Yesterday,

Charlie and a few of her chicks from the squad showed up to my house with a few invitations."

I looked at Renée, heart pounding harder than ever in my chest. "Invitations to what, Renée?"

"The engagement party, Ne'Vaeh! The bitch is having the party Thanksgiving Day!" Renée exclaimed. She reached in her purse and pulled out a beige, sparkly invitation, handing it to me. "Here."

It had my name on it. I laughed a little. I knew Charlie was going to invite me just to rub it in. If she knew about my three-night stand with her boyfriend, she sure as hell was playing it off really well. She hadn't called. She hadn't come to hunt me down at school. She hadn't tried to fight me. She hadn't showed any signs that she knew about anything that happened between her fiancé and me. Yeah, she had plans for me.

"Well, *that* ruined my day." I laughed at Charlie's ignorance, handing the invitation back to Renée.

Renée shook her head at me. "Sweetie, I know this shit is devastating, but you gotta do what you gotta do to move on. I'm pretty sure you fucked that muthafucka's brains out those days you were with him in Virginia. And no sooner than a few hours after he's home, he's back to fuckin' *Charlie's* ass! It's sad that you're in love with this dude and know nothing about him or his stuck-up-ass rich family. I know that boy loves you. Shit, *Charlie* knows that boy loves you! But they are having a baby, and they are getting married, and that's that."

I sat back in my chair, mind racing in all sorts of directions.

"So, with that being said, *Jamie* also gave me an invitation to give to you." Renée reached into her purse again, pulling out a purple and gold invitation.

I looked at her, rolling my eyes, taking the invitation from her hand. "Renée, I can't even believe you're handing me this shit. What is this?"

"An invitation to *Jamie's* Ravens' party! It's tonight at ten-thirty! Don't tell me you haven't heard the dude just signed with the Ravens yesterday! Yeah, come spring, he's training with the Ravens!" Renée was definitely more excited than I was to hear that Jamie was coming back to town.

I shook my head, looking at the bitch as if she'd lost her fuckin' mind. "I'm not going to this shit. This invitation is just as fucked up as Charlie's invitation!"

Renée shook her head back at me, "Well, boo-boo, you *will* be ready to roll at ten o'clock tonight when I come back to get you. And if you're not, I swear to goodness, I will tell Jamie which dorm room you stay in. You know the muthafucka is fine. One of these thirsty bitches would let him in your dorm!"

I rolled my eyes, handing the invitation back to her. "Renée, that's fucked up! My heart is in no condition to go out to no fuckin' party, especially a party where Jamie Green's ass is gonna be! He broke my heart! You think I really wanna go around him right now?"

Renée sighed. "Girl, you gotta let it go. I know it's too soon to say some shit like that to you, but it's reality. You got the chance to be with Aaron for a few days. You got the chance to feel what it was like to know that he loves you. I know that feeling was snatched from you too soon, but I *told* you to leave that situation alone! Jamie Green is back, the boy you used to love with all of your heart. He's leaving Sunday to go back to Memphis to finish his semester in school; then he's back in Baltimore. He personally gave me this invitation to give to you, which means he wants you to come."

I fought back any old feelings that I may have felt for Jamie. "I really don't give a fuck, Renée. And you're wrong for doing this to me!"

Renée got up from the table, "Okay, whatever, Ne'Vaeh. I expect to see you waiting outside your dorm tonight wearing something purple and sexy. The party is at Purple Panties. We gonna have a ball, girl!" She came around the table to hug me. "Everything is gonna be okay, boo, you'll see."

Seemed like nothing fit right that night. It was too soon to be going to a got-damn party. It was too soon to have any fun. It was too soon to see Jamie's face. I prayed that the club would be so crowded that Jamie wouldn't be able to spot me. He knew everybody, so I knew the club would be crowded beyond capacity. Renée must have called me a million damn times that day, just to make sure that I was getting ready. She even sent over our cousin Jennel to do my hair and makeup. I was in no mood to be pretty, so I could give a damn if I wore a wife beater and sweatpants. Jennel flat ironed my hair, put makeup on my face, and even brought over a sexy, tight, purple dress with matching heels for me to wear. The bitch even brought me a purple silk bra and bikini panties set. Why the hell did I need to match my underwear with my damn clothes? I don't know whom Renée called herself trying to impress. I couldn't care less how Jamie thought I looked. That muthafucka.

"Done! I sure can beat a face!" Jennel said, after applying the last coat of mascara. She smiled, dark eyes searching my face for any flaws with my makeup. "Girl, I am a *beast* in the cosmetic department! Not that you needed any makeup with your perfect-skin-havin' ass, but yeah, you look like a beauty queen!" She gave me a hand mirror.

I grinned a little, looking at my reflection in the mirror. I admit, she *did* have skills, but I wasn't in the mood to go out anywhere. My smile quickly faded. "Jennel, I am *not* in the mood to go out tonight." I handed the mirror back to her. "Y'all know how Jamie did me. *Why* would I wanna celebrate with him? And you know this whole being drafted-to-the-Ravens thing is bullshit, right? Jamie doesn't even *like* the Ravens! Remember when he said they were dried up—he used to call them the Baltimore *Raisins!*"

Jennel shook her head, putting all of her makeup back in her Chanel makeup case. "Girl, shut up. Renée means well, and you know it. She is your *biggest* fan. Always has been, always will be. You're like a sister to her, the little sister she never had! A bunch of us ran into Jamie last night at the mall. He told her to bring everybody out to the club tonight for his party. *You* were the only one he had an invitation for. The only reason we are gettin' in is because *you* got an invite!"

I sighed. "Why did she have to match my underwear with my outfit? What the fuck kind of party do y'all have me going to?"

Jennel laughed aloud. "Girl, *you'll* see!"

Renée, along with about ten of her friends, picked me up that night in a stretch Hummer. Renée always rolled deep, if you haven't noticed. All of her friends were dressed to impress, looking like a bunch of black Playboy models. Renée was excited to see that Jennel had done such a good job with my hair and makeup. She went on and on about how I was going to win. Win what? I had no idea.

Once we got to Purple Panties, we stepped out of the limo. The line was wrapped all the way around the damn building. I didn't want to skip everyone, because I really didn't want to go to the party in the first damn place. But Alisha's ass was already standing in the door, wearing a skimpy silk purple dress that barely touched the bottom of her butt cheeks. You could see her purple push-up bra and thong through her dress. Her long hair was swept up into a bun.

She squealed when she saw the thirteen of us walking toward her, prancing down the red carpet. She nudged the security guard, whispering something to him. He looked at us, then unhooked the rope, letting us in.

Alisha quickly rushed over to me, throwing her arms around me. "Cutie, you made it!"

I faked a smile. "Hey, girl."

"Ooohhh, look at *you!*" Alisha smacked me on the butt. "Look at the rest of y'all, lookin' like a bunch'a raisins with all that got-damn purple on! C'mon, girls, we got a few booths in the back of the club." She grabbed my arm, pulling me behind her, leading me into the club.

Alisha led us through the crowded club over to the section in the back of the club where a few other girls in the squad were sitting. Most of the girls were just dressed in purple stilettos, purple sequined bras, and boy shorts. Others were dressed in white, glowing under the white lights. Our crew spread out among the booths.

"What's up, ladies? Let's get these drinks flowing!" Kristina exclaimed. I hated going to the club with her because her drinking almost always led to a fight.

"Hey, y'all missin' a few dancers, aren'tcha?" Renée put her arm over my shoulder.

I looked at her, rolling my eyes. She was referring to Charlie, who was the only dancer that wasn't there at the moment. I looked at Alisha to see her reaction. Alisha laughed a little, shooting me a quick look. "Girl, you know Charlie hates this damn club, but there's no way she'd let Aaron come here unaccompanied tonight. She knows Jamie's party is tonight. She knows anybody who's anybody is gonna be up in the spot tonight, including Cutie."

My heart skipped a beat or ten. I sighed. I really was in no mood for any bullshit tonight. "Look, the only reason I came to this damn club is because Renée talked me into this bullshit. Now, I'm not with the damn reality TV, drama shit tonight. So, if some shit is about to go down, y'all can just take me back to where the fuck you picked me up at."

Alisha took me by the hand, leading me to the corner booth that she was sitting in. "Girl, chill, no worries. You know we got your back. We're here to have some fun, get drunk, get crunk, and get *fucked* up!"

I sighed, sitting down next to her at the booth. "I'm tellin' you, any shit, and I'm out."

"Girl, whateva. Stop trippin'. Eh!"

Kelissa hollered across the room, taking a wad of one-dollar bills out of her bra, "Where them strippers at?"

Yeah, it did get live in Purple Panties that night. The party was jumpin' before Jamie and his crew even showed up. The strippers stayed in our section most of the night. Many admired Alisha's dancers. They were sexy, they were fit, they were flexible, and they were fashionable. Strippers didn't have shit on the Morgan Girls.

Alisha was right. Charlie *did* show up with Aaron that night around eleven-thirty. I had already been drinkin' a few Long Island Iced Teas, so their presence didn't bother me the way it would have if I had been sober. The two split up at the door. Aaron went over to what I call the basketball section, and Charlie made her way over to her squad. I remained as calm as I could when she came over to my booth and sat right across from me. My heart nearly shot out of my chest, but still, I remained silent.

"What's up, Charlie?" Renée turned to her in her seat.

Charlie looked at Renée, eyes sparkling under the club lights. "What's up?" She looked at me. "Can we talk in private?"

Before I could open my mouth to say anything, Renée opened hers. "Nah, she's cool right *here*. Anything you can say to her alone, you can say in front of us. Ain't gonna be no *shit* tonight. We came to chill."

Charlie rolled her eyes at Renée. "Renée, mind your business. Look," she looked at me, "I ain't here for all that. Me and you have been friends for a long time, Ne'Vaeh, and I'll be damned if I let a man come between us."

I just looked at her, lips trembling, not sure what to say.

She put her hand up, showing off the huge rock on her finger. The ring nearly blinded all of us girls who sat with her at the booth. She grinned, watching the hurt expression on my face. "Ya know, when I found the receipt to that dress you had on at your birthday party in his pocket, the first thought in my mind was beating your ass right in front of him. When I called him for three days straight and he didn't answer, I tracked him down. Turns out, a few people saw him at the Marriott Hotel in Virginia with you. Again, I plotted all sorts of ways to end your life in my head. My own best friend fucked my man." Charlie laughed to herself. "After all that I have done for you, you're gonna go and fuck with Aaron? What makes you think that he would leave me for something like *you?*"

"Charlie, you really need to back the fuck off." Kelissa stood from the table.

Charlie laughed. "I mean, really, you got my engagement party invitation, didn't you? Didn't anyone tell you that groupies get nothing but the dick? Groupies get no love, bitch. You should know that. You *were* Jamie's groupie for two years, *weren't* you?"

Renée almost went across the table on Charlie's ass, but Kristina and I pulled her back. "Bitch, you better watch your mouth before I wrap your ass around one of these muthafuckin' poles! Who the fuck do you think you are? You got my cousin fucked up! You got some nerve steppin' to her like this! Did Aaron tell you that they fucked? Did you hear that shit from *his* mouth? If not, then you need to back the fuck up. Me and you already talked about this earlier this week. You need to let the shit go."

Charlie looked at me. She was so angry that her lips and jawbone were trembling. "I wanna hear the words come out of *Ne'Vaeh's* mouth."

All eyes were on me. What difference did it make what I said? She had in her mind the way that she felt about me. According to her, I wasn't shit but one of the many girls who were drooling over an athlete. She knew Aaron loved me. I saw it all over her face. She knew the only reason they were getting married was because she was pregnant. She knew he didn't love her and probably never would, and she hated me for that. To hear her say those words to me stung like bees. Yes, I was wrong for what I had done, but it wasn't as if I went after her man. Aaron came after me, even when I told him no. But what use was it to explain that to Charlie, when she already had in her head that I was a groupie after her man?

I laughed a little to cover the pain and embarrassment that I was feeling. I really didn't feel like stooping to her level that night. "You know, it really doesn't matter what I say to you right now, because you have in your head that something happened between us. In your mind, you think I'm some random chick who fucked your man behind your back. You won, Charlie. You're having his baby, and you're getting married, and you get to do the shit right smack in front of my face. Yeah, he bought me a dress. I tried to give it back, and he wouldn't take the shit back. Yeah, he told me that he had feelings for me, and I told him there was no way that we could be together when his girlfriend was my *best* friend. Did he tell you that, while you're over here calling *me* a groupie? If you think I fucked your man, if you think I want your man, if you think your man wants *me*, then why are you marrying him?"

Charlie's lips trembled.

I shook my head. "You let everyone here know the first time you laid eyes on Aaron that he was yours, and that hasn't changed. Whatever you think happened between me and Aaron doesn't change that either. I won't deny that I have feelings for him. That may be inappropriate, but I missed my chance, so congratulations on the baby and on the engagement, Charlie."

Charlie looked at me, face red as hell. "You got me *fucked* up, Ne'Vaeh. If I catch you so much as *looking* at him the wrong way, I will *kill* you, girl. Do you hear me? I'm not fuckin' stupid, Ne'Vaeh, so don't think for one fuckin' second that you can play a playa! Stay the *fuck* away from him." Charlie got up from the table and walked away, shouting, "See you at the engagement party, *groupie*."

Everyone looked at me like I had been touched by an angel.

"Girl, I thought she was gonna dust the *floor* with your ass!" Kristina exclaimed.

Renée shook her head at me. "Y'all bitches crazy! I need another drink."

I looked at Alisha. "See, that's the shit I'm talkin' about, Alisha. I didn't come here to be called a fuckin' groupie. A muthafuckin' *groupie?* After fuckin' and suckin' hundreds—no—*thousands* of dudes *and* females in high school, she has the nerve to call *me* a fuckin' groupie?"

Alisha shook her head. "Man, don't even sweat Charlie. She's got problems bigger than you fuckin' her man, *trust* me."

That little conversation put a small damper in my night, but the party continued, and I soon found out why Renée was so adamant about me wearing purple panties. At around twelve-thirty, purple lights flashed all around the room, and every lady in the club, except for me, who was clueless about what was going on, and the strippers, who were already naked, of course, stripped down to their purple panties.

My heart pounded in my chest. "What the fuck is goin' on?" I asked Dana who didn't even have on a bra but just purple thongs. Titties and ass cheeks were flappin' *everywhere*.

"Girl, we about to do the pole-dancing contest! How could you *not* know about this?" Dana looked me up and down. She rolled her eyes. "Girl, I almost forgot how lame you were. Always got your nose buried in some book somewhere. You never get out. If you did, you'd know that on Fridays, the guests at the club compete with the strippers to see who's got it and who doesn't. Tonight, the winner gets a date with Jamie G.!"

I rolled my eyes. "Been there, done that shit, so I'll pass." I sat back in the corner booth, sipping on my daiquiri.

Every—and I mean just about *every*—woman up in the club took center stage that night, working the hell out of that pole. Asses shakin', twerkin', bouncin', droppin', poppin'. I know them dudes were lovin' that shit. I, on the other hand, was regretting my decision to come out tonight.

After the last dancer hit the stage, Jamie's childhood friend and teammate at Memphis State, Jerry King, got onstage. "So, is that it? No more titties?" he asked.

"No, that's *not* it!" The Morgan Girls pointed to me.

My eyes widened, and I shook my head frantically as Renée and Alisha pulled me up from my seat. "Oh, hell nah!" I squealed.

"Jerry King, baby, we have another one!" Alisha pulled my arm, pulling me behind her up to the stage.

A stripper held out her hand, helping me onto the stage. I stood alongside Alisha, the strippers, and Jerry. My heart pounded in my chest. I looked over to the corner of the room where Jamie sat in the VIP section with his teammates. He was grinning from ear to ear. I looked around the room and caught sight of Aaron and his teammates in the basketball section. Aaron just sat back in his chair, leaned back, smoking

and looking at me as if he couldn't believe I let
the girls talk me into coming to Jamie's party.
Charlie sat right on his lap, arms folded, looking
at me as if she wanted to cut me.

I swallowed hard as a stripper attempted to
untie my dress from around my neck. I turned
to her, stopping her from doing that. "Hold up,
now. Get your got-damn hands off me." I put my
hands up. "Nah, I don't strip."

The crowd booed.

Jerry laughed into the microphone. "Well,
then, what *do* you do, shorty?"

As I took the microphone from his hands, I
looked down into Renée's face as she stood at
the front of the stage, cheering me on. Then I
looked at Alisha who was standing beside me
in her bra and panties. She nodded at me to do
what she knew I was about to do.

I took a deep breath, putting the microphone
to my lips and I started to sing. *"I've been
drinkin', I've been drinkin' . . ."*

The crowd went wild as I sang a cappella to the
only sexy song I could think of at the moment. I
didn't intend on singing it, but that was the first
song that came to my mind because I could still
feel the coldness of the kitchen floor on my back.
I could still feel Aaron's lips all over me. Every
time I closed my eyes, I could see him sucking

the wine from my lips. I'm pretty sure Aaron knew I was singing that song to him. He couldn't help but grin before he got up and walked out of the club, Charlie following behind him.

The look on Jamie's face let me know that he knew I was singing to Aaron as well. He grinned, shaking his head at me, but he clapped and cheered along with everyone else. I couldn't finish the song fast enough when Alisha and Renée cheered me on, grabbing on me, hugging me as if *they* had just struck gold or something.

"This is *my* cousin, y'all! *Whew!*" Renée squealed at the top of her lungs. "Hollywood, here we come!"

I rolled my eyes as she dragged me offstage and back over to the table with the dancers. Everyone cheered me on, talking among themselves. Though I was in the choir, I'm pretty sure most of them had no clue that I could really sing. They thought the only thing I could do was homework. Dana sat there stunned.

"Humph, not so lame *now*, am I, Dana? Choke on *that* shit, bitch." I rolled my eyes at her as I sat down at the corner booth with Renée and Alisha.

"Girl, I know Charlie wants to whup your *ass* right about now! She knew you were singin' to her man! And look at *Jamie's* fine ass over there droolin'!" Kelissa laughed aloud.

The football players picked their favorite ten girls from those who danced that night and lined them up onstage. Just when I thought I was out of the running, Jamie called me to the stage. I was reluctant to get back up there, but Renée . . . Man, that bitch just wouldn't give up. She practically dragged me up onstage and stood beside me, arm around me, preventing me from running back off the stage. The winner was chosen, and guess who won the date with Jamie Green? Yeah . . . me.

After the humiliation was over, I sat alone at the bar.

"Why are you sittin' over here alone, shorty?" I heard Jamie's voice over my shoulder.

I rolled my eyes at him as he sat down next to me. "Because maybe I *want* to be alone, Jamie."

He laughed to himself. "So, where you wanna go on our date tomorrow night?"

"I don't know, but do you want me to tell you which part of hell that *you* can go to?" I took a sip from my rum and Coke.

Jamie laughed aloud. "Shorty, do you really hate me *that* much?"

I didn't answer. My eyes were drenched in tears. It took all my strength to hold the tears back. "What are you doing here, Jamie?" I managed to say.

"What do you mean?" he asked.

I looked up into his face. Oh, I had almost forgotten that face. I had almost forgotten how just one look, one word, one touch from Jamie could just set my soul on fire. He was so sexy and so charming. He was so fuckin' arrogant too, and a small part of me always liked that about him.

"What do I *mean?* Jamie, you could have picked any team you wanted to go to. I'm pretty sure that the Ravens aren't the only team who wanted you, right? Don't try to play me like I'm stupid." I took a sip from my drink.

He shrugged. "Shorty, you're the first person to know how much I hate Maryland or anything to do with this muthafucka, but shit, they need a nigga like me on their team. Who else they got on their team that can play like me?"

I rolled my eyes.

"Nah, the Ravens weren't my first choice, but trust me, they *are* payin' your boy quite a bit of bread. But honestly, this was my opportunity to come back to Maryland, so I took it. I already bought a house here, shorty, in Southern Maryland. You wanna see it tomorrow night?" His eyes searched mine.

I looked at him. "No, not really, Jamie. You know good and fuckin' well that every last one of those girls onstage tonight did a hell of a lot better stripping than I did singing! Those girls got completely naked for you, basically having sex with that pole! And you chose me *why?*"

Jamie laughed to himself. "Man, I missed you, shorty." He signaled the bartender to fix him a drink. "I almost forgot how muthafuckin' sexy you are. I almost forgot how beautiful your voice is. I heard your cousin's wife offered you a job singin' with her. Man, you crazy as hell for not takin' her up on her offer. Do you know how *big* Anastasia is right now?"

I looked at him, watching him as he took a sip from his glass. It would have been easier to hate him if he wasn't so damn nonchalant about my attitude. I believe he knew it was a front for being hurt. He knew I still felt something for him, but he knew I was mad at him for leaving me. He knew what I had been through in my life. He knew that he left me when I needed him the most. He knew it wasn't going to be easy gaining my trust back.

Jamie looked up at me. "To answer your questions about these girls twerkin' their asses off for me onstage, that shit was just for show. I've seen every last one of these girls who showed up tonight naked. If I wasn't the one havin' sex with them, trust me, I *saw* them having sex with someone else."

I rolled my eyes. "Yeah, they say you turned into a ho."

He laughed aloud. "Nah, I guess I just wanted a li'l appetizer while I was waiting on the main course."

I couldn't help but laugh at his ignorance. "What desperate kinda woman would wait around for you until you got tired of fuckin' groupies, Jamie? I hope you don't think that I was sitting around waiting on you, because I wasn't, asshole."

"Oh, trust me, shorty, I know."

I looked at him, my heartbeat starting to accelerate in my chest. "No, you *think* you know."

Jamie smirked. "*Think* I know? Shorty, do you think I'm stupid? Man, the muthafucka couldn't leave this club fast enough once you started singin' to him."

I rolled my eyes. "Singin' to *him?* What makes you think I was singing to Aaron?"

Jamie grinned. His grill was gleaming under the club lights. "You ain't gotta lie to me, Ne'Vaeh. My man seen your ass with dude at the hotel, shorty. You must'a really put it on him. Probably got the dude having flashbacks of whatever it is that you did to the muthafucka. Remember, I have *been* with you, so I know the magic you can do. You put your heart in it."

I just sipped on my drink, heart pounding in my chest. "I don't know what the fuck you're talking about, Jamie."

Jamie nodded, eyes sparkling under the club lights. "Yeah, you do, shorty. I'm sorry that I hurt you, okay? But you didn't have to go and fuck with Charlie's boyfriend. You think she don't know that you was with her man at the hotel for all those days, shorty? Sleepin' with your best friend's man, shorty? She's been your rider for *years*, Ne'Vaeh. Fuckin' her man, and then havin' the nerve to sing to dude in her *face? That's* fucked up."

I looked at him. "Fucked up? Are you serious? First of all, this shit is none of your fuckin' business! Second of all, he came after *me, not* the other way around! And third, if *you* would have never left me, he would have *never* gotten to me! Never!" I got up from the stool, nearly stumbling over my own two feet. Yeah, I was drunk as fuck, and I really didn't want the jerk to see that I still felt some type of way about him. Up until that point, *I* didn't even realize that I still felt anything toward him. I forced myself to forget Jamie and the feelings that I once had for him. Apparently, my heart hadn't gotten the message.

Jamie got up from the bar, taking the glass from my hands. "Shorty, you shouldn't even be drinkin', man. What the fuck, yo? Since when did you start drinkin'? Since when did you start dressing like this? Since when did you start going to strip clubs? Since when did you fuck your own friend's boyfriend? Are you high, yo? You've been smokin' too? Man, this is not the Ne'Vaeh that *I* used to know."

"Well, I know I'm drunk, but if I remember correctly, *you* invited me to this club, Jamie!" I pushed him in his chest. "Yeah, I drink, I smoke, and I go to the clubs every now and then. Do you think I meant to fall in love with Charlie's boyfriend? I waited for you, Jamie! I hadn't had sex in *four* fuckin' years! So before you go thinkin' I turned into some fuckin' ho when you left, I didn't! I fell in love with Aaron, yes, but he pursued *me*, not the other way around! You wanna judge me, then go ahead, Jamie. But remember, *your* shit stinks too, muthafucka! You and Charlie wanna sit here and judge me, but if I can remember correctly, you two were professional hoes back in high school! There wasn't a guy Charlie *hadn't* fucked back then! And *you* started having sex around the age of thirteen! Charlie was the one sleeping around, chasin' niggas before Aaron came along, but *I'm* the groupie? Jamie, she called me your fuckin' *groupie!* A groupie?" I laughed aloud. I was so pissed off.

Jamie shook his head at me. "Shorty, you're drunk. Let me take you home."

"Was I really your groupie, Jamie?" I looked into his face.

He shook his head, lookin' down at me. "You gonna let what Charlie said to you out of anger have you questioning what you *know* you meant to me?"

"What I *know* I meant to you? Are you serious? Jamie, you left me the day your father came in town! You didn't even say good-bye! You just left, then tried to explain to me over the *phone* why you left me! You talked me into having sex with you, when you knew I wasn't ready; then you just up and bounced!" I pushed him in his chest.

Jamie sighed. "There's more to it and you know it, shorty. My father was sick. He had just come into my life. I hadn't seen him since I was about three years old. He needed help. He needed me to stay with him. My father, who I had never known, wanted to get to know me, so I left. I tried explaining the situation, but you wouldn't listen. I know you needed me, but my father needed me too. What was I supposed to do?"

I didn't know his father was sick. He never told me. He never mentioned anything about his father coming to get him. When he called me on the phone and tried to explain why he left me, I really didn't even give him the chance to explain. All I knew was that when I woke up the morning after we had sex, he wasn't lying next to me. Whatever reason he had for leaving me alone in his bed, staring at an empty closet, I couldn't have cared less back then.

I shook my head at him. "Follow your heart, which is exactly what you did."

Jamie shook his head back at me. "Ne'Vaeh, you know what you meant to me back then. I have known you since we were in day care. We were the *best* of homies for years before we started dating, shorty. Yeah, I messed around with a few females before we started officially dating. Yeah, I had a few girls still trying to holla, even when they knew me and you were dating. Yeah, I know I didn't make it easy for you to be with me. Yeah, I know I left you when you had a lot goin' on, but I had a lot goin' on too, shorty. You meant the fuckin' world to me."

I shook my head, trying to walk away from him, but he grabbed my arm, pulling me back to him. I looked into his face.

Jamie's eyes searched mine. "I had a lot of pressure comin' from all angles back then, so don't think I just up and left you because I wanted to leave. I never knew my father, and he was askin' me to come and stay with him. He was sick and doctors were saying he wasn't gonna make it past a year. It was a blessing that Pops lived a lot longer than doctors said that he would. He's hangin' on by a thread, but he's still here with me. Ne'Vaeh, you know, I have never had the support I needed from my family. You may not have had your mom's support, but you had support from your aunts, your cousins, and Charlie's family. Shit, even Darrick Allan and his wife have been helping you ever since he found out that y'all were related. I didn't have that shit, Ne'Vaeh. I always had to work ten times harder than anyone else to have anything, and you know that."

I looked up into his face.

Jamie held my face in his hands. "I'm goin' through a lot right now, shorty, and I need you, Ne'Vaeh."

My heart jumped in my chest. I took his hands from my face. His touch always sent a jolt of energy straight to my heart. My heart and mind were already in conflict enough. I didn't need Jamie confusing me any more than I already was. I turned to walk away.

Jamie caught my hand, pulling me back to him just when the DJ played "Heart Attack." "C'mon, shorty, let's dance." He held my hand, leading me out onto the dance floor.

I tried to pull from him, but he pulled me close against his chest. Oh my goodness, his smell was still intoxicating. He wrapped his hands around my waist. I was reluctant to glide to the music along with him, but he really gave me no choice. The people around us, cheering us on, really didn't help much either. Seemed as though every guy followed suit, grabbing a girl, bringing her out onto the dance floor. I wrapped my arms around Jamie's body, just in time to see Charlie and Aaron coming onto the dance floor. That damn song was the perfect theme song to my emotions at that moment. I felt like I was having a heart attack. I could feel Jamie's heart beating in his chest. I could hear the air circulating in his lungs. Aaron caught sight of me in Jamie's arms. Our eyes met for a few seconds before looking away.

"Shorty, I missed you," Jamie whispered softly in my ear, lips grazing against my skin a little.

Chills trickled up and down my spine. I looked up at him. I had to get out of there. Aaron's presence was something I really couldn't handle at the moment, and there I was, embraced by Jamie's arms, still feeling like I was in Aaron's.

Jamie looked down at me, looking at the uncomfortable expression on my face. He looked up, in Aaron's direction. He laughed a little to himself. "So, you're in love with your best friend's boyfriend? How's that working out for you?"

Oh my goodness, he always had such a smart-ass mouth. What really made me mad about some of the rude shit he said was that there was always some truth to his statements.

"Why do you say the shit that you say, Jamie? Are you laughing at my pain?" I shook my head at him, looking up into his pretty brown eyes.

Jamie shook his head. "Nah, shorty, I'm not laughing at you. I'm pissed when I really shouldn't be. The nigga would have never even gotten the chance to steal what was mine if I wouldn't have left you here. I should have taken you with me. I must've been real stupid thinkin' that one of the finest girls in our high school was gonna sit around, waiting on me, trying to figure out whether I was ever gonna come back. I just thought that I held the only key to your heart, but I guess you had a spare."

I knew Aaron was watching me. I could just feel him staring at me, but I refused to look. I quickly dried my face. I started to feel pressure in my chest, but I tried to ignore it. "I shut everyone off when you left, Jamie. I didn't want anything to do with love. Love feels like a fuckin' heart attack, especially when the one you love leaves you when you need him most, when the one you love is in a relationship with someone else, or when the one you love kills your brother!" I held my hand over my heart, feeling the room beginning to spin around me. My knees started to tremble, and my body grew weaker. Suddenly, I couldn't breathe.

Jamie looked down into my face, feeling my weight on him as my knees gave out from under me. "Ne'Vaeh, shorty, are you okay?" He held my body tightly up against his.

I shook my head, words slurring. "Help me."

Chapter 11

His Place

Ne'Vaeh

The next thing I remember, I was waking up to the sound of beeping. I was in a triage in the emergency room. A nurse stood over me typing on a computer. I looked to the right to see Renée, Alisha, Jamie, Kristina, and Kelissa. I sat up in the bed. Renée rushed over to my side once she saw that I was awake.

"OMG, cuz!" She threw her arms around me. "You scared me, passing out on the dance floor! Twice in one week, Ne'Vaeh? You gotta start taking care of yourself!"

I looked over her shoulder at Jamie, who sat in a chair looking right back at me, eyes dampened.

"I'm okay, Renée," I whispered.

Renée let go of me, looking into my face. She shook her head. "No, sweetie, you're not. You haven't been taking your medication, you've been drinkin' your ass off all week, and you've been stressed! I should have never taken you to that fuckin' party. I'm sorry! I don't know *what* I was thinkin'!"

I looked up at the nurse. "Ma'am, I'm fine. Can I please go back to my dorm?"

The nurse looked at me, shaking her head. "No, honey, I'm afraid the doctor is admitting you for further testing. Your blood pressure is extremely high. Sweetie, you're already aware that you have a weak heart. You *have* to take it easy. You have had numerous surgeries to repair the holes in your heart, but your heart is still weak. Your left atrium isn't working properly, which puts even more pressure on the right side of your heart. We're ordering a stress test for you in the morning. Depending on the results, that will determine on how long you will be here. Sweetie, the blood is not flowing through your heart properly. Your friends sitting here with you now really care about you. They brought you here tonight. Just be thankful they did."

My eyes watered as I sat back in the bed. I knew my health was coasting downhill. I often ignored my doctors. I had stopped taking the heart medication and started drinking. My heart was broken, literally. Story of my fuckin' life.

The nurse left the room after getting a technician to start an IV. I was admitted to the hospital that night and moved to another room. Kristina and Kelissa had to leave that morning around 4:30, but Renée, Alisha, and Jamie stayed. I really need to be alone and wasn't in the mood to talk to anyone, but they wouldn't leave me. My stress test was that morning. It was abnormal. Apparently, my heart was still weak, even after numerous surgeries. See what I mean—once the heart is broken, it can never be completely repaired.

Renée was so upset, she couldn't stop crying. Alisha tried to console her. Jamie sat on the sofa, leaned back in the chair, not really sure what to say to me. The doctors debated whether to keep me in the hospital for a few weeks, or send me home under a nurse's supervision. The only problem was that home was my college campus dorm room.

"Ne'Vaeh, I think you should move back in with me." Renée dried her face. "I'm moving into a new apartment this week, and we should move in together. You need someone to help you with your medication."

I shook my head at her. "No, I don't, Renée. The doctors just said that I could stay here in the hospital for a few weeks to be monitored. I really don't wanna stay in an apartment with you. I don't feel like dealing with you and that dude of yours making out and damn near fuckin' in front of me, Renée!"

Renée shook her head at me, drying her tears. "Ne'Vaeh, me and Russell ain't that fuckin' bad. Okay, so we may kiss and touch a little, but no clothes ever came off in front of you!"

I rolled my eyes. "Renée, I'm *not* moving in with you!"

"I don't give a fuck what you say, Ne'Vaeh. By the time you leave this hospital, your shit is gonna be at my mama's house!" she exclaimed.

I sat up in the bed, furious with her. "Renée, oh my goodness! I am so sick and tired of you acting like you're my fuckin' mom! You're *not* my mother! Got-damn, I don't *need* a fuckin' mother! I need fuckin' space! I am so tired of everyone telling me what I need! I'm tired of everyone telling me what they think I should do! How about everyone get their lives straight before they go trying to straighten up mine! You can't undo the holes in my heart, Renée! The damage has already been done! You're twenty-six years old. You need to worry about trying to get and *keep* a man instead of trying to live vicariously through your nineteen-year-old cousin! I love you, Renée, but you are *smothering* me! I don't need a fuckin' babysitter! I need you to back the fuck off! Get a life of your own and stay the *fuck* out of mine!"

Renée's eyes swelled up with tears. She stood from the chair.

Alisha grabbed her arm. "Renée, she didn't mean it. It's all these pain meds they have her on." Alisha looked at me. "Nobody could really be *that* ungrateful after *everything* that you've done for her. Cutie, what's wrong with you?"

I didn't mean to make my cousin cry. "I appreciate everything, Renée, you know I do. But you have to stop trying to run my life," I exclaimed.

"Life? You call this a *life?* You sittin' here, heart bleeding over your best friend's boyfriend! He used the girl to get to you, instead of steppin' to you like a real man!" Renée exclaimed. "You push everyone away in your life who gives a fuck about you! I may be a little hard on you. I may be a little overprotective of my baby cousin. I may push you to be the very best that you can be. I know I'm not your mother. Shit, your damn *mama* isn't your fuckin' mother! I helped raise you, Ne'Vaeh, so don't you *ever* in your fuckin' life disrespect me again!"

"I'm sorry!" I apologized.

Renée dried her face. "I'm goin' to your dorm room to get your shit. Now you can either give me the key now, or I'll just go home and get the copy I made a few months ago."

"Renée?" Jamie spoke up.

"What?" she snapped, going over to the night-stand to pick up her purse.

Jamie looked at me.

I looked up at him.

"She can stay at my crib."

Renée's eyes lit up. "With you? Aren't you goin' back to Memphis tomorrow?"

Jamie shook his head. "Nah, I mean, I don't *have* to go, shorty."

Alisha rolled her eyes. "Jamie, please. Why you wanna stay here in Maryland three months before you're supposed to be here? You tryin' to keep tabs on Ne'Vaeh or somethin'?"

Jamie just looked at her, not feeling the need to respond.

"Mr. Panty Dropper, won't your groupies be mad if you have a girl living up in your house? Oh no, forget the groupies—what about Pamela, your *girlfriend?*" Alisha folded her arms.

I looked at her. Oh, she was "Team Aaron" all the way. She never really cared for Jamie too much. She always thought he had too many hoes.

Jamie laughed to himself. "You know, Alisha, you always were a fuckin' instigator. You know it was over with Pamela months ago."

Alisha rolled her eyes. "Whateva, nigga. I just call 'em how I see 'em. You want Ne'Vaeh to stay with you, why? Just so you can keep an eye on her? Just so you can make sure she doesn't go tiptoeing back to Aaron?"

"Shorty, you need to mind your own fuckin' business. I know you don't like me, and I really don't give a fuck. But this isn't about me. This isn't about you. It's about *her*. I haven't seen shorty in four years, and the day that I actually get to talk to her again, she passes out in my arms, man. Come to find out she stopped taking her heart medication. Alisha, *I* was the one who held her hand six years ago before she went into heart surgery. *I* was the one who held her hand in eighth grade when they told her that her heart was failing. I cried *for* her because she was too numb to cry about it herself. She's been hurt her entire life by the people that she loved the most, myself included." Jamie sounded sincere, as if he really cared about me, as if he was really sorry for what he had done.

I bit my lip to keep from crying out.

Jamie looked at me. "I just wanna be here for you, shorty. I already have two live-in nurses scheduled to move in the house this week, preparing for my dad to get here tonight. He was sick of Memphis and wanted to come up here a few months early. You're welcome to stay, shorty. You won't even know I'm there, I promise. This is the least I can do, shorty. C'mon."

I looked at Renée.

She nodded. Of course, she would be all for it. She always was a fan of Jamie's. To tell you the truth, if she was a few years younger, she probably would've been all on him. "I see no problem with that," Renée shrugged.

Alisha rolled her eyes. "Oh my goodness." She grabbed her purse. "Renée? *Really?*"

Renée rolled her eyes back, going over to my purse to get my dorm room key. "What the fuck you mean 'really'? Yeah, *really*. What, you expect *Aaron* to drop by and take her back to his crib? How would Charlie feel about that? A man who'd fuck his girl's best friend is *no* fuckin' hero. I don't see anything wrong with Jamie helping Ne'Vaeh. They have known each other forever. Yeah, he left her, but now he's back, just in time. She needs him."

I looked at Jamie.

"Y'all muthafuckas crazy! 'She *needs* him'? Are you serious? I don't think she's gonna need a house full of bitches every night! This isn't sweet,

high school, popular Jamie. This is star quarter-
back, fuck-you-you-you-*and*-you Jamie! Y'all
are making a huge mistake!" Alisha exclaimed.

Jamie couldn't care less about Alisha's attitude problem. "I just wanna take care of you,
Ne'Vaeh. Fuck that shit Alisha's talkin' about.
I've known you since we were in day care, shorty.
I know I haven't been here in a while, but I'm
here now. I'm not trying to disrupt your life or
control your life in any way. I just wanna be here
for you. Can I do that?"

I hesitated, not sure how to respond.

Renée looked at me, hoping I'd respond to
Jamie before he changed his mind. "C'mon, cuz,
say something! The doctor says that you need
help. We're here to help you. You have a weak
heart, you have fluid around your heart, and
you can't keep trying to take care of yourself
by yourself. You don't have to when you have
friends who love and care about you." Renée's
cell phone rang in her purse. "I know that's
Mom calling." She looked at me. "Just let me
know where you want me to take your stuff. I'm
gonna head over to your dorm tonight to pack
everything up. On Monday, I'll go talk to your
professors to let them know what's going on. I
have all the medical paperwork that they need.

I'm going to see how they can accommodate you while you're on bed rest these next few weeks." Renée came over to kiss me on the forehead. "Love you, cuz. I'll call you later." She looked over at Jamie. "Take care of my baby, will you?"

He nodded.

Alisha sighed, getting up from the chair. "I'm sorry to ruin the moment, but there are two people in Maryland that I don't trust, and that's Charlie's and Jamie's triflin' asses. So if I were you, I wouldn't trust Jamie. I'm sorry, Cutie, but you know I'm team Aaron all the way. Jamie is nothing but trouble. I'm tellin' you, Charlie has plans for you, and I'm warning you, her plans include *him*."

Renée rolled her eyes, pulling Alisha by the arm. "Okay, Alisha, you said what you had to say, so let's go. Later, guys."

Alisha and Renée left the room, leaving Jamie and me there alone.

We sat there in awkward silence. I had so much to say to him, but had no idea where to start. I'd forced myself to forget about Jamie over the past four years. It hurt like hell being in his presence, seeing his face again.

"Jamie, my heart is broken, literally," I whispered.

He just looked at me.

"I'm really—I mean, *really*—vulnerable right now. I haven't been taking care of myself for some time. I've done some things that I normally wouldn't do, because I'm tired of being lonely. I'm stubborn, I know. I just have been doing things my way, on my own, for so long. My heart is really confused right now, so whatever you do, don't play games with it. This heart of mine refuses to let you break it again. I don't wanna love you again, Jamie. My heart can't take it." I shook my head at him.

Jamie looked at me earnestly.

"If I stay with you for a little while, it's just as a houseguest. I'm not your girl; you're not my man. Just keep doin' you, groupies and all." I dried my tears. "It is what it is, Jamie, so don't try to make it something that it's not. I don't wanna love you, so don't try to make me," I whispered, watching him gathering my personal belongings. He wasn't really listening to me once he heard that I agreed to go home with him.

Needless to say, Jamie's home in the countryside was spectacular. It didn't feel anything like being in Maryland. I felt so at home, so at peace, so comfortable. His home looked like it sat right in the middle of the Garden of Eden. There were gardeners all around the home, planting flowers, watering the grass, trimming the hedges. He had an outside pool, tennis court, basketball court, a pool house, and two guesthouses behind the mansion. Jamie had about seven sports cars and two antique cars lining the driveway. He finally did it, and I hate to admit it, but I was really proud of him. He wasn't lying when he said he didn't have it easy. His life was just as painful as mine was.

Jamie had to leave the hospital while I was waiting to be discharged. He had one of his nurses pick me up at the hospital that afternoon. She was about twenty-four years old, sexy, cute, brown-skinned, shapely, and dimply. Her name was Helen. She was going to be my personal nurse for the next two weeks. I rode to Jamie's mansion with her in her new black 2015 Mercedes-Benz, probably paid for in full by Jamie. Helen didn't say much to me until we pulled up into Jamie's driveway and she saw the awestruck look on my face as I stared out the window in wonder at Jamie's world.

"So," Helen's voice broke my trance, "*you're* that lady that's making it hard for everyone else? Wow, it's nice to finally meet that special someone who keeps Mr. Green from settling down."

I looked at her. "Wh-what?" I was still stunned by my surroundings, including her.

Helen grinned, one dimple piercing her left cheek. "I've seen a lot of girlfriends come and go. I've been working for Jamie for the past two-and-a-half years. Jamie is a pretty closed book. He doesn't open up to anyone. Pamela Rhodes was his last girlfriend. They dated for about a year. She loved that boy, despite all of his women, but she got tired of competing with those women and with football. I must say, you're the first girl who's ever lived with him."

I shook my head frantically. "Helen, no, we're not living together. Oh my goodness. My cousin thinks that I need someone to make sure I take my medications. The doctors wouldn't let me leave unless I was under a nurse's supervision. Jamie volunteered to let me stay here for a while until I was released from bed rest."

"And why do you think that is?" Helen took off her seat belt.

I looked at her.

She looked at me. "You've known Jamie a long time?"

I nodded, my eyes growing misty, tears already lining my lashes. I hated reminiscing. "Yeah, ummm, since we were about three years old. He stayed with his aunt and older sister on

Fort Meade. He spent the school year here in Maryland, and the summer and holidays back in Memphis. We were, umm . . . He was my best friend. It hurt when he left me. I loved him for a long time."

A sympathetic look swept across Helen's face. "Well, the fact that he's here says a lot. He wasn't supposed to even move back to Maryland for another three months, and he wasn't supposed to move into this house until around March. He completely changed his life plans to include you, sweetie, so please remember that."

I looked at her. She felt some type of way about me. I wasn't crazy. She was more than Jamie's father's nurse. She had feelings for him. "You know, you're one nosy nurse," I whispered, taking my seat belt off.

Helen laughed a little. "Oh, sweetie, I'm *much* more than a nurse. You shall see." She popped the trunk open to her car, then opened her door to help me out.

I sighed, running my fingers through my hair. "What the *fuck* was I thinking coming here?" I said aloud to myself as I opened the door.

Helen closed the trunk. I heard the sound of tiny wheels rolling against the concrete. She pushed a wheelchair over to my side.

I looked up at her.

She smiled, holding out her hand to help me out of the car. "Your chariot awaits."

I sighed, taking her hand, as she helped me out of the car.

I felt like I was in a fancy hotel room. Maids brought me fresh warm towels. They washed my clothes and even brought me pajamas to put on. African maids washed, brushed, and styled my hair. The Jamaican cook brought my plate to my room. Jamie even had a massage therapist give me an hour-long massage. Helen sat with me while I had my back, shoulders, arms, and legs massaged. My blood pressure was watched all through the day. I wasn't doing well. It was nowhere near going down.

It was 8:30 that Saturday night. I lay back in the bed, eating fresh fruit, watching reruns of *Martin* on the 42-inch, flat-screen TV. Renée had been texting me all day and messaging me on Facebook. Charlie unfriended me on Facebook and blocked me from looking at her page. Aaron messaged me on Facebook. "I miss you." That's what he had the nerve to say. I tossed my cell in the corner of the room, sighed, and ran my fingers through my hair. It was raining cats and dogs outside. It matched my situation, because it was raining cats and dogs in my life.

There was a knock at my bedroom door.

"Come in." I sat up in bed.

The door slowly opened, and Jamie entered the room. I could smell his cologne from the door. He was dressed in all blue from head to toe, looking like he was about to head to the club. He was blinged out from his ears to his wrists.

I sighed as he walked into my room.

"What's up, shorty?" he asked, coming over to the bed, sitting down at my side.

I looked at him, not really sure what else to say but, "Thank you."

Jamie looked at me, nodding. "No need to thank me. It's the least I can do. You deserve someone to take care of you. You deserve the best, and I'm here to give it to you."

I looked him up and down a little. He looked just like a bottle of vintage wine. Time sure did change that boy for the better. I hesitated, "You gotta date or something?"

Jamie laughed. "A date? Nah, I had to meet my agent in D.C. You know I dress to impress wherever I go, shorty. I haven't changed that much." He looked at me. "You had a bath? You eat good? Helen treating you right?"

I nodded. "Yes to all of the above."

Jamie's eyes searched mine. "I started not to come in your room. I promised you that you wouldn't know I'm here, but my dad is flying in from Tennessee in a few hours on a medical plane. I just wanted to make sure you were okay with meeting him. He's been asking about you."

I wasn't really sure what to say to him. His father was the reason that he left me.

Jamie held my face in his hands, knowing that hearing about his father was going to have me emotional.

I pushed him off me. "Don't touch me, Jamie!"

He instantly put his hands up. "I'm sorry." His eyes glistened.

There was a tap at the bedroom door before Helen entered the room. She grinned when she saw Jamie sitting there with me. "Time for your meds." She came over to my side with a glass of cold water and a medicine cup full of pills. She handed them to me and watched as I swallowed all the pills, washing them down with the entire glass of water. She nodded at me as I handed her the empty glass and pill cup. "Don't you two have a date tonight?" she asked.

I looked at Jamie, who sat there laughing to himself. I looked back at Helen. "Ummm, my blood pressure is already high enough. Don't get me started, okay?"

Helen grinned. "Well, to get the ball rolling, I found something." She reached into her pocket and pulled out a photo, handing it to me.

I looked down at the photo, immediately covering my mouth in astonishment. It was a picture of Jamie, my sister, my brother, Jamie's cousin Fred, and his cousin Janet at my eighth birthday party. My pretty lace dress was covered in dirt. I think Jamie and I had gotten into a fight that day over a game of tag. He was always claiming someone cheated whenever he didn't win at a game. He always was a sore loser. Regardless of my soiled dress, I was happy. There I was, on Jamie's back, legs wrapped around his waist. We all had the biggest smiles on our faces. We were happy. My mom had OD'ed the night before and was not at my party, but Aunt Joyce threw the party for me at her house. I don't know why Charlie wasn't there, but I do remember that the biggest present on the table was from her: my Barbie Dream House.

"Oh my goodness, Helen! Where did you find this?" I exclaimed.

"Oh, in one of Jamie's photo albums. There's a lot more of these in the family room." Helen glanced at Jamie. "Well, I'm going to head out to the guesthouse to get some sleep before Mr. James Green shows up and shows out." Then she exited the room.

I just sat there with the picture held tightly against my chest, over my heart. Tears slid down my face. "Oh my goodness, this picture brings back *so* many memories!" I cried to myself.

"I never meant to break your heart, shorty." Jamie responded, after watching me embrace the picture.

I looked at him, drying my face, heart beating strong in my chest, even though I could feel it trembling. I shook my head at him. "Jamie," I handed the picture to him, "I told you no reminiscing. No more confusion, okay?"

"I just wanna help, shorty. I'm supposed to be at an event tonight in Baltimore. I'm late actually. My agent, Rodney, is gonna kill me." Jamie laughed to himself.

"Then maybe you should go. You have your career to think about. Your staff will take care of me. This hasn't been your job for four years, Jamie," I whispered.

He looked at me. "But *I* wanna take care of you." He placed his warm hand on my thigh.

A surge of energy soared through my body. His hands were so strong, so warm, so gentle, so soothing. My heart was racing. No, no, I couldn't let him get to my heart. I pushed his hand off my thigh.

"J-Jamie, you-you should go. Please," I begged him.

His eyes searched my face. "Do you remember our first kiss?"

I looked at him, my lips trembling. Why was he torturing me?

Our first kiss was in my aunt's backyard. I was thirteen. That was also the night Jamie wanted to try "other" things. He snuck me into his room at his older sister's house, at around 1:00 in the morning. He asked to shave my coochie. I was so scared, but let him do it. I wasn't ready for sex. We were too young. But when he asked to kiss my pussy, I let him, not knowing what he actually meant. He kissed it all right—he sucked it, licked it, and he chewed on it. He made my pussy explode in his mouth. I didn't have a problem feeling on him, jacking him off, or sucking on him. That was our thing. Before we officially started dating, we were having oral sex. That was our way of being intimate for about three years. Yeah, I was young and in love with that boy.

"How could I forget?" I rolled my eyes, playing off the fact that I still held on to that kiss.

"Shorty, you know I have been with a lot of girls, but none of them felt quite like you. I miss your lips, your hands, your skin, your touch."

Jamie licked his lips. "I know I can't take anything back that I have done, but I mean it when I say that I *miss* you. I don't know what I have to do to make it up to you, but can I just start by taking you on a date? I know you can't leave the house, but I have something set up in a room down the hallway."

I shook my head. He already had my whole body trembling. I wasn't sure how much more of him I could handle tonight. "Jamie, no, I can't. This is already too much. I can't handle any more surprises."

Jamie held my hand, gently lifting me from the bed. "Nah, shorty, I think you'll like this surprise." He felt my hand trembling in his. "Want me to carry you?"

I hesitated as he scooped me up in arms, carrying me over to the wheelchair. He wheeled me down the long hallway to another room. He opened the door, and we went inside. It was a recording studio. My mouth dropped open as he shut the door behind him.

"A *recording* studio, Jamie!" I exclaimed.

He laughed to himself as he helped me out of the wheelchair. "Just another one of my money-makers. I have a few artists already scheduled to record records starting next week, shorty. I would love to get *your* voice recorded."

I shook my head. "No, Jamie, I don't think so."

He chuckled. "Shorty, don't act like you're shy. You just sang in front of hundreds of people last night at the club. Not to mention you're the star soloist in the Gospel choir at your school. You should do something with that voice. C'mon, shorty. I even wrote a song for your cousin, D-Allan."

I laughed a little. Of all the skills Jamie had, writing wasn't one of them. He suffered from dyslexia. Fortunately for technology, Jamie made it through school by talking into a microphone connected to his Mac desktop computer to complete his homework assignments, projects, and book reports. If he did write a song, he probably used the microphone on his cell phone to write it. As hard as it must have been for Jamie to adjust to a life without being able to read, his memory was amazing. I would help him memorize book reports in school. I'm talking book reports ranging from five to ten pages. The boy had skills.

"Okay, let me hear it." I sat in a chair in front of the equipment.

Jamie looked at me. "Why you gotta laugh, yo? You think that I'm lyin'?" He sat in a chair, facing me. "Why would I lie about writing a song for someone, shorty?"

"I wanna hear the song." I looked at him.

He sighed. "Okay, shorty, you got me. It's not finished because I can't get the hook down."

"Well, what's the song about?" I hesitated.

He looked at me. "About this girl that he loved but lost because he did something stupid. The song describes everything that he likes about the girl, from her hair all the way down to her toes. Any nigga who's been in love with a girl can feel me on this song."

I looked at Jamie. "So, *this* is why you brought me into your studio? To help you with lyrics to your song? I'm really not in the mood for any singing tonight, sweetie."

He grinned, turning on his equipment. Everything lit up. "Do you remember our first dance?" he asked.

I looked at him, heart fluttering in my chest, as my favorite song started playing.

Our first dance was when I was fourteen, the summer before tenth grade, at Jamie's fifteenth birthday party. The song was "Slow Down." I held on to him tight. He held my hips, gripping my dress in his hands, and he whispered in my ear, telling me that that night, he wanted to make love. He knew I wasn't ready, but he said he would take care of me. That he wouldn't hurt me. That night over at his sister's house, in his bedroom, Jamie talked me out of my panties. I cried the entire time. He practically ripped my panties off that night. I bled all over his sheets. I must have had a hundred hickies all over my body. He kissed and sucked all the way from my forehead to my pinky toe. Our bodies were drenched in sweat and tears. He sucked my nipples, neck, back, stomach, thighs, and clit until they were throbbing. My body was sensitive to touch for weeks afterward. We cried in each other's arms that night. No birth control, no condoms, no contraceptives. Getting pregnant was the furthest thing from my mind. I think I even *wanted* the boy's child at that young age, that's how sprung he had me back in high school. The very next morning, I woke up to an empty room. He was gone and that was the last time that I saw his face up until my nineteenth birthday.

"How could I forget our first dance? That was also the night that we made love for four hours straight. The very next morning, you left me, Jamie!" I exclaimed.

Jamie dug in his pocket. "Yeah, I left with these." He took what looked like pink silk cloth out of his pocket.

I snatched it from him. "What the hell is—" I stopped when I held it in my hand, noticing what it was the panties I'd worn that night. I blushed, handing them back to him. "Jamie, that's gross. Why the hell do you still have these?"

He laughed.

I rolled my eyes, trying to play off my embarrassment. "Another pair to add to the collection, huh?"

He shook his head. "Nah, what collection? I took this pair from you so that I could always remember that night. I felt like I was in heaven with you, shorty. I didn't wanna leave you, baby, I swear I didn't. My sister woke me up that morning, cursing me the fuck out about having you in my room. We were both drunk, butt naked, and lying on *top* of the covers! My dad was outside waiting. I didn't get a chance to explain. I didn't even get the chance to shower or pack. My sister had my shit downstairs, in two black duffle bags. Not only was she tired of me getting into trouble, but my dad wanted to know me too, so she sent me to stay with him."

"I cried for *two* whole years after you left, Jamie. I really missed you." I shook my head at him.

"I missed you, too."

"I waited for you as long as I could. Four years, Jamie—four long-ass, muthafuckin' years! You made me feel like I was special that night, Jamie.

You held me, you kissed me, you touched me, you made love to me—then you just left! It took a long time to shake the sensation of you kissing me and humpin' me. I felt you inside of me for a long time. You remember the way you beat it up, Jamie." My eyes searched his face. "You didn't care that I was a virgin. You ignored my whimpering and crying. You were *not* gentle at all."

Jamie laughed a little. "Hey, I waited all of my life to get it, shorty. I wasn't playin' no games, was I?"

I shook my head at him. "Jamie, this is not a joke."

Jamie's eyes traced my lips. "I also knew that I was leaving and I probably would never get it again. I cried in your arms that night, Ne'Vaeh. I wasn't crying just because you felt amazing—I was crying because I knew I was leaving you when you needed me the most."

My chest began to hurt. I stood from the chair. The song was bringing back hurtful memories. It was bringing back moments that were bittersweet. Moments that I wasn't ready to relive. "Jamie, can you just turn this song off? I can't do this." I tried my hardest not to let the memories of us make me break down and cry over him. "I really don't wanna relive the past, okay? I told you at the hospital that you need to keep the sentimental shit to yourself."

Jamie stood from his chair and reached for my wrist, pulling me to him. "Ne'Vaeh, you have to forgive me."

I shook my head. "I don't have to do *anything* tonight. And don't you have some place to be, Jamie?"

Jamie nodded, pulling my body up against his. "Yeah, right here." He looked down into my face.

I looked up into his face, lips trembling. "I'm . . . I'm supposed to be in bed."

Jamie grinned a little. "Well, let's go then."

I shook my head, but Jamie scooped me up into his arms. I thought he was taking me into his bedroom, but he was taking me to the spa room. He gently let my feet down to the floor. Scented candles were lit all around the room. I faced Jamie as he removed his jewelry. He unbuttoned his shirt. He removed it, then pulled me closer to him by the drawstring of my pajama pants. My entire body trembled against his as he slid his hands around my waist.

"Strip." His voice serenaded my heart.

I looked up at him, "What?"

"*Strip,*" he repeated.

I shook my head, trying to back away. "Jamie, now, if you think—"

He laughed a little. "I'm not trying to fuck you, shorty. I just wanna make you feel good. Your doctor says you need to ease your mind. I'm about to help you do that. Besides, you owe me a date."

I hesitated.

Jamie laughed to himself, standing there in his wife beater. Chest, muscles, chocolaty skin exposed. He was driving me crazy when I was trying my best to hate his guts. "C'mon, shorty. Take off them clothes and get up on the bed. It ain't like I haven't seen you naked before. You remember it was *me* who showed you how to use a tampon. I even helped you find the muthafucka the day you 'lost the string.' There's nothing on your body that I haven't seen already—I have seen your *everything,* shorty."

I blushed a little as I pulled the drawstring to my pants and dropped them to the floor, stepping out of them. I slipped my tank top over my head, then stood there in my panties, arms across my chest. I was embarrassed and nervous as hell.

Jamie couldn't help but burst out laughing.

"What? Oh my goodness, this situation is awkward enough, Jamie! Why the hell are you laughing at me?" I exclaimed.

"I mean, c'mon. You standing there covering up your titties like I never seen them. I mean, I *have* seen a naked girl before, shorty. You are fine as hell, I'm not gonna lie. But I'm not here for that tonight. C'mon, take your panties off and get on the table."

I slipped my panties off and climbed onto the bed, lying on my stomach. I braced myself as Jamie stood alongside the table. He placed his warm hands on my toes. He worked his way from my toes to my calves. It took everything I had not to scream out in pleasure that night. His fingertips dug into my skin as if he was kneading dough. I mean, there wasn't a part of my body that Jamie didn't touch that night. My whole body was paralyzed as he stroked the insides of my thighs. His thumbs grazed against my pussy lips as he kneaded my butt cheeks. My whole body was in heat. I was coated in sweat by the time he started massaging my lower back. As he massaged the middle of my back, his hands slid under each breast. Purposely, he grazed his fingers across my nipples. I was on fire. I couldn't take anymore.

"Jamie, stop!" I squealed, sitting up from the bed. I had to have had at least two or three mental orgasms from his touch. My thighs, toes, pussy, and nipples were tingling and throbbing.

Jamie looked at me. He was breathing rapidly as he watched me get up from the bed, barely able to stand on my own two feet. He watched me grab my clothes from the floor and struggle to slide into my panties.

"Shorty." He grabbed my hands.

I looked up into his eyes, chest heaving in and out. "Jamie, this is too much. I can't handle shit like this! You *know* I can't handle shit like this!" I exclaimed, sliding my hands from his. I put on my tank top, which was sticking to my skin. I was sweaty as hell and needed a shower, but I knew I was too weak to stand. I braced my body up against the massage bed.

Jamie grinned, bending over to pick my pants off the floor. "Felt good, huh?"

I looked up at him, snatching the pants from him. "You said you weren't trying to fuck. Well, *that* sure as hell *felt* like fuckin' to me, Jamie!"

He laughed. "I still got it, huh?"

I shook my head. "Jamie, please. Stop, okay? Why are you doing this?"

His eyes searched mine.

"You know I'm not this kind of girl. I made some pretty irrational choices these past few weeks, I'll admit to that. But I'm not about to make any more. Don't try to change your lifestyle just because you *think* you got me back in your life again. I'm not about to have a NSA relationship with you, and you damn sure know I'm not about to be your girl again after all of these years." I struggled to get back into my pants. "I have heart failure, Jamie. I need someone who will help heal my heart, not break the muthafucka!"

"Ne'Vaeh, you're the only girl I wanna be with. You know I love sex. You know I love pussy. I love *your* pussy. You know I never cheated on you when we were together. I'd *never* cheat on you. I *can* take care of your heart, Ne'Vaeh. You remember how it felt when we were together. I can bring that feeling back—and then some. I can make you forget that I ever left. When you want me, shorty, just let me know." Jamie backed away a little.

I wasn't sure what to say.

"You need help back to your room?" He hesitated.

I shook my head, "No, Jamie. I'll just walk slowly. Please, just leave me alone."

He nodded. "All right. Well, I'm gonna go meet Rodney. Welcome home, shorty." Jamie grabbed his shirt and jewelry and walked out of the room.

Chapter 12

The Funeral

Ne'Vaeh

I don't think I slept that entire night. Helen came into my room at least every hour, checking my vitals, which hadn't improved. Once Jamie's father arrived with the other live-in nurse, the house was buzzing again. Paramedics wheeled Mr. James Green to his room. I stood in the doorway of my room watching as they wheeled him down the hallway early that morning, around 2:45. Jamie hadn't arrived back at home yet. Mr. James looked at me as they wheeled him down the hallway to his room. He didn't wave or say hello, but he winked his eye at me.

I sat in my bed that night and found myself waiting up for Jamie, and it seemed that Helen was waiting for him as well. She paced the floor for about two hours. When she checked my blood pressure around 3:30 that morning, I had to find out a little more about her.

"You're kinda sexy for a nurse. How did you even meet Jamie?" I asked after she swept the thermometer across my forehead.

"Girl, you are burning up! Here, take these ibuprofens." She handed me two pills.

I looked at her as she handed me a glass of water.

She watched as I swallowed the pills, then chased them down with cold water.

I handed her the glass, wiping the water from my lips.

Helen looked at me. "My girlfriend and I had a threesome with Jamie about three years ago at a frat party while I was in nursing school."

My mouth dropped open a little. I don't think I was prepared for that answer. "Seriously?"

Helen laughed. "Seriously. Whenever Jamie wants a threesome, I hook him up. I go after the girls *with* him."

"Wow. You really *are* the head nurse." I shook my head.

Helen laughed aloud. "Whatever Jamie wants, he gets. He's payin', so I'll provide the service. We have fun, honey. No strings attached. Yeah, I have sucked on his dick with a few chicks, but

I don't let him penetrate me. I'm more into women, to be honest. They'll do anything to be with him, even if that includes being with me too. He fucks the pussy. I eat the pussy, but not before they have a full physical."

Jamie was living the life, that's for damn sure.

Helen looked at me. "You're not upset?"

I looked at her. "Why should I be? Did you *expect* me to be? Jamie is *not* my man."

Helen grinned. "Then why are you waiting up for him?"

I looked at her, rolling my eyes. "Why are *you* waiting up for him?"

She laughed to herself. "I'm just hoping he has a surprise for me when he gets back, that's all. It's been a few weeks since I had some pussy. My girlfriend is back in Tennessee. She doesn't come up for another few weeks. And Jamie tells me you're off-limits, so—"

I laughed aloud. "Oh my goodness! Girl, I needed that laugh! If I wanted to play with some pussy, I can play with my own, thank you very much!"

Helen laughed too. "You don't have to worry about me and Jamie, sweetie. I'm expendable, just like the rest of 'em."

My eyes sparkled. It was going to be a long two weeks.

***

For nearly a whole week, Jamie had pool parties. I stayed in my room the entire time, only coming out to go to the masseuse. I had a full-sized bathroom in my room. Breakfast, lunch, and dinner were brought to me in bed. I can't tell you how many nights I heard females giggling, tiptoeing past my room and down the hallway, at all times of the night. I'm pretty sure Helen was happy. She was glowing all weeklong. I don't think there was a day that she wasn't smiling from ear to ear.

Jamie hadn't spoken to me all week. In fact, he didn't step within five feet of my bedroom door. He didn't care that I knew that there were at least three or four female voices coming past my room every night. He didn't care that I could see the pool from my bedroom window. At least twice that week, I saw him having sex with someone in his pool. I tried not to let it bother me because *I* was the one who told him to do him. He was mad at me. He was upset with me for being in love with Aaron. He knew that was part of the reason why I didn't want to fall back in love with him again.

It had only been two weeks since I'd had sex with Aaron. Aaron had messaged me about fourteen times on Facebook. I guess he didn't get it. He was engaged. It was bad enough that

Charlie was pregnant. It was even worse that they were getting married. He had me fucked up if he thought that after all of the drama that had happened over the course of two weeks, I would even want to message him on social media. I was detoxing off him. I was clearing every trace of Aaron from my system, and I wasn't about to replace one addiction with another.

The following week, on day ten, I decided to leave my room and pay Mr. James a visit. I tiptoed down the hallway to his room. It was about 10:15 at night. When I arrived at his room, Helen and the other nurse, Kristen, were changing his IVs.

Helen looked up at me as I entered the room. Her eyes sparkled, and she shook her head at me.

"He . . . He's not doing well."

I hesitated to ask, already having a gut feeling of what the answer would be.

Helen shook her head. "He has a fever that refuses to go down. We're taking him to the hospital tonight."

Mr. James looked at me, his eyes watering. "Hello, young lady," he whispered, his voice shaking. He couldn't have been over fifty-five. He looked like death, literally.

"Mr. James, what happened to you?" I had to know.

Mr. James looked away from me. "Life," he struggled to say. "Whatever you do, don't let it get to you." He looked back up at me. "He didn't mean to leave you. Don't think it was easy for my son, because it wasn't."

I looked at him.

"I needed my son. I never got the chance to know him because his mother and aunts kept him from me. When I finally found out where he was, I just showed up at his doorstep. I told him I was dying of kidney failure. I drank and smoked my life away, sweetheart. Turns out, I had lung cancer too. And six months ago, I was diagnosed with liver cancer." His chest heaved in and out. You could hear the guttural sounds from within his chest. "I-I guess it's my time."

My eyes watered. I looked up at Helen and Kristen. "Has anyone called Jamie?"

Helen nodded. "Yes. He's on his way. But we can't wait for him."

Sirens wailed outside of the bedroom window.

Kristen's light eyes focused on me. She was a petite, white girl with tan skin, blond hair, and blue eyes. She was Helen's roommate in college. "That's the paramedics," she spoke with a country twang. She left Mr. James's side and hurried off to meet them.

Mr. James reached for my hand. "If I'm not here when Jamie gets to the hospital, you tell him that I love him and—" Mr. James coughed violently.

"Stop talking, Mr. Green!" Helen exclaimed.

Mr. James shook his head. "Marry my son," he begged me.

I looked at him, shaking my head at him. "Mr. James, Jamie isn't ready for me."

He smiled. "*Make* him ready."

Paramedics rushed into the room, pushing their way past me. Helen held my arm, gently pulling me out of the way and out of the room.

Tears slid down my face as we watched the paramedics wheel Mr. James out of the room.

"He's not going to make it, is he?" I whispered.

Helen shook her head. "No, he's not, and I don't think Jamie is going to make it back in time to say good-bye either. He's coming from Virginia Beach, and he's about an hour away." Helen looked at me. "Your vitals are pretty good today. Your blood pressure has gone down to normal. You only have to be here about two more days to be monitored. But I don't want you at the hospital with us. You're still pretty fragile, sweetie."

I looked at her.

"I really wanna be there with Mr. James tonight. But if you need me here—" Helen burst out crying.

I shook my head, rubbing her shoulder. "I'll be okay. You should go with them."

Helen threw her arms around me, hugging me tightly, before hurrying down the hallway after the paramedics.

I stayed up all night, until around 4:00, waiting on a phone call or someone to come home. I sat up, wide awake, when there was a knock at my bedroom door. I looked up to see Jamie entering my room. I stood from the bed, my heart pounding in my chest as he walked toward me.

Jamie's face was flushed. His eyes were puffy. He shook his head before throwing his arms around me. I surrounded him in my arms, running my hands across his head, and he cried like a baby in my arms. "He's gone!" He wailed, his face buried in my neck.

He cried himself to sleep in my arms that night. I didn't get any more than maybe fifteen or twenty minutes of sleep that night. I lay on my bed, arms around Jamie, his face buried in between my breasts. My shirt was soaked in tears. I wasn't ready for Mr. James's death any more than Jamie was. I knew in my heart that

Jamie wanted me to go with him to his father's funeral. My heart was still recovering from the nightmares of going to my little brother's funeral. There was no way I could handle going with Jamie to see his father being buried.

Jamie awoke that morning, looking into my face.

I looked down at him, eyes moist.

"Was it a dream?" he whispered.

I shook my head. "No, Jamie."

Jamie lifted his head from my chest, sitting up in bed.

I looked at him, then took his hand in mine.

Jamie looked at me. "I knew this was coming, but I guess I wasn't prepared."

"You can't prepare yourself for your father's death, sweetie. I can only imagine what you're going through. I still see my brother's blue face, lying lifeless in his bed." Tears trickled down my face.

Jamie's eyes were coated in tears. "I don't know how you do it, shorty. I don't even know how I'm gonna get through this. I was just gettin' to know Pops. I gotta take him back to Memphis this week to bury him. I gotta get my agent or my manager to let everyone know about Pop's funeral. Everybody loved him, man. You would have loved him too."

I hesitated to tell him what his father told me before he died. "I talked to him last night before the paramedics arrived."

Jamie looked at me, tears sliding down his face. "Yeah? What did he say to you?"

"That . . . that he loves you very much," I whispered.

His eyes searched my face. "Did he say anything else, shorty?"

I hesitated before I shook my head. "No."

Jamie exhaled deeply before getting up from the bed.

I knew it wasn't the time to confront him about the women, but before he asked me to go with him to Memphis, I had to let him know that I saw him in the pool. "I saw you with those girls in the pool, Jamie," I blurted out before I lost my nerve to confront him.

He looked at me.

"Jamie, it *hurt* to see those girls with you in the pool," I admitted.

His eyes dampened.

"You have a live-in freak who is down for whatever! You have girls tiptoeing past my room every night! I can hear the headboard knocking against the damn wall for fuckin' *hours!* You fucked the *shit* out of that little Puerto Rican girl in the pool the other night! You had hoes lined up around the pool, waiting on you as you fucked the person in front of them! I *watched* this shit, Jamie!" I pushed him in his chest.

Jamie laughed a little to himself to hide his pain. "Are they still here?"

"Is who still here, Jamie?" I asked.

"The hoes," he replied. "Are they still here? I only see one female standing here, sleeping in my house, getting waited on hand and foot by people who work for me. This is *my* world that you're in, Ne'Vaeh. There is nobody here with me but *you*."

I shook my head at him, not really feeling like hearing his twisted reasoning for why he did the things that he did.

"Helen is a down-ass chick. Yeah, she'd do whatever for me. She takes care of me mentally and sexually. Nah, we haven't had actual intercourse, but she's done some things with me to other women. She's my friend, but if you said you wanted her gone, she'd be dismissed. Ne'Vaeh, you pissed me the fuck off when I found out you were fuckin' Charlie's man, yo!" Jamie exclaimed.

"So, you didn't wait for me, yet you thought I was supposed to wait for *you*?" I questioned.

He nodded. "Yeah, I know I'm an asshole for saying that, but, yes, I expected you to wait for me! I'm not gonna lie. I have cravings, but none of it compares to my feelings for you. When I'm with the other girls, I'm always thinking about you, shorty. My father died, and you steppin' to me about hoes and shit, Ne'Vaeh? If you want me, then I'll leave it all alone. But until then, shorty, you can really stay the fuck out of my business."

Damn, that hurt like hell.

I laughed to myself, trying my damnedest not to cry. "Well, Helen said that I was gonna be okay to leave in a few days since my blood pressure has improved. She says I can go back to my regularly scheduled program, so I called Renée and she's coming to get me on Friday morning. So, sweetie, I'd be *glad* to 'stay the fuck out of your business.'"

Jamie's eyes just searched my face. He looked at me as if he was expecting me to stay with him permanently.

I shook my head, looking up at him. "Jamie, I can't live with you. I love it out here in the country, in your beautiful home, but I can't stay here and watch groupies fuck you in your outdoor pool. I'm sorry if I'm being inconsiderate of your feelings, I'm sorry if your father just passed away, but I've held this in for nearly a week and a half. I can't be your friend, Jamie. We're not friends anymore. I can't trust you to be here for me when I need you. All I can trust you to do is hurt me. I know you just lost your father and you need some comfort right now, but I can't do it. Why don't you ask Helen? I'm sure she wouldn't mind going with you." I walked past him, but Jamie caught my arm, pulling me back.

I looked up at him as he let go of my arm.

"I need you in Tennessee with me, shorty. You *know* I need you." Tears slid down his face. I hated seeing him upset. Seeing Jamie cry was breaking my heart. He was always so carefree and nonchalant about everything. Seeing that he still had a heart gave mine a little boost.

My eyes moistened. "Jamie, no, I can't. I'm sorry, but I can't."

"Ne'Vaeh, I know I wasn't here for you when you needed me, but, shorty, I *need* you to be here with me. Please. I'll do anything just to have you there. Don't leave me."

How could I look him in that face and walk away from him? He needed me. I was so angry with him, but I had to let go of my own selfish feelings and be there to hold his hand.

I had never been to Memphis, Tennessee. Up until that point, the only people I had met in Jamie's family were his oldest sister and his aunt Bethany. The family church was crowded beyond capacity. I had no idea Jamie's family was so huge. His father's side of the family was on one side of the church. His mother and her side of the family were on the other side of the church. I'm sure there were some of Jamie's groupies scattered in there somewhere. Helen and her family were there. Kristen and her family were there. Jamie's entire college football team was there to support him. A few of his new Ravens teammates were there to support him. His agent and old and new coaches were there. Friends from our high school in Maryland were there, including Alisha and the entire cheerleading squad from our high school. Renée showed up with a few of her friends. I shouldn't have been shocked to see Charlie there with a few of her family members. She grew up with Jamie, just as I did, but what did shock me was when she showed up with Aaron. It was too much for my heart to handle at the moment. Jamie needed me, and I had no time to get wrapped up in my confused feelings for Aaron.

I sat with Jamie on the first row, on the side of the church where his father's family sat. His father's family was the only side of the family that supported him outside of his oldest sister

Angelina and his Aunt Bethany. His mother barely looked at him while we were there, though she couldn't keep her evil glare off me. Jamie gave his father a great homecoming with the best Gospel choir in Memphis. I had to hold my composure as the ceremony closed and we walked past his open casket upon leaving the church. I held Jamie's hand tightly as we left the church, and Jamie broke down right there in front of his father. I never let go of his hand.

I can't see how people can eat after funerals. I lose my appetite as soon as I see the dead body in the casket. Jamie would not let my hand go the entire time that we were at the reception afterward. I had to basically pry his hand from mine when his agent called him over to talk with a few of his colleagues.

Renée made her way over to me, throwing her arms around me. "Cuz, are you okay?"

I was still shook from the entire event. "No, Renée, I'm not, but it's not about me, it's about Jamie."

She grinned a little. "C'mon, let's go sit with the girls. I thought Jamie would *never* let your hand go. I think a part of that has to do with Aaron being here, but I'll keep my thoughts to myself."

I rolled my eyes at her as she pulled me off to the table with her friends and my schoolmates.

It didn't take Charlie five minutes to make her way over to our table. I looked up at her as she approached, dressed in a peach Versace dress. "Ne'Vaeh, can we talk?" she asked.

Alisha rolled her eyes. "C'mon, Charlie, we're at a funeral. Are you serious?"

Charlie ignored her. "I didn't mean it when I called you a groupie."

I looked at her. "You know what, Charlie? I'm over that, I really am. You were upset, and you said the first thing to me that you knew would really hurt."

Her eyes sparkled. "Well, it's nice to see you and Jamie back together again."

I looked at her. The only reason she even spoke to me was that she thought that Jamie and I were a couple. She just knew that since Jamie was back in the picture; that meant Aaron wasn't. I shook my head at her, but before I could clarify, she walked away.

"Oh my goodness!" I put my hand on my head in frustration. "Who is saying this shit? Who the hell started the rumor that me and Jamie are back together?"

"It wasn't me!" Kelissa assured me, in her shaggy voice.

Alisha looked at me. "It's nice what you are doing for Jamie, but I heard about him and the parties at his place this week. You stayed with that nigga in the midst of all of that shit?"

I rolled my eyes. "Okay, now *who's* acting inappropriate at a funeral?"

Alisha shook her head, "I'm just saying. Shiddd, if I saw my boyfriend in the pool fuckin' a bitch, I'd be ready to cut a muthafucka's dick off in that bitch. I'd be like, 'You wanna fuck, nigga? With *what* dick, nigga?'"

Everyone burst out laughing.

Alisha had no fuckin' chill whatsoever.

I rolled my eyes. "Look, let me clear the air for *all* of you—Jamie and me are *not* back together. He just lost his father, and as you could see, his entire family on his mother's side, *including* his own damn mama, hasn't said a word to him all day. I know what it's like not to have your mother or father around. Jamie needs someone who cares, so it might as well be me." My heart beat rapidly in my chest. "The man's father just died, and y'all bitches are *still* with this drama shit? This is *exactly* why I don't hang with y'all anymore!"

Renée looked at me, watching the tears sliding down my cheeks. "Sweetie, you know Alisha is your girl. Her timing is whack as fuck, but you know she didn't mean any harm."

Alisha looked at me. "Girl, you know I got love for you. I just don't trust him. A nigga like that will murder your heart, girl, I'm tellin' you. I'm just looking out for you, Cutie. Stay the fuck away from him!"

Renée touched my hand. "You gonna be okay, cuz?"

I shook my head. "I'm . . . I'm gonna go outside to get some air." I got up from the table, hurrying outside, gasping for air.

I exhaled as soon as I reached the outside of the church—only to run dead into Aaron. His eyes lit up a little when he saw me. I started to turn around and go back into the church.

"Heaven," he called out to my heart.

I sighed, turning back around, facing him as he approached me.

He smiled a little. "Well, look at you in your Christian Dior."

I rolled my eyes. "Hi, Aaron."

"'Hi, Aaron'? That's *all* I get?"

I shrugged. "What more do you expect? Your *fiancée* already threatened to kill me if she saw me *'so much as look at you in the wrong way.'* I really ain't in the mood for her shit today. I don't wanna have to fight a pregnant chick, but I will if I have to."

Aaron laughed a little. "How are you? How have you been?"

I looked at him. I knew he'd heard where I had been the last two weeks. "Well taken care of, thank you for asking. What about you?"

He replied, "You call fuckin' bitches in your face being well-taken care of? Shorty, what are you doin' with him?"

I folded my arms. "Aaron, we're at a funeral. He was my best friend since I was in fuckin' day care. Do you actually think I *wouldn't* come to his father's funeral with him?"

Aaron looked at me, eyes tracing my face. "You held his hand for the past three hours. Dude cried in your arms, on your shoulder, in your hair. Took dude until his agent called him over to let you out of his sight. I saw the way that he looked at you. I saw the way that he held you. Dude still has feelings for you. And after the way that he did you, the fact that you found it in your heart to come with the dude proves that you still love him too."

It took everything in me to fight away the tears. "Aaron, you need to mind your own damn business because you don't know what you're talking about."

He laughed a little. "I don't? So you're not living with dude?"

I looked at him. "First of all, Aaron, I'm not *with* Jamie. Second, if I *was* with Jamie, it would really be none of your fuckin' business. And third, *stop* sending me messages on Facebook telling me how much you miss me! *Stop* fuckin' with my heart, Aaron! We both agreed that things between us were over, so *stop* trying to reach out to me! What are you even doing here? You don't even know Jamie. You just came here to fuck with me!"

Aaron looked at me. "You didn't answer me—are you living with him?"

I rolled my eyes. "Since you heard so much shit, Aaron, did you hear that I have fuckin' heart failure? He has the money and the nurses to provide home care for me so that I don't have to sit alone in a fuckin' hospital. You need to be worrying about your pregnant fiancée, instead of being overly concerned with shit that *shouldn't* even concern you."

Aaron said, "I heard about your heart condition, and I've been worried about you."

I scoffed, rolling my eyes. "Aaron, *please*."

His eyes traced my lips for a few seconds. "My feelings for you haven't changed, Heaven."

I looked up into his face. "Your 'feelings' for me? Let's get something straight—there is *no* us. There never has been, and there never will be!

I can't help that as soon as you decided to build up the nerve to finally talk to me, Charlie decides to tell you that you're gonna be a daddy. You need to concentrate on being a father to that baby and a support system for her. We did our wrong, Aaron. It's *over*, Aaron."

His eyes searched my face. "You really feeling this dude? How much could he really care about you if he's fuckin' other females in your face, shorty?"

I pushed him in his chest. "Isn't that what *you* were doing to me for two years, Aaron?"

He shook his head in disagreement. "I didn't know how you felt about me until a few weeks ago, Heaven. Do you think I would actually be with Charlie if I knew how you felt about me? You can't compare what Jamie's doing to that, and you know it. You feeling him, Heaven? *That's* the type of nigga you wanna be with? *That's* the shit that you think you deserve?"

"If I recall correctly, wasn't it *you* who told me that I couldn't give up on love? I thought *you* were the one who told me that I needed to give it a shot with him, that I needed someone to take care of me, that I needed love, that I couldn't push everyone away who tries to love me," I exclaimed.

Aaron looked at me. "That was before I knew exactly what type of dude he is. Jamie doesn't love you, shorty, at least not the way that he should. And you can't love yourself all that much either if you can watch the dude fuck females in a pool outside of your window. One minute, you love me; then the next, you love him. Yeah, my niggas was right in high school when they told me that I was just gonna be a rebound if I ended up fuckin' around with you, Heaven. I didn't believe it, but turns out, they were right. One night, you're suckin' my dick, then the next, you're suckin' his."

"Go to hell, do you hear me!" I cried, as I turned from him to walk away. Aaron caught my hand, pulling me back to him.

I pulled away. "Don't touch me!" I cried. "Don't you *ever* touch me!"

"Yo." I heard Jamie's voice over my shoulder.

I turned around to see Jamie and his crew walking toward us.

I sighed, backing away from Aaron. "Jamie, please, don't start—everything is fine."

"Yo," Jamie approached my side, face-to-face with Aaron. "Charlie's not out here, dawg. Maybe you should go find her."

"Bruh, I didn't come here for any drama. I came to give my condolences for your loss." Aaron looked Jamie dead in his face.

Jamie shook his head. "Nah, you came here to fuck with Ne'Vaeh. Your chances with her have come and gone, muthafucka, so you need to go find your girl and stay the fuck away from mine."

My mouth dropped open. I can't believe the asshole was claiming me. I looked up at Jamie, then looked back up at Aaron.

Aaron grinned a little, shaking his head at me. He backed up and walked away. He would respect Jamie at his father's funeral. I wasn't so sure he was going to respect him after that point, especially after he had heard about the events at Jamie's house that past week.

Jamie grabbed my hand, pulling me along with him away from the church.

"Why did you tell Aaron that I was your girl? You basically implied that we had gotten back together, Jamie!" I exclaimed that afternoon at his hotel room. "Are *you* the one spreading these fuckin' rumors?"

Jamie stood in the mirror removing his tie. He was heading out with his family members to some sort of football event at his college. "Shorty, you comin' with me to Memphis State or what?"

"Jamie! I know you heard my question! Why would you do that? Everybody at that funeral heard about your fuckin' orgy in your fuckin' pool! Do you think that if we were together I would put up with that type of shit?" I yelled.

He turned around, facing me. "Why the fuck do you even care what he thinks, shorty?"

I was trying to hold back the tears so hard that my lips were trembling. "What?"

"No matter if he thinks you're my girl, why does it matter to you?" He hesitated before saying, "You still wanna be with that nigga, is that it?"

I pushed him in his chest. "Jamie, I don't want people thinking that me and you are together and you're fuckin' around on me! I've looked stupid enough as it is! Just three weeks ago, I was sleeping with my best friend's boyfriend and now, I'm—" I broke down and cried, "I'm with my ex-boyfriend at his father's funeral. I'm staying in the house with my ex-boyfriend who thinks it's cool to fuck females right in front of my face!"

His eyes sparkled. "Shorty, I wasn't trying to make you look stupid." He hesitated. "It hurt seeing you talking to Aaron, shorty. I didn't know what else to say."

I just looked at him. "I'm coming back to my senses, Jamie. I'm flushing Aaron out of my system. You never have to worry about anything *ever* happening with him again. I came here with *you*, Jamie, nobody else."

"I couldn't let your hand go today at the funeral. I thought my heart was gonna stop when I saw my dad lying there in the casket. I needed your support. You saw my mama didn't give a fuck about me. She probably only came to the funeral to actually make sure Pops was really dead." Jamie tossed his tie on the bed.

I shook my head. "Jamie, I'm so sorry about all of this." I approached him, looking up into his face. "I wasn't entirely truthful the other night when you asked me what your father said to me."

He looked at me. "What do you mean?"

"He—" I laughed to myself nervously, "he told me to marry you."

Jamie's eyes glistened. "He did? He told us to get married?"

I nodded, wiping my tears, "Yeah," I grabbed my purse off of the bed, "but *I* told him that you weren't ready. He seems to think that I can *make* you ready."

"Ne'Vaeh . . ." He reached for me because he knew I was seconds away from leaving the room.

I pulled away from him. "What, Jamie? What do you have to say about that?"

"Baby, you *know* you can make me ready." He looked at me earnestly. "Shit, I'm already ready."

I shook my head. "No, you're not ready for me. The only thing you're ready for is a different freak every night. I don't think you had sex with the same girl twice these past few days, Jamie! That's the lifestyle you're used to! One girl could *never* satisfy you!"

Jamie shook his head, "Nah, you have it all wrong. It takes *all* those girls just to satisfy my craving for *you*, shorty." He held my hands in his. "Ne'Vaeh, you know I don't care about any of them girls."

"Jamie, you're not thinking clearly. You just lost your dad. That feeling has you ready to settle down. This isn't how you really feel, Jamie!" I cried.

"Baby, I wanna be with you." His eyes watered.

I shook my head. "No, Jamie! We're not doing this again! We need to move forward, not backward! It's too late to start over!"

"Why is it too late? Don't you still love me?" He paused a moment. "You used to love me."

I cried aloud as he pulled me closer. I couldn't escape his kiss, or maybe I didn't even resist. His lips embraced mine for a few seconds before I pulled away, backing away from him. "Jamie, no! Not again!" I cried. "Please don't do this to my heart!"

Tears slid down his face. He pulled my body up against his again and gently kissed my lips again. "I miss you. I need you. I still love you. I never stopped loving you, Ne'Vaeh. Please, give me you. *Please*," he whispered.

I sighed as he kissed me repeatedly. The next thing I knew, he was unbuttoning his shirt and I was unzipping my dress. In seconds, it seems, we were completely naked on top of the bed, kissing, touching, rubbing, and sucking.

"*Fuck*, I missed this!" he cried out, sucking on my neck, yanking on my hair. He held my body oh so tight against his. "I just wanna hold you for a few minutes, *please*." He tried to calm himself.

I held on to him, crying on his shoulder. His dick was throbbing between my legs, rubbing against my clit. He felt so good, he smelled so good, and to my surprise, I missed him too.

"Jamie, I missed you too. I missed you *so* much," I whispered.

He looked into my face, tears sliding down his cheeks.

I nodded. "I did." I cried. "You just—you just hurt me, so I wanted to forget you."

Jamie ran his fingers through my hair. "I'm here, Ne'Vaeh. I won't leave you again, I promise." He gently kissed my lips.

I took in a deep breath between kisses as Jamie held my thighs and dug his way inside of me. I cried out as he began to stroke, biting down on my neck. My pussy was a little tense. She tightened around his dick, and he dug into it.

"This is *my* pussy, Ne'Vaeh," Jamie moaned with a fistful of my hair. "*Say* it's mine, shorty."

I cried, shaking my head.

He dug deeper, pulling my hair tighter. "Say it, shorty. Tell me this is *my* pussy."

I cried out, digging my nails into his back.

He dug his nails into my thighs. He stroked my pussy until she started to fart, squirt, and whistle. Even though my mouth wasn't telling him the pussy was his, my *pussy* was telling him, "I'm all yours."

"Oh!" I cried out, as my pussy tightened.

Jamie looked down into my face, and he stopped pumping.

I looked into his face, chest heaving in and out. I wanted to come, and he wouldn't let me until I gave myself to him. "Jamie, please," I cried, "Don't stop. Keep going."

He shook his head. "Is it mine?" He pulled out of me. "Baby, tell me it's mine. What do I gotta do to make you mine?" He got up from the bed, pulling me up with him. He held my face in his hands, gently kissing my lips.

My body was on fire. He wasn't playing fair. I shook my head. "*Please*. I gotta release this tension that you just built up inside of me, Jamie!" I cried.

He turned my body around, pressing my back down so that my chest rested on the bed and my ass was in the air. Again, he grabbed a handful of hair and gripped my ass with the other hand. He thrust his way inside of me as he pulled my hair. "Are you gonna tell me it's mine?" he said as he started to stroke.

My lips trembled. I couldn't even talk. Tears slid down my face as Jamie worked my soul from the inside out. He worked my body until my legs gave out. My knees buckled, and my body fell to the bed. He still didn't stop. He sucked on my neck, running his fingers through my hair, gripping my hips as he dug through me.

I couldn't take it anymore. He owned it. I squealed out his name as he sucked on my ear. "Jamie, it's yours!" I cried, biting the pillow.

"It's mine?" He pumped a little deeper, stronger, and faster. "It's really mine? You sure about that? Then throw it back, ma."

"Just take it," I cried, propping up on my elbows a little as I worked my hips and ass, throwing it back on him a little, matching my thrusts with his.

"I'm taking it." He bit down on my neck, gripping my hips.

I gripped the sheets in my hands as Jamie hit all types of spots. He gripped my pussy in his hand, pumping in and out, causing her to make all types of sounds. He growled in my ear and after about a good ten or fifteen minutes, his body trembled as he exploded inside of me. Then, all of his weight rested on top of me as I fell back down on the bed. It was a quickie, but it felt *so* fuckin' good, so good that I burst out crying.

I buried my face in the pillow. "Oh my goodness. What am I thinking?"

Jamie pulled his body from mine, lying beside me on the bed. "Shorty, look at me."

I shook my head, tears saturating the pillow. "No."

He slid his hand over my waist, pulling my body closer to his.

I felt so good in his arms. I turned to him, drying my face. "What did we just do? What does this mean?"

He just looked at me.

"Does this mean we're back together?" I whispered.

"It's your call," Jamie whispered back.

I shook my head. "I hate answers like that."

He laughed a little. "Shorty, I already told you that if you wanted me, I was all yours."

"Jamie, you got too many hoes." My eyes searched his face.

Jamie nodded. "True."

Tears slid down my face. "I swear, I never intended on sleeping with Aaron. Charlie has been my best friend since I was six years old, and over some guy, our friendship is over! I never meant to hurt her. I just needed love. I haven't felt love in so long. I thought I'd never see you again. When Aaron told me he loved me, I believed it. I made a horrible mistake that cost me the best friend that I ever had."

Jamie said, "Shorty, when I left Maryland, I was on a mission. I was gonna do something great. I was gonna have something to show for leaving the best friend that I ever had. You know the shit I've been through in my family. I was the only one out of twelve kids who was given up at birth. I was tossed around from house to house all my life. I was forced to do all types of shit when I stayed with my mom during the summer. No food to eat, nothing to drink, abused, misused . . . Nobody understood. I worked my ass off to make a career out of football. When my father found me, he invested so much money in my career to make sure that I achieved greatness.

He did a lot for me to make sure that I never had to ask my mother for anything again." Jamie's eyes glistened. "I tried talking to her today, and she wouldn't even look at me. She always told me that I wasn't gonna be shit. And now that I *am* something, she won't even allow herself to be proud of me."

Tears slid down my face. I felt his pain.

Jamie's eyes searched mine. "Because of her, I have trust issues. I have relationship issues. I have a hard time trusting a woman. I haven't showed *any* woman any love for some years. I swear. I have had sex with at least ten girls a week for the past four years. I'm not gonna lie, Ne'Vaeh, I have done some wild shit. I have lived my life to the fullest. I may have over-compensated for the love I didn't have from my mom and for the pain of leaving you behind. I will admit, I have done wrong. Trust me. I don't mind giving up the hoes. I'm not gonna say that they will never confront you, because you know how bitches are these days. But I will say that I told each and every one how it was from jump—I told them before we had sex that if they were looking for love, they could leave."

I shook my head, pushing my hair from my face. "I have been through *so* much shit, Jamie.

I'm sick and tired of being sick and tired. I need love, and I'm not even sure that you know how to give it to me anymore. You say you can give up all that pussy, but I'm not too sure that you can, and I'm not gonna force you either, Jamie. You have to show me that I'm the only one, and maybe, *then,* I can give this a shot. I can't go through any more pain, Jamie. And I already know that fuckin' around with you is gonna have me *insane.*"

Jamie's eyes traced my lips. "I'm not here to hurt you. Hopefully, I can heal some of those wounds that I caused."

"I'm not sure if I'm ready to be your one and only, Jamie. I'm not even sure that I wanna feel weak again. You make my heart weak. You always had me wide open, ready to do whatever for you. I don't wanna be sprung, doing shit that I would never do. I'm not over the pain yet, Jamie. I haven't healed well enough to forgive you, and I can't forgive myself for allowing my emotions to get the best of me. I was drunk the entire time that I was sleeping with that boy! I knew what I was doing was wrong! I should have never let him touch me! What was I thinking?" I cried.

Jamie gently kissed my lips. "We all have made mistakes. I've done shit that I'm not proud of too,

Ne'Vaeh, so don't think you're the only one who has some cleaning up to do." He held my face in his hands, pressing his lips against my forehead. "I know you have been through a lot, shorty. I'm here. The storm is over."

I shook my head. "It's not over—it just started, Jamie."

He shook his head back at me. "I got my baby back. I swear, I'm never letting go. It's you and me forever, baby. It may be raining a little, but the worst is over. I'll dance in the rain with you, shorty. A little rain never hurt anybody."

THE RAZOR'S EDGE

William Somerset Maugham was born in 1874 and lived in Paris until he was ten. He was educated at King's School, Canterbury, and at Heidelberg University. He afterwards walked the wards of St Thomas's Hospital with a view to practice in medicine, but the success of his first novel, *Liza of Lambeth* (1897), won him over to letters. Something of his hospital experience is reflected, however, in the first of his masterpieces, *Of Human Bondage* (1915), and with *The Moon and Sixpence* (1919) his reputation as a novelist was assured.

His position as one of the most successful playwrights on the London stage was being consolidated simultaneously. His first play, *A Man of Honour* (1903), was followed by a procession of successes just before and after the First World War. (At one point only Bernard Shaw had more plays running at the same time in London.) His theatre career ended with *Sheppey* (1933).

His fame as a short-story writer began with *The Trembling of a Leaf*, sub-titled *Little Stories of the South Sea Islands*, in 1921, after which he published more than ten collections.

Somerset Maugham's general books are fewer in number. They include travel books, such as *On a Chinese Screen* (1922) and *Don Fernando* (1935), essays, criticism, and the self-revealing *The Summing Up* (1938) and *A Writer's Notebook* (1949).

Somerset Maugham lived latterly on the Riviera, from which he retired temporarily during the war. During his life he travelled in almost every part of the world. He became Companion of Honour in 1954, and died in 1965.

W. Somerset Maugham

THE RAZOR'S EDGE

PENGUIN BOOKS

PENGUIN BOOKS

Published by the Penguin Group
Penguin Books Ltd, 27 Wrights Lane, London W8 5TZ, England
Viking Penguin, a division of Penguin Books USA Inc.
375 Hudson Street, New York, New York 10014, USA
Penguin Books Australia Ltd, Ringwood, Victoria, Australia
Penguin Books Canada Ltd, 2801 John Street, Markham, Ontario, Canada L3R 1B4
Penguin Books (NZ) Ltd, 182–190 Wairau Road, Auckland 10, New Zealand

Penguin Books Ltd, Registered Offices: Harmondsworth, Middlesex, England

First published in Great Britain by William Heinemann Ltd 1944
Published in Penguin Books 1963
Published in Penguin Books in the United States of America
by arrangement with Doubleday & Company, Inc.
25 27 29 30 28 26 24

Printed in England by Clays Ltd, St Ives plc
Set in Linotype Times

*The sharp edge of a razor is difficult to pass over;
thus the wise say the path to Salvation is hard.*

KATHA-UPANISHAD

1

I HAVE never begun a novel with more misgiving. If I call it a novel it is only because I don't know what else to call it. I have little story to tell and I end neither with a death nor a marriage. Death ends all things and so is the comprehensive conclusion of a story, but marriage finishes it very properly too and the sophisticated are ill-advised to sneer at what is by convention termed a happy ending. It is a sound instinct of the common people which persuades them that with this all that needs to be said is said. When male and female, after whatever vicissitudes you like, are at last brought together they have fulfilled their biological function and interest passes to the generation that is to come. But I leave my reader in the air. This book consists of my recollections of a man with whom I was thrown into close contact only at long intervals, and I have little knowledge of what happened to him in between. I suppose that by the exercise of invention I could fill the gaps plausibly enough and so make my narrative more coherent; but I have no wish to do that. I only want to set down what I know of my own knowledge.

Many years ago I wrote a novel called *The Moon and Six-pence*. In that I took a famous painter, Paul Gauguin, and, using the novelist's privilege, devised a number of incidents to illustrate the character I had created on the suggestions afforded me by the scanty facts I knew about the French artist. In the present book I have attempted to do nothing of the kind. I have invented nothing. To save embarrassment to people still living I have given to the persons who play a part in this story names of my own contriving, and I have in other ways taken pains to make sure that no one should recognize them. The man I am writing about is not famous. It may be that he never will be. It may be that when his life at last comes to an end he will leave no more trace of his sojourn on earth than a stone thrown into a river leaves on the surface of the water. Then my

7

book, if it is read at all, will be read only for what intrinsic interest it may possess. But it may be that the way of life that he has chosen for himself and the peculiar strength and sweetness of his character may have an ever-growing influence over his fellow men so that, long after his death perhaps, it may be realized that there lived in this age a very remarkable creature. Then it will be quite clear of whom I write in this book and those who want to know at least a little about his early life may find in it something to their purpose. I think my book, within its acknowledged limitations, will be a useful source of information to my friend's biographers.

I do not pretend that the conversations I have recorded can be regarded as verbatim reports. I never kept notes of what was said on this or the other occasion, but I have a good memory for what concerns me, and though I have put these conversations in my own words they faithfully represent, I believe, what was said. I remarked a little while back that I have invented nothing; I want now to modify that statement. I have taken the liberty that historians have taken from the time of Herodotus to put into the mouths of the persons of my narrative speeches that I did not myself hear and could not possibly have heard. I have done this for the same reasons as the historians have, to give liveliness and verisimilitude to scenes that would have been ineffective if they had been merely recounted. I want to be read and I think I am justified in doing what I can to make my book readable. The intelligent reader will easily see for himself where I have used this artifice, and he is at perfect liberty to reject it.

Another reason that has caused me to embark upon this work with apprehension is that the persons I have chiefly to deal with are American. It is very difficult to know people and I don't think one can ever really know any but one's own countrymen. For men and women are not only themselves; they are also the region in which they were born, the city apartment or the farm in which they learnt to walk, the games they played as children, the old wives' tales they overheard, the food they ate, the schools they attended, the sports they followed, the poets they read, and the God they believed in. It is all these things that have made them what they are, and these are the things that you can't come to know by hearsay, you can only know them if you have lived them. You can only know them if you are them. And because you cannot know persons of a nation foreign to you except from observation, it is difficult to give them credibility in the pages of a book. Even so subtle and careful an observer as Henry James, though he lived in England for forty years, never managed to create an Englishman who was through and through English. For my part, except in a few short stories, I have never attempted to deal with any but my own countrymen, and if I have ventured to do otherwise in short stories it is because in them you can treat your characters more summarily. You give the reader broad indications and leave him to fill in the details. It may be asked why, if I turned Paul Gauguin into an Englishman, I could not do the same with the persons of this book. The answer is simple: I couldn't. They would not then have been the people they are. I do not pretend that they are American as Americans see themselves; they are American seen through an English eye. I have not attempted to reproduce the peculiarities of their speech. The mess English writers make when they try to do this is only equalled by the mess American writers make when they try to reproduce English as spoken in England. Slang is the great pitfall. Henry James in his English stories made constant use of it, but never quite as the English do, so that instead of getting the colloquial effect he was after, it too often gives the English reader an uncomfortable jolt.

2

In 1919 I happened to be in Chicago on my way to the Far East, and for reasons that have nothing to do with this narrative I was staying there for two or three weeks. I had recently brought out a successful novel and being for the moment news, I had no sooner arrived than I was interviewed. Next morning my telephone rang. I answered.

'Elliott Templeton speaking.'

'Elliott? I thought you were in Paris.'

'No, I'm visiting with my sister. We want you to come along and lunch with us today.'

'I should love to.'

9

He named the hour and gave me the address.

I had known Elliott Templeton for fifteen years. He was at this time in his late fifties, a tall, elegant man with good features and thick waving dark hair only sufficiently greying to add to the distinction of his appearance. He was always beautifully dressed. He got his haberdashery at Charvet's, but his suits, his shoes, and his hats in London. He had an apartment in Paris on the Rive Gauche in the fashionable Rue St Guillaume. People who did not like him said he was a dealer, but this was a charge that he resented with indignation. He had taste and knowledge, and he did not mind admitting that in bygone years, when he first settled in Paris, he had given rich collectors who wanted to buy pictures the benefit of his advice; and when through his social connexions he heard that some impoverished nobleman, English or French, was disposed to sell a picture of first-rate quality he was glad to put him in touch with the directors of American museums who, he happened to know, were on the lookout for a fine example of such and such a master. There were many old families in France and some in England whose circumstances compelled them to part with a signed piece of Buhl or a writing-table made by Chippendale himself if it could be done quietly, and they were glad to know a man of great culture and perfect manners who could arrange the matter with discretion. One would naturally suppose that Elliott profited by the transactions, but one was too well bred to mention it. Unkind people asserted that everything in his apartment was for sale and that after he had invited wealthy Americans for an excellent lunch, with vintage wines, one or two of his valuable drawings would disappear, or a marquetry commode would be replaced by one in lacquer. When he was asked why a particular piece had vanished he very plausibly explained that he hadn't thought it quite up to his mark and had exchanged it for one of much finer quality, He added that it was tiresome always to look at the same things.

'*Nous autres Américains*, we Americans,' he said, 'like change. It is at once our weakness and our strength.'

Some of the American ladies in Paris, who claimed to know all about him, said that his family was quite poor and if he was able to live in the way he did it was only because he had

10

been very clever. I do not know how much money he had, but his ducal landlord certainly made him pay a lot for his apartment and it was furnished with objects of value. On the walls were drawings by the great French masters, Watteau, Fragonard, Claude Lorraine and so on; Savonnerie and Aubusson rugs displayed their beauty on the parquet floors; and in the drawing-room there was a Louis Quinze suite in *petit point* of such elegance that it might well have belonged, as he claimed, to Madame de Pompadour. Anyhow he had enough to live in what he considered was the proper style for a gentleman without trying to earn money, and the method by which he had done so in the past was a matter which, unless you wished to lose his acquaintance, you were wise not to refer to. Thus relieved of material cares he gave himself over to the ruling passion of his life, which was social relationships. His business connexions with the impecunious great both in France and in England had secured the foothold he had obtained on his arrival in Europe as a young man with letters of introduction to persons of consequence. His origins recommended him to the American ladies of title to whom he brought letters, for he was of an old Virginian family and through his mother traced his descent from one of the signatories of the Declaration of Independence. He was well-favoured, bright, a good dancer, a fair shot, and a fine tennis player. He was an asset at any party. He was lavish with flowers and expensive boxes of chocolates, and though he entertained little, when he did it was with an originality that pleased. It amused these rich ladies to be taken to bohemian restaurants in Soho or *bistros* in the Latin Quarter. He was always prepared to make himself useful, and there was nothing, however tiresome, that you asked him to do for you that he would not do with pleasure. He took an immense amount of trouble to make himself agreeable to ageing women, and it was not long before he was the *ami de la maison*, the household pet, in many an imposing mansion. His amiability was extreme; he never minded being asked at the last moment because someone had thrown you over and you could put him next to a very boring old lady and count on him to be as charming and amusing with her as he knew how.

In two or more years, both in London to which he went for

the last part of the season and to pay a round of country house visits in the early autumn, and in Paris, where he had settled down, he knew everyone whom a young American could know. The ladies who had first introduced him into society were surprised to discover how wide the circle of his acquaintance had grown. Their feelings were mixed. On the one hand they were pleased that their young protégé had made so great a success, and on the other a trifle nettled that he should be on intimate terms with persons with whom their own relations had remained strictly formal. Though he continued to be obliging and useful to them, they were uneasily conscious that he had used them as stepping-stones to his social advancement. They were afraid he was a snob. And of course he was. He was a colossal snob. He was a snob without shame. He would put up with any affront, he would ignore any rebuff, he would swallow any rudeness to get asked to a party he wanted to go to or to make a connexion with some crusty old dowager of great name. He was indefatigable. When he had fixed his eye on his prey he hunted it with the persistence of a botanist who will expose himself to dangers of flood, earthquake, fever, and hostile natives to find an orchid of peculiar rarity. The war of 1914 gave him his final chance. When it broke out he joined an ambulance corps and served first in Flanders and then in the Argonne; he came back after a year with a red ribbon in his buttonhole and secured a position in the Red Cross in Paris. By then he was in affluent circumstances and he contributed generously to the good works patronized by persons of consequence. He was always ready with his exquisite taste and his gift for organization to help in any charitable function that was widely publicized. He became a member of the two most exclusive clubs in Paris. He was *ce cher Elliott* to the greatest ladies in France. He had finally arrived.

3

When I first met Elliott I was just a young author like another and he took no notice of me. He never forgot a face and when I ran across him here or there he shook hands with me cordially, but showed no desire to further our acquaintance; and if I saw him at the opera, say, he being with a person of high rank, he was apt not to catch sight of me. But then I happened to make a somewhat startling success as a playwright, and presently I became aware that Elliott regarded me with a warmer feeling. One day I received a note from him asking me to lunch at Claridge's, where he lived when in London. It was a small party and not a very smart one, and I conceived the notion that he was trying me out. But from then on, since my success had brought me many new friends, I began to see him more frequently. Shortly after this I spent some weeks of the autumn in Paris and met him at the house of a common acquaintance. He asked me where I was staying and in a day or two I received another invitation to lunch, this time at his apartment; when I arrived I was surprised to see that it was a party of considerable distinction. I giggled to myself. I knew that with his perfect sense of social relations he had realized that in English society as an author I was not of much account, but that in France, where an author just because he is an author has prestige, I was. During the years that followed our acquaintance became fairly intimate without ever developing into friendship. I doubt whether it was possible for Elliott Templeton to be a friend. He took no interest in people apart from their social position. When I chanced to be in Paris or he in London, he continued to ask me to parties when he wanted an extra man or was obliged to entertain travelling Americans. Some of these were, I suspected, old clients and some were strangers sent to him with letters of introduction. They were the cross of his life. He felt he had to do something for them and yet was unwilling to have them meet his grand friends. The best way of disposing of them of course was to give them dinner and take them to a play, but that was often difficult when he was engaged every evening for three weeks ahead, and also he had an inkling that they would scarcely be satisfied with that. Since I was an author and so of little consequence he didn't mind telling me his troubles on this matter.

'People in America are so inconsiderate in the way they give letters. It's not that I'm not delighted to see the people who are sent to me, but I really don't see why I should inflict them on my friends.'

He sought to make amends by sending them great baskets of

roses and huge boxes of chocolates, but sometimes he had to do more. It was then, somewhat naïvely after what he had told me, that he asked me to come to the party he was organizing.

'They want to meet you so much,' he wrote to flatter me. 'Mrs So-and-so is a very cultivated woman and she's read every word you've written.'

Mrs So-and-so would then tell me she'd so much enjoyed my book *Mr Perrin and Mr Traill* and congratulate me on my play *The Mollusc*. The first of these was written by Hugh Walpole and the second by Hubert Henry Davies.

4

If I have given the reader an impression that Elliott Templeton was a despicable character I have done him an injustice.

He was for one thing what the French call *serviable*, a word for which, so far as I know, there is no exact equivalent in English. The dictionary tells me that *serviceable* in the sense of helpful, obliging, and kind is archaic. That is just what Elliott was. He was generous, and though early in his career he had doubtless showered flowers, candy, and presents on his acquaintance from an ulterior motive, he continued to do so when it was no longer necessary. It caused him pleasure to give. He was hospitable. His chef was as good as any in Paris and you could be sure at his table of having set before you the earliest delicacies of the season. His wine proved the excellence of his judgement. It is true that his guests were chosen for their social importance rather than because they were good company, but he took care to invite at least one or two for their powers of entertainment, so that his parties were almost always amusing. People laughed at him behind his back and called him a filthy snob, but nevertheless accepted his invitations with alacrity. His French was fluent and correct and his accent perfect. He had taken great pains to adopt the manner of speech as it is spoken in England and you had to have a very sensitive ear to catch now and then an American intonation. He was a good talker if only you could keep him off the subject of dukes and duchesses, but even about them, now that his position was unassailable, he allowed himself, especially when you were alone with him, to be amusing. He had a pleasantly malicious tongue and there was no scandal about these exalted personages that did not reach his ears. From him I learnt who was the father of the Princess X's last child and who was the mistress of the Marquis de Y. I don't believe even Marcel Proust knew more of the inner life of the aristocracy than Elliott Templeton.

When I was in Paris we used often to lunch together, sometimes at his apartment and sometimes at a restaurant. I like to wander about the antiquity shops, occasionally to buy but more often to look, and Elliott was always enchanted to go with me. He had knowledge and a real love of beautiful objects. I think he knew every shop of the kind in Paris and was on familiar terms with the proprietor. He adored haggling and when we started out would say to me:

'If there's anything you want don't try to buy it yourself. Just give me a hint and let me do the rest.'

He would be delighted when he had got for me something I fancied for half the asking price. It was a treat to watch him bargain. He would argue, cajole, lose his temper, appeal to the seller's better nature, ridicule him, point out the defects of the object in question, threaten never to cross his threshold again, sigh, shrug his shoulders, admonish, start for the door in frowning anger, and when finally he had won his point shake his head sadly as though he accepted defeat with resignation. Then he would whisper to me in English.

'Take it with you. It would be cheap at double the money.'

Elliott was a zealous Catholic. He had not lived long in Paris before he met an abbé who was celebrated for his success in bringing infidels and heretics back to the fold. He was a great diner-out and a noted wit. He confined his ministrations to the rich and the aristocratic. It was inevitable that Elliott should be attracted by a man who, though of humble origins, was a welcome guest in the most exclusive houses, and he confided to a wealthy American lady who was one of the abbé's recent converts that, though his family had always been Episcopalian, he had for long been interested in the Catholic Church. She asked Elliott to meet the abbé at dinner one evening, just three of them, and the abbé was scintillating. Elliott's hostess brought the conversation around to Catholicism and the abbé spoke of it with unction, but without pedantry, as a man of the world, though a priest, speaking to another man of the world. Elliott was flattered to discover that the abbé knew all about him.

'The Duchesse de Vendôme was speaking of you the other day. She told me that she thought you highly intelligent.'

Elliott flushed with pleasure. He had been presented to Her Royal Highness, but it had never occurred to him that she would give him a second thought. The abbé spoke of the faith with wisdom and benignity; he was broad-minded, modern in his outlook, and tolerant. He made the Church seem to Elliott very like a select club that a well-bred man owed it to himself to belong to. Six months later he was received into it. His conversion, combined with the generosity he showed in his contributions to Catholic charities, opened several doors that had been closed to him before.

It may be that his motives in abandoning the faith of his fathers were mixed, but there could be no doubt of his devoutness when he had done so. He attended Mass every Sunday at the church frequented by the best people, went to confession regularly, and made periodical visits to Rome. In course of time he was rewarded for his piety by being made a papal chamberlain, and the assiduity with which he performed the duties of his office was rewarded by the order of, I think, the Holy Sepulchre. His career as a Catholic was in fact no less successful than his career as an *homme du monde*.

I often asked myself what was the cause of the snobbishness that obsessed this man who was so intelligent, so kindly, and so cultivated. He was no upstart. His father had been president of one of the southern universities and his grandfather a divine of some eminence. Elliott was too clever not to see that many of the persons who accepted his invitations did so only to get a free meal and that of these some were stupid and some worthless. The glamour of their resounding titles blinded him to their faults. I can only guess that to be on terms of intimate familiarity with these gentlemen of ancient lineage, to be the faithful retainer of their ladies, gave him a sensation of triumph that never palled; and I think that at the back of it all was a passionate romanticism that led him to see in the weedy little

French duke the crusader who had gone to the Holy Land with Saint Louis, and in the blustering, fox-hunting English earl the ancestor who had attended Henry the Eighth to the Field of the Cloth of Gold. In the company of such as these he felt that he lived in a spacious and gallant past. I think when he turned the pages of the *Almanach de Gotha* his heart beat warmly as one name after another brought back to him recollections of old wars, historic sieges, and celebrated duels, diplomatic intrigues, and the love affairs of kings. Such anyhow was Elliott Templeton.

5

I was having a wash and a brush-up before starting out to go to the luncheon Elliott had invited me to, when they rang up from the desk to say that he was below. I was a little surprised, but as soon as I was ready went down.

'I thought it would be safer if I came and fetched you,' he said as we shook hands. 'I don't know how well you know Chicago.'

He had the feeling I have noticed in some Americans who have lived many years abroad that America is a difficult and even dangerous place in which the European cannot safely be left to find his way about by himself.

'It's early yet. We might walk part of the way,' he suggested.

There was a slight nip in the air, but not a cloud in the sky, and it was pleasant to stretch one's legs.

'I thought I'd better tell you about my sister before you meet her,' said Elliott as we walked along. 'She's stayed with me once or twice in Paris, but I don't think you were there at the time. It's not a big party, you know. Only my sister and her daughter Isabel and Gregory Brabazon.'

'The decorator?' I asked.

'Yes. My sister's house is awful, and Isabel and I want her to have it done over. I happened to hear that Gregory was in Chicago and so I got her to ask him to lunch today. He's not quite a gentleman, of course, but he has taste. He did Raney Castle for Mary Olifant and St Clement Talbot for the St Erths. The duchess was delighted with him. You'll see Louisa's house for yourself. How she can have lived in it all these years

I shall never understand. For the matter of that, how she can live in Chicago I shall never understand either.'

It appeared that Mrs Bradley was a widow with three children, two sons and a daughter; but the sons were much older and married. One was in a government post in the Philippines, and the other, in the diplomatic service as his father had been, was at Buenos Aires. Mrs Bradley's husband had occupied posts in various parts of the world, and after being first secretary in Rome for some years was made minister to one of the republics on the west coast of South America and had there died.

'I wanted Louisa to sell the house in Chicago when he passed over,' Elliott went on, 'but she had a sentiment about it. It had been in the Bradley family for quite a long while. The Bradleys are one of the oldest families in Illinois. They came from Virginia in 1839 and took up land about sixty miles from what is now Chicago. They still own it.' Elliott hesitated a little and looked at me to see how I would take it. 'The Bradley who settled here was what I suppose you might call a farmer. I'm not sure whether you know, but about the middle of last century, when the Middle West began to be opened up, quite a number of Virginians, younger sons of good family, you know, were tempted by the lure of the unknown to leave the fleshpots of their native state. My brother-in-law's father, Chester Bradley, saw that Chicago had a future and entered a law office here. At all events he made enough money to leave his son very adequately provided for.'

Elliott's manner, rather than his words, suggested that perhaps it was not quite the thing for the late Chester Bradley to have left the stately mansion and the broad acres he had inherited to enter an office, but the fact that he had amassed a fortune at least partly compensated for it. Elliott was none too pleased when on a later occasion Mrs Bradley showed me some snapshots of what he called their 'place' in the country, and I saw a modest frame house with a pretty little garden, but with a barn and a cowhouse and hog pens within a stone's throw, surrounded by a desolate waste of flat fields. I couldn't help thinking that Mr Chester Bradley knew what he was about when he abandoned this to make his way in the city.

18

Presently we hailed a taxi. It put us down before a brown-stone house. Narrow and rather high, and you ascended to the front door by a flight of steep steps. It was in a row of houses, in a street that led off Lake Shore Drive, and its appearance, even on that bright autumn day, was so drab that you wondered how anyone could feel any sentiment about it. The door was opened by a tall and stout Negro butler with white hair, and we were ushered into the drawing-room. Mrs Bradley got up from her chair as we came in and Elliott presented me to her. She must have been a handsome woman when young, for her features, though on the large side, were good, and she had fine eyes. But her sallowish face, almost agressively desti-tute of make-up, had sagged, and it was plain that she had lost the battle with the corpulence of middle age. I surmised that she was unwilling to accept defeat, for when she sat down she sat very erect in a straight-backed chair which the cruel armour of her corsets doubtless made more comfortable than an up-holstered one. She wore a blue gown, heavily braided, and her high collar was stiff with whalebone. She had a fine head of white hair tightly marcelled and intricately dressed. Her other guest had not arrived and while waiting for him we talked of one thing and another.

'Elliott tells me that you came over by the southern route,' said Mrs Bradley. 'Did you stop in Rome?'

'Yes, I spent a week there.'

'And how is dear Queen Margherita?'

Somewhat surprised by her question, I said I didn't know.

'Oh, didn't you go and see her? Such a very nice woman. She was so kind to us when we were in Rome. Mr Bradley was first secretary. Why didn't you go and see her? You're not like Elliott, so black that you can't go to the Quirinal?'

'Not at all,' I smiled. 'The fact is I don't know her.'

'Don't you?' said Mrs Bradley as though she could hardly believe her ears. 'Why not?'

'To tell you the truth authors don't hobnob with kings and queens as a general rule.'

'But she's such a sweet woman,' Mrs Bradley expostulated, as though it were very hoity-toity of me not to know that royal personage. 'I'm sure you'd like her.'

19

At this moment the door was opened and the butler ushered in Gregory Brabazon.

Gregory Brabazon, notwithstanding his name, was not a romantic creature. He was a short, very fat man, as bald as an egg except for a ring of black curly hair round his ears and at the back of his neck, with a red, naked face that looked as though it were on the point of breaking out into a violent sweat, quick grey eyes, sensual lips, and a heavy jowl. He was an Englishman and I had sometimes met him at bohemian parties in London. He was very jovial, very hearty, and laughed a great deal, but you didn't have to be a great judge of character to know that his noisy friendliness was merely cover for a very astute man of business. He had been for some years the most successful decorator in London. He had a great booming voice and little fat hands that were wonderfully expressive. With telling gestures, with a spate of excited words he could thrill the imagination of a doubting client so that it was almost impossible to withhold the order he seemed to make it a favour to accept.

The butler came in again with a tray of cocktails.

'We won't wait for Isabel,' said Mrs Bradley as she took one.

'Where is she?' asked Elliott.

'She went to play golf with Larry. She said she might be late.' Elliott turned to me.

'Larry is Laurence Darrell. Isabel is supposed to be engaged to him.'

'I didn't know you drank cocktails, Elliott,' I said.

'I don't,' he answered grimly, as he sipped the one he had taken, 'but in this barbarous land of prohibition what can one do?' He sighed. 'They're beginning to serve them in some houses in Paris. Evil communications corrupt good manners.'

'Stuff and nonsense, Elliott,' said Mrs Bradley.

She said it good-naturedly enough, but with a decision that suggested to me that she was a woman of character, and I suspected from the look she gave him, amused but shrewd, that she had no illusions about him. I wondered what she would make of Gregory Brabazon. I had caught the professional look he gave the room as he came in and the involuntary lifting of his bushy eyebrows. It was indeed an amazing room. The paper on the walls, the cretonne of the curtains and on the up-holstered furniture were of the same pattern; on the walls were oil paintings in massive gold frames that the Bradleys had evidently bought when they were in Rome. Virgins of the school of Raphael, Virgins of the school of Guido Reni, landscapes of the school of Zuccarelli, ruins of the school of Pannini. There were trophies of their sojourn in Peking, blackwood tables too profusely carved, huge cloisonné vases, and there were the purchases they had made in Chile or Peru, obese figures in hard stone and earthenware vases. There was a Chippendale writing-table and a marquetry vitrine. The lamp-shades were of white silk on which some ill-advised artist had painted shepherds and shepherdesses in Watteau costumes. It was hideous and yet, I don't know why, agreeable. It had a homely, lived-in air, and you felt that that incredible jumble had a significance. All those incongruous objects belonged together because they were part of Mrs Bradley's life.

We had finished our cocktails when the door was flung open and a girl came in, followed by a boy.

'Are we late?' she asked. 'I've brought Larry back. Is there anything for him to eat?'

'I expect so,' smiled Mrs Bradley. 'Ring the bell and tell Eugene to put another place.'

'He opened the door for us. I've already told him.'

'This is my daughter Isabel,' said Mrs Bradley, turning to me. 'And this is Laurence Darrell.'

Isabel gave me a rapid handshake and turned impetuously to Gregory Brabazon.

'Are you Mr Brabazon? I've been crazy to meet you. I love what you've done for Clementine Dormer. Isn't this room terrible? I've been trying to get Mamma to do something about it for years and now you're in Chicago it's our chance. Tell me honestly what you think of it.'

I knew that was the last thing Brabazon would do. He gave Mrs Bradley a quick glance, but her impassive face told him nothing. He decided that Isabel was the person who counted and broke into a boisterous laugh.

'I'm sure it's very comfortable and all that,' he said, 'but if you ask me point-blank, well, I do think it's pretty awful.'

21

Isabel was a tall girl with the oval face, straight nose, fine eyes, and full mouth that appeared to be characteristic of the family. She was comely though on the fat side, which I ascribed to her age, and I guessed that she would fine down as she grew older. She had strong, good hands, though they also were a trifle fat, and her legs, displayed by her short skirt, were fat too. She had a good skin and a high colour, which exercise and the drive back in an open car had doubtless heightened. She was sparkling and vivacious. Her radiant health, her playful gaiety, her enjoyment of life, the happiness you felt in her were exhilarating. She was so natural that she made Elliott, for all his elegance, look rather tawdry. Her freshness made Mrs Bradley, with her pasty, lined face, look tired and old.

We went down to lunch. Gregory Brabazon blinked when he saw the dining-room. The walls were papered with a dark red paper that imitated stuff and hung with portraits of grim, sour-faced men and women, very badly painted, who were the immediate forebears of the late Mr Bradley. He was there, too, with a heavy moustache, very stiff in a frock coat and a white starched collar. Mrs Bradley, painted by a French artist of the nineties, hung over the chimney-piece in full evening dress of pale blue satin with pearls around her neck and a diamond star in her hair. With one bejewelled hand she fingered a lace scarf so carefully painted that you could count every stitch and with the other negligently held an ostrich-feather fan. The furniture, of black oak, was overwhelming.

'What do you think of it?' asked Isabel of Gregory Brabazon as we sat down.

'I'm sure it cost a great deal of money,' he answered.

'It did,' said Mrs Bradley. 'It was given to us as a wedding present by Mr Bradley's father. It's been all over the world with us. Lisbon, Peking, Quito, Rome. Dear Queen Margherita admired it very much.'

'What would you do if it was yours?' Isabel asked Brabazon, but before he could answer, Elliott answered for him.

'Burn it,' he said.

The three of them began to discuss how they would treat the room. Elliot was all for Louis Quinze, while Isabel wanted a refectory table and Italian chairs. Brabazon thought Chippendale would be more in keeping with Mrs Bradley's personality.

'I always think that's so important,' he said, 'a person's personality.' He turned to Elliott. 'Of course you know the Duchess of Olifant?'

'Mary? She's one of my most intimate friends.'

'She wanted me to do her dining-room and the moment I saw her I said George the Second.'

'How right you were. I noticed the room the last time I dined there. It's in perfect taste.'

So the conversation went on. Mrs Bradley listened, but you could not tell what she was thinking. I said little, and Isabel's young man, Larry, I'd forgotten his surname, said nothing at all. He was sitting on the other side of the table between Brabazon and Elliott and every now and then I glanced at him. He looked very young. He was about the same height as Elliott, just under six feet, thin and loose-limbed. He was a pleasant-looking boy, neither handsome nor plain, rather shy and in no way remarkable. I was interested in the fact that though, so far as I could remember, he hadn't said half a dozen words since entering the house, he seemed perfectly at ease and in a curious way appeared to take part in the conversation without opening his mouth. I noticed his hands. They were long, but not large for his size, beautifully shaped and at the same time strong. I thought that a painter would be pleased to paint them. He was slightly built but not delicate in appearance; on the contrary I should have said he was wiry and resistant. His face, grave in repose, was tanned, but otherwise there was little colour in it, and his features, though regular enough, were undistinguished. He had rather high cheekbones and his temples were hollow. He had dark brown hair with a slight wave in it. His eyes looked larger than they really were because they were deep set in the orbits and his lashes were thick and long. His eyes were peculiar, not of the rich hazel that Isabel shared with her mother and her uncle, but so dark that the iris made one colour with the pupil, and this gave them a peculiar intensity. He had a natural grace that was attractive and I could see why Isabel had been taken by him. Now and again her glance rested on him for a moment and I seemed to see in her expression not only love but fondness. Their eyes met and there was in his a tenderness that was beautiful to see. There is nothing more touching than the sight of young love, and I, a middle-aged man then, envied them, but at the same time, I couldn't imagine why, I felt sorry for them. It was silly because, so far as I knew, there was no impediment to their happiness; their circumstances seemed easy and there was no reason why they should not marry and live happily ever afterwards.

Isabel, Elliott, and Gregory Brabazon went on talking of the redecoration of the house, trying to get out of Mrs Bradley a least an admission that something should be done, but she only smiled amiably.

'You mustn't try to rush me. I want to have time to think it over.' She turned to the boy. 'What do you think of it all, Larry?'

He looked round the table, a smile in his eyes.

'I don't think it matters one way or the other,' he said.

'You beast, Larry,' cried Isabel. 'I particularly told you to back us up.'

'If Aunt Louisa is happy with what she's got, what is the object of changing?'

His question was so much to the point and so sensible that it made me laugh. He looked at me then and smiled.

'And don't grin like that just because you've made a very stupid remark,' said Isabel.

But he only grinned the more, and I noticed then that he had small and white and regular teeth. There was something in the look he gave Isabel that made her flush and catch her breath. Unless I was mistaken she was madly in love with him, but I don't know what it was that gave me the feeling that in her love for him there was also something maternal. It was a little unexpected in so young a girl. With a soft smile on her lips she directed her attention once more to Gregory Brabazon.

'Don't pay any attention to him. He's very stupid and entirely uneducated. He doesn't know anything about anything except flying.'

'Flying?' I said.

'He was an aviator in the war.'

'I should have thought he was too young to have been in the war.'

24

'He was. Much too young. He behaved very badly. He ran away from school and went to Canada. By lying his head off he got them to believe he was eighteen and got into the air corps. He was fighting in France at the time of the armistice.'

'You're boring your mother's guests, Isabel,' said Larry.

'I've known him all my life, and when he came back he looked lovely in his uniform, with all those pretty ribbons on his tunic, so I just sat on his doorstep, so to speak, till he consented to marry me just to have a little peace and quiet. The competition was awful.'

'Really, Isabel,' said her mother.

Larry leant over towards me.

'I hope you don't believe a word she says. Isabel isn't a bad girl really, but she's a liar.'

Luncheon was finished and soon after Elliott and I left. I had told him before that I was going to the museum to look at the pictures and he said he would take me. I don't particularly like going to a gallery with anyone else, but I could not say I would sooner go alone, so I accepted his company. On our way we spoke of Isabel and Larry.

'It's rather charming to see two young things so much in love with one another,' I said.

'They're much too young to marry.'

'Why? It's such fun to be young and in love and to marry.'

'Don't be ridiculous. She's nineteen and he's only just twenty. He hasn't got a job. He has a tiny income, three thousand a year Louisa tells me, and Louisa's not a rich woman by any manner of means. She needs all she has.'

'Well, he can get a job.'

'That's just it. He's not trying to. He seems to be quite satisfied to do nothing.'

'I dare say he had a pretty rough time in the war. He may want a rest.'

'He's been resting for a year. That's surely long enough.'

'I thought he seemed a nice sort of boy.'

'Oh, I have nothing against him. He's quite well born and all that sort of thing. His father came from Baltimore. He was assistant professor of Romance languages at Yale or something like that. His mother was a Philadelphian of old Quaker stock.'

'You speak of them in the past. Are they dead?'

'Yes, his mother died in childbirth and his father about twelve years ago. He was brought up by an old college friend of his father's who's a doctor at Marvin. That's how Louisa and Isabel knew him.'

'Where's Marvin?'

'That's where the Bradley place is. Louisa spends the summer there. She was sorry for the child. Dr Nelson's a bachelor and didn't know the first thing about bringing up a boy. It was Louisa who insisted that he should be sent to St Paul's and she always had him out here for his Christmas vacation.' Elliott shrugged a Gallic shoulder. 'I should have thought she would foresee the inevitable result.'

We had now arrived at the museum and our attention was directed to the pictures. Once more I was impressed by Elliott's knowledge and taste. He shepherded me around the rooms as though I were a group of tourists, and no professor of art could have discoursed more instructively than he did. Making up my mind to come again by myself when I could wander at will and have a good time, I submitted; after a while he looked at his watch.

'Let us go,' he said. 'I never spend more than one hour in a gallery. That is as long as one's power of appreciation persists. We will finish another day.'

I thanked him warmly when we separated. I went my way perhaps a wiser but certainly a peevish man.

When I was saying good-bye to Mrs Bradley she told me that next day Isabel was having a few of her young friends in to dinner and they were going on to dance afterwards, and if I would come Elliott and I could have a talk when they had gone.

'You'll be doing him a kindness,' she added. 'He's been abroad so long, he feels rather out of it here. He doesn't seem able to find anyone he has anything in common with.'

I accepted and before we parted on the museum steps Elliott told me he was glad I had.

'I'm like a lost soul in this great city,' he said. 'I promised Louisa to spend six weeks with her, we hadn't seen one another since 1912, but I'm counting the days till I can get back to Paris. It's the only place in the world for a civilized man to live. My dear fellow, d'you know how they look upon me here? They look upon me as a freak. Savages.'

I laughed and left.

<h1 style="text-align:center">6</h1>

The following evening, having refused Elliott's telephoned offer to fetch me, I arrived quite safely at Mrs Bradley's house. I had been delayed by someone who had come to see me and was a trifle late. So much noise came from the sitting-room as I walked upstairs that I thought it must be a large party and I was surprised to find that there were, including myself, only twelve people. Mrs Bradley was very grand in green satin with a dog-collar of seed pearls round her neck, and Elliott in his well-cut dinner jacket looked elegant as he alone could look. When he shook hands with me my nostrils were assailed by all the perfumes of Arabia. I was introduced to a stoutish, tall man with a red face who looked somewhat ill at ease in evening clothes. He was a Dr Nelson, but at the moment that meant nothing to me. The rest of the party consisted of Isabel's friends, but their names escaped me as soon as I heard them. The girls were young and pretty and the men young and upstanding. None of them made any impression on me except one boy and that only because he was so tall and so massive. He must have been six foot three or four and he had great broad shoulders. Isabel was looking very pretty; she was dressed in white silk, with a long, hobbled skirt that concealed her fat legs; the cut of her frock showed that she had well-developed breasts; her bare arms were a trifle fat, but her neck was lovely. She was excited and her fine eyes sparkled. There was no doubt about it, she was a very pretty and desirable young woman, but it was obvious that unless she took care she would develop an unbecoming corpulence.

At dinner I found myself placed between Mrs Bradley and a shy drab girl who seemed even younger than the others. As we sat down, to make the way easier Mrs Bradley explained that her grandparents lived at Marvin and that she and Isabel had been at school together. Her name, the only one I heard mentioned, was Sophie. A lot of chaff was bandied across the table, everyone talked at the top of his voice and there was a great deal of laughter. They seemed to know one another very well. When I was not occupied with my hostess I attempted to make conversation with my neighbour, but I had no great success. She was quieter than the rest. She was not pretty, but she had an amusing face, with a little tilted nose, a wide mouth, and greenish blue eyes; her hair, simply done, was of a sandy brown. She was very thin and her chest was almost as flat as a boy's. She laughed at the badinage that went on, but in a manner that was a little forced so that you felt she wasn't as much amused as she pretended to be. I guessed that she was making an effort to be a good sport. I could not make out if she was a trifle stupid or only painfully timid and, having tried various topics of conversation only to have them dropped, for want of anything better to say I asked her to tell me who all the people at table were.

'Well, you know Dr Nelson,' she said, indicating the middle-aged man who was opposite me on Mrs Bradley's other side. 'He's Larry's guardian. He's our doctor at Marvin. He's very clever, he invents gadgets for planes that no one will have anything to do with, and when he isn't doing that he drinks.'

There was a gleam in her pale eyes as she said this that made me suspect that there was more in her than I had at first supposed. She went on to give me the names of one young thing after another, telling me who their parents were, and in the case of the men what college they had been to and what work they did. It wasn't very illuminating.

'She's very sweet,' or: 'He's a very good golfer.'

'And who is that big fellow with the eyebrows?'

'That? Oh, that's Gray Maturin. His father's got an enormous house on the river at Marvin. He's our millionaire. We're very proud of him. He gives us class. Maturin, Hobbes, Rayner, and Smith. He's one of the richest men in Chicago and Gray's his only son.'

She put such a pleasant irony into that list of names that I gave her an inquisitive glance. She caught it and flushed.

'Tell me more about Mr Maturin.'

'There's nothing to tell. He's rich. He's highly respected. He built us a new church at Marvin and he's given a million dollars to the University of Chicago.'

28

'His son's a fine-looking fellow.'

'He's nice. You'd never think his grandfather was shanty Irish and his grandmother a Swedish waitress in an eating house.'

Gray Maturin was striking rather than handsome. He had a rugged, unfinished look; a short blunt nose, a sensual mouth, and the florid Irish complexion; a great quantity of raven black hair, very sleek, and under heavy eyebrows clear, very blue eyes. Though built on so large a scale he was finely proportioned, and stripped he must have been a fine figure of a man. He was obviously very powerful. His virility was impressive. He made Larry who was sitting next to him, though only three or four inches shorter, look puny.

'He's very much admired,' said my shy neighbour. 'I know several girls who would stop at nothing short of murder to get him. But they haven't a chance.'

'Why not?'

'You don't know anything, do you?'

'How should I?'

'He's so much in love with Isabel, he can't see straight, and Isabel's in love with Larry.'

'What's to prevent him from setting to and cutting Larry out?'

'Larry's his best friend.'

'I suppose that complicates matters.'

'If you're as high-principled as Gray is.'

I was not sure whether she said this in all seriousness or whether there was in her tone a hint of mockery. There was nothing saucy in her manner, forward or pert, and yet I got the impression that she was lacking neither in humour nor in shrewdness. I wondered what she was really thinking while she made conversation with me, but that I knew I should never find out. She was obviously unsure of herself and I conceived the notion that she was an only child who had lived a secluded life with people a great deal older than herself. There was a modesty, an unobtrusiveness about her that I found engaging, but if I was right in thinking that she had lived much alone I guessed that she had quietly observed the older persons she lived with and had formed decided opinions upon them. We who are of mature age seldom suspect how unmercifully and yet with what insight the very young judge us. I looked again into her greenish blue eyes.

'How old are you?' I asked.

'Seventeen.'

'Do you read much?' I asked at a venture.

But before she could answer, Mrs Bradley, attentive to her duties as a hostess, drew me to her with some remark and before I could disengage myself dinner was at an end. The young people went off at once to wherever they were going and the four of us who were left went up to the sitting-room.

I was surprised that I had been asked to this party, for after a little desultory conversation they began to talk of a matter that I should have thought they would have preferred to discuss in private. I could not make up my mind whether it would be more discreet in me to get up and go or whether, as a disinterested audience of one, I was useful to them. The question at issue was Larry's odd disinclination to go to work, and it had been brought to a point by an offer from Mr Maturin, the father of the boy who had been at dinner, to take him into his office. It was a fine opportunity. With ability and industry Larry could look forward to making in due course a great deal of money. Young Gray Maturin was eager for him to take it.

I cannot remember all that was said, but the gist of it is clear in my memory. On Larry's return from France Dr Nelson, his guardian, had suggested that he should go to college, but he had refused. It was natural that he should want to do nothing for a while; he had had a hard time and had been twice, though not severely, wounded. Dr Nelson thought that he was still suffering from shock and it seemed a good idea that he should rest till he had completely recovered. But the weeks passed into months and now it was over a year since he'd been out of uniform. It appeared that he had done well in the air corps and on his return he cut something of a figure in Chicago, the result of which was that several business men offered him positions. He thanked them, but refused. He gave no reason except that he hadn't made up his mind what he wanted to do. He became engaged to Isabel. This was no surprise to Mrs Bradley since they had been inseparable for years and she knew that Isabel was in love with him. She was fond of him and thought he would make Isabel happy.

'Her character's stronger than his. She can give him just what he lacks.'

Though they were both so young Mrs Bradley was quite willing that they should marry at once, but she wasn't prepared for them to do so until Larry had gone to work. He had a little money of his own, but even if he had had ten times more than he had she would have insisted on this. So far as I could gather, what she and Elliott wished to find out from Dr Nelson was what Larry intended to do. They wanted him to use his influence to get him to accept the job that Mr Maturin offered him.

'You know I never had much authority over Larry,' he said. 'Even as a boy he went his own way.'

'I know. You let him run wild. It's a miracle he's turned out as well as he has.'

Dr Nelson, who had been drinking quite heavily, gave her a sour look. His red face grew a trifle redder.

'I was very busy. I had my own affairs to attend to. I took him because there was nowhere else for him to go and his father was a friend of mine. He wasn't easy to do anything with.'

'I don't know how you can say that,' Mrs Bradley answered tartly. 'He has a very sweet disposition.'

'What are you to do with a boy who never argues with you, but does exactly what he likes and when you get mad at him just says he's sorry and lets you storm? If he'd been my own son I could have beaten him. I couldn't beat a boy who hadn't got a relation in the world and whose father had left him to me because he thought I'd be kind to him.'

'That's neither here nor there,' said Elliott, somewhat irritably. 'The position is this: he's dawdled around long enough; he's got a fine chance of a position in which he stands to make a lot of money, and if he wants to marry Isabel he must take it.'

'He must see that in the present state of the world', Mrs Bradley put in, 'a man has to work. He's perfectly strong and well now. We all know how after the war between the States, there were men who never did a stroke after they came back

31

from it. They were a burden to their families and useless to the community.'

Then I added my word.

'But what reason does he give for refusing the various offers that are made him?'

'None. Except that they don't appeal to him.'

'But doesn't he want to do anything?'

'Apparently not.'

Dr Nelson helped himself to another highball. He took a long drink and then looked at his two friends.

'Shall I tell you what my impression is? I dare say I'm not a great judge of human nature, but at any rate after thirty-odd years of practice I think I know something about it. The war did something to Larry. He didn't come back the same person that he went. It's not only that he's older. Something happened that changed his personality.'

'What sort of thing?' I asked.

'I wouldn't know. He's very reticent about his war experiences.' Dr Nelson turned to Mrs Bradley. 'Has he ever talked to you about them, Louisa?'

She shook her head.

'No. When he first came back we tried to get him to tell us some of his adventures, but he only laughed in that way of his and said there was nothing to tell. He hasn't even told Isabel. She's tried and tried, but she hasn't got a thing out of him.'

The conversation went on in this unsatisfactory way and presently Dr Nelson, looking at his watch, said he must go. I prepared to leave with him, but Elliott pressed me to stay. When he had gone, Mrs Bradley apologized for troubling me with their private affairs and expressed her fear that I had been bored.

'But you see it's all very much on my mind,' she finished.

'Mr Maugham is very discreet, Louisa; you needn't be afraid of telling him anything. I haven't the feeling that Bob Nelson and Larry are very close, but there are some things that Louisa and I thought we'd better not mention to him.'

'Elliott.'

'You've told him so much, you may as well tell him the rest. I don't know whether you noticed Gray Maturin at dinner?'

'He's so big, one could hardly fail to.'

'He's a beau of Isabel's. All the time Larry was away he was very attentive. She likes him, and if the war had lasted much longer she might very well have married him. He proposed to her. She didn't accept and she didn't refuse. Louisa guessed she didn't want to make up her mind till Larry came home.'

'How is it that he wasn't in the war?' I asked.

'He strained his heart playing football. It's nothing serious, but the army wouldn't take him. Anyhow when Larry came home he had no chance. Isabel turned him down flat.'

I didn't know what I was expected to say to that, so I said nothing. Elliott went on. With his distinguished appearance and his Oxford accent he couldn't have been more like an official of high standing at the Foreign Office.

'Of course Larry's a very nice boy and it was damned sporting of him to run away and join the air corps, but I'm a pretty good judge of character. . . .' He gave a knowing little smile and made the only reference I ever heard him make to the fact that he had made a fortune by dealing in works of art. 'Otherwise I shouldn't have at this moment a tidy sum in gilt-edged securities. And my opinion is that Larry will never amount to very much. He has no money to speak of and no standing. Gray Maturin is a very different proposition. He has a good old Irish name. They've had a bishop in the family, and a dramatist and several distinguished soldiers and scholars.'

'How do you know all that?' I asked.

'It's the sort of thing one knows,' he answered casually. 'As a matter of fact I happened to be glancing through the *Dictionary of National Biography* the other day at the club and I came across the name.'

I didn't think it was my business to repeat what my neighbour at dinner had told me of the shanty Irishman and the Swedish waitress who were Gray's grandfather and grandmother. Elliott proceeded.

'We've all known Henry Maturin for many years. He's a very fine man and a very rich one. Gray's stepping into the best brokerage house in Chicago. He's got the world at his feet. He wants to marry Isabel and one can't deny that from her point of view it would be a very good match. I'm all in favour of it myself and I know Louisa is too.'

'You've been away from America so long, Elliott,' said Mrs Bradley, with a dry smile, 'you've forgotten that in this country girls don't marry because their mothers and their uncles are in favour of it.'

'That is nothing to be proud of, Louisa,' said Elliott sharply. 'As the result of thirty years' experience I may tell you that a marriage arranged with proper regard to position, fortune, and community of circumstances has every advantage over a love match. In France, which after all is the only civilized country in the world, Isabel would marry Gray without thinking twice about it; then, after a year or two, if she wanted it, she'd take Larry as her lover, Gray would install a prominent actress in a luxurious apartment, and everyone would be perfectly happy.'

Mrs Bradley was no fool. She looked at her brother with sly amusement.

'The objection to that, Elliott, is that as the New York plays only come here for limited periods, Gray could only hope to keep the tenants of his luxurious apartment for a very uncertain length of time. That would surely be very unsettling for all parties.'

Elliott smiled.

'Gray could buy a seat on the New York stock exchange. After all, if you must live in America I can't see any object in living anywhere but in New York.'

I left soon after this, but before I did Elliott, I hardly know why, asked me if I would lunch with him to meet the Maturins, father and son.

'Henry is the best type of the American businessman,' he said, 'and I think you ought to know him. He's looked after our investments for many years.'

I hadn't any particular wish to do this, but no reason to refuse, so I said I would be glad to.

7

I had been put up for the length of my stay at a club which possessed a good library, and next morning I went there to look at one or two of the university magazines that for the person who does not subscribe to them have always been rather hard to come by. It was early and there was only one other person there. He was seated in a big leather chair absorbed in a book. I was surprised to see it was Larry. He was the last person I should have expected to find in such a place. He looked up as I passed, recognized me and made as if to get up.

'Don't move,' I said, and then almost automatically: 'What are you reading?'

'A book,' he said, with a smile, but a smile so engaging that the rebuff of his answer was in no way offensive.

He closed it and looking at me with his peculiarly opaque eyes held it so that I couldn't see the title.

'Did you have a good time last night?' I asked.

'Wonderful. Didn't get home till five.'

'It's very strenuous of you to be here so bright and early.'

'I come here a good deal. Generally I have the place to myself at this time.'

'I won't disturb you.'

'You're not disturbing me,' he said, smiling again, and now it occurred to me that he had a smile of great sweetness. It was not a brilliant, flashing smile, it was a smile that lit his face as with an inner light. He was sitting in an alcove made by jutting out shelves and there was a chair next to him. He put his hand on the arm. 'Won't you sit down for a minute?'

'All right.'

He handed me the book he was holding.

'That's what I was reading.'

I looked at it and saw it was William James's *Principles of Psychology*. It is, of course, a standard work and important in the history of the science with which it deals; it is moreover exceedingly readable; but it is not the sort of book I should have expected to see in the hands of a very young man, an aviator, who had been dancing till five in the morning.

'Why are you reading this?' I asked.

'I'm very ignorant.'

'You're also very young,' I smiled.

He did not speak for so long a time that I began to find the silence awkward and I was on the point of getting up and looking for the magazines I had come to find. But I had a feeling that he wanted to say something. He looked into vacancy,

35

his face grave and intent, and seemed to meditate. I waited. I was curious to know what it was all about. When he began to speak it was as though he were continuing the conversation without awareness of that long silence.

'When I came back from France they all wanted me to go to college. I couldn't. After what I'd been through I felt I couldn't go back to school. I learnt nothing at my prep school anyway. I felt I couldn't enter into a freshman's life. They wouldn't have liked me. I didn't want to act a part I didn't feel. And I didn't think the instructors would teach me the sort of things I wanted to know.'

'Of course I know this is no business of mine,' I answered, 'but I'm not convinced you were right. I think I understand what you mean and I can see that, after being in the war for two years, it would have been rather a nuisance to become the sort of glorified schoolboy an undergraduate is during his first and second years. I can't believe they wouldn't have liked you. I don't know much about American universities, but I don't believe American undergraduates are very different from English ones, perhaps a little more boisterous and a little more inclined to horse-play, but on the whole very decent, sensible boys, and I take it that if you don't want to lead their lives they're quite willing, if you exercise a little tact, to let you lead yours. I never went to Cambridge as my brothers did. I had the chance, but I refused it. I wanted to get out into the world. I've always regretted it. I think it would have saved me a lot of mistakes. You learn more quickly under the guidance of experienced teachers. You waste a lot of time going down blind alleys if you have no one to lead you.'

'You may be right. I don't mind if I make mistakes. It may be that in one of the blind alleys I may find something to my purpose.'

'What is your purpose?'

He hesitated a moment.

'That's just it. I don't quite know it yet.'

I was silent, for there didn't seem to be anything to say in answer to that. I, who from a very early age have always had before me a clear and definite purpose, was inclined to feel impatient, but I chid myself; I had what I can only call an intuition that there was in the soul of that boy some confused striving, whether of half-thought-out ideas or of dimly felt emotions I could not tell, which filled him with a restlessness that urged him he did not know whither. He strangely excited my sympathy. I had never before heard him speak much and it was only now that I became conscious of the melodiousness of his voice. It was very persuasive. It was like balm. When I considered that, his engaging smile, and the expressiveness of his very black eyes I could well understand that Isabel was in love with him. There was indeed something very lovable about him. He turned his head and looked at me without embarrassment, but with an expression in his eyes that was at once scrutinizing and amused.

'Am I right in thinking that after we all went off to dance last night you talked about me?'

'Part of the time.'

'I thought that was why Uncle Bob had been pressed to come to dinner. He hates going out.'

'It appears that you've got the offer of a very good job.'

'A wonderful job.'

'Are you going to take it?'

'I don't think so.'

'Why not?'

'I don't want to.'

I was butting into an affair that was no concern of mine, but I had a notion that just because I was a stranger from a foreign country Larry was not disinclined to talk to me about it.

'Well, you know when people are no good at anything else they become writers,' I said, with a chuckle.

'I have no talent.'

'Then what do you want to do?'

He gave me his radiant, fascinating smile.

'Loaf,' he said.

I had to laugh.

'I shouldn't have thought Chicago the best place in the world to do that in,' I said. 'Anyhow, I'll leave you to your reading. I want to have a look at the *Yale Quarterly*.'

I got up. When I left the library Larry was still absorbed in William James's book. I lunched by myself at the club and since it was quiet in the library went back there to smoke my cigar and idle an hour or two away, reading and writing letters. I was surprised to see Larry still immersed in his book. He looked as if he hadn't moved since I left him. He was still there when about four I went away. I was struck by his evident power of concentration. He had neither noticed me go nor come. I had various things to do during the afternoon and did not go back to the Blackstone till it was time to change for the dinner party I was going to. On my way I was seized with an impulse of curiosity. I dropped into the club once more and went into the library. There were quite a number of people there then, reading the papers and what not. Larry was still sitting in the same chair, intent on the same book. Odd!

8

Next day Elliott asked me to lunch at the Palmer House to meet the elder Maturin and his son. We were only four. Henry Maturin was a big man, nearly as big as his son, with a red fleshy face and a great jowl, and he had the same blunt aggressive nose, but his eyes were smaller than his son's, not so blue and very, very shrewd. Though he could not have been much more than fifty he looked ten years older and his hair, rapidly thinning, was snow-white. At first sight he was not preposessing. He looked as though for many years he had done himself too well, and I received the impression of a brutal, clever, competent man who, in business matters at all events, would be pitiless. At first he said little and I had a notion that he was taking my measure. I could not but perceive that he looked upon Elliott as something of a joke. Gray, amiable and polite, was almost completely silent, and the party would have been sticky if Elliott, with his perfect social tact, hadn't kept up a flow of easy conversation. I guessed that in the past he had acquired a good deal of experience in dealing with Middle Western businessmen who had to be cajoled into paying a fancy price for an old master. Presently Mr Maturin began to feel more at his ease and he made one or two remarks that showed he was brighter than he looked and indeed had a dry sense of humour. For a while the conversation turned on stocks and shares. I should have been surprised to discover that Elliott was very knowledgeable on the subject if I had not long been aware that for all his nonsense he was nobody's fool. It was then that Mr Maturin remarked:

'I had a letter from Gray's friend Larry Darrell this morning.'

'You didn't tell me, Dad,' said Gray.

Mr Maturin turned to me.

'You know Larry, don't you?' I nodded. 'Gray persuaded me to take him into my business. They're great friends. Gray thinks the world of him.'

'What did he say, Dad?'

'He thanked me. He said he realized it was a great chance for a young fellow and he'd thought it over very carefully and come to the conclusion he'd have been a disappointment to me and thought it better to refuse.'

'That's very foolish of him,' said Elliott.

'It is,' said Mr Maturin.

'I'm awfully sorry, Dad,' said Gray. 'It would have been grand if we could have worked together.'

'You can lead a horse to the water, but you can't make him drink.'

Mr Maturin looked at his son while he said this and his shrewd eyes softened. I realized that there was another side to the hard businessman; he doted on this great hulking son of his. He turned to me once more.

'D'you know, that boy did our course in two under par on Sunday. He beat me seven and six. I could have brained him with my niblick. And to think that I taught him to play golf myself.'

He was brimming over with pride. I began to like him.

'I had a lot of luck, Dad.'

'Not a bit of it. Is it luck when you get out of a bunker and lay your ball six inches from the hole? Thirty-five yards if it was an inch, the shot was. I want him to go into the amateur championship next year.'

'I shouldn't be able to spare the time.'

'I'm your boss, ain't I?'

'Don't I know it! The hell you raise if I'm a minute late at the office.'

Mr Maturin chuckled.

'He's trying to make me out a tyrant,' he said to me. 'Don't you believe him. I'm my business, my partners are no good, and I'm very proud of my business. I've started this boy of mine at the bottom and I expect him to work his way up just like any young fellow I've hired, so that when the time comes for him to take my place he'll be ready for it. It's a great responsibility, a business like mine. I've looked after the investments of some of my clients for thirty years and they trust me. To tell you the truth, I'd rather lose my own money than see them lose theirs.'

Gray laughed.

'The other day when an old girl came in and wanted to invest a thousand dollars in a wildcat scheme that her minister had recommended he refused to take the order, and when she insisted he gave her such hell that she went out sobbing. And then he called up the minister and gave him hell too.'

'People say a lot of hard things about us brokers, but there are brokers and brokers. I don't want people to lose money, I want them to make it, and the way they act, most of them, you'd think their one object in life was to get rid of every cent they have.'

'Well, what did you think of him?' Elliott asked me as we walked away after the Maturins had left us to go back to the office.

'I'm always glad to meet new types. I thought the mutual affection of father and son was rather touching. I don't know that that's so common in England.'

'He adores that boy. He's a queer mixture. What he said about his clients was quite true. He's got hundreds of old women, retired service men, and ministers whose savings he looks after. I'd have thought they were more trouble than they're worth, but he takes pride in the confidence they have in him. But when he's got some big deal on and he's up against powerful interests there isn't a man who can be harder and more ruthless. There's no mercy in him then. He wants his pound of flesh and there's nothing much he'll stop at to get it. Get on the wrong side of him and he'll not only ruin you, but get a big laugh out of doing it.'

On getting home Elliott told Mrs Bradley that Larry had refused Henry Maturin's offer. Isabel had been lunching with girl friends and came in while they were still talking about it. They told her. I gathered from Elliott's account of the conversation that ensued that he had expressed himself with considerable eloquence. Though he had certainly not done a stroke of work for ten years, and the work by which he had amassed an ample competence had been far from arduous, he was firmly of opinion that for the run of mankind industry was essential. Larry was a perfectly ordinary young fellow, of no social consequence, and there was no possible reason why he shouldn't conform to the commendable customs of his country. It was evident to a man as clear-sighted as Elliott that America was entering upon a period of prosperity such as it had never known. Larry had a chance of getting in on the ground floor, and if he kept his nose to the grindstone he might well be many times a millionaire by the time he was forty. If he wanted to retire then and live like a gentleman, in Paris, say, with an apartment in the Avenue du Bois and a château in Touraine, he (Elliott) would have nothing to say against it. But Louisa Bradley was more succinct and more unanswerable.

'If he loves you, he ought to be prepared to work for you.'

I don't know what Isabel answered to all this, but she was sensible enough to see that her elders had reason on their side. All the young men of her acquaintance were studying to enter some profession or already busy in an office. Larry could hardly expect to live the rest of his life on his distinguished record in the air corps. The war was over, everyone was sick of it and anxious only to forget about it as quickly as possible. The result of the discussion was that Isabel agreed to have the matter out with Larry once and for all. Mrs Bradley suggested that Isabel should ask him to drive her down to Marvin. She was ordering new curtains for the living-room and had mislaid the measurements, so she wanted Isabel to take them again.

'Bob Nelson will give you luncheon,' she said.

'I have a better plan than that,' said Elliott. 'Put up a luncheon basket for them and let them lunch on the stoop and after lunch they can talk.'

'That would be fun,' said Isabel.

'There are few things so pleasant as a picnic lunch eaten in perfect comfort,' Elliott added sententiously. 'The old Duchesse d'Uzès used to tell me that the most recalcitrant male becomes amenable to suggestion in these conditions. What will you give them for luncheon?'

'Stuffed eggs and a chicken sandwich.'

'Nonsense. You can't have a picnic without *pâté de foie gras*. You must give them curried shrimps to start with, breast of chicken in aspic, with a heart-of-lettuce salad for which I'll make the dressing myself, and after the *pâté* if you like, as a concession to your American habits, an apple pie.'

'I shall give them stuffed eggs and a chicken sandwich, Elliott,' said Mrs Bradley with decision.

'Well, mark my words, it'll be a failure and you'll only have yourself to blame.'

'Larry eats very little, Uncle Elliott,' said Isabel, 'and I don't believe he notices what he eats.'

'I hope you don't think that is to his credit, my poor child,' her uncle returned.

But what Mrs Bradley said they should have was what they got. When Elliott later told me the outcome of the excursion he shrugged his shoulders in a very French way.

'I told them it would be a failure. I begged Louisa to put in a bottle of the Montrachet I sent her just before the war, but she wouldn't listen to me. They took a thermos of hot coffee and nothing else. What would you expect?'

It appeared that Louisa Bradley and Elliott were sitting by themselves in the living-room when they heard the car stop at the door and Isabel came into the house. It was just after dark and the curtains were drawn. Elliott was lounging in an arm-chair by the fireside reading a novel and Mrs Bradley was at work on a piece of tapestry that was to be made into a fire-screen. Isabel did not come in, but went on up to her room. Elliott looked over his spectacles at his sister.

'I expect she's gone to take off her hat. She'll be down in a minute,' she said.

But Isabel did not come. Several minutes passed.

'Perhaps she's tired. She may be lying down.'

'Wouldn't you have expected Larry to have come in?'

'Don't be exasperating, Elliott.'

'Well, it's your business, not mine.'

He returned to his book. Mrs Bradley went on working. But when half an hour had gone by she got up suddenly.

'I think perhaps I'd better go up and see that she's all right. If she's resting I won't disturb her.'

She left the room, but in a very short while came down again.

'She's been crying. Larry's going to Paris. He's going to be away for two years. She's promised to wait for him.'

'Why does he want to go to Paris?'

'It's no good asking me questions, Elliott. I don't know. She won't tell me anything. She says she understands and she isn't going to stand in his way. I said to her, "If he's prepared to leave you for two years he can't love you very much." "I can't help that," she said, "the thing that matters is that I love *him* very much." "Even after what's happened today?" I said. "Today's made me love him more than ever I did," she said, "and he does love me, Mamma. I'm sure of that."'

Elliott reflected for a while.

'And what's to happen at the end of two years?'

'I tell you I don't know, Elliott.'

'Don't you think it's very unsatisfactory?'

'Very.'

'There's only one thing to be said and that is that they're both very young. It won't hurt them to wait two years and in that time a lot may happen.'

They agreed that it would be better to leave Isabel in peace. They were going out to dinner that night.

'I don't want to upset her,' said Mrs Bradley. 'People would only wonder if her eyes were all swollen.'

But next day after luncheon, which they had by themselves, Mrs Bradley brought the subject up again. But she got little out of Isabel.

'There's really nothing more to tell you than I've told you already, Mamma,' she said.

'But what does he want to do in Paris?'

Isabel smiled, for she knew how preposterous her answer would seem to her mother.

'Loaf.'

'Loaf? What on earth do you mean?'

'That's what he told me.'

'Really I have no patience with you. If you had any spirit you'd have broken off your engagement there and then. He's just playing with you.'

Isabel looked at the ring she wore on her left hand.

'What can I do? I love him.'

Then Elliott entered the conversation. He approached the matter with his famous tact, 'Not as if I was her uncle, my dear fellow, but as a man of the world speaking to an inexperienced girl,' but he did no better than her mother had done. I received the impression that she had told him, no doubt politely but quite unmistakably, to mind his own business. Elliott told me all this later on in the day in the little sitting-room I had at the Blackstone.

'Of course Louisa is quite right,' he added. 'It's all very unsatisfactory, but that's the sort of thing you run up against when young people are left to arrange their marriages on no better basis than mutual inclination. I've told Louisa not to worry; I think it'll turn out better than she expects. With Larry out of the way and young Gray Maturin on the spot – well, if I know anything about my fellow-creatures the outcome is fairly obvious. When you're eighteen your emotions are violent, but they're not durable.'

'You're full of worldly wisdom, Elliott,' I smiled.

'I haven't read my La Rochefoucauld for nothing. You know what Chicago is; they'll be meeting all the time. It flatters a girl to have a man so devoted to her, and when she knows there isn't one of her girl friends who wouldn't be only too glad to marry him – well, I ask you, is it in human nature to resist the temptation of cutting out everyone else? I mean it's like going to a party where you know you'll be bored to distraction and the only refreshments will be lemonade and biscuits; but you go because you know your best friends would give their eye-teeth to and haven't been asked.'

'When does Larry go?'

'I don't know. I don't think that's been decided yet.' Elliott took a long, thin cigarette case in platinum and gold out of his pocket and extracted an Egyptian cigarette. Not for him were

Fatimas, Chesterfields, Camels, or Lucky Strikes. He looked at me with a smile full of insinuation. 'Of course I wouldn't care to say so to Louisa, but I don't mind telling you that I have a sneaking sympathy for the young fellow. I understand that he got a glimpse of Paris during the war, and I can't blame him if he was captivated by the only city in the world fit for a civilized man to live in. He's young and I have no doubt he wants to sow his wild oats before he settles down to married life. Very natural and very proper. I'll keep an eye on him. I'll introduce him to the right people; he has nice manners and with a hint or two from me he'll be quite presentable; I can guarantee to show him a side of French life that very few Americans have a chance of seeing. Believe me, my dear fellow, the average American can get into the kingdom of heaven much more easily than he can get into the Boulevard St Germain. He's twenty and he has charm. I think I could probably arrange a liaison for him with an older woman. It would form him. I always think there's no better education for a young man than to become the lover of a woman of a certain age and of course if she is the sort of person I have in view, a *femme du monde*, you know, it would immediately give him a situation in Paris.'

'Did you tell that to Mrs Bradley?' I asked, smiling.

Elliott chuckled.

'My dear fellow, if there's one thing I pride myself on it's my tact. I did not tell her. She wouldn't understand, poor dear. It's one of the things I've never understood about Louisa; though she's lived half her life in diplomatic society, in half the capitals of the world, she's remained hopelessly American.'

9

That evening I went to dine at a great stone house on Lake Shore Drive which looked as though the architect had started to build a medieval castle and then, changing his mind in the middle, had decided to turn it into a Swiss chalet. It was a huge party and I was glad when I got into the vast and sumptuous drawing-room, all statues, palms, chandeliers, old masters, and overstuffed furniture, to see that there were at least a few people I knew. I was introduced by Henry Maturin to his thin, raddled, frail wife. I said how d'you do to Mrs Bradley and

Isabel. Isabel was looking very pretty in a red silk dress that suited her dark hair and rich hazel eyes. She appeared to be in high spirits and no one could have guessed that she had so recently gone through a harassing experience. She was talking gaily to the two or three young men, Gray among them, who surrounded her. She sat at dinner at another table and I could not see her, but afterwards, when we men, after lingering interminably over our coffee, liqueurs, and cigars, returned to the drawing-room, I had a chance to speak to her. I knew her too little to say anything directly about what Elliott had told me, but I had something to say that I thought she might be glad to hear.

'I saw your young man the other day in the club,' I remarked casually.

'Oh, did you?'

She spoke as casually as I had, but I perceived that she was instantly alert. Her eyes grew watchful and I thought I read in them something like apprehension.

'He was reading in the library. I was very much impressed by his power of concentration. He was reading when I went in soon after ten, he was still reading when I went back after lunch, and he was reading when I went in again on my way out to dinner. I don't believe he'd moved from his chair for the best part of ten hours.'

'What was he reading?'

'William James's *Principles of Psychology*.'

She looked down so that I had no means of knowing how what I had said affected her, but I had a notion that she was at once puzzled and relieved. I was at that moment fetched by my host who wanted me to play bridge and by the time the game broke up Isabel and her mother had gone.

10

A couple of days later I went to say good-bye to Mrs Bradley and Elliott. I found them sitting over a cup of tea. Isabel came in shortly after me. We talked about my approaching journey, I thanked them for their kindness to me during my stay in Chicago and after a decent interval got up to go.

'I'll walk with you as far as the drugstore,' said Isabel. 'I've just remembered there's something I want to get.'

The last words Mrs Bradley said to me were, 'You will give my love to dear Queen Margherita the next time you see her, won't you?'

I had given up disclaiming any acquaintance with that august lady and answered glibly that I would be sure to.

When we got into the street Isabel gave me a sidelong smiling glance.

'D'you think you could drink an ice-cream soda?' she asked me.

'I could try,' I answered prudently.

Isabel did not speak till we reached the drugstore, and I, having nothing to say, said nothing. We went in and sat at a table on chairs with twisted wire backs and twisted wire legs. They were very uncomfortable. I ordered two ice-cream sodas. There were a few people at the counters buying; two or three couples were seated at other tables, but they were busy with their own concerns; and to all intents and purposes we were alone. I lit a cigarette and waited while Isabel with every appearance of satisfaction sucked at a long straw. I had a notion that she was nervous.

'I wanted to talk to you,' she said abruptly.

'I gathered that,' I smiled.

For a moment or two she looked at me reflectively.

'Why did you say that about Larry at the Satterthwaites' the night before last?'

'I thought it would interest you. It occurred to me that perhaps you didn't quite know what his idea of loafing was.'

'Uncle Elliott's a terrible gossip. When he said he was going to the Blackstone to have a chat with you I knew he was going to tell you all about everything.'

'I've known him a good many years, you know. He gets a lot of fun out of talking about other people's business.'

'He does,' she smiled. But it was only a gleam. She looked at me steadily and her eyes were serious. 'What do you think of Larry?'

'I've only seen him three times. He seems a very nice boy.'

'Is that all?'

There was a note of distress in her voice.

'No, not quite. It's hard for me to say; you see, I know him

47

so little. Of course, he's attractive. There's something modest and friendly and gentle in him that is very appealing. He's got a lot of self-possession for so young a man. He isn't quite like any of the other boys I've met here.'

While I was thus fumblingly trying to put into words an impression that was not distinct in my own mind, Isabel looked at me intently. When I had finished she gave a little sigh, as if of relief, and then flashed a charming, almost roguish smile at me.

'Uncle Elliott says he's often been surprised at your power of observation. He says nothing much escapes you, but that your great asset as a writer is your common sense.'

'I can think of a quality that would be more valuable,' I answered dryly. 'Talent, for instance.'

'You know, I have no one to talk this over with. Mamma can only see things from her own point of view. She wants my future to be assured.'

'That's natural, isn't it?'

'And Uncle Elliott only looks at it from the social side. My own friends, those of my generation, I mean, think Larry's a washout. It hurts terribly.'

'Of course.'

'It's not that they're not nice to him. One can't help being nice to Larry. But they look upon him as a joke. They josh him a lot and it exasperates them that he doesn't seem to care. He only laughs. You know how things are at present?'

'I only know what Elliott has told me.'

'May I tell you exactly what happened when we went down to Marvin?'

'Of course.'

I have reconstructed Isabel's account partly from my recollection of what she then said to me and partly with the help of my imagination. But it was a long talk that she and Larry had, and I have no doubt that they said a great deal more than I now propose to relate. I suspect that as people do on these occasions they not only said much that was irrelevant, but said the same things over and over again.

When Isabel awoke and saw that it was a fine day she gave Larry a ring and, telling him that her mother wanted her to go to Marvin to do something for her, asked him to drive her down. She took the precaution to add a thermos of martinis to the thermos of coffee her mother had told Eugene to put in the basket. Larry's roadster was a recent acquisition and he was proud of it. He was a fast driver and the speed at which he went exhilarated them both. When they arrived, Isabel, with Larry to write down the figures, measured the curtains that were to be replaced. Then they set out the luncheon on the stoop. It was sheltered from any wind there was and the sun of the Indian summer was good to bask in. The house, on a dirt road, had none of the elegance of the old frame houses of New England, and the best you could say of it was that it was roomy and comfortable, but from the stoop you had a pleasing view of a great red barn with a black roof, a clump of old trees, and beyond them, as far as the eye could reach, brown fields. It was a dull landscape, but the sunshine and the glowing tints of the waning year gave it that day an intimate loveliness. There was an exhilaration in the great space that was spread before you. Cold, bleak, and dreary as it must have been in winter, dry, sunbaked, and oppressive as it may have been in the dog days, just then it was strangely exciting, for the vastness of the view invited the soul to adventure.

They enjoyed their lunch like the healthy young things they were and they were happy to be together. Isabel poured out the coffee and Larry lit his pipe.

'Now go right ahead, darling,' he said, with an amused smile in his eyes.

Isabel was taken aback.

'Go right ahead about what?' she asked with as innocent a look as she could assume.

He chuckled.

'Do you take me for a perfect fool, honey? If your mother didn't know perfectly well the measurements of the living-room windows I'll eat my hat. That isn't why you asked me to drive you down here.'

Recovering her self-assurance, she gave him a brilliant smile.

'It might be that I thought it would be nice if we spent a day together by ourselves.'

'It might be, but I don't think it is. My guess is that Uncle

49

Elliott has told you that I've turned down Henry Maturin's offer.'

He spoke gaily and lightly and she found it convenient to continue in the same tone.

'Gray must be terribly disappointed. He thought it would be grand to have you in the office. You must get down to work some time, and the longer you leave it the harder it'll be.'

He puffed at his pipe and looked at her, tenderly smiling, so that she could not tell if he was serious or not.

'Do you know, I've got an idea that I want to do more with my life than sell bonds.'

'All right then. Go into a law office or study medicine.'

'No, I don't want to do that either.'

'What do you want to do then?'

'Loaf,' he replied calmly.

'Oh, Larry, don't be funny. This is desperately serious.'

Her voice quivered and her eyes filled with tears.

'Don't cry, darling. I don't want to make you miserable.'

He went and sat down beside her and put his arm round her. There was a tenderness in his voice that broke her and she could no longer hold back her tears. But she dried her eyes and forced a smile to her lips.

'It's all very fine to say you don't want to make me miserable. You are making me miserable. You see, I love you.'

'I love you too, Isabel.'

She sighed deeply. Then she disengaged herself from his arm and drew away from him.

'Let's be sensible. A man must work, Larry. It's a matter of self-respect. This is a young country, and it's a man's duty to take part in its activities. Henry Maturin was saying only the other day that we were beginning an era that would make the achievements of the past look like two bits. He said he could see no limit to our progress and he's convinced that by 1930 we shall be the richest and greatest country in the world. Don't you think that's terribly exciting?'

'Terribly.'

'There's never been such a chance for a young man. I should have thought you'd be proud to take part in the work that lies before us. It's such a wonderful adventure.'

He laughed lightly.

'I dare say you're right. The Armours and the Swifts will pack more and better meat, the McCormicks will make more and better harvesters, and Henry Ford will turn out more and better cars. And everyone'll get richer and richer.'

'And why not?'

'As you say, and why not? Money just doesn't happen to interest me.'

Isabel giggled.

'Darling, don't talk like a fool. One can't live without money.'

'I have a little. That's what gives me the chance to do what I want.'

'Loaf?'

'Yes,' he answered, smiling.

'You're making it so difficult for me, Larry,' she sighed.

'I'm sorry. I wouldn't if I could help it.'

'You can help it.'

He shook his head. He was silent for a while, lost in thought. When at last he spoke it was to say something that startled her.

'The dead look so terribly dead when they're dead.'

'What do you mean exactly?' she asked, troubled.

'Just that.' He gave her a rueful smile. 'You have a lot of time to think when you're up in the air by yourself. You get odd ideas.'

'What sort of ideas?'

'Vague,' he said, smiling. 'Incoherent. Confused.'

Isabel thought this over for a while.

'Don't you think if you took a job they might sort themselves out and you'd know where you were?'

'I've thought of that. I had a notion that I might go to work with a carpenter or in a garage.'

'Oh, Larry, people would think you were crazy.'

'Would that matter?'

'To me, yes.'

Once more silence fell upon them. It was she who broke it. She sighed.

'You're so different from what you were before you went out to France.'

'That's not strange. A lot happened to me then, you know.'

'Such as?'

'Oh, just the ordinary casual run of events. My greatest friend in the air corps was killed saving my life. I didn't find that easy to get over.'

'Tell me, Larry.'

He looked at her with deep distress in his eyes.

'I'd rather not talk about it. After all, it was only a trivial incident.'

Emotional by nature, Isabel's eyes again filled with tears.

'Are you unhappy, darling?'

'No,' he answered, smiling. 'The only thing that makes me unhappy is that I'm making you unhappy.' He took her hand and there was something so friendly in the feel of his strong firm hand against hers, something so intimately affectionate, that she had to bite her lips to prevent herself from crying. 'I don't think I shall ever find peace till I make up my mind about things,' he said gravely. He hesitated. 'It's very difficult to put into words. The moment you try to you feel embarrassed. You say to yourself: "Who am I that I should bother my head about this, that, and the other? Perhaps it's only because I'm a conceited prig. Wouldn't it be better to follow the beaten track and let what's coming to you come?" And then you think of a fellow who an hour before was full of life and fun, and he's lying dead; it's all so cruel and so meaningless. It's hard not to ask yourself what life is all about and whether there's any sense to it or whether it's all a tragic blunder of blind fate.'

It was impossible not to be moved when Larry, with that wonderfully melodious voice of his, spoke, haltingly as though he forced himself to say what he would sooner have left unsaid and yet with such an anguished sincerity; and for a while Isabel did not trust herself to speak.

'Would it help you if I went away for a bit?'

She put the question with a sinking heart. He took a long time to answer.

'I think so. You try to be indifferent to public opinion, but it's not easy. When it's antagonistic it arouses antagonism in you and that disturbs you.'

'Why don't you go then?'

'Well, on account of you.'

'Let's be frank with one another, darling. There's no place for me in your life just now.'

'Does that mean you don't want to be engaged to me any more?'

She forced a smile to her trembling lips.

'No, foolish, it means I'm prepared to wait.'

'It may be a year. It may be two.'

'That's all right. It may be less. Where'd you want to go?'

He looked at her intently as though he were trying to see into her innermost heart. She smiled lightly to hide her deep distress.

'Well, I thought I'd start by going to Paris. I know no one there. There'd be no one to interfere with me. I went to Paris several times on leave. I don't know why, but I've got it into my head that there everything that's muddled in my mind would grow clear. It's a funny picture, it gives you the feeling that there you can think out your thoughts to the end without let or hindrance. I think there I may be able to see my way before me.'

'And what's to happen if you don't?'

He chuckled.

'Then I shall fall back on my good American horse sense, give it up as a bad job and come back to Chicago and take any work I can get.'

The scene had affected Isabel too much for her to be able to tell it to me without getting somewhat emotional, and when she finished she looked at me pitifully.

'Do you think I did right?'

'I think you did the only thing you could do, but what's more I think you've been wonderfully kind, generous, and understanding.'

'I love him and I want him to be happy. And you know, in a way I'm not sorry he should go. I want him to be out of this hostile atmosphere, and that not only for his sake, but for mine too. I can't blame people when they say he'll never amount to anything; I hate them for it, and yet all the time deep down in

53

me I have an awful fear that they're right. But don't say I'm understanding. I don't begin to understand what he's after.'

'Perhaps you understand with your heart rather than with your reason.' I smiled. 'Why don't you marry him right away and go off to Paris with him?'

The shadow of a smile came into her eyes.

'There's nothing I'd like to do more. But I couldn't. And you know, though I hate to acknowledge it, I do really think he's better off without me. If Dr Nelson is right and he's suffering from delayed shock surely new surroundings and new interests will cure him, and when he's got his balance again he'll come back to Chicago and go into business like everybody else. I wouldn't want to marry an idler.'

Isabel had been brought up in a certain way and she accepted the principles that had been instilled into her. She did not think of money, because she had never known what it was not to have all she needed, but she was instinctively aware of its importance. It meant power, influence, and social consequence. It was the natural and obvious thing that a man should earn it. That was his plain life's work.

'It doesn't surprise me that you don't understand Larry,' I said, 'because I'm pretty sure he doesn't understand himself. If he's reticent about his aims it may be that it's because they're obscure to him. Mind you, I hardly know him and this is only guesswork: isn't it possible that he's looking for something, but what it is he doesn't know, and perhaps he isn't even sure it's there? Perhaps whatever it is that happened to him during the war has left him with a restlessness that won't let him be. Don't you think he may be pursuing an ideal that is hidden in a cloud of unknowing – like an astronomer looking for a star that only a mathematical calculation tells him exists?'

'I feel that something's troubling him.'

'His soul? It may be that he's a little frightened of himself. It may be that he has no confidence in the authenticity of the vision that he dimly perceives in his mind's eye.'

'He gives me such an odd impression sometimes; he gives me the impression of a sleep-walker who's suddenly wakened in a strange place and can't think where he is. He was so normal before the war. One of the nice things about him was his enormous zest for life. He was so scatter-brained and gay, it was wonderful to be with him; he was so sweet and ridiculous. What can have happened to change him so much?'

'I wouldn't know. Sometimes a very small thing will have an effect on you out of all proportion to the event. It depends on the circumstances and your mood at the time. I remember going to mass on All Saints' Day, which the French called the Day of the Dead, in a village church that the Germans had knocked about a bit on their first advance into France. It was filled with soldiers and with women in black. In the graveyard were rows of little wooden crosses and as the sad, solemn service went on, and women wept and men too, I had a feeling that perhaps those men who lay under the little crosses were better off than we who lived. I told a friend what I felt and he asked me what I meant. I couldn't explain and I saw that he thought me a perfect damned fool. And I remember after a battle seeing a pile of dead French soldiers heaped upon one another. They looked like the marionettes in a bankrupt puppet show that had been cast pell-mell into a dusty corner because they were of no use any more. I thought then just what Larry said to you: the dead look so awfully dead.'

I do not want the reader to think I am making a mystery of whatever it was that happened to Larry during the war that so profoundly affected him, a mystery that I shall disclose at a convenient moment. I don't think he ever told anybody. He did, however, many years later tell a woman, Suzanne Rouvier, whom Larry and I both knew, about the young airman who had met his death saving his life. She repeated it to me and so I can only relate it at second hand. I have translated it from her French. Larry had apparently struck up a great friendship with another boy in his squadron. Suzanne knew him only by the ironical nickname by which Larry spoke of him.

'He was a little chap with red hair, an Irishman. We used to call him Patsy,' Larry said, 'and he had more vitality than anyone I've ever known. Gosh, he was a live wire. He had a funny face and a funny grin, so that it made you laugh just to look at him. He was a harum-scarum devil and he'd do the craziest things; he was always getting hell from the higher-ups. He was absolutely without fear and when he'd escaped death by a hair's breadth he'd grin all over his face as if it was the best joke in the world. But he was a natural-born flyer and up in the air he was cool and wary. He taught me a lot. He was a bit older than me and he took me under his wing; it was rather comic really, because I was a good six inches taller than he was and if it had come to a scrap I could have knocked him out cold. Once in Paris when he was drunk and I was afraid he was going to get into trouble I did.

'I felt a bit out of it when I joined the squadron and I was afraid I wouldn't make good, but he just joshed me into having confidence in myself. He was funny about the war, he had no feeling of hatred for the Jerries; he loved a scrap and to fight them tickled him to death. He simply couldn't look upon bringing down one of their planes as anything but a practical joke. He was impudent and wild and irresponsible, but there was something so genuine about him that you couldn't help liking him. He'd give you his last penny as freely as he'd take yours. And if you were lonely or homesick or scared, and I was sometimes, he'd see it and with his ugly little face puckered up with laughter he'd say just the right thing to make you feel all right again.'

Larry puffed at his pipe and Suzanne waited for him to go on.

'We used to wangle it so that we could get our leave together, and when we were in Paris he went wild. We had a grand time. We were due for a spot of leave early in March, in 'eighteen that was, and we made our plans beforehand. There wasn't a thing we weren't going to do. The day before we were to go we were sent up to fly over the enemy lines and bring back reports of what we saw. Suddenly we came bang up against some German planes, and before we knew where we were we were in the middle of a dogfight. One of them came after me, but I got in first. I took a look to see if he was going to crash and then out of the corner of my eye I saw another plane on my tail. I dived to get away from him, but he was on to me like a flash and I thought I was done for; then I saw Patsy come down on him like a streak of lightning and give him all he'd got. They'd had enough and sheered off and we made for home. My machine had got pretty well knocked about and I only just made it. Patsy got in before me. When I got out of my plane they'd just got him out of his. He was lying on the ground and they were waiting for the ambulance to come up. When he saw me he grinned.

' "I got that blighter who was on your tail," he said.

' "What's the matter, Patsy?" I asked.

' "Oh, it's nothing. He winged me."

'He was looking deathly white. Suddenly a strange look came over his face. It had just come to him that he was dying, and the possibility of death had never so much as crossed his mind. Before they could stop him he sat up and gave a laugh.

' "Well I'm jiggered," he said.

'He fell back dead. He was twenty-two. He was going to marry a girl in Ireland after the war.'

The day after my talk with Isabel I left Chicago for San Francisco, where I was to take ship for the Far East.

II

1

I DID not see Elliott till he came to London towards the end of June in the following year. I asked him whether Larry had after all gone to Paris. He had. I was faintly amused at Elliott's exasperation with him.

'I had a kind of sneaking sympathy for the boy. I couldn't blame him for wanting to spend a couple of years in Paris and I was prepared to launch him. I told him to let me know the moment he arrived, but it was only when Louisa wrote and told me he was there that I knew he'd come. I wrote to him care of the American Express, which was the address she gave me, and asked him to come and dine to meet some of the people I thought he ought to know; I thought I'd try him out first with the Franco-American set, Emily de Montadour and Gracie de Château-Gaillard and so on, and d'you know what he answered? He said he was sorry he couldn't come, but he hadn't brought any evening clothes with him.'

Elliott looked me full in the face to see the stupefaction with which he expected this communication to fill me. He raised a supercilious eyebrow when he observed that I took it with calm.

'He replied to my letter on a sheet of nasty paper with the heading of a café in the Latin Quarter and when I wrote back I asked him to let me know where he was staying. I felt I must do something about him for Isabel's sake, and I thought perhaps he was shy – I mean I couldn't believe that any young fellow in his senses could come to Paris without evening clothes, and in any case there are tolerable tailors there, so I asked him to lunch and said it would be quite a small party, and would you believe it, not only did he ignore my request to give me some other address than the American Express, but he said he never ate luncheon. That finished him as far as I was concerned.'

'I wonder what he's been doing with himself.'

'I don't know, and to tell you the truth I don't care. I'm afraid he's a thoroughly undesirable young man and I think it would be a great mistake for Isabel to marry him. After all, if he led a normal sort of life I'd have run across him at the Ritz bar or at Fouquet's or somewhere.'

I go sometimes to these fashionable places myself, but I go to others also, and it happened that I spent several days in Paris early in the autumn of that year on my way to Marseilles, where I was proposing to take one of the Messagerie ships for Singapore. I dined one evening with friends in Montparnasse and after dinner we went to the Dôme to drink a glass of beer. Presently my wandering eye caught sight of Larry sitting by himself at a little marble-topped table on the crowded terrace. He was looking idly at the people who strolled up and down enjoying the coolness of the night after a sultry day. I left my party and went up to him. His face lit up when he saw me and he gave me an engaging smile. He asked me to sit down, but I said I couldn't as I was with a party.

'I just wanted to say how d'you do to you,' I said.

'Are you staying here?' he asked.

'Only for a very few days.'

'Will you lunch with me tomorrow?'

'I thought you never lunched.'

He chuckled.

'You've seen Elliott. I don't generally. I can't afford the time, I just have a glass of milk and a brioche, but I'd like you to lunch with me.'

'All right.'

We arranged to meet at the Dôme next day to have an apéritif and eat at some place on the boulevard. I rejoined my friends. We sat on talking. When next I looked for Larry he had gone.

2

I spent the next morning very pleasantly. I went to the Luxembourg and passed an hour looking at some pictures I liked. Then I strolled in the gardens, recapturing the memories of my youth. Nothing had changed. They might have been the same students who walked along the gravel paths in pairs, eagerly discussing the writers who excited them. They might have been the same children who trundled the same hoops under the watchful eyes of the same nurses. They might have been the same old men who basked in the sunshine, reading the morning paper. They might have been the same middle-aged women in mourning who sat on the free benches and gossiped with one another about the price of food and the misdeeds of servants. Then I went to the Odéon and looked at the new books in the galleries and I saw the lads who like myself thirty years before were trying under the petulant eyes of the smock-frocked attendants to read as much as they could of books they could not afford to buy. Then I strolled leisurely along those dear, dingy streets till I came to the Boulevard du Montparnasse and so to the Dôme. Larry was waiting. We had a drink and walked along to a restaurant where he could lunch in the open air.

He was perhaps a little paler than I remembered him and this made his very dark eyes, in their deep orbits, more striking; but he had the same self-possession, curious in one so young, and the same ingenuous smile. When he ordered his lunch I noticed that he spoke French fluently and with a good accent. I congratulated him on it.

'I knew a certain amount of French before, you know,' he explained. 'Aunt Louisa had a French governess for Isabel, and when they were at Marvin she used to make us talk French with her all the time.'

I asked him how he liked Paris.

'Very much.'

'D'you live in Montparnasse?'

'Yes,' he said, after a moment's hesitation which I interpreted into a disinclination to tell exactly where he lived.

'Elliott was rather put out that the only address you gave was the American Express.'

Larry smiled but did not answer.

'What do you do with yourself all the time?'

'I loaf.'

'And you read?'

'Yes, I read.'

'Do you ever hear from Isabel?'

'Sometimes. We're neither of us great letter-writers. She's having a grand time in Chicago. They're coming over next year to stay with Elliott.'

'That'll be nice for you.'

'I don't believe Isabel's ever been to Paris. It'll be fun taking her around.'

He was curious to know about my journey in China and listened attentively to what I told him; but when I tried to get him to talk about himself, I failed. He was so uncommunicative that I was forced to the conclusion that he had asked me to lunch with him merely to enjoy my company. I was pleased, but baffled. We had no sooner finished our coffee than he called for the bill, paid it, and got up.

'Well, I must be off,' he said.

We parted. I knew no more of what he was up to than before. I did not see him again.

3

I was not in Paris in the spring when, sooner than they had planned, Mrs Bradley and Isabel arrived to stay with Elliott; and again I have to eke out my knowledge of what passed during the few weeks they spent there by the exercise of my imagination. They landed at Cherbourg, and Elliott, always considerate, went to meet them. They passed through the customs. The train started. Elliott with some complacency told them that he had engaged a very good lady's maid to look after them and when Mrs Bradley said that was quite unnecessary, since they didn't need one, he was very sharp with her.

'Don't be tiresome the moment you arrive, Louisa. No one can be well turned out without a maid, and I've engaged Antoinette not only for your sake and Isabel's but for mine. It would mortify me that you shouldn't be perfectly dressed.'

He gave the clothes they were wearing a disparaging glance.

'Of course you'll want to buy some new frocks. On mature consideration I've come to the conclusion that you can't do better than Chanel.'

'I always used to go to Worth,' said Mrs Bradley.

She might as well not have spoken, for he took no notice.

'I've talked to Chanel myself and I've made an appointment for you tomorrow at three. Then there are hats. Obviously Reboux.'

'I don't want to spend a lot of money, Elliott.'

'I know. I am proposing to pay for everything myself. I'm determined that you shall be a credit to me. Oh, and Louisa, I've arranged several parties for you and I've told my French friends that Myron was an ambassador, which, of course, he would have been if he'd lived a little longer, and it makes a better effect. I don't suppose it'll come up, but I thought I'd better warn you.'

'You're ridiculous, Elliott.'

'No, I'm not. I know the world. I know that the widow of an ambassador has more prestige than the widow of a minister.'

As the train steamed into the Gare du Nord, Isabel, who was standing at the window, called out:

'There's Larry.'

It had hardly stopped when she sprang out and ran to meet him. He threw his arms around her.

'How did he know you were coming?' Elliott asked his sister acidly.

'Isabel wirelessed him from the ship.'

Mrs Bradley kissed him affectionately, and Elliott gave him a limp hand to shake. It was ten o'clock at night.

'Uncle Elliott, can Larry come to lunch tomorrow?' cried

Isabel, her arm in the young man's, her face eager and her eyes shining.

'I should be charmed, but Larry has given me to understand that he doesn't eat lunch.'

'He will tomorrow, won't you, Larry?'

'I will,' he smiled.

'I shall look forward to seeing you at one o'clock then.'

He stretched out his hand once more, intending to dismiss him, but Larry grinned at him impudently.

'I'll help with the luggage and get a cab for you.'

'My car is waiting and my man will see to the luggage,' said Elliott with dignity.

'That's fine. Then all we've got to do is to go. If there's room for me I'll come as far as your door with you.'

'Yes, do, Larry,' said Isabel.

They walked down the platform together, followed by Mrs Bradley and Elliott. Elliott's face bore a look of frigid disapproval.

'Quelles manières,' he said to himself, for in certain circumstances he felt he could express his sentiments more forcibly in French.

Next morning at eleven, having finished dressing, for he was not an early riser, he sent a note to his sister, via his man Joseph and her maid Antoinette, to ask her to come to the library so that they could have a talk. When she appeared he closed the door carefully and, putting a cigarette into an immensely long agate holder, lit it and sat down.

'Am I to understand that Isabel and Larry are still engaged?' he asked.

'So far as I know.'

'I'm afraid I haven't a very good account to give you of the young man.' He told her then how he had been prepared to launch him in society and the plans he had made to establish him in a fit and proper manner. 'I even had my eye on a *rez-de-chaussée* that would have been the very thing for him. It belongs to the young Marquis de Rethel and he wanted to sublet it because he'd been appointed to the embassy at Madrid.'

But Larry had refused his invitations in a manner that made it quite clear that he did not want his help.

'What the object of coming to Paris is if you're not going to take advantage of what Paris has to give you is beyond my comprehension. I don't know what he does with himself. He doesn't seem to know anybody. Do you know where he lives?'

'The only address we've ever had is the American Express.'

'Like a travelling salesman or a school-teacher on vacation. I shouldn't be surprised if he was living with some little trollop in a studio in Montmartre.'

'Oh, Elliott.'

'What other explanation can there be for the mystery he's making of his dwelling place and for his refusal to consort with people of his own class?'

'It doesn't sound like Larry. And last night, didn't you get the impression that he was just as much in love with Isabel as ever? He couldn't be so false.'

Elliott by a shrug of the shoulders gave her to understand that there was no limit to the duplicity of men.

'What about Gray Maturin? Is he still in the picture?'

'He'd marry Isabel tomorrow if she'd have him.'

Mrs Bradley told him then why they had come to Europe sooner than they had at first intended. She had found herself in ill-health, and the doctors had informed her that she was suffering from diabetes. It was not serious, and by attention to her diet and taking moderate doses of insulin there was no reason why she should not live for a good many years, but the knowledge that she had an incurable disease made her anxious to see Isabel settled. They had talked the matter over. Isabel was sensible. She had agreed that if Larry refused to come back to Chicago at the end of the two years in Paris they had agreed upon and get a job, there was only one thing to do and that was to break with him. But it offended Mrs Bradley's sense of personal dignity that they should wait till the appointed time and then come to fetch him, like a fugitive from justice, back to his own country. She felt that Isabel would put herself in a humiliating position. But it was very natural that they should spend the summer in Europe, where Isabel had not been since she was a child. After their visit in Paris they could go to some watering-place suitable to Mrs Bradley's complaint, then on to the Austrian Tyrol for a while and from there travel slowly through Italy. Mrs Bradley's intention was to ask Larry to accompany them, so that he and Isabel could see whether the long separation had left their feelings unchanged. It would be manifest in due course whether Larry, having had his fling, was prepared to accept the responsibilities of life.

'Henry Maturin was sore with him for turning down the position he offered him, but Gray has talked him round, and he can go into the business the moment he comes back to Chicago.'

'Gray's a very nice fellow.'

'He certainly is.' Mrs Bradley sighed. 'I know he'd make Isabel happy.'

Elliott then told her what parties he had arranged for them. He was giving a big luncheon on the following day and at the end of the week a grand dinner party. He was taking them to a reception at the Château-Gaillards and he had got cards for them to a ball that the Rothschilds were giving.

'You'll ask Larry, won't you?'

'He tells me he hasn't any evening clothes,' Elliott sniffed.

'Well, ask him all the same. After all, he is a nice boy, and it wouldn't help to give him the cold shoulder. It would only make Isabel obstinate.'

'Of course I'll ask him if you wish it.'

Larry came to lunch at the appointed time, and Elliott, whose manners were admirable, was pointedly cordial to him. It was not difficult, since Larry was so gay, in such high spirits that it would have needed a much more ill-natured man than Elliott not to be charmed with him. The conversation dealt with Chicago and their common friends there, so that there was not much for Elliott to do other than to look amiable and pretend to be interested in the concerns of persons whom he thought of no social consequence. He did not mind listening; indeed, he thought it rather touching to hear them tell of this young couple's engagement, that young couple's marriage, and another young couple's divorce. Who had ever heard of them? *He* knew that the pretty little Marquise de Clinchant had tried to poison herself because her lover, the Prince de Colombey, had left her to marry the daughter of a South American millionaire. That *was* something to talk about. Looking at Larry, he was obliged to admit that there was something peculiarly attractive in him; with his deep-set strangely black eyes, his high cheekbones, pale skin, and mobile mouth he reminded Elliott of a portrait by Botticelli, and it occurred to him that if he were dressed in the costume of the period he would look extravagantly romantic. He remembered his notion of getting him off with a distinguished Frenchwoman and he smiled slyly on reflecting that he was expecting at dinner on Saturday Marie Louise de Florimond, who combined irreproachable connexions with notorious immorality. She was forty, but looked ten years younger; she had the delicate beauty of her ancestress painted by Nattier which, owing to Elliott himself, now hung in one of the great American collections; and her sexual voracity was insatiable. Elliott decided to put Larry next to her. He knew she would waste no time in making her desires clear to him. He had already invited a young attaché at the British embassy whom he thought Isabel might like. Isabel was very pretty, and as he was an Englishman, and well off, it wouldn't matter that she had no fortune. Mellowed by the excellent Montrachet with which they had started lunch and by the fine Bordeaux that followed, Elliott thought with tranquil pleasure of the possibilities that presented themselves to his mind. If things turned out as he thought they very well might, dear Louisa would have no more cause for anxiety. She had always slightly disapproved of him; poor dear, she was very provincial; but he was fond of her. It would be a satisfaction to him to arrange everything for her by help of his knowledge of the world.

To waste no time, Elliott had arranged to take his ladies to look at clothes immediately after lunch, so as they got up from table he intimated to Larry with the tact of which he was a master that he must make himself scarce, but at the same time he asked him with pressing affability to come to the two grand parties he had arranged. He need hardly have taken so much trouble, since Larry accepted both invitations with alacrity.

But Elliott's plan failed. He was relieved when Larry appeared at the dinner party in a very presentable dinner-jacket, for he had been a little nervous that he would wear the same blue suit that he had worn at lunch; and after dinner, getting

Marie Louise de Florimond into a corner, he asked her how she had liked his young American friend.

'He has nice eyes and good teeth.'

'Is that all? I put you beside him because I thought he was just your cup of tea.'

She looked at him suspiciously.

'He told me he was engaged to your pretty niece.'

'*Voyons, ma chère,* the fact that a man belongs to another woman has never prevented you from taking him away from her if you could.'

'Is that what you want me to do? Well, I'm not going to do your dirty work for you, my poor Elliott.'

Elliott chuckled.

'The meaning of that, I presume, is that you tried your stuff and found there was nothing doing.'

'Why I like you, Elliott, is that you have the morals of a bawdy-house keeper. You don't want him to marry your niece. Why not? He is well bred and quite charming. But he's really too innocent. I don't think he had the least suspicion of what I meant.'

'You should have been more explicit, dear friend.'

'I have enough experience to know when I'm wasting my time. The fact is that he has eyes only for your little Isabel, and between you and me, she has twenty years advantage over me. And she's sweet.'

'Do you like her dress? I chose it for her myself.'

'It's pretty and it's suitable. But of course she has no chic.'

Elliott took this as a reflection on himself, and he was not prepared to let Madame de Florimond get away without a dig. He smiled genially.

'One has to have reached your ripe maturity to have *your* chic, dear friend,' he said.

Madame de Florimond wielded a bludgeon rather than a rapier. Her retort made Elliott's Virginian blood boil.

'But I'm sure that in your fair land of gangsters [*votre beau pays d'apaches*] they will hardly miss something that is so subtle and so inimitable.'

But if Madame de Florimond carped, the rest of Elliott's friends were delighted both with Isabel and with Larry. They liked her fresh prettiness, her abounding health, and her vitality; they liked his picturesque appearance, his good manners, and his quiet, ironic humour. Both had the advantage of speaking good and fluent French. Mrs Bradley, after living so many years in diplomatic circles, spoke it correctly enough but with an unabashed American accent. Elliott entertained them lavishly. Isabel, pleased with her new clothes and her new hats, amused by all the gaiety Elliott provided, and happy to be with Larry, thought she had never enjoyed herself so much.

4

Elliott was of opinion that breakfast was a meal that you should share only with total strangers, and then only if there was no help for it, so Mrs Bradley, somewhat against her will, and Isabel, far from displeased, were obliged to have theirs in their bedrooms. But Isabel, when she awoke, sometimes told Antoinette, the grand maid Elliott had engaged for them, to take her *café au lait* into her mother's room so that she could talk to her while she had it. In the busy life she led it was the only moment of the day in which she could be alone with her. One such morning, when they had been in Paris nearly a month, after Isabel had done narrating the events of the previous night, most of which she and Larry had spent going the rounds of the night clubs with a party of friends, Mrs Bradley let fall the question she had had in mind to ask ever since their arrival.

'When is he coming back to Chicago?'

'I don't know. He hasn't spoken of it.'

'Haven't you asked him?'

'No.'

'Are you scared to?'

'No, of course not.'

Mrs Bradley, lying on a chaise longue, in a modish dressing-gown that Elliott had insisted on giving her, was polishing her nails.

'What do you talk about all the time when you're alone?'

'We don't talk all the time. It's nice to be together. You know, Larry was always rather silent. When we talk I think I do most of the talking.'

'What has he been doing with himself?'

'I don't really know. I don't think anything very much. I suppose he's been having a good time.'

'And where is he living?'

'I don't know that either.'

'He seems very reticent, doesn't he?'

Isabel lit a cigarette and, as she blew a cloud of smoke from her nostrils, looked coolly at her mother.

'What exactly do you mean by that, Mamma?'

'Your uncle Elliott thinks he has an apartment and is living there with a woman.'

Isabel burst out laughing.

'You don't believe that, do you?'

'No. I honestly don't.' Mrs Bradley looked reflectively at her nails. 'Don't you ever talk to him about Chicago?'

'Yes, a lot.'

'Hasn't he given any sort of indication that he intends to come back?'

'I can't say he has.'

'He will have been gone two years next October.'

'I know.'

'Well, it's your business, dear, and you must do what you think right. But things don't get any easier by putting them off.' She glanced at her daughter, but Isabel would not meet her eyes. Mrs Bradley gave her an affectionate smile. 'If you don't want to be late for lunch you'd better go and have your bath.'

'I'm lunching with Larry. We're going to some place in the Latin Quarter.'

'Enjoy yourself.'

An hour later Larry came to fetch her. They took a cab to the Pont St Michel and sauntered up the crowded boulevard till they came to a café they liked the look of. They sat down on the terrace and ordered a couple of Dubonnets. Then they took another cab and went to a restaurant. Isabel had a healthy appetite and she enjoyed the good things Larry ordered for her. She enjoyed looking at the people sitting cheek by jowl with them, for the place was packed, and it made her laugh to see the intense pleasure they so obviously took in their food; but she enjoyed above all sitting at a tiny table alone with Larry. She loved the amusement in his eyes while she chattered away gaily. It was enchanting to feel so much at home with him. But at the back of her mind was a vague disquiet, for though he seemed very much at home too, she felt it was not so much with her as with the surroundings. She had been faintly disturbed by what her mother had said, and though seeming to prattle so guilelessly she observed his every expression. He was not quite the same as when he had left Chicago, but she couldn't tell in what the difference lay. He looked exactly as she remembered him, as young, as frank, but his expression was changed. It was not that he was more serious, his face in repose had always been serious, it had a calmness that was new to her; it was as though he had settled something with himself and were at ease in a way he had never been before.

When they had finished lunch he suggested that they should take a stroll through the Luxembourg.

'No, I don't want to go and look at pictures.'

'All right then, let's go and sit in the gardens.'

'No, I don't want to do that either. I want to go and see where you live.'

'There's nothing to see. I live in a scrubby little room in a hotel.'

'Uncle Elliott says you've got an apartment and are living in sin with an artist's model.'

'Come on then and see for yourself,' he laughed. 'It's only a step from here. We can walk.'

He took her through narrow, tortuous streets, dingy notwithstanding the streak of blue sky that showed between the high houses, and after a while stopped at a small hotel with a pretentious façade.

'Here we are.'

Isabel followed him into a narrow hall, on one side of which was a desk and behind it a man in shirt-sleeves, with a waistcoat in thin black and yellow stripes and a dirty apron, reading a paper. Larry asked for his key, and the man handed it to him from the rack immediately behind him. He gave Isabel an inquisitive glance that turned into a knowing smirk. It was clear that he thought she was going to Larry's room for no honest purpose.

They climbed up two flights of stairs, on which was a threadbare red carpet, and Larry unlocked his door. Isabel entered a smallish room with two windows. They looked out on the grey apartment house opposite, on the ground floor of which was a stationer's shop. There was a single bed in the room, with a night table beside it, a heavy wardrobe with a large mirror, an upholstered but straight-backed armchair, and a table between the windows on which were a typewriter, papers, and a number of books. The chimney-piece was piled with paper-bound volumes.

'You sit in the armchair. It's not very comfortable, but it's the best I can offer.'

He drew up another chair and sat down.

'Is this where you live?' asked Isabel.

He chuckled at the look on her face.

'It is. I've been here ever since I came to Paris.'

'But why?'

'It's convenient. It's near the Bibliothèque Nationale and the Sorbonne.' He pointed to a door she had not noticed. 'It's got a bathroom. I can get breakfast here and I generally dine at that restaurant where we had lunch.'

'It's awfully sordid.'

'Oh no, it's all right. It's all I want.'

'But what sort of people live here?'

'Oh, I don't know. Up in the attics a few students. Two or three old bachelors in government offices and a retired actress at the Odéon; the only other room with a bath is occupied by a kept woman whose gentleman friend comes to see her every other Thursday; I suppose a few transients. It's a very quiet and respectable place.'

Isabel was a trifle disconcerted and because she knew Larry noticed it and was amused she was half inclined to take offence.

'What's that great big book on the table?' she asked.

'That? Oh, that's my Greek dictionary.'

'Your what?' she cried.

'It's all right. It won't bite you.'

'Are you learning Greek?'

'Yes.'

'Why?'

'I thought I'd like to.'

70

He was looking at her with a smile in his eyes and she smiled back at him.

'Don't you think you might tell me what you've been up to all the time you've been in Paris?'

'I've been reading a good deal. Eight or ten hours a day. I've attended lectures at the Sorbonne. I think I've read everything that's important in French literature and I can read Latin, at least Latin prose, almost as easily as I can read French. Of course Greek's more difficult. But I have a very good teacher. Until you came here I used to go to him three evenings a week.'

'And what is that going to lead to?'

'The acquisition of knowledge,' he smiled.

'It doesn't sound very practical.'

'Perhaps it isn't and on the other hand perhaps it is. But it's enormous fun. You can't imagine what a thrill it is to read the Odyssey in the original. It makes you feel as if you had only to get on tiptoe and stretch out your hands to touch the stars.'

He got up from his chair, as though impelled by an excitement that seized him, and walked up and down the small room.

'I've been reading Spinoza the last month or two. I don't suppose I understand very much of it yet, but it fills me with exultation. It's like landing from your plane on a great plateau in the mountains. Solitude, and an air so pure that it goes to your head like wine and you feel like a million dollars.'

'When are you coming back to Chicago?'

'Chicago? I don't know. I haven't thought of it.'

'You said that if you hadn't got what you wanted after two years you'd give it up as a bad job.'

'I couldn't go back now. I'm on the threshold. I see vast lands of the spirit stretching out before me, beckoning, and I'm eager to travel them.'

'What do you expect to find in them?'

'The answers to my questions.' He gave her a glance that was almost playful, so that except that she knew him so well, she might have thought he was speaking in jest. 'I want to make up my mind whether God is or God is not. I want to find out why evil exists. I want to know whether I have an immortal soul or whether when I die it's the end.'

Isabel gave a little gasp. It made her uncomfortable to hear

Larry say such things, and she was thankful that he spoke so lightly, in the tone of ordinary conversation, that it was possible for her to overcome her embarrassment.

'But Larry,' she smiled. 'People have been asking those questions for thousands of years. If they could be answered, surely they'd have been answered by now.'

Larry chuckled.

'Don't laugh as if I'd said something idiotic,' she said sharply.

'On the contrary I think you've said something shrewd. But on the other hand you might say that if men have been asking them for thousands of years it proves that they can't help asking them and have to go on asking them. Besides, it's not true that no one has found the answers. There are more answers than questions, and lots of people have found answers that were perfectly satisfactory for them. Old Ruysbroek for instance.'

'Who was he?'

'Oh, just a guy I didn't know at college,' Larry answered flippantly.

Isabel didn't know what he meant, but passed on.

'It all sounds so adolescent to me. Those are the sort of things sophomores get excited about and then when they leave college they forget about them. They have to earn a living.'

'I don't blame them. You see, I'm in the happy position that I have enough to live on. If I hadn't I'd have had to do like everybody else and make money.'

'But doesn't money mean anything to you?'

'Not a thing,' he grinned.

'How long d'you think all this is going to take you?'

'I wouldn't know. Five years. Ten years.'

'And after that? What are you going to do with all this wisdom?'

'If I ever acquire wisdom I suppose I shall be wise enough to know what to do with it.'

Isabel clasped her hands passionately and leant forwards in her chair.

'You're so wrong, Larry. You're an American. Your place isn't here. Your place is in America.'

'I shall come back when I'm ready.'

'But you're missing so much. How can you bear to sit here in a backwater just when we're living through the most wonderful adventure the world has ever known? Europe's finished. We're the greatest, the most powerful people in the world. We're going forward by leaps and bounds. We've got everything. It's your duty to take part in the development of your country. You've forgotten, you don't know how thrilling life is in America today. Are you sure you're not doing this because you haven't the courage to stand up to the work that's before every American now? Oh, I know you're working in a way, but isn't it just an escape from your responsibilities? Is it more than just a sort of laborious idleness? What would happen to America if everyone shirked as you're shirking?'

'You're very severe, honey,' he smiled. 'The answer to that is that everyone doesn't feel like me. Fortunately for themselves, perhaps, most people are prepared to follow the normal course; what you forget is that I want to learn as passionately as – Gray, for instance, wants to make pots of money. Am I really a traitor to my country because I want to spend a few years educating myself? It may be that when I'm through I shall have something to give that people will be glad to take. It's only a chance, of course, but if I fail I shall be no worse off than a man who's gone into business and hasn't made a go of it.'

'And what about me? Am I of no importance to you at all?'

'You're of very great importance. I want you to marry me.'

'When? In ten years?'

'No. Now. As soon as possible.'

'On what? Mamma can't afford to give me anything. Besides, she wouldn't if she could. She'd think it wrong to help you to live without doing anything.'

'I wouldn't want to take anything from your mother,' said Larry. 'I've got three thousand a year. That's plenty in Paris. We could have a little apartment and a *bonne à tout faire*. We'd have such a lark, darling.'

'But, Larry, one can't live on three thousand a year.'

'Of course one can. Lots of people live on much less.'

'But I don't want to live on three thousand a year. There's no reason why I should.'

73

'I've been living on half that.'

'But how!'

She looked at the dingy little room with a shudder of distaste.

'It means I've got a bit saved up. We could go down to Capri for our honeymoon and then in the fall we'd go to Greece. I'm crazy to go there. Don't you remember how we used to talk about travelling all over the world together?'

'Of course I want to travel. But not like that. I don't want to travel second-class on steamships and put up at third-rate hotels, without a bathroom, and eat at cheap restaurants.'

'I went all through Italy last October like that. I had a wonderful time. We could travel all over the world on three thousand a year.'

'But I want to have babies, Larry.'

'That's all right. We'll take them along with us.'

'You're so silly,' she laughed. 'D'you know what it costs to have a baby? Violet Tomlinson had one last year and she did it as cheaply as she could and it cost her twelve hundred and fifty. And what d'you think a nurse costs?' She grew more vehement as one idea after another occurred to her. 'You're so impractical. You don't know what you're asking me to do. I'm young, I want to have fun. I want to do all the things that people do. I want to go to parties, I want to go to dances, I want to play golf and ride horseback. I want to wear nice clothes. Can't you imagine what it means to a girl not to be as well dressed as the rest of her crowd? D'you know what it means, Larry, to buy your friends' old dresses when they're sick of them and be thankful when someone out of pity makes you a present of a new one? I couldn't even afford to go to a decent hairdresser to have my hair properly done. I don't want to go about in street-cars and omnibuses; I want to have my own car. And what d'you suppose I'd find to do with myself all day long while you were reading at the Library? Walk about the streets window-shopping or sit in the Luxembourg Garden seeing that my children didn't get into mischief? We wouldn't have any friends.'

'Oh, Isabel,' he interrupted.

'Not the sort of friends I'm used to. Oh yes, Uncle Elliott's friends would ask us now and then for his sake, but we couldn't go because I wouldn't have the clothes to go in, and we wouldn't go because we couldn't afford to return their hospitality. I don't want to know a lot of scrubby, unwashed people; I've got nothing to say to them and they've got nothing to say to me. I want to live, Larry.' She grew suddenly conscious of the look in his eyes, tender as it always was when fixed on her, but gently amused. 'You think I'm silly, don't you? You think I'm being trivial and horrid.'

'No, I don't. I think what you say is very natural.'

He was standing with his back to the fireplace, and she got up and went up to him so that they were face to face.

'Larry, if you hadn't a cent to your name and got a job that brought you in three thousand a year I'd marry you without a minute's hesitation. I'd cook for you, I'd make the beds, I wouldn't care what I wore, I'd go without anything, I'd look upon it as wonderful fun, because I'd know that it was only a question of time and you'd make good. But this means living in a sordid beastly way all our lives with nothing to look forward to. It means that I should be a drudge to the day of my death. And for what? So that you can spend years trying to find answers to questions that you say yourself are insoluble. It's so wrong. A man ought to work. That's what he's here for. That's how he contributes to the welfare of the community.'

'In short it's his duty to settle down in Chicago and enter Henry Maturin's business. Do you think that by getting my friends to buy the securities that Henry Maturin is interested in I should add greatly to the welfare of the community?'

'There must be brokers and it's a perfectly decent and honourable way of earning a living.'

'You've drawn a very black picture of life in Paris on a moderate income. You know, it isn't really like that. One can dress very nicely without going to Chanel. And all the interesting people don't live in the neighbourhood of the Arc de Triomphe and the Avenue Foch. In fact few interesting people do, because interesting people generally don't have a lot of money. I know quite a number of people here, painters and writers and students, French, English, American, and what not, whom I think you'd find much more amusing than Elliott's

75

seedy marquises and long-nosed duchesses. You've got a quick mind and a lively sense of humour. You'd enjoy hearing them swap ideas across the dinner table even though the wine was only *vin ordinaire* and you didn't have a butler and a couple of footmen to wait on you.'

'Don't be stupid, Larry. Of course I would. You know I'm not a snob. I'd love to meet interesting people.'

'Yes, in a Chanel dress. D'you think they wouldn't catch on to it that you looked upon it as a sort of cultured slumming? They wouldn't be at their ease, any more than you would, and you wouldn't get anything out of it except to tell Emily de Montadour and Gracie de Château-Gaillard afterwards what fun you'd had meeting a lot of weird bohemians in the Latin Quarter.'

Isabel slightly shrugged her shoulders.

'I dare say you're right. They're not the sort of people I've been brought up with. They're not the sort of people I have anything in common with.'

'Where does that leave us?'

'Just where we started. I've lived in Chicago ever since I can remember. All my friends are there. All my interests are there. I'm at home there. It's where I belong and it's where you belong. Mamma's ill and she's never going to get any better. I couldn't leave her even if I wanted to.'

'Does that mean that unless I'm prepared to come back to Chicago you don't want to marry me?'

Isabel hesitated. She loved Larry. She wanted to marry him. She wanted him with all the power of her senses. She knew that he desired her. She couldn't believe that when it came to a showdown he wouldn't weaken. She was afraid, but she had to risk it.

'Yes, Larry, that's just what it does mean.'

He struck a match on the chimney-piece, one of those old-fashioned French sulphur matches that fill your nostrils with an acrid odour, and lit his pipe. Then, passing her, he went over and stood by one of the windows. He looked out. He was silent for what seemed an endless time. She stood as she had stood before, when she was facing him, and looked in the mirror over the chimney-piece, but she did not see herself. Her

76

heart was beating madly and she was sick with apprehension. He turned at last.

'I wish I could make you see how much fuller the life I offer you is than anything you have a conception of. I wish I could make you see how exciting the life of the spirit is and how rich in experience. It's illimitable. It's such a happy life. There's only one thing like it, when you're up in a plane by yourself, high, high, and only infinity surrounds you. You're intoxicated by the boundless space. You feel such a sense of exhilaration that you wouldn't exchange it for all the power and glory in the world. I was reading Descartes the other day. The ease, the grace, the lucidity. Gosh!'

'But Larry,' she interrupted him desperately, 'don't you see you're asking something of me that I'm not fitted for, that I'm not interested in and don't want to be interested in? How often have I got to repeat to you that I'm just an ordinary, normal girl. I'm twenty, in ten years I shall be old, I want to have a good time while I have the chance. Oh, Larry, I do love you so terribly. All this is just trifling. It's not going to lead you anywhere. For your own sake I beseech you to give it up. Be a man, Larry, and do a man's work. You're just wasting the precious years that others are doing so much with. Larry, if you love me you won't give me up for a dream. You've had your fling. Come back with us to America.'

'I can't, darling. It would be death to me. It would be the betrayal of my soul.'

'Oh, Larry, why d'you talk in that way? That's the way hysterical, highbrow women talk. What does it mean? Nothing. Nothing. Nothing.'

'It happens to mean exactly what I feel,' he answered, his eyes twinkling.

'How can you laugh? Don't you realize this is desperately serious? We've come to the cross-roads and what we do now is going to affect our whole lives.'

'I know that. Believe me, I'm perfectly serious.'

She sighed.

'If you won't listen to reason there's nothing more to be said.'

'But I don't think it's reason. I think you've been talking the most terrible nonsense all the time.'

'I?' If she hadn't been so miserable she would have laughed. 'My poor Larry, you're as crazy as a coot.'

She slowly slipped her engagement ring off her finger. She placed it on the palm of her hand and looked at it. It was a square-cut ruby set in a thin platinum band and she had always liked it.

'If you loved me you wouldn't make me so unhappy.'

'I do love you. Unfortunately sometimes one can't do what one thinks is right without making someone else unhappy.'

She stretched out her hand on which the ruby was resting and forced a smile to her trembling lips.

'Here you are, Larry.'

'It's no good to me. Won't you keep it as a memento of our friendship? You can wear it on your little finger. Our friendship needn't stop, need it?'

'I shall always care for you, Larry.'

'Then keep it. I should like you to.'

She hesitated for an instant, then put it on the finger of her right hand.

'It's too large.'

'You can have it altered. Let's go to the Ritz bar and have a drink.'

'All right.'

She was a trifle taken aback that it had all gone so easily. She had not cried. Nothing seemed to be changed except that now she wasn't going to marry Larry. She could hardly believe that everything was over and done with. She resented a little the fact that they hadn't had a terrific scene. They had talked it all over almost as coolly as though they had been discussing the taking a house. She felt let down, but at the same time was conscious of a slight sense of satisfaction because they had behaved in such a civilized way. She would have given a lot to know exactly what Larry was feeling. But it was always difficult to know that; his smooth face, his dark eyes were a mask that she was aware even she, who had known him for so many years, could not penetrate. She had taken off her hat and laid it on the bed. Now, standing before the mirror, she put it on again.

'Just as a matter of interest,' she said, arranging her hair, 'did you want to break our engagement?'

'No.'

'I thought it might be a relief to you.' He made no reply. She turned round with a gay smile on her lips. 'Now I'm ready.'

Larry locked the door behind him. When he handed the key to the man at the desk he enveloped them both in a look of conniving archness. It was impossible for Isabel not to guess what he thought they had been up to.

'I don't believe that old fellow would bet much on my virginity,' she said.

They took a taxi to the Ritz and had a drink. They spoke of indifferent things, without apparent constraint, like two old friends who saw one another every day. Though Larry was naturally silent, Isabel was a talkative girl, with an ample fund of chit-chat, and she was determined that no silence should fall between them that might be hard to break. She wasn't going to let Larry think she felt any resentment towards him and her pride constrained her to act so that he should not suspect that she was hurt and unhappy. Presently she suggested that he should drive her home. When he dropped her at the door she said to him gaily:

'Don't forget that you're lunching with us tomorrow.'

'You bet your life I won't.'

She gave him her cheek to kiss and passed through the *porte cochère*.

5

When Isabel entered the drawing-room she found that some people had dropped in to tea. There were two American women who lived in Paris, exquisitely gowned, with strings of pearls round their necks, diamond bracelets on their wrists, and costly rings on their fingers. Though the hair of one was darkly hennaed and that of the other unnaturally golden they were strangely alike. They had the same heavily mascaraed eyelashes, the same brightly painted lips, the same rouged cheeks, the same slim figures, maintained at the cost of extreme mortification, the same clear, sharp features, the same hungry restless eyes; and you could not but be conscious that their lives were a desperate struggle to maintain their fading charms. They talked with inanity in a loud, metallic voice without a moment's pause, as though afraid that if they were silent for an instant the machine would run down and the artificial construction which was all they were would fall to pieces. There was also a secretary from the American Embassy, suave, silent, for he could not get a word in, and very much the man of the world, and a small dark Rumanian prince, all bows and servility, with little darting black eyes and a clean-shaven swarthy face, who was for ever jumping up to hand a teacup, pass a plate of cakes, or light a cigarette, and who shamelessly dished out to those present the most flattering, the most gross compliments. He was paying for all the dinners he had received from the objects of his adulation and for all the dinners he hoped to receive.

Mrs Bradley, seated at the tea table and dressed to please Elliott somewhat more grandly than she thought suitable to the occasion, performed her duties as hostess with her usual civil but rather indifferent composure. What she thought of her brother's guests I can only imagine. I never knew her more than slightly and she was a woman who kept herself to herself. She was not a stupid woman; in all the years she had lived in foreign capitals she had met innumerable people of all kinds and I think she summed them up shrewdly enough according to the standards of the small Virginian town where she was born and bred. I think she got a certain amount of amusement from observing their antics, and I don't believe she took their airs and graces any more seriously than she took the aches and pains of the characters in a novel which she knew from the beginning (otherwise she wouldn't have read it) would end happily. Paris, Rome, Peking had had no more effect on her Americanism that Elliott's devout Catholicism on her robust, but not inconvenient, Presbyterian faith.

Isabel, with her youth, her strapping good looks, and her vitality, brought a breath of fresh air into that meretricious atmosphere. She swept in like a young earth goddess. The Rumanian prince leapt to his feet to draw forward a chair for her and with ample gesticulation did his shift. The two American ladies, with shrill amiabilities on their lips, looked her up and down, took in the details of her dress, and perhaps in their hearts felt a pang of dismay at being confronted with her exuberant youth. The American diplomat smiled to himself as he saw how false and haggard she made them look. But Isabel thought they were grand; she liked their rich clothes and expensive pearls and felt a twinge of envy for their sophisticated poise. She wondered if she would ever achieve that supreme elegance. Of course the little Rumanian was quite ridiculous, but he was rather sweet and even if he didn't mean the charming things he said it was nice to listen to them. The conversation which her entrance had interrupted was resumed, and they talked so brightly, with so much conviction that what they were saying was worth saying, that you almost thought they were talking sense. They talked of the parties they had been to and the parties they were going to. They gossiped about the latest scandal. They tore their friends to pieces. They bandied great names from one to the other. They seemed to know everybody. They were in on all the secrets. Almost in a breath they touched upon the latest play, the latest dressmaker, the latest portrait painter, and the latest mistress of the latest premier. One would have thought there was nothing they didn't know. Isabel listened with ravishment. It all seemed to her wonderfully civilized. This really was life. It gave her a thrilling sense of being in the midst of things. This was real. The setting was perfect. That spacious room with the Savonnerie carpet on the floor, the lovely drawings on the richly-panelled walls, the *petit-point* chairs on which they sat, the priceless pieces of marquetry, commodes and occasional tables, every piece worthy to go into a museum; it must have cost a fortune, that room, but it was worth it. Its beauty, its discretion struck her as never before because she had still so vividly in her mind the shabby little hotel room, with its iron bed and that hard, comfortless chair in which he had sat, that room that Larry saw nothing wrong in. It was bare, cheerless, and horrid. It made her shudder to remember it.

The party broke up and Isabel was left with her mother and Elliott.

'Charming women,' said Elliott when he came back from seeing the two poor painted drabs to the door. 'I knew them when they first settled in Paris. I never dreamt they'd turn out as well as they have. It's amazing, the adaptability of our women. You'd hardly know now they were Americans and Middle West into the bargain.'

Mrs Bradley, raising her eyebrows, without speaking gave him a look which he was too quick-witted not to understand.

'No one could ever say that of you, my poor Louisa,' he continued half acidly and half affectionately. 'Though heaven knows, you've had every chance.'

Mrs Bradley pursed her lips.

'I'm afraid I've been a sad disappointment to you, Elliott, but to tell you the truth I'm very satisfied with myself as I am.'

'*Tous les goûts sont dans la nature,*' Elliott murmured.

'I think I ought to tell you that I'm no longer engaged to Larry,' said Isabel.

'Tut,' cried Elliott. 'That'll put my luncheon table out for tomorrow. How on earth am I going to get another man at this short notice?'

'Oh, he's coming to lunch all right.'

'After you've broken off your engagement? That sounds very unconventional.'

Isabel giggled. She kept her gaze on Elliott, for she knew her mother's eyes were fixed upon her and she didn't want to meet them.

'We haven't quarrelled. We talked it over this afternoon and came to the conclusion we'd made a mistake. He doesn't want to come back to America; he wants to stop on in Paris. He's talking of going to Greece.'

'What on earth for? There's no society in Athens. As a matter of fact I never thought so much of Greek art myself. Some of that Hellenistic stuff has a certain decadent charm that's rather attractive. But Phidias: no, no.'

'Look at me, Isabel,' said Mrs Bradley.

Isabel turned and with a faint smile on her lips faced her mother. Mrs Bradley gave her a scrutinizing stare, but all she said was, 'H'm.' The girl hadn't been crying, that she saw; she looked calm and composed.

'I think you're well out of it, Isabel,' said Elliott. 'I was prepared to make the best of it, but I never thought it a good match. He wasn't really up to your mark, and the way he's been behaving in Paris is a pretty clear indication that he'll

never amount to anything. With your looks and your connexions you can aspire to something better than that. I think
you've behaved in a very sensible manner.'

Mrs Bradley gave her daughter a glance that was not devoid
of anxiety.

'You haven't done this on my acount, Isabel?'

Isabel shook her head decidedly.

'No, darling, I've done it entirely on my own.'

6

I had come back from the East and was spending some time in
London just then. It was perhaps a fortnight after the events
I have just related that Elliott called me up one morning. I was
not surprised to hear his voice, for I knew that he was in the
habit of coming to England to enjoy the fag end of the season.
He told me that Mrs Bradley and Isabel were with him and if
I would drop in that evening at six for a drink they would be
glad to see me. They were, of course, staying at Claridge's. I
was at that time living not far from there, so I strolled down
Park Lane and through the quiet, dignified streets of Mayfair
till I came to the hotel. Elliott had his usual suite. It was
panelled in brown wood like the wood of a cigar box and
furnished with quiet sumptuousness. He was alone when I was
ushered in. Mrs Bradley and Isabel had gone shopping and he
was expecting them at any minute. He told me that Isabel had
broken her engagement to Larry.

Elliott with his romantic and highly conventional sense of
how people should comport themselves under given circumstances had been disconcerted by the young people's behaviour.
Not only had Larry come to lunch the very day after the break,
but he had acted as though his position were unchanged. He
was as pleasant, attentive, and soberly gay as usual. He treated
Isabel with the same comradely affectionateness with which he
had always treated her. He seemed neither harassed, upset, nor
woe-begone. Nor did Isabel appear dispirited. She looked as
happy, she laughed as lightly, she jested as merrily as though
she had not just taken a decisive and surely searing step in
her life. Elliott could not make head or tail of it. From such
scraps of their conversation as he caught he gathered that they

had no intention of breaking any of the dates they had made. On the first opportunity he talked it over with his sister.

'It's not decent,' he said. 'They can't run around together as if they were still engaged. Larry really should have more sense of propriety. Besides, it damages Isabel's chances. Young Fotheringham, that boy at the British Embassy, is obviously taken with her; he's got money and he's very well connected; if he knew the coast was clear I wouldn't be at all surprised if he made her an offer. I think you ought to talk to her about it.'

'My dear, Isabel's twenty and she has a technique for telling you to mind your own business without offensiveness which I've always found very difficult to cope with.'

'Then you've brought her up extremely badly, Louisa. And besides, it is your business.'

'That is a point on which you and she would certainly differ.'

'You're trying my patience, Louisa.'

'My poor Elliott, if you'd ever had a grown-up daughter you'd know that by comparison a bucking steer is easy to manage. And as to knowing what goes on inside her – well, it's much better to pretend you're the simple, innocent old fool she almost certainly takes you for.'

'But you have talked the matter over with her?'

'I tried to. She laughed at me and told me there was really nothing to tell.'

'Is she cut up?'

'I wouldn't know. All I do know is that she eats well and sleeps like a child.'

'Well, take my word for it, if you let them go on like this they'll go off one of these days and get married without saying a word to anybody.'

Mrs Bradley permitted herself to smile.

'It must be a relief to you to think that at present we're living in a country where every facility is afforded to sexual irregularity and every obstacle put in the way of marriage.'

'And quite rightly. Marriage is a serious matter on which rest the security of the family and the stability of the state.

But marriage can only maintain its authority if extraconjugal relations are not only tolerated but sanctioned. Prostitution, my poor Louisa –'

'That'll do, Elliott,' interrupted Mrs Bradley. 'I'm not interested in your views on the social and moral values of promiscuous fornication.'

It was then he put forward a scheme that would interrupt Isabel's continued intercourse with Larry, which was so repugnant to his sense of what was fitting. The Paris season was drawing to a close and all the best people were arranging to go to watering places or to Deauville before repairing for the rest of the summer to their ancestral *châteaux* in Touraine, Anjou, or Brittany. Ordinarily Elliott went to London at the end of June, but his family feeling was strong and his affection for his sister and Isabel sincere; he had been quite ready to sacrifice himself and remain in Paris, if they wished it, when no one who was anyone was there; but he found himself now in the agreeable situation of being able to do what was best for others and at the same time what was convenient to himself. He proposed to Mrs Bradley that the three of them should go to London immediately, where the season was still in full swing and where new interests and new friends would distract Isabel's mind from her unfortunate entanglement. According to the papers the great specialist on Mrs Bradley's disease was then in the British capital, and the desirability of consulting him would reasonably account for their precipitate departure and override any disinclination to leave Paris that Isabel might have. Mrs Bradley fell in with the plan. She was puzzled by Isabel. She could not make up her mind whether she was as carefree as she seemed or whether, hurt, angry, or heartsick, she was putting on a bold front to conceal her wounded feelings. Mrs Bradley could only agree with Elliott that it would do Isabel good to see new people and new places.

Elliot got busy on the telephone and when Isabel, who had been spending the day at Versailles with Larry, came home, he was able to tell her that he had made an appointment for her mother to see the celebrated doctor three days from then, that he had engaged a suite at Claridge's and that they were starting on the next day but one. Mrs Bradley watched her daughter

85

while this intelligence was being somewhat smugly imparted to her by Elliott, but she did not turn a hair.

'Oh, darling, I'm so glad you're going to see that doctor,' she cried with her usual rather breathless impetuosity. 'Of course, you mustn't miss the chance. And it'll be grand going to London. How long are we going to stay?'

'It would be useless to come back to Paris,' said Elliott. 'There won't be a soul here in a week. I want you to stay with me at Claridge's for the rest of the season. There are always some good balls in July and of course there's Wimbledon. And then Goodwood and Cowes. I'm sure the Ellinghams will be glad to have us on their yacht for Cowes and the Bantocks always have a large party for Goodwood.'

Isabel appeared to be delighted and Mrs Bradley was reassured. It looked as though she were not giving Larry a thought.

Elliott had just finished telling me all this when mother and daughter came in. I had not seen them for more than eighteen months. Mrs Bradley was a little thinner than before and more pasty-faced; she looked tired and none too well. But Isabel was blooming. With her high colour, the rich brown of her hair, her shining hazel eyes, her clear skin, she gave an impression of such youth, of so much enjoyment of the mere fact of being alive, that you felt half inclined to laugh with delight. She gave me the rather absurd notion of a pear, golden and luscious, perfectly ripe and simply asking to be eaten. She radiated warmth so that you thought that if you held out your hands you could feel its comfort. She looked taller than when I had last seen her, whether because she wore higher heels or because the clever dressmaker had cut her frock to conceal her youthful plumpness I don't know, and she held herself with the graceful ease of a girl who has played outdoor games since childhood. She was in short sexually a very attractive young woman. Had I been her mother I should have thought it high time she was married.

Glad of the opportunity to repay some of the kindness I had received from Mrs Bradley in Chicago, I asked them all three to come to a play with me one evening. I arranged to give a luncheon for them.

'You'll be wise to get in at once, my dear fellow,' said Elliott.

'I've already let my friends know we're here and I presume that in a day or two we shall be fixed up for the rest of the season.'

I understood by this that Elliott meant that then they would have no time for the likes of me and I laughed. Elliott gave me a glance in which I discerned a certain hauteur.

'But of course you'll generally find us here about six o'clock and we shall always be glad to see you,' he said graciously, but with the evident intention of putting me, as an author, in my humble place.

But the worm sometimes turns.

'You must try to get in touch with the St Olpherds,' I said. 'I hear they want to dispose of their Constable of Salisbury Cathedral.'

'I'm not buying any pictures just now.'

'I know, but I thought you might dispose of it for them.'

A steely glitter came into Elliott's eyes.

'My dear fellow, the English are a great people, but they have never been able to paint and never will be able to paint. I am not interested in the English school.'

7

During the next four weeks I saw little of Elliott and his relations. He did them proud. He took them for a week-end to a grand house in Sussex and for another week-end to an even grander one in Wiltshire. He took them to the royal box at the opera as guests of a minor princess of the House of Windsor. He took them to lunch and dine with the great. Isabel went to several balls. He entertained at Claridge's a series of guests whose names made a fine show in the paper next day. He gave supper parties at Ciro's and the Embassy. In fact he did all the right things and Isabel would have had to be much more sophisticated than she was not to have been a trifle dazzled by the splendour and elegance he provided for her delectation. Elliott could flatter himself that he was taking all this trouble from the purely unselfish motive of distracting Isabel's mind from an unfortunate love affair; but I had a notion he got besides a good deal of satisfaction out of letting his sister see with her own eyes how familiar he was with the illustrious and fashionable. He was an admirable host and he took a delight in displaying his virtuosity.

I went to one or two of his parties myself and now and again I dropped in at Claridge's at six o'clock. I found Isabel surrounded by strapping young men in beautiful clothes who were in the Household Brigade or by elegant young men in less beautiful clothes from the Foreign Office. It was on one of these occasions that she drew me aside.

'I want to ask you something,' she said. 'Do you remember that evening we went to a drugstore and had an ice-cream soda?'

'Perfectly.'

'You were very nice and helpful then. Will you be nice and helpful again?'

'I'll do my best.'

'I want to talk to you about something. Couldn't we lunch one day?'

'Almost any day you like.'

'Somewhere quiet.'

'What d'you say to driving down to Hampton Court and lunching there? The gardens should be at their best just now and you could see Queen Elizabeth's bed.'

The notion suited her and we fixed a day. But when the day came the weather, which had been fine and warm, broke; the sky was grey and a drizzling rain was falling. I called up and asked her if she wouldn't prefer to lunch in town.

'We shouldn't be able to sit in the gardens and the pictures will be so dark, we shan't see a thing.'

'I've sat in lots of gardens and I'm fed to the teeth with old masters. Let's go anyway.'

'All right.'

I fetched her and we drove down. I knew a small hotel where one ate tolerably and we went straight there. On the way Isabel talked with her usual vivacity of the parties she had been to and the people she had met. She had been enjoying herself, but her comments on various acquaintances she had made suggested to me that she had shrewdness and a quick eye for the absurd. The bad weather kept visitors away and we were the only occupants of the dining-room. The hotel specialized in homely English fare and we had a cut off a leg of excellent

lamb with green peas and new potatoes and a deep-dish apple
pie with Devonshire cream to follow. With a tankard of pale
ale it made an excellent lunch. When we had finished I suggested that we should go into the empty coffee-room where
there were armchairs in which we could sit in comfort. It was
chilly in there, but the fire was laid, so I put a match to it. The
flames made the dingy room more companionable.

'That's that,' I said. 'Now tell me what you want to talk to
me about.'

'It's the same as last time,' she chuckled. 'Larry.'

'So I guessed.'

'You know that we've broken off our engagement.'

'Elliott told me.'

'Mamma's relieved and he's delighted.'

She hesitated for a moment and then embarked upon the
account of her talk with Larry of which I have done my best
faithfully to inform the reader. It may surprise the reader that
she should have chosen to tell so much to someone whom she
knew so little. I don't suppose I had seen her a dozen times
and, except for that one occasion at the drugstore, never alone.
It did not surprise me. For one thing, as any writer will tell
you, people do tell a writer things that they don't tell others.
I don't know why, unless it is that having read one or two of
his books they feel on peculiarly intimate terms with him; or it
may be that they dramatize themselves and, seeing themselves
as it were as characters in a novel, are ready to be as open with
him as they imagine the characters of his invention are. And I
think that Isabel felt that I liked Larry and her, and that their
youth touched me, and that I was sympathetic to their dis-
tresses. She could not expect to find a friendly listener in Elliott
who was disinclined to trouble himself with a young man who
had spurned the best chance a young man ever had of getting
into society. Nor could her mother help her. Mrs Bradley had
high principles and common sense. Her common sense assured
her that if you wanted to get on in this world you must accept
its conventions, and not to do what everybody else did clearly
pointed to instability. Her high principles led her to believe
that a man's duty was to go to work in a business where by
energy and initiative he had a chance of earning enough money

to keep his wife and family in accordance with the standards of his station, give his sons such an education as would enable them on reaching man's estate to make an honest living, and on his death leave his widow adequately provided for.

Isabel had a good memory and the various turns of the long discussion had engraved themselves upon it. I listened in silence till she had finished. She only interrupted herself once to ask me a question.

'Who was Ruysdael?'

'Ruysdael? He was a Dutch landscape painter. Why?'

She told me that Larry had mentioned him. He had said that Ruysdael at least had found an answer to the questions he was asking, and she repeated to me his flippant reply when she had inquired who he was.

'What d'you suppose he meant?'

I had an inspiration.

'Are you sure he didn't say Ruysbroek?'

'He might have. Who was he?'

'He was a Flemish mystic who lived in the fourteenth century.'

'Oh,' she said with disappointment.

It meant nothing to her. But it meant something to me. That was the first indication I had of the turn Larry's reflection was taking, and while she went on with her story, though still listening attentively, part of my mind busied itself with the possibilities that reference of his had suggested. I did not want to make too much of it, for it might be that he had only mentioned the name of the Ecstatic Teacher to make an argumentative point; it might also have a significance that had escaped Isabel. When he answered her question by saying Ruysbroek was just a guy he hadn't known in college he evidently meant to throw her off the scent.

'What do you make of it all?' she asked when she had come to an end.

I paused before replying.

'D'you remember his saying that he was just going to loaf? If what he tells you is true his loafing seems to involve some very strenuous work.'

'I'm sure it's true. But don't you see that if he'd worked as

90

hard at any productive form of work he'd be earning a decent income?'

'There are people who are strangely constituted. There are criminals who'll work like beavers to contrive schemes that land them in prison and they no sooner get out than they start all over again and again land in prison. If they put as much industry, as much cleverness, resource, and patience into honest practices they could make a handsome living and occupy important positions. But they're just made that way. They like crime.'

'Poor Larry,' she giggled. 'You're not going to suggest that he's learning Greek to cook up a bank robbery.'

I laughed too.

'No, I'm not. What I'm trying to tell you is that there are men who are possessed by an urge so strong to do some particular thing that they can't help themselves, they've got to do it. They're prepared to sacrifice everything to satisfy their yearning.'

'Even the people who love them?'

'Oh, yes.'

'Is that anything more than plain selfishness?'

'I wouldn't know,' I smiled.

'What can be the possible use of Larry's learning dead languages?'

'Some people have a disinterested desire for knowledge. It's not an ignoble desire.'

'What's the good of knowledge if you're not going to do anything with it?'

'Perhaps he is. Perhaps it will be sufficient satisfaction merely to know, as it's a sufficient satisfaction to an artist to produce a work of art. And perhaps it's only a step towards something further.'

'If he wanted knowledge why couldn't he go to college when he came back from the war? It's what Dr Nelson and Mamma wanted him to do.'

'I talked to him about that in Chicago. A degree would be of no use to him. I have an inkling that he had a definite idea of what he wanted and felt he couldn't get it at a university. You know, in learning there's the lone wolf as well as the wolf who runs in the pack. I think Larry is one of those persons who can go no other way than their own.'

'I remember once asking him if he wanted to write. He laughed and said he had nothing to write about.'

'That's the most inconclusive reason for not writing that I've ever heard,' I smiled.

Isabel made a gesture of impatience. She was in no mood even for the mildest jest.

'What I can't make out is why he should have turned out like this. Before the war he was just like everybody else. You wouldn't think it, but he plays a very good game of tennis and he's quite a decent golfer. He used to do all the things the rest of us did. He was a perfectly normal boy and there was no reason to suppose he wouldn't become a perfectly normal man. After all you're a novelist, you ought to be able to explain it.'

'Who am I to explain the infinite complexities of human nature?'

'That's why I wanted to talk to you today,' she added, taking no notice of what I said.

'Are you unhappy?'

'No, not exactly unhappy. When Larry isn't there I'm all right; it's when I'm with him that I feel so weak. Now it's just a sort of ache, like the stiffness you get after a long ride when you haven't been on a horse for months; it's not pain, it's not at all unbearable, but you're conscious of it. I shall get over it all right. I hate the idea of Larry making such a mess of his life.'

'Perhaps he won't. It's a long, arduous road he's starting to travel, but it may be that at the end of it he'll find what he's seeking.'

'What's that?'

'Hasn't it occurred to you? It seems to me that in what he said to you he indicated it pretty plainly. God.'

'God!' she cried. But it was an exclamation of incredulous surprise. Our use of the same word, but in such a different sense, had a comic effect, so that we were obliged to laugh. But Isabel immediately grew serious again and I felt in her whole attitude something like fear. 'What on earth makes you think that?'

'I'm only guessing. But you asked me to tell you what I

thought as a novelist. Unfortunately you don't know what experience he had in the war that so profoundly moved him. I think it was some sudden shock for which he was unprepared. I suggest to you that whatever it was that happened to Larry filled him with a sense of the transiency of life, and an anguish to be sure that there was a compensation for the sin and sorrow of the world.'

I could see that Isabel didn't like the turn I had given the conversation. It made her feel shy and awkward.

'Isn't all that awfully morbid? One has to take the world as it comes. If we're here, it's surely to make the most of life.'

'You're probably right.'

'I don't pretend to be anything but a perfectly normal, ordinary girl. I want to have fun.'

'It looks as though there were complete incompatibility of temper between you. It's much better that you should have found it out before marriage.'

'I want to marry and have children and live –'

'In that state of life in which a merciful Providence has been pleased to place you,' I interrupted, smiling.

'Well, there's no harm in that, is there? It's a very pleasant state and I'm quite satisfied with it.'

'You're like two friends who want to take their holiday together, but one of them wants to climb Greenland's icy mountains while the other wants to fish off India's coral strand. Obviously it's not going to work.'

'Anyway, I might get a sealskin coat off Greenland's icy mountains, and I think it's very doubtful if there are any fish off India's coral strand.'

'That remains to be seen.'

'Why d'you say that?' she asked, frowning a little. 'All the time you seem to be making some sort of mental reservation. Of course I know that I'm not playing the star part in this. Larry's got that. He's the idealist, he's the dreamer of a beautiful dream, and even if the dream doesn't come true, it's rather thrilling to have dreamt it. I'm cast for the hard, mercenary, practical part. Common sense is never very sympathetic, is it? But what you forget is that it's I who'd have to pay. Larry would sweep along, trailing clouds of glory, and all there'd be left for me would be to tag along and make both ends meet. I want to live.'

'I don't forget that at all. Years ago, when I was young, I knew a man who was a doctor, and not a bad one either, but he didn't practise. He spent years burrowing away in the library of the British Museum and at long intervals produced a huge pseudo-scientific, pseudo-philosophical book that nobody read and that he had to publish at his own expense. He wrote four or five of them before he died and they were absolutely worthless. He had a son who wanted to go into the army, but there was no money to send him to Sandhurst, so he had to enlist. He was killed in the war. He had a daughter too. She was very pretty and I was rather taken with her. She went on the stage, but she had no talent and she traipsed around the provinces playing small parts in second-rate companies at a miserable salary. His wife, after years of dreary, sordid drudgery, broke down in health and the girl had to come home and nurse her and take on the drudgery her mother no longer had the strength for. Wasted, thwarted lives and all to no purpose. It's a toss-up when you decide to leave the beaten track. Many are called but few are chosen.'

'Mother and Uncle Elliott approve of what I've done. Do you approve too?'

'My dear, what can that matter to you? I'm almost a stranger to you.'

'I look upon you as a disinterested observer,' she said, with a pleasant smile. 'I should like to have your approval. You do think I've done right, don't you?'

'I think you've done right for you,' I said, fairly confident that she would not catch the slight distinction I made in my reply.

'Then why have I a bad conscience?'

'Have you?'

With a smile still on her lips, but a slightly rueful smile now, she nodded.

'I know it's only horse sense. I know that every reasonable person would agree that I've done the only possible thing. I know that from every practical standpoint, from the standpoint of worldly wisdom, from the standpoint of common decency, from the standpoint of what's right and wrong, I've done what I ought to do. And yet at the bottom of my heart I've got an uneasy feeling that if I were better, if I were more disinterested, more unselfish, nobler, I'd marry Larry and lead his life. If I only loved him enough I'd think the world well lost.'

'You might put it the other way about. If he loved you enough he wouldn't have hesitated to do what you want.'

'I've said that to myself too. But it doesn't help. I suppose it's more in woman's nature to sacrifice herself than in a man's.' She chuckled. 'Ruth and the alien corn and all that sort of thing.'

'Why don't you risk it?'

We had been talking quite lightly, almost as if we were having a casual conversation about people we both knew but in whose affairs we were not intimately concerned, and even when she narrated to me her talk with Larry, Isabel had spoken with a sort of breezy gaiety, enlivening it with humour, as if she did not want me to take what she said too seriously. But now she went pale.

'I'm afraid.'

For a while we were silent. A chill went down my spine as it strangely does when I am confronted with deep and genuine human emotion. I find it terrible and rather awe-inspiring.

'Do you love him very much?' I asked at last.

'I don't know. I'm impatient with him. I'm exasperated with him. I keep longing for him.'

Silence again fell upon us. I didn't know what to say. The coffee-room in which we sat was small, and heavy lace curtains over the window shut out the light. On the walls, covered with yellow marbled paper, were old sporting prints. With its mahogany furniture, its shabby leather chairs, and its musty smell, it was strangely reminiscent of a coffee-room in a Dickens novel. I poked the fire and put more coal on it. Isabel suddenly began to speak.

'You see, I thought when it came to a showdown he'd knuckle under. I knew he was weak.'

'Weak?' I cried. 'What made you think that? A man who for a year withstood the disapproval of all his friends and associates because he was determined to go his own way.'

'I could always do anything I wanted with him. I could turn him round my little finger. He was never a leader in the things we did. He just tagged along with the crowd.'

I had lit a cigarette and watched the smoke ring I had made. It grew larger and larger and then faded away into the air.

'Mamma and Elliott thought it very wrong of me to go about with him afterwards as though nothing had happened, but I didn't take it very seriously. I kept on thinking up to the end that he'd yield. I couldn't believe that when he'd got it into his thick head that I meant what I said he wouldn't give in.' She hesitated and gave me a smile of roguish, playful malice. 'Will you be awfully shocked if I tell you something?'

'I think it very unlikely.'

'When we decided to come to London I called Larry and asked him if we couldn't spend my last evening in Paris together. When I told them, Uncle Elliott said it was most improper and Mamma said she thought it unnecessary. When Mamma says something is unnecessary it means she thoroughly disapproves. Uncle Elliott asked me what the idea was and I said we were going to dine somewhere and then make a tour of the night clubs. He told Mamma she ought to forbid me to go. Mamma said, "Will you pay any attention if I forbid you to go?" "No, darling," I said, "none." Then she said, "That is what I imagined. In that case there doesn't seem to be much point in my forbidding it." '

'Your mother appears to be a woman of enormous sense.'

'I don't believe she misses much. When Larry called for me I went into her room to say good night to her. I'd made up a bit; you know, you have to in Paris or else you look so naked, and when she saw the dress I had on, I had an uneasy suspicion from the way she took me in from top to toe that she had a pretty shrewd idea what I was after. But she didn't say anything. She just kissed me and said she hoped I'd have a good time.'

'What were you after?'

Isabel looked at me doubtfully, as though she couldn't quite decide how frank she was prepared to be.

'I didn't think I was looking too bad and it was my last chance. Larry had reserved a table at Maxim's. We had lovely things to eat, all the things I particularly liked, and we had champagne. We talked our heads off, at least I did, and I made Larry laugh. One of the things I've liked about him is that I can always amuse him. We danced. When we'd had enough of that we went on to the Château de Madrid. We found some people we knew and joined them and we had more champagne. Then we all went to the Acacia. Larry dances quite well, and we fit. The heat and the music and the wine – I was getting a bit light-headed. I felt absolutely reckless. I danced with my face against Larry's and I knew he wanted me. God knows I wanted him. I had an idea. I suppose it had been at the back of my mind all the time. I thought I'd get him to come home with me and once I'd got him there, well, it was almost inevitable that the inevitable should happen.'

'Upon my word you couldn't put it more delicately.'

'My room was quite a way from Uncle Elliott's and Mamma's, so I knew there was no risk. When we were back in America I thought I'd write and say I was going to have a baby. He'd be obliged to come back and marry me, and when I'd got him home I didn't believe it would be hard to keep him there, especially with Mamma ill. "What a fool I am not to have thought of that before," I said to myself. "Of course that'll settle everything." When the music stopped I just stayed there in his arms. Then I said it was getting late and we had to take the train at noon, so we'd better go. We got into a taxi. I nestled close to him and he put his arms around me and kissed me. He kissed me, he kissed me – oh, it was heaven. It hardly seemed a moment before the taxi stopped at the door. Larry paid it.

' "I shall walk home," he said.

'The taxi rattled off and I put my arms round his neck.

' "Won't you come up and have one last drink?" I said.

' "Yes, if you like," he said.

'He'd rung the bell and the door swung open. He switched on the light as we stepped in. I looked into his eyes. They were so trusting, so honest, so – so guileless; he so obviously hadn't the smallest idea that I was laying a trap for him; I felt I couldn't play him such a dirty trick. It was like taking candy off a child. D'you know what I did? I said, "Oh well, perhaps

97

you'd better not. Mamma's not very well tonight and if she's fallen asleep I don't want to wake her up. Good night." I put my face up for him to kiss and pushed him out of the door. That was the end of that.'

'Are you sorry?' I asked.

'I'm neither pleased nor sorry. I just couldn't help myself. It wasn't me that did what I did. It was just an impulse that took possession of me and acted for me.' She grinned. 'I suppose you'd call it my better nature.'

'I suppose you would.'

'Then my better nature must take the consequences. I trust in the future it'll be more careful.'

That was in effect the end of our talk. It may be that it was some consolation to Isabel to have been able to speak to someone with entire freedom, but that was all the good I had been able to do her. Feeling I had been inadequate, I tried to say at least some small thing that would give her comfort.

'You know, when one's in love,' I said, 'and things go all wrong, one's terribly unhappy and one thinks one won't ever get over it. But you'll be astounded to learn what the sea will do.'

'What do you mean?' she smiled.

'Well, love isn't a good sailor and it languishes on a sea voyage. You'll be surprised when you have the Atlantic between you and Larry to find how slight the pang is that before you sailed seemed intolerable.'

'Do you speak from experience?'

'From the experience of a stormy past. When I suffered from the pangs of unrequited love I immediately got on an ocean liner.'

The rain showed no sign of letting up, so we decided that Isabel could survive without seeing the noble pile of Hampton Court or even Queen Elizabeth's bed, and drove back to London. I saw her two or three times after that, but only when other people were present, and then, having had enough of London for a while, I set off for the Tyrol.

III

1

FOR ten years after this I saw neither Isabel nor Larry. I continued to see Elliott, and indeed, for a reason that I shall tell later, more frequently than before, and from time to time I learnt from him what was happening to Isabel. But of Larry he could tell me nothing.

'For all I know he's still living in Paris, but I'm not likely to run across him. We don't move in the same circles,' he added, not without complacency. 'It's very sad that he should have gone so completely to seed. He comes of a very good family. I'm sure I could have made something of him if he'd put himself in my hands. Anyhow it was a lucky escape for Isabel.'

My circle of acquaintance was not so restricted as Elliott's and I knew a number of persons in Paris whom he would have thought eminently undesirable. On my brief but not infrequent sojourns I asked one or other of them whether he had run across Larry or had news of him; a few knew him casually, but none could claim any intimacy with him and I could find nobody to give me news of him. I went to the restaurant at which he habitually dined, but found he had not been there for a long time, and they thought he must have gone away. I never saw him at any of the cafés on the Boulevard du Montparnasse which people who live in the neighbourhood are apt to go to.

His intention, after Isabel left Paris, was to go to Greece, but this he abandoned. What he actually did he told me himself many years later, but I will relate it now because it is more convenient to place events as far as I can in chronological order. He stayed on in Paris during the summer and worked without a break till autumn was well advanced.

'I thought I needed a rest from books then,' he said, 'I'd been working from eight to ten hours a day for two years. So I went to work in a coal mine.'

'You did what?' I cried.

He laughed at my astonishment.

'I thought it would do me good to spend a few months in manual labour. I had a notion it would give me an opportunity to sort my thoughts and come to terms with myself.'

I was silent. I wondered whether that was the only reason for this unexpected step or whether it was connected with Isabel's refusal to marry him. The fact was, I didn't know at all how deeply he loved her. Most people when they're in love invent every kind of reason to persuade themselves that it's only sensible to do what they want. I suppose that's why there are so many disastrous marriages. They are like those who put their affairs in the hands of someone they know to be a crook, but who happens to be an intimate friend because, unwilling to believe that a crook is a crook first and a friend afterwards, they are convinced that, however dishonest he may be with others, he won't be so with them. Larry was strong enough to refuse to sacrifice for Isabel's sake the life that he thought was the life for him, but it may be that to lose her was bitterer to endure than he had expected. It may be that like most of us he wanted to eat his cake and have it.

'Well, go on,' I said.

'I packed my books and my clothes in a couple of trunks and got the American Express to store them. Then I put an extra suit and some linen in a grip and started off. My Greek teacher had a sister who was married to the manager of a mine near Lens and he gave me a letter to him. D'you know Lens?'

'No.'

'It's in the North of France, not far from the Belgian border. I only spent a night there, at the station hotel, and next day I took a local to the place where the mine was. Ever been to a mining village?'

'In England.'

'Well, I suppose it's much the same. There's the mine and the manager's house, rows and rows of trim little two-storey houses, all alike, exactly alike, and it's so monotonous it makes your heart sink. There's a newish, ugly church and several bars. It was bleak and cold when I got there and a thin rain was falling. I went to the manager's office and sent in my letter. He was a little, fat man with red cheeks and the look of a guy who enjoys his food. They were short of labour, a lot of miners had been killed in the war, and there were a good many Poles working there, two or three hundred, I should think. He asked me one or two questions, he didn't much like my being an American, he seemed to think it rather fishy, but his brother-in-law's letter spoke well of me and anyhow he was glad to have me. He wanted to give me a job on the surface, but I told him I wanted to work down below. He said I'd find it hard if I wasn't used to it, but I told him I was prepared for that, so then he said I could be helper to a miner. That was boy's work really, but there weren't enough boys to go round. He was a nice fellow; he asked me if I'd done anything about finding a lodging, and when I told him I hadn't he wrote an address on a piece of paper and said that if I went there the woman of the house would let me have a bed. She was the widow of a miner who'd been killed and her two sons were working in the mine.

'I took up my grip and went on my way. I found the house, and the door was opened for me by a tall, gaunt woman with greying hair and big, dark eyes. She had good features and she must have been nice-looking once. She wouldn't have been bad then in a haggard way except for two missing front teeth. She told me she hadn't a room, but there were two beds in a room she'd let to a Pole and I could have the other one. Her two sons had one of the upstairs rooms and she had the other. The room she showed me was on the ground floor and supposed, I imagined, to be the living-room; I should have liked a room to myself, but I thought I'd better not be fussy; and the drizzle had turned into a steady, light rain and I was wet already. I didn't want to go farther and get soaked to the skin. So I said that would suit me and I settled in. They used the kitchen as a living-room. It had a couple of rickety armchairs in it. There was a coal shed in the yard which was also the bath-house. The two boys and the Pole had taken their lunch with them, but she said I could eat with her at midday. I sat in the kitchen afterwards smoking and while she went on with her work she told me all about herself and her family. The others came in at the end of their shift. The Pole first and then the two boys. The Pole passed through the kitchen, nodded to me without speaking when our landlady told him I was to share his room, took a great kettle off the hob and went off to wash himself in the shed. The two boys were tall good-looking fellows notwithstanding the grime on their faces, and seemed inclined to be friendly. They looked upon me as a freak because I was American. One of them was nineteen, off to his military service in a few months, and the other eighteen.

'The Pole came back and then they went to clean up. The Pole had one of those difficult Polish names, but they called him Kosti. He was a big fellow, two or three inches taller than me, and heavily built. He had a pale fleshy face with a broad short nose and a big mouth. His eyes were blue and because he hadn't been able to wash the coal dust off his eyebrows and eyelashes he looked as if he was made up. The black lashes made the blue of his eyes almost startling. He was an ugly, uncouth fellow. The two boys after they'd changed their clothes went out. The Pole sat on in the kitchen, smoking a pipe and reading the paper. I had a book in my pocket, so I took it out and began reading too. I noticed that he glanced at me once or twice and presently he put his paper down.

' "What are you reading?" he asked

'I handed him the book to see for himself. It was a copy of the *Princesse de Clèves* that I'd bought at the station in Paris because it was small enough to put in my pocket. He looked at it, then at me, curiously, and handed it back. I noticed an ironical smile on his lips.

' "Does it amuse you?"

' "I think it's very interesting – even absorbing."

' "I read it at school at Warsaw. It bored me stiff." He spoke very good French, with hardly a trace of Polish accent. "Now I don't read anything but the newspaper and detective stories."

'Madame Leclerc, that was our old girl's name, with an eye on the soup that was cooking for supper, sat at the table darning socks. She told Kosti that I had been sent to her by the manager of the mine and repeated what else I had seen fit to tell her. He listened, puffing away at his pipe, and looked at me with brilliantly blue eyes. They were hard and shrewd. He asked me a few questions about myself. When I told him I had never worked in a mine before his lips broke again into an ironical smile.

' "You don't know what you're in for. No one would go to work in a mine who could do anything else. But that's your affair and doubtless you have your reasons. Where did you live in Paris?"

'I told him.

' "At one time I used to go to Paris every year, but I kept to the Grands Boulevards. Have you ever been to Larue's? It was my favourite restaurant."

'That surprised me a bit because, you know, it's not cheap.'

'Far from it.'

'I fancy he saw my surprise, for he gave me once more his mocking smile, but evidently didn't think it necessary to explain further. We went on talking in a desultory fashion and then the two boys came in. We had supper and when we'd finished Kosti asked me if I'd like to come to the *bistro* with him and have a beer. It was just a rather large room with a bar at one end of it and a number of marble-topped tables with wooden chairs around them. There was a mechanical piano and some-one had put a coin in the slot and it was braying out a dance tune. Only three tables were occupied besides ours. Kosti asked me if I played *belote*. I'd learnt it with some of my student friends, so I said I did and he proposed that we should play for the beer. I agreed and he called for cards. I lost a beer and a second beer. Then he proposed that we should play for money. He had good cards and I had bad luck. We were playing for very small stakes, but I lost several francs. This and the beer put him in a good humour and he talked. It didn't take me long to guess both by his way of expressing himself and by his manners, that he was a man of education. When he spoke again of Paris it was to ask me if I knew So-and-so and So-and-so, American women I had met at Elliott's when Aunt Louisa and Isabel were staying with him. He appeared to know them better than I did and I wondered how it was that he found himself in his present position. It wasn't late, but we had to get up at the crack of dawn.

' "Let's have one more beer before we go," said Kosti.

'He sipped it and peered at me with his shrewd little eyes.

I knew what he reminded me of then, an ill-tempered pig.

' "Why have you come here to work in this rotten mine?" he asked me.

' "For the experience."

' "*Tu es fou, mon petit,*" he said.

' "And why are you working in it?"

'He shrugged his massive, ungainly shoulders.

' "I entered the nobleman's cadet school when I was a kid, my father was a general under the Czar and I was a cavalry officer in the last war. I couldn't stand Pilsudski. We arranged to kill him, but someone gave us away. He shot those of us he caught. I managed to get across the frontier just in time. There was nothing for me but the Foreign Legion or a coal mine. I chose the lesser of two evils."

'I had already told Kosti what job I was to have in the mine and he had said nothing, but now, putting his elbow on the marble-topped table, he said:

' "Try to push my hand back."

'I knew the old trial of strength and I put my open palm against his. He laughed. "Your hand won't be as soft as that in a few weeks." I pushed with all my might, but I could make no effect against his huge strength and gradually he pressed my hand back and down to the table.

' "You're pretty strong," he was good enough to say. "There aren't many men who keep up as long as that. Listen, my helper's no good, he's a puny little Frenchman, he hasn't got the strength of a louse. You come along with me tomorrow and I'll get the foreman to let me have you instead."

' "I'd like that," I said. "D'you think he'll do it?"

' "For a consideration. Have you got fifty francs to spare?"

'He stretched out his hand and I took a note out of my wallet. We went home and to bed. I'd had a long day and I slept like a log.'

'Didn't you find the work terribly hard?' I asked Larry.

'Back-breaking at first,' he grinned. 'Kosti worked it with the foreman and I was made his helper. At that time Kosti was working in a space about the size of a hotel bathroom and one got to it through a tunnel so low that you had to crawl through it on your hands and knees. It was as hot as hell in there and we worked in nothing but our pants. There was something terribly repulsive in that great white fat torso of Kosti's; he looked like a huge slug. The row of the pneumatic cutter in that narrow space was deafening. My job was to gather the blocks of coal that he hacked away and load a basket with them and drag the basket through the tunnel to its mouth, where it could be loaded into a truck when the train came along at intervals on its way to the elevators. It's the only coal mine I've ever known, so I don't know if that's the normal practice. It seemed amateurish to me and it was damned hard work. At half time we knocked off for a rest and ate our lunch and smoked. I wasn't sorry when we were through for the day, and gosh, it was good to have a bath. I thought I'd never get my feet clean; they were as black as ink. Of course my hands blistered and they got as sore as the devil, but they healed. I got used to the work.'

'How long did you stick it out?'

'I was only kept on that job for a few weeks. The trucks that carried the coal to the elevators were hauled by a tractor and the driver was a poor mechanic and the engine was always breaking down. Once he couldn't get it going and he didn't seem to know what to do. Well, I'm a pretty good mechanic, so I had a look at it and in half an hour I got it working. The foreman told the manager and he sent for me and asked me if I knew about cars. The result was that he gave me the mechanic's job; of course it was monotonous, but it was easy, and because they didn't have any more engine trouble they were pleased with me.

'Kosti was as sore as hell at my leaving him. I suited him and he'd got used to me. I got to know him pretty well, working with him all day, going to the *bistro* with him after supper, and sharing a room with him. He was a funny fellow. He was the sort of man who'd have appealed to you. He didn't mix with the Poles and we didn't go to the cafés they went to. He couldn't forget he was a nobleman and had been a cavalry officer and he treated them like dirt. Naturally they resented it, but they couldn't do anything about it; he was as strong as an ox, and if it had ever come to a scrap, knives or no knives, he'd have been a match for half a dozen of them together. I got to know some of them all the same, and they told me he'd been a cavalry officer all right in one of the smart regiments, but it was a lie about his having left Poland for political reasons. He'd been kicked out of the Officers' Club at Warsaw and cashiered because he'd been caught cheating at cards. They warned me against playing with him. They said that was why he fought so shy of them, because they knew too much about him and wouldn't play with him.

'I'd been losing to him consistently, not much, you know, just a few francs a night, but when he won he always insisted on paying for drinks, so it didn't amount to anything really. I thought I was just having a run of bad luck or that I didn't play as well as he did. But after that I kept my eyes skinned and I was dead sure he was cheating, but d'you know, for the life of me I couldn't see how he did it. Gosh, he was clever. I knew he simply couldn't have the best cards all the time. I watched him like a lynx. He was as cunning as a fox and I guess he saw I'd been put wise to him. One night, after we'd been playing for a while, he looked at me with that rather cruel, sarcastic smile of his which was the only way he knew how to smile, and said:

' "Shall I show you a few tricks?"

'He took the pack of cards and asked me to name one. He shuffled them and he told me to choose one; I did, and it was the card I'd named. He did two or three more tricks and then he asked me if I played poker. I said I did and he dealt me a hand. When I looked at it I saw I'd got four aces and a king.

' "You'd be willing to bet a good deal on that hand, wouldn't you?" he asked.

' "My whole stack," I answered.

' "You'd be silly." He put down the hand he'd dealt himself. It was a straight flush. How it was done I don't know. He laughed at my amazement. "If I weren't an honest man I'd have had your shirt by now."

' "You haven't done so badly as it is," I grinned.

' "Chicken feed. Not enough to buy a dinner at Larue's."

'We continued to play pretty well every night. I came to the conclusion that he cheated not so much for the money as for the fun of it. It gave him a queer satisfaction to know that he was making a fool of me, and I think he got a lot of amusement out of knowing that I was on to what he was doing and couldn't see how it was done.

'But that was only one side of him and it was the other side that made him so interesting to me. I couldn't reconcile the two. Though he boasted he never read anything but the paper and detective stories he was a cultivated man. He was a good talker, caustic, harsh, cynical, but it was exhilarating to listen to him. He was a devout Catholic and had a crucifix hanging over his bed, and he went to Mass every Sunday regularly. On Saturday nights he used to get drunk. The *bistro* we went to was crammed jammed full then, and the air was heavy with smoke. There were quiet, middle-aged miners with their families, and there were groups of young fellows kicking up a hell of a row, and there were men with sweaty faces round tables playing *belote* with loud shouts, while their wives sat by, a little behind them, and watched. The crowd and the noise had a strange effect on Kosti and he'd grow serious and start talking – of all unlikely subjects – of mysticism. I knew nothing of it then but an essay of Maeterlinck's on Ruysbroek that I'd read in Paris. But Kosti talked of Plotinus and Denis the Areopagite and Jacob Boehme the shoemaker and Meister Eckhart. It was fantastic to hear that great hulking bum, who'd been thrown out of his own world, that sardonic, bitter down-and-out, speaking of the ultimate reality of things and the blessedness of union with God. It was all new to me and I was confused and excited. I was like someone who's lain awake in a darkened room and suddenly a chink of light shoots through the curtains and he knows he only has to draw them and there the country will be spread before him in the glory of the dawn. But if I tried to get him on the subject when he was sober he got mad at me. His eyes were spiteful.

' "How should I know what I was talking about when I didn't know what I was saying?" he snapped.

'But I knew he was lying. He knew perfectly well what he was talking about. He knew a lot. Of course he was soused, but the look in his eyes, the rapt expression on his ugly face, weren't due only to drink. There was more to it than that. The first time he talked in that way he said something that I've never forgotten, because it horrified me; he said that the world isn't a creation, for out of nothing nothing comes; but a manifestation of the eternal nature; well, that was all right, but then he added that evil is as direct a manifestation of the divine as good. They were strange words to hear in that sordid, noisy café, to the accompaniment of dance tunes on the mechanical piano.'

2

To give the reader a moment's rest I am starting here upon a new section, but I am doing it only for his convenience; the conversation was uninterrupted. I may take this opportunity to say that Larry spoke without haste, often choosing his words with care, and though of course I do not pretend to report them exactly, I have tried to reproduce not only the matter, but the manner of his discourse. His voice, rich in tone, had a musical quality that was grateful to the ear; and as he talked without gesticulation of any kind, puffing away at his pipe and stopping now and again to relight it, he looked you in the face with a pleasant, often whimsical expression in his dark eyes.

'Then the spring came, late in that flat, dismal part of the country, cold and rainy still; but sometimes a fine warm day made it hard to leave the world above ground and go down hundreds of feet in a rickety elevator, crowded with miners in their grimy overalls, into the bowels of the earth. It was spring all right, but it seemed to come shyly in that grim and sordid landscape as though unsure of a welcome. It was like a flower, a daffodil or a lily, growing in a pot on the window-sill of a slum dwelling and you wondered what it did there. One Sunday morning we were lying in bed, we always slept late on Sunday morning, and I was reading, when Kosti said to me out of a blue sky:

' "I'm getting out of here. D'you want to come with me?"

'I knew a lot of the Poles went back to Poland in the summer to get the harvest in, but it was early for that, and besides, Kosti couldn't go back to Poland.

' "Where are you going?" I asked.

' "Tramping. Across Belgium and into Germany and down

the Rhine. We could get work on a farm that would see us through the summer."

'It didn't take a minute to make up my mind.

' "It sounds fine," I said.

'Next day we told the foreman we were through. I found a fellow who was willing to take my grip in exchange for a rucksack. I gave the clothes I didn't want or couldn't carry on my back to the younger of Madame Leclerc's sons who was about my size. Kosti left a bag, packed what he wanted in his rucksack and the day after, as soon as the old girl had given us our coffee, we started off.

'We weren't in any hurry as we knew we couldn't get taken on at a farm at least until the hay was ready to cut, and so we dawdled along through France and Belgium by way of Namur and Liège and got into Germany through Aachen. We didn't do more than ten or twelve miles a day. When we liked the look of a village we stopped there. There was always some kind of an inn where we could get beds and an alehouse where we could get something to eat and beer to drink. On the whole we had fine weather. It was grand to be out in the open air after all those months in the mine. I don't think I'd ever realized before how good a green meadow is to look at and how lovely a tree is when the leaves aren't out yet, but the branches are veiled in a faint green mist. Kosti started to teach me German and I believe he spoke it as well as he spoke French. As we trudged along he would tell me the German for the various objects we passed, a cow, a horse, a man and so on, and then make me repeat simple German sentences. It made the time pass and by the time we got into Germany I could at least ask for the things I wanted.

'Cologne was a bit out of our way, but Kosti insisted on going there, on account of the Eleven Thousand Virgins, he said, and when we got there he went on a bat. I didn't see him for three days and when he turned up at the room we'd taken in a sort of workmen's rooming-house he was very surly. He'd got in a fight and he had a black eye and a cut on his lip. He wasn't a pretty object, I can tell you. He went to bed for twenty-four hours, and then we started to walk down the valley of the Rhine towards Darmstadt, where he said the country was good and we stood the best chance of getting work.

'I never enjoyed anything more. The fine weather held and we wandered through towns and villages. When there were sights to see we stopped off and looked at them. We put up where we could and once or twice we slept in a loft on the hay. We ate at wayside inns, and when we got in the wine country we turned from beer to wine. We made friends with the people in the taverns we drank in. Kosti had a sort of rough joviality that inspired them with confidence and he'd play *skat* with them, that's a German card game, and skin them with such bluff good humour, with the earthy jokes they appreciated, that they hardly minded losing their pfennigs to him. I practised my German on them. I'd bought a little English–German conversation grammar at Cologne and I was getting on pretty well. And then at night, when he'd got a couple of litres of white wine inside him, Kosti would talk in a morbid way of the flight from the Alone to the Alone, of the Dark Night of the Soul and of the final ecstasy in which the creature becomes one with the Beloved. But when in the early morning, as we walked through the smiling country, with the dew still on the grass, I tried to get him to tell me more, he grew so angry that he could have hit me.

' "Shut up, you fool," he said. "What do you want with all that stuff and nonsense? Come, let's get on with our German."

'You can't argue with a man who's got a fist like a steam hammer and wouldn't think twice about using it. I'd seen him in a rage. I knew he was capable of laying me out cold and leaving me in a ditch and I wouldn't have put it past him to empty my pockets while I was out. I couldn't make head or tail of him. When wine had loosened his tongue and he spoke of the Ineffable, he shed the rough obscene language that he ordinarily used, like the grimy overalls he wore in the mine, and he was well-spoken and even eloquent. I couldn't believe he wasn't sincere. I don't know how it occurred to me, but I got the idea somehow that he'd taken on that hard, brutal labour of the mine to mortify his flesh. I thought he hated that great, uncouth body of his and wanted to torture it, and that his cheating and his bitterness and his cruelty were the revolt of his will against – oh, I don't know what you'd call it – against a deep-

110

rooted instinct of holiness, against a desire for God that terrified and yet obsessed him.

'We'd taken our time, the spring was pretty well over and the trees were in full leaf. The grapes in the vineyards were beginning to fill out. We kept to the dirt roads as much as we could and they were getting dusty. We were in the neighbourhood of Darmstadt, and Kosti said we'd better start looking for a job. Our money was getting short. I had half a dozen travellers' cheques in my pocket, but I'd made up my mind not to use them if I could possibly help it. When we saw a farmhouse that looked promising we stopped and asked if they wanted a couple of hands. I dare say we didn't look very inviting. We were dusty and sweaty and dirty. Kosti looked a terrible ruffian and I don't suppose I looked much better either. We were turned down time after time. At one place the farmer said he'd take Kosti but couldn't do with me and Kosti said we were buddies and wouldn't separate. I told him to go ahead, but he wouldn't. I was surprised. I knew Kosti had taken a fancy to me, though I couldn't imagine why, as I didn't begin to be the kind of guy he had any use for, but I would never have thought he liked me well enough to refuse a job on my account. I felt rather conscience-stricken as we walked on, because I didn't really like him, in fact I found him rather repulsive, but when I tried to say something to show I was pleased with what he'd done, he bit my head off.

'But at last our luck turned. We'd just gone through a village in a hollow and we came to a rambling farmhouse that didn't look so bad. We knocked at the door and a woman opened it. We offered ourselves as usual. We said we didn't want any wages, but were willing to work for our board and lodging, and to my surprise instead of slamming the door in our face, she told us to wait. She called to someone inside the house and presently a man came out. He had a good stare at us and asked us where we came from. He asked to see our papers. He gave me another stare when he saw I was American. He didn't seem to like it very much, but anyhow he asked us to come in and have a glass of wine. He took us into the kitchen and we sat down. The woman brought a flagon and some glasses. He told us that his hired man had been gored by a bull and was

111

in hospital and wouldn't be fit for anything till after the harvest was in. With so many men killed, and others going into the factories that were springing up along the Rhine, it was the devil's own job to get labour. We knew that and had been counting on it. Well, to make a long story short he said he'd take us. There was plenty of room in the house, but I suppose he didn't fancy having us there; anyway he told us there were two beds in the hayloft and that was where we were to sleep.

'The work wasn't hard. There were the cows to look after and the hogs; the machinery was in a bad way, and we had to do something about that; but I had some leisure. I loved the sweet-smelling meadows and in the evenings I used to wander about and dream. It was a good life.

'The household consisted of old Becker, his wife, his widowed daughter-in-law, and her children. Becker was a heavy, grey-haired man in his late forties; he'd been through the war and still limped from a wound in the leg. It hurt him a lot and he drank to kill the pain. He was generally high by the time he got to bed. Kosti got on with him fine and they used to go down to the inn together after supper to play *skat* and swill wine. Frau Becker had been a hired girl. They'd got her out of an orphanage and Becker had married her soon after his wife's death. She was a good many years younger than he was, rather handsome in a way, full-blown, with red cheeks and fair hair and a hungry sensual look. It didn't take Kosti long to come to the conclusion that there was something doing there. I told him not to be a fool. We had a good job and we didn't want to lose it. He only jeered at me; he said Becker wasn't satisfying her and she was asking for it. I knew it was useless to appeal to his sense of decency, but I told him to be careful; it might be that Becker wouldn't see what he was after, but there was his daughter-in-law, and she wasn't missing anything.

'Ellie, that was her name, was a thickset, big young woman, well under thirty, with black eyes and black hair, a sallow square face and a sullen look. She still wore mourning for her husband killed at Verdun. She was very devout and on Sunday mornings trudged down to the village to early Mass and again in the afternoon to vespers. She had three children, one of whom had been born after her husband's death, and she never spoke at meals except to scold them. She did little work on the farm, but spent most of her time looking after the kids, and in the evening sat by herself in the sitting-room, with the door open so that she could hear if one of them was crying, and read novels. The two women hated one another. Ellie despised Frau Becker because she was a foundling and had been a servant, and bitterly resented her being the mistress of the house and in a position to give orders.

'Ellie was the daughter of a prosperous farmer and had brought a good dowry with her. She hadn't gone to the village school, but to Zwingenberg, the nearest town, where there was a girl's *gymnasium*, and she'd got quite a good education. Poor Frau Becker had come to the farm when she was fourteen and if she could read and write that's about all she could do. That was another cause of discord between the two women. Ellie lost no opportunity of showing off her knowledge, and Frau Becker, red in the face with anger, would ask what use it was to a farmer's wife. Then Ellie would look at her husband's identification disc which she wore on a steel chain round her wrist and with a bitter look on her sullen face say:

' "Not a farmer's wife. Only a farmer's widow. Only the widow of a hero who gave his life for his country."

'Poor old Becker had his work cut out to keep the peace between them.'

'But what did they make of you?' I interrupted Larry.

'Oh, they thought I'd deserted from the American Army and couldn't go back to America or I'd be put in jail. That's how they explained that I didn't care to go down to the inn and drink with Becker and Kosti. They thought I didn't want to attract attention to myself and have the village constable asking questions. When Ellie found out I was trying to learn German she brought out her old schoolbooks and said she'd teach me. So after supper she and I would go into the sitting-room, leaving Frau Becker in the kitchen, and I'd read aloud to her while she corrected my accent and tried to make me understand words I couldn't get the sense of. I guessed she was doing it not so much to help me as to put something over on Frau Becker.

'All this time Kosti was trying to make Frau Becker and wasn't getting anywhere. She was a jolly, merry woman and quite prepared to joke and laugh with him, and he had a way with him with women. I guess she knew what he was after and I dare say she was flattered, but when he started pinching her she told him to keep his hands to himself and smacked his face. And I bet it was a good hard smack.'

Larry hesitated a little and smiled rather shyly.

'I've never been the sort who thinks women are after me, but it occurred to me that – well, that Frau Becker had fallen for me. It made me rather uncomfortable. For one thing she was a lot older than me, and then old Becker had been very decent to us. She dished out the food at table and I couldn't help noticing that she helped me more liberally than the others, and she seemed to me to look for opportunities of being alone with me. She'd smile at me in what I suppose you'd call a provocative manner. She'd ask me if I had a girl, and say that a young fellow like me must suffer for the want of it in a place like that. You know the sort of thing. I only had three shirts and they were pretty well worn. Once she said it was a disgrace that I should wear such rags and if I'd bring them along she'd mend them. Ellie heard her and next time we were alone said that if I had anything to mend she'd do it. I said it didn't matter. But a day or two later I found that my socks had been darned and my shirts patched and put back on the bench in the loft on which we kept our things; but which of them had done it I don't know. Of course I didn't take Frau Becker seriously; she was a good-natured old soul and I thought it might be just motherliness on her part; but then one day Kosti said to me:

' "Listen, it's not me she wants; it's you. I haven't got a chance."

' "Don't talk such nonsense," I said to him. "She's old enough to be my mother."

' "What of it? You go ahead, my boy, I won't stand in your way. She's not so young as she might be, but she's a fine figure of a woman."

' "Oh, shut up."

' "Why d'you hesitate? Not on my account, I hope. I'm a philosopher and I know there are as good fish in the sea as ever came out. I don't blame her. You're young. I've been young too. *Jeunesse ne dure qu'un moment.*"

'I wasn't too pleased that Kosti was so sure of what I didn't want to believe. I didn't quite know how to deal with the situation, and then I recalled various things that hadn't struck me at the time. Things said by Ellie that I hadn't paid much attention to. But now I understood them and I was pretty sure that she too knew what was happening. She'd turn up suddenly in the kitchen when Frau Becker and I happened to be alone. I got the impression that she was watching us. I didn't like it. I thought she was out to catch us. I knew she hated Frau Becker, and if she had half a chance she'd make trouble. Of course I knew she couldn't catch us, but she was a malevolent creature and I didn't know what lies she mightn't invent and pour into old Becker's ears. I didn't know what to do except to pretend I was such a fool I didn't see what the old girl was up to. I was happy at the farm and enjoying the work and I didn't want to go till after we'd got the harvest in.'

I couldn't help smiling. I could imagine what Larry had looked like then, in his patched shirt and shorts, his face and neck burnt brown by the hot sun of the Rhine valley, with his lithe slim body, and his black eyes in their deep sockets. I could well believe that the sight of him set the matronly Frau Becker, so blonde, so full-breasted, all of a flutter with desire.

'Well, what happened?' I asked.

'Well, the summer wore on. We worked like demons there. We cut and stacked the hay. Then the cherries were ripe, Kosti and I got up on ladders and picked them, and the two women put them in great baskets and old Becker took them into Zwingenberg and sold them. Then we cut the rye. And of course there were always the animals to look after. We were up before dawn and we didn't stop work till nightfall. I supposed Frau Becker had given me up as a bad job; as far as I could without offending her, I kept her at arm's length. I was too sleepy to read much German in the evenings and soon after supper I'd take myself off to our loft and fall into bed. Most evenings Becker and Kosti went to the inn down in the village, but I was fast asleep by the time Kosti came back. It was hot in the loft and I slept naked.

'One night I was awakened. At the first moment I couldn't make out what it was; I was only half awake. I felt a hot hand on my mouth and I realized somebody was in bed with me. I tore the hand away and then a mouth was pressed to mine, two arms were thrown round me, and I felt Frau Becker's great breasts against my body.

' "*Sei still*," she whispered. "Be quiet."

'She pressed up against me and kissed my face with hot full lips and her hands travelled over my body and she twined her legs in mine.'

Larry stopped. I giggled.

'What did you do?'

He gave me a deprecating smile. He even flushed a little.

'What could I do? I could hear Kosti breathing heavily in his sleep in the bed next to mine. The situation of Joseph has always seemed to me faintly ridiculous. I was only just twenty-three. I couldn't make a scene and kick her out. I didn't want to hurt her feelings. I did what was expected of me.

'Then she slipped out of bed and tiptoed out of the loft. I can tell you, I heaved a sigh of relief. You know, I'd been scared. "Gosh," I said, "what a risk to take!" I thought it likely that Becker had come home drunk and fallen asleep in a stupor, but they slept in the same bed, and it might be that he'd woken up and seen his wife wasn't there. And there was Ellie. She always said she didn't sleep well. If she'd been awake she'd have heard Frau Becker go downstairs and out of the house. And then, suddenly, something struck me. When Frau Becker was in bed with me I'd felt a piece of metal against my skin. I'd paid no attention, you know one doesn't in those circumstances, and I'd never thought of asking myself what the devil it was. And now it flashed across me. I was sitting on the side of my bed thinking and worrying about the consequences of all this and it was such a shock that I jumped up. The piece of metal was Ellie's husband's identification disc that she wore round her wrist and it wasn't Frau Becker that had been in bed with me. It was Ellie.'

I roared with laughter. I couldn't stop.

'It may seem funny to you,' said Larry. 'It didn't seem funny to me.'

'Well, now you look back on it, don't you think there is just a faint element of the humorous about it?'

An unwilling smile played on his lips.

'Perhaps. But it was an awkward situation. I didn't know what it was going to lead to. I didn't like Ellie. I thought her a most unpleasant female.'

'But how could you mistake one for the other?'

'It was pitch dark. She never said a word except to tell me to keep my trap shut. They were both big stout women. I thought Frau Becker had her eye on me. It never occurred to me for a moment that Ellie gave me a thought. She was always thinking of her husband. I lit a cigarette and thought the position over and the more I thought of it the less I liked it. It seemed to me that the best thing I could do was to get out.

'I'd often cursed Kosti because he was so hard to wake. When we were at the mine I used to have to shake the life out of him to get him up in time to go to work. But I was thankful now that he slept so heavily. I lit my lantern and dressed, bundled my things into my rucksack – I hadn't got much, so it didn't take a minute – and slipped my arms through the straps. I walked across the loft in my stocking feet and didn't put my shoes on till I got to the bottom of the ladder. I blew out the lantern. It was a dark night, with no moon, but I knew my way to the road and I turned in the direction of the village. I walked fast as I wanted to get through it before anyone was up and about. It was only twelve miles to Zwingenberg and I got there just as it was stirring. I shall never forget that walk. There wasn't a sound except my footsteps on the road and now and then the crowing of a cock in a farm. Then the first greyness when it wasn't yet light and not quite dark, and the first hint of dawn, and the sunrise with the birds all starting to sing, and that lush green country, meadows and woods and the wheat in the fields silvery gold in the cool light of the beginning day. I got a cup of coffee at Zwingenberg and a roll, then I went to the post office and sent a wire to the American Express to have my clothes and my books sent to Bonn.'

'Why Bonn?' I interrupted.

'I'd taken a fancy to it when we stopped off there on our tramp down the Rhine. I liked the way the light shone on the roofs and the river, and its old narrow streets, and its villas and gardens and avenues of chestnut trees and the rococo buildings

117

of the university. It struck me then it wouldn't be a bad place to stay in for a bit. But I thought I'd better present a respectable appearance when I got there, I looked like a tramp and I didn't think I'd inspire much confidence if I went to a pension and asked for a room, so I took a train to Frankfurt and bought myself a grip and a few clothes. I stayed in Bonn off and on for a year.'

'And did you get anything out of your experience, at the mine, I mean, and on the farm?'

'Yes,' said Larry, nodding his head and smiling.

But he didn't tell me what it was and I knew him well enough by then to know that when he felt like telling you something he did, but when he didn't he would turn off questions with a cool pleasantry that made it useless to insist. For I must remind the reader that he narrated all this to me ten years after it happened. Till then, when I once more came in contact with him, I had no notion where he was or how he was engaged. For all I knew he might be dead. Except for my friendship with Elliott, who kept me posted with the course of Isabel's life and so reminded me of Larry, I should doubtless have forgotten his existence.

3

Isabel was married to Gray Maturin early in the June of the year after the termination of her engagement to Larry. Though Elliott hated leaving Paris at a moment when the season was at its height and he must miss a number of grand parties, his family feeling was too strong to allow him to neglect what he thought a social duty. Isabel's brothers were unable to leave their distant posts and so it behoved him to make the irksome journey to Chicago to give his niece away. Remembering that French aristocrats had gone to the guillotine in all their finery, he made a special journey to London to get himself a new morning coat, a dove-grey double-breasted waistcoat, and a silk hat. On his return to Paris he invited me to come and see them on. He was in a state of perturbation because the grey pearl he usually wore in his necktie would not make any sort of effect against the pale grey tie he had chosen as suitable to the festive occasion. I suggested his emerald-and-diamond pin.

118

'If I were a guest – yes,' he said. 'But in the particular position I shall occupy I *feel* that a pearl is indicated.'

He was much pleased with the marriage, which concorded with all his ideas of propriety, and he spoke of it with the unctuousness of a dowager duchess expressing herself on the suitability of a union between a scion of the La Rochefoucaulds with a daughter of the Montmorencys. As a visible mark of his satisfaction he was taking over as a wedding present, sparing no expense, a fine portrait by Nattier of a princess of the House of France.

It appeared that Henry Maturin had bought for the young couple a house in Astor Street so that they should be close to where Mrs Bradley lived and not too far from his own palatial residence on Lake Shore Drive. By a happy chance, in which I suspected the deft complicity of Elliott, Gregory Brabazon was in Chicago at the time the purchase was made and the decoration was entrusted to him. When Elliott returned to Europe and, throwing in his hand so far as the season in Paris was concerned, came straight to London, he brought photographs of the result. Gregory Brabazon had let himself go. In the drawing-room he had gone all George the Second and it was very grand. In the library, which was to be Gray's den, he had been inspired by a room in the Amalienburg Palace at Munich, and except that there was no place in it for books it was perfect. Save for the twin beds, Louis Quinze visiting Madame de Pompadour would have found himself perfectly at home in the bedroom Gregory had provided for this young American couple, but Isabel's bathroom would have been an eye-opener to him; it was all glass – walls, ceiling and bath – and on the walls silver fish meandered profusely among gilded aquatic plants.

'Of course it's a tiny house,' said Elliott, 'but Henry told me the decoration set him back a hundred thousand dollars. A fortune to some people.'

The ceremony was performed with such pomp as the Episcopalian church could afford.

'Not like a wedding at Notre Dame,' he told me complacently, 'but for a Protestant affair it didn't lack style.'

The press had behaved very handsomely and Elliott negligently tossed the cuttings to me. He showed me photographs of Isabel, hefty but handsome in her wedding-dress, and Gray, a massive but fine figure of a man, a trifle self-conscious in his formal clothes. There was a group of the young couple with bridesmaids and another group with Mrs Bradley in a sumptuous garment and Elliott holding his new top-hat with a grace that only he could have achieved. I asked how Mrs Bradley was.

'She's lost a good deal of weight and I don't like her colour, but she's pretty well. Of course the whole thing was a strain on her, but now it's all over she'll be able to rest up.'

A year later Isabel was delivered of a daughter, to whom, following the fashion of the moment, she gave the name of Joan; and after an interval of two years she had another daughter whom, following another fashion, she called Priscilla.

One of Henry Maturin's partners died and the other two under pressure soon afterwards retired, so that he entered into sole possession of the business over which he had always exercised despotic control. He realized the ambition he had long entertained and took Gray into partnership with him. The firm had never been so prosperous.

'They're making money hand over fist, my dear fellow,' Elliott told me. 'Why, Gray at the age of twenty-five is making fifty thousand a year, and that's only a beginning. The resources of America are inexhaustible. It isn't a boom, it's just the natural development of a great country.'

His chest swelled with an unwonted patriotic fervour.

'Henry Maturin can't live for ever, high blood pressure, you know, and by the time Gray's forty he should be worth twenty million dollars. Princely, my dear fellow, princely.'

Elliott kept up a fairly regular correspondence with his sister and from time to time as the years went on passed on to me what she told him. Gray and Isabel were very happy, and the babies were sweet. They lived in a style that Elliott gladly admitted was eminently suitable; they entertained lavishly and were lavishly entertained; he told me with satisfaction that Isabel and Gray hadn't dined by themselves once in three months. Their whirl of gaiety was interrupted by the death of Mrs Maturin, that colourless, highborn lady whom Henry

Maturin had married for her connexions when he was making a place for himself in the city to which his father had come as a country bumpkin; and out of respect for her memory for a year the young couple never entertained more than six people to dinner.

'I've always said that eight was the perfect number,' said Elliott, determined to look on the bright side of things. 'It's intimate enough to permit of general conversation and yet large enough to give the impression of a party.'

Gray was wonderfully generous to his wife. On the birth of their first child he gave her a square-cut diamond ring and on the birth of her second a sable coat. He was too busy to leave Chicago much, but such holidays as he could take they spent at Henry Maturin's imposing house at Marvin. Henry could deny nothing to the son whom he adored and one Christmas gave him a plantation in South Carolina so that he could get a fortnight's duck-shooting in the season.

'Of course our merchant princes correspond to those great patrons of the arts of the Italian Renaissance who made fortunes by commerce. The Medici, for instance. Two kings of France were not too proud to marry the daughters of that illustrious family and I foresee the day when the crowned heads of Europe will seek the hands of our dollar princesses. What was it Shelley said? "The world's great age begins anew, the golden years return." '

Henry Maturin had for many years looked after Mrs Bradley's and Elliott's investments and they had a well-justified confidence in his acumen. He had never countenanced speculation and had put their money into sound securities, but with the great increase in values they found their comparatively modest fortunes increased in a manner that both surprised and delighted them. Elliott told me that, without stirring a finger, he was nearly twice as rich in 1926 as he had been in 1918. He was sixty-five, his hair was grey, his face lined, and there were pouches under his eyes, but he bore his years gallantly; he was as slim and held himself as erectly as ever; he had always been moderate in his habits and taken care of his appearance. He had no intention of submitting to the ravages of time so long as he could have his clothes made by the best tailor in London, his hair dressed and his face shaved by his own particular barber, and a masseur to come in every morning to keep his elegant body in perfect condition. He had long forgotten that he had ever so far demeaned himself as to engage in a trade, and without ever saying so outright, for he was not so stupid as to tell a lie that might be found out, he was inclined to suggest that in his youth he had been in the diplomatic service. I must admit that if I had ever had occasion to draw a portrait of an ambassador I should without hesitation have chosen Elliott as my model.

But things were changing. Such of the great ladies who had advanced Elliott's career as were still alive were well along in years. The English peeresses, having lost their lords, had been forced to surrender their mansions to daughters-in-law, and had retired to villas at Cheltenham or to modest houses in Regent's Park. Stafford House was turned into a museum, Curzon House became the seat of an organization, Devonshire House was for sale. The yacht on which Elliott had been in the habit of staying at Cowes had passed into other hands. The fashionable persons who occupied the stage had no use for the elderly man that Elliott now was. They found him tiresome and ridiculous. They were still willing to come to his elaborate luncheon parties at Claridge's but he was quick-witted enough to know that they came to meet one another rather than to see him. He could no longer pick and choose among the invitations that once had littered his writing-table, and much more often than he would have liked anyone to know he suffered the humiliation of dining by himself in the privacy of his suite. Women of rank in England, when a scandal has closed the doors of society to them, develop an interest in the arts and surround themselves with painters, writers and musicians. Elliott was too proud thus to humiliate himself.

'The death duties and the war profiteers have ruined English society,' he told me. 'People don't seem to mind who they know. London still has its tailors, its bootmakers, and its hatters, and I trust they'll last my time, but except for them it's finished. My dear fellow, do you know that the St Erth's have women to wait at table?'

This he said when we were walking away from Carlton House

Terrace after a luncheon party at which an unfortunate incident had occurred. Our noble host had a well-known collection of pictures, and a young American who was there, Paul Barton by name, expressed a desire to see them.

'You've got a Titian, haven't you?'

'We had. It's in America now. Some old Jew offered us a packet of money for it and we were damned hard up at the time, so my governor sold it.'

I noticed that Elliott, bristling, threw a venomous glance at the jovial marquess, and guessed that it was he who had bought the picture. He was furious at hearing himself, Virginian born and the descendant of a signatory of the Declaration, thus described. He had never in his life suffered so great an affront. And what made it worse was that Paul Barton was the object of his virulent hatred. He was a young man who had appeared in London soon after the war. He was twenty-three, blond, very good-looking, charming, a beautiful dancer, and had an ample fortune. He had brought a letter of introduction to Elliott, who with the kindness of heart natural to him had presented him to several of his friends. Not content with this he had given him some valuable hints on conduct. Delving back into his own experience, he had shown him how it was possible, by paying small attentions to old ladies and by lending a willing ear to distinguished men, however tedious, for a stranger to make his way in society.

But it was a different world that Paul Barton entered from that into which, a generation before, Elliott Templeton had penetrated by means of dogged perseverance. It was a world bent on amusing itself. Paul Barton's high spirits, pleasing exterior, and engaging manner did for him in a few weeks what Elliott had achieved only after years of industry and determination. Soon he no longer needed Elliott's help and took small pains to conceal the fact. He was pleasant to him when they met, but in an offhand way that deeply offended the older man. Elliott did not ask people to a party because he liked them, but because they helped to make it go, and since Paul Barton was popular he continued to invite him on occasion to his weekly luncheons; but the successful young man was generally engaged and twice he threw Elliott over at the last moment.

Elliott had done this himself too often not to know it was because he had just had a more tempting invitation.

'I don't ask you to believe it,' Elliott told me, fuming, 'but it's God's truth that when I see him now he patronizes me. ME. Titian. Titian,' he spluttered. 'He wouldn't know a Titian if he saw one.'

I had never seen Elliott so angry and I guessed his wrath was caused by his belief that Paul Barton had asked about the picture maliciously, having somehow learnt that Elliott had bought it, and would make a funny story at his expense out of the noble lord's reply.

'He's nothing but a dirty little snob, and if there's one thing in the world I detest and despise it's snobbishness. He'd have been nowhere except for me. Would you believe it, his father makes office furniture. Office furniture.' He put withering scorn into the two words. 'And when I tell people he simply doesn't exist in America, his origins couldn't be more humble, they don't seem to care. Take my word for it, my dear fellow, English society is as dead as the dodo.'

Nor did Elliott find France much better. There the great ladies of his youth, if still alive, were given over to bridge (a game he loathed), piety, and the care of their grandchildren. Manufacturers, Argentines, Chileans, American women separated or divorced from their husbands, inhabited the stately houses of the aristocracy and entertained with splendour, but at their parties Elliott was confounded to meet politicians who spoke French with a vulgar accent, journalists whose table manners were deplorable, and even actors. The scions of princely families thought it no shame to marry the daughters of shopkeepers. It was true Paris was gay, but with what a shoddy gaiety! The young, devoted to the mad pursuit of pleasure, thought nothing more amusing than to go from one stuffy little night club to another, drinking champagne at a hundred francs a bottle and dancing close-packed with the riff-raff of the town till five o'clock in the morning. The smoke, the heat, the noise made Elliott's head ache. This was not the Paris that he had accepted thirty years before as his spiritual home. This was not the Paris that good Americans went to when they died.

But Elliott had a flair. An inner monitor suggested to him that the Riviera was on the point of becoming once more the resort of rank and fashion. He knew the coast well from having often spent a few days in Monte Carlo at the Hôtel de Paris on his way back from Rome, whither his duties at the papal court had called him, or at Cannes in the villa of one or the other of his friends. But that was in the winter, and of late rumours had reached him that it was beginning to be well spoken of as a summer resort. The big hotels were remaining open; their summer visitors were listed in the social columns of the *Paris Herald* and Elliott read the familiar names with approval.

'The world is too much with me,' he said. 'I have now reached a time of life when I am prepared to enjoy the beauties of nature.'

The remark may seem obscure. It isn't really. Elliott had always felt that nature was an impediment to the social life, and he had no patience with people who could bother to go to see a lake or a mountain when they had before their eyes a Regency commode or a painting by Watteau. He had at the time a considerable sum of money to spend. Henry Maturin, urged by his son and exasperated by the sight of his friends on the stock exchange who were making fortunes overnight, had surrendered at last to the current of events and, abandoning little by little his old conservatism, had seen no reason why he too should not get on the band wagon. He wrote to Elliott that he was as much opposed to gambling as he had ever been, but this was not gambling, it was an affirmation of his belief in the inexhaustible resources of the country. His optimism was based on common sense. He could see nothing to halt the progress of America. He ended by saying that he had bought on margin a number of sound securities for dear Louisa Bradley and was glad to be able to tell Elliott that she now had a profit of twenty thousand dollars. Finally, if Elliott wanted to make a little money and would allow him to act according to his judgement, he was confident that he would not be disappointed. Elliott, apt to use hackneyed quotations, remarked that he could resist anything but temptation; the consequence of which was that from then on, instead of turning to the social intelligence as he had done for many years when the *Herald* was brought him with his breakfast, he gave his first attention to the reports of the stock market. So successful were Henry Maturin's transactions on his behalf that now Elliott found himself with the tidy sum of fifty thousand dollars which he had done nothing to earn.

He decided to take his profit and buy a house on the Riviera. As a refuge from the world he chose Antibes, which held a strategic position between Cannes and Monte Carlo so that it could be conveniently reached from either; but whether it was the hand of Providence or his own sure instinct that led him to choose a spot that was soon to become the centre of fashion, it is impossible to say. To live in a villa with a garden had a suburban vulgarity that revolted his fastidious taste, so he acquired two houses in the old town looking on the sea, knocked them into one, and installed central heating, bathrooms, and the sanitary conveniences that American example has forced on a recalcitrant Europe. Pickling was all the rage just then, so he furnished the house with old Provençal furniture duly pickled and, surrendering discreetly to modernity, with modern fabrics. He was still unwilling to accept such painters as Picasso and Braque – 'horrors, my dear fellow, horrors' – whom certain misguided enthusiasts were making such a fuss about, but felt himself at long last justified in extending his patronage to the Impressionists and so adorned his walls with some very pretty pictures. I remember a Monet of people rowing on a river, a Pissaro of a quay and a bridge on the Seine, a Tahitian landscape by Gauguin, and a charming Renoir of a young girl in profile with long yellow hair hanging down her back. His house when finished was fresh and gay, unusual, and simple with that simplicity that you knew could only have been achieved at great expense.

Then began the most splendid period of Elliott's life. He brought his excellent chef down from Paris and it was soon acknowledged that he had the best cuisine on the Riviera. He dressed his butler and his footman in white with gold straps on their shoulders. He entertained with a magnificence that never overstepped the bounds of good taste. The shores of the

Mediterranean were littered with royalties from all parts of Europe: some lured there on account of the climate, some in exile, and some because a scandalous past or an unsuitable marriage made it more convenient for them to inhabit a foreign country. There were Romanoffs from Russia, Hapsburgs from Austria, Bourbons from Spain, the two Sicilys, and Parma; there were princes of the House of Windsor and princes of the House of Bragança; there were Royal Highnesses from Sweden and Royal Highnesses from Greece: Elliott entertained them. There were princes and princesses not of royal blood, dukes and duchesses, marquesses and marchionesses, from Austria, Italy, Spain, Russia, and Belgium: Elliott entertained them. In winter the King of Sweden and the King of Denmark made sojourns on the coast; now and then Alfonso of Spain paid a hurried visit: Elliott entertained them. I never ceased to admire the way in which, while he bowed with courtly grace to those exalted personages, he managed to maintain the independent demeanour of the citizen of a country where all men are said to be born equal.

I had then, after some years of travel, bought a house on Cap Ferrat and thus saw a good deal of Elliott. I had risen so high in his good graces that sometimes he invited me to his very grandest parties.

'Come as a favour to me, my dear fellow,' he would say. 'Of course I know just as well as you do that royalties ruin a party. But other people like to meet them and I think one owes it to oneself to show the poor things some attention. Though heaven knows they don't deserve it. They're the most ungrateful people in the world; they'll use you, and when they have no further use for you they'll cast you aside like a frayed shirt; they'll accept innumerable favours from you, but there's not one of them who'd cross the road to do the smallest thing for you in return.'

Elliott had taken pains to get on good terms with the local authorities, and the prefect of the district and the bishop of the diocese, accompanied by his vicar general, often graced his table. The bishop had been a cavalry officer before entering the Church and in the war had commanded a regiment. He was a rubicund, stoutish man, who affected the rough-and-ready language of the barracks, and his austere, cadaverous vicar general was always on pins and needles lest he should say something scandalous. He listened with a deprecating smile when his superior told his favourite stories. But the bishop conducted his diocese with remarkable competence, and his eloquence in the pulpit was no less moving than his sallies at the luncheon table were amusing. He approved of Elliott for his pious generosity to the Church and liked him for his amiability and the good food he provided; and the two became good friends. Elliott could thus flatter himself that he was making the best of both worlds and, if I may venture so to put it, effecting a very satisfactory working arrangement between God and Mammon.

Elliott was house-proud and he was anxious to show his new house to his sister; he had always felt a certain reserve in her approval of him and he wanted her to see the style in which he now lived and the friends he hobnobbed with. It was the definitive answer to her hesitations. She would have to admit that he had made good. He wrote and asked her to come over with Gray and Isabel, not to stay with him, for he had no room, but to stay as his guests at the near-by Hôtel du Cap. Mrs Bradley replied that her travelling days were over, for her health was indifferent and she thought she was better off at home; and in any case it was impossible for Gray to absent himself from Chicago; business was booming and he was making a great deal of money and had to stay put. Elliott was attached to his sister and her letter alarmed him. He wrote to Isabel. She replied by cable that, though her mother was so far from well that she had to stay in bed one day a week, she was in no immediate danger and indeed with care might be expected to live a long time yet; but that Gray needed a rest and, with his father there to look after things, there was no reason why he should not take a holiday; so, not that summer but the next, she and Gray would come over.

On October the 23rd, 1929, the New York market broke.

4

I was in London then and at first we in England did not realize how grave the situation was nor how distressing its results would be. For my own part, though chagrined at losing a con-

128

siderable sum, it was for the most part paper profits that I lost, and when the dust had settled I found myself little the poorer in cash. I knew that Elliott had been gambling heavily and feared that he was badly hit, but I did not see him till we both returned to the Riviera for Christmas. He told me then that Henry Maturin was dead and Gray ruined.

I know little of business matters and I dare say that my account of the events, given me by Elliott, will seem confused. So far as I could make out the catastrophe that had befallen the firm was due in part to Henry Maturin's self-will and in part to Gray's rashness. Henry Maturin at first would not believe that the break was serious, but persuaded himself that it was a plot of the New York brokers to put a quick one over their provincial brethren, and setting his teeth he poured forth money to support the market. He raged against the Chicago brokers who were letting themselves be stampeded by those scoundrels in New York. He had always prided himself on the fact that none of his smaller clients, widows with settled incomes, retired officers and such like, had ever lost a penny by following his advice, and now, instead of letting them take a loss, he supported their accounts out of his own pocket. He said he was prepared to go broke, he could make another fortune, but he could never hold up his head again if the little people who trusted him lost their all. He thought he was magnanimous; he was only vain. His great fortune melted and one night he had a heart attack. He was in his sixties, he had always worked hard, played hard, eaten too much, and drunk heavily; after a few hours of agony he died of coronary thrombosis.

Gray was left to deal with the situation alone. He had been speculating extensively on the side, without the knowledge of his father, and was personally in the greatest difficulty. His efforts to extricate himself failed. The banks would not lend him money; older men on the exchange told him that the only thing was to throw up the sponge. I am not clear about the rest of the story. He was unable to meet his obligations and was, I understand, declared bankrupt; he had already mortgaged his own house and was glad to hand it over to the mortgagees; his father's house on Lake Shore Drive and the house at Marvin were sold for what they would fetch; Isabel

129

sold her jewels: all that was left them was the plantation in South Carolina, which was settled on Isabel and for which a purchaser could not be found. Gray was wiped out.

'And what about you, Elliott?' I asked.

'Oh, I'm not complaining,' he answered airily. 'God tempers the wind to the shorn lamb.'

I did not question him further, for his financial affairs were no business of mine, but whatever his losses were I presumed that like the rest of us he had suffered.

The depression did not at first hit the Riviera badly. I heard of two or three people who had lost a good deal, many villas remained closed for the winter and several were put up for sale. The hotels were far from full and the Casino at Monte Carlo complained that the season was poor. But it was not for a couple of years that the draught made itself felt. Then an estate agent told me that on the stretch of coast that reaches from Toulon to the Italian border there were forty-eight thousand properties, large and small, to be sold. The shares of the Casino slumped. The great hotels put down their prices in a vain attempt to attract. The only foreigners to be seen were those who had always been so poor that they couldn't be poorer, and they spent no money because they had no money to spend. The shopkeepers were in despair. But Elliott neither diminished his staff nor lessened their wages as many did; he continued to provide choice food and choice wines to royal and titled persons. He bought himself a large new car, which he imported from America and on which he had to pay a heavy duty. He gave generously to the charity the bishop had organized to provide free meals for the families of the workless. In fact he lived as though there had never been a crisis and half the world were not staggering from its effects.

I discovered the reason by chance: Elliott had by this time ceased to go to England except for a fortnight once a year to buy clothes, but he still transferred his establishment to his apartment in Paris for three months in the autumn and for May and June, these being the periods when the Riviera was deserted by Elliott's friends; he liked the summer there, partly on account of the bathing, but chiefly, I think, because the hot weather gave him the opportunity to indulge in a gaiety of dress that his sense of decorum had always forced him to eschew. He would appear then in trousers of startling colour, red, blue, green, or yellow, and with them wear singlets of contrasting hue, mauve, violet, puce, or harlequin, and would accept the compliments his attire clamoured for with the deprecating grace of an actress who is told that she has played a new role divinely.

I happened to be spending a day in Paris in the spring on my way back to Cap Ferrat and had asked Elliott to lunch with me. We met in the Ritz bar, no longer thronged with college boys come from America to have a good time, but as deserted as a playwright after the first night of an unsuccessful play. We had a cocktail, a transatlantic habit to which Elliott had at last become reconciled, and ordered our lunch. When we had finished, he suggested that we should go round the curio shops, and though I told him I had no money to spend I was glad enough to accompany him. We walked through the Place Vendôme and he asked if I would mind going in to Charvet's for a moment; he had ordered some things and wanted to know if they were ready. It appeared that he was having some vests made, and some drawers, and he was having his initials embroidered on them. The vests had not come in yet, but the drawers were there and the shop assistant asked Elliott if he would like to see them.

'I would,' said he, and when the man had gone to fetch them added to me: 'I have them made to order on a pattern of my own.'

They were brought, and to me, except that they were of silk, looked exactly like the drawers I had frequently bought for myself at Macy's; but what caught my eye was that above the intertwined E. T. of the initials was a count's crown. I did not say a word.

'Very nice, very nice,' said Elliott. 'Well, when the undershirts are ready you'll send them along.'

We left the shop and Elliott, as he walked away, turned to me with a smile.

'Did you notice the crown? To tell you the truth, I'd forgotten about it when I asked you to come in to Charvet's. I don't think I've had occasion to tell you that His Holiness has been graciously pleased to revive in my favour my old family title.'

'Your what?' I said, startled out of my politeness.

Elliott raised a disapproving eyebrow.

'Didn't you know? I am descended in the female line from the Count de Lauria who came over to England in the suite of Philip the Second and married a maid of honour of Queen Mary's.'

'Our old friend Bloody Mary?'

'That, I believe, is what heretics call her,' Elliott answered stiffly. 'I don't think I ever told you that I spent September of 'twenty-nine in Rome. I thought it a bore having to go because Rome is empty then, but it was fortunate for me that my sense of duty prevailed over my desire for worldly pleasures. My friends at the Vatican told me that the crash was coming and strongly advised me to sell all my American securities. The Catholic Church has the wisdom of twenty centuries behind it and I didn't hesitate for a moment. I cabled to Henry Maturin to sell everything and buy gold, and I cabled to Louisa to tell her to do the same. Henry cabled back asking me if I was crazy and said he'd do nothing until I confirmed the instructions. I immediately cabled in the most peremptory manner, telling him to carry them out and to cable me that he had done so. Poor Louisa paid no attention to my advice and suffered for it.'

'So when the crash came you were sitting pretty?'

'An Americanism, my dear fellow, which I see no occasion for you to use, but it expresses my situation with a good deal of accuracy. I lost nothing; in fact I had made what you would probably call a packet. I was able some time later to buy back my securities for a fraction of their original cost, and since I owed it all to what I can only describe as the direct interposition of Providence I felt it only right and proper that I should do something for Providence in return.'

'Oh, and how did you set about that?'

'Well, you know the Duce has been reclaiming great tracts of land in the Pontine Marshes and it was represented to me that His Holiness was gravely concerned at the lack of places of worship for the settlers. So, to cut a long story short, I built a little Romanesque church, an exact copy of one I knew in

Provence, and perfect in every detail, which, though I say it myself, is a gem. It is dedicated to St Martin because I was lucky enough to find an old stained-glass window representing St Martin in the act of cutting his cloak in two to give half of it to a naked beggar, and as the symbolism seemed so apt I bought it and placed it over the high altar.'

I didn't interrupt Elliott to ask him what connexion he saw between the Saint's celebrated action and the rake-off on the pretty penny he had made by selling out in the nick of time which, like an agent's commission, he was paying to a higher power. But to a prosaic person like me symbolism is often obscure. He went on.

'When I was privileged to show the photographs to the Holy Father, he was gracious enough to tell me that he could see at a glance that I was a man of impeccable taste, and he added that it was a pleasure to him to find in this degenerate age someone who combined devotion to the Church with such rare artistic gifts. A memorable experience, my dear fellow, a memorable experience. But no one was more surprised than I when shortly afterwards it was intimated to me that he had been pleased to confer a title upon me. As an American citizen I feel it more modest not to use it, except of course at the Vatican, so I have forbidden my Joseph to address me as *Monsieur le Comte*, and I trust you will respect my confidence. I don't wish it bruited abroad. But I would not like His Holiness to think that I do not value the honour that he has done me and it is purely out of respect for him that I have the crown embroidered on my personal linen. I don't mind telling you that I take a modest pride in concealing my rank under the sober pin-stripe of an American gentleman.'

We parted. Elliott told me he would come down to the Riviera at the end of June. He did not do so. He had just made his arrangements to transfer his staff from Paris, intending to drive down leisurely in his car so that everything should be in perfect order on his arrival, when he received a cable from Isabel to say that her mother had suddenly taken a turn for the worse. Elliott, besides being fond of his sister, had, as I have said, a strong strain of family feeling. He took the first ship out of Cherbourg and from New York went to Chicago.

He wrote to tell me that Mrs Bradley was very ill and grown so thin that it was a shock to him. She might last a few weeks longer or even a few months, but in any case he felt it his sad duty to remain with her till the end. He said he found the great heat more supportable than he had expected, but the lack of congenial society only tolerable because at such a moment he had in any case no heart for it. He said he was disappointed with the way his fellow-countrymen had reacted to the depression; he would have expected them to take their misfortune with more equanimity. Knowing that nothing is easier than to bear other people's calamities with fortitude, I thought that Elliott, richer now than he had ever been in his life, was perhaps hardly entitled to be severe. He ended by giving me messages for several of his friends and bade me by no means forget to explain to everyone I met why it was that his house must remain closed for the summer.

Little more than a month later I received another letter from him to tell me that Mrs Bradley had died. He wrote with sincerity and emotion. I should never have thought him capable of expressing himself with such dignity, real feeling, and simplicity, had I not long known that notwithstanding his snobbishness and his absurd affectations Elliott was a kindly, affectionate, and honest man. In the course of this letter he told me that Mrs Bradley's affairs appeared to be in some disorder. Her elder son, a diplomatist, being *chargé d'affaires* in Tokyo during the absence of the ambassador, had been of course unable to leave his post. Her second son, Templeton, who had been in the Philippines when I first knew the Bradleys, had been in due course recalled to Washington and occupied a responsible position in the State Department. He had come with his wife to Chicago when his mother's condition was recognized as hopeless, but had been obliged to return to the capital immediately after the funeral. In these circumstances Elliott felt that he must remain in America until things were straightened out. Mrs Bradley had divided her fortune equally between her three children, but it appeared that her losses in the crash of 'twenty-nine had been substantial. Fortunately they had found a purchaser for the farm at Marvin. Elliott in his letter referred to it as dear Louisa's country place.

'It is always sad when a family has to part with its ancestral home,' he wrote, 'but of late years I have seen this forced upon so many of my English friends that I feel that my nephews and Isabel must accept the inevitable with the same courage and resignation that *they* have. *Noblesse oblige.*'

They had been lucky too in disposing of Mrs Bradley's house in Chicago. There had long been a scheme afoot to tear down the row of houses in one of which Mrs Bradley lived and build in their stead a great block of apartments, but it had been held up by her obstinate determination to die in the house in which she had lived. But no sooner was the breath out of her body than the promoters came forward with an offer and it was promptly accepted. Yet even at that Isabel was left very ill provided for.

After the crash Gray had tried to get a job, even as a clerk in the office of such of the brokers as had weathered the storm, but there was no business. He applied to his old friends to give him something to do, however humble and however badly paid, but he applied in vain. His frenzied efforts to stave off the disaster that finally overwhelmed him, the burden of anxiety, the humiliation, resulted in a nervous breakdown, and he began to have headaches so severe that he was incapacitated for twenty-four hours and as limp as a wet rag when they ceased. It had appeared to Isabel that they could not do better than go down with the children to the plantation in South Carolina till Gray regained his health. In its day it had brought in a hundred thousand dollars a year for its rice crop, but for long now had been no more than a wilderness of marsh and gum-wood, useful only to sportsmen who wanted to shoot duck, and no purchaser could be found for it. There they had lived off and on since the crash and there they proposed to return till conditions improved and Gray could find employment.

'I couldn't allow that,' Elliott wrote. 'Why, my dear fellow, they live like pigs. Isabel without a maid, no governess for the children, and only a couple of coloured women to look after them. So I've offered them my apartment in Paris and proposed that they should stay there till things change in this fantastic country. I shall provide them with a staff, as a matter of fact my kitchen-maid is a very good cook, so I shall leave her with them and I can easily find someone to take her place. I shall arrange to settle the accounts myself so that Isabel can spend her small income on her clothes and the *menus plaisirs* of the family. This means of course that I shall spend much more of my time on the Riviera and so hope to see a great deal more of you, my dear fellow, than I have in the past. London and Paris being now what they are, I'm really more at home on the Riviera. It's the only place remaining where I can meet people who speak my own language. I dare say I shall go to Paris now and then for a few days, but when I do, I don't in the least mind pigging it at the Ritz. I'm glad to say that I've at long last persuaded Gray and Isabel to accede to my wishes and I'm bringing them all over as soon as the necessary arrangements can be made. The furniture and the pictures (very poor in quality, my dear fellow, and of the most doubtful authenticity) are being sold the week after next and meanwhile, as I thought to live in the house till the last moment would be painful to them, I have brought them to stay with me at the Drake. I shall settle them in when we get to Paris and then come down to the Riviera. Don't forget to remember me to your royal neighbour.'

Who could deny that Elliott, that arch-snob, was also the kindest, most considerate and generous of men?

IV

1

ELLIOTT, having installed the Maturins in his spacious apartment on the Left Bank, returned to the Riviera at the end of the year. He had planned his house to suit his own convenience and there was no room in it for a family of four, so that, even if he had wanted to, he could not have had them to stay with him there. I do not think he regretted it. He was well aware that as a man by himself he was a more desirable asset than if he must be accompanied by a niece and a nephew, and he could hardly expect to arrange his own distinguished little parties (a matter over which he took immense trouble) if he had to count invariably on the presence of two house guests.

'It's much better for them to settle down in Paris and accustom themselves to civilized life. Besides, the two girls are old enough to go to school and I've found one not far from my apartment which I'm assured is very select.'

In consequence of this I did not see Isabel till the spring when, because I had some work to do that made it desirable for me to spend some weeks there, I went to Paris and took a couple of rooms in a hotel just out of the Place Vendôme. It was a hotel I frequented, not only for its convenient situation, but because it had an air. It was a big old house built around a courtyard and it had been an inn for close upon two hundred years. The bathrooms were far from luxurious and the plumbing far from satisfactory; the bedrooms with their iron beds, painted white, their old-fashioned white counterpanes, and their huge *armoires à glace* had a poverty-stricken look; but the parlours were furnished with fine old furniture. The sofa, the armchairs, dated from the gaudy reign of Napoleon the Third, and, though I could not say they were comfortable, they had a florid charm. In that room I lived in the past of the French novelists. When I looked at the Empire clock under its glass case I thought that a pretty woman in ringlets and a flounced dress might have watched the minute hand move as she waited for a visit from Rastignac, the well-born adventurer whose career in novel after novel Balzac followed from his humble beginnings to his ultimate grandeur. Dr Bianchon, the physician who was so real to Balzac that when he lay dying he said: 'Only Bianchon can save me,' might well have come into that room to feel the pulse and look at the tongue of a noble dowager from the provinces who had come to Paris to see an attorney about a lawsuit and had called in a doctor for a passing ailment. At that bureau a lovesick woman in a crinoline, her hair parted in the middle, may have written a passionate letter to her faithless lover, or a peppery old gentleman in a green frock coat and a stock indited an angry epistle to his extravagant son.

The day after my arrival I called up Isabel and asked if she would give me a cup of tea if I came along at five. It was ten years since I'd seen her. She was reading a French novel when I was ushered into the drawing-room by a staid butler, and getting up she took both my hands and greeted me with a warm and winning smile. I had never seen her more than a dozen times, and only twice alone, but she made me feel at once that we were not casual acquaintances but old friends. The ten years that had passed had reduced the gulf that separated the young girl from the middle-aged man and I was no longer conscious of the disparity of age between us. With the delicate flattery of a woman of the world she treated me as if I were her contemporary, and in five minutes we were chatting as frankly and as unconstrainedly as though we were playmates who had been in the habit of meeting without interruption. She had acquired ease, self-possession, and assurance.

But what chiefly struck me was the change in her appearance. I remembered her as a pretty, bouncing girl who threatened to run to fat; I do not know whether, realizing this, she had taken heroic measures to reduce her weight or whether it was an unusual, though happy, accident of childbearing; but now she was as slender as anyone could wish. The mode of the moment accentuated this. She was in black, and at a glance I noticed that her silk dress, neither too plain nor too fancy, had been made by one of the best dressmakers in Paris, and she wore it with the careless confidence of a woman to whom it is second nature to wear expensive clothes. Ten years before, even with Elliott to advise, her frocks had been somewhat on the showy side and she had worn them as though she were not quite at home in them. Marie Louise de Florimond could not have said now that she lacked chic. She had chic to the tips of her rose-painted nails. Her features had fined down and it occurred to me that she had as pretty and as straight a nose as I had ever seen on a woman's face. There was not a line on her forehead or under her hazel eyes, and though her skin had lost the fresh bloom of extreme youth, its texture was as fine as ever; it obviously owed something now to lotions, creams, and massage, but they had given it a soft, transparent delicacy that was singularly attractive. Her thin cheeks were very faintly rouged and her mouth was painted with discretion. She wore her bright brown hair bobbed as was the fashion of the moment and marcelled. She had no rings on her fingers, and I remembered that Elliott had told me that she had sold her jewellery; her hands, though not remarkably small, were well made. At that period women wore short frocks in the day-time and I saw that her legs in champagne-coloured stockings were shapely, long, and slender. Legs are the undoing of many a comely woman; Isabel's legs, as a girl her most unfortunate trait, were now uncommonly good. In fact from the pretty girl whose glowing health, high spirits, and brilliant colour had given her attractiveness she was become a beautiful woman. That she owed her beauty in some degree to art, discipline, and mortification of the flesh did not seem to matter. The result was vastly satisfactory. It might be that the grace of her gestures, the felicity of her carriage, had been acquired by taking thought, but they had a look of perfect spontaneity. I conceived the notion that these four months in Paris had put the finishing touches to a work of conscious art that had been years in the making. Elliott, even in his most censorious mood, could not but have approved of her; I, a person less difficult to please, found her ravishing.

Gray had gone to Mortefontaine to play golf, but she told me he would be in presently.

'And you must see my two little girls. They've gone to the Tuileries Gardens, but they ought to be in soon. They're sweet.'

We talked of one thing and another. She liked being in Paris and they were very comfortable in Elliott's apartment. Before leaving them he had made them acquainted with such of his friends as he thought they would like and they had already a pleasant circle of acquaintances. He had pressed them to entertain as abundantly as he had been in the habit of doing.

'You know, it tickles me to death to think that we're living like quite rich people when really we're absolutely broke.'

'Is it as bad as that?'

She chuckled, and now I remembered the light, gay laugh that I had found so pleasing in her ten years before.

'Gray hasn't a penny and I have almost exactly the income Larry had when he wanted me to marry him and I wouldn't because I thought we couldn't possibly live on it and now I've got two children besides. It's rather funny, isn't it?'

'I'm glad you can see the joke of it.'

'What news have you of Larry?'

'I? None. I haven't set eyes on him since before you were

last in Paris. I knew slightly some of the people he used to know and I did ask them what had become of him, but that was years ago. No one seemed to know anything about him. He just vanished.'

'We know the manager of the bank in Chicago where Larry has his account and he told us that every now and then he got a draft from some queer place. China, Burma, India. He seems to have been getting around.'

I did not hesitate to put the question that came to the tip of my tongue. After all, if you want to know something the best way is to ask.

'D'you wish now that you had married him?'

She smiled engagingly.

'I've been very happy with Gray. He's been a wonderful husband. You know, until the crash came we had a grand time together. We like the same people, and we like doing the same things. He's very sweet. And it's nice being adored; he's just as much in love with me now as when we first married. He thinks I'm the most wonderful girl in the world. You can't imagine how kind and considerate he is. It was quite absurd how generous he was; you see, he thought nothing was too good for me. D'you know, he's never said an unkind or harsh thing to me all these years we've been married. Oh, I've been very lucky.'

I asked myself if she thought she'd answered my question. I changed the conversation.

'Tell me about your little girls.'

As I spoke the doorbell rang.

'Here they are. You shall see for yourself.'

In a moment they came in followed by a nursery governess and I was introduced first to Joan, the elder, and then to Priscilla. Each in turn gave a polite little knick as she took my hand. One was eight and the other six. They were tall for their age; Isabel of course was tall, and Gray, I remembered, was immense; but they were pretty only in the way all children are pretty. They looked frail. They had their father's black hair and their mother's hazel eyes. The presence of a stranger did not make them shy, and they talked eagerly to her of their doings in the gardens. They cast eager eyes on the dainties

140

Isabel's cook had provided for tea, but which neither of us had touched, and being given permission to have one thing were thrown into a small agony of doubt as to which to choose. It was pleasant to see the demonstrative affection they had for their mother and the three of them clustered together made a charming picture. When they had eaten the little cake each had selected, Isabel sent them away and they went without a word of expostulation. I received the impression that she was bringing them up to do as they were told.

When they were gone I said the usual things one says to a mother about her children and Isabel accepted my compliments with evident, but somewhat casual, pleasure. I asked her how Gray was liking Paris.

'Well enough. Uncle Elliott left us a car so he can go and play golf almost every day and he's joined the Traveller's Club and he plays bridge there. Of course, Uncle Elliott's offer to support us in this apartment has been a godsend. Gray's nerves went all to pieces and he still has those terrible headaches; even if he could get a job he isn't really fit to take it; and naturally that worries him. He wants to work, he feels he ought to, and it humiliates him not to be wanted. You see, he feels it's a man's business to work and if he can't work he may just as well be dead. He can't bear his feeling of being a drug on the market, and I only got him to come here by persuading him that rest and change would bring him back to normalcy. But I know he won't be happy till he gets back into harness.'

'I'm afraid you've had a very rough time these last two and a half years.'

'Well, you know, when the crash came at first I simply couldn't believe it. It seemed inconceivable to me that we should be ruined. I could understand that other people should be ruined, but that we should be – well, it just seemed impossible. I went on thinking that something would happen to save us at the last moment. And then, when the final blow came, I felt that life wasn't worth living any more, I didn't think I could face the future; it was too black. For a fortnight I was absolutely miserable. God, it was awful, having to part with everything, knowing there wouldn't be any fun any more, having to do without everything I liked – and then at the end of a fortnight I said : "Oh, to hell with it, I'm not going to give it another thought," and I promise you I never have. I don't regret anything. I had a lot of fun while it lasted and now it's gone, it's gone.'

'It's obvious that ruin is easier to bear in a luxurious apartment in a fashionable quarter, with a competent butler and an excellent cook free and for nothing, and when one can cover one's haggard bones with a dress by Chanel, isn't it?'

'Lanvin,' she giggled. 'I see you haven't changed much in ten years. I don't suppose you'll believe me, being a cynical brute, but I'm not sure if I'd have accepted Uncle Elliott's offer except for Gray and the children. On my twenty-eight hundred a year we could have managed perfectly well on the plantation and we'd have grown rice and rye and corn and kept pigs. After all I was born and raised on a farm in Illinois.'

'In a manner of speaking,' I smiled, knowing that in point of fact she had been born in an expensive clinic in New York.

At this point Gray came in. It is true that I had only seen him two or three times twelve years before, but I had seen a photograph of him with his bride (Elliott kept it in a splendid frame on his piano along with signed photographs of the King of Sweden, the Queen of Spain, and the Duc de Guise) and I had a fair recollection of him. I was taken aback. His hair had receded on the temples and there was a small bald patch on the crown, his face was puffy and red, and he had a double chin. He had put on a lot of weight during years of good living and hard drinking, and only his great height saved him from being grossly obese. But the thing I most noticed was the expression of his eyes. I remembered quite well the trusting, open frankness of their Irish blue, when the world was before him and he hadn't a care in the world; now I seemed to see in them a sort of puzzled dismay, and even if I hadn't known the facts I think I might have guessed that something had occurred to destroy his confidence in himself and in the ordered course of events. I felt a kind of diffidence in him, as though he had done wrong, though unwittingly, and were ashamed. It was plain that his nerve was shaken. He greeted me with pleasant cordiality and indeed seemed as glad to see me as if I were an old friend, but I had the impression that his rather noisy heartiness was a habit of manner that scarcely corresponded with his inner feeling.

Drinks were brought in and he mixed us a cocktail. He'd played a couple of rounds of golf and was satisfied with his game. He went into somewhat verbose detail over the difficulties he had surmounted over one of the holes and Isabel listened with an appearance of lively interest. After a few minutes, having made a date to take them to dine and see a play, I left.

2

I fell into the habit of dropping in to see Isabel three or four times a week in the afternoon after my day's work was over. She was generally alone at that hour and glad to have a gossip. The persons to whom Elliott had introduced her were much older than she and I discovered that she had few friends of her own generation. Mine were for the most part busy till dinnertime and I found it more agreeable to talk with Isabel than to go to my club and play bridge with rather grouchy Frenchmen who did not particularly welcome the intrusion of a stranger. Her charming way of treating me as if she and I were of an age made conversation easy and we joked and laughed and chaffed one another, chatting now about ourselves, now about our common acquaintances, now about books and pictures, so that the time passed very agreeably. One of the defects of my character is that I can never grow used to the plainness of people; however sweet a disposition a friend of mine may have, years of intimacy can never reconcile me to his bad teeth or lopsided nose: on the other hand I never cease to delight in his comeliness and after twenty years of familiarity I am still able to take pleasure in a well-shaped brow or the delicate line of a cheekbone. So I never came into Isabel's presence without feeling anew a little thrill of pleasure in the perfection of her oval face, in the creamy delicacy of her skin, and in the bright warmth of her hazel eyes.

Then a very unexpected thing happened.

3

In all big cities there are self-contained groups that exist without intercommunication, small worlds within a greater world that lead their lives, their members dependent upon one another for companionship, as though they inhabited islands separated from each other by an unnavigable strait. Of no city, in my experience, is this more true than of Paris. There high society seldom admits oustiders into its midst, the politicians live in their own corrupt circle, the bourgeoisie, great and small, frequent one another, writers congregate with writers (it is remarkable in André Gide's *Journal* to see with how few people he seems to have been intimate who did not follow his own calling), painters hobnob with painters and musicians with musicians. The same thing is true of London, but in a less marked degree; there birds of a feather flock much less together, and there are a dozen houses where at the same table you may meet a duchess, an actress, a painter, a member of Parliament, a lawyer, a dressmaker, and an author.

The events of my life have led me at one time and another to dwell transitorily in pretty well all the worlds of Paris, even (through Elliott) in the closed world of the Boulevard St Germain; but that which I liked best, better than the discreet circle that has its centre in what is now called the Avenue Foch, better than the cosmopolitan crew that patronize Larue's and the Café de Paris, better than the noisy sordid gaiety of Montmartre, is that section of which the artery is the Boulevard du Montparnasse. In my youth I spent a year in a tiny apartment near the Lion de Belfort, on the fifth floor, from which I had a spacious view of the cemetery. Montparnasse has still for me the tranquil air of a provincial town that was characteristic of it then. When I pass through the dingy narrow Rue d'Odessa I remember with a pang the shabby restaurant where we used to foregather to dine, painters and illustrators and sculptors, I, but for Arnold Bennett on occasion, the only writer, and sit late discussing excitedly, absurdly, angrily, painting and literature. It is still a pleasure to me to stroll down the boulevard and look at the young people who are as young as I was then and invent stories for myself about them. When I have nothing better to do I take a taxi and go and sit in the old Café du Dôme. It is no longer what it was then, the meeting place exclusively of Bohemia; the small tradesmen of the neighbourhood have taken to visiting it, and strangers from the other side of the Seine come to it in the hope of seeing a world that has ceased to exist. Students come to it still, of course, painters and writers, but most of them are foreigners; and when you sit there you hear around you as much Russian, Spanish, German, and English as French. But I have a notion that they are saying very much the same sort of things as we said forty years ago, only they speak of Picasso instead of Manet and of André Breton instead of Guillaume Apollinaire. My heart goes out to them.

When I had been in Paris about a fortnight I was sitting one evening at the Dôme and since the terrace was crowded I had been forced to take a table in the front row. It was fine and warm. The plane trees were just bursting into leaf and there was in the air that sense of leisure, lightheartedness, and alacrity that was peculiar to Paris. I felt at peace with myself, but not lethargically, with exhilaration rather. Suddenly a man walking past me, stopped and with a grin that displayed a set of very white teeth said: 'Hello!' I looked at him blankly. He was tall and thin. He wore no hat and he had a mop of dark brown hair that badly needed cutting. His upper lip and his chin were concealed by a thick brown beard. His forehead and his neck were deeply tanned. He wore a frayed shirt, without a tie, a brown, threadbare coat, and a pair of shabby grey slacks. He looked a bum and to the best of my belief I had never seen him before. I put him down for one of those good-for-nothings who have gone to the devil in Paris and I expected him to pull a hard-luck story to wheedle a few francs out of me for a dinner and a bed. He stood in front of me, his hands in his pockets, showing his white teeth, with a look of amusement in his dark eyes.

'You don't remember me?' he said.

'I've never set eyes on you in my life.'

I was prepared to give him twenty francs, but I wasn't prepared to let him get away with the bluff that we knew one another.

'Larry,' he said.

'Good God! Sit down.' He chuckled, stepped forward and took the empty chair at my table. 'Have a drink.' I beckoned to the waiter. 'How could you expect me to recognize you with all that hair on your face?'

The waiter came and he ordered an orangeade. Now that I looked at him I remembered the peculiarity of his eyes, which came from the black of the iris being as black as that of the pupil and which gave them at once intensity and opaqueness.

'How long have you been in Paris?' I asked.

'A month.'

'Are you going to stay?'

'For a while.'

While I asked these questions my mind was busy. I noticed that the cuffs of his trousers were ragged and that there were holes in the elbows of his coat. He looked as destitute as any beachcomber I had ever met in an Eastern port. It was hard in those days to forget the depression and I wondered whether the crash of 'twenty-nine had left him penniless. I didn't much like the thought of that and not being a person to beat about the bush I asked outright:

'Are you down and out?'

'No, I'm all right. What makes you think that?'

'Well, you look as if you could do with a square meal and the things you've got on are only fit for the garbage can.'

'Are they as bad as all that? I never thought about it. As a matter of fact I have been meaning to get myself a few odds and ends, but I never seem able to get down to it.'

I thought he was shy or proud and I didn't see why I should put up with that sort of nonsense.

'Don't be a fool, Larry. I'm not a millionaire, but I'm not poor. If you're short of cash let me lend you a few thousand francs. That won't break me.'

He laughed outright.

'Thanks a lot, but I'm not short of cash. I've got more money than I can spend.'

'Notwithstanding the crash?'

'Oh, that didn't affect me. Everything I had was in government bonds. I don't know whether they went down in value, I never inquired, but I do know that Uncle Sam went on paying up on the coupons like the decent old party he is. In point of fact I've been spending so little during the last few years, I must have quite a bit in hand.'

146

'Where have you come from now then?'

'India.'

'Oh, I heard you'd been there. Isabel told me. She apparently knows the manager of your bank in Chicago.'

'Isabel? When did you last see her?'

'Yesterday.'

'She's not in Paris?'

'She is indeed. She's living in Elliott Templeton's apartment.'

'That's grand. I'd love to see her.'

Though I was watching his eyes pretty closely while we were exchanging these remarks I could discern only a natural surprise and pleasure, but no feeling more complicated.

'Gray's there too. You know they're married?'

'Yes, Uncle Bob – Dr Nelson, my guardian – wrote and told me, but he died some years ago.'

It occurred to me that with this break in what appeared his only link with Chicago and his friends there he probably knew nothing of what had happened. I told him of the birth of Isabel's two daughters, of the death of Henry Maturin and Louisa Bradley, of Gray's ruin and of Elliott's generosity.

'Is Elliott here too?'

'No.'

For the first time in forty years Elliott was not spending the spring in Paris. Though looking younger he was now seventy and as usual with men of that age there were days when he felt tired and ill. Little by little he had given up taking any but walking exercise. He was nervous about his health and his doctor came to see him twice a week to thrust into an alternate buttock a hypodermic needle with the fashionable injection of the moment. At every meal, at home or abroad, he took from his pocket a little gold box from which he extracted a tablet which he swallowed with the reserved air of one performing a religious rite. His doctor had recommended him to take the cure at Montecatini, a watering-place in the north of Italy, and after this he proposed to go to Venice to look for a font of a design suitable to his Romanesque church. He was less unwilling to leave Paris unvisited since each year he found it socially more unsatisfactory. He did not like old people, and resented it when he was invited to meet only persons of his own age, and the young he found vapid. The adornment of the church he had built was now a main interest of his life and here he could indulge his ineradicable passion for buying works of art with the comfortable assurance that he was doing it to the glory of God. He had found in Rome an early altar of honey-coloured stone and had been dickering in Florence for six months for a triptych of the Siennese school to put over it.

Then Larry asked me how Gray was liking Paris.

'I'm afraid he's feeling rather lost here.'

I tried to explain to him how Gray had struck me. He listened to me with his eyes fixed on my face in a meditative, unblinking gaze that suggested to me, I don't know why, that he was listening to me not with his ears, but with some inner more sensitive organ of hearing. It was queer and not very comfortable.

'But you'll see for yourself,' I finished.

'Yes, I'd love to see them. I suppose I shall find the address in the phone book.'

'But if you don't want to scare them out of their wits and drive the children into screaming hysterics, I think you'd be wise to have your hair cut and your beard shaved.'

He laughed.

'I've been thinking of it. There's no object in making myself conspicuous.'

'And while you're about it you might get yourself a new outfit.'

'I suppose I am a bit shabby. When I came to leave India I found that I had nothing but the clothes I stand up in.'

He looked at the suit I was wearing, and asked me who my tailor was. I told him, but added that he was in London and so couldn't be of much use to him. We dropped the subject and he began to talk again of Gray and Isabel.

'I've been seeing quite a lot of them,' I said. 'They're very happy together. I've never had a chance of talking to Gray alone, and anyway I dare say he wouldn't talk to me about Isabel, but I know he's devoted to her. His face is rather sullen in repose and his eyes are harassed, but when he looks at Isabel such a gentle, kind look comes into them, it's rather moving. I have a notion that all through their trouble she stood by him like a rock and he never forgets how much he owes her. You'll find Isabel changed.' I didn't tell him she was beautiful as she had never been before. I wasn't sure he had the discernment to see how the pretty, strapping girl had made herself into the wonderfully graceful, delicate, and exquisite woman. There are men who are affronted by the aids that art can supply to feminine nature. 'She's very good to Gray. She's taking infinite pains to restore his confidence in himself.'

But it was growing late and I asked Larry if he would come along the boulevard and dine with me.

'No, I don't think I will, thanks,' he answered. 'I must be off.'

He got up, nodded in a friendly way, and stepped out on to the pavement.

4

I saw Gray and Isabel next day and told them that I had seen Larry. They were as much surprised as I had been.

'It'll be wonderful to see him,' said Isabel. 'Let's call him up at once.'

Then I remembered that I hadn't thought of asking him where he was staying. Isabel gave me hell.

'I'm not sure he'd have told me if I had,' I protested, laughing. 'Probably my subconscious had something to do with it. Don't you remember, he never liked telling people where he lived. It was one of his oddities. He may walk in at any moment.'

'That would be like him,' said Gray. 'Even in the old days you could never count on his being where you expected him to be. He was here today and gone tomorrow. You'd see him in a room and think in a moment you'd go and say hello to him and when you turned round he'd disappeared.'

'He always was the most exasperating fellow,' said Isabel. 'It's no good denying that. I suppose we shall just have to wait till it suits him to turn up.'

He didn't come that day, nor the next, nor the day after. Isabel accused me of having invented the story to annoy. I promised her I hadn't and sought to give her reasons why he hadn't shown up. But they were implausible. Within myself I wondered whether on thinking it over he hadn't made up his mind that he just didn't want to see Gray and Isabel and had wandered off somewhere or other away from Paris. I had a feeling already that he never took root anywhere, but was always prepared at a moment's notice, for a reason that seemed good to him or on a whim, to move on.

He came at last. It was a rainy day and Gray hadn't gone to Mortefontaine. The three of us were together, Isabel and I drinking a cup of tea, Gray sipping a whisky and Perrier, when the butler opened the door and Larry strolled in. Isabel with a cry sprang to her feet and throwing herself into his arms kissed him on both cheeks. Gray, his fat red face redder than ever, warmly wrung his hand.

'Gee, I'm glad to see you, Larry,' he said, his voice choked with emotion.

Isabel bit her lip and I saw she was constraining herself not to cry.

'Have a drink, old man,' said Gray unsteadily.

I was touched by their delight at seeing the wanderer. It must have been pleasant for him to perceive how much he meant to them. He smiled happily. It was plain to me that he was, however, completely self-possessed. He noticed the tea things.

'I'll have a cup of tea,' he said.

'Oh, gosh, you don't want tea,' cried Gray. 'Let's have a bottle of champagne.'

'I'd prefer tea,' smiled Larry.

His composure had on the others the effect he may have intended. They calmed down, but looked at him still with fond eyes. I don't mean to suggest that he responded to their natural exuberance with an ungracious coldness; on the contrary, he was as cordial and charming as one could wish; but I was conscious in his manner of something that I could only describe as remoteness and I wondered what it signified.

'Why didn't you come and see us at once, you horror?' cried Isabel, with a pretence of indignation. 'I've been hanging out of the window for the last five days to see you coming and every time the bell rang my heart leapt to my mouth and I had all I could do to swallow it again.'

Larry chuckled.

'Mr M. told me I looked so tough that your man would

never let me through the door. I flew over to London to get some clothes.'

'You needn't have done that,' I smiled. 'You could have got a reach-me-down at the Printemps or the Belle Jardinière.'

'I thought if I was going to do it at all, I'd better do the thing in style. I haven't bought any European clothes for ten years. I went to your tailor and said I wanted a suit in three days. He said it would take a fortnight, so we compromised on four. I got back from London an hour ago.'

He wore a blue serge that nicely fitted his slim figure, a white shirt with a soft collar, a blue silk tie, and brown shoes. He had had his hair cut short and shaved off the hair on his face. He looked not only neat, but well-groomed. It was a transformation. He was very thin; his cheekbones were more prominent, his temples hollower, and his eyes in the deep sockets larger than I remembered them; but notwithstanding he looked very well; he looked, indeed, with his deeply sunburnt, unlined face, amazingly young. He was a year younger than Gray, they were both in their early thirties, but whereas Gray looked ten years more than his age, Larry looked ten years less. Gray's movements, owing to his great bulk, were deliberate and rather heavy; but Larry's were light and easy. His manner was boyish, gay, and debonair, but withal it had a serenity that I was peculiarly conscious of and that I did not recollect in the lad I had known before. And as the conversation proceeded, flowing without difficulty as was natural in old friends with so many common memories, with bits of news about Chicago thrown in by Gray and Isabel, trivial gossip, one thing leading to another, with airy laughter, my impression persisted that in Larry, though his laughter was frank and he listened with evident pleasure to Isabel's breezy chatter, there was a very singular detachment. I didn't feel that he was playing a part, he was too natural for that and his sincerity was obvious; I felt that there was something within him, I don't know whether to call it awareness or a sensibility or a force, that remained strangely aloof.

The children were brought in and made known to Larry, and gave him their polite little knicks. He held out his hand, looking at them with an engaging tenderness in his soft eyes, and they took it, staring at him gravely. Isabel brightly told him they were getting on nicely with their lessons, gave them a cookie each, and sent them away.

'I'll come and read to you for ten minutes when you're in bed.'

She did not at that moment want to be interrupted in her pleasure at seeing Larry. The little girls went up to say good night to their father. It was charming to see the love that lit up the red face of that gross man as he took them in his arms and kissed them. No one could help seeing that he proudly adored them and when they were gone he turned to Larry and with a sweet slow smile on his lips said:

'They're not bad kids, are they?'

Isabel gave him an affectionate glance.

'If I let Gray have his way he'd spoil them to death. He'd let me starve, that great brute would, to feed the children on caviare and *pâté de foie gras.*'

He looked at her with a smile and said: 'You're a liar and you know it. I worship the ground you tread on.'

There was a responsive smile in Isabel's eyes. She knew that and was glad of it. A happy couple.

She insisted that we should stay to dinner. I, thinking they would prefer to be by themselves, made excuses, but she would not listen to them.

'I'll tell Marie to put another carrot in the soup and there'll be plenty for four. There's a chicken, and you and Gray can eat the legs while Larry and I eat the wings, and she can make the *soufflé* large enough for all of us.'

Gray too seemed to want me to stay, so I let myself be persuaded to do what I wanted to.

While we waited Isabel told Larry at length what I had already told him in brief. Though she narrated the lamentable story as gaily as possible Gray's face assumed an expression of sullen melancholy. She tried to cheer him up.

'Anyhow, it's all over now. We've fallen on our feet and we've got the future before us. As soon as things improve, Gray's going to get a splendid job and make millions.'

Cocktails were brought in and a couple did something to raise the poor fellow's spirits. I saw that Larry, though he took

152

one, scarcely touched it, and when Gray, unobservant, offered him another he refused. We washed our hands and sat down to dinner. Gray had ordered a bottle of champagne, but when the butler began to fill Larry's glass he told him he didn't want any.

'Oh, but you must have some,' cried Isabel. 'It's Uncle Elliott's best and he only gives it to very special guests.'

'To tell you the truth I prefer water. After having been in the East so long it's a treat to drink water that's safe.'

'This is an occasion.'

'All right, I'll drink a glass.'

The dinner was excellent, but Isabel noticed, as I did too, that Larry ate very little. It struck her, I suppose, that she had been doing all the talking and that Larry had had no chance to do more than listen, so now she began to question him on his actions during the ten years since she had seen him. He answered with his cordial frankness, but so vaguely as not to tell us much.

'Oh, I've been loafing around, you know. I spent a year in Germany and some time in Spain and Italy. And I knocked about the East for a bit.'

'Where have you just come from now?'

'India.'

'How long were you there?'

'Five years.'

'Did you have fun?' asked Gray. 'Shoot any tigers?'

'No,' Larry smiled.

'What on earth were you doing with yourself in India for five years?' said Isabel.

'Playing about,' he answered, with a smile of kindly mockery.

'What about the Rope Trick?' asked Gray. 'Did you see that?'

'No, I didn't.'

'What did you see?'

'A lot.'

I put a question to him then.

'Is it true that the Yogis acquire powers that would seem to us supernatural?'

'I wouldn't know. All I can tell you is that it's commonly believed in India. But the wisest don't attach any importance

153

to powers of that sort; they think they're apt to hinder spiritual progress. I remember one of them telling me of a Yogi who came to the bank of a river; he hadn't the money to pay the ferryman to take him across and the ferryman refused to take him for nothing, so he stepped on the water and walked upon its surface to the other side. The Yogi who told me shrugged his shoulders rather scornfully. "A miracle like that," he said "is worth no more than the penny it would have cost to go on the ferryboat." '

'But d'you think the Yogi really walked over the water?' asked Gray.

'The Yogi who told me believed it implicitly.'

It was a pleasure to hear Larry talk, because he had a wonderfully melodious voice; it was light, rich without being deep, and with a singular variety of tone. We finished dinner and went back to the drawing-room to have our coffee. I had never been to India and was eager to hear more of it.

'Did you come in contact with any writers and thinkers?' I asked.

'I notice that you make a distinction between the two,' said Isabel to tease me.

'I made it my business to,' Larry answered.

'How did you communicate with them? In English?'

'The most interesting, if they spoke at all, didn't speak it very well and understood less. I learnt Hindustani. And when I went south I picked up enough Tamil to get along pretty well.'

'How many languages d'you know now, Larry?'

'Oh, I don't know. Half a dozen or so.'

'I want to know more about the Yogis,' said Isabel. 'Did you get to know any of them intimately?'

'As intimately as you can know persons who pass the best part of their time in the Infinite,' he smiled. 'I spent two years in the Ashrama of one.'

'Two years? What's an Ashrama?'

'Well, I suppose you might call it a hermitage. There are holy men who live alone, in a temple, in the forest, or on the slopes of the Himalayas. There are others who attract disciples. A charitable person to acquire merit builds a room, large or small, to lodge a Yogi whose piety has impressed him, and the disciples live with him, sleeping on the veranda or in the cookhouse if there is one or under the trees. I had a tiny hut in the compound just big enough for my camp bed, a chair and a table, and a bookshelf.'

'Where was this?' I inquired.

'In Travancore, a beautiful country of green hills and valleys and soft-flowing rivers. Up in the mountains there are tigers, leopards, elephants, and bison, but the Ashrama was on a lagoon and all around it grew coconuts and areca palms. It was three or four miles from the nearest town, but people used to come from there, and even from much farther, on foot or by bullock cart, to hear the Yogi talk when he was inclined to, or just to sit at his feet and share with one another the peace and blessedness that were radiated from his presence as fragrance is wafted upon the air by a tuberose.'

Gray moved uneasily in his chair. I guessed that the conversation was taking a turn that he found uncomfortable.

'Have a drink?' he said to me.

'No, thanks.'

'Well, I'm going to have one. What about you Isabel?'

He raised his great weight from the chair and went over to the table on which stood whisky and Perrier and glasses.

'Were there other white men there?'

'No. I was the only one.'

'How could you stand it for two years?' cried Isabel.

'They passed like a flash. I've spent days that seemed to be unconscionably longer.'

'What did you do with yourself all the time?'

'I read. I took long walks. I went out in a boat on the lagoon. I meditated. Meditation is very hard work; after two or three hours of it you're as exhausted as if you'd driven a car five hundred miles, and all you want to do is to rest.'

Isabel frowned slightly. She was puzzled and I'm not sure that she wasn't a trifle scared. I think she was beginning to have a notion that the Larry who had entered the room a few hours before, though unchanged in appearance and seemingly as open and friendly as he had ever been, was not the same as the Larry, so candid, easy, and gay, wilful to her mind but delightful, that she had known in the past. She had lost him before, and on seeing him again, taking him for the old Larry, she had a feeling that, however altered the circumstances, he was still hers; and now, as though she had sought to catch a sunbeam in her hand and it slipped through her fingers as she grasped it, she was a trifle dismayed. I had looked at her a good deal that evening, which was always a pleasant thing to do, and had seen the fondness in her eyes as they rested on his trim head, with the small ears close to the skull, and how the expression in them changed when they dwelt on his hollow temples and the thinness of his cheek. She glanced at his long lean hands, which notwithstanding their emaciation were strong and virile. Then her gaze lingered on his mobile mouth, well shaped, full without being sensual, and on his serene brow and clean-cut nose. He wore his new clothes not with the bandbox elegance of Elliott, but with a sort of loose carelessness as though he had worn them every day for a year. I felt that he aroused in Isabel motherly instincts I had never felt in her relation with her children. She was an experienced woman; he still looked a boy; and I seemed to read in her air the pride of a mother for her grown-up son because he is talking intelligently and others are listening to him as if he made sense. I don't think the import of what he said penetrated her consciousness.

But I was not done with my questioning.

'What was your Yogi like?'

'In person, d'you mean? Well, he wasn't tall, neither thin nor fat, palish brown in colour and clean-shaven, with close-cropped white hair. He never wore anything but a loincloth, and yet he managed to look as trim and neat and well dressed as a young man in one of Brooks Brothers' advertisements.'

'And what had he got that particularly attracted you?'

Larry looked at me for a full minute before answering. His eyes in their deep sockets seemed as though they were trying to pierce to the depths of my soul.

'Saintliness.'

I was slightly disconcerted by his reply. In that room, with its fine furniture, with those lovely drawings on the walls, the word fell like a plop of water that has seeped through the ceiling from an overflowing bath.

'We've read all about the saints, St Francis, St John of the Cross, but that was hundreds of years ago. I never thought it possible to meet one who was alive now. From the first time I saw him I never doubted that he was a saint. It was a wonderful experience.'

'And what did you gain from it?'

'Peace,' he said casually, with a light smile. Then, abruptly, he rose to his feet. 'I must go.'

'Oh, not yet, Larry,' cried Isabel. 'It's quite early.'

'Good night,' he said, smiling still, taking no notice of her expostulation. He kissed her on the cheek. 'I'll see you again in a day or two.'

'Where are you staying? I'll call you.'

'Oh, don't bother to do that. You know how difficult it is to get a call through in Paris, and in any case our telephone is generally out of order.'

I laughed inwardly at the neatness with which Larry had got out of giving an address. It was a queer kink of his to make a secret of his abode. I suggested that they should all dine with me next evening but one in the Bois de Boulogne. It was very pleasant in that balmy spring weather to eat out-of-doors, under the trees, and Gray could drive us there in the coupé. I left with Larry and would willingly have walked some way with him, but as we got into the street he shook hands with me and walked quickly off. I got into a taxi.

5

We had arranged to meet at the apartment and have a cocktail before starting. I arrived before Larry. I was taking them to a very smart restaurant and expected to find Isabel arrayed for the occasion; with all the women dressed up to the nines I was confident she would not wish to be outshone. But she had on a plain woollen frock.

'Gray's got one of his headaches,' she said. 'He's in agony. I can't possibly leave him. I told the cook she could go out when she'd given the children their supper and I must make something for him myself and try to get him to take it. You and Larry had better go alone.'

'Is Gray in bed?'

'No, he won't ever go to bed when he has his headaches. God knows, it's the only place for him, but he won't. He's in the library.'

This was a little panelled room, brown and gold, that Elliott had found in an old château. The books were protected from anyone who wanted to read them by gilt latticework, and locked up, but this was perhaps as well, as they consisted for the most part of illustrated pornographic works of the eighteenth century. In their contemporary morocco, however, they made a very pretty effect. Isabel led me in. Gray was sitting humped up in a big leather chair, with picture papers scattered on the floor beside him. His eyes were closed and his usually red face had a grey pallor. It was evident that he was in great pain. He tried to get up, but I stopped him.

'Have you given him any aspirin?' I asked Isabel.

'That never does any good. I have an American prescription, but that doesn't help either.'

'Oh, don't bother, darling,' said Gray. 'I shall be all right tomorrow.' He tried to smile. 'I'm sorry to make such a nuisance of myself,' he said to me. 'You all go out to the Bois.'

'I wouldn't dream of it,' said Isabel. 'D'you think I should enjoy myself when I knew you were suffering the tortures of the damned?'

'Poor slut, I think she loves me,' said Gray, his eyes closed.

Then his face was suddenly contorted and you could almost see the lancinating pain that pierced his head. The door was softly opened and Larry stepped in. Isabel told him what was the matter.

'Oh, I am sorry,' he said, giving Gray a look of commiseration. 'Isn't there anything one can do to relieve him?'

'Nothing,' said Gray, his eyes still closed. 'The only thing you can any of you do for me is to leave me alone; go off and have a good time by yourselves.'

I thought myself that was the only sensible course to take, but I didn't suppose Isabel could square it with her conscience.

'Will you let me see if I can help you?' asked Larry.

'No one can help me,' said Gray wearily. 'It's just killing me and sometimes I wish to God it would.'

'I was wrong in saying that perhaps I could help you. What

158

I meant was that perhaps I could help you to help yourself.'

Gray slowly opened his eyes and looked at Larry.

'How can you do that?'

Larry took what looked like a silver coin out of his pocket and put it in Gray's hand.

'Close your fingers on it tightly and hold your hand palm downwards. Don't fight against me. Make no effort, but hold the coin in your clenched fist. Before I count twenty your hand will open and the coin will drop out of it.'

Gray did as he was told. Larry seated himself at the writing-table and began to count. Isabel and I remained standing. One, two, three, four. Till he got up to fifteen there was no movement in Gray's hand, then it seemed to tremble a little and I had the impression, I can hardly say I saw, that the clenched fingers were loosening. The thumb moved away from the fist. I distinctly saw the fingers quiver. When Larry reached nineteen the coin fell out of Gray's hand and rolled to my feet. I picked it up and looked at it. It was heavy and misshapen, and in bold relief on one side of it was a youthful head which I recognized as that of Alexander the Great. Gray stared at his hand with perplexity.

'I didn't let the coin drop,' he said. 'It fell of itself.'

He was sitting with his right arm resting on the arm of the leather chair.

'Are you quite comfortable in that chair?' asked Larry.

'As comfortable as I can be when my head's giving me hell.'

'Well, let yourself go quite slack. Take it easy. Do nothing. Don't resist. Before I count twenty your right arm will rise from the arm of the chair until your hand is above your head. One, two, three, four.'

He spoke the numbers slowly in that silver-toned, melodious voice of his, and when he had reached nine we saw Gray's hand rise, only just perceptibly, from the leather surface on which it rested until it was perhaps an inch above it. It stopped for a second.

'Ten, eleven, twelve.'

There was a little jerk and then slowly the whole arm began to move upwards. It wasn't resting on the chair any more. Isabel, a little scared, took hold of my hand. It was a curious

159

effect. It had no likeness to a voluntary movement. I've never seen a man walking in his sleep, but I can imagine that he would move in just the same strange way that Gray's arm moved. It didn't look as though the will were the motive power. I should have thought it would be hard to raise the arm so slowly and so evenly by a conscious effort. It gave the impression that a subconscious force, independent of the mind, was raising it. It was the same sort of movement as that of a piston moving very slowly back and forth in a cylinder.

'Fifteen, sixteen, seventeen.'

The words fell, slow, slow, slow, like drops of water in a basin from a defective tap. Gray's arm rose, rose, till his hand was above his head, and as Larry reached the number he had said it fell of its own weight on to the arm of the chair.

'I didn't lift my arm,' said Gray. 'I couldn't help its rising like that. It did it of its own accord.'

Larry faintly smiled.

'It's of no consequence. I thought it might give you confidence in me. Where's that Greek coin?'

I gave it to him.

'Hold it in your hand.' Gray took it. Larry glanced at his watch. 'It's thirteen minutes past eight. In sixty seconds your eyelids will grow so heavy that you'll be obliged to close them and then you'll sleep. You'll sleep for six minutes. At eight twenty you'll wake and you'll have no more pain.'

Neither Isabel nor I spoke. Our eyes were on Larry. He said nothing more. He fixed his gaze on Gray, but did not seem to look at him; he seemed rather to look through and beyond him. There was something eerie in the silence that fell upon us; it was like the silence of flowers in a garden at nightfall. Suddenly I felt Isabel's hand tighten. I glanced at Gray. His eyes were closed. He was breathing easily and regularly; he was asleep. We stood there for a time that seemed interminable. I badly wanted a cigarette, but did not like to light one. Larry was motionless. His eyes looked into I knew not what distance. Except that they were open he might have been in a trance. Suddenly he appeared to relax; his eyes took on their normal expression and he looked at his watch. As he did so, Gray opened his eyes.

160

'Gosh,' he said, 'I believe I dropped off to sleep.' Then he started. I noticed that his face had lost its ghastly pallor. 'My headache's gone.'

'That's fine,' said Larry. 'Have a cigarette and then we'll all go out to dinner.'

'It's a miracle. I feel perfectly swell. How did you do it?'

'I didn't do it. You did it yourself.'

Isabel went to change and meanwhile Gray and I drank a cocktail. Though it was plain that Larry did not wish it, Gray insisted on talking of what had just happened. He couldn't make it out at all.

'I didn't believe you could do a thing, you know,' he said. 'I just gave in because I felt too lousy to argue.'

He went on to describe the onset of his headaches, the anguish he endured, and the wreck he was when the attack subsided. He could not understand how it was that just then he felt his usual robust self. Isabel came back. She was wearing a dress I had not seen before; it reached to the ground, a white sheath of what I think is called marocain, with a flare of black tulle, and I could not but think she would be a credit to us.

It was very gay at the Château de Madrid and we were in high spirits. Larry talked amusing nonsense in a way I had not heard him do before and he made us laugh. I had a notion he was doing this with the idea of diverting our minds from the exhibition of his unexpected power. But Isabel was a determined woman. She was prepared to play ball with him as long as it suited her convenience, but she did not lose sight of her desire to satisfy her curiosity. When we had finished dinner and were drinking coffee and liqueurs and she might well have supposed that the good food, the one glass of wine he drank, and the friendly talk had weakened his defences she fixed her bright eyes on Larry.

'Now tell us how you cured Gray's headache.'

'You saw for yourself,' he answered, smiling.

'Did you learn to do that sort of thing in India?'

'Yes.'

'He suffers agonies. D'you think you could cure him permanently?'

'I don't know. I might be able to.'

'It would make a difference to his whole life. He couldn't expect to hold a decent job when he may be incapacitated for forty-eight hours. He'll never be happy till he's at work again.'

'I can't work miracles, you know.'

'But it was a miracle. I saw it with my own eyes.'

'No, it wasn't. I merely put an idea in old Gray's head and he did the rest himself.' He turned to Gray. 'What are you doing tomorrow?'

'Playing golf.'

'I'll look in at six and we'll have a talk.' Then, giving Isabel his winning smile: 'I haven't danced with you for ten years, Isabel. Would you care to see if I still know how to?'

6

After that we saw a good deal of Larry. For the next week he came to the apartment every day and for half an hour shut himself up with Gray in the library. It appeared that he wanted to persuade him – that was how he smilingly put it – out of having those shattering megrims, and Gray conceived a child-like trust in him. From the little Gray said I got the idea that he was trying besides to restore his broken confidence in himself. About ten days later Gray had another headache, and it so happened that Larry was not to come till the evening. It was not a very bad one, but Gray was so confident now in Larry's odd power that he thought if Larry could be got hold of he could take it away in a few minutes. But neither I, whom Isabel called on the phone, nor they knew where he lived. When Larry at last came and relieved Gray of his pain, Gray asked him for his address so that in case of need he could summon him at once. Larry smiled.

'Call the American Express and leave a message. I'll call them every morning.'

Isabel asked me later why Larry made a secret of his address. He had done that before and then it had turned out that he lived without any mystery in a third-rate hotel in the Latin Quarter.

'I haven't a notion,' I said in answer. 'I can only suggest something very fanciful and there's probably nothing in it. It may be that some queer instinct urges him to carry over to his dwelling-place some privacy of his spirit.'

'What in God's name d'you mean by that?' she cried irritably.

'Hasn't it struck you that when he's with us, easy as he is to get on with, friendly and sociable, one's conscious of a sort of detachment in him, as though he weren't giving all of himself, but withheld in some hidden part of his soul something, I don't know what it is – a tension, a secret, an aspiration, a knowledge – that sets him apart?'

'I've known Larry all my life,' she said impatiently.

'Sometimes he reminds me of a great actor playing perfectly a part in a trumpery play. Like Eleanora Duse in *La Locandiera*.'

Isabel pondered over this for a moment.

'I suppose I know what you mean. One's having fun, and one thinks he's just like one of us, just like everybody else, and then suddenly you have the feeling that he's escaped you like a smoke ring that you try to catch in your hands. What do you think it can be that makes him so queer?'

'Perhaps something so commonplace that one simply doesn't notice it.'

'Such as?'

'Well, goodness, for instance.'

Isabel frowned.

'I wish you wouldn't say things like that. It gives me a nasty feeling in the pit of my stomach.'

'Or is it a little pain in the depth of your heart?'

Isabel gave me a long look as though she were trying to read my thoughts. She took a cigarette from the table beside her and, lighting it, leant back in her chair. She watched the smoke curl up into the air.

'Do you want me to go?' I asked.

'No.'

I was silent for a moment, watching her, and I took my pleasure in the contemplation of her shapely nose and the exquisite line of her jaw.

'Are you very much in love with Larry?'

'God damn you, I've never loved anyone else in all my life.'

'Why did you marry Gray?'

'I had to marry somebody. He was mad about me and

163

Mamma wanted me to marry him. Everybody told me I was well rid of Larry. I was very fond of Gray; I'm very fond of him still. You don't know how sweet he is. No one in the world could be so kind and so considerate. He looks as though he had an awful temper, doesn't he? With me he's always been angelic. When we had money, he wanted me to want things so that he could have the pleasure of giving them to me. Once I said it would be fun if we could have a yacht and go round the world, and if the crash hadn't come he'd have bought one.'

'He sounds almost too good to be true,' I murmured.

'We had a grand time. I shall always be grateful to him for that. He made me very happy.'

I looked at her but did not speak.

'I suppose I didn't really love him, but one can get on all right without love. At the bottom of my heart I hankered for Larry, but as long as I didn't see him it didn't really bother me. D'you remember saying to me that with three thousand miles of ocean between, the pangs of love become quite tolerable? I thought it a cynical remark then, but of course it's true.'

'If it's a pain to see Larry, don't you think it would be wiser not to see him?'

'But it's a pain that's heaven. Besides, you know what he is. Any day he may vanish like a shadow when the sun goes in and we may not see him again for years.'

'Have you never thought of divorcing Gray?'

'I've got no reason for divorcing him.'

'That doesn't prevent your countrywomen from divorcing their husbands when they have a mind to.'

She laughed.

'Why d'you suppose they do it?'

'Don't you know? Because American women expect to find in their husbands a perfection that English women only hope to find in their butlers.'

Isabel gave her head such a haughty toss that I wondered she didn't get a crick in the neck.

'Because Gray isn't articulate you think there's nothing to him.'

'You're wrong there,' I interrupted quickly. 'I think there's something rather moving about him. He has a wonderful faculty of love. One has only to glance at his face when he's looking at you to see how deeply, how devotedly he's attached to you. He loves his children much more than you do.'

'I suppose you're going to say now that I'm not a good mother.'

'On the contrary I think you're an excellent mother. You see that they're well and happy. You watch over their diet and take care that their bowels act regularly. You teach them to behave nicely and you read to them and make them say their prayers. If they were sick you'd send for a doctor at once and nurse them with care. But you're not wrapped up in them as Gray is.'

'It's unnecessary that one should be. I'm a human being and I treat them as human beings. A mother only does her children harm if she makes them the only concern of her life.'

'I think you're quite right.'

'And the fact remains that they worship me.'

'I've noticed that. You're their ideal of all that's graceful and beautiful and wonderful. But they're not cosy and at their ease with you as they are with Gray. They worship you, that's true; but they love him.'

'He's very lovable.'

I liked her for saying that. One of her most amiable traits was that she was never affronted by the naked truth.

'After the crash Gray went all to pieces. For weeks he worked at the office till midnight. I used to sit at home in an agony of fear, I was afraid he'd blow his brains out, he was so ashamed. You see, they'd been so proud of the firm, his father and Gray, they were proud of their integrity and the sureness of their judgement. It wasn't so much that we'd lost all our money, what he couldn't get over was that all those people who'd trusted him had lost theirs. He felt that he ought to have had more foresight. I couldn't get him to see that he wasn't to blame.'

Isabel took a lipstick out of her bag and painted her lips.

'But that's not what I wanted to tell you. The one thing we had left was the plantation and I felt that the only chance for Gray was to get away, so we parked the children with Mamma and went down there. He'd always liked it, but we'd never

165

been there by ourselves; we'd taken a crowd with us and had a
grand time. Gray's a good shot, but he hadn't the heart to
shoot then. He used to take a boat and go out on the marsh by
himself for hours at a time and watch the birds. He'd wander
up and down the canals with the pale rushes on each side of him
and only the blue sky above. On some days the canals are as
blue as the Mediterranean. He used not to say much when he
came back. He'd say it was swell. But I could see what he felt.
I knew that his heart was moved by the beauty and the vastness and the stillness. There's a moment just before sunset when
the light on the marsh is lovely. He used to stand and look at
it and it filled him with bliss. He took long rides in those soli-
tary, mysterious woods; they're like the woods in a play of
Maeterlinck's, so grey, so silent, it's almost uncanny; and there's
a moment in spring – it hardly lasts more than a fortnight –
when the dogwood bursts into flower, and the gum trees burst
into leaf, and their young fresh green against the grey Spanish
moss is like a song of joy; the ground is carpeted with great
white lilies and wild azalea. Gray couldn't say what it meant
to him, but it meant the world. He was drunk with the loveliness of it. Oh, I know I don't put it well, but I can't tell you
how moving it was to see that great hulk of a man uplifted by
an emotion so pure and so beautiful that it made me want to
cry. If there is a God in heaven Gray was very near Him then.'

Isabel had grown a trifle emotional while she told me this
and taking a tiny handkerchief she carefully wiped away a tear
that glistened at the corner of each eye.

'Aren't you romanticizing?' I said, smiling. 'I have a notion
that you're ascribing to Gray thoughts and emotions that you
would have expected him to have.'

'How should I have seen them if they hadn't been there? You
know what I am. I'm never really happy unless I feel the
cement of a sidewalk under my feet and there are large plate-
glass windows all along the street with hats to look at and fur
coats and diamond bracelets and gold-mounted dressingcases.'

I laughed and we were silent for a moment. Then she went
back to what we had been talking of before.

'I'd never divorce Gray. We've been through too much together. And he's absolutely dependent upon me. It's rather

flattering, you know, and it gives you a sense of responsibility. And besides ...'

'Besides what?'

She gave me a sidelong glance and there was a roguish twinkle in her eyes. I had a notion she didn't quite know how I would take what she had in mind to say.

'He's wonderful in bed. We've been married for ten years and he's as passionate a lover as he was at the beginning. Didn't you say in a play once that no man wants the same woman longer than five years? Well, you didn't know what you were talking about. Gray wants me as much as when we were first married. He's made me very happy in that way. Although you wouldn't think it to look at me, I'm a very sensual woman.'

'You're quite wrong, I would think it.'

'Well, it's not an unattractive trait, is it?'

'On the contrary.' I gave her a searching look. 'Do you regret you didn't marry Larry ten years ago?'

'No. It would have been madness. But of course if I'd known then what I know now I'd have gone away and lived with him for three months, and then I'd have got him out of my system for good and all.'

'I think it's lucky for you you didn't make the experiment; you might have found yourself bound to him by bonds you couldn't break.'

'I don't think so. It was merely a physical attraction. You know, often the best way to overcome desire is to satisfy it.'

'Has it ever struck you that you're a very possessive woman? You've told me that Gray has a deep strain of poetic feeling and you've told me that he's an ardent lover; and I can well believe that both mean a lot to you; but you haven't told me what means much more to you than both of them put together – your feeling that you hold him in the hollow of that beautiful but not so small hand of yours. Larry would always have escaped you. D'you remember that *Ode* of Keats's? "Bold Lover, never, never canst thou kiss, though winning near the goal." '

'You often think you know a great deal more than you do,' she said, a trifle acidly. 'There's only one way a woman holds a man and you know it. And let me tell you this: it's not the first time she goes to bed with him that counts, it's the second. If she holds him then she holds him for good.'

'You do pick up the most extraordinary bits of information.'

'I get around and I keep my eyes and ears open.'

'May I inquire how you acquired that one?'

She gave me her most teasing smile.

'From a woman I made friends with at a dress show. The *vendeuse* told me she was the smartest kept woman in Paris, so I made up my mind I'd get to know her. Adrienne de Troye. Ever heard of her?'

'Never.'

'How your education has been neglected! She's forty-five and not even pretty, but she looks much more distinguished than any of Uncle Elliott's duchesses. I sat down beside her and put on my impulsive little-American-girl act. I told her I had to speak to her because I'd never seen anyone more ravishing in my life. I told her she had the perfection of a Greek cameo.'

'The nerve you've got.'

'She was rather stiff at first and stand-offish, but I ran on in my simple naïve way and she thawed. Then we had quite a nice little chat. When the show was over I asked her if she wouldn't come to lunch with me at the Ritz one day. I told her I'd always admired her wonderful chic.'

'Had you ever seen her before?'

'Never. She wouldn't lunch with me, she said they had such malicious tongues in Paris, it would compromise me, but she was pleased that I'd asked her, and when she saw my mouth quiver with disappointment she asked me if I wouldn't come and lunch with her in her house. She patted my hand when she saw I was simply overwhelmed by her affability.'

'And did you go?'

'Of course I went. She has a dear little house off the Avenue Foch and we were waited on by a butler who's the very image of George Washington. I stayed till four o'clock. We took our hair down and our stays off, and had a thorough girls' gossip. I learnt enough that afternoon to write a book.'

'Why don't you? It's just the sort of thing to suit the *Ladies' Home Journal*.'

'You fool,' she laughed.

I was silent for a moment. I pursued my thoughts.

'I wonder if Larry was ever *really* in love with you,' I said presently.

She sat up. Her expression lost its amenity. Her eyes were angry.

'What are you talking about? Of course he was in love with me. D'you think a girl doesn't know when a man's in love with her?'

'Oh, I dare say he was in love with you after a fashion. He didn't know any girl so intimately as he knew you. You'd played around together since you were children. He expected himself to be in love with you. He had the normal sexual instinct. It seemed such a natural thing that you should marry. There wouldn't have been any particular difference in your relations except that you lived under the same roof and went to bed together.'

Isabel, to some exent mollified, waited for me to go on and, knowing that women are always glad to listen when you discourse upon love, I went on.

'Moralists try to persuade us that the sexual instinct hasn't got so very much to do with love. They're apt to speak of it as if it were an epiphenomenon.'

'What in God's name is that?'

'Well, there are psychologists who think that consciousness accompanies brain processes and is determined by them, but doesn't itself exert any influence on them. Something like the reflection of a tree in water; it couldn't exist without the tree, but it doesn't in any way affect the tree. I think it's all stuff and nonsense to say that there can be love without passion; when people say love can endure after passion is dead they're talking of something else, affection, kindliness, community of taste and interest, and habit. Especially habit. Two people can go on having sexual intercourse from habit in just the same way as they grow hungry at the hour they're accustomed to have their meals. Of course there can be desire without love. Desire isn't passion. Desire is the natural consequence of the sexual instinct and it isn't of any more importance than any other function of the human animal. That's why women are foolish

169

to make a song and dance if their husbands have an occasional flutter when the time and the place are propitious.'

'Does that apply only to men?'

I smiled.

'If you insist I'll admit that what is sauce for the gander is sauce for the goose. The only thing to be said against it is that with a man a passing connexion of that sort has no emotional significance, while with a woman it has.'

'It depends on the woman.'

I wasn't going to let myself be interrupted.

'Unless love is passion, it's not love, but something else; and passion thrives not on satisfaction, but on impediment. What d'you suppose Keats meant when he told the lover on his Grecian urn not to grieve? "Forever wilt thou love, and she be fair!" Why? Because she was unattainable, and however madly the lover pursued she still eluded him. For they were both imprisoned in the marble of what I suspect was an indifferent work of art. Your love for Larry and his for you were as simple and natural as the love of Paolo and Francesca or Romeo and Juliet. Fortunately for you it didn't come to a bad end. You made a rich marriage and Larry roamed the world to find out what song the Sirens sang. Passion didn't enter into it.'

'How d'you know?'

'Passion doesn't count the cost. Pascal said that the heart has its reasons that reason takes no account of. If he meant what I think, he meant that when passion seizes the heart it invents reasons that seem not only plausible but conclusive to prove that the world is well lost for love. It convinces you that honour is well sacrificed and that shame is a cheap price to pay. Passion is destructive. It destroyed Antony and Cleopatra, Tristan and Isolde, Parnell and Kitty O'Shea. And if it doesn't destroy it dies. It may be then that one is faced with the desolation of knowing that one has wasted the years of one's life, that one's brought disgrace upon oneself, endured the frightful pang of jealousy, swallowed every bitter mortification, that one's expended all one's tenderness, poured out all the riches of one's soul on a poor drab, a fool, a peg on which one hung one's dreams, who wasn't worth a stick of chewing gum.'

170

Before I finished this harangue I knew very well that Isabel wasn't paying any attention to me, but was occupied with her own reflections. But her next remark surprised me.

'Do you think Larry is a virgin?'

'My dear, he's thirty-two.'

'I'm certain he is.'

'How can you be?'

'That's the kind of thing a woman knows instinctively.'

'I knew a young man who had a very prosperous career for some years by convincing one beautiful creature after another that he'd never had a woman. He said it worked like a charm.'

'I don't care what you say. I believe in my intuition.'

It was growing late, Gray and Isabel were dining with friends, and she had to dress. I had nothing to do, so I walked in the pleasant spring evening up the Boulevard Raspail. I have never believed very much in women's intuition; it fits in too neatly with what they want to believe to persuade me that it is trustworthy; and as I thought of the end of my long talk with Isabel I couldn't help but laugh. It put me in mind of Suzanne Rouvier and it occurred to me that I hadn't seen her for several days. I wondered if she was doing anything. If not, she might like to dine with me and go to a movie. I stopped a prowling taxi and gave the address of her apartment.

7

I mentioned Suzanne Rouvier at the beginning of this book. I had known her for ten or twelve years and at the date which I have now reached she must have been not far from forty. She was not beautiful; in fact she was rather ugly. She was tall for a Frenchwoman, with a short body, long legs, and long arms, and she held herself gawkily as though she didn't know how to cope with the length of her limbs. The colour of her hair changed according to her whim, but most often it was a reddish brown. She had a small square face, with very prominent cheekbones vividly rouged, and a large mouth with heavily-painted lips. None of this sounds attractive, but it was; it is true that she had a good skin, strong white teeth, and big, vividly blue eyes. They were her best feature, and she made the most of them by painting her eyelashes and her eyelids. She had a

171

shrewd, roving, friendly look and she combined great good nature with a proper degree of toughness. In the life she had led she needed to be tough. Her mother, the widow of a small official in the government, had on his death returned to her native village in Anjou to live on her pension, and when Suzanne was fifteen she apprenticed her to a dressmaker in the neighbouring town, which was near enough for her to be able to come home on Sundays. It was during her fortnight's holiday, when she had reached the age of seventeen, that she was seduced by an artist who was spending his summer in the village to paint landscape. She already knew very well that without a penny to bless herself with her chance of marriage was remote and when the painter, at the end of the summer, proposed taking her to Paris she consented with alacrity. He took her to live with him in a rabbit-warren of studios in Montmartre, and she spent a very pleasant year in his company.

At the end of this he told her that he had not sold a single canvas and could no longer afford the luxury of a mistress. She had been expecting the news for some time and was not disconcerted by it. He asked her if she wanted to go home and when she said she didn't, told her that another painter in the same block would be glad to have her. The man he named had made a pass at her two or three times and though she had rebuffed him it had been with so much good humour that he was not affronted. She did not dislike him and so accepted the proposition with placidity. It was convenient that she did not have to go to the expense of taking a taxi to transport her trunk. Her second lover, a good deal older than the first, but still presentable, painted her in every conceivable position, clothed and in the nude; and she passed two happy years with him. She was proud to think that with her as a model he had made his first real success and she showed me a reproduction cut out of an illustrated paper of the picture that had brought it about. It had been purchased by an American gallery. It was a nude, life-size, and she was lying in something of the same position as Manet's Olympe. The artist had been quick to see that there was something modern and amusing in her proportions, and, fining down her thin body to emaciation, he had elongated her long legs and arms, he had emphasized her high cheekbones and made her blue eyes extravagantly large. From the reproduction I naturally could not tell what the colour was like, but I was sensible of the elegance of the design. The picture brought him sufficient notoriety to enable him to marry an admiring widow with money, and Suzanne, well aware that a man had to think of his future, accepted the rupture of their cordial relations without acrimony.

For by now she knew her value. She liked the artistic life, it amused her to pose, and after the day's work was over she found it pleasant to go to the café and sit with painters, their wives and mistresses, while they discussed art, reviled dealers, and told bawdy stories. On this occasion, having seen the break coming, she had made her plans. She picked out a young man who was unattached and who, she thought, had talent. She chose her opportunity when he was alone at the café, explained the circumstances, and without further preamble suggested that they should live together.

'I'm twenty and a good housekeeper. I'll save you money there and I'll save you the expense of a model. Look at your shirt, it's a disgrace, and your studio is a mess. You want a woman to look after you.'

He knew she was a good sort. He was amused at her proposal and she saw he was inclined to accept.

'After all, there's no harm in trying,' she said. 'If it doesn't work we shall neither of us be worse off than we are now.'

He was a non-representative artist and he painted portraits of her in squares and oblongs. He painted her with one eye and no mouth. He painted her as a geometrical arrangement in black and brown and grey. He painted her in a criss-cross of lines through which you vaguely saw a human face. She stayed with him for a year and a half and left him of her own accord.

'Why?' I asked her. 'Didn't you like him?'

'Yes, he was a nice boy. I didn't think he was getting any further. He was repeating himself.'

She found no difficulty in discovering a successor. She remained faithful to artists.

'I've always been in painting,' she said. 'I was with a sculptor for six months, but I don't know why, it said nothing to me.'

She was pleased to think that she had never separated from a

173

lover with unpleasantness. She was not only a good model, but a good housewife. She loved working about the studio she happened for a while to be living in and took pride in keeping it in apple-pie order. She was a good cook and could turn out a tasty meal at the smallest possible cost. She mended her lovers' socks and sewed buttons on their shirts.

'I never saw why because a man was an artist he shouldn't be neat and tidy.'

She only had one failure. This was a young Englishman who had more money than anyone she had known before and he had a car.

'But it didn't last long,' she said. 'He used to get drunk and then he was tiresome. I wouldn't have minded that if he'd been a good painter, but, my dear, it was grotesque. I told him I was going to leave him and he began to cry. He said he loved me.

' "My poor friend," I said to him. "Whether you love me or not isn't of the smallest consequence. What is of consequence is that you have no talent. Return to your own country and go into the grocery business. That is all you're fit for." '

'What did he say to that?' I asked.

'He flew into a passion and told me to get out. But it was good advice I gave him, you know. I hope he took it, he wasn't a bad fellow; only a bad artist.'

Common sense and good nature will do a lot to make the pilgrimage of life not too difficult to a light woman, but the profession Suzanne had adopted had its ups and downs like any other. There was the Scandinavian for instance. She was so imprudent as to fall in love with him.

'He was a god, my dear,' she told me. 'He was immensely tall, as tall as the Eiffel Tower, with great broad shoulders and a magnificent chest, a waist that you could almost put your hands round, a belly flat, but flat like the palm of my hand, and muscles like a professional athlete's. He had golden, wavy hair and a skin of honey. And he didn't paint badly. I liked his brush work, it was bold and dashing, and he had a rich vivid palette.'

She made up her mind to have a child by him. He was against it, but she told him she would take the responsibility.

'He liked it well enough when it was born. Oh, such a lovely baby, rosy, fair-haired and blue-eyed like her papa. It was a girl.'

Suzanne lived with him for three years.

'He was a little stupid and sometimes he bored me, but he was very sweet and so beautiful that I didn't really mind.'

Then he got a telegram from Sweden to say his father was dying and he must come back at once. He promised to return, but she had a premonition that he never would. He left her all the money he had. She didn't hear from him for a month and then she got a letter from him saying that his father had died, leaving his affairs in confusion, and that he felt it his duty to remain by his mother and go into the lumber business. He enclosed a draft for ten thousand francs. Suzanne was not the woman to give way to despair. She came to the conclusion very quickly that a child would hamper her activities, so she took the baby girl down to her mother's and left her, along with the ten thousand francs, in her care.

'It was heart-rending, I adored that child, but in life one has to be practical.'

'What happened then?' I asked.

'Oh, I got along. I found a friend.'

But then came her typhoid. She always spoke of it as 'my typhoid' as a millionaire might speak of 'my place at Palm Beach' or 'my grouse moor'. She nearly died of it and was in the hospital for three months. When she left she was nothing but skin and bone, as weak as a rat, and so nervous that she could do nothing but cry. She wasn't much use to anyone then, she wasn't strong enough to pose and she had very little money.

'*Oh la, la*,' she said, 'I passed through some hard times. Luckily I had good friends. But you know what artists are, it's a struggle for them to make both ends meet, anyway. I was never a pretty woman, I had something of course, but I wasn't twenty any more. Then I ran into the cubist I'd been with; he'd been married and divorced since we lived together, he'd given up cubism and become a surrealist. He thought he could use me and said he was lonely; he said he'd give me board and lodgings and I promise you, I was glad to accept.'

Suzanne stayed with him till she met her manufacturer. The manufacturer was brought to the studio by a friend on the chance that he might buy one of the ex-cubist's pictures, and Suzanne, anxious to effect a sale, set herself out to be as agreeable to him as she knew how. He could not make up his mind to buy on the spur of the moment, but said he would like to come and see the pictures again. He did, a fortnight later, and this time she received the impression that he had come to see her rather than works of art. When he left, still without buying, he pressed her hand with unnecessary warmth. Next day the friend who had brought him waylaid her when she was on her way to market to buy the day's provisions and told her that the manufacturer had taken a fancy to her and wanted to know if she would dine with him next time he came to Paris, because he had a proposition to make to her.

'What does he see in me, d'you suppose?' she asked.

'He's an amateur of modern art. He's seen portraits of you. You intrigue him. He's a provincial and a businessman. You represent Paris to him, art, romance, everything that he misses in Lille.'

'Has he money?' she asked in her sensible way.

'Plenty.'

'Well, I'll dine with him. There's no harm hearing what he's got to say.'

He took her to Maxim's, which impressed her; she had dressed very quietly, and she felt as she looked at the women around her that she could pass very well for a respectable married woman. He ordered a bottle of champagne, and this persuaded her that he was a gentleman. When they came to coffee he put his proposition before her. She thought it very handsome. He told her that he came to Paris regularly once a fortnight to attend a board meeting, and it was tiresome in the evening to dine alone and if he felt the need of feminine society to go to a brothel. Being a married man with two children, he thought that an unsatisfactory arrangement for a man in his position. Their common friend had told him all about her and he knew she was a woman of discretion. He was no longer young and he had no wish to get entangled with a giddy girl. He was something of a collector of the modern school and her connexion with it was sympathetic to him. Then he came down to brass tacks. He was prepared to take an apartment for her and furnish it and provide her with an income of two thousand francs a month. In return for this he wished to enjoy her company for one night every fourteen days. Suzanne had never had the spending of so much money in her life, and she quickly reckoned that on such a sum she could not only live and dress as such an advancement in the world evidently demanded, but provide for her daughter and put away something for a rainy day. But she hesitated for a moment. She had always been 'in painting', as she put it, and there was no doubt in her mind that it was a come-down to be the mistress of a businessman.

'*C'est à prendre ou à laisser,*' he said. 'You can take it or leave it.'

He was not repulsive to her and the rosette of the Legion of Honour in his buttonhole proved that he was a man of distinction. She smiled.

'*Je prends,*' she replied. 'I'll take it.'

8

Though Suzanne had always lived in Montmartre, she decided that it was necessary to break with the past, so she took an apartment in Montparnasse in a house just off the boulevard. It consisted of two rooms, a tiny kitchen, and a bathroom; it was on the sixth floor, but there was a lift. To her a bathroom and a lift, even though it only held two persons and moved at a snail's pace and you had to walk downstairs, represented not only luxury but style.

For the first few months of their union Monsieur Achille Gauvain, for such was his name, put up at a hotel on his fortnightly visits to Paris and, after spending such part of the night with Suzanne as his amorous inclination demanded, returned to it to sleep by himself till it was time for him to get up and catch his train to return to his business affairs and the sober pleasures of family life; but then Suzanne pointed out to him that he was throwing away money to no purpose and it would be both more economical and more comfortable if he stayed in the apartment till morning. He could not but see the force of this. He was flattered at Suzanne's thoughtfulness for his comfort – it was true, there was nothing agreeable in going out into the street and finding a taxi on a cold winter night –

and he approved of her disinclination to put him to useless expense. It was a good woman who counted not only her own pennies but her lover's.

Monsieur Achille had every reason to feel pleased with himself. In general they went to dine at one of the better restaurants in Montparnasse, but now and then Suzanne prepared dinner for him in the apartment. The tasty food she gave him was very much to his liking. On warm evenings he would dine in his shirt-sleeves and feel deliciously wanton and bohemian. He had always had an inclination for buying pictures, but Suzanne would let him buy nothing that she did not approve of, and he soon found reason to trust her judgement. She would have no truck with dealers, but took him to the studios of the painters and thus enabled him to buy pictures for half the money he would otherwise have had to pay. He knew that she was putting something aside, and when she told him that year by year she was buying a bit of land in her native village, he felt a thrill of pride. He knew the desire to own land that is in the heart of every person of French blood, and his esteem for her was increased because she possessed it too.

On her side Suzanne was well satisfied. She was neither faithful to him nor unfaithful; that is to say, she took care not to form any permanent connexion with another man, but if she came across one who took her fancy she was not averse from going to bed with him. But it was a point of honour with her not to let him stay all night. She felt she owed that to the man of means and position who had settled her life in such an assured and respectable manner.

I had come to know Suzanne when she was living with a painter who happened to be an acquaintance of mine and had often sat in his studio while she posed; I continued to see her now and then at irregular intervals, but did not enter upon terms of any intimacy with her till she moved to Montparnasse. It appeared that Monsieur Achille, for this was how she always spoke of him and how she addressed him, had read one or two of my books in translation, and one evening he invited me to dine with them at a restaurant. He was a little man, half a head shorter than Suzanne, with iron-grey hair and a neat grey moustache. He was on the plump side, and he had a pot-belly, but only to the extent of giving him an air of substance. He walked with the short fat man's strut and it was plain that he was not displeased with himself. He gave me a fine dinner. He was very polite. He told me he was glad I was a friend of Suzanne's, he could see at a glance that I was *comme il faut* and he would be glad to think that I should see something of her. His affairs, alas! kept him tied to Lille and the poor girl was too often alone; it would be a comfort to him to know that she was in touch with a man of education. He was a business-man, but he had always admired artists.

'*Ah, mon cher monsieur*, art and literature have always been the twin glories of France. Along with her military prowess, of course. And I, a manufacturer of woollen goods, have no hesitation in saying that I put the painter and the writer on a level with the general and the statesman.'

No one could say handsomer than that.

Suzanne would not hear of having a maid to do the house-work, partly for economy's sake and partly because (for reasons best known to herself) she didn't want anyone poking her nose into what was nobody's business but her own. She kept the tiny apartment, furnished in the most modern style of the moment, clean and neat, and she made all her own under-clothes. But even then, now that she no longer posed, time hung heavily on her hands, for she was an industrious woman; and presently the idea occurred to her that, after having sat to so many painters, there was no reason why she should not paint too. She bought canvases, brushes, and paints and forthwith set to work. Sometimes when I was to take her out to dinner I would go early and find her in a smock busily at work. Just as the embryo in the womb recapitulates in brief the evolution of the species, so did Suzanne recapitulate the styles of all her lovers. She painted landscape like the landscape painter, abstractions like the cubist, and with the help of picture postcards sailing-boats lying at anchor like the Scandinavian. She could not draw, but she had an agreeable sense of colour, and if her pictures were not very good she got a lot of fun out of painting them.

Monsieur Achille encouraged her. It gave him a sense of satisfaction that his mistress should be an artist. It was on his insistence that she sent a canvas to the autumn salon and they were both very proud when it was hung. He gave her one bit of good advice.

'Don't try to paint like a man, my dear,' he said. 'Paint like a woman. Don't aim to be strong; be satisfied to charm. And be honest. In business sharp practice sometimes succeeds, but in art honesty is not only the best but the only policy.'

At the time of which I write the connexion had lasted for five years to their mutual content.

'Evidently he doesn't thrill me,' said Suzanne. 'But he's intelligent and in a good position. I've reached an age when it's necessary for me to think of my situation.'

She was sympathetic and understanding and Monsieur Achille conceived a high opinion of her judgement. She lent a willing ear when he discussed with her his business and domestic affairs. She condoled with him when his daughter failed in an examination and rejoiced with him when his son got engaged to a girl with money. He had himself married the only child of a man in his own line of business and the amalgamation of two rival firms had been a source of profit to both parties. It was naturally a satisfaction to him that his son was sensible enough to see that the soundest basis of a happy marriage is community of financial interests. He confided to Suzanne his ambition to marry his daughter into the aristocracy.

'And why not, with her fortune?' said Suzanne.

Monsieur Achille made it possible for Suzanne to send her own daughter to a convent where she would receive a good education, and he promised that at the proper age he would pay to have her suitably trained to earn her living as a typist and stenographer.

'She's going to be a beauty when she grows up,' Suzanne told me, 'but evidently it won't hurt her to have an education and to be able to pound a typewriter. She's so young it's too soon to tell, but it may be that she'll have no temperament.'

Suzanne had delicacy. She left it to my intelligence to infer her meaning. I inferred it all right.

A week or so after I had so unexpectedly run into Larry,
Suzanne and I one night, having dined together and gone to a
movie, were sitting in the Sélect on the Boulevard du Montparnasse, having a glass of beer, when he strolled in. She gave a
gasp and to my surprise called out to him. He came up to the
table, kissed her, and shook hands with me. I could see that
she could hardly believe her eyes.

'May I sit down?' he said. 'I haven't had any dinner and I'm
going to have something to eat.'

'Oh, but it's good to see you, *mon petit*,' she said, her eyes
sparkling. 'Where have you sprung from? And why have you
given no sign of life all these years? My God, how thin you
are! For all I knew you might have been dead.'

'Well, I wasn't,' he answered, his eyes twinkling. 'How is
Odette?'

That was the name of Suzanne's daughter.

'Oh, she's growing a big girl. And pretty. She still remembers
you.'

'You never told me you knew Larry,' I said to her.

'Why should I? I never knew you knew him. We're old
friends.'

Larry ordered himself eggs and bacon. Suzanne told him
all about her daughter and then about herself. He listened in
his smiling, charming way while she chattered. She told him
that she had settled down and was painting. She turned to me.

'I'm improving, don't you think? I don't pretend I'm a
genius, but I have as much talent as many of the painters I've
known.'

'D'you sell any pictures,' asked Larry.

'I don't have to,' she answered airily. 'I have private means.'

'Lucky girl.'

'No, not lucky: clever. You must come and see my pictures.'

She wrote down her address on a piece of paper and made
him promise to go. Suzanne, excited, went on talking nineteen
to the dozen. Then Larry asked for his bill.

'You're not going?' she cried.

'I am,' he smiled.

He paid and with a wave of the hand left us. I laughed. He had a way that always amused me of being with you one moment and without explanation gone the next. It was so abrupt; it was almost as if he had faded into the air.

'Why did he want to go away so quickly?' said Suzanne, with vexation.

'Perhaps he's got a girl waiting for him,' I replied mockingly.

'That's an idea like another.' She took her compact out of her bag and powdered her face. 'I pity any woman who falls in love with him. *Oh la, la.*'

'Why do you say that?'

She looked at me for a minute with a seriousness I had not often seen in her.

'I very nearly fell in love with him myself once. You might as well fall in love with a reflection in the water or a ray of sunshine or a cloud in the sky. I had a narrow escape. Even now when I think of it I tremble at the danger I ran.'

Discretion be blowed. It would have been inhuman not to want to know what this was all about. I congratulated myself that Suzanne was a woman who had no notion of reticence.

'How on earth did you ever get to know him?' I asked.

'Oh, it was years ago. Six years, seven years, I forget. Odette was only five. He knew Marcel when I was living with him. He used to come to the studio and sit while I was posing. He'd take us out to dinner sometimes. You never knew when he'd come. Sometimes not for weeks and then two or three days running. Marcel used to like to have him there; he said he painted better when he was there. Then I had my typhoid. I went through a bad time when I came out of the hospital.' She shrugged her shoulders. 'But I've already told you all that. Well, one day I'd been round the studios trying to get work and no one wanted me, and I'd had nothing but a glass of milk and a croissant all day and I didn't know how I was going to pay for my room, and I met him accidentally on the Boulevard Clichy. He stopped and asked me how I was and I told him about my typhoid, and then he said to me: "You look as if you could do with a square meal." And there was something in his voice and in the look of his eyes that broke me; I began to cry.

'We were next door to La Mère Mariette and he took me by

182

the arm and sat me down at a table. I was so hungry I was ready to eat an old boot, but when the omelette came I felt I couldn't eat a thing. He forced me to take a little and he gave me a glass of burgundy. I felt better then and I ate some asparagus. I told him all my troubles. I was too weak to hold a pose. I was just skin and bone and I looked terrible; I couldn't expect to get a man. I asked him if he'd lend me the money to go back to my village. At least I'd have my little girl there. He asked me if I wanted to go, and I said of course not, Mamma didn't want me, she could hardly live on her pension with prices the way they were, and the money I'd sent for Odette had all been spent, but if I appeared at the door she would hardly refuse to take me in, she'd see how ill I looked. He looked at me for a long time, and I thought he was going to say he couldn't lend me anything. Then he said:

' "Would you like me to take you down to a little place I know in the country, you and the kid? I want a bit of a holiday."

'I could hardly believe my ears. I'd known him for ages and he'd never made a pass at me.

' "In the condition I'm in?" I said. I couldn't help laughing. "My poor friend," I said, "I'm no use to any man just now."

'He smiled at me. Have you ever noticed what a wonderful smile he's got? It's as sweet as honey.

' "Don't be so silly," he said. "I'm not thinking of that."

'I was crying so hard by then, I could hardly speak. He gave me money to fetch the child and we all went to the country together. Oh, it was charming, the place he took us to.'

Suzanne described it to me. It was three miles from a little town the name of which I have forgotten, and they took a car out to the inn. It was a ramshackle building on a river with a lawn that ran down to the water. There were plane trees on the lawn and they had their meals in their shade. In summer artists came there to paint, but it was early for that yet and they had the inn to themselves. The fare was famous, and on Sundays people used to drive from here and there to lunch with abandon, but on week-days their peace was seldom disturbed. With the rest and the food and wine, Suzanne grew stronger, and she was happy to have her child with her.

'He was sweet with Odette and she adored him. I had to prevent her from making a nuisance of herself, but he never seemed to mind how much she pestered him. It used to make me laugh, they were like two children together.'

'What did you do with yourselves?' I asked.

'Oh, there was always something to do. We used to take a boat and fish and sometimes we'd get the *patron* to lend us his Citroën and we'd go into town. Larry liked it. The old houses and the *place*. It was so quiet that your footsteps on the cobblestones were the only sound you heard. There was a Louis Quatorze *hôtel de ville* and an old church, and at the edge of the town was the château with a garden by Le Nôtre. When you sat at the café on the *place* you had the feeling that you had stepped back three hundred years and the Citroën at the kerb didn't seem to belong to this world at all.'

It was after one of these outings that Larry told her the story of the young airman which I narrated at the beginning of this book.

'I wonder why he told you,' I said.

'I haven't an idea. They'd had a hospital in the town during the war and in the cemetery there were rows and rows of little crosses. We went to see it. We didn't stay long, it gave me the creeps – all those poor boys lying there. Larry was very silent on the way home. He never ate much, but at dinner he hardly touched a thing. I remember so well, it was a beautiful, starry night and we sat on the riverbank, it was pretty with the poplars silhouetted against the darkness, and he smoked his pipe. And suddenly, *à propos de bottes*, he told me about his friend and how he died to save him.' Suzanne took a swig of beer. 'He's a strange creature. I shall never understand him. He used to like to read to me. Sometimes in the daytime, while I sewed things for the little one, and in the evening after I'd put her to bed.'

'What did he read?'

'Oh, all sorts of things. Letters of Madame de Sévigné and bits of Saint-Simon. *Imagine-toi*, I who'd never read anything before but the newspaper and now and then a novel when I heard them talk about it in the studios and didn't want them to think me a fool! I had no idea reading could be so interesting. Those old writers weren't such fatheads as one would think.'

'Who would think?' I chuckled.

'Then he made me read with him. We read *Phèdre* and *Bérénice*. He took the men's parts and I took the women's. You can't think how amusing it was,' she added naïvely. 'He used to look at me so strangely when I cried at the pathetic parts. Of course it was only because I hadn't got my strength. And you know, I've still got the books. Even now I can't read some of the letters of Madame de Sévigné that he read to me without hearing his lovely voice and without seeing the river flowing so quietly and the poplars on the opposite bank, and sometimes I can't go on, it gives me such a pain in my heart. I know now that those were the happiest weeks I ever spent in my life. That man, he's an angel of sweetness.'

Suzanne felt she was growing sentimental and feared (wrongly) that I should laugh at her. She shrugged her shoulders and smiled.

'You know, I've always made up my mind that when I've reached the canonical age and no man wants to sleep with me any more I shall make my peace with the Church and repent of my sins. But the sins I committed with Larry nothing in the world will ever induce me to repent of. Never, never, never!'

'But as you've described it I can see nothing you can possibly have to repent of.'

'I haven't told you the half of it yet. You see, I have a naturally good constitution and being out in the air all day, eating well, sleeping well, with not a care in the world, in three or four weeks I was as strong as ever I'd been. And I was looking well; I had colour in my cheeks and my hair had recovered its sheen. I felt twenty. Larry swam in the river every morning and I used to watch him. He has a beautiful body, not an athlete's like my Scandinavian, but strong and of an infinite grace.

'He'd been very patient while I was so weak, but now that I was perfectly well I saw no reason to keep him waiting any longer. I gave him a hint or two that I was ready for anything, but he didn't seem to understand. Of course you Anglo-Saxons are peculiar, you're brutal and at the same time you're sentimental; there's no denying it, you're not good lovers. I said to myself, "Perhaps it's his delicacy, he's done so much for me, he's let me have the child here, it may be that he hasn't the heart to ask me for the return that is his right." So one night, as we were going to bed, I said to him, "D'you want me to come to your room tonight?" '

I laughed.

'You put it a bit bluntly, didn't you?'

'Well, I couldn't ask him to come to mine, because Odette was sleeping there,' she answered ingenuously. 'He looked at me with those kind eyes of his for a moment, then he smiled. "D'you want to come?" he said.

' "What do you think – with that fine body of yours?"

' "All right, come then."

'I went upstairs and undressed and then I slipped along the passage to his room. He was lying in bed reading and smoking a pipe. He put down his pipe and his book and moved over to make room for me.'

Suzanne was silent for a while and it went against my grain to ask her questions. But after a while she went on.

'He was a strange lover. Very sweet, affectionate and even tender, virile without being passionate, if you understand what I mean, and absolutely without vice. He loved like a hot-blooded schoolboy. It was rather funny and rather touching. When I left him I had the feeling that I should be grateful to him rather than he to me. As I closed the door I saw him take up his book and go on reading from where he had left off.'

I began to laugh.

'I'm glad it amuses you,' she said a trifle grimly. But she was not without a sense of humour. She giggled. 'I soon discovered that if I waited for an invitation I might wait indefinitely, so when I felt like it I just went into his room and got into bed. He was always very nice. He had in short natural human instincts, but he was like a man so preoccupied that he forgets to eat, yet when you put a good dinner before him he eats it with appetite. I know when a man's in love with me, and I should have been a fool if I'd believed that Larry loved me, but I thought he'd get into the habit of me. One has to be practical in life and I said to myself that it would suit me very well if when we went back to Paris he took me to live with him.

I knew he'd let me have the child and I should have liked that. My instinct told me I'd be silly to fall in love with him, you know women are very unfortunate, so often when they fall in love they cease to be lovable, and I made up my mind to be on my guard.'

Suzanne inhaled the smoke of her cigarette and blew it out through her nose. It was growing late and many of the tables were now empty, but there was still a group of people hanging around the bar.

'One morning, after breakfast, I was sitting on the river-bank sewing, and Odette was playing with some bricks he'd bought her when Larry came up to me.

' "I've come to say good-bye to you," he said.

' "Are you going somewhere?" I said, surprised.

' "Yes."

' "Not for good?" I said.

' "You're quite well now. Here's enough money to keep you for the rest of the summer and to start you off when you get back to Paris."

'For a moment I was so upset I didn't know what to say. He stood in front of me, smiling in that candid way of his.

' "Have I done something to displease you?" I asked him.

' "Nothing. Don't think that for a moment. I've got work to do. We've had a lovely time down here. Odette, come and say good-bye to your uncle."

'She was too young to understand. He took her up in his arms and kissed her; then he kissed me and walked back into the hotel; in a minute I heard the car drive away. I looked at the banknotes I had in my hand. Twelve thousand francs. It came so quickly I hadn't time to react. "*Zut alors*," I said to myself. I had at least one thing to be thankful for, I hadn't allowed myself to fall in love with him. But I couldn't make head or tail of it.'

I was obliged to laugh.

'You know, at one time I made quite a little reputation for myself as a humorist by the simple process of telling the truth. It came as such a surprise to most people that they thought I was being funny.'

'I don't see the connexion.'

'Well, Larry is, I think, the only person I've ever met who's completely disinterested. It makes his actions seem peculiar. We're not used to persons who do things simply for the love of God whom they don't believe in.'

Suzanne stared at me.

'My poor friend, you've had too much to drink.'

V

1

I DAWDLED over my work in Paris. It was very agreeable in the springtime, with the chestnuts in the Champs Élysées in bloom and the light in the streets so gay. There was pleasure in the air, a light transitory pleasure, sensual without grossness, that made your step more springy and your intelligence more alert. I was happy in the various company of my friends and, my heart filled with amiable memories of the past, I regained in spirit at least something of the glow of youth. I thought I should be a fool to allow work to interfere with a delight in the passing moment that I might never enjoy again so fully.

Isabel, Gray, Larry, and I went for excursions to places of interest within convenient distance. We went to Chantilly and Versailles, to St Germain and Fontainebleau. Wherever we went, we lunched well and copiously. Gray ate largely to satisfy his enormous frame and was apt to drink a little too much. His health, whether owing to Larry's treatment or merely to the course of time, was certainly improved. He ceased to have racking headaches and his eyes were losing the look of bewilderment that when first I saw him on coming to Paris had been so distressing. He did not talk much except now and then to tell a long-winded story, but laughed with great loud guffaws at the nonsense Isabel and I talked. He enjoyed himself. Though not amusing, he was so good-humoured and so easily pleased that it was impossible not to like him. He was the kind of man with whom one would have hesitated to pass a lonely evening, but with whom one might cheerfully have looked forward to spending six months.

His love for Isabel was a delight to see; he adored her beauty and thought her the most brilliant, fascinating creature in the world; and his devotion, his doglike devotion to Larry was touching. Larry appeared to enjoy himself too; I had a notion that he looked upon this time as a holiday that he was taking from whatever projects he had in mind and was serenely making the most of it. He didn't talk very much either, but it didn't matter, his company was sufficient conversation; he was so easy, so pleasantly cheerful that you didn't ask more of him than what he gave, and I well knew that if the days we spent together were so happy it was due to his being with us. Though he never said a brilliant or a witty thing, we should have been dull without him.

It was on the return from one of these jaunts that I witnessed a scene that somewhat startled me. We had been to Chartres and were on our way back to Paris. Gray was driving and Larry was sitting beside him; Isabel and I were at the back. We were tired after the long day. Larry sat with his arm stretched out along the top of the front seat. His shirt-cuff was pulled back by his position and displayed his slim, strong wrist and the lower part of his brown arm lightly covered with fine hairs. The sun shone goldenly upon them. Something in Isabel's immobility attracted my attention, and I glanced at her. She was so still you might have thought her hypnotized. Her breath was hurried. Her eyes were fixed on the sinewy wrist with its little golden hairs and on that long, delicate, but powerful hand, and I have never seen on a human countenance such a hungry concupiscence as I saw then on hers. It was a mask of lust. I should never have believed that her beautiful features could assume an expression of such unbridled sensuality. It was animal rather than human. The beauty was stripped from her face; the look upon it made her hideous and frightening. It horribly suggested the bitch in heat and I felt rather sick. She was unconscious of my presence; she was conscious of nothing but the hand, lying along the rim so negligently, that filled her with frantic desire. Then as it were a spasm twitched across her face, she gave a shudder and shutting her eyes sank into the corner of the car.

'Give me a cigarette,' she said in a voice I hardly recognized, it was so raucous.

I got one out of my case and lit it for her. She smoked it greedily. For the rest of the drive she looked out of the window and never said a word.

When we arrived at their house Gray asked Larry to drive me back to my hotel and then take the car to the garage. Larry got into the driver's seat and I sat myself beside him. As they crossed the pavement Isabel took Gray's arm and, snuggling up to him, gave him a look which I could not see, but whose sense I could divine. I guessed that he would have a passionate bed-fellow that night, but would never know to what prickings of conscience he owed her ardour.

June was approaching its end and I had to get back to the Riviera. Friends of Elliott's, who were going to America, had lent the Maturins their villa at Dinard and they were going there with the children as soon as their school closed. Larry was staying in Paris to work, but was buying himself a second-hand Citroën and had promised to spend a few days with them in August. On my last night in Paris I asked the three of them to dine with me.

It was on that night that we met Sophie Macdonald.

2

Isabel had conceived the desire to make a tour of the tough joints, and because I had some acquaintance with them she asked me to be their guide. I did not much like the notion, because in places of that sort in Paris they are apt to make their disapproval of sightseers from another world unpleasantly obvious. But Isabel insisted. I warned her that it would be very boring and begged her to dress plainly. We dined late, went to the Folies-Bergère for an hour, and then set out. I took them first to a cellar near Notre Dame frequented by gangsters and their molls where I knew the proprietor, and he made room for us at a long table at which were sitting some very disreputable people, but I ordered wine for all of them and we drank one another's healths. It was hot, smoky, and dirty. Then I took them to the Sphynx where women, naked under their smart, tawdry evening dresses, their breasts, nipples and all, exposed, sit in a row on two benches opposite one another and when the band strikes up dance together listlessly with their eyes on the lookout for the men who sit round the dance hall at marble-topped tables. We ordered a bottle of warm champagne. Some of the women gave Isabel the eye as they passed us and I wondered if she knew what it meant.

Then we went on to the Rue de Lappe. It is a dingy, narrow street, and even as you enter it you get the impression of sordid lust. We went into a café. There was the usual young man, pale and dissipated, playing the piano, while another man, old and tired, scraped away on a fiddle, and a third made discordant noises on a saxophone. The place was packed and it looked as though there wasn't a vacant table, but the *patron*, seeing that we were customers with money to spend, unceremoniously turned a couple out, making them take seats at a table already occupied, and settled us down. The two persons who were hustled away did not take it well, and they made remarks about us that were far from complimentary. A lot of people were dancing, sailors with the red pompon on their hats, men mostly with their caps on and handkerchiefs round their necks, women of mature age, and young girls, painted to the eyes, bareheaded, in short skirts and coloured blouses. Men danced with podgy boys with made-up eyes; gaunt, hard-featured women danced with fat women with dyed hair; men danced with women. There was a frowst of smoke and liquor and of sweating bodies. The music went on interminably and that unsavoury mob proceeded round the room, the sweat shining on their faces, with a solemn intensity in which there was something horrible. There were a few big men of brutal aspect, but for the most part they were puny and ill-nourished. I watched the three who were playing. They might have been robots, so mechanical was their performance, and I asked myself if it was possible that at one time, when they were setting out, they had thought they might be musicians whom people would come from far to hear and to applaud. Even to play the violin badly you must take lessons and practise: did that fiddler go to all that trouble just to play fox-trots till the small hours of the morning in that stinking squalor? The music stopped and the pianist wiped his face with a dirty handkerchief. The dancers slouched or sidled or squirmed back to their tables. Suddenly we heard an American voice:

'For Christ's sake.'

A woman got up from one of the tables across the room. The man she was with tried to stop her, but she pushed him aside and staggered across the floor. She was very drunk. She came up to our table and stood in front of us, swaying a little and grinning stupidly. She seemed to find the sight of us vastly amusing. I glanced at my companions. Isabel was staring at her blankly, Gray had a sullen frown on his face, and Larry gazed as though he couldn't believe his eyes.

'Hello,' she said.

'Sophie,' said Isabel.

'Who the hell did you think it was?' she gurgled. She grabbed the waiter who was passing. 'Vincent, fetch me a chair.'

'Fetch one yourself,' he said, snatching himself away.

'*Salaud*,' she cried, spitting at him.

'*T'en fais pas, Sophie*,' said a big fat fellow with a great head of greasy hair, who was sitting next to us in his shirt-sleeves. 'Here's a chair.'

'Fancy meeting you all like this,' she said, still swaying. 'Hello, Larry. Hello, Gray.' She sank into the chair which the man who had spoken placed behind her. 'Let's all have a drink. *Patron*,' she screamed.

I had noticed that the proprietor had his eye on us and now he came up.

'You know these people, Sophie?' he asked, addressing her in the familiar second person singular.

'*Ta gueule*,' she laughed drunkenly. 'They're my childhood friends. I'm buying a bottle of champagne for them. And don't you bring us any *urine de cheval*. Bring us something one can swallow without vomiting.'

'You're drunk, my poor Sophie,' he said.

'To hell with you.'

He went off, glad enough to sell a bottle of champagne – we for safety's sake had been drinking brandy and soda – and Sophie stared at me dully for a moment.

'Who's your friend, Isabel?'

Isabel told her my name.

'Oh? I remember, you came to Chicago once. Bit of a stuffed shirt, aren't you?'

'Maybe,' I smiled.

I had no recollection of her, but that was not surprising, since I had not been to Chicago for more than ten years and had met a great many people then and a great many since.

She was quite tall and, when standing, looked taller still, for she was very thin. She wore a bright green silk blouse, but it was crumpled and spotted, and a short black skirt. Her hair, cut short and loosely curled, but tousled, was brightly hennaed. She was outrageously made up, her cheeks rouged to the eyes, and her eyelids, upper and lower, heavily blued; her eyebrows and eyelashes were thick with mascara and her mouth scarlet with lipstick. Her hands, with their painted nails, were dirty. She looked more of a slut than any woman there and I had a suspicion that she was not only drunk but doped. But one couldn't deny that there was a certain vicious attractiveness about her; she held her head with an arrogant tilt and her make-up accentuated the startling greenness of her eyes. Sodden with drink as she was, she had a bold-faced shamelessness that I could well imagine appealed to all that was base in men. She embraced us in a sardonic smile.

'I can't say you seem so terribly pleased to see me,' she said.

'I heard you were in Paris,' said Isabel lamely, a chilly smile on her face.

'You might have called me. I'm in the phone-book.'

'We haven't been here very long.'

Gray came to the rescue.

'Are you having a good time over here, Sophie?'

'Fine. You went bust, Gray, didn't you?'

His face flushed a deeper red.

'Yes.'

'Tough on you. I guess it's pretty grim in Chicago right now. Lucky for me I got out when I did. For Christ's sake why doesn't that bastard bring us something to drink?'

'He's just coming,' I said, seeing the waiter threading his way through the tables with glasses and wine on a tray.

My remark drew her attention to me.

'My loving in-laws kicked me out of Chicago. Said I was gumming up their f— reputations.' She giggled savagely. 'I'm a remittance man.'

The champagne came and was poured out. With a shaking hand she raised a glass to her lips.

'To hell with stuffed shirts,' she said. She emptied the glass and glanced at Larry. 'You don't seem to have much to say for yourself, Larry.'

He had been looking at her with an impassive face. He had not taken his eyes off her since she had appeared. He smiled amiably.

'I'm not a very talkative guy.'

The music struck up again and a man came over to us. He was a tallish fellow and well built, with a great hooked nose, a mat of shining black hair, and great sensual lips. He looked like an evil Savonarola. Like most of the men there he wore no collar and his tight-fitting coat was closely buttoned to give him a waist.

'Come on, Sophie. We're going to dance.'

'Go away. I'm busy. Can't you see I'm with friends?'

'*J' m'en fous de tes amis.* To hell with your friends. You're dancing.'

He took hold of her arm but she snatched it away.

'*Fous-moi la paix, espèce de con,*' she cried, with sudden violence.

'*Merde.*'

'*Mange.*'

Gray did not understand what they were saying, but I saw that Isabel, with that strange knowledge of obscenity that the most virtuous woman seems to possess, understood perfectly, and her face went hard with a frown of disgust. The man raised his arm with his hand open, the horny hand of a workman, and was about to slap her, when Gray half raised himself from his chair.

'*Allaiz vous ong,*' he shouted, with his execrable accent.

The man stopped and threw Gray a furious glance.

'Take care, Coco,' said Sophie, with a bitter laugh. 'He'll lay you out cold.'

The man took in Gray's great height and weight and strength. He shrugged his shoulders sullenly and, throwing a filthy word at us, slunk off. Sophie giggled drunkenly. The rest of us were silent. I refilled her glass.

'You living in Paris, Larry?' she asked after she had drained it.

'For the present.'

It's always difficult to make conversation with a drunk, and there's no denying it, the sober are at a disadvantage with him. We went on talking for a few minutes in a dreary, embarrassed way. Then Sophie pushed back her chair.

'If I don't go back to my boy friend he'll be as mad as hell. He's a sulky brute, but Christ, he's a good screw.' She staggered to her feet. 'So long, folks. Come again. I'm here every night.'

She pushed her way through the dancers and we lost sight of her in the crowd. I almost laughed at the icy scorn on Isabel's classic features. None of us said a word.

'This is a foul place,' said Isabel suddenly. 'Let's go.'

I paid for our drinks and for Sophie's champagne and we trooped out. The crowd was on the dance floor and we got out without remark. It was after two, and to my mind time to go to bed, but Gray said he was hungry, so I suggested that we should go to Graf's in Montmartre and get something to eat. We were silent as we drove up. I sat beside Gray to direct him. We reached the garish restaurant. There were still people sitting on the terrace. We went in and ordered bacon and eggs and beer. Isabel, outwardly at least, had regained her composure. She congratulated me, somewhat ironically perhaps, on my acquaintance with the more disreputable parts of Paris.

'You asked for it,' I said.

'I've thoroughly enjoyed myself. I've had a grand evening.'

'Hell,' said Gray. 'It stank. And Sophie.'

Isabel shrugged an indifferent shoulder.

'D'you remember her at all?' she asked me. 'She sat next to you the first night you came to dinner with us. She hadn't got that awful red hair then. Its natural colour is dingy beige.'

I threw my mind back. I had a recollection of a very young girl with blue eyes that were almost green and an attractive tilt to her head. Not pretty, but fresh and ingenuous with a mixture of shyness and pertness that I found amusing.

'Of course I remember. I liked her name. I had an aunt called Sophie.'

'She married a boy called Bob Macdonald.'

'Nice fellow,' said Gray.

'He was one of the best-looking boys I ever saw. I never understood what he saw in her. She married just after I did. Her parents were divorced and her mother married a Standard Oil man in China. She lived with her father's people at Marvin and we used to see a lot of her then, but after she married she dropped out of our crowd somehow. Bob Macdonald was a lawyer, but he wasn't making much money, and they had a walk-up apartment on the North Side. But it wasn't that. They didn't want to see anybody. I never saw two people so crazy about one another. Even after they'd been married two or three years and had a baby they'd go to the pictures and he'd sit with his arm round her waist and she with her head on his shoulder just like lovers. They were quite a joke in Chicago.'

Larry listened to what Isabel said, but made no comment. His face was inscrutable.

'What happened then?' I asked.

'One night they were driving back to Chicago in a little open car of theirs, and they had the baby with them. They always had to take the baby along because they hadn't any help. Sophie did everything herself, and, anyway, they worshipped it. And a bunch of drunks in a great sedan driving at eighty miles an hour crashed into them head on. Bob and the baby were killed outright, but Sophie only had concussion and a rib or two broken. They kept it from her as long as they could that Bob and the baby were dead, but at last they had to tell her. They say it was awful. She nearly went crazy. She shrieked the place down. They had to watch her night and day and once she nearly succeeded in jumping out of the window. Of course we did all we could, but she seemed to hate us. After she came out of the hospital they put her in a sanatorium and she was there for months.'

'Poor thing.'

'When they let her go she started to drink, and when she was drunk she'd go to bed with anyone who asked her. It was terrible for her in-laws. They're very nice quiet people and they hated the scandal. At first we all tried to help her, but it was impossible; if you asked her to dine she'd arrive plastered and she was quite likely to pass out before the evening was

196

over. Then she got in with a rotten crowd and we had to drop her. She was arrested once for driving a car when she was drunk. She was with a dago she'd picked up in a speak-easy and it turned out that he was wanted by the cops.'

'But had she money?' I asked.

'There was Bob's insurance; the people who owned the car that smashed into them were insured and she got something from them. But it didn't last long. She spent it like a drunken sailor and in two years she was broke. Her grandmother wouldn't have her back at Marvin. Then her in-laws said they'd make her an allowance if she'd go and live abroad. I suppose that's what she's living on now.'

'The wheel comes full circle,' I remarked. 'There was a time when the black sheep of the family was sent from my country to America; now apparently he's sent from your country to Europe.'

'I can't help feeling sorry for her,' said Gray.

'Can't you?' said Isabel coolly. 'I can. Of course it was a shock and no one could have sympathized with Sophie more than I did. We'd known one another always. But a normal person recovers from a thing like that. If she went to pieces it's because there was a rotten streak in her. She was naturally unbalanced; even her love for Bob was exaggerated. If she'd had character she'd have been able to make something of life.'

'If pots and pans ... Aren't you very hard, Isabel?' I murmured.

'I don't think so. I have common sense and I see no reason to be sentimental about Sophie. God knows, no one could be more devoted to Gray and the babes than I am, and if they were killed in a motor accident I should go out of my mind, but sooner or later I'd pull myself together. Isn't that what you'd wish me to do, Gray, or would you prefer me to get blind every night and go to bed with every apache in Paris?'

Gray then came as near to making a humorous remark as I ever heard him.

'Of course I'd prefer you to hurl yourself on my funeral pyre in a new Molyneux dress, but as that's not done any more, I guess the best thing you could do would be to take the bridge. And I'd like you to remember not to go an original

197

no-trump on less than three and a half to four quick tricks.'

It was not the occasion for me to point out to Isabel that her love for her husband and her children, though sincere enough, was scarcely passionate. Perhaps she read the thought that was passing through my mind, for she addressed me somewhat truculently.

'What have you got to say?'

'I'm like Gray, I'm sorry for the girl.'

'She's not a girl. She's thirty.'

'I suppose it was the end of the world for her when her husband and her baby were killed. I suppose she didn't care what became of her and flung herself into the horrible degradation of drink and promiscuous copulation to get even with life that had treated her so cruelly. She'd lived in heaven and when she lost it she couldn't put up with the common earth of common men, but in despair plunged headlong into hell. I can imagine that if she couldn't drink the nectar of the gods any more she thought she might as well drink bathroom gin.'

'That's the sort of thing you say in novels. It's nonsense and you know it's nonsense. Sophie wallows in the gutter because she likes it. Other women have lost their husbands and children. It wasn't that that made her evil. Evil doesn't spring from good. The evil was there always. When that motor accident broke her defences it set her free to be herself. Don't waste your pity on her; she's now what at heart she always was.'

All this time Larry had remained silent. He seemed to be in a brown study and I thought he hardly heard what we were saying. Isabel's words were followed by a brief silence. He began to speak, but in a strange, toneless voice, as though not to us, but to himself; his eyes seemed to look into the dim distance of past time.

'I remember her when she was fourteen with her long hair brushed back off her forehead and a black bow at the back, with her freckled, serious face. She was a modest, high-minded, idealistic child. She read everything she could get hold of and we used to talk about books.'

'When?' asked Isabel, with a slight frown.

'Oh, when you were out being social with your mother. I used to go up to her grandfather's and we'd sit under a great elm

198

they had there and read to one another. She loved poetry and wrote quite a lot herself.'

'Plenty of girls do that at that age. It's pretty poor stuff.'

'Of course it's a long time ago and I dare say I wasn't a very good judge.'

'You couldn't have been more than sixteen yourself.'

'Of course it was imitative. There was a lot of Robert Frost in it. But I have a notion it was rather remarkable for so young a girl. She had a delicate ear and a sense of rhythm. She had a feeling for the sounds and scents of the country, the first softness of spring in the air and the smell of the parched earth after rain.'

'I never knew she wrote poetry,' said Isabel.

'She kept it a secret, she was afraid you'd all laugh at her. She was very shy.'

'She's not that now.'

'When I came back from the war she was almost grown-up. She'd read a lot about the condition of the working classes and she'd seen something of it for herself in Chicago. She'd got on to Carl Sandburg and was writing savagely in free verse about the misery of the poor and the exploitation of the working classes. I dare say it was rather commonplace, but it was sincere and it had pity in it and aspiration. At that time she wanted to become a social worker. It was moving, her desire for sacrifice. I think she was capable of a great deal. She wasn't silly or mawkish, but she gave one the impression of a lovely purity and a strange loftiness of soul. We saw a lot of one another that year.'

I could see that Isabel listened to him with growing exasperation. Larry had no notion that he was driving a dagger in her heart and with his every detached word twisting it in the wound. But when she spoke it was with a smile on her lips.

'How did she come to choose you for her confidant?'

Larry looked at her with his trustful eyes.

'I don't know. She was a poor girl among all of you who had plenty of dough, and I didn't belong. I was there just because Uncle Bob practised at Marvin. I suppose she felt that gave us something in common.'

Larry had no relations. Most of us have at least cousins

199

whom we may hardly know, but who at least give us a sense that we are part of the human family. Larry's father had been an only son, his mother an only daughter; his grandfather on one side, the Quaker, had been lost at sea when a young man and his grandfather on the other side had neither brother nor sister. No one could be more alone in the world than Larry.

'Did it ever occur to you that Sophie was in love with you?' asked Isabel.

'Never,' he smiled.

'Well, she was.'

'When he came back from the war as a wounded hero half the girls in Chicago had a crush on Larry,' said Gray in his bluff way.

'This was more than a crush. She worshipped you, my poor Larry. D'you mean to say you didn't know it?'

'I certainly didn't and I don't believe it.'

'I suppose you thought she was too high-minded.'

'I can still see that skinny little girl with the bow in her hair and her serious face whose voice trembled with tears when she read that ode of Keats's because it was so beautiful. I wonder where she is now.'

Isabel gave a very slight start and threw him a suspicious inquiring glance.

'It's getting frightfully late and I'm so tired I don't know what to do. Let's go.'

3

On the following evening I took the Blue Train to the Riviera and two or three days later went over to Antibes to see Elliott and give him news of Paris. He looked far from well. The cure at Montecatini had not done him the good he expected, and his subsequent wanderings had exhausted him. He found a baptismal font in Venice and then went on to Florence to buy the triptych he had been negotiating for. Anxious to see these objects duly placed, he went down to the Pontine Marshes and put up at a miserable inn where the heat had been hard to bear. His precious purchases were a long time on the way, but determined not to leave till he had accomplished his purpose, he stayed on. He was delighted with the effect when at last everything was in order, and he showed me with pride the photographs he had taken. The church, though small, had dignity, and the restrained richness of the interior was proof of Elliott's good taste.

'I saw an early Christian sarcophagus in Rome that took my fancy and I deliberated a long time about buying it, but in the end I thought better of it.'

'What on earth did you want with an early Christian sarcophagus, Elliott?'

'To put myself in it, my dear fellow. It was of a very good design, and I thought it would balance the font on the other side of the entrance, but those early Christians were stumpy little fellows and I shouldn't have fitted in. I wasn't going to lie there till the Last Trump with my knees doubled up to my chin like a foetus. Most uncomfortable.'

I laughed, but Elliott was serious.

'I had a better idea. I've made all arrangements, with some difficulty, but that was to be expected, to be buried in front of the altar at the foot of the chancel steps, so that when the poor peasants of the Pontine Marshes come up to take the Sacrament they'll clump over my bones with their heavy shoes. Rather chic, don't you think? Just a plain stone slab with my name on it and a couple of dates. *Si monumentum quaeris, circumspice*. If you seek his monument, look around, you know.'

'I do know enough Latin to understand a hackneyed quotation, Elliott,' I said tartly.

'I beg your pardon, my dear fellow. I'm so accustomed to the crass ignorance of the upper classes, I forgot for the moment that I was talking to an author.'

He scored.

'But what I wanted to say to you was this,' he continued. 'I've left proper instructions in my will, but I want you to see they're carried out. I will *not* be buried on the Riviera among a lot of retired colonels and middle-class French people.'

'Of course I'll do what you wish, Elliott, but I don't think we need plan for anything like that for many years to come.'

'I'm getting on, you know, and to tell you the truth I shan't be sorry to go. What are those lines of Landor's? "I've warmed both hands ..."'

201

Though I have a bad verbal memory, the poem is very short and I was able to repeat it.

> *'I strove with none, for none was worth my strife.*
> *Nature I loved, and, next to Nature, Art;*
> *I warmed both hands before the fire of Life;*
> *It sinks, and I am ready to depart.'*

'That's it,' he said.

I could not but reflect that it was only by a violent stretch of the imagination that Elliott could fit the epigram to himself.

'It expresses my sentiments exactly,' he said, however. 'The only thing I could add to it is that I've always moved in the best society in Europe.'

'It would be difficult to squeeze that into a quatrain.'

'Society is dead. At one time I had hopes that America would take the place of Europe and create an aristocracy that the *hoi polloi* would respect, but the depression has destroyed any chance of that. My poor country is becoming hopelessly middle-class. You wouldn't believe it, my dear fellow, but last time I was in America a taxi driver addressed me as brother.'

But though the Riviera, still shaken by the crash of 'twenty-nine, was not what it had been, Elliott continued to give parties and go to parties. He had never frequented Jews, making an exception only for the family of Rothschild, but the grandest parties were being given now by members of the chosen race, and when there was a party Elliott could not bear not to go to it. He wandered through these gatherings, graciously shaking the hand of one or kissing that of another, but with a kind of forlorn detachment like an exiled royalty who felt a trifle embarrassed to find himself in such company. The exiled royalties, however, had the time of their lives, and to meet a film star seemed the height of their ambitions. Nor had Elliott ever looked with approval on the modern practice of treating members of the theatrical profession as persons whom you met socially; but a retired actress had built herself a sumptuous residence in his immediate neighbourhood and kept open house. Cabinet ministers, dukes, great ladies stayed with her for weeks on end. Elliott became a constant visitor.

'Of course it's a very mixed crowd,' he told me, 'but one

doesn't have to talk to people one doesn't want to. She's a compatriot of mine and I feel I ought to help her out. It must be a relief to her house guests to find someone who can talk their own language.'

Sometimes he was obviously so far from well that I asked him why he didn't take things more easily.

'My dear fellow, at my age one can't afford to fall out. You don't think I've moved in the highest circles for nearly fifty years without realizing that if you're not seen everywhere you're forgotten.'

I wondered if he realized what a lamentable confession he was then making. I had not the heart to laugh at Elliott any more; he seemed to me a profoundly pathetic object. Society was what he lived for, a party was the breath of his nostrils, not to be asked to one was an affront, to be alone was a mortification; and, an old man now, he was desperately afraid.

So the summer passed. Elliott spent it scurrying from one end of the Riviera to the other, lunching in Cannes, dining in Monte Carlo, and exercising all his ingenuity to fit in a tea party here and a cocktail party there; and however tired he felt, taking pains to be affable, chatty, and amusing. He was full of gossip and you could trust him to know the details of the latest scandal before anyone but the parties immediately concerned. He would have stared at you with frank amazement had you suggested to him that his existence was futile. He would have thought you distressingly plebeian.

4

The autumn came and Elliott decided to go to Paris for a while, partly to see how Isabel, Gray, and the children were getting on, and partly to make what he called *acte de présence* in the capital. Then he meant to go to London to order some new clothes and incidentally to look up some old friends. My own plan was to go straight to London, but he asked me to drive up with him to Paris, and since that is an agreeable thing to do I consented and, having done so, saw no reason why I should not spend at least a few days in Paris myself. We made the journey by easy stages, stopping at places where the food was good; Elliott had something the matter with his kidneys and drank nothing but Vichy, but always insisted on choosing my half-bottle of wine for me and, too good-natured to grudge me a pleasure he could not share, got a genuine satisfaction out of my enjoyment of a fine vintage. He was so generous that I had difficulty in persuading him to let me pay my share of the expenses. Though I grew a little tired of his stories of the great whom he had known in the past I liked the trip. Much of the country we drove through, just touched with the beginning of its autumn beauty, was very lovely. Having lunched at Fontainebleau, we did not arrive in Paris till afternoon. Elliott dropped me at my modest, old-fashioned hotel and went round the corner to the Ritz.

We had warned Isabel of our arriving, so I was not surprised to find a note from her awaiting me, but I was surprised at its contents:

Come round the moment you get in. Something terrible has happened. Don't bring Uncle Elliott. For God's sake come as soon as you can.

I am not less curious than anyone else, but I had to have a wash and put on a clean shirt; then I took a taxi and went round to the apartment in the Rue St Guillaume. I was shown into the drawing-room. Isabel sprang to her feet.

'Where have you been all this time? I've been waiting for hours.'

It was five o'clock and, before I could answer, the butler brought in the tea-things. Isabel, her hands clenched, watched him with impatience. I couldn't imagine what was the matter.

'I've only just arrived. We dawdled over lunch at Fontainebleau.'

'God, how slow he is. Maddening!' said Isabel.

The man placed the salver with the teapot and the sugar basin and the cups on the table and with what really was exasperating deliberation arranged around it plates of bread and butter, cakes, and cookies. He went out and closed the door behind him.

'Larry's going to marry Sophie Macdonald.'

'Who's she?'

'Don't be so stupid,' cried Isabel, her eyes flashing with anger.

'That drunken slut we met at that filthy café you took us to. God knows why you took us to a place like that. Gray was disgusted.'

'Oh, you mean your Chicago friend?' I said, ignoring her unjust reproach. 'How d'you know?'

'How should I know? He came and told me himself yesterday afternoon. I've been frantic ever since.'

'Supposing you sat down, gave me a cup of tea, and told me all about it.'

'Help yourself.'

She sat behind the tea-table and watched me irritably while I poured myself out a cup. I made myself comfortable on a small sofa by the fireplace.

'We haven't seen so much of him lately, since we came back from Dinard, I mean; he came up there for a few days, but wouldn't stay with us, he stayed at a hotel. He used to come down to the beach and play with the children. They're crazy about him. We played golf at St Briac. Gray asked him one day if he'd seen Sophie again.

' "Yes, I've seen her several times," he said.

' "Why?" I asked.

' "She's an old friend," he said.

' "If I were you I wouldn't waste my time on her," I said.

'Then he smiled. You know how he smiles, as though he thought what you'd said funny, though it isn't funny at all.

' "But you're not me," he said.

'I shrugged my shoulders and changed the conversation. I never gave the matter another thought. You can imagine my horror when he came here and told me they were going to be married.

' "You can't, Larry," I said. "You can't."

' "I'm going to," he said as calmly as if he was going to have a second helping of potatoes. "And I want you to be very nice to her, Isabel."

' "That's asking too much," I said. "You're crazy. She's bad, bad, bad." '

'What makes you think that?' I interrupted.

Isabel looked at me with flashing eyes.

'She's soused from morning till night. She goes to bed with every tough who asks her.'

'That doesn't mean she's bad. Quite a number of highly respected citizens get drunk and have a liking for rough trade. They're bad habits, like biting one's nails, but I don't know that they're worse than that. I call a person bad who lies and cheats and is unkind.'

'If you're going to take her part I'll kill you.'

'How did Larry meet her again?'

'He found her address in the phone-book. He went to see her. She was sick, and no wonder, with the life she leads. He got a doctor and had someone in to look after her. That's how it started. He says she's given up drink; the damned fool thinks she's cured.'

'Have you forgotten what Larry did for Gray? He's cured him, hasn't he?'

'That's different. Gray wanted to be cured. She doesn't.'

'How d'you know?'

'Because I know women. When a woman goes to pieces like that she's done for; she can never get back. If Sophie's what she is, it's because she was like that always. D'you think she'll stick to Larry? Of course not. Sooner or later she'll break out. It's in her blood. It's a brute she wants, that's what excites her, and it's a brute she'll go after. She'll lead Larry a hell of a life.'

'I think it's very probable, but I don't know what you can do about it. He's going into this with his eyes open.'

'*I* can do nothing about it, but you can.'

'I?'

'Larry likes you and he listens to what you say. You're the only person who has any influence over him. You know the world. Go to him and tell him that he can't make such a fool of himself. Tell him that it'll ruin him.'

'He'll only tell me that it's no business of mine and he'll be quite right.'

'But you like him, at least you're interested in him, you can't sit by and let him make a hopeless mess of his life.'

'Gray's his oldest and most intimate friend. I don't think it'll do any good, but I should have thought Gray was the best person to speak to him.'

'Oh, Gray,' she said impatiently.

'You know it may not turn out so badly as you think. I've known two or three fellows, one in Spain and two in the East, who married whores, and they made them very good wives. They were grateful to their husbands, for the security they gave them, I mean, and they of course knew what pleases a man.'

'You make me tired. D'you think I sacrificed myself to let Larry fall into the hands of a raging nymphomaniac?'

'How did *you* sacrifice yourself?'

'I gave Larry up for the one and only reason that I didn't want to stand in his way.'

'Come off it, Isabel. You gave him up for a square-cut diamond and a sable coat.'

The words were hardly out of my mouth when a plate of bread and butter came flying at my head. By sheer luck I caught the plate, but the bread and butter was scattered on the floor. I got up and put the plate back on the table.

'Your uncle Elliott wouldn't have thanked you if you'd broken one of his Crown Derby plates. They were made for the third Duke of Dorset and they're almost priceless.'

'Pick up the bread and butter,' she snapped.

'Pick it up yourself,' I said, seating myself again on the sofa.

She got up and, fuming, picked up the scattered pieces.

'And you call yourself an English gentleman,' she exclaimed, savagely.

'No, that's a thing I've never done in all my life.'

'Get the hell out of here. I never want to see you again. I hate the sight of you.'

'I'm sorry for that, because the sight of you always gives me pleasure. Have you ever been told that your nose is exactly like that of the Psyche in the museum of Naples, and that's the loveliest representation of virginal beauty that ever existed. You've got exquisite legs, so long and shapely, and I never cease to be surprised at them, because they were thick and lumpy when you were a girl. I can't imagine how you've managed it.'

'An iron will and the grace of God,' she said angrily.

'But of course your hands are your most fascinating feature. They're so slim and so elegant.'

'I was under the impression you thought them too big.'

'Not for your height and build. I'm always amazed at the infinite grace with which you use them. Whether by nature or by art you never make a gesture without imparting beauty to it. They're like flowers sometimes and sometimes like birds on the wing. They're more expressive than any words you can say. They're like the hands of El Greco's portraits; in fact, when I look at them I'm inclined to believe Elliott's highly improbable story of your having an ancestor who was a Spanish grandee.'

She looked up crossly.

'What are you talking about? That's the first I've heard of it.'

I told her about the Count de Lauria and Queen Mary's maid of honour from whose issue in the female line Elliott traced his descent. Meanwhile Isabel contemplated her long fingers and her manicured painted nails with complacency.

'One must be descended from someone,' she said. Then with a tiny chuckle, giving me a mischievous look in which no trace of rancour remained, she added: 'You lousy bastard.'

So easy is it to make a woman see reason if you only tell her the truth.

'There are moments when I don't positively dislike you,' said Isabel.

She came and sat on the sofa beside me and, slipping her arm through mine, leant over to kiss me. I withdrew my cheek.

'I will not have my face smeared with lipstick,' I said. 'If you want to kiss me, kiss me on the lips, which is what merciful Providence intended them for.'

She giggled and, her hand turning my head towards her, with her lips pressed a thin layer of paint on mine. The sensation was far from unpleasant.

'Now you've done that, perhaps you'll tell me what it is you want.'

'Advice.'

'I'm quite willing to give you that, but I don't think for a moment you'll take it. There's only one thing you can do and that is to make the best of a bad job.'

Flaring up again, she snatched her arm away and, getting up, flung herself into a chair on the other side of the fireplace.

'I'm not going to sit by and let Larry ruin himself. I'll stick at nothing to prevent him from marrying that slut.'

'You won't succeed. You see, he's enthralled by one of the most powerful emotions that can beset the human breast.'

'You don't mean to say you think he's in love with her?'

'No. That would be trifling in comparison.'

'Well?'

'Have you ever read the New Testament?'

'I suppose so.'

'D'you remember how Jesus was led into the wilderness and fasted forty days? Then, when he was a-hungered, the devil came to him and said: If thou be the son of God, command that these stones be made bread. But Jesus resisted the temptation. Then the devil set him on a pinnacle of the temple and said to him: If thou be the son of God, cast thyself down. For angels had charge of him and would bear him up. But again Jesus resisted. Then the devil took him into a high mountain and showed him the kingdoms of the world and said that he would give them to him if he would fall down and worship him. But Jesus said: Get thee hence, Satan. That's the end of the story according to the good simple Matthew. But it wasn't. The devil was sly and he came to Jesus once more and said: If thou wilt accept shame and disgrace, scourging, a crown of thorns and death on the cross, thou shalt save the human race, for greater love hath no man than this, that a man lay down his life for his friends. Jesus fell. The devil laughed till his sides ached, for he knew the evil men would commit in the name of their redeemer.'

Isabel looked at me indignantly.

'Where on earth did you get that?'

'Nowhere. I've invented it on the spur of the moment.'

'I think it's idiotic and blasphemous.'

'I only wanted to suggest to you that self-confidence is a passion so overwhelming that beside it even lust and hunger are trifling. It whirls its victim to destruction in the highest affirmation of his personality. The object doesn't matter; it may be worth while or it may be worthless. No wine is so intoxicating, no love so shattering, no vice so compelling. When he sacrifices himself man for a moment is greater than God, for how can God, infinite and omnipotent, sacrifice himself? At best he can only sacrifice his only begotten son.'

'Oh, Christ, how you bore me,' said Isabel.

I paid no attention.

'How can you suppose that common sense or prudence will have any effect on Larry when he's in the grip of a passion like that? You don't know what he's been seeking all these years. I don't know either, I only suspect. All these years of labour, all these experiences he garnered weigh nothing in the balance now they're set against his desire – oh, it's more than a desire, his urgent, clamorous need to save the soul of a wanton woman whom he'd known as an innocent child. I think you're right, I think he's undertaking a hopeless job; with his acute sensibility he'll suffer the tortures of the damned; his life's work, whatever it may be, will remain undone. The ignoble Paris killed Achilles by shooting an arrow in his heel. Larry lacks just that touch of ruthlessness that even the saint must have to win his halo.'

'I love him,' said Isabel. 'God knows, I ask nothing of him. I expect nothing. No one could love anyone more unselfishly than I love him. He's going to be so unhappy.'

She began to cry and, thinking it would do her good, I let her be. I diverted myself idly with the idea that had sprung so unexpectedly into my mind. I played with it. I couldn't but surmise that the devil, looking at the cruel wars that Christianity has occasioned, the persecutions, the tortures Christian has inflicted on Christian, the unkindness, the hypocrisy, the intolerance, must consider the balance sheet with complacency. And when he remembers that it has laid upon mankind the bitter burden of the sense of sin that has darkened the beauty of the starry night and cast a baleful shadow on the passing pleasures of a world to be enjoyed, he must chuckle as he murmurs: give the devil his due.

Presently Isabel took a handkerchief from her bag and a mirror and, looking at herself, carefully wiped the corner of her eyes.

'Damned sympathetic, aren't you?' she snapped.

I looked at her pensively, but did not answer. She powdered her face and painted her lips.

'You said just now you suspected what he's been after all these years. What did you mean?'

'I can only guess, you know, and I may be quite wrong. I think he's been seeking for a philosophy, or maybe a religion, and a rule of life that'll satisfy both his head and his heart.'

Isabel considered this for a moment. She sighed.

'Don't you think it's very strange that a country boy from Marvin, Illinois, should have a notion like that?'

'No stranger than that Luther Burbank who was born on a farm in Massachusetts should have produced a seedless orange or that Henry Ford who was born on a farm in Michigan should have invented a Tin Lizzie.'

'But those are practical things. That's in the American tradition.'

I laughed.

'Can anything in the world be more practical than to learn how to live to best advantage?'

Isabel gave a gesture of lassitude.

'You don't want to lose Larry altogether, do you?'

She shook her head.

'You know how loyal he is: if you won't have anything to do with his wife he won't have anything to do with you. If you've got any sense you'll make friends with Sophie. You'll forget the past and be as nice to her as you can be when you like. She's going to be married and I suppose she's buying some clothes. Why don't you offer to go shopping with her? I think she'd jump at it.'

Isabel listened to me with narrowed eyes. She seemed intent upon what I was saying. For a moment she pondered, but I could not guess what was passing through her mind. Then she surprised me.

'Will you ask her to lunch? It would be rather awkward for me after what I said to Larry yesterday.'

'Will you behave if I do?'

'Like an angel of light,' she answered with her most engaging smile.

'I'll fix it up right away.'

There was a phone in the room. I soon found Sophie's number, and after the usual delay which those who use the

French telephone learn to put up with patiently, I got her. I mentioned my name.

'I've just arrived in Paris,' I said, 'and heard that you and Larry are going to be married. I want to congratulate you. I hope you'll be very happy.' I smothered a cry as Isabel, who was standing by me, gave the soft of my arm a vicious pinch. 'I'm only here for a very short time and I wonder if you and Larry will come and lunch with me the day after tomorrow at the Ritz. I'm asking Gray and Isabel and Elliott Templeton.'

'I'll ask Larry. He's here now.' There was a pause. 'Yes, we shall be glad to.'

I fixed an hour, made a civil remark, and replaced the receiver on its stand. I caught an expression in Isabel's eyes that caused me some misgiving.

'What are you thinking?' I asked her. 'I don't quite like the look of you.'

'I'm sorry; I thought that was the one thing about me you did like.'

'You haven't got some nefarious scheme that you're hatching, Isabel?'

She opened her eyes very wide.

'I promise you I haven't. As a matter of fact I'm terribly curious to see what Sophie looks like now Larry has reformed her. All I hope is that she won't come to the Ritz with a mask of paint on her face.'

5

My little party did not go too badly. Gray and Isabel arrived first; Larry and Sophie Macdonald five minutes later. Isabel and Sophie kissed each other warmly and Isabel and Gray congratulated her on her engagement. I caught the appraising sweep of the eyes with which Isabel took in Sophie's appearance. I was shocked at it. When I saw her in that dive in the Rue de Lappe, outrageously painted, with hennaed hair, in the bright green coat, though she looked outrageous and was very drunk, there was something provocative and even basely alluring in her; but now she looked drab and, though certainly a year or two younger than Isabel, much older. She still had that gallant tilt of her head, but now, I don't know why, it was pathetic.

She was letting her hair go back to its natural colour and it had the slatternly look that hair has when it has been dyed and left to grow. Except for a streak of red on her lips she had no make-up on. Her skin was rough and it had an unhealthy pallor. I remembered how vividly green her eyes had looked, but now they were pale and grey. She wore a red dress, obviously brand-new, with hat, shoes, and bag to match; I don't pretend to know anything about women's clothes, but I had a feeling that it was fussy and too elaborate for the occasion. On her breast was a piece of showy artificial jewellery such as you buy in the Rue de Rivoli. Beside Isabel, in black silk, with a string of cultured pearls round her neck and in a very smart hat, she looked cheap and dowdy.

I ordered cocktails, but Larry and Sophie refused them. Then Elliott arrived. His progress through the vast foyer was, how-ever, impeded by the hands he had to shake and the hands he had to kiss as he saw one person after the other whom he knew. He behaved as though the Ritz were his private house and he were assuring his guests of his pleasure that they had been able to accept his invitation. He had been told nothing about Sophie except she had lost her husband and child in a motor accident and was now going to marry Larry. When at last he reached us he congratulated them both with the elaborate graciousness of which he was a master. We went in to the dining-room and since we were four men and two women I placed Isabel and Sophie opposite one another at the round table, with Sophie between Gray and myself; but the table was small enough for the conversation to be general. I had already ordered the lun-cheon and the wine waiter came along with the wine card.

'You don't know anything about wine, my dear fellow,' said Elliott. 'Give me the wine card, Albert.' He turned over the pages. 'I drink nothing but Vichy myself, but I can't bear to see people drink wine that isn't perfect.'

He and Albert, the wine waiter, were old friends and after an animated discussion they decided on the wine I should give my guests. Then he turned to Sophie.

'And where are you going for your honeymoon, my dear?'

He glanced at her dress and an almost imperceptible raising

of his eyebrows showed me that he had formed an unfavourable opinion of it.

'We're going to Greece.'

'I've been trying to get there for ten years,' said Larry, 'but somehow I've never been able to manage it.'

'It ought to be lovely at this time of the year,' said Isabel, with a show of enthusiasm.

She remembered, as I remembered, that that was where Larry proposed to take her when he wanted her to marry him. It seemed to be an *idée fixe* with Larry to go to Greece on a honeymoon.

The conversation flowed none too easily and I should have found it a difficult row to hoe if it hadn't been for Isabel. She was on her best behaviour. Whenever silence seemed to threaten us and I racked my brain for something fresh to talk about, she broke in with facile chatter. I was grateful to her. Sophie hardly spoke except when she was spoken to and then it seemed an effort to her. The spirit had gone out of her. You would have said that something had died in her and I asked myself if Larry wasn't putting her to a strain greater than she could support. If as I suspected she had doped as well as drunk, the sudden deprivation must have worn her nerves to a frazzle. Sometimes I intercepted a look between them. In his I saw tenderness and encouragement, but in hers an appeal that was pathetic. It may be that Gray with his sweetness of disposition instinctively felt what I thought I saw, for he began to tell her how Larry had cured him of the headaches that had incapacitated him and went on to say how much he had depended on him and how much he owed him.

'Now I'm fit as a flea,' he continued. 'As soon as ever I can get a job I'm going back to work. I've got several irons in the fire and I'm hoping to land something before long. Gosh, it'll be good to be back home again.'

Gray meant well, but what he had said was perhaps not very tactful if, as I supposed, Larry to cure Sophie of her aggravated alcoholism had used with her the same method of suggestion – for that to my mind was what it was – that had been successful with Gray.

'You never have headaches now, Gray?' asked Elliott.

214

'I haven't had one for three months and if I think one's coming on I take hold of my charm and I'm all right.' He fished out of his pocket the ancient coin Larry had given him. 'I wouldn't sell it for a million dollars.'

We finished luncheon and coffee was served. The wine waiter came up and asked whether we wanted liqueurs. We all refused except Gray, who said he would have a brandy. When the bottle was brought Elliott insisted on looking at it.

'Yes, I can recommend it. That'll do you no harm.'

'A little glass for Monsieur?' asked the waiter.

'Alas, it's forbidden me.'

Elliott told him at some length that he was having trouble with his kidneys and that his doctor would not allow him to drink alcohol.

'A tear of zubrovka could do Monsieur no harm. It's well known to be very good for the kidneys. We have just received a consignment from Poland.'

'Is that true? It's hard to get nowadays. Let me have a look at a bottle.'

The wine waiter, a portly, dignified creature with a long silver chain round his neck, went away to fetch it, and Elliott explained that it was the Polish form of vodka but in every way superior.

'We used to drink it at the Radziwills when I stayed with them for the shooting. You should have seen those Polish princes putting it away; I'm not exaggerating when I tell you that they'd drink it by the tumbler without turning a hair. Good blood, of course; aristocrats to the tips of their fingers. Sophie, you must try it, and you too, Isabel. It's an experience no one can afford to miss.'

The wine waiter brought the bottle. Larry, Sophie, and I refused to be tempted, but Isabel said she would like to try it. I was surprised, for habitually she drank very little and she had had two cocktails and two or three glasses of wine. The waiter poured out a glass of pale green liquid and Isabel sniffed it.

'Oh, what a lovely smell.'

'Hasn't it?' cried Elliott. 'That's the herbs they put in it; it's they that give it its delicate taste. Just to keep you company I'll have a drop. It can't hurt me for once.'

'It tastes divine,' said Isabel. 'It's like mother's milk. I've never tasted anything so good.'

Elliott raised his glass to his lips.'

'Oh, how it brings back the old days! You people who never stayed with the Radziwills don't know what living is. That was the grand style. Feudal, you know. You might have thought yourself back in the Middle Ages. You were met at the station by a carriage with six horses and postilions. And at dinner a footman in livery behind every person.'

He went on to describe the magnificence and luxury of the establishment and the brilliance of the parties; and the suspicion, doubtless unworthy, occurred to me that the whole thing was a put-up job between Elliott and the wine waiter to give Elliott an opportunity to discourse upon the grandeur of this princely family and the host of Polish aristocrats he hobnobbed with in their castle. There was no stopping him.

'Another glass, Isabel?'

'Oh, I daren't. But it is heavenly. I'm so glad to know about it; Gray, we must get some.'

'I'll have some sent round to the apartment.'

'Oh, Uncle Elliott, would you?' cried Isabel enthusiastically. 'You are so kind to us. You must try it, Gray; it smells of freshly mown hay and spring flowers, of thyme and lavender, and it's soft on the palate and so comfortable, it's like listening to music by moonlight.'

It was unlike Isabel to gush inordinately and I wondered if she was a trifle tight. The party broke up. I shook hands with Sophie.

'When are you going to be married?' I asked her.

'The week after next. I hope you'll come to the wedding.'

'I'm afraid I shan't be in Paris. I'm leaving for London tomorrow.'

While I was saying good-bye to the rest of my guests Isabel took Sophie aside and talked to her for a minute, then turned to Gray.

'Oh, Gray, I'm not coming home just yet. There's a dress show at Molyneux's and I'm taking Sophie to it. She ought to see the new models.'

'I'd love to,' said Sophie.

We parted. I took Suzanne Rouvier out to dinner that night and next morning started for England.

Elliott arrived at Claridge's a fortnight later and shortly afterwards I dropped in to see him. He had ordered himself several suits of clothes and at what I thought excessive length told me in detail what he had chosen and why. When at last I could get a word in I asked him how the wedding had gone off.

'It didn't go off,' he answered grimly.

'What *do* you mean?'

'Three days before it was to take place Sophie disappeared. Larry hunted everywhere for her.'

'What an extraordinary thing! Did they have a row?'

'No. Far from it. Everything had been arranged. I was going to give her away. They were taking the Orient Express immediately after the wedding. If you ask me, I think Larry's well out of it.'

I guessed that Isabel had told Elliott everything.

'What exactly happened?' I asked.

'Well, you remember that day we lunched at the Ritz with you. Isabel took her to Molyneux's. D'you remember the dress Sophie wore? Deplorable. Did you notice the shoulders? That's how you tell if a dress is well made, by the way it fits over the shoulders. Of course, poor girl, she couldn't afford Molyneux's prices, and Isabel, you know how generous she is, and after all they've known one another since they were children, Isabel offered to give her a dress so that at least she'd have something decent to be married in. Naturally she jumped at it. Well, to cut a long story short, Isabel asked her to come to the apartment one day at three so that they could go together for the final fitting. Sophie came all right, but unfortunately Isabel had to take one of the children to the dentist's and didn't get in till after four and by that time Sophie had gone. Isabel thought she'd got tired of waiting and had gone on to Molyneux's, so she went there at once, but she hadn't come. At last she gave her up and went home again. They were all going to dine together and Larry came along at dinner-time and the first thing she asked him was where Sophie was.

217

'He couldn't understand it and he rang up her apartment, but there was no reply, so he said he'd go down there. They held dinner up as long as they could, but neither of them turned up and so they had dinner by themselves. Of course you know what Sophie's life was before you ran into her in the Rue de Lappe; that was a most unfortunate idea of yours to take them down there. Well, Larry spent all night going around her old haunts, but couldn't find her anywhere. He went to the apartment time after time, but the *concierge* said she hadn't been in. He spent three days hunting for her. She'd just vanished. Then on the fourth day he went to the apartment again and the *concierge* told him she'd been in and packed a bag and gone away in a taxi.'

'Was Larry awfully upset?'

'I didn't see him. Isabel tells me he was rather.'

'She didn't write or anything?'

'Nothing.'

I thought it over.

'What do you make of it?' I said.

'My dear fellow, exactly what you make of it. She couldn't stick it out. She went on the booze again.'

That was obvious, but for all that it was strange. I couldn't see why she had chosen just that moment to skip.

'How is Isabel taking it?'

'Of course she's sorry, but she's a sensible girl and she told me she always thought it would be a disaster if Larry married a woman like that.'

'And Larry?'

'Isabel's been very kind to him. She says that what makes it difficult is that he won't discuss it. He'll be all right, you know; Isabel says he was never in love with Sophie. He was only marrying her out of a sort of misguided chivalry.'

I could see Isabel putting a brave face on a turn of events that was certainly causing her a great deal of satisfaction. I well knew that next time I saw her she would not fail to point out to me that she had known all along what would happen.

But it was nearly a year before I saw her again and though by that time I could have told her something about Sophie that would have set her thinking, the circumstances were such that

I had no inclination to. I stayed in London till nearly Christmas and then, wanting to get home, went straight down to the Riviera without stopping in Paris. I set to work on a novel and for the next few months lived in retirement. I saw Elliott now and then. It was obvious that his health was failing, and it pained me that he persisted notwithstanding in leading a social life. He was vexed with me because I would not drive thirty miles to go to the constant parties he continued to give. He thought it very conceited of me to prefer to sit at home and work.

'It's an unusually brilliant season, my dear fellow,' he told me. 'It's a crime to shut yourself up in your house and miss everything that's going on. And why you had to choose a part of the Riviera to live in that's completely out of fashion I shan't be able to understand if I live to be a hundred.'

Poor nice silly Elliott; it was very clear that he would live to no such age.

By June I had finished the rough draft of my novel and thought I deserved a holiday, so, packing a bag, I got on the cutter from which in summer we used to bathe in the Baie des Fosses and set sail along the coast towards Marseilles. There was only a fitful breeze and for the most part we chugged along with the motor auxiliary. We spent a night in the harbour at Cannes, another at Sainte Maxime, and a third at Sanary. Then we got to Toulon. That is a port I have always had an affection for. The ships of the French fleet give it an air at once romantic and companionable, and I am never tired of wandering about its old streets. I can linger for hours on the quay, watching the sailors on shore leave strolling about in pairs or with their girls, and the civilians who saunter back and forth as though they had nothing in the world to do but enjoy the pleasant sunshine. Because of all these ships and the ferry-boats that take the bustling crowd to various points of the vast harbour, Toulon gives you the effect of a terminal on which all the ways of the wide world converge; and as you sit in a café, your eyes a little dazzled by the brightness of sea and sky, your fancy takes golden journeys to the uttermost parts of the earth. You land in a longboat on a coral beach, fringed with coconut palms, in the Pacific; you step off the gangway on to the dock at Rangoon and get into a rickshaw; you watch from the upper deck the noisy, gesticulating crowd of Negroes as your ship is made fast to the pier at Port au Prince.

We got in latish in the morning and towards the middle of the afternoon I landed and walked along the quay, looking at the shops, at the people who passed me, and at the people sitting under the awning in the cafés. Suddenly I saw Sophie and at the same moment she saw me. She smiled and said hello. I stopped and shook hands with her. She was by herself at a small table with an empty glass before her.

'Sit down and have a drink,' she said.

'You have one with me,' I replied, taking a chair.

She wore the striped blue-and-white jersey of the French sailor, a pair of bright red slacks, and sandals through which protruded the painted nails of her big toes. She wore no hat, and her hair, cut very short and curled, was of so pale a gold that it was almost silver. She was as heavily made up as when we had run across her at the Rue de Lappe. She had had a drink or two as I judged from the saucers on the table, but she was sober. She did not seem displeased to see me.

'How are all the folks in Paris?' she asked.

'I think they're all right. I haven't seen any of them since that day we all lunched together at the Ritz.'

She blew a great cloud of smoke from her nostrils and began to laugh.

'I didn't marry Larry after all.'

'I know. Why not?'

'Darling, when it came to the point I couldn't see myself being Mary Magdalen to his Jesus Christ. No, sir.'

'What made you change your mind at the last moment?'

She looked at me mockingly. With that audacious tilt of the head, with her small breasts and narrow flanks, in that get-up, she looked like a vicious boy; but I must admit that she was much more attractive than in the red dress, with its dismal air of provincial smartness, in which I had last seen her. Face and neck were deeply burnt by the sun, and though the brownness of her skin made the rouge on her cheeks and the black of her eyebrows more aggressive, the effect in its vulgar way was not without lure.

'Would you like me to tell you?'

I nodded. The waiter brought the beer I had ordered for myself and the brandy and seltzer for her. She lit a *caporal* from one she had just finished.

'I hadn't had a drink for three months. I hadn't had a smoke.' She saw my faint look of surprise and laughed. 'I don't mean cigarettes. Opium. I felt awful. You know, sometimes when I was alone I'd shriek the place down; I'd say, "I can't go through with it, I can't go through with it." It wasn't so bad when I was with Larry, but when he wasn't there it was hell.'

I was looking at her and when she mentioned opium I scanned her more sharply; I noticed the pin-point pupils that showed she was smoking it now. Her eyes were startlingly green.

'Isabel was giving me my wedding dress. I wonder what's happened to it now. It was a peach. We'd arranged that I should pick her up and we'd go to Molyneux's together. I will say this for Isabel, what she doesn't know about clothes isn't worth knowing. When I got to the apartment their man said she'd had to take Joan to the dentist's and had left a message that she'd be in directly. I went into the living-room. The coffee things were still on the table and I asked the man if I could have a cup. Coffee was the only thing that kept me going. He said he'd bring me some and took the empty cups and the coffee-pot away. He left a bottle on the tray. I looked at it, and it was that Polish stuff you'd all talked about at the Ritz.'

'Zubrovka. I remember Elliott saying he'd send Isabel some.'

'You'd all raved how good it smelt and I was curious. I took out the cork and had a sniff. You were quite right; it smelt damned good. I lit a cigarette and in a few minutes the man came in with the coffee. That was good too. They talk a lot about French coffee, they can have it; give me American coffee. That's the only thing I miss here. But Isabel's coffee wasn't bad, I was feeling lousy, and after I'd had a cup I felt better. I looked at that bottle standing there. It was a terrible temptation, but I said, "To hell with it, I won't think of it," and I lit another cigarette. I thought Isabel would be in any minute, but she didn't come. I got frightfully nervous; I hate being kept waiting and there was nothing to read in the room. I started walking about and looking at the pictures, but I kept on seeing that damned bottle. Then I thought I'd just pour out a glass and look at it. It had such a pretty colour.'

'Pale green.'

'That's right. It's funny, its colour is just like its smell. It's like that green you sometimes see in the heart of a white rose. I *had* to see if it tasted like that, I thought just a taste couldn't hurt me; I only meant to take a sip and then I heard a sound, I thought it was Isabel coming in and I swallowed the glassful because I didn't want her to catch me. But it wasn't Isabel after all. Gosh, it made me feel good, I hadn't felt like that since I'd gone on the wagon. I really began to feel alive again. If Isabel had come in then I suppose I'd be married to Larry now. I wonder how it would have turned out.'

'And she didn't come in?'

'No, she didn't. I was furious with her. Who did she think she was, keeping me waiting like that? And then I saw that the liqueur glass was full again; I suppose I must have poured it out without thinking, but, believe it or not, I didn't know I had. It seemed silly to pour it back again, so I drank it. There's no denying it, it was delicious. I felt a different woman; I felt like laughing and I hadn't felt like that for three months. D'you remember that old cissie saying he'd seen fellas in Poland drink it by the tumbler without turning a hair? Well, I thought I could take what any Polish son of a bitch could take and you may as well be hanged for a sheep as a lamb, so I emptied the dregs of my coffee in the fireplace and filled the cup to the brim. Talk of mother's milk – my arse. Then I don't quite know what happened, but I don't believe there was much left in the bottle by the time I was through. Then I thought I'd get out before Isabel came in. She nearly caught me. Just as I got out of the front door I heard Joanie's voice. I ran up the stairs and waited till they were safely in the apartment and then I dashed down and got into a taxi. I told the driver to drive like hell and when he asked where to I burst out laughing in his face. I felt like a million dollars.'

'Did you go back to your apartment?' I asked, though I knew she hadn't.

'What sort of a damn fool d'you take me for? I knew Larry

222

would come and look for me. I didn't dare go to any of the places I used to go to, so I went to Hakim's. I knew Larry'd never find me there. Besides, I wanted a smoke.'

'What's Hakim's?'

'Hakim's? Hakim's an Algerian and he can always get you opium if you've got the dough to pay for it. He was quite a friend of mine. He'll get you anything you want, a boy, a man, a woman, or a nigger. He always has half a dozen Algerians on tap. I spent three days there. I don't know how many men I didn't have.' She began to giggle. 'All shapes, sizes, and colours. I made up for lost time all right. But you know, I was scared. I didn't feel safe in Paris, I was afraid Larry'd find me, besides I hadn't got any money left, those bastards you have to pay them to go to bed with you, so I got out, I went back to the apartment and gave the *concierge* a hundred francs and told her if anyone came and asked for me to say I'd gone away. I packed my things and that night I took the train to Toulon. I didn't feel really safe till I got here.'

'And have you been here ever since?'

'You betcha, and I'm going to stay here. You can get all the opium you want, the sailors bring it back from the East, and it's good stuff, not that muck they sell you in Paris. I've got a room at the hotel. You know, the Commerce et la Marine. When you go in there at night the corridors just reek of it.' She sniffed voluptuously. 'Sweet and acrid, and you know they're smoking in their rooms, and it gives you a nice homey feeling. And they don't mind who you take in with you. They come and thump at your door at five in the morning to get the sailors up to go back to their ships, so you don't have to worry about that.' And then, without transition: 'I saw a book of yours in the store just along the quay; if I'd known I was going to see you I'd have bought it and got you to sign it.'

When passing the bookshop I had stopped to look in the window and had noticed among other new books the translation of a novel of mine that had recently appeared.

'I don't suppose it would have amused you much,' I said.

'I don't know why it shouldn't. I *can* read, you know.'

'And you can write too, I believe.'

She gave me a rapid glance and began to laugh.

'Yeah, I used to write poetry when I was a kid. I guess it was pretty terrible, but I thought it fine. I suppose Larry told you.' She hesitated for a moment. 'Life's hell anyway, but if there is any fun to be got out of it, you're only a god-damn fool if you don't get it.' She threw back her head defiantly. 'If I buy that book will you write in it?'

'I'm leaving tomorrow. If you really want it, I'll get you a copy and leave it at your hotel.'

'That'd be swell.'

Just then a naval launch came up to the quay and a crowd of sailors tumbled out of it. Sophie embraced them with a glance.

'That'll be my boy friend.' She waved her arm at someone. 'You can stand him a drink and then you better scram. He's a Corsican and as jealous as our old friend Jehovah.'

A young man came up to us, hesitated when he saw me, but on a beckoning gesture came up to the table. He was tall, swarthy, clean-shaven, with splendid dark eyes, an aquiline nose, and raven black, wavy hair. He did not look more than twenty. Sophie introduced me as an American friend of her childhood.

'Dumb but beautiful,' she said to me.

'You like 'em tough, don't you?'

'The tougher the better.'

'One of these days you'll get your throat cut.'

'I wouldn't be surprised,' she grinned. 'Good riddance to bad rubbish.'

'One's going to speak French, isn't one?' the sailor said sharply.

Sophie turned upon him a smile in which there was a trace of mockery. She spoke a fluent and slangy French, with a strong American accent, but this gave the vulgar and obscene colloquialisms that she commonly used a comic tang, so that you could not help but laugh.

'I was telling him that you were beautiful, but to spare your modesty I was saying it in English.' She addressed me. 'And he's strong. He has the muscles of a boxer. Feel them.'

The sailor's sullenness was dispelled by the flattery and with a complacent smile he flexed his arm so that the biceps stood out.

'Feel it,' he said. 'Go on, feel it.'

I did so and expressed a proper admiration. We chatted for a few minutes. I paid for the drinks and got up.

'I must be going.'

'It's nice to have seen you. Don't forget the book.'

'I won't.'

I shook hands with them both and strolled off. On my way I stopped at the bookshop, bought the novel, and wrote Sophie's name and my own. Then, because it suddenly occurred to me I could think of nothing else, I wrote the first line of Ronsard's lovely little poem which is in all the anthologies:

Mignonne, allons voir si la rose. . . .

I left it at the hotel. It is on the quay and I have often stayed there because when you are awakened at dawn by the clarion that calls the men on night leave back to duty the sun rising mistily over the smooth water of the harbour invests the wraith-like ships with a shrouded loveliness. Next day we sailed for Cassis, where I wanted to buy some wine, and then to Marseilles to take up a new sail that we had ordered. A week later I got home.

7

I found a message from Joseph, Elliott's manservant, to tell me that Elliott was ill in bed and would be glad to see me, so next day I drove over to Antibes. Joseph, before taking me up to see his master, told me that Elliott had had an attack of uraemia and that his doctor took a grave view of his condition. He had come through it and was getting better, but his kidneys were diseased and it was impossible that he should ever completely recover. Joseph had been with Elliott for forty years and was devoted to him, but though his manner was regretful it was impossible not to notice the inner satisfaction with which, like so many members of his class, catastrophe in the house filled him.

'*Ce pauvre monsieur*,' he sighed. 'Evidently he had his manias but at bottom he was good. Sooner or later he must die.'

He spoke already as though Elliott were at his last gasp.

'I'm sure he's provided for you, Joseph,' I said grimly.

'One must hope it,' he said mournfully.

I was surprised when he ushered me into the bedroom to find Elliott very spry. He was pale and looked old, but was in good spirits. He was shaved and his hair was neatly brushed. He wore pale blue silk pyjamas, on the pocket of which were embroidered his initials surmounted by his count's crown. These, much larger and again with the crown, were heavily embroidered on the turned-down sheet.

I asked him how he felt.

'Perfectly well,' he said cheerfully. 'It's only a temporary indisposition. I shall be up and about again in a few days. I've got the Grand Duke Dimitri lunching with me on Saturday, and I've told my doctor he must put me to rights by then at all costs.'

I spent half an hour with him, and on my way out asked Joseph to let me know if Elliott had a relapse. I was astonished a week later when I went to lunch with one of my neighbours to find him there. Dressed for a party, he looked like death.

'You oughtn't to be out, Elliott,' I told him.

'Oh, what nonsense, my dear fellow. Frieda is expecting the Princess Mafalda. I've known the Italian royal family for years, ever since poor Louisa was *en poste* at Rome, and I couldn't let poor Frieda down.'

I did not know whether to admire his indomitable spirit or to lament that at his age, stricken with mortal illness, he should still retain his passion for society. You would never have thought he was a sick man. Like a dying actor when he has the grease paint on his face and steps on the stage, who forgets for the time being his aches and pains, Elliott played his part of the polished courtier with his accustomed assurance. He was infinitely amiable, flatteringly attentive to the proper people, and amusing with that malicious irony at which he was an adept. I think I had never see him display his social gift to greater advantage. When the Royal Highness had departed (and the grace with which Elliott bowed, managing to combine respect for her exalted rank with an old man's admiration for a comely woman, was a sight to see) I was not surprised to hear our hostess tell him that he had been the life and soul of the party.

A few days later he was in bed again and his doctor forbade him to leave his room. Elliott was exasperated.

'It's too bad this should happen just now. It's a particularly brilliant season.'

He reeled off a long list of persons of importance who were spending the summer on the Riviera.

I went to see him every three or four days. Sometimes he was in bed, but sometimes he lay on a chaise longue in a gorgeous dressing-gown. He seemed to have an inexhaustible supply of them, for I do not remember that I ever saw him in the same one twice. On one of these occasions, it was the beginning of August by now, I found Elliott unusually quiet. Joseph had told me when he let me into the house that he seemed a little better so I was surprised that he was so listless. I tried to amuse him with such gossip of the coast as I had picked up, but he was plainly uninterested. There was a slight frown between his eyes, and a sullenness in his expression that was unusual with him.

'Are you going to Edna Novemali's party?' he asked me suddenly.

'No, of course not.'

'Has she asked you?'

'She's asked everybody on the Riviera.'

The Princess Novemali was an American of immense wealth who had married a Roman prince, but not an ordinary prince such as go for two a penny in Italy, but the head of a great family and the descendant of a *condottiere* who had carved out a principality for himself in the sixteenth century. She was a woman of sixty, a widow, and since the Fascist regime demanded too large a slice of her American income to suit her, she had left Italy and built herself, on a fine estate behind Cannes, a Florentine villa. She had brought marble from Italy with which to line the walls of her great reception rooms and imported painters to paint the ceilings. Her pictures, her bronzes, were uncommonly fine and even Elliott, though he didn't like Italian furniture, was obliged to admit that hers was magnificent. The gardens were lovely and the swimming-pool must have cost a small fortune. She entertained largely and you never sat down less than twenty at table. She had arranged to give a fancy-dress party on the night of the August full moon, and although it was still three weeks ahead nothing else was being talked of on the Riviera. There were to be fireworks and she was bringing down a coloured orchestra from Paris. The exiled royalties were telling one another with envious admiration that it would cost her more than they had to live on for a year.

'It's princely,' they said.

'It's crazy,' they said.

'It's in bad taste,' they said.

'What are you going to wear?' Elliott asked me.

'But I told you, Elliott, I'm not going. You don't think I'm going to dress myself up in fancy dress at my time of life.'

'She hasn't asked me,' he said hoarsely.

He looked at me with haggard eyes.

'Oh, she will,' I said coolly. 'I dare say all the invitations haven't gone out yet.'

'She's not going to ask me.' His voice broke. 'It's a deliberate insult.'

'Oh, Elliott, I can't believe that. I'm sure it's an oversight.'

'I'm not a man that people overlook.'

'Anyhow, you wouldn't have been well enough to go.'

'Of course I should. The best party of the season! If I were on my deathbed I'd get up for it. I've got the costume of my ancestor, the Count de Lauria, to wear.'

I did not quite know what to say and so remained silent.

'Paul Barton was in to see me just before you came,' Elliott said suddenly.

I cannot expect the reader to remember who this was, since I had to look back myself to see what name I had given him. Paul Barton was the young American whom Elliott had introduced into London society and who had aroused his hatred by dropping him when he no longer had any use for him. He had been somewhat in the public eye of late, first because he had adopted British nationality and then because he had married the daughter of a newspaper magnate who had been raised to the peerage. With this influence behind him and with his own

228

adroitness it was evident that he would go far. Elliott was very bitter.

'Whenever I wake up in the night and hear a mouse scratching away in the wainscoat I say: "That's Paul Barton climbing." Believe me, my dear fellow, he'll end up in the House of Lords. Thank God I shan't be alive to see it.'

'What did he want?' I asked, for I knew as well as Elliott that this young man did nothing for nothing.

'I'll tell you what he wanted,' said Elliott, snarling. 'He wanted to borrow my Count de Lauria costume.'

'Nerve!'

'Don't you see what it means? It means he knew Edna hadn't asked me and wasn't going to ask me. She put him up to it. The old bitch. She'd never have got anywhere without me. I gave parties for her. I introduced her to everyone she knows. She sleeps with her chauffeur; you knew that of course. Disgusting! He sat there and told me that she's having the whole garden illuminated and there are going to be fireworks. I love fireworks. And he told me that Edna was being pestered by people who were asking for invitations, but she had turned them all down because she wanted the party to be really brilliant. He spoke as though there were no question of my being invited.'

'And are you lending him the costume?'

'I'd see him dead and in hell first. I'm going to be buried in it.' Elliott, sitting up in bed, rocked to and fro like a woman distraught. 'Oh, it's so unkind,' he said. 'I hate them, I hate them all. They were glad enough to make a fuss of me when I could entertain them, but now I'm old and sick they have no use for me. Not ten people have called to inquire since I've been laid up, and all this week only one miserable bunch of flowers. I've done everything for them. They've eaten my food and drunk my wine. I've run their errands for them. I've made their parties for them. I've turned myself inside out to do them favours. And what have I got out of it? Nothing, nothing, nothing. There's not one of them who cares if I live or die. Oh, it's so cruel.' He began to cry. Great heavy tears trickled down his withered cheeks. 'I wish to God I'd never left America.'

It was lamentable to see that old man, with the grave yawning in front of him, weep like a child because he hadn't been asked to a party: shocking and at the same time almost intolerably pathetic.

'Never mind, Elliott,' I said, 'it may rain on the night of the party. That'll bitch it.'

He caught at my words like the drowning man we've all heard about at a straw. He began to giggle through his tears.

'I've never thought of that. I'll pray to God for rain as I've never prayed before. You're quite right; that'll bitch it.'

I managed to divert his frivolous mind into another channel and left him, if not cheerful, at least composed. But I was not willing to let the matter rest, so on getting home I called up Edna Novemali and, saying I had to come to Cannes next day, asked if I could lunch with her. She sent a message that she'd be pleased but there'd be no party. Nevertheless when I arrived I found ten people there besides herself. She was not a bad sort, generous and hospitable, and her only grave fault was her malicious tongue. She could not help saying beastly things about even her intimate friends, but she did this because she was a stupid woman and knew no other way to make herself interesting. Since her slanders were repeated she was often not on speaking terms with the objects of her vemon, but she gave good parties and most of them found it convenient after a while to forgive her. I did not want to expose Elliott to the humiliation of asking her to invite him to her big do, so waited to see how the land lay. She was excited about it and the conversation at luncheon was concerned with nothing else.

'Elliott will be delighted to have an opportunity to wear his Philip the Second costume,' I said as casually as I could.

'I haven't asked him,' she said.

'Why not?' I replied, with an air of surprise.

'Why should I? He doesn't count socially any more. He's a bore and a snob and a scandalmonger.'

Since these accusations could with equal truth be brought against her, I thought this a bit thick. She was a fool.

'Besides,' she added, 'I want Paul to wear Elliott's costume. He'll look simply divine in it.'

I said nothing more, but determined by hook or by crook to get poor Elliott the invitation he hankered after. After luncheon

Edna took her friends out into the garden. That gave me the chance I was looking for. On one occasion I had stayed in the house for a few days and knew its arrangement. I guessed that there would still be a number of invitation cards left over and that they would be in the secretary's room. I whipped along there, meaning to slip one in my pocket, write Elliott's name on it, and post it. I knew he was much too ill to go, but it would mean a great deal to him to receive it. I was taken aback when I opened the door to find Edna's secretary at her desk. I had expected her to be still at lunch. She was a middle-aged Scotch woman, called Miss Keith, with sandy hair, a freckled face, pince-nez, and an air of determined virginity. I collected myself.

'The Princess is taking the crowd around the garden, so I thought I'd come in and smoke a cigarette with you.'

'You're welcome.'

Miss Keith spoke with a Scotch burr and when she indulged in the dry humour which she reserved for her favourites she so broadened it as to make her remarks extremely amusing, but when you were overcome with laughter she looked at you with pained surprise as though she thought you daft to see anything funny in what she said.

'I suppose this party is giving you a hell of a lot of work, Miss Keith,' I said.

'I don't know whether I'm standing on my head or on my heels.'

Knowing I could trust her, I went straight to the point.

'Why hasn't the old girl asked Mr Templeton?'

Miss Keith permitted a smile to cross her grim features.

'You know what she is. She's got a down on him. She crossed his name out on the list herself.'

'He's dying, you know. He'll never leave his bed again. He's awfully hurt at being left out.'

'If he wanted to keep in with the Princess he'd have been wiser not to tell everyone that she goes to bed with her chauffeur. And him with a wife and three children.'

'And does she?'

Miss Keith looked at me over her pince-nez.

'I've been a secretary for twenty-one years, my dear sir, and

231

I've made it a rule to believe all my employers as pure as the driven snow. I'll admit that when one of my ladies found herself three months gone in the family way when his lordship had been shooting lions in Africa for six, my faith was sorely tried, but she took a little trip to Paris, a very expensive little trip it was too, and all was well. Her ladyship and I shared a deep sigh of relief.'

'Miss Keith, I didn't come here to smoke a cigarette with you, I came to snitch an invitation card and send it to Mr Templeton myself.'

'That would have been a very unscrupulous thing to do.'

'Granted. Be a good sport, Miss Keith. Give me a card. He won't come and it'll make the poor old man happy. You've got nothing against him, have you?'

'No, he's always been very civil to me. He's a gentleman, I will say that for him, and that's more than you can say for most of the people who come here and fill their fat bellies at the Princess's expense.'

All important persons have about them someone in a subordinate position who has their ear. These dependents are very susceptible to slights, and, when they are not treated as they think they should be, will by well-directed shafts, constantly repeated, poison the minds of their patrons against those who have provoked their animosity. It is well to keep in with them. This Elliott knew better than anybody and he had always a friendly word and a cordial smile for the poor relation, the old maidservant, or the trusted secretary. I was sure he had often exchanged pleasant badinage with Miss Keith and at Christmas had not forgotten to send her a box of chocolates, a vanity case, or a handbag.

'Come on, Miss Keith, have a heart.'

Miss Keith fixed her pince-nez more firmly on her prominent nose.

'I am sure you wish me to do nothing disloyal to my employer, Mr Maugham, besides which the old cow would fire me if she found out I'd disobeyed her. The cards are on the desk in their envelopes. I am going to look out of the window, partly to stretch my legs which are cramped from sitting too long in one position and also to observe the beauty of the prospect. What happens when my back is turned neither God nor man can hold me responsible for.'

When Miss Keith resumed her seat the invitation was in my pocket.

'It's been nice to see you, Miss Keith,' I said, holding out my hand. 'What are you wearing at the fancy-dress party?'

'I am a minister's daughter, my dear sir,' she replied. 'I leave such foolishness to the upper classes. When I have seen that the representatives of the *Herald* and the *Mail* get a good supper and a bottle of our second-best champagne, my duties will be terminated and I shall retire to the privacy of my bed-chamber with a detective story.'

8

A couple of days later, when I went to see Elliott, I found him beaming.

'Look,' he said, 'I've had my invitation. It came this morning.'

He took the card out from under his pillow and showed it to me.

'It's what I told you,' I said. 'You see, your name begins with a T. The secretary has evidently only just reached you.'

'I haven't answered yet. I'll do it tomorrow.'

I had a moment's fright at that.

'Would you like me to answer it for you? I could post it when I leave you.'

'No, why should you? I'm quite capable of answering invitations myself.'

Fortunately, I thought, the envelope would be opened by Miss Keith and she would have the sense to suppress it. Elliott rang the bell.

'I want to show you my costume.'

'You're not thinking of going, Elliott?'

'Of course I am. I haven't worn it since the Beaumont's ball.'

Joseph answered the bell and Elliott told him to bring the costume. It was in a large flat box, wrapped in tissue paper. There were long white silk hose, padded trunks of cloth of gold lashed with white satin, a doublet to match, a cloak, a ruff to wear round the neck, a flat velvet cap, and a long gold chain from which hung the order of the Golden Fleece. I recognized it as a copy of the gorgeous dress worn by Philip the Second in Titian's portrait at the Prado, and when Elliott told me it was exactly the costume the Count de Lauria had worn at the wedding of the King of Spain with the Queen of England I could not but think that he was giving rein to his imagination.

On the following morning while I was having breakfast I was called to the telephone. It was Joseph to tell me that Elliott had had another bad attack during the night and the doctor hurriedly summoned, doubted whether he would last through the day. I sent for the car and drove over to Antibes. I found Elliott unconscious. He had resolutely refused to have a nurse but I found one there, sent for by the doctor from the English hospital between Nice and Beaulieu, and was glad to see her. I went out and telegraphed to Isabel. She and Gray were spending the summer with the children at the inexpensive seaside resort of La Baule. It was a long journey and I was afraid they would not get to Antibes in time. Except for her two brothers whom he had not seen for years, she was Elliott's only living relative.

But the will to live was strong in him, or it may be that the doctor's medicaments were effective, for during the course of the day he rallied. Though shattered, he put on a bold front and amused himself by asking the nurse indecent questions about her sex life. I stayed with him most of the afternoon and next day, on going to see him again, found him, though very weak, sufficiently cheerful. The nurse would only let me stay with him a short time. I was worried at not having received an answer to my telegram. Not knowing Isabel's address at La Baule I had sent it to Paris and feared that the *concierge* had delayed to forward it. It was not till two days later that I got a reply to say that they were starting at once. As ill luck would have it, Gray and Isabel were on a motor trip in Brittany and had only just had my wire. I looked up the trains and saw that they could not arrive for at least thirty-six hours.

Early next morning Joseph called me again to tell me that Elliott had had a very bad night and was asking for me. I hurried over. When I arrived Joseph took me aside.

'Monsieur will excuse me if I speak to him on a delicate

234

subject,' he said to me. 'I am of course a freethinker and believe all religion is nothing but a conspiracy of the priests to gain control over the people, but Monsieur knows what women are. My wife and the chambermaid insist that the poor gentleman should receive the last sacraments and evidently the time is growing short.' He looked at me in rather a shamefaced way. 'And the fact remains, one never knows, perhaps it is better, if one's got to die, to regularize one's situation with the Church.'

I understood him perfectly. However freely they mock, most Frenchmen, when the end comes, prefer to make their peace with the faith that is part of their blood and bones.

'Do you want me to suggest it to him?'

'If Monsieur would have the goodness.'

It was not a job I much fancied, but after all Elliott had been for many years a devout Catholic, and it was fitting that he should conform to the obligations of his faith. I went up to his room. He was lying on his back, shrivelled and wan, but perfectly conscious. I asked the nurse to leave us alone.

'I'm afraid you're very ill, Elliott,' I said. 'I was wondering, I was wondering if you wouldn't like to see a priest?'

He looked at me for a minute without answering.

'D'you mean to say I'm going to die?'

'Oh, I hope not. But it's just as well to be on the safe side.'

'I understand.'

He was silent. It is a terrible moment when you have to tell someone what I had just told Elliott. I could not look at him. I clenched my teeth because I was afraid I was going to cry. I was sitting on the edge of the bed, facing him, with my arm outstretched for support.

He patted my hand.

'Don't be upset, my dear fellow. *Noblesse oblige,* you know.'

I laughed hysterically.

'You ridiculous creature, Elliott.'

'That's better. Now call up the bishop and say that I wish to make my confession and receive Extreme Unction. I would be grateful if he'd send the Abbé Charles. He's a friend of mine.'

The Abbé Charles was the bishop's vicar general whom I had occasion to mention before. I went downstairs and telephoned. I spoke to the bishop himself.

'Is it urgent?' he asked.

'Very.'

'I will attend to it at once.'

The doctor arrived and I told him what I had done. He went up with the nurse to see Elliott and I waited on the ground floor in the dining-room. It is only twenty minutes' drive from Nice to Antibes and little more than half an hour later a black sedan drew up at the door. Joseph came to me.

'*C'est Monseigneur en personne, Monsieur,*' he said in a flurry. 'It's the bishop himself.'

I went out to receive him. He was not as usual accompanied by his vicar general, but, why I did not know, by a young abbé who bore a basket that contained, I supposed, the utensils needed to administer the sacrament. The chauffeur followed with a shabby black valise. The bishop shook hands with me and presented his companion.

'How is our poor friend?'

'I'm afraid he's very ill, Monseigneur.'

'Will you be so obliging as to show us into a room where we can enrobe?'

'The dining-room is here, Monseigneur, and the drawing-room is on the next floor.'

'The dining-room will do very well.'

I ushered him in. Joseph and I waited in the hall. Presently the door opened and the bishop came out, followed by the abbé holding in both hands the chalice surmounted by a little platter on which lay the consecrated wafer. They were covered by a cambric napkin so fine that it was transparent. I had never seen the bishop but at a dinner or luncheon party, and a very good trencherman he was, who enjoyed his food and a glass of good wine, telling funny and sometimes ribald stories with verve. He had struck me then as a sturdy, thickset man of no more than average height. Now, in surplice and stole, he looked not only tall, but stately. His red face, puckered as a rule with malicious yet kindly laughter, was grave. There was in his appearance nothing left of the cavalry officer he had once been; he looked, what indeed he was, a great dignitary of the Church. I was hardly surprised to see Joseph cross himself. The bishop inclined his head in a slight bow.

'Conduct me to the sick man,' he said.

I made way for him to ascend the stairs before me, but he bade me precede him. We went up in solemn silence. I entered Elliott's room.

'The bishop has come himself, Elliott.'

Elliott struggled to raise himself to a sitting position.

'Monseigneur, this is an honour I did not venture to expect.'

'Do not move, my friend.' The bishop turned to the nurse and me. 'Leave us.' And then to the abbé: 'I will call you when I am ready.'

The abbé glanced around and I guessed that he was looking for a place to set down the chalice. I pushed aside the tortoise-shell-backed brushes on the dressing-table. The nurse went downstairs and I led the abbé into the adjoining room which Elliott used as a study. The windows were open to the blue sky and he went over and stood by one of them. I sat down. A race of Stars was in progress and their sails gleamed dazzling white against the azure. A big schooner with a black hull, her red sails spread, was beating up against the breeze towards the harbour. I recognized her for a lobster boat, bringing a catch from Sardinia to supply the gala dinners at the casinos with a fish course. Through the closed door I could hear the muffled murmur of voices. Elliott was making his confession. I badly wanted a cigarette, but feared the abbé would be shocked if I lit one. He stood motionless, looking out, a slender young man, and his thick waving black hair, his fine dark eyes, his olive skin revealed his Italian origin. There was the quick fire of the South in his aspect and I asked myself what urgent faith, what burning desire had caused him to abandon the joys of life, the pleasures of his age, and the satisfaction of his senses, to devote himself to the service of God.

Suddenly the voices in the next room were still and I looked at the door. It was opened and the bishop appeared.

'*Venez,*' he said to the priest.

I was left alone. I heard the bishop's voice once more and I knew he was saying the prayers that the Church has ordained should be said for the dying. Then there was another silence and I knew that Elliott was partaking of the body and the blood of Christ. From I know not what feeling, inherited, I suppose, from far-away ancestors, though not a Catholic I can never attend Mass without a sense of tremulous awe when the little tinkle of the servitor's bell informs me of the Elevation of the Host; and now, similarly, I shivered as though a cold wind ran through me, I shivered with fear and wonder. The door was opened once more.

'You may come in,' said the bishop.

I entered. The abbé was spreading the cambric napkin over the cup and the little gilt plate on which the consecrated wafer had lain. Elliott's eyes shone.

'Conduct Monseigneur to his car,' he said.

We descended the stairs. Joseph and the maids were waiting in the hall. The maids were crying. There were three of them and one after the other they came forward and, dropping to their knees, kissed the bishop's ring. He blessed them with two fingers. Joseph's wife nudged him and he advanced, fell to his knees too, and kissed the ring. The bishop smiled faintly.

'You are a freethinker, my son?'

I could see Joseph making an effort over himself.

'Yes, Monseigneur.'

'Do not let it trouble you. You have been a good and faithful servant to your master. God will overlook the errors of your understanding.'

I went out into the street with him and opened the door of his car. He gave me a bow as he stepped in and smiled indulgently.

'Our poor friend is very low. His defects were of the surface; he was generous of heart and kindly towards his fellow men.'

9

Thinking that Elliott might want to be alone after the ceremony in which he had taken part, I went up to the drawing-room and began to read, but no sooner had I settled myself than the nurse came in to tell me that he wanted to see me. I climbed the flight of stairs to his room. Whether owing to a shot that the doctor had given him to help him to support the ordeal before him or whether from the excitement of it, he was calmly cheerful and his eyes were bright.

'A great honour, my dear fellow,' he said. 'I shall enter the

238

kingdom of heaven with a letter of introduction from a prince of the Church. I fancy that all doors will be open to me.'

'I'm afraid you'll find the company very mixed,' I smiled.

'Don't you believe it, my dear fellow. We know from Holy Writ that there are class distinctions in heaven just as there are on earth. There are seraphim and cherubim, archangels and angels. I have always moved in the best society in Europe and I have no doubt that I shall move in the best society in heaven. Our Lord has said: The House of my Father hath many mansions. It would be highly unsuitable to lodge the *hoi polloi* in a way to which they're entirely unaccustomed.'

I suspected that Elliott saw the celestial habitations in the guise of the châteaux of a Baron de Rothschild with eighteenth-century panelling on the walls, Buhl tables, marquetry cabinets, and Louis Quinze suites covered with their original *petit-point*.

'Believe me, my dear fellow,' he went on after a pause, 'there'll be none of this damned equality in heaven.'

He dropped off quite suddenly into a doze. I sat down with a book. He slept off and on. At one o'clock the nurse came in to tell me that Joseph had luncheon ready for me. Joseph was subdued.

'Fancy Monseigneur the Bishop coming himself. It is a great honour he has done our poor gentleman. You saw me kiss his ring?'

'I did.'

'It's not a thing I would have done of myself! I did it to satisfy my poor wife.'

I spent the afternoon in Elliott's room. In the course of it a telegram came from Isabel to say that she and Gray would arrive by the Blue Train next morning. I could hardly hope they would be in time. The doctor came. He shook his head. Towards sunset Elliott awoke and was able to take a little nourishment. It seemed to give him a momentary strength. He beckoned to me and I went up to the bed. His voice was very weak.

'I haven't answered Edna's invitation.'

'Oh, don't bother about that now, Elliott.'

'Why not? I've always been a man of the world; there's no

reason why I should forget my manners as I'm leaving it. Where is the card?'

It was on the chimney piece and I put it in his hand, but I doubt whether he could see it.

'You'll find a pad of writing paper in my study. If you'll get it I'll dictate my answer.'

I went into the next room and came back with writing materials. I sat down by the side of his bed.

'Are you ready?'

'Yes.'

His eyes were closed, but there was a mischievous smile on his lips and I wondered what was coming.

'Mr Elliot Templeton regrets that he cannot accept Princess Novemali's kind invitation owing to a previous engagement with his Blessed Lord.'

He gave a faint, ghostly chuckle. His face was of a strange blue-white, ghastly to behold, and he exhaled the nauseating stench peculiar to his disease. Poor Elliott who had loved to spray himself with the perfumes of Chanel and Molyneux. He was still holding the purloined invitation card and, thinking it incommoded him, I tried to take it out of his hand, but he tightened his grip on it. I was startled to hear him speak quite loudly.

'The old bitch,' he said.

These were the last words he spoke. He sank into a coma. The nurse had been up with him all the previous night and looked very tired, so I sent her to bed, promising to call her if necessary, and said I would sit up. There was indeed nothing to do. I lit a shaded lamp and read till my eyes ached and then, turning it off, I sat in darkness. The night was warm and the windows wide open. At regular intervals the flash of the lighthouse swept the room with a passing glimmer. The moon, which when full would look upon the vacuous, noisy gaiety of Edna Novemali's fancy-dress party, set, and in the sky, a deep, deep blue, the countless stars shone with their terrifying brilliance. I think I may have dropped off into a light sleep, but my senses were still awake, and I was suddenly startled into intense consciousness by a hurried, angry sound, the most awe-inspiring sound anyone can hear, the death rattle. I went over to the bed and by the gleam of the lighthouse felt Elliott's pulse. He was dead. I lit the lamp by his bedside and looked at him. His jaw had fallen. His eyes were open and before closing them I stared into them for a minute. I was moved and I think a few tears trickled down my cheeks. An old, kind friend. It made me sad to think how silly, useless, and trivial his life had been. It mattered very little now that he had gone to so many parties and had hobnobbed with all those princes, dukes, and counts. They had forgotten him already.

I saw no reason to wake the exhausted nurse, so I returned to my chair by the window. I was asleep when she came in at seven. I left her to do whatever she thought fit and had breakfast, then I went to the station to meet Gray and Isabel. I told them that Elliott was dead, and since there was no room for them at his house asked them to stay with me, but they preferred to go to a hotel. I went back to my own house to have a bath, shave, and change.

In the course of the morning Gray called me to say that Joseph had given them a letter addressed to me that Elliott had entrusted to him. Since it might contain something for my eyes alone I said I would drive over at once, and so less than an hour later I once more entered the house. The letter, marked on the envelope: *To be delivered immediately after my death,* contained instructions for his obsequies. I knew that he had set his heart on being buried in the church that he had built and I had already told Isabel. He wished to be embalmed and mentioned the name of the firm to which the commission should be given. 'I have made inquiries,' he continued, 'and I am informed that they make a very good job of it. I trust you to see that it is not scamped. I desire to be dressed in the dress of my ancestor the Count de Lauria, with his sword by my side and the order of the Golden Fleece on my breast. I leave the choice of my coffin to you. It should be unpretentious but suitable to my position. In order to give no one unnecessary trouble I desire that Thomas Cook and Son should make all arrangements for the transportation of my remains and that one of their men should accompany the coffin to its final resting-place.'

I remembered that Elliott had said he wanted to be buried in that fancy dress of his, but I had taken it for a passing whim and hadn't thought he meant it seriously. Joseph was insistent that his wishes be carried out and there seemed no reason why they should not be. The body was duly embalmed and then I went with Joseph to dress it in those absurd clothes. It was a gruesome business. We slipped his long legs into the white silk hose and pulled the cloth-of-gold over them. It was a job to get his arms through the sleeves of the doublet. We fixed the great starched ruff and draped the satin cape over his shoulders. Finally we placed the flat velvet cap on his head and the collar of the Golden Fleece round his neck. The embalmer had rouged his cheeks and reddened his lips. Elliott, the costume too large now for his emaciated frame, looked like a chorus man in an early opera of Verdi's. The sad Don Quixote of a worthless purpose. When the undertaker's men had put him in the coffin I laid the property sword down the length of his body, between his legs, with his hands on the pommel as I have seen the sword laid on the sculptured tomb of a Crusader.

Gray and Isabel went to Italy to attend the funeral.

VI

1

I FEEL it right to warn the reader that he can very well skip this chapter without losing the thread of such story as I have to tell, since for the most part it is nothing more than the account of a conversation that I had with Larry. I should add, however, that except for this conversation I should perhaps not have thought it worth while to write this book.

2

That autumn, a couple of months after Elliott's death, I spent a week in Paris on my way to England. Isabel and Gray, after their grim journey to Italy, had returned to Brittany, but were now once more settled in the apartment in the Rue St Guillaume. She told me the details of his will. He had left a sum of money for Masses to be said for his soul in the church he had built and a further sum for its upkeep. He had bequeathed a handsome amount to the Bishop of Nice to be spent on charitable purposes. He had left me the equivocal legacy of his eighteenth-century pornographic library and a beautiful drawing by Fragonard of a satyr engaged with a nymph on a performance that is usually conducted in private. It was too indecent to hang on my walls and I am not one to gloat upon obscenity in private. He had provided generously for his servants. His two nephews were to have ten thousand dollars each, and the residue of his estate went to Isabel. What this amounted to she did not tell me and I did not inquire; I gathered from her complacency that it was quite a lot of money.

For long, ever since he had regained his health, Gray had been impatient to go back to America and get to work again, and though Isabel was comfortable enough in Paris, his restlessness had affected her too. He had for some time been in communication with his friends, but the best opening that presented itself was contingent on his putting in a considerable amount of capital. That he had not got, but Elliott's death had put Isabel in possession of very much more than was needed; and Gray with her approval was starting negotiations with the view, if everything turned out as well as it was presented, of leaving Paris and going to look into the matter for himself. But before that was possible there was much to attend to. They had to come to a reasonable agreement with the French Treasury over the inheritance tax. They had to get rid of the house at Antibes and the apartment in the Rue St Guillaume. They had to arrange for a sale at the Hôtel Drouot of Elliott's furniture, pictures, and drawings. These were valuable and it seemed wise to wait till spring when the great collectors were likely to be in Paris. Isabel was not sorry to spend another winter there; the children by now could chatter French as easily as they could chatter English and she was glad to let them have a few more months at a French school. They had grown in three years and were now long-legged, skinny, vivacious little creatures, with little at present of their mother's beauty, but with nice manners and an insatiable curiosity.

So much for that.

I met Larry by chance. I had asked Isabel about him and she told me that since their return from La Baule they had seen little of him. She and Gray had by now made a number of friends for themselves, people of their own generation, and they were more often engaged than during the pleasant weeks when the four of us were so much together. One evening I went to the Théâtre Français to see *Bérénice*. I had read it of course, but had never seen it played, and since it is seldom given I was unwilling to miss the opportunity. It is not one of Racine's best plays, for the subject is too tenuous to support five acts, but it is moving and contains passages that are justly famous. The story is founded on a brief passage in Tacitus: Titus, who loved Bérénice, Queen of Palestine, with passion and who had even, as was supposed, promised her marriage, for reasons of state sent her away from Rome during the first days of his reign in despite of his desires and in despite of hers. For the Senate and the people of Rome were violently opposed to their Emperor's alliance with a foreign queen. The play is concerned with the struggle in his breast between love and duty, and when he falters, it is Bérénice who in the end, assured that he loves her, confirms his purpose and separates herself from him for ever.

I suppose only a Frenchman can appreciate to the full the grace and grandeur of Racine and the music of his verse, but even a foreigner, once he has accustomed himself to the peri-wigged formality of the style, can hardly fail to be moved by his passionate tenderness and by the nobility of his sentiment. Racine knew as few have done how much drama is contained in the human voice. To me at all events the roll of those melli-fluous Alexandrines is a sufficient substitute for action, and I find the long speeches, worked up with infinite skill to the ex-pected climax, every bit as thrilling as any hair-raising adven-ture of the movies.

There was an interval after the third act and I went out to smoke a cigarette in the foyer over which presides Houdon's Voltaire with his toothless, sardonic grin. Someone touched me on the shoulder. I turned round, perhaps with a slight movement of annoyance, for I wanted to be left with the exaltation with which those sonorous lines had filled me, and saw Larry. As always, I was glad to see him. It was a year since I had set eyes on him, and I suggested that at the end of the play we should meet and have a glass of beer together. Larry said he was hungry, for he had had no dinner, and proposed that we should go to Montmartre. We found one another in due course and stepped out into the open. The Théâtre Français has a musty fug that is peculiar to it. It is impregnated with the body odour of those unnumbered generations of sour-faced, unwashed women called *ouvreuses* who show you to your seat and domineeringly await their tip. It was a relief to get into the fresh air, and since the night was fine we walked. The arc lamps in the Avenue de l'Opéra glared so defiantly that the stars above, as though too proud to compete, shrouded their brightness in the dark of their infinite distance. As we walked we spoke of the performance we had just seen. Larry was disappointed. He would have liked it to be more natural, the lines spoken as people naturally speak and the gestures less theatrical. I thought his point of view mistaken. It was rhetoric, magnificent rhetoric, and I had a notion that it should be spoken rhetorically. I liked the regular thump of the rhymes; and the stylized gestures, handed down in a long tradition, seemed to me to suit the temper of that formal act. I could not but think that that was how Racine would have wished his play to be played. I had admired the way in which the actors had contrived to be human, passionate, and true within the limitations that confined them. Art is triumphant when it can use convention as an instrument of its own purpose.

We reached the Avenue de Clichy and went into the Brasserie Graf. It was not long past midnight and the room was crowded, but we found a table and ordered ourselves eggs and bacon. I told Larry I had seen Isabel.

'Gray will be glad to get back to America,' he said. 'He's a fish out of water here. He won't be happy till he's at work again. I dare say he'll make a lot of money.'

'If he does it'll be due to you. You not only cured him in body, but in spirit as well. You restored his confidence in himself.'

'I did very little. I merely showed him how to cure himself.'

'How did you learn to do that little?'

'By accident. It was when I was in India. I'd been suffering from insomnia and happened to mention it to an old Yogi I knew and he said he'd soon settle that. He did just what you saw me do with Gray and that night I slept as I hadn't slept for months. And then, a year later it must have been, I was in the Himalayas with an Indian friend of mine and he sprained his ankle. It was impossible to get a doctor and he was in great pain. I thought I'd try to do what the old Yogi had done, and it worked. You can believe it or not, he was completely relieved of the pain.' Larry laughed. 'I can assure you, no one was more surprised than I. There's nothing to it really; it only means putting the idea into the sufferer's mind.'

'Easier said than done.'

'Would it surprise you if your arm raised itself from the table without any volition of yours?'

'Very much.'

'It will. My Indian friend told people what I'd done when we got back to civilization and he brought others to see me. I hated doing it, because I couldn't quite understand it, but they insisted. Somehow or other I did them good. I found I was able to relieve people not only of pain but of fear. It's strange how many people suffer from it. I don't mean fear of closed spaces and fear of heights, but fear of death and, what's worse, fear of life. Often they're people who seem in the best of health, prosperous, without any worry, and yet they're tortured by it. I've sometimes thought it was the most besetting humour of men, and I asked myself at one time if it was due to some deep animal instinct that man has inherited from that primeval something that first felt the thrill of life.'

I was listening to Larry with expectation, for it was not often that he spoke at any length, and I had an inkling that for once he felt communicative. Perhaps the play we had just seen had released some inhibition and the rhythm of its sonorous cadences, as music will, had overcome his instinctive reserve. Suddenly I realized that something was happening to my hand. I had not given another thought to Larry's half-laughing question. I was conscious that my hand no longer rested on the

246

table, but was raised an inch above it without my willing it. I was taken aback. I looked at it and saw that it trembled slightly. I felt a queer tingling in the nerves of my arm, a little jerk, and my hand and forearm lifted of themselves, I to the best of my belief neither aiding nor resisting, until they were several inches from the table. Then I felt my whole arm being raised from the shoulder.

'This is very odd,' I said.

Larry laughed. I made the slightest effort of will and my hand fell back on to the table.

'It's nothing,' he said. 'Don't attach any importance to it.'

'Were you taught that by the Yogi you spoke to us about when you first came back from India?'

'Oh no, he had no patience with that kind of thing. I don't know whether he believed that he possessed the powers that some Yogis claim to have, but he would have thought it puerile to exercise them.'

Our eggs and bacon arrived and we ate them with good appetite. We drank our beer. Neither of us spoke. Larry was thinking of I knew not what and I was thinking of him. We finished. I lit a cigarette and he lit a pipe.

'What made you go to India in the first place?' I asked abruptly.

'Chance. At least I thought so at the time. Now I'm inclined to think it was the inevitable outcome of my years in Europe. Almost all the people who've had most effect on me I seem to have met by chance, yet looking back it seems as though I couldn't but have met them. It's as if they were waiting there to be called upon when I needed them. I went to India because I wanted a rest. I'd been working very hard and wished to sort out my thoughts. I got a job as a deck hand on one of those pleasure-cruise ships that go around the world. It was going to the East and through the Panama Canal to New York. I hadn't been to America for five years and I was homesick. I was depressed. You know how ignorant I was when we first met in Chicago all those years ago. I'd read an awful lot in Europe and seen a lot, but I was no nearer than when I started to what I was looking for.'

I wanted to ask him what that was, but had a feeling that

247

he'd just laugh, shrug his shoulders, and say it was a matter of no consequence.

'But why did you go as a deck hand?' I asked instead. 'You had money.'

'I wanted the experience. Whenever I've got water-logged spiritually, whenever I've absorbed all I can for the time, I've found it useful to do something of that sort. That winter, after Isabel and I broke off our engagement, I worked in a coal-mine near Lens for six months.'

It was then that he told me of those incidents that I have narrated in a previous chapter.

'Were you sore when Isabel threw you over?'

Before he answered he looked at me for some time with those strangely black eyes of his that seemed then to look inwards rather than out.

'Yes. I was very young. I'd made up my mind that we were going to marry. I'd made plans for the life that we were going to lead together. I expected it to be lovely.' He laughed faintly. 'But it takes two to make a marriage just as it takes two to make a quarrel. It had never occurred to me that the life I offered Isabel was a life that filled her with dismay. If I'd had any sense I'd never have suggested it. She was too young and ardent. I couldn't blame her. I couldn't yield.'

It's just possible that the reader will remember that on his flight from the farm, after that grotesque encounter with the farmer's widowed daughter-in-law, he had gone to Bonn. I was anxious to get him to continue, but knew I must be careful not to ask more direct questions than I could help.

'I've never been to Bonn,' I said. 'When I was a boy I spent some time as a student at Heidelberg. It was, I think, the happiest time of my life.'

'I liked Bonn. I spent a year there. I got a room in the house of the widow of one of the professors at the university who took in a couple of boarders. She and her two daughters, both of them middle-aged, did the cooking and the house-work. I found my fellow boarder was a Frenchman and I was disappointed at first because I wanted to speak nothing but German; but he was an Alsatian and he spoke German, if not more fluently, with a better accent than he spoke French. He was dressed like a German pastor and I was surprised to find out after a few days that he was a Benedictine monk. He's been granted leave of absence from his monastery to make researches at the university library. He was a very learned man, but he didn't look it any more than he looked like my idea of a monk. He was a tall, stout fellow, with sandy hair, prominent blue eyes, and a red, round face. He was shy and reserved and didn't seem to want to have anything much to do with me, but he was very polite in a rather elaborate way and always took a civil part in the conversation at table; I only saw him then; as soon as we had finished dinner he went back to work at the library, and after supper, when I sat in the parlour improving my German with whichever of the two daughters wasn't washing up, he retired to his room.

'I was surprised when one afternoon, after I'd been there at least a month, he asked me if I'd care to take a walk with him. He said he could show me places in the neighbourhood that he didn't think I'd be likely to discover for myself. I'm a pretty good walker, but he could outwalk me any day. We must have covered a good fifteen miles on that first walk. He asked me what I was doing in Bonn, and I said I'd come to learn German and get to know something about German literature. He talked very intelligently. He said he'd be glad to help me in any way he could. After that we went for walks two or three times a week. I discovered that he'd taught philosophy for some years. When I was in Paris I'd read a certain amount, Spinoza and Plato and Descartes, but I hadn't read any of the great German philosophers and I was only too glad to listen while he talked about them. One day, when we'd made an excursion across the Rhine and were sitting in a beer-garden drinking a glass of beer, he asked me if I was a Protestant.

' "I suppose so," I said.

'He gave me a quick look and I thought I saw in his eyes the glimmer of a smile. He began to talk about Aeschylus; I'd been learning Greek, you know, and he knew the great tragedians as I could never hope to know them. It was inspiring to hear him. I wondered why he'd suddenly asked me that question. My guardian, Uncle Bob Nelson, was an agnostic, but he went to church regularly because his patients expected it of him and sent me to Sunday school for the same reason. Martha, our help, was a rigid Baptist and she used to frighten my childhood by telling me of the hell fire to which the sinner would be condemned to all eternity. She took a real delight in picturing to me the agonies that would be endured by the various people in the village whom for some reason or other she had had it in for.

'By winter I'd got to know Father Ensheim very well. I think he was rather a remarkable man. I never saw him vexed. He was good-natured and kindly, far more broadminded than I would have expected, and wonderfully tolerant. His erudition was prodigious and he must have known how ignorant I was, but he used to talk to me as though I were as learned as he. He was very patient with me. He seemed to want nothing but to be of service to me. One day, I don't know why, I had an attack of lumbago, and Frau Grabau, my landlady, insisted on putting me to bed with hot-water-bottles. Father Ensheim, hearing I was laid up, came into my room to see me, after supper. Except that I was in a good deal of pain I felt perfectly well. You know what bookish people are, they're inquisitive about books, and as I put down the book I was reading when he came in, he took it up and looked at the title. It was a book about Meister Eckhart that I'd found at a bookseller's in the town. He asked me why I was reading it, so I said that I'd been going through a certain amount of mystical literature and told him about Kosti and how he'd aroused my interest in the subject. He surveyed me with his prominent blue eyes and there was a look in them that I can only describe as amused tenderness. I had the feeling that he found me rather ridiculous, but felt so much loving-kindness towards me that he didn't like me any the less. Anyhow, I've never much minded if people thought me a bit of a fool.

' "What are you looking for in these books?" he asked me.

' "If I knew that," I answered, "I'd at least be on the way to finding it."

' "Do you remember my asking you if you were a Protestant? You said you supposed so. What did you mean by that?"

' "I was brought up as one," I said.

' "Do you believe in God?" he asked.

250

'I don't like personal questions and my first impulse was to tell him that was no business of his. But there was so much goodness in his aspect that I felt it impossible to affront him. I didn't know what to say; I didn't want to answer yes and I didn't want to answer no. It may have been the pain I was suffering that enabled me to speak or it may have been something in him. Anyhow, I told him about myself.'

Larry hesitated for a moment, and when he went on I knew he wasn't speaking to me but to the Benedictine monk. He had forgotten me. I don't know what there was in the time or the place that enabled him to speak, without my prompting, of what his natural reticence had so long concealed.

'Uncle Bob Nelson was very democratic and he sent me to the high school at Marvin. It was only because Louisa Bradley nagged him into it that when I was fourteen he let me go to St Paul's. I wasn't very good at anything, either at work or games, but I fitted in all right. I think I was an entirely normal boy. I was crazy about aviation. Those were the early days of flying and Uncle Bob was as excited about it as I was. He knew some of the airmen, and when I said I wanted to learn to fly he said he'd fix it for me. I was tall for my age and when I was sixteen I could easily pass for eighteen. Uncle Bob made me promise to keep it a secret, because he knew everyone would be down on him like a ton of bricks for letting me go, but as a matter of fact he helped me to get over to Canada and gave me a letter to someone he knew, and the result was that by the time I was seventeen I was flying in France.

'They were terrible gimcrack planes we flew in then, and you practically took your life in your hands each time you went up. The heights we got to were absurd, judged by present standards, but we didn't know any better and thought it wonderful. I loved flying. I couldn't describe the feeling it gave me, I only knew I felt proud and happy. In he air, 'way up, I felt that I was part of something very great and very beautiful. I didn't know what it was all about, I only knew that I wasn't alone any more, by myself as I was, two thousand feet up, but that I belonged. I can't help it if it sounds silly. When I was flying above the clouds and they were like an enormous flock of sheep below me I felt that I was at home with infinitude.'

Larry paused. He gazed at me from the caverns of his impenetrable eyes, but I did not know whether he saw me.

'I'd known that men had been killed by the hundred thousand, but I hadn't seen them killed. It didn't mean very much to me. Then I saw a dead man with my own eyes. The sight filled me with shame.'

'Shame?' I exclaimed involuntarily.

'Shame, because that boy, he was only three or four years older than me, who'd had such energy and daring, who a moment before had had so much vitality, who'd been so good, was now just mangled flesh that looked as if it had never been alive.'

I didn't say anything. I had seen dead men when I was a medical student and I had seen many more during the war. What had dismayed me was how trifling they looked. There was no dignity in them. Marionettes that the showman had thrown into the discard.

'I didn't sleep that night. I cried. I wasn't frightened for myself; I was indignant; it was the wickedness of it that broke me. The war came to an end and I went home. I'd always been keen on mechanics, and if there was nothing doing in aviation, I'd intended to get into an automobile factory. I'd been wounded and had to take it easy for a while. Then they wanted me to go to work. I couldn't do the sort of work they wanted me to do. It seemed futile. I'd had a lot of time to think. I kept on asking myself what life was for. After all it was only by luck that I was alive; I wanted to make something of my life, but I didn't know what. I'd never thought much about God. I began to think about Him now. I couldn't understand why there was evil in the world. I knew I was very ignorant; I didn't know anyone I could turn to and I wanted to learn, so I began to read at haphazard.

'When I told Father Ensheim all this he asked me: "Then you've been reading for four years? Where have you got?"

' "Nowhere," I said.

'He looked at me with such an air of radiant benignity that I was confused. I didn't know what I'd done to arouse so much feeling in him. He softly drummed his fingers on the table as though he were turning a notion over in his mind.

' "Our wise old Church," he said then, "has discovered that if you will act as if you believed belief will be granted to you; if you pray with doubt, but pray with sincerity, your doubt will be dispelled; if you will surrender yourself to the beauty of that liturgy the power of which over the human spirit has been proved by the experience of the ages, peace will descend upon you. I am returning to my monastery in a little while. Why don't you come and spend a few weeks with us? You can work in the fields with our lay brothers; you can read in our library. It will be an experience no less interesting than working in a coal mine or on a German farm."

' "Why do you suggest it?" I asked.

' "I've been observing you for three months," he said. "Perhaps I know you better than you know yourself. The distance that separates you from faith is no greater than the thickness of a cigarette paper."

'I didn't say anything to that. It gave me a funny sort of feeling, as though someone had got hold of my heartstrings and were giving them a tug. At last I said I'd think about it. He dropped the subject. For the rest of Father Ensheim's stay in Bonn we never spoke of anything connected with religion again, but as he was leaving he gave me the address of his monastery and told me if I made up my mind to come I had only to write him a line and he'd make arrangements. I missed him more than I expected. The year wore on and it was midsummer. I liked it well enough in Bonn. I read Goethe and Schiller and Heine. I read Hölderlin and Rilke. Still I wasn't getting anywhere. I thought a lot of what Father Ensheim had said, and at last I decided to accept his offer.

'He met me at the station. The monastery was in Alsace and the country was pretty. Father Ensheim presented me to the abbot and then showed me to the cell that had been assigned to me. It had a narrow iron bed, a crucifix on the wall, and by way of furniture only the barest necessities. The dinner bell rang and I made my way to the refectory. It was a huge vaulted chamber. The abbot stood at the door with two monks, one of whom held a basin and the other a towel, and the abbot sprinkled a few drops of water on the hands of the guests by way of washing them and dried them with the towel one of the two monks handed him. There were three guests besides myself, two priests who were passing that way and had stopped off for dinner and an elderly, grouchy Frenchman who was making a retreat.

'The abbot and the two priors, senior and junior, sat at the head of the room, each at his separate table; the fathers along two sides of the walls, while the novices, the lay brothers, and the guests sat at tables in the middle. Grace was said and we ate. A novice took up his position near the refectory door and in a monotonous voice read from an edifying work. When we had finished grace was said again. The abbot, Father Ensheim, the guests, and the monk in charge of them went into a small room where we had coffee and talked of casual things. Then I went back to my cell.

'I stayed there three months. I was very happy. The life exactly suited me. The library was good and I read a great deal. None of the fathers tried in any way to influence me, but they were glad to talk to me. I was deeply impressed by their learning, their piety, and their unworldliness. You mustn't think it was an idle life they led. They were constantly occupied. They farmed their own land and worked it themselves and they were glad to have my help. I enjoyed the splendour of the services, but the one I liked best of all was Matins. It was at four in the morning. It was wonderfully moving to sit in the church with the night all around you while the monks, mysterious in their habits, their cowls drawn over their heads, sang with their strong male voices the plain-song of the liturgy. There was something reassuring in the regularity of the daily round, and notwithstanding all the energy that was displayed, notwithstanding the activity of thought, you had an abiding sense of repose.'

Larry smiled a trifle ruefully.

'Like Rolla, I've come too late into a world too old. I should have been born in the Middle Ages when faith was a matter of course; then my way would have been clear to me and I'd have sought to enter the order. I couldn't believe, I wanted to believe, but I couldn't believe in a God who wasn't better than the ordinary decent man. The monks told me that God had created the world for his glorification. That didn't seem to me a very worthy object. Did Beethoven create his symphonies for his glorification? I don't believe it. I believe he created them because the music in his soul demanded expression and then all he tried to do was to make them as perfect as he knew how.

'I used to listen to the monks repeating the Lord's Prayer; I wondered how they could continue to pray without misgiving to their heavenly father to give them their daily bread. Do children beseech their earthly father to give them sustenance? They expect him to do it, they neither feel nor need to feel gratitude to him for doing it, and we have only blame for a man who brings children into the world that he can't or won't provide for. It seemed to me that if an omnipotent creator was not prepared to provide his creatures with the necessities of existence, material and spiritual, he'd have done better not to create them.'

'Dear Larry,' I said, 'I think it's just as well you weren't born in the Middle Ages. You'd undoubtedly have perished at the stake.'

He smiled.

'You've had a great deal of success,' he went on. 'Do you want to be praised to your face?'

'It only embarrasses me.'

'That's what I should have thought. I couldn't believe that God wanted it either. We didn't think much in the air corps of a fellow who wangled a cushy job out of his C.O. by buttering him up. It was hard for me to believe that God thought much of a man who tried to wangle salvation by fulsome flattery. I should have thought the worship most pleasing to him was to do your best according to your lights.

'But that wasn't the chief thing that bothered me: I couldn't reconcile myself with that preoccupation with sin which, so far as I could tell, was never entirely absent from the monks' thoughts. I'd known a lot of fellows in the air corps. Of course they got drunk when they got a chance, and had a girl whenever they could, and used foul language; we had one or two bad hats: one fellow was arrested for passing rubber cheques and was sent to prison for six months; it wasn't altogether his fault; he'd never had any money before, and when he got more than he'd ever dreamt of having, it went to his head. I'd known bad men in Paris, and when I got back to Chicago I knew more, but for the most part their badness was due to heredity, which they couldn't help, or to their environment, which they didn't choose: I'm not sure that society wasn't more responsible for their crimes than they were. If I'd been God I couldn't have brought myself to condemn one of them, not even the worst, to eternal damnation. Father Ensheim was broad-minded; he thought that hell was the deprivation of God's presence, but if that is such an intolerable punishment that it can justly be called hell, can one conceive that a good God can inflict it? After all, He created men: if He so created them that it was possible for them to sin, it was because He willed it. If I trained a dog to fly at the throat of any stranger who came into my back yard, it wouldn't be fair to beat him when he did so.

'If an all-good and all-powerful God created the world, why did He create evil? The monks said, so that man by conquering the wickedness in him, by resisting temptation, by accepting pain and sorrow and misfortune as the trials sent by God to purify him, might at long last be made worthy to receive His grace. It seemed to me like sending a fellow with a message to some place and just to make it harder for him you constructed a maze that he had to get through, then dug a moat that he had to swim, and finally built a wall that he had to scale. I wasn't prepared to believe in an all-wise God who hadn't common sense. I didn't see why you shouldn't believe in a God who hadn't created the world, but had to make the best of the bad job he'd found, a being enormously better, wise, and greater than man, who strove with the evil he hadn't made and who you hoped might in the end overcome it. But on the other hand, I didn't see why you should.

'Those good fathers had no answers that satisfied either my head or my heart to the questions that perplexed me. My place was not with them. When I went to say good-bye to Father Ensheim he didn't ask me whether I had profited by the experience in the way he had been so sure I would. He looked at me with inexpressible kindness.

' "I'm afraid I've been a disappointment to you, Father," I said.

' "No," he answered. "You are a deeply religious man who

256

doesn't believe in God. God will seek you out. You'll come back. Whether here or elsewhere only God can tell."

'I settled down in Paris for the rest of the winter. I knew nothing of science, and I thought the time had come when I must acquire at least a nodding acquaintance with it. I read a lot. I don't know that I learnt much except that my ignorance was abysmal. But I knew that before. When the spring came I went to the country and stayed at a little inn on a river near one of those beautiful old French towns where life doesn't seem to have moved for two hundred years.'

I guessed that this was the summer Larry had spent with Suzanne Rouvier, but I did not interrupt him.

'After that I went to Spain. I wanted to see Velasquez and El Greco. I wondered if art could point out the way to me that religion hadn't. I wandered about a bit and then came to Seville. I liked it and thought I'd spend the winter there.'

I had myself been to Seville when I was twenty-three and I, too, had liked it. I liked its white, tortuous streets, its cathedral, and the wide-spreading plain of the Guadalquivir; but I liked also those Andalusian girls with their grace and their gaiety, with their dark shining eyes, the carnation in their hair stressing its blackness and by the contrast itself more vivid; I liked the rich colour of their skins and the inviting sensuality of their lips. Then indeed to be young was very heaven. When Larry went there he was only a little older than I had been and I could not but ask myself whether it was possible that he had remained indifferent to the lure of those enchanting creatures. He answered my unspoken question.

'I ran across a French painter I'd known in Paris, a fellow called Auguste Cottet, who'd kept Suzanne Rouvier at one time. He'd come to Seville to paint and was living with a girl he'd picked up there. He asked me to go with them one evening to Eretania to listen to a *flamenco* singer and they brought along with them a friend of hers. She was the prettiest little thing you ever saw. She was only eighteen. She'd got into trouble with a boy and had had to leave her native village because she was going to have a baby. The boy was doing his military service. After she had the baby she put it out to nurse and got a job in the tobacco factory. I took her home with me. She was very gay and very sweet, and after a few days I asked her if she'd like to come and live with me. She said she would, so we took a couple of rooms in a *casa de huéspedes,* a bedroom and a sitting-room. I told her she could leave her job, but she didn't want to, and that suited me because it left me my days to myself. We had the run of the kitchen, so she used to make my breakfast for me before she went to work and then at midday she'd come back and cook the lunch and in the evening we'd dine at a restaurant and go to a movie or to some place to dance. She looked upon me as a lunatic because I had a rubber bath and insisted on having a cold sponge every morning. The baby was farmed out in a village a few miles from Seville and we used to go and see it on Sundays. She made no secret of the fact that she was living with me to make enough money to furnish the lodging in a tenement they were going to take when her boy friend was through with his military service. She was a dear little thing and I'm sure she's made her Paco a good wife. She was cheerful, good-tempered, and affectionate. She looked upon what you delicately call sexual congress as a natural function of the body like any other. She took pleasure in it and she was happy to give pleasure. She was of course a little animal, but a very nice, attractive, domesticated animal.

'Then one evening she told me that she'd had a letter from Paco in Spanish Morocco, where he was doing his service, to say that he was to be released and would arrive in Cadiz in a couple of days. She packed her belongings next morning and slipped her money in her stocking and I took her to the station. She gave me a hearty kiss as I put her into the railway carriage, but she was too excited at the thought of seeing her lover again to have a thought for me and I'm sure that before the train was out of the station she'd forgotten my existence.

'I stayed on in Seville and in the fall I set out on the journey that landed me in India.'

5

It was getting late. The crowd had thinned out and only a few tables were occupied. The people who had been sitting there because they had nothing else to do had gone home. Those who had been to a play or a picture and had come to have a drink or a bite to eat had left. Now and then latecomers straggled in. I saw a tall man, evidently an Englishman, come in with a young rough. He had the long, washed-out face with thinning wavy hair of the British intellectual and evidently suffered from the delusion common to many that when you are abroad no one you know at home can possibly recognize you. The young rough greedily ate a great plate of sandwiches while his companion watched him with amused benevolence. What an appetite! I saw one man whom I knew by sight because he went to the same barber's at Nice. He was stout, elderly, and grey-haired, with a puffy red face and heavy pouches under his eyes. He was a Middle Western banker who had left his native city after the crash rather than face an investigation. I do not know whether he had committed any crime; if he had, he was perhaps too small fry to put the authorities to the trouble of getting him extradited. He had a pompous manner and the false heartiness of a cheap politician, but his eyes were frightened and unhappy. He was never quite drunk and never quite sober. He was always with some harlot who was obviously getting all she could out of him, and he was now with two painted middle-aged women who treated him with a mockery they didn't trouble to conceal while he, only half understanding what they said, giggled fatuously. The gay life! I wondered if he wouldn't have done better to stay at home and take his medicine. One day his women would have squeezed him dry and then there would be nothing left for him but the river or an overdose of veronal.

Between two and three there was a slight increase of custom and I supposed that the night clubs were closing their doors. A bunch of young Americans strolled in, very drunk and noisy, but they didn't stay long. Not far from us two fat, sombre women, tightly fitted into mannish clothes, sat side by side, drinking whiskies and sodas in gloomy silence. A party in evening dress put in an appearance, what they call in French *gens du monde*, who had evidently been doing the rounds and now wanted a spot of supper to finish up with. They came and went. My curiosity had been excited by a little man, quietly dressed, who had been sitting there for an hour or more with a glass of beer in front of him reading the paper. He had a neat black beard and wore pince-nez. At last a woman came in and joined him. He gave her a nod devoid of friendliness and I conjectured that he was annoyed because she had kept him waiting. She was young, rather shabby, but heavily painted, and looked very tired. Presently I noticed her take something out of her bag and hand it to him. Money. He looked at it and his face darkened. He addressed her in words I could not hear, but from her manner I guessed they were abusive, and she seemed to be making excuses. Suddenly he leant over and gave her a resounding smack on the cheek. She gave a cry and began to sob. The manager, drawn by the disturbance, came up to see what was the matter. It looked as if he were telling them to get out if they couldn't behave. The girl turned on him and shrilly, so that one heard every word, told him in foul language to mind his own business.

'If he slapped my face it's because I deserved it,' she cried.

Women! I had always thought that to live on a woman's immoral earnings you must be a strapping flashy fellow with sex appeal, ready with your knife or your gun; it was astonishing that such a puny creature, who might have been a lawyer's clerk from his appearance, could get a footing in such an overcrowded profession.

6

The waiter who had served us was going off duty and to get his tip presented the bill. We paid and ordered coffee.

'Well?' I said.

I felt that Larry was in the mood to talk and I knew that I was in the mood to listen.

'Aren't I boring you?'

'No.'

'Well, we got to Bombay. The ship was stopping there for three days to give the tourists a chance to see the sights and make excursions. On the third day I got the afternoon off and went ashore. I walked about for a while, looking at the crowd: what a conglomeration! Chinese, Mohammedans, Hindus, Tamils as black as your hat; and those great humped bullocks with their long horns that draw the carts! Then I went to Elephanta to see the caves. An Indian had joined us at Alexandria for the passage to Bombay and the tourists were rather sniffy about him. He was a fat little man with a brown round face and he wore a thick tweed suit of black and green check and a clerical collar. I was having a breath of air on deck one night and he came up and spoke to me. I didn't want to talk to anyone just then, I wanted to be alone; he asked me a lot of questions and I'm afraid I was rather short with him. Anyhow I told him I was a student working my passage back to America.

' "You should stop off in India," he said. "The East has more to teach the West than the West conceives."

' "Oh yes?" I said.

' "At any rate," he went on, "be sure you go and see the caves at Elephanta. You'll never regret it." ' Larry interrupted himself to ask me a question. 'Have you ever been to India?'

'Never.'

'Well, I was looking at the colossal image with its three heads which is the great sight at Elephanta and wondering what it was all about when I heard someone behind me say: "I see you've taken my advice." I turned round and it took me a minute to realize who it was that had spoken to me. It was the little man in the heavy check suit and the clerical collar, but now he was wearing a long saffron robe, the robe, I knew later, of the Ramakrishna Swamis; and instead of the funny, spluttering little guy he'd been before, he was dignified and rather splendid. We both stared at the colossal bust.

' "Brahma, the Creator," he said. "Vishnu the Preserver, and Siva the Destroyer. The three manifestations of the Ultimate Reality."

' "I'm afraid I don't quite understand," I said.

' "I'm not surprised," he answered, with a little smile on his lips and a twinkle in his eyes, as though he were gently mocking me. "A God that can be understood is no God. Who can explain the Infinite in words?"

'He joined the palms of his hands together and with just the indication of a bow strolled on. I stayed looking at those three mysterious heads. Perhaps because I was in a receptive mood,

261

I was strangely stirred. You know how sometimes you try to recall a name; it's on the tip of your tongue, but you just can't get it: that was the feeling I had then. When I came out of the caves I sat for a long while on the steps and looked at the sea. All I knew about Brahminism were those verses of Emerson's and I tried to remember them. It exasperated me that I couldn't and when I went back to Bombay I went into a bookshop to see if I could find a volume of poetry that had them in. They're in the *Oxford Book of English Verse*. D'you remember them?

> 'They reckon ill who leave me out;
> When me they fly, I am the wings;
> I am the doubter and the doubt,
> And I the hymn the Brahmin sings.

'I had supper in a native eating-house and then, as I didn't have to be on board till ten, I went and walked on the Maidan and looked at the sea. I thought I'd never seen so many stars in the sky. The cool was delicious after the heat of the day. I found a public garden and sat on a bench. It was very dark there and silent white figures flitted to and fro. That wonderful day, with the brilliant sunshine, the coloured, noisy crowds, the smell of the East, acrid and aromatic, enchanted me; and like an object, a splash of colour that a painter puts in to pull his composition together, those three enormous heads of Brahma, Vishnu, and Siva gave a mysterious significance to it all. My heart began to beat like mad, because I'd suddenly become aware of an intense conviction that India had something to give me that I had to have. It seemed to me that a chance was offered to me and I must take it there and then or it would never be offered me again. I made up my mind quickly. I decided not to go back to the ship. I'd left nothing there but a few things in a grip. I walked slowly back to the native quarter and looked about for a hotel. I found one after a while and took a room. I had the clothes I stood up in, some loose cash, my passport, and my letter of credit. I felt so free, I laughed out loud.

'The ship was sailing at eleven and just to be on the safe side I stayed in my room till then. I went down to the quay and

262

watched her pull out. After that I went to the Ramakrishna Mission and routed out the Swami who'd spoken to me at Elephanta. I didn't know his name, but I explained that I wanted to see the Swami who'd just arrived from Alexandria. I told him I'd decided to stay in India and asked him what I ought to see. We had a long talk and at last he said he was going to Benares that night and asked me if I'd like to go with him. I jumped at it. We went third-class. The carriage was full of people eating and drinking and talking and the heat was terrific. I didn't get a wink of sleep and next morning I was pretty tired, but the Swami was as fresh as a daisy. I asked him how come and he said: "By meditation on the formless one; I found rest in the Absolute." I didn't know what to think, but I could see with my own eyes that he was as alert and wide awake as though he'd had a good night's sleep in a comfortable bed.

'When at last we got to Benares a young man of my own age came to meet my companion and the Swami asked him to find me a room. His name was Mahendra and he was a teacher at the university. He was a nice, kindly, intelligent fellow and he seemed to take as great a fancy to me as I took to him. That evening he took me out in a boat on the Ganges; it was a thrill for me, very beautiful with the city crowding down to the water's edge, and awe-inspiring; but next morning he had something better to show me, he fetched me at my hotel before dawn and took me out on the river again. I saw something I could never have believed possible, I saw thousands upon thousands of people come down to take their lustral bath and pray. I saw one tall gaunt fellow, with a mass of tangled hair and a great ragged beard, with nothing but a jock-strap to cover his nakedness, stand with his long arms outstretched, his head up, and in a loud voice pray to the rising sun. I can't tell you what an impression it made on me. I spent six months in Benares and I went over and over again on the Ganges at dawn to see that strange sight. I never got over the wonder of it. Those people believed not halfheartedly, not with reservation or uneasy doubt, but with every fibre of their being.

'Everyone was very kind to me. When they discovered I hadn't come to shoot tigers or to buy or sell anything, but only to learn, they did everything to help me. They were pleased that I should wish to learn Hindustani, and found teachers for me. They lent me books. They were never tired of answering my questions. Do you know anything about Hinduism?'

'Very little,' I answered.

'I should have thought it would interest you. Can there be anything more stupendous than the conception that the universe has no beginning and no end, but passes everlastingly from growth to equilibrium, from equilibrium to decline, from decline to dissolution, from dissolution to growth, and so on to all eternity?'

'And what do the Hindus think is the object of this endless recurrence?'

'I think they'd say that such is the nature of the Absolute. You see, they believe that the purpose of creation is to serve as a stage for the punishment or reward of the deeds of the soul's earlier existences.'

'Which presupposes belief in the transmigration of souls.'

'It's a belief held by two thirds of the human race.'

'The fact that a great many people believe something is no guarantee of its truth.'

'No, but at least it makes it worthy of consideration. Christianity absorbed so much of Neo-Platonism, it might very easily have absorbed that too, and in point of fact there was an early Christian sect that believed in it, but it was declared heretical. Except for that Christians would believe in it as confidently as they believe in the resurrection of Christ.'

'Am I right in thinking that it means that the soul passes from body to body in an endless course of experience occasioned by the merit or demerit of previous works?'

'I think so.'

'But you see, I'm not only my spirit but my body, and who can decide how much I, my individual self, am conditioned by the accident of my body? Would Byron have been Byron but for his club foot, or Dostoyevsky Dostoyevsky without his epilepsy?'

'The Indians wouldn't speak of an accident. They would answer that it's your actions in previous lives that have determined your soul to inhabit an imperfect body.' Larry drummed

264

idly on the table and, lost in thought, gazed into space. Then, with a faint smile on his lips and a reflective look in his eyes, he went on. 'Has it occurred to you that transmigration is at once an explanation and a justification of the evil of the world? If the evils we suffer are the result of sins committed in our past lives we can bear them with resignation and hope that if in this one we strive towards virtue our future lives will be less afflicted. But it's easy enough to bear our own evils, all we need for that is a little manliness; what's intolerable is the evil, often so unmerited in appearance, that befalls others. If you can persuade yourself that it is the inevitable result of the past you may pity, you may do what you can to alleviate, and you should, but you have no cause to be indignant.'

'But why didn't God create a world free from suffering and misery at the beginning when there was neither merit nor demerit in the individual to determine his actions?'

'The Hindus would say that there was no beginning. The individual soul, co-existent with the universe, has existed from all eternity and owes its nature to some prior existence.'

'And does the belief in the transmigration of souls have a practical effect on the lives of those who believe it? After all, that is the test.'

'I think it has. I can tell you of one man I knew personally on whose life it certainly had a very practical effect. The first two or three years I was in India I lived mostly in native hotels, but now and then someone asked me to stay with him and once or twice I lived in grandeur as the guest of a maharajah. Through one of my friends in Benares I got an invitation to stay in one of the smaller northern states. The capital was lovely: *a rose-red city half as old as time.* I was recommended to the Minister of Finance. He'd had a European education and had been to Oxford. When you talked to him you got the impression of a progressive, intelligent, and enlightened man; and he had the reputation of being an extremely efficient minister and a clever, astute politician. He wore European clothes and was very natty in appearance. He was rather a nice-looking fellow, a little on the stout side as Indians tend to become in middle age, with a close-cropped, neat moustache. He often asked me to go to his house. He had a large garden and we'd sit under the shade of great trees and talk. He had a wife and two grown-up children. You'd have taken him for just the ordinary, rather commonplace Anglicized Indian and I was staggered when I found out that in a year, when he reached the age of fifty, he was going to resign his profitable position, dispose of his property to his wife and children, and go out into the world as a wandering mendicant. But the most surprising part was that his friends, and the maharajah, accepted it as a settled thing and looked upon it not as an extraordinary proceeding but as a natural one.

'One day I said to him: "You, who are so liberal, who know the world, who've read so much, science, philosophy, literature – do you in your heart of hearts believe in reincarnation?"

'His whole face changed. It became the face of a visionary.

' "My dear friend," he said, "if I didn't believe in it life would have no meaning for me." '

'And do you believe in it, Larry?' I asked.

'That's a very difficult question to answer. I don't think it's possible for us Occidentals to believe in it as implicitly as these Orientals do. It's in their blood and bones. With us it can only be an opinion. I neither believe in it nor disbelieve in it.'

He paused for a moment and with his face resting on his hand looked down at the table. Then he leant back.

'I should like to tell you of a very strange experience I had once. I was practising meditation one night in my little room at the Ashrama as my Indian friends had taught me to do. I had lit a candle and was concentrating my attention on its flame, and after a time, through the flame, but quite clearly, I saw a long line of figures one behind the other. The foremost was an elderly lady in a lace cap with grey ringlets that hung down over her ears. She wore a tight black bodice and a black silk flounced skirt – the sort of clothes, I think, they wore in the seventies – and she was standing full face to me in a gracious, diffident attitude, her arms hanging straight down her sides with the palms towards me. The expression on her lined face was kindly, sweet, and mild. Immediately behind her, but sideways so that I saw his profile, with a great hooked nose and thick lips, was a tall gaunt Jew in a yellow gabardine with a yellow skullcap on his thick dark hair. He had the studious look of a scholar and an air of grim and at the same time passionate austerity. Behind him, but facing me and as distinct as though there were no one between us, was a young man with a cheerful ruddy countenance, whom you couldn't have taken for anything but an Englishman of the sixteenth century. He stood firmly on his feet, his legs a little apart, and he had a bold, reckless, wanton look. He was dressed all in red, grandly as though it were a court dress, with broad-toed velvet shoes on his feet and a flat velvet cap on his head. Behind those three there was an endless chain of figures, like a queue outside a movie house, but they were dim and I couldn't see what they looked like. I was only aware of their vague shapes and of the movement that passed through them like wheat waving in a summer breeze. In a little while, I don't know whether it was in a minute, or five, or ten, they faded slowly into the darkness of the night and there was nothing but the steady flame of the candle.'

Larry gave a little smile.

'Of course it may be that I'd fallen into a doze and dreamt. It may be that my concentration on that feeble flame had induced a sort of hypnotic condition in me and that those three figures that I saw as distinctly as I see you were recollections of pictures preserved in my subconscious. But it may be that they were myself in past lives. It may be that I was not so very long ago an old lady in New England and before that a Levantine Jew and somewhere back, soon after Sebastian Cabot had sailed from Bristol, a gallant at the Court of Henry Prince of Wales.'

'What eventually happened to your friend of the rose-red city?'

'Two years later I was down south at a place called Madura. One night in the temple someone touched me on the arm. I looked round and saw a bearded man with long black hair, dressed in nothing but a loincloth, with the staff and the begging-bowl of the holy man. It was not till he spoke that I recognized him. It was my friend. I was so astounded that I didn't know what to say. He asked me what I'd been doing and I told him; he asked me where I was going and I said to Travancore; he told me to go and see Shri Ganesha. "He will give you

267

what you're looking for," he said. I asked him to tell me about him, but he smiled and said I'd find out all that was necessary for me to know when I saw him. I'd got over my surprise by then and asked him what he was doing in Madura. He said he was making a pilgrimage on foot to the holy places of India. I asked him how he ate and how he slept. He told me that when anyone offered him shelter he slept on the veranda, but otherwise under a tree or in the precincts of a temple; and as for food, if people offered him a meal he ate it and if they didn't he went without. I looked at him: "You've lost weight," I said. He laughed and answered that he felt all the better for it. Then he said good-bye to me – it was funny to hear that guy in a loincloth say, "Well, so long, old chap" – and stepped into that part of the temple where I couldn't follow him.

'I stayed in Madura for some time. I think it's the only temple in India in which the white man can walk about freely so long as he doesn't enter the holy of holies. At nightfall it was packed with people. Men, women, and children. The men, stripped to the waist, wore dhoties, and their foreheads, and often their chests and arms, were thickly smeared with the white ash of burnt cow dung. You saw them making obeisance at one shrine or another and sometimes lying full length on the ground, face downwards, in the ritual attitude of prostration. They prayed and recited litanies. They called to one another, quarrelled with one another, heatedly argued with one another. There was an ungodly row, and yet in some mysterious way God seemed to be near and living.

'You pass through long halls, the roof supported by sculptured columns, and at the foot of each column a religious mendicant is seated; each has in front of him a bowl for offerings or a small mat on which the faithful now and again throw a copper coin. Some are clad; some are almost naked. Some look at you vacantly as you pass; some are reading, silently or aloud, and appear unconscious of the streaming throng. I looked for my friend among them; I never saw him again. I suppose he proceeded on the journey to his goal.'

'And what was that?'

'Liberation from the bondage of rebirth. According to the Vedantists the self, which they call the atman and we call the soul, is distinct from the body and its senses, distinct from the mind and its intelligence; it is not part of the Absolute, for the Absolute, being infinite, can have no parts, but the Absolute itself. It is uncreated; it has existed from eternity and when at last it has cast off the seven veils of ignorance will return to the infinitude from which it came. It is like a drop of water that has arisen from the sea and in a shower has fallen into a puddle, then drifts into a brook, finds its way into a stream, after that into a river, passing through mountain gorges and wide plains, winding this way and that, obstructed by rocks and fallen trees, till at last it reaches the boundless sea from which it rose.'

'But that poor little drop of water, when it has once more become one with the sea, has surely lost its individuality.'

Larry grinned.

'You want to taste sugar, you don't want to become sugar. What is individuality but the expression of our egoism? Until the soul has shed the last trace of that it cannot become one with the Absolute.'

'You talk very familiarly of the Absolute, Larry, and it's an imposing word. What does it actually signify to you?'

'Reality. You can't say what it is; you can only say what it isn't. It's inexpressible. The Indians call it Brahman. It's no-where and everywhere. All things imply and depend upon it. It's not a person, it's not a thing, it's not a cause. It has no qualities. It transcends permanence and change; whole and part, finite and infinite. It is eternal because its completeness and perfection are unrelated to time. It is truth and freedom.'

'Golly!' I said to myself, but to Larry: 'But how can a purely intellectual conception be a solace to the suffering human race? Men have always wanted a personal God to whom they can turn in distress for comfort and encouragement.'

'It may be that at some far distant day greater insight will show them that they must look for comfort and encouragement in their own souls. I myself think that the need to worship is no more than the survival of an old remembrance of cruel gods that had to be propitiated. I believe that God is within me or nowhere. If that's so, whom or what am I to worship – myself? Men are on different levels of spiritual development, and so the imagination of India has evolved the manifestations of the Absolute that are known as Brahma, Vishnu, Siva, and by a hundred other names. The Absolute is in Isvara, the creator and ruler of the world, and it is in the humble fetish before which the peasant in his sun-baked field places the offering of a flower. The multitudinous gods of India are but expedients to lead to the realization that the self is one with the supreme self.'

I looked at Larry reflectively.

'I wonder just what it was that attracted you to this austere faith,' I said.

'I think I can tell you. I've always felt that there was something pathetic in the founders of religion who made it a condition of salvation that you should believe in them. It's as though they needed your faith to have faith in themselves. They remind you of those old pagan gods who grew wan and faint if they were not sustained by the burnt offerings of the devout. Advaita doesn't ask you to take anything on trust; it asks only that you should have a passionate craving to know Reality; it states that you can experience God as surely as you can experience joy or pain. And there are men in India today – hundreds of them for all I know – who have the certitude that they have done so. I found something wonderfully satisfying in the notion that you can attain Reality by knowledge. In later ages the sages of India in recognition of human infirmity admitted that salvation may be won by the way of love and the way of works, but they never denied that the noblest way, though the hardest, is the way of knowledge, for its instrument is the most precious faculty of man, his reason.'

7

I must interrupt myself to make it plain that I am not attempting here to give anything in the nature of a description of the philosophical system known as Vedanta. I have not the knowledge to do so, but even if I had this would not be the proper place for it. Our conversation was a long one and Larry told me a great deal more than I have felt it possible to set down in what after all purports to be a novel. My concern is with Larry. I should not have touched on such an intricate subject at all except that it seemed to me that without at least some slight account of his speculations and the singular experiences that were perhaps occasioned by them I could not give plausibility to the line of conduct which he was led to adopt and with which I shall presently acquaint the reader. It irks me that I cannot hope with any words of mine to give an idea of the pleasantness of his voice that invested even his most casual utterances with persuasiveness, or of the constant change in his expression, from grave to gently gay, from reflective to playful, that accompanied his thoughts like the ripple of a piano when the violins with a great sweep sing the several themes of a concerto. Although he spoke of serious things he spoke of them quite naturally, in a conversational tone, with a certain diffidence, perhaps, but without any more constraint than if he had been speaking of the weather and the crops. If I have given the impression that there was anything didactic in his manner the fault is mine. His modesty was as evident as his sincerity.

There was no more than a sprinkling of people in the café. The roisterers had long since departed. The sad creatures who make a business of love had gone to their sordid dwellings. Now and then a tired-looking man came in to have a glass of beer and a sandwich, or one, who seemed only half awake, for a cup of coffee. White-collar workers. One had been on a night shift and was going home to bed; the other, roused by the call of an alarm clock, was on his unwilling way to the long day's labour. Larry appeared as unconscious of the time as of the surroundings. I have found myself in the course of my life in many strange situations. More than once I have been within a hair's breadth of death. More than once I have touched hands with romance and known it. I have ridden a pony through Central Asia along the road that Marco Polo took to reach the fabulous lands of Cathay; I have drunk a glass of Russian tea in a prim parlour in Petrograd while a soft-spoken little man in a black coat and striped trousers told me how he had assassinated a grand duke. I have sat in a drawing-room in Westminster and listened to the serene geniality of a piano trio of Haydn's while the bombs were crashing without; but I do not think I have ever found myself in a stranger situation than when I sat on the red-plush seats of that garish restaurant for hour after hour while Larry talked of God and eternity, of the Absolute and the weary wheel of endless becoming.

8

Larry had been silent for a few minutes, and unwilling to hurry him, I waited. Presently he gave me a friendly little smile as though he had suddenly once more become aware of me.

'When I got down to Travancore I found I needn't have asked for information about Shri Ganesha. Everyone knew of him. For many years he'd lived in a cave in the hills, but finally he'd been persuaded to move down to the plain where some charitable person had given him a plot of land and had built a little adobe house for him. It was a long way from Trivandrum, the capital, and it took me all day, first by train and then by bullock cart, to get to the Ashrama. I found a young man at the entrance of the compound and asked him if I could see the Yogi. I'd brought with me the basket of fruit which is the customary gift to offer. In a few minutes the young man came back and led me into a long hall with windows all around it. In one corner Shri Ganesha sat in the attitude of meditation on a raised dais covered with a tiger skin. "I've been expecting you," he said. I was surprised, but supposed my friend of Madura had told him something about me. But he shook his head when I mentioned his name. I presented my fruit and he told the young man to take it away. We were left alone and he looked at me without speaking. I don't know how long the silence lasted. It might have been for half an hour. I've told you what he looked like; what I haven't told you is the serenity that he irradiated, the goodness, the peace, the selflessness. I was hot and tired after my journey, but gradually I began to feel wonderfully rested. Before he'd said another word I knew that this was the man I'd been seeking.'

'Did he speak English?' I interrupted.

'No. But, you know, I'm pretty quick at languages, I'd picked up enough Tamil to understand and make myself understood in the South. At last he spoke.

' "What have you come here for?" he asked.

'I began to tell him how I'd come to India and how I'd

272

passed my time for three years; how, on report of their wisdom and sanctity, I'd gone to one holy man after another and had found no one to give me what I looked for. He interrupted me.

' "All that I know. There is no need to tell me. What have you come here for?"

' "So that you may be my Guru," I answered.

' "Brahman alone is the Guru," he said.

'He continued to look at me with a strange intensity and then suddenly his body became rigid, his eyes seemed to turn inwards, and I saw that he'd fallen into the trance which the Indians call Samadhi and in which they hold the duality of subject and object vanishes and you become Knowledge Absolute. I was sitting cross-legged on the floor, in front of him, and my heart beat violently. After how long a time I don't know he sighed and I realized that he had recovered normal consciousness. He gave me a glance sweet with loving-kindness.

' "Stay," he said. "They will show you where you may sleep."

'I was given as a dwelling-place the shack in which Shri Ganesha had lived when first he came down to the plain. The hall in which he now passed both day and night had been built when disciples gathered around him and more and more people, attracted by his fame, came to visit him. So that I mightn't be conspicuous I adopted the comfortable Indian dress and I got so sunburnt that unless your attention was drawn to me you might have taken me for a native. I read a great deal. I meditated. I listened to Shri Ganesha when he chose to talk; he didn't talk very much, but he was always willing to answer questions and it was wonderfully inspiring to listen to him. It was like music in your ears. Though in his youth he had himself practised very severe austerities he did not enjoin them on his disciples. He sought to wean them from the slavery of self-hood, passion, and sense, and told them that they could acquire liberation by tranquillity, restraint, renunciation, resignation, by steadfastness of mind and by an ardent desire for freedom. People used to come from the nearby town three or four miles away, where there was a famous temple to which great crowds flocked once a year for a festival; they came from Trivandrum and from far-off places to tell him their troubles, to ask his advice, to listen to his teaching; and all went away strengthened

273

in soul and at peace with themselves. What he taught was very simple. He taught that we are all greater than we know and that wisdom is the means to freedom. He taught that it is not essential to salvation to retire from the world, but only to renounce the self. He taught that work done with no selfish interest purifies the mind and that duties are opportunities afforded to man to sink his separate self and become one with the universal self. But it wasn't his teaching that was so remarkable; it was the man himself, his benignity, his greatness of soul, his saintliness. His presence was a benediction. I was very happy with him. I felt that at last I had found what I wanted. The weeks, the months passed with unimaginable rapidity. I proposed to stay either till he died, and he told us that he did not intend very much longer to inhabit his perishable body, or till I received illumination, the state when you have at last burst the bonds of ignorance, and know with a certainty there is no disputing that you and the Absolute are one.'

'And then?'

'Then, if what they say is true, there is nothing more. The soul's course on earth is ended and it will return no more.'

'And is Shri Ganesha dead?' I asked.

'Not so far as I know.'

As he spoke he saw what was implied in my question and gave a light laugh. He went on after a moment's hesitation, but in such a manner as led me at first to suppose that he wished to avoid answering the second question that he well knew was on the tip of my tongue, the question, of course, whether he had received illumination.

'I didn't stay at the Ashrama continuously. I was lucky enough to make the acquaintance of a native forestry officer whose permanent residence was on the outskirts of a village at the foot of the mountains. He was a devotee of Shri Ganesha and when he could get away from his work came and spent two or three days with us. He was a nice fellow and we had long talks. He liked to practise his English on me. After I'd known him for some time, he told me that the forestry service had a bungalow up in the mountains and if ever I wanted to go there to be by myself he would give me the key. I went there now and then. It was a two-day journey; first you had to go

274

by bus to the forestry officer's village, then you had to walk, but when you got there it was magnificent in its grandeur and its solitude. I took what I could in a knapsack on my back and hired a bearer to carry provisions for me, and I stayed till they were exhausted. It was only a log cabin with a cookhouse behind it and for furniture there was nothing but a trestle bed on which to put your sleeping-mat, a table, and a couple of chairs. It was cool up there and at times it was pleasant to light a fire at night. It gave me a wonderful thrill to know that there wasn't a living soul within twenty miles of me. At night I used often to hear the roar of a tiger or the racket of elephants as they crashed through the jungle. I used to take long walks in the forest. There was one place where I loved to sit because from it I saw the mountains spread before me and below, a lake to which at dusk the wild animals, deer, pig, bison, elephant, leopard came to drink.

'When I'd been at the Ashrama just two years I went up to my forest retreat for a reason that'll make you smile. I wanted to spend my birthday there. I got there the day before. Next morning I awoke before dawn and I thought I'd go and see the sunrise from the place I've just told you about. I knew the way blindfold. I sat down under a tree and waited. It was night still, but the stars were pale in the sky, and day was at hand. I had a strange feeling of suspense. So gradually that I was hardly aware of it light began to filter through the darkness, slowly, like a mysterious figure slinking between the trees. I felt my heart beating as though at the approach of danger. The sun rose.'

Larry paused and a rueful smile played on his lips.

'I have no descriptive talent, I don't know the words to paint a picture; I can't tell you, so as to make you see it, how grand the sight was that was displayed before me as the day broke in its splendour. Those mountains with their deep jungle, the mist still entangled in the treetops, and the bottomless lake far below me. The sun caught the lake through a cleft in the heights and it shone like burnished steel. I was ravished with the beauty of the world. I'd never known such exaltation and such a transcendent joy. I had a strange sensation, a tingling that arose in my feet and travelled up to my head, and I felt as though I were suddenly released from my body and as pure spirit partook of a loveliness I had never conceived. I had a sense that a knowledge more than human possessed me, so that everything that had been confused was clear and everything that had perplexed me was explained. I was so happy that it was pain and I struggled to release myself from it, for I felt that if it lasted a moment longer I should die; and yet it was such rapture that I was ready to die rather than forgo it. How can I tell you what I felt? No words can tell the ecstasy of my bliss. When I came to myself I was exhausted and trembling. I fell asleep.

'It was high noon when I woke. I walked back to the bungalow, and I was so light at heart that it seemed to me that I hardly touched the ground. I made myself some food, gosh, I was hungry, and I lit my pipe.'

Larry lit his pipe now.

'I dared not think that this was illumination that I, Larry Darrell of Marvin, Illinois, had received when others striving for it for years, with austerity and mortification, still waited.'

'What makes you think that it was anything more than a hypnotic condition induced by your state of mind combined with the solitude, the mystery of the dawn, and the burnished steel of your lake?'

'Only my overwhelming sense of its reality. After all it was an experience of the same order as the mystics have had all over the world through all the centuries, Brahmins in India, Sufis in Persia, Catholics in Spain, Protestants in New England; and so far as they've been able to describe what defies description they've described it in similar terms. It's impossible to deny the fact of its occurrence; the only difficulty is to explain it. If I was for a moment one with the Absolute or if it was an inrush from the subconscious of an affinity with the universal spirit which is latent in all of us, I wouldn't know.'

Larry paused for an instant and threw me a quizzical glance.

'By the way, can you touch your little finger with your thumb?' he asked.

'Of course,' I said with a laugh, proving it with the appropriate action.

'Are you aware that that's something that only man and the primates can do? It's because the thumb is opposable to the

276

other digits that the hand is the admirable instrument it is. Isn't it possible that the opposable thumb, doubtless in a rudimentary form, was developed in the remote ancestor of man and the gorilla in certain individuals, and was a characteristic that only became common to all after innumerable generations? Isn't it at least possible that these experiences of oneness with Reality that so many diverse persons have had point to a development in the human consciousness of a sixth sense which in the far, far future will be common to all men so that they may have as direct a perception of the Absolute as we have now of the objects of sense?'

'And how would you expect that to affect them?' I asked.

'I can as little tell you that as the first creature that found it could touch its little finger with its thumb could have told you that infinite consequences were entailed in that insignificant action. So far as I'm concerned I can only tell you that the intense sense of peace, joy, and assurance that possessed me in that moment of rapture abides with me still and that the vision of the world's beauty is as fresh and vivid now as when first my eyes were dazzled by it.'

'But Larry, surely your idea of the Absolute forces you to believe that the world and its beauty are merely an illusion – the fabric of Maya.'

'It's a mistake to think that the Indians look upon the world as an illusion; they don't; all they claim is that it's not real in the same sense as the Absolute. Maya is only a speculation devised by those ardent thinkers to explain how the Infinite could produce the Finite. Samkara, the wisest of them all, decided that it was an insoluble mystery. You see, the difficulty is to explain why Brahman, which is Being, Bliss, and Intelligence, which is unalterable, which ever is and forever maintains itself in rest, which lacks nothing and needs nothing and so knows neither change nor strife, which is perfect, should create the world. Well, if you ask that question the answer you're generally given is that the Absolute created the world in sport without reference to any purpose. But when you think of flood and famine, of earthquake and hurricane and all the ills that flesh is heir to, your moral sense is outraged at the idea that so much that is shocking can have been created in play. Shri Ganesha had too much kindliness of heart to believe that; he looked upon the world as the expression of the Absolute and as the overflow of its perfection. He taught that God cannot help creating and that the world is the manifestation of his nature. When I asked how, if the world was a manifestation of the nature of a perfect being, it should be so hateful that the only reasonable aim man can set before him is to liberate himself from its bondage, Shri Ganesha answered that the satisfactions of the world are transitory and that only the Infinite gives enduring happiness. But endless duration makes good no better, nor white any whiter. If the rose at noon has lost the beauty it had at dawn, the beauty it had then was real. Nothing in the world is permanent, and we're foolish when we ask anything to last, but surely we're still more foolish not to take delight in it while we have it. If change is of the essence of existence one would have thought it only sensible to make it the premiss of our philosophy. We can none of us step into the same river twice, but the river flows on and the other river we step into is cool and refreshing too.

'The Aryans when they first came down into India saw that the world we know is but an appearance of the world we know not; but they welcomed it as gracious and beautiful; it was only centuries later, when the exhaustion of conquest, when the debilitating climate had sapped their vitality so that they became a prey to invading hordes, that they saw only evil in life and craved for liberation from its return. But why should we of the West, we Americans especially, be daunted by decay and death, hunger and thirst, sickness, old age, grief, and delusion? The spirit of life is strong in us. I felt more alive then, as I sat in my log cabin smoking my pipe, than I had ever felt before. I felt in myself an energy that cried out to be expended. It was not for me to leave the world and retire to a cloister, but to live in the world and love the objects of the world, not indeed for themselves, but for the Infinite that is in them. If in those moments of ecstasy I had indeed been one with the Absolute, then, if what they said was true, nothing could touch me and when I had worked out the karma of my present life I should return no more. The thought filled me with dismay. I wanted to live again and again. I was willing to accept every sort of life, no matter what its pain and sorrow; I felt that only life after life, life after life could satisfy my eagerness, my vigour, and my curiosity.

'Next morning I started down the mountain and the day after arrived at the Ashrama. Shri Ganesha was surprised to see me in European clothes. I'd put them on at the forestry officer's bungalow when I started uphill because it was colder there and hadn't thought to change them.

' "I've come to bid you farewell, master," I said. "I am going back to my own people."

'He did not speak. He was sitting, as ever, cross-legged on the tiger skin on the dais. A stick of incense burnt in the brazier before it and scented the air with its faint fragrance. He was alone as he had been on the first day I saw him. He looked at me with an intensity so piercing that I had the impression he saw into the deepest recesses of my being. I know he knew what had happened.

' "It is well," he said. "You have been gone long enough."

'I went down on my knees and he gave me his blessing. When I rose to my feet my eyes were filled with tears. He was a man of noble and saintly character. I shall always look upon it as a privilege to have known him. I said good-bye to the devotees. Some had been there for years; some had come after me. I left my few belongings and my books, thinking they might be useful to someone, and with my knapsack on my back, in the same old slacks and brown coat I had arrived in, a battered topee on my head, I trudged back to the town. A week later I boarded a ship at Bombay and landed at Marseilles.'

Silence fell upon us as we pursued our separate reflections; but, tired though I was, there was one more point which I very much wanted to put to him, and it was I who finally spoke.

'Larry, old boy,' I said, 'this long quest of yours started with the problem of evil. It was the problem of evil that urged you on. You've said nothing all this time to indicate that you've reached even a tentative solution of it.'

'It may be that there is no solution or it may be that I'm not clever enough to find it. Ramakrishna looked upon the world as the sport of God. "It is like a game," he said. "In this

279

game there are joy and sorrow, virtue and vice, knowledge and ignorance, good and evil. The game cannot continue if sin and suffering are altogether eliminated from the creation." I would reject that with all my strength. The best I can suggest is that when the Absolute manifested itself in the world evil was the natural correlation of good. You could never have had the stupendous beauty of the Himalayas without the unimaginable horror of a convulsion of the earth's crust. The Chinese craftsman who makes a vase in what they call eggshell porcelain can give it a lovely shape, ornament it with a beautiful design, stain it a ravishing colour, and give it a perfect glaze, but from its very nature he can't make it anything but fragile. If you drop it on the floor it will break into a dozen fragments. Isn't it possible in the same way that the values we cherish in the world can only exist in combination with evil?'

'It's an ingenious notion, Larry. I don't think it's very satisfactory.'

'Neither do I,' he smiled. 'The best to be said for it is that when you've come to the conclusion that something is inevitable all you can do is to make the best of it.'

'What are your plans now?'

'I've got a job of work to finish here and then I shall go back to America.'

'What to do?'

'Live.'

'How?'

He answered very coolly, but with an impish twinkle in his eyes, for he knew very well how little I expected such a reply.

'With calmness, forbearance, compassion, selflessness, and continence.'

'A tall order,' I said. 'And why continence? You're a young man; is it wise to attempt to suppress what with hunger is the strongest instinct of the human animal?'

'I am in the fortunate position that sexual indulgence with me has been a pleasure rather than a need. I know by personal experience that in nothing are the wise men of India more dead right than in their contention that chastity intensely enhances the power of the spirit.'

'I should have thought that wisdom consisted in striking a

balance between the claims of the body and the claims of the spirit.'

'That is just what the Indians maintain that we in the West haven't done. They think that we with our countless inventions, with our factories and machines and all they produce, have sought happiness in material things, but that happiness rests not in them, but in spiritual things. And they think the way we have chosen leads to destruction.'

'And are you under the impression that America is a suitable place to practise the particular virtues you mentioned?'

'I don't see why not. You Europeans know nothing about America. Because we amass large fortunes you think we care for nothing but money. We care nothing for it; the moment we have it we spend it, sometimes well, sometimes ill, but we spend it. Money is nothing to us; it's merely the symbol of success. We are the greatest idealists in the world; I happen to think that we've set our ideal on the wrong objects; I happen to think that the greatest ideal man can set before himself is self-perfection.'

'It's a noble one, Larry.'

'Isn't it worth while to try to live up to it?'

'But can you for a moment imagine that you, one man, can have any effect on such a restless, busy, lawless, intensely individualistic people as the people of America? You might as well try to hold back the waters of the Mississippi with your bare hands.'

'I can try. It was one man who invented the wheel. It was one man who discovered the law of gravitation. Nothing that happens is without effect. If you throw a stone in a pond the universe isn't quite the same as it was before. It's a mistake to think that those holy men of India lead useless lives. They are a shining light in the darkness. They represent an ideal that is a refreshment to their fellows; the common run may never attain it, but they respect it and it affects their lives for good. When a man becomes pure and perfect the influence of his character spreads so that they who seek truth are naturally drawn to him. It may be that if I lead the life I've planned for myself it may affect others; the effect may be no greater than the ripple caused by a stone thrown in a pond, but one ripple causes another, and that one a third; it's just possible that a few people will see that my way of life offers happiness and peace, and that they in their turn will teach what they have learnt to others.'

'I wonder if you have any idea what you're up against, Larry. You know, the Philistines have long since discarded the rack and stake as a means of suppressing the opinions they feared: they've discovered a much more deadly weapon of destruction – the wisecrack.'

'I'm a pretty tough guy,' smiled Larry.

'Well, all I can say is that it's damned lucky for you that you have a private income.'

'It's been of great use to me. Except for that I shouldn't have been able to do all I've done. But my apprenticeship is over. From now on it can only be a burden to me. I shall rid myself of it.'

'That would be very unwise. The only thing that may make the kind of life you propose possible is financial independence.'

'On the contrary, financial independence would make the life I propose meaningless.'

I couldn't restrain a gesture of impatience.

'It may be all very well for the wandering mendicant in India; he can sleep under a tree and the pious are willing enough to acquire merit by filling his begging-bowl with food. But the American climate is far from suitable for sleeping out in the open, and though I don't pretend to know much about America, I do know that if there's one thing your countrymen are agreed upon it is that if you want to eat you must work. My poor Larry, you'd be sent to the workhouse as a vagrant before ever you got into your stride.'

He laughed.

'I know. One must adapt oneself to one's environment and of course I'd work. When I get to America I shall try to get a job in a garage. I'm a pretty good mechanic and I don't think it ought to be difficult.'

'Wouldn't you then be wasting energy that might be more usefully employed in other ways?'

'I like manual labour. Whenever I've got waterlogged with study I've taken a spell of it and found it spiritually invigorating. I remember reading a biography of Spinoza and thinking how silly the author was to look upon it as a terrible hardship that in order to earn his scanty living Spinoza had to polish lenses. I'm sure it was a help to his intellectual activity, if only because it diverted his attention for a while from the hard work of speculation. My mind is free when I'm washing a car or tinkering with a carburettor and when the job's done I have the pleasant sensation of having accomplished something. Naturally I wouldn't want to stay in a garage indefinitely. It's many years since I was in America and I must learn it afresh. I shall try to get work as a truck driver. In that way I should be able to travel from end to end of the country.'

'You've forgotten perhaps the most important use of money. It saves time. Life is so short, and there's so much to do, one can't afford to waste a minute; and just think how much you waste, for instance, in walking from place to place instead of going by bus and in going by bus instead of by taxi.'

Larry smiled.

'True enough and I hadn't thought of it, but I could cope with that difficulty by having my own taxi.'

'What d'you mean by that?'

'Eventually I shall settle in New York, among other reasons because of its libraries; I can live on very little, I don't mind where I sleep and I'm quite satisfied with one meal a day; by the time I've seen all I want to of America I should be able to have saved enough to buy a taxi and become a taxi driver.'

'You ought to shut up, Larry. You're as crazy as a loon.'

'Not at all. I'm very sensible and practical. As an owner-driver I would need to work only for as many hours as would provide for my board and lodging and for the depreciation on the car. The rest of my time I could devote to other work and if I wanted to go anywhere in a hurry I could always go in my taxi.'

'But, Larry, a taxi is just as much of a possession as a government bond,' I said, to tease him. 'As an owner-driver you'd be a capitalist.'

He laughed.

'No. My taxi would be merely the instrument of my labour.

283

It would be an equivalent to the staff and the begging-bowl of the wandering mendicant.'

On this note of banter our conversation ended. I had noticed for some time that people were coming into the café with greater frequency. One man in evening dress sat down not far from us and ordered himself a substantial breakfast. He had the tired but satisfied mien of one who looks back with complacency upon a night of amorous dalliance. A few old gentlemen, early risers because old age needs little sleep, were drinking their *café au lait* with deliberation while through thick-lensed spectacles they read the morning paper. Younger men, some of them neat and spruce, others in threadbare coats, hurried in to devour a roll and swallow a cup of coffee on their way to a shop or an office. An old crone entered with a pile of newspapers and went round offering them for sale, vainly as far as I could see, at the various tables. I looked out of the great plate glass windows and saw that it was broad daylight. A minute or two later the electric light was turned off except at the rear of the huge restaurant. I looked at my watch. It was past seven o'clock.

'What about a spot of breakfast?' I said.

We had croissants, all crisp and hot from the baker's, and *café au lait*. I was tired and listless, and felt certain I looked like the wrath of God, but Larry seemed as fresh as ever. His eyes were shining, there wasn't a line on his smooth face, and he didn't look a day more than twenty-five. The coffee revived me.

'Will you allow me to give you a piece of advice, Larry? It's not a thing I give often.'

'It's not a thing I take often,' he answered with a grin.

'Will you think very carefully before you dispossess yourself of your very small fortune? When it's gone, it's gone for ever. A time may come when you'll want money very badly, either for yourself or for somebody else, and then you'll bitterly regret that you were such a fool.'

There was a glint of mockery in his eyes as he answered, but it was devoid of malice.

'You attach more importance to money than I do.'

'I can well believe it,' I answered tartly. 'You see, you've always had it and I haven't. It's given me what I value almost more than anything else in life – independence. You can't think what a comfort it's been to me to think that if I wanted to I could tell anyone in the world to go to hell.'

'But I don't want to tell anyone in the world to go to hell, and if I did the lack of a bank balance wouldn't prevent me. You see, money to you means freedom; to me it means bondage.'

'You're an obstinate brute, Larry.'

'I know. I can't help it. But in any case I have plenty of time to change my mind if I want to. I'm not going back to America till next spring. My friend Auguste Cottet, the painter, has lent me a cottage at Sanary and I'm going to spend the winter there.'

Sanary is an unpretentious seaside resort on the Riviera, between Bandol and Toulon, and it is frequented by artists and writers who do not care for the garish mummery of St Tropez.

'You'll like it if you don't mind its being as dull as ditchwater.'

'I have work to do. I've collected a lot of material and I'm going to write a book.'

'What's it about?'

'You'll see when it comes out,' he smiled.

'If you'd like to send it to me when it's finished I think I can get it published for you.'

'You needn't bother about that. I have some American friends who run a small press in Paris and I've arranged with them to print it for me.'

'But you can't expect a book brought out like that to have any sale and you won't get any reviews.'

'I don't care if it's reviewed and I don't expect it to sell. I'm only printing enough copies to send to my friends in India and the few people I know in France who might be interested in it. It's of no particular importance. I'm only writing it to get all that material out of the way, and I'm publishing it because I think you can only tell what a thing's like when you see it in print.'

'I see the point of both those reasons.'

We had finished our breakfast by now and I called the waiter for the bill. When it came I passed it over to Larry.

'If you're going to chuck your money down the drain you can damn well pay for my breakfast.'

He laughed and paid. I was stiff from sitting so long and as we walked out of the restaurant my sides ached. It was good to get into the fresh clean air of the autumn morning. The sky was blue, and the Avenue de Clichy, a sordid thoroughfare by night, had a mild jauntiness, like a painted, haggard woman walking with a girl's springy step, that was not displeasing. I signalled a passing taxi.

'Can I give you a lift?' I asked Larry.

'No. I shall walk down to the Seine and have a swim at one of the baths, then I must go to the Bibliothèque, I've got some research to do there.'

We shook hands and I watched him cross the road with his loose, long-legged stride. I, being made of stuff less stern, stepped into a taxi and returned to my hotel. When I got into my sitting-room I noticed that it was after eight.

'This is a nice hour for an elderly gentleman to get home,' I remarked disapprovingly to the nude lady (under a glass case) who had since the year 1813 been lying on top of the clock in what I should have thought was a position of extreme discomfort.

She continued to look at her gilt bronze face in a gilt bronze mirror, and all the clock said was: tick, tick. I turned on a hot bath. When I had lain in it till it was tepid, I dried myself, swallowed a sleeping-tablet, and taking to bed with me Valéry's *Le Cimetière marin*, which happened to be on the night table, read till I fell asleep.

VII

1

ONE morning, six months later, in April, I was busy writing in my study on the roof of my house at Cap Ferrat when a servant came up to say that the police of St Jean (my neighbouring village) were below and wished to see me. I was vexed at being interrupted and could not imagine what they wanted.

My conscience was at ease and I had already given my subscription to the Benevolent Fund. In return I had received a card, which I kept in my car so that if I was stopped for exceeding the speed limit or found parked on the wrong side of a street I could unostentatiously let it be seen while producing my driving licence and so escape with an indulgent caution. I thought it more likely then that one of my servants had been the victim of an anonymous denunciation, that being one of the amenities of French life, because her papers were not in order; but being on good terms with the local cops, whom I never allowed to leave my house without a glass of wine to speed them on their way, I anticipated no great difficulty. But they, for they worked in pairs, had come on a very different errand.

After we had shaken hands and inquired after our respective healths, the senior of the two – he was called a *brigadier* and had one of the most imposing moustaches I ever saw – fished a notebook out of his pocket. He turned over the pages with a dirty thumb.

'Does the name Sophie Macdonald say something to you?' he asked.

'I know a person of that name,' I replied cautiously.

'We have just been in telephonic communication with the police station at Toulon and the chief inspector requests you to betake yourself there (*vous prie de vous y rendre*) without delay.'

'For what reason?' I asked. 'I am only slightly acquainted with Mrs Macdonald.'

I jumped to the conclusion that she had got into trouble, probably connected with opium, but I didn't see why I should be mixed up in it.

'That is not my affair. There is no doubt that you have had dealings with this woman. It appears that she has been missing from her lodgings for five days and a body has been fished out of the harbour which the police have reason to believe is hers. They want you to identify it.'

A cold shiver passed through me. I was not, however, too much surprised. It was likely enough that the life she led would incline her in a moment of depression to put an end to herself.

287

'But surely she can be identified by her clothes and her papers.'

'She was found stark naked with her throat cut.'

'Good God!' I was horrified. I reflected for an instant. For all I knew the police could force me to go and I thought I had better submit with good grace. 'Very well. I will take the first train I can.'

I looked up a timetable and found that I could catch one that would get me to Toulon between five and six. The *brigadier* said he would phone the chief inspector to that effect and asked me on my arrival to go straight to the police station. I did no more work that morning. I packed a few necessary things in a suitcase and after luncheon drove to the station.

2

On presenting myself at the headquarters of the Toulon police I was immediately ushered into the room of the chief inspector. He was sitting at a table, a heavy, swarthy man of saturnine appearance whom I took to be a Corsican. He threw me, perhaps from force of habit, a suspicious glance; but noticing the ribbon of the Legion of Honour, which I had taken the precaution to put in my buttonhole, with an unctuous smile asked me to sit down and proceeded to make profuse apologies for having been obliged to incommode a person of my distinction. Adopting a similar tone, I assured him that nothing could make me happier than to be of service to him. Then we got down to brass tacks and he resumed his brusque, rather insolent manner. Looking at some papers before him, he said:

'This is a dirty business. It appears that the woman Macdonald had a very bad reputation. She was a drunkard, a dope fiend, and a nymphomaniac. She was in the habit of sleeping not only with sailors off the ships, but with the riffraff of the town. How does it happen that a person of your age and respectability should be acquainted with such a character?'

I was inclined to tell him that it was no business of his, but from a diligent perusal of hundreds of detective stories I have learnt that it is well to be civil with the police.

'I knew her very little. I met her when she was a girl in Chicago, where she afterwards married a man of good position. I met her again in Paris a year or so ago through friends of hers and mine.'

I had been wondering how on earth he had ever connected me with Sophie, but now he pushed forward a book.

'This volume was found in her room. If you will kindly look at the dedication you will see that it hardly suggests that your acquaintance with her was as slight as you claim.'

It was the translation of that novel of mine that she had seen in the bookshop window and asked me to write in. Under my own name I had written *'Mignonne, allons voir si la rose,'* because it was the first thing that occurred to me. It certainly looked a trifle familiar.

'If you are suggesting that I was her lover, you are mistaken.'

'It would be no affair of mine,' he replied, and then with a gleam in his eye: 'And without wishing to say anything offensive to you I must add that from what I have heard of her proclivities I should not say you were her type. But it is evident that you would not address a perfect stranger as *mignonne.'*

'That line, *monsieur le commissaire,* is the first line of a celebrated poem by Ronsard, whose works I am certain are familiar to a man of your education and culture. I wrote it because I felt sure she knew the poem and would recall the following lines, which might suggest to her that the life she was leading was, to say the least of it, indiscreet.'

'Evidently I have read Ronsard at school, but with all the work I have to do I confess that the lines you refer to have escaped my memory.'

I repeated the first stanza and knowing very well he had never heard the poet's name till I mentioned it, had no fear that he would recall the last one which can hardly be taken as an incitement to virtue.

'She was apparently a woman of some education. We found a number of detective stories in her room and two or three volumes of poetry. There was a Baudelaire and a Rimbaud and an English volume by someone called Eliot. Is he known?'

'Widely.'

'I have no time to read poetry. In any case I cannot read

289

English. If he is a good poet it is a pity he doesn't write in French, so that educated people could read him.'

The thought of my chief inspector reading *The Waste Land* filled me with pleasure. Suddenly he pushed a snapshot towards me.

'Have you any idea who that is?'

I immediately recognized Larry. He was in bathing trunks, and the photograph, a recent one, had been taken, I guessed, during the summer part of which he had spent with Isabel and Gray at Dinard. My first impulse was to say I did not know, for I wanted nothing less than to get Larry mixed up in this hateful business, but I reflected that if the police discovered his identity my assertion would look as if I thought there was something to hide.

'He's an American citizen called Laurence Darrell.'

'It was the only photograph found among the woman's effects. What was the connexion between them?'

'They both came from the same village near Chicago. They were childhood friends.'

'But this photograph was taken not long ago, I suspect at a seaside resort in the North or on the West of France. It would be easy to discover the exact place. What is he, this individual?'

'An author,' I said boldly. The inspector slightly raised his bushy eyebrows and I guessed that he did not attribute high morality to members of my calling. 'Of independent means,' I added to make it sound more respectable.

'Where is he now?'

Again I was tempted to say I didn't know, but again decided it would only make things awkward if I did. The French police may have many faults, but their system enables them to find anyone they want without delay.

'He's living at Sanary.'

The inspector looked up and it was clear that he was interested.

'Where?'

I had remembered Larry telling me that Auguste Cottet had lent him his cottage and on my return at Christmas I had written to ask him to come and stay with me for a while, but as I fully expected he had refused. I gave the inspector his address

'I'll telephone to Sanary and have him brought here. It might be worth while to question him.'

I could not but see that the inspector thought that here might be a suspect, but I was only inclined to laugh; I was convinced that Larry could easily prove that he had nothing to do with the affair. I was anxious to hear more about Sophie's lamentable end, but the inspector only told me in somewhat greater detail what I already knew. Two fishermen had brought the body in. It was a romantic exaggeration of my local policeman's that it was stark naked. The murderer had left girdle and brassière. If Sophie had been dressed in the same way as I had seen her he had had to strip her only of her slacks and her jersey. There was nothing to identify her and the police had inserted a description in the local paper. This had brought a woman to the station who kept a small rooming-house in a back street, what the French call a *maison de passe,* to which men could bring women or boys. She was an agent of the police, who liked to know who frequented her house and what for. Sophie had been turned out of the hotel on the quay at which she was living when I ran across her because her conduct was more scandalous than even the tolerant proprietor could put up with. She had offered to engage a room with a tiny sitting-room beside it in the house of the woman I have just mentioned. It was more profitable to let it two or three times a night for short periods, but Sophie offered to pay so handsomely that the woman consented to rent it to her by the month. She came to the police station now to state that her tenant had been absent for several days, she had not bothered, thinking she had gone for a trip to Marseilles or to Villefranche, where ships of the British fleet had lately arrived, an event that always attracted women, young and old, from all along the coast; but she had read the description of the deceased in the paper and thought it might apply to her tenant. She had been taken to see the body and after a trifling hesitation declared it was that of Sophie Macdonald.

'But if the body's been identified, what do you want me for?'

'Madame Bellet is a woman of high honourability and excellent character,' said the inspector, 'but she may have reasons

291

for identifying the dead woman that we do not know; and in any case I think she should be seen by someone who was more closely connected with her so that the fact may be confirmed.'

'Do you think you have any chance of catching the murderer?'

The inspector shrugged his massive shoulders.

'Naturally we are making inquiries. We have questioned a number of persons at the bars she used to go to. She may have been killed out of jealousy by a sailor whose ship has already left the port, or by a gangster for whatever money she had on her. It appears that she always had on her a sum that would seem large to a man of that sort. It may be that some people have a strong suspicion who the culprit is, but in the circles she moved it is unlikely that anyone will speak unless it is to his advantage. Consorting with the bad characters she did, such an end as she has come to was only too probable.'

I had nothing to say to this. The inspector asked me to come next morning at nine o'clock, by which time he would have seen 'this gentleman of the photograph', after which a policeman would take us to the nearest morgue to see the body.

'And how about burying her?'

'If after identifying the body you claim it as friends of the deceased and are prepared to undertake the expense of the funeral yourselves, you will receive the necessary authorization.'

'I'm sure that Mr Darrell and I would like to have it as soon as possible.'

'I quite understand. It is a sad story and it is better that the poor woman should be laid to rest without delay. And that reminds me that I have here the card of an undertaker who will arrange the matter for you on reasonable terms and with dispatch. I will just write a line on it so that he may give you every attention.'

I was pretty sure he would get a rake-off on the amount paid, but I thanked him warmly, and when he had ushered me out with every expression of esteem I went forthwith to the address on the card. The undertaker was brisk and businesslike. I chose a coffin, neither the cheapest nor the most expensive, accepted his offer to get me two or three wreaths from a florist of his acquaintance – 'to save monsieur a painful duty and out of respect for the dead,' he said – and arranged for the hearse to be at the morgue at two o'clock next day. I could not but admire his efficiency when he told me that I need not trouble to see about a grave, he would do all that was necessary, and 'Madame was a Protestant, I assume,' furthermore he would, if I wished it, have a pastor waiting at the cemetery to read the burial service. But since I was a stranger and a foreigner he was sure that I would not take it amiss if he asked me to be good enough to give him a cheque in advance. He named a larger sum than I had foreseen, evidently expecting me to beat him down, and I discerned a look of surprise, perhaps even of disappointment, on his face when I took out my cheque-book and wrote out a cheque without demur.

I took a room at an hotel and next morning returned to the police station. I was kept waiting for some time and then was bidden to go into the chief inspector's office. I found Larry, looking grave and distressed, sitting in the chair I had sat in the day before. The inspector greeted me with joviality. I might have been a long-lost brother.

'Well, *mon cher monsieur,* your friend has answered all the questions it was my duty to put him with the utmost frankness. I have no reason to disbelieve his statement that he had not seen this poor woman for eighteen months. He has accounted for his movements during the last week in a perfectly satisfactory manner as well as for the fact that his photograph was found in her room. It was taken at Dinard and he happened to have it in his pocket one day when he was lunching with her. I have had excellent reports of the young man from Sanary and I am besides, I say it without vanity, a good judge of character myself; I am convinced that he is incapable of committing a crime of this nature. I have ventured to offer him my sympathy that a friend of his childhood, brought up with all the advantages of a healthy family life, should have turned out so badly. But such is life. And now, my dear gentlemen, one of my men will accompany you to the morgue and when you have identified the body, your time is at your own disposal. Go and have a good lunch. I have a card here of the best restaurant in Toulon and I will just write a word on it which will assure you of the *patron*'s best attention. A good bottle of wine will do you both good after this harrowing experience.'

He was by now positively beaming with good will. We walked to the mortuary with a policeman. They were not doing a lively business in that establishment. There was a body on one slab only. We went up to it and the mortuary attendant uncovered the head. It was not a pleasant sight. The sea water had taken the curl out of the dyed silvery hair and it was plastered dankly on the skull. The face was horribly swollen and it was ghastly to look at, but there was no doubt that it was Sophie's. The attendant drew the covering sheet down to show us what we both would rather not have seen, the horrid gash across the throat that stretched from ear to ear.

We went back to the station. The chief inspector was busy, but we said what we had to say to an assistant; he left us and presently returned with the necessary papers. We took them to the undertaker.

'Now let's have a drink,' I said.

Larry hadn't uttered a word since we left the police station to go to the mortuary except on our return there to declare that he identified the body as that of Sophie Macdonald. I led him down to the quay and we sat in the café in which I had sat with her. A strong mistral was blowing and the harbour, usually so smooth, was flecked with white foam. The fishing-boats were gently rocking. The sun shone brightly and, as always happens with a mistral, every object in sight had a peculiar sparkling sharpness as though you looked at it through glasses focused with more than common accuracy. It imparted a nerve-racking, throbbing vitality to everything in sight. I drank a brandy and soda, but Larry never touched the one I had ordered for him. He sat in moody silence and I did not disturb him.

Presently I looked at my watch.

'We'd better go and have something to eat,' I said. 'We've got to be at the mortuary at two.'

'I'm hungry, I didn't have any breakfast.'

Having judged from his appearance that the chief inspector knew where the food was good, I took Larry to the restaurant he had told us of. Knowing that Larry seldom ate meat, I

ordered an omelette and a grilled lobster and then, asking for
the wine list, chose, again following the policeman's counsel, a
vintage wine. When it appeared I poured out a glass for Larry.

'You damn well drink it,' I said. 'It may suggest a topic of
conversation to you.'

He obediently did as I bade him.

'Shri Ganesha used to say that silence also is conversation,'
he murmured.

'That suggests a jolly social gathering of intellectual dons at
the University of Cambridge.'

'I'm afraid you'll have to stand the racket of this funeral by
yourself,' he said. 'I haven't any money.'

'I'm quite prepared to do that,' I answered. Then the impli-
cation of his remark hit me. 'You haven't been and gone and
done it really?'

He did not answer for a moment. I noticed the whimsical,
teasing glint in his eyes.

'You haven't got rid of your money?'

'Every cent except what I need to last me till my ship comes
in.'

'What ship?'

'The man who has the next cottage to mine at Sanary is the
Marseilles agent of a line of freighters that run from the Near
East to New York. They've cabled him from Alexandria that
they've had to put off a couple of sick men there from a ship
that's coming on to Marseilles and asked him to get two more
to take their place. He's a buddy of mine and he's promised to
get me on. I'm giving him my old Citroën as a parting present.
When I step on board I shall have nothing but the clothes I
stand up in and a few things in a grip.'

'Well, it's your own money. You're free, white, and twenty-
one.'

'Free is the right word. I've never been happier or felt more
independent in my life. When I get to New York I shall have
my wages and they'll carry me on till I can get a job.'

'What about your book?'

'Oh, it's finished and printed. I made a list of people I
wanted it sent to — you ought to get a copy in a day or two.'

'Thank you.'

There was not much more to say and we finished our meal in amiable silence. I ordered coffee. Larry lit a pipe and I a cigar. I looked at him thoughtfully. He felt my eyes upon him and threw me a glance; his own were lit with an impish twinkle.

'If you feel like telling me I'm a damned fool, don't hesitate. I wouldn't in the least mind.'

'No, I don't particularly feel like that. I was only wondering if your life wouldn't have fallen into a more perfect pattern if you'd married and had children like everybody else.'

He smiled. I must have remarked twenty times on the beauty of his smile, it was so cosy, trustful, and sweet, it reflected the candour, the truthfulness of his charming nature; but I must do so once again, for now, besides all that, there was in it something rueful and tender.

'It's too late for that now. The only woman I've met whom I could have married was poor Sophie.'

I looked at him with amazement.

'Can you say that after all that's happened?'

'She had a lovely soul, fervid, aspiring, and generous. Her ideals were greathearted. There was even at the end a tragic nobility in the way she sought destruction.'

I was silent. I did not know what to make of these strange assertions.

'Why didn't you marry her then?' I asked.

'She was a child. To tell you the truth, it never occurred to me when I used to go over to her grandfather's and we read poetry together under the elm tree that there was in that skinny brat the seed of spiritual beauty.'

I could not but think it surprising that at this juncture he made no mention of Isabel. He could not have forgotten that he had been engaged to her and I could only suppose that he regarded the episode as a foolishness without consequence of two young things not old enough to know their own minds. I was ready to believe that the suspicion had never so much as fugitively crossed his mind that ever since she had been eating her heart out for him.

It was time for us to go. We walked to the square where Larry had left his car, very shabby now, and drove to the mortuary. The undertaker was as good as his word. The businesslike efficiency with which everything was accomplished, under that garish sky, with the violent wind bending the cypresses of the cemetery, added a last note of horror to the proceedings. When it was all over the undertaker shook hands with us cordially.

'Well, gentlemen, I hope you were satisfied. It went very well.'

'Very well,' I said.

'Monsieur will not forget that I am always at his disposition if he has need of my services. Distance is no object.'

I thanked him. When we came to the gate of the cemetery Larry asked me if there was anything further I wanted him for.

'Nothing.'

'I'd like to get back to Sanary as soon as possible.'

'Drop me at my hotel, will you?'

We spoke never a word as we drove. When we arrived I got out. We shook hands and he went off. I paid my bill, got my bag, and took a taxi to the station. I too wanted to get away.

3

A few days later I started for England. My intention had been to go straight through, but after what had happened I particularly wanted to see Isabel, so I decided to stop in Paris for twenty-four hours. I wired to her to ask if I could come in late in the afternoon and stay to dinner; when I reached my hotel I found a note from her to say that she and Gray were dining out, but that she would be very glad to see me if I would come not before half past five as she had a fitting.

It was chilly and raining off and on quite heavily, so that I presumed Gray would not have gone to Mortefontaine to play golf. This did not suit me very well, since I wanted to see Isabel alone, but when I arrived at the apartment the first thing she said was that Gray was at the Travellers playing bridge.

'I told him not to be too late if he wanted to see you, but we're not dining till nine, which means we needn't get there before nine-thirty, so we've got plenty of time for a good talk. I've got all sorts of things to tell you.'

They had sublet the apartment, and the sale of Elliott's collection was to take place in a fortnight. They wanted to attend and were moving into the Ritz. Then they were sailing. Isabel was selling everything except the modern pictures that Elliott had had in his house at Antibes. Though she didn't care much for them she thought quite rightly that they would be a prestige item in their future home.

'It's a pity poor Uncle Elliott wasn't more advanced. Picasso, Matisse, and Rouault, you know. I suppose his pictures are good in their way, but I'm afraid they'll seem rather old-fashioned.'

'I wouldn't bother about that if I were you. Other painters will come along in a few years and Picasso and Matisse won't seem any more up to date than your Impressionists.'

Gray was in process of concluding his negotiations and with the capital provided by Isabel was to enter a flourishing business as vice-president. It was connected with oil and they were to live at Dallas.

'The first thing we shall have to do is to find a suitable house. I want a nice garden so that Gray can have somewhere to potter about when he comes home from work and I must have a really large living-room so that I can entertain.'

'I wonder you don't take Elliott's furniture over with you.'

'I don't think it would be very suitable. I shall make it all modern, with perhaps just a little touch of Mexican here and there to give it a note. As soon as I get to New York I'll find out who is the decorator everyone's going to now.'

Antoine, the manservant, brought in a tray with an array of bottles, and Isabel, always tactful, knowing that nine men out of ten are convinced they can mix a better cocktail than any woman (and they are right), asked me to shake a couple. I poured out the gin and the Noilly-Prat and added the dash of absinthe that transforms a dry Martini from a nondescript drink to one for which the gods of Olympus would undoubtedly have abandoned their home-brewed nectar, a beverage that I have always thought must have been rather like Coca-Cola. I noticed a book on the table as I handed Isabel her glass.

'Hello!' I said. 'Here's Larry's book.'

'Yes, it came this morning, but I've been so busy, I had a thousand things to do before lunch and I was lunching out and I was at Molyneux's this afternoon. I don't know when I shall have a moment to get down to it.'

I thought with melancholy how an author spends months writing a book, and may be puts his heart's blood into it, and then it lies about unread till the reader has nothing else in the world to do. It was a volume of three hundred pages nicely printed and neatly bound.

'I suppose you know Larry has been in Sanary all the winter. Did you see him by any chance?'

'Yes, we were at Toulon together only the other day.'

'Were you? What were you doing there?'

'Burying Sophie.'

'She's not dead?' cried Isabel.

'If she hadn't been we'd have had no plausible reason to bury her.'

'That's not funny.' She paused for a second. 'I'm not going to pretend I'm sorry. A combination of drink and dope, I suppose.'

'No, she had her throat cut and was thrown into the sea stark naked.'

Like the *brigadier* at St Jean I found myself impelled a trifle to exaggerate her undress.

'How horrible! Poor thing. Of course leading the life she did she was bound to come to a bad end.'

'That's what the *commissaire de police* at Toulon said.'

'Do they know who did it?'

'No, but I do. I think you killed her.'

She gave me a stare of amazement.

'What *are* you talking about?' Then with the ghost of a chuckle: 'Guess again; I have a cast-iron alibi.'

'I ran across her at Toulon last summer. I had a long talk with her.'

'Was she sober?'

'Sufficiently. She told me how it happened that she'd disappeared so unaccountably just a few days before she was going to be married to Larry.'

I noticed Isabel's face stiffen. I proceeded to tell her exactly what Sophie had told me. She listened warily.

'I've thought of her story a good deal since then and the more I've thought about it the more convinced I am that there's something fishy about it. I've lunched here twenty times and

299

'you never have liqueurs for luncheon. You'd been lunching alone. Why should there have been a bottle of zubrovka on the tray with the coffee-cup?'

'Uncle Elliott had just sent it to me. I wanted to see if I liked it as much as when I'd had it at the Ritz.'

'Yes, I remember how you raved about it then. I was surprised, as you never drink liqueurs anyway; you're much too careful of your figure for that. I had at the time an impression that you were trying to tantalize Sophie. I thought it was just malice.'

'Thank you.'

'On the whole you're very good at keeping appointments. Why should you have gone out when you were expecting Sophie for something so important to her and interesting to you as a fitting of her wedding dress?'

'She told you that herself. I wasn't happy about Joan's teeth. Our dentist is very busy and I just had to take the time he could give me.'

'When one goes to a dentist one makes the next appointment before leaving.'

'I know. But he called me up in the morning and said he had to break it, but could give me three o'clock that afternoon instead, so of course I jumped at it.'

'Couldn't the governess have taken Joan.'

'She was scared, poor darling, I felt she'd be happier if I went with her.'

'And when you came back and found the bottle of zubrovka three parts empty and Sophie gone, weren't you rather surprised?'

'I thought she'd got tired of waiting and gone on to Molyneux's by herself. I couldn't make it out when I went there and they told me she hadn't been.'

'And the zubrovka?'

'Well, I did notice that a good deal had been drunk. I thought Antoine had drunk it and I very nearly spoke to him about it, but Uncle Elliott was paying for him and he was a friend of Joseph's, so I thought I'd better ignore it. He's a very good servant and if he takes a little nip now and then who am I to blame him?'

300

'What a liar you are, Isabel.'

'Don't you believe me?'

'Not for a moment.'

Isabel got up and walked over to the chimney-piece. There was a wood fire and it was pleasant on that dreary day. She stood with one elbow on the mantel-shelf in a graceful attitude which it was one of her most charming gifts to be able to assume without any appearance of intention. Like most French women of distinction she dressed in black in the daytime, which peculiarly suited her rich colouring, and on this occasion she wore a dress the expensive simplicity of which displayed her slender figure to advantage. She puffed at her cigarette for a minute.

'There's no reason why I shouldn't be perfectly frank with you. It was most unfortunate that I had to go out and of course Antoine should never have left the liqueur and the coffee-things in the room. They ought to have been taken away when I went out. When I came back and saw the bottle was nearly empty of course I knew what had happened, and when Sophie disappeared I guessed she'd gone off on a bat. I didn't say anything about it because I thought it would only distress Larry, and he was worried enough as it was.'

'Are you sure the bottle wasn't left there on your explicit instructions?'

'Quite.'

'I don't believe you.'

'Don't then.' She flung the cigarette viciously into the fire. Her eyes were dark with anger. 'All right, if you want the truth you can have it and to hell with you. I did it and I'd do it again. I told you I'd stick at nothing to prevent her from marrying Larry. You wouldn't do a thing, either you or Gray. You just shrugged your shoulders and said it was a terrible mistake. You didn't care a damn. I did.'

'If you'd left her alone she'd be alive now.'

'Married to Larry and he'd be utterly miserable. He thought he'd make a new woman of her. What fools men are! I knew that sooner or later she'd break down. It stuck out a mile. You saw yourself when we were all lunching together at the Ritz how jittery she was. I noticed you looking at her when she

301

was drinking her coffee; her hand was shaking so, she was afraid to take the cup with one hand, she had to put both her hands to it to get it up to her mouth. I noticed her watching the wine when the waiter filled our glasses; she followed the bottle with those horrible washed-out eyes of hers like a snake following the fluttering of a new-fledged chick and I knew she'd give her soul for a drink.'

Isabel faced me now, her eyes flashing with passion, and her voice was harsh. She couldn't get the words out quickly enough.

'The idea came to me when Uncle Elliott made all that fuss about that damned Polish liqueur. I thought it beastly, but I pretended it was the most wonderful stuff I'd ever tasted. I was certain that if she got a chance she'd never have the strength to resist. That's why I took her to the dress show. That's why I offered to make her a present of her wedding dress. That day, when she was going to have the last fitting, I told Antoine I'd have the zubrovka after lunch and then I told him I was expecting a lady and to ask her to wait and offer her some coffee and to leave the liqueur in case she fancied a glass. I did take Joan to the dentist's, but of course we hadn't an appointment and he couldn't see us, so I took her to a newsreel. I'd made up my mind that if I found Sophie hadn't touched the stuff I'd make the best of things and try to be friends with her. That's true, I swear it. But when I got home and saw the bottle I knew I'd been right. She'd gone and I'd have bet any money in the world she'd gone for good.'

Isabel was actually panting when she finished.

'That's more or less what I imagined had happened,' I said. 'You see, I was right; you cut her throat as surely as if you'd drawn the knife across it with your own hands.'

'She was bad, bad, bad. I'm glad she's dead.' She threw herself into a chair. 'Give me a cocktail, damn you.'

I went over and mixed another.

'You are a mean devil,' she said as she took it from me. Then she allowed herself to smile. Her smile was like a child's that knows it's been naughty, but thinks it can wheedle you by its ingenuous charm not to be cross. 'You won't tell Larry, will you?'

'I wouldn't dream of it.'

'Cross your heart? Men are so untrustworthy.'

'I promise you I won't. But even if I wanted to, I shouldn't have an opportunity as I don't suppose I shall ever see him again in my life.'

She sat bolt upright.

'What *do* you mean?'

'At this moment, he's on a freighter, either as a deck hand or a stoker, on his way to New York.'

'You don't mean that? What a strange creature he is! He was up here a few weeks ago for something to do with his book that he had to look up at the public library, but he never said a word about going to America. I'm glad; that means we shall see him.'

'I doubt it. His America will be as remote from your America as the Gobi desert.'

Then I told her what he had done and what he intended to do. She listened to me open-mouthed. Consternation was written on her face. She interrupted me now and then with an interjection 'He's crazy. He's crazy.' When I had finished she hung her head and I saw two tears trickle down her cheeks.

'Now I really have lost him.'

She turned away from me and wept, leaning her face against the back of the chair. Her lovely face was twisted with the grief she did not care to hide. There was nothing I could do. I didn't know what vain, conflicting hopes she had cherished that my tidings had finally shattered. I had a vague notion that to see him occasionally, at least to know that he was part of her world, had been a bond of union, however tenuous, that his action had finally severed so that she knew herself for ever bereft. I wondered what unavailing regret afflicted her. I thought it would do her good to cry. I picked up Larry's book and looked at the table of contents. My copy had not arrived when I left the Riviera and I could not now hope to get it for several days. It was not in the least the sort of thing I expected. It was a collection of essays of about the same length as those in Lytton Strachey's *Eminent Victorians*, upon a number of famous persons. The choice he had made puzzled me. There was one on Sulla, the Roman dictator who, having achieved absolute power, resigned it to return to private life; there was one on Akbar, the Mogul conqueror who won an empire; there was one on Rubens, there was one on Goethe, and there was one on the Lord Chesterfield of the *Letters*. It was obvious that each of the essays had needed a tremendous amount of reading and I was no longer surprised that it had taken Larry so long to produce this book, but I could not see why he had thought it worth while to give it so much time or why he had chosen those particular men to study. Then it occurred to me that every one of them in his own way had made a supreme success of life and I guessed that this was what had interested Larry. He was curious to see what in the end it amounted to.

I skimmed a page to see how he wrote. His style was scholarly, but lucid and easy. There was nothing in it of the pretentiousness or the pedantry that too often characterizes the writing of the amateur. One could tell that he had frequented the best authors as assiduously as Elliott Templeton frequented the nobility and gentry. I was interrupted by a sigh from Isabel. She sat up and finished with a grimace the cocktail which was now luke-warm.

'If I don't stop crying my eyes'll be terrible and we're going out to dinner tonight.' She took a mirror out of her bag and looked at herself anxiously. 'Yes, half an hour with an ice bag over my eyes, that's what I want.' She powdered her face and reddened her lips. Then she looked at me reflectively. 'Do you think any the worse of me for what I did?'

'Would you care?'

'Strange as it may seem to you, I would. I want you to think well of me.'

I grinned.

'My dear, I'm a very immoral person,' I answered. 'When I'm really fond of anyone, though I deplore his wrongdoing it doesn't make me less fond of him. You're not a bad woman in your way and you have every grace and every charm. I don't enjoy your beauty any the less because I know how much it owes to the happy combination of perfect taste and ruthless determination. You only lack one thing to make you completely enchanting.'

She smiled and waited.

'Tenderness.'

The smile died on her lips and she gave me a glance that was totally lacking in amenity, but before she could collect herself to reply Gray lumbered into the room. In the three years he had been in Paris Gray had put on a good many pounds, his face had grown redder, and his hair was thinning rapidly, but he was in rude health and in high spirits. He was unaffectedly pleased to see me. Gray's conversation was composed of clichés. However shop-worn, he uttered them with an obvious conviction that he was the first person to think of them. He never went to bed, but hit the hay, where he slept the sleep of the just; if it rained, it rained to beat the band and to the very end Paris to him was Gay Paree. But he was so kindly, so unselfish, so upright, so reliable, so unassuming that it was impossible not to like him. I had a real affection for him. He was excited now over their approaching departure.

'Gosh, it'll be great to get into harness again,' he said. 'I'm feeling my oats already.'

'Is it all settled then?'

'I haven't signed on the dotted line yet, but it's on ice. The fella I'm going in with was a room-mate of mine at college, and he's a good scout, and I'm dead sure he wouldn't hand me a lemon. But as soon as we get to New York I'll fly down to Texas to give the outfit the once-over, and you bet I'll keep my eyes peeled for a nigger in the woodpile before I cough up any of Isabel's dough.'

'Gray's a very good businessman, you know,' she said.

'I wasn't raised in a barn,' he smiled.

He went on to tell me at somewhat excessive length about the business he was entering, but I understood little of such matters and the only concrete fact I gathered was that he stood a good chance of making a lot of money. He grew so interested in what he was saying that presently he turned to Isabel and said:

'Look here, why shouldn't we cut this lousy party and us three go and have a slap-up dinner at the Tour d'Argent by ourselves?'

'Oh, darling, we can't do that. They're giving the party for us.'

'Anyhow, I couldn't come now,' I interrupted. 'When I heard you were fixed up this evening I called up Suzanne Rouvier and arranged to take her out.'

'Who's Suzanne Rouvier?' asked Isabel.

'Oh, one of Larry's gals,' I said to tease her.

'I always suspected Larry had a little floozie tucked away somewhere,' said Gray, with a fat chuckle.

'Nonsense,' snapped Isabel. 'I know all about Larry's sex life. There isn't any.'

'Well, let's have one more drink before we part,' said Gray.

We had it and then I said good-bye to them. They came into the hall with me and while I was putting on my coat Isabel slipped her arm through Gray's and, nestling up to him, looked into his eyes with an expression that imitated very well the tenderness I had accused her of lacking.

'Tell me, Gray – frankly – do you think I'm hard-boiled?'

'No, darling, far from it. Why, has anybody been saying you were?'

'No.'

She turned her head away so that he shouldn't see, and in a manner that Elliott would certainly have thought very unlady-like put out her tongue at me.

'It's not the same thing,' I murmured as I stepped out of the door and closed it behind me.

4

When I passed through Paris again the Maturins had gone and other people lived in Elliott's apartment. I missed Isabel. She was good to look at and easy to talk to. She was quick on the uptake and bore no malice. I have never seen her since. I am a poor and dilatory correspondent and Isabel was no letter writer. If she could not communicate with you by telephone or telegram she did not communicate with you. I had a Christmas card from her that Christmas with a pretty picture on it of a house with a Colonial portico surrounded by live oaks, which I took to be the house of the plantation that they had been unable to sell when they wanted the money and which now they were probably willing to keep. The postmark showed that it had been posted at Dallas, so I concluded that the deal had gone through satisfactorily and they were settled there. I have never been to Dallas, but I suppose that, like other American cities I know, it has a residential district within easy motoring distance of the business section and the country club where the affluent have fine houses in large gardens with a handsome view of hill or dale from the living-room windows. In such a district and in such a house, furnished from cellar to attic in the latest mode by the most fashionable decorator in New York, Isabel certainly dwells. I can only hope that her Renoir, her flower piece by Manet, her landscape by Monet, and her Gauguin do not look too dated. The dining-room is doubtless of a convenient size for the women's luncheons which she gives at frequent intervals and at which the wine is good and the food superlative. Isabel learnt a great deal in Paris. She would not have settled on the house unless she had seen at a glance that the living-room would do very well for the sub-deb dances which it would be her pleasant duty to give as her daughters grew older. Joan and Priscilla must be now of a marriageable age. I am sure that they have been admirably brought up; they have been sent to the best schools and Isabel has taken care that they should acquire the accomplishments that must make them desirable in the eyes of eligible young men. Though I suppose Gray by now is still a little redder in the face, more jowly, balder, and a good deal heavier, I can't believe that Isabel has changed. She is still more beautiful than her daughters. The Maturins must be a great asset to the community and I have little doubt that they are as popular as they deserve to be. Isabel is entertaining, gracious, complaisant, and tactful; Gray, of course, is the quintessence of the Regular Guy.

5

I continued to see Suzanne Rouvier from time to time until an unexpected change in her condition caused her to leave Paris and she too went out of my life. One afternoon, roughly two years after the events that I have just related, having spent an hour pleasantly browsing over the books in the galleries of the Odéon and with nothing to do for a while, I thought I would call on Suzanne. I had not seen her for six months. She opened the door, a palette on her thumb and a paintbrush between her teeth, clad in a smock covered with paint.

'Ah, c'est vous, cher ami. Entrez, je vous en prie.'

I was a little surprised at this formal address, for generally we spoke to one another in the second person singular, but I stepped into the small room that served both as living-room and studio. There was a canvas on the easel.

'I'm so busy, I don't know which way to turn, but sit down and I will go on with my work. I haven't a moment to waste. You wouldn't believe it, but I'm giving a one-man show at Meyerheim's, and I have to get thirty canvases ready.'

'At Meyerheim's? That's wonderful. How on earth have you managed that?'

For Meyerheim is not one of those fly-by-night dealers in the Rue de la Seine who have a small shop that is always on the verge of closing for lack of money to pay the rent. Meyerheim has a fine gallery on the moneyed side of the Seine and he has an international reputation. An artist whom he takes up is well on the way to fortune.

'Monsieur Achille brought him to see my work and he thinks I have a lot of talent.'

'À d'autres, ma vieille,' I replied, which I think can best be translated by: 'Tell that to the marines, old girl.'

She threw me a glance and giggled.

'I'm going to be married.'

'To Meyerheim?'

'Don't be an idiot.' She put down her brushes and her palette. 'I've been working all day and I deserve a rest. Let us have a little glass of porto and I'll tell you all about it.'

One of the less agreeable features of French life is that you are apt to be pressed to drink a glass of vinegary port at an unseasonable hour. You must resign yourself to it. Suzanne fetched a bottle and two glasses, filled them, and sat down with a sigh of relief.

'I've been standing for hours and my varicose veins are aching. Well, it's like this. Monsieur Achille's wife died at the beginning of this year. She was a good woman and a good Catholic, but he did not marry her from inclination, he married her because it was good business, and though he esteemed and respected her it would be an exaggeration to say that her death left him inconsolable. His son is suitably married and is doing well in the firm and now a marriage has been arranged between his daughter and a count. Belgian it is true, but authentic, with a very pretty château in the neighbourhood of Namur. Monsieur Achille thought his poor wife would not wish the happiness of two young people to be deferred on her account, so the marriage, notwithstanding that they are in mourning, is to take place as soon as the financial arrangements are completed. Evidently Monsieur Achille will be lonely in that large house at Lille, and needs a woman not only to minister to his comfort, but also to run the important establishment necessary to his position. To cut a long story short, he has asked me to take the place of his poor wife, for as he very reasonably said: "I married for the first time to eliminate competition between two rival firms, and I do not regret it, but there is no reason why I should not marry the second time to please myself." '

'I congratulate you,' said I.

'Evidently I shall miss my liberty. I have enjoyed it. But one has to think of the future. Between ourselves, I don't mind telling you that I shall never see forty again. Monsieur Achille is at a dangerous age; where should I be if he suddenly took it into his head to run after a girl of twenty? And then there is my daughter to think of. She is now sixteen and promises to be as beautiful as her father. I have given her a good education. But it is no good denying facts that stare you in the face; she has neither the talent to be an actress nor the temperament to be a whore like her poor mother: I ask you then, what has she to look forward to? A secretaryship or a job in the post office. Monsieur Achille has very generously agreed that she should live with us and has promised to give her a handsome *dot* so that she can make a good marriage. Believe me, my dear friend, people can say what they like, but marriage still remains the most satisfactory profession a woman can adopt. Obviously when my daughter's welfare was concerned I could not hesitate to accept a proposition even at the cost of certain satisfactions which in any case, as the years go by, I should find it more difficult to obtain; for I must tell you that when I am married I propose to be of a ferocious virtue (*d'une vertu farouche*), for my long experience has convinced me that the only basis of a happy marriage is complete fidelity on both sides.'

'A highly moral sentiment, my pretty,' I said. 'And will Monsieur Achille continue to make his fortnightly visits to Paris on business?'

'*Oh, la la,* for whom do you take me, my little one? The first thing I said to Monsieur Achille when he asked for my hand was: "Now listen, my dear, when you come to Paris for your board meetings it is understood that I come too. I am not going to trust you here by yourself." "You cannot imagine that I am capable of committing follies at my age," he answered. "Monsieur Achille," I said to him, "you are a man in the prime of life and no one knows better than I that you have a passionate temperament. You have a fine presence and a distinguished air. You have everything to please a woman; in short I think it better that you should not be exposed to temptation." In the end he agreed to give up his place on the board to his son, who will come to Paris instead of his father. Monsieur Achille pretended to think me unreasonable, but he was in point of fact enormously flattered.' Suzanne gave a sigh of satisfaction. 'Life would be even harder for us poor women than it is if it were not for the unbelievable vanity of men.'

'All that is very fine, but what has it got to do with your having a one-man show at Meyerheim's?'

'You are a little stupid today, my poor friend. Have I not told you for years that Monsieur Achille is a highly intelligent man? He has his position to think of and the people of Lille are censorious. Monsieur Achille wishes me to take the place in society which as the wife of a man of his importance it will be my right to occupy. You know what these provincials are, they love to poke their long noses in other people's affairs, and the first thing they will ask is: who is Suzanne Rouvier? Well, they will have their answer. She is the distinguished painter whose recent show at the Meyerheim Gallery had a remarkable and well-deserved success. "Madame Suzanne Rouvier, the widow of an officer in the colonial infantry, has with the courage characteristic of our Frenchwomen for some years supported herself and a charming daughter deprived too soon of a father's care by means of her talent, and we are happy to know that the general public will soon have the opportunity to appreciate the delicacy of her touch and the soundness of her technique at the galleries of the ever perspicacious Monsieur Meyerheim." '

'What gibberish is that?' I said, pricking up my ears.

'That, my dear, is the advance publicity that Monsieur Achille is putting out. It will appear in every paper in France of any consequence. He has been magnificent. Meyerheim's terms were onerous, but Monsieur Achille accepted them as if they were a bagatelle. There will be a *champagne d'honneur* at the private view and the Minister of Fine Arts, who is under an obligation to Monsieur Achille, will open the exhibition with an eloquent speech in which he will dwell upon my virtues as a woman and my talent as a painter and which he will end with the declaration that the state, whose duty and privilege it is to reward merit, has bought one of my pictures for the national collections. All Paris will be there and Meyerheim is looking after the critics himself. He has guaranteed that their notices will be not only favourable but lengthy. Poor devils, they earn so little, it is a charity to give them an opportunity of making something on the side.'

'You've deserved it all, my dear. You've always been a good sort.'

'*Et ta sœur*,' she replied, which is untranslatable. 'But that's not all. Monsieur Achille has bought in my name a villa on the coast at St Rafael, so I shall take my place in Lille society not only as a distinguished artist, but as a woman of property. In two or three years he is going to retire and we shall live on the Riviera like gentlefolks (*comme des gens bien*). He can paddle in the sea and catch shrimps while I devote myself to my art. Now I will show you my pictures.'

Suzanne had been painting for several years and she had worked through the manner of her various lovers to arrive at a style of her own. She still could not draw, but she had acquired a pretty sense of colour. She showed me landscapes that she had painted while staying with her mother in the province of Anjou, bits of the gardens at Versailles and the forest at Fontainebleau, street scenes that had taken her fancy in the suburbs of Paris. Her painting was vaporous and unsubstantial, but it

311

had a flowerlike grace and even a certain careless elegance. There was one picture that took my fancy and because I thought she would be pleased I offered to buy it. I cannot remember whether it was called *A Glade in the Forest* or *The White Scarf* and subsequent examination has left me uncertain to this day. I asked the price, which was reasonable, and said I would take it.

'You're an angel,' she cried. 'My first sale. Of course you can't have it till after the show, but I'll see that it gets into the papers that you've bought it. After all, a little publicity can do you no harm. I'm glad you've chosen that one, I think it's one of my best.' She took a hand mirror and looked at the picture in it. 'It has charm,' she said, screwing up her eyes. 'No one can deny that. Those greens – how rich they are and yet how delicate! And that white note in the middle, that is a real find; it ties the picture together, it has distinction. There's talent there, there can be no doubt of it, there's real talent.'

I saw that she was already a long way on the road to being a professional painter.

'And now, my little one, we've gossiped long enough, I must get back to work.'

'And I must be going,' I said.

'*À propos,* is that poor Larry still among the Redskins?'

For that was the disrespectful way in which she was accustomed to refer to the inhabitants of God's Own Country.

'So far as I know.'

'It must be hard for someone like him who is so sweet and gentle. If one can believe the movies life is terrible over there with all those gangsters and cowboys and Mexicans. Not that those cowboys haven't physical attraction which says something to you. *Oh, la la!* But it appears that it is *excessively* dangerous to go out into the streets of New York without a revolver in your pocket.'

She came to the door to see me out and kissed me on both cheeks.

'We've had some good times together. Keep a good recollection of me.'

312

This is the end of my story. I have heard nothing of Larry, nor indeed did I expect to. Since he generally did what he proposed, I think it likely that on his return to America he got a job in a garage and then drove a truck till he had acquired the knowledge he wanted of the country from which he had for so many years absented himself. When he had done that he may very well have carried out his fantastic suggestion of becoming a taxi driver: true, it was only a random idea thrown across a café table in jest, but I shouldn't be altogether surprised if he had put it into effect; and I have never since taken a taxi in New York without glancing at the driver on the chance that I might meet Larry's gravely smiling, deep-set eyes. I never have. War broke out. He would have been too old to fly, but he may be once more driving a truck, at home or abroad; or he may be working in a factory. I should like to think that in his leisure hours he is writing a book in which he is trying to set forth whatever life has taught him and the message he has to deliver to his fellow-men; but if he is, it may be long before it is finished. He has plenty of time, for the years have left no mark on him and to all intents and purposes he is still a young man.

He is without ambition and he has no desire for fame; to become anything of a public figure would be deeply distasteful to him; and so it may be that he is satisfied to lead his chosen life and be no more than just himself. He is too modest to set himself up as an example to others; but it may be he thinks that a few uncertain souls, drawn to him like moths to a candle, will be brought in time to share his own glowing belief that ultimate satisfaction can only be found in the life of the spirit, and that by himself following with selflessness and renunciation the path of perfection he will serve as well as if he wrote books or addressed multitudes.

But this is conjecture. I am of the earth, earthy; I can only admire the radiance of such a rare creature, I cannot step into his shoes and enter into his innermost heart as I sometimes think I can do with persons more nearly allied to the common run of men. Larry has been absorbed, as he wished, into that tumultuous conglomeration of humanity, distracted by so many conflicting interests, so lost in the world's confusion, so wishful of good, so cocksure on the outside, so diffident within, so kind, so hard, so trustful, and so cagey, so mean and so generous, which is the people of the United States. That is all I can tell of him: I know it is very unsatisfactory; I can't help it. But as I was finishing this book, uneasily conscious that I must leave my reader in the air and seeing no way to avoid it, I looked back with my mind's eye on my long narrative to see if there was any way in which I could devise a more satisfactory ending; and to my intense surprise it dawned upon me that without in the least intending to I had written nothing more or less than a success story. For all the persons with whom I have been concerned got what they wanted: Elliott social eminence; Isabel an assured position backed by a substantial fortune in an active and cultured community; Gray a steady and lucrative job, with an office to go to from nine till six every day; Suzanne Rouvier security; Sophie death; and Larry happiness. And however superciliously the highbrows carp, we the public in our heart of hearts all like a success story; so perhaps my ending is not so unsatisfactory after all.

FOR THE BEST IN PAPERBACKS, LOOK FOR THE 🐧

In every corner of the world, on every subject under the sun, Penguin represents quality and variety – the very best in publishing today.

For complete information about books available from Penguin – including Puffins, Penguin Classics and Arkana – and how to order them, write to us at the appropriate address below. Please note that for copyright reasons the selection of books varies from country to country.

In the United Kingdom: Please write to *Dept E.P., Penguin Books Ltd, Harmondsworth, Middlesex, UB7 0DA.*

If you have any difficulty in obtaining a title, please send your order with the correct money, plus ten per cent for postage and packaging, to *PO Box No 11, West Drayton, Middlesex*

In the United States: Please write to *Dept BA, Penguin, 299 Murray Hill Parkway, East Rutherford, New Jersey 07073*

In Canada: Please write to *Penguin Books Canada Ltd, 2801 John Street, Markham, Ontario L3R 1B4*

In Australia: Please write to the *Marketing Department, Penguin Books Australia Ltd, P.O. Box 257, Ringwood, Victoria 3134*

In New Zealand: Please write to the *Marketing Department, Penguin Books (NZ) Ltd, Private Bag, Takapuna, Auckland 9*

In India: Please write to *Penguin Overseas Ltd, 706 Eros Apartments, 56 Nehru Place, New Delhi, 110019*

In the Netherlands: Please write to *Penguin Books Netherlands B.V., Postbus 195, NL–1380AD Weesp*

In West Germany: Please write to *Penguin Books Ltd, Friedrichstrasse 10–12, D–6000 Frankfurt/Main 1*

In Spain: Please write to *Longman Penguin España, Calle San Nicolas 15, E–28013 Madrid*

In Italy: Please write to *Penguin Italia s.r.l., Via Como 4, I-20096 Pioltello (Milano)*

In France: Please write to *Penguin Books Ltd, 39 Rue de Montmorency, F-75003 Paris*

In Japan: Please write to *Longman Penguin Japan Co Ltd, Yamaguchi Building, 2-12-9 Kanda Jimbocho, Chiyoda-Ku, Tokyo 101*

W. Somerset Maugham

COLLECTED SHORT STORIES

W. Somerset Maugham's short stories are masterpieces of the art. No more need be said, except that in their precision of form and beauty of expression, they are jewels of their kind.

VOLUME 1

Of the thirty stories in this volume some take place on Pacific islands, and some in England, Spain, and France. They include 'Rain', the sardonic tragedy of Mr Davidson, the prudish missionary, and Sadie Thompson, the prostitute.

VOLUME 2

These twenty-four stories are set in and around Malaya, in America, and in England and include that famous story 'The Vessel of Wrath'.

ASHENDEN

This volume contains the famous Ashenden series of stories. These are stories of espionage in the First World War, told by Ashenden, a Secret Service Agent, who, Maugham has stated, can be taken as a flattering self-portrait of himself.

VOLUME 4

Most of the thirty stories in this final volume are set in Malaya and Southeast Asia, always favourite Maugham territory. The author brings home the charged atmosphere of remote colonial stations. 'The Outstation' immortalizes in Warburton a significant type of colonial administrator.

W. Somerset Maugham

CAKES AND ALE

Of all W. Somerset Maugham's novels, *Cakes and Ale* is the gayest. The entrancing character of Rosie, a barmaid with a history and a heart of gold, places the book, as creative literature, on a level with *Of Human Bondage*.

CHRISTMAS HOLIDAY

Charley Mason's father would certainly never have given his son a Christmas trip to Paris had he known the underworld of sin, sensuality, and expiation to which he was introducing him — for Paris, on the eve of the Second World War, was a city dark in spirit. . . .

LIZA OF LAMBETH

Into London's East End of the 1890s came a young medical student; from this experience of life that was hard, unpredictable, and sordid emerged one of the greatest novelists of this century. This is his first novel: the story of strong-willed Liza, who overstepped the conventions of her world.

THE MAGICIAN

Evil for evil's sake is the theme, and Paris of the 1900s the place. The sinister and repulsive Richard Haddo gradually brings a happily engaged young English girl under his hypnotic spell, a spell from which the efforts of her fiancé and friends cannot save her.

W. Somerset Maugham

THE MOON AND SIXPENCE

A disturbing study of single-minded genius, *The Moon and Sixpence* confirmed W. Somerset Maugham's reputation as a novelist and is probably his best-known book.

MRS CRADDOCK

'Extremely daring' was the publisher's verdict in 1900. Today's readers, though they are unlikely to share that opinion, will certainly find Maugham's story of a woman who 'marries beneath her' still has the power to move and surprise.

THE NARROW CORNER

The Narrow Corner recalls the best of Maugham's short stories in its location in the Far East, its subtlety, and its wry penetration of human nature. Money talked the shifty Captain Nichols into whisking a young Australian over the horizon for a discreet period, but it was love that lured the luckless Fred Blake into disaster. Ultimately it is money that ironically winds up this partnership of gamblers in a book that utters a tart comment on the futility of idealism.

OF HUMAN BONDAGE

Of Human Bondage is generally considered to be Maugham's masterpiece in a long, versatile, and extremely distinguished literary career. First published in 1915, the book was described by Maugham as an autobiographical novel in which fact and fiction are inextricably mixed. Philip Carey, a handicapped orphan, is brought up by a self-indulgent Victorian clergyman. Shedding his religious faith as a young man, he begins to study art in Paris but finally returns to London to become a doctor.

W. Somerset Maugham

THE PAINTED VEIL

The Painted Veil is probably the only novel that W. Somerset Maugham based on a story rather than a character. Nevertheless, on publication in 1925 it was twice threatened with libel actions. Maugham gives a modern setting to the curious plot, which was suggested by a few lines of Dante. Detected in an affair with the Assistant Colonial Secretary of Hong Kong, Kitty Fane is forced by her husband, a bacteriologist, to accompany him to the heart of a cholera epidemic. In the course of this harsh penance she learns the true meaning of love, but her discovery comes too late.

THE SUMMING UP

The Summing Up might aptly be described as the *Religio Medici* of a great modern writer (who, as it happens, ascribes much of his literary success to his medical training). Maugham had already completed the bulk of his best work when, in 1938, he published this personal statement. Here is Maugham's impartial judgement on Maugham, a considered comment on life and on his own life's work, a careful weighing of religion, philosophy, and the arts. On every page the reader is charmed by the directness, the lucidity, and the sincerity of the author's tone.

UP AT THE VILLA

Up at the Villa so shocked the New York editor who commissioned it that it never appeared as the magazine serial it was intended to be, but, in the end, it proved to be one of the most popular books Maugham ever wrote. A short novel, *Up at the Villa* tells the story of a beautiful woman who, though she could have chosen at will from the highly eligible men who courted her, gives herself to a comparative stranger — and tragedy follows. . . .

W. Somerset Maugham

A WRITER'S NOTEBOOK

Maugham's *Notebook* provides a fascinating insight into the life
and times of one of the great twentieth-century writers.

From 1892 to 1949, Somerset Maugham recorded his thoughts
and observations in this journal, which confirms his acute vision
and his outstanding ability as a creative artist. *A Writer's
Notebook* contains his notes while a medical student in London
and follows his career as he travelled around the world developing his incomparable talent.

At times light-hearted, and occasionally barbed, this is a revealing and curiously intimate collection of the sketches and ideas of
one of literature's most compelling personalities.